The Catalan House

by
Susana Cory-Wright

Bloomington, IN　　Milton Keynes, UK

AuthorHouse™
1663 Liberty Drive, Suite 200
Bloomington, IN 47403
www.authorhouse.com
Phone: 1-800-839-8640

AuthorHouse™ *UK Ltd.*
500 Avebury Boulevard
Central Milton Keynes, MK9 2BE
www.authorhouse.co.uk
Phone: 08001974150

© *2006 Susana Cory-Wright. All rights reserved.*

No part of this book may be reproduced, stored in a retrieval system, or transmitted by any means without the written permission of the author.

First published by AuthorHouse 10/24/2006

ISBN: 1-4259-6466-4 (sc)

Printed in the United States of America
Bloomington, Indiana

This book is printed on acid-free paper.

For Maria Luisa and in memory of Oriol

Family Tree of Isabel de Roble

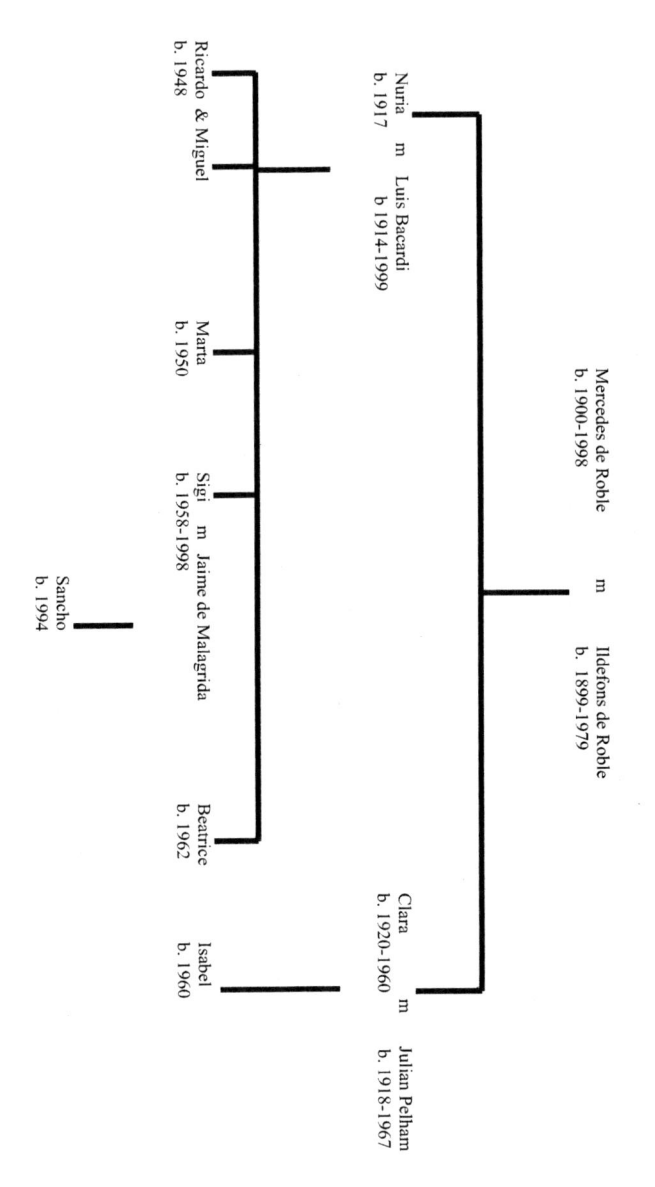

Mercedes de Roble (b. 1900-1998) m Ildefons de Roble (b. 1899-1979)

Children:
- Nuria (b. 1917) m Luis Bacardi (b. 1914-1999)
  - Ricardo & Miguel (b. 1948)
  - Marta (b. 1950)
  - Sigi (b. 1958-1998) m Jaime de Malagrida
    - Sancho (b. 1994)
  - Beatrice (b. 1962)
- Clara (b. 1920-1960) m Julian Pelham (b. 1918-1967)
  - Isabel (b. 1960)

"The permanent temptation of life is to confuse dreams with reality. The permanent defeat of life comes when dreams are surrendered to reality."
Goethe

"Que veas los hijos de tus hijos hasta la tercera y la cuarta generacion."

May you live to see your children's children to the third and fourth generation.
From the old marriage liturgy

Prologue

Isabel
Winchester
Winter 1997

 Last night Isabel Pelham dreamt of her cousin Ricardo. In those brief seconds before waking and while clinging to sleep, she once again felt the scorching sun on her back and his hands as they brushed her shoulder. Unsure if she was still dreaming, she could smell the overpowering perfume of gardenia that hovers in the heat after a sudden downpour. Raindrops slid to her face from the palm trees above and she watched, half fearful, as small scorpions scuttled towards the shade. Willing herself to stay asleep, to place her lips against his smooth dark neck, she was reluctantly dragged to wakefulness.
 Intermittently over the years and often after a long absence, Ricardo appeared in her dreams as if to make sure he was not forgotten. In the morning, Isabel would wake with a face that was wet with tears, yet strangely comforted and while she knew that the dream was delicious and left her with a delicious feeling, she could never remember what it had actually been about - the tears she could only conclude, were tears of longing. It was uncanny but Ricardo seemed to know just when he was needed and she would wake feeling completely enveloped by his being, comforted after an inexplicable hurt, as if healing hands had reached into her very soul. But the shockwaves such dreams left behind resounded in her for a while after and were unsettling. For a few days after a Ricardo dream, Isabel found it difficult to concentrate on anything, darting from one project to another, unable to shake off the persistent feeling that she should be somewhere else. And while she could not allow herself to really think about him, to remember everything, longing for Val Negra, her grandmother and cousins

and the house in which they had spent so much time together, gnawed at her heart. Sometimes the yearning to be with Ricardo was so great she thought she would go mad. But then, after a few days, the strange restlessness would pass and in time the longing too subsided.

Did Ricardo ever dream of Val Negra she often wondered. Did his body physically yearn as hers did, to revisit their childhood and take in the unearthly beauty of Val Negra with its vineyards purple against grey hills? Did he hope to hold on to that memory while it was still intact before they all grew up and were damaged?

Did he ever dream of her?

Chapter 1

Isabel
Winchester
Winter 1997

"Anyone here to sign?"

Isabel looked up from her computer at the sight of the leather clad biker as he weaved his way through the crowded office, past the 2 metre mock ups of coca cola bottles, airplane seats and oversize lipsticks- all work in progress. She sincerely hoped he didn't have anything for her. She was running late as it was, to meet her boyfriend for a drink and her stomach told her at every opportunity that it was tapas time. At the thought of a dwarf size plate of manchego cheese and pan tomacat, Isabel literally licked her lips. A strong whiff of petrol jolted her back to reality.

"Yes?"

The biker was standing in front of her, pushing up his visor. He dropped a large jiffy bag onto her cluttered desk which sent stray papers fluttering to the floor. She bent double to pick them up.

"Sorry," he muttered. "You Ruble?" he added pushing a clipboard under her face. She took the offered pen.

"Roble," she corrected rolling the r, coming up breathless.

"Whatever." The biker motioned to the room. "You guys don't have homes or something?"

Apparently not, thought Isabel watching as a team of giggling Americans took it in turn to wear the giant sized sunglasses they'd constructed from wine corks. The biker snapped closed his helmet and creaked out of the office. She rested the package on her lap irritated that anything should arrive so late. She glanced at the franking with disinterest. It was probably just another proposal. Her work station was already cluttered with the like.

Most came from Spanish wine companies but there were brochures and paperwork of every description. There was also a clay bull with a copper ring through its nose which she used as a paperweight and a hideous flamenco doll with dust ingrained in the folds of its synthetic skirt, neither of which she could quite bring herself to get rid of.

Lolling in her chair, a foot anchored sideways on a drawer, she tore open the jiffy bag to reveal a heavy cardboard box. She lifted the lid on swathes of tissue paper. Delving in between the crisp folds she pulled out an album sized book, beautifully bound in buff coloured suede. She pushed herself upright. The proposals her company Archid, generally received, were A4 printouts. This couldn't have been more different and had clearly cost a fortune to produce. She traced patterns on the delicate leather with the tip of her index finger and then ran the palm of her hand over the whole. In the centre, discretely carved into the leather, was what Isabel assumed to be the company logo. At first sight, it appeared to be a letter but examining it more closely, Isabel saw that it was actually a bloated scorpion. She frowned, her heart beginning to thump with inexplicable excitement and the niggling feeling that she knew that scorpion from before. Puzzled, she continued to run her fingers absentmindedly over the soft leather as curiosity rumbled in her stomach.

"So you've seen it then?"

Isabel's boss, Mike Fagan had a disconcerting habit of creeping up on her and no matter how hard she tried to be on her guard, he always succeeded in surprising her. Now he stood before her rocking his large frame on small, expensive shoes. He leaned over her desk so that his suit jacket gaped over a pregnant looking belly.

"I'm sorry?"

Mike reached over Isabel's computer his hand brushing her arm. She recoiled instinctively.

"It's from a new client - well *potential* client and as you can probably guess from that-" he motioned to the layers of tissue paper. "One we really, really want."

Isabel placed the book carefully in its box, pushing it to one side.

"Why's that then?" she said trying to avoid eye contact and making every effort to appear as if she were ready to leave.

Mike's silence forced Isabel to look at him. She concentrated on the hairline of his immaculately dyed, black hair but his next words startled her into meeting his lustful gaze.

"Well they're a Catalan concern for one thing and they're cava producers for another. Just up your street I'd have thought. I want you to go out there, pay them a visit. I can't stress how much I want this… for the firm. We could of course…" he paused lowering his voice for effect. "Discuss this over dinner…"

Isabel's eyes widened.

"No!" she said forcibly but when she saw, that rather than discourage him, the stern tone of her voice served only to make his eyes sparkle with renewed interest, did she add more reasonably, "What I mean is… I doubt very much that a Catalan firm would even consider us. Catalans consider themselves to be at the fore of design technology, and as confident of course as I am in Archid's abilities - I'm sorry Mike just a minute - " Out of the corner of her eye, Isabel spied her secretary, Sam, sidling towards the front door.

"Oh Sam!" she called making her voice deliberately dulcet-like.

There was a momentary silence, then a scrape as Sam reluctantly sashayed into her office. To Isabel's amusement, Sam had managed to find the one winter jacket that afforded almost no visible protection and seemingly little warmth. A fat bandage of skin was still clearly exposed around her midriff. Isabel did her best to avoid staring at the pierced belly but was acutely aware of the other rings through Sam's nose, eyebrows and when she spoke, tongue. Mike looked at her distastefully.

"Did you fax the Spanish Wine Board?" asked Isabel making a mental inventory and trusting that she hadn't had anything more pierced during her lunch break.

Sam nodded, making a bolt for the door. Sam wasn't generally light of foot except when it was time to go home.

"Sam, this proposal …"

Sam did a double take, like a deer caught in the headlights. A frown creased the piercing near her left eyebrow.

"Er… I heard about the engagement. You and Tim. Congratulations."

Mike shot Isabel a questioning, not altogether friendly look.

"Tim?" he said sharply.

"My boyfriend," said Isabel impatiently and glancing at her watch added, "who I was supposed to be meeting ten minutes ago."

Ignoring Mike's hostile expression, she turned to Sam.

"We're not engaged," she said. "Besides, that wasn't quite what I meant."

Sam looked predictably blank. "Yeah ... well, office gossip I guess... You said I could leave early today. I'm going to the cinema."

Mike raised an eyebrow as if to question Isabel's authority. He resumed his rocking and his hands thrust deep into trouser leg pockets, jangled his keys. Irritated, Isabel motioned to the box.

"We'll answer these people in the morning then Sam. Off you go. I'm almost done here myself."

Sam nodded and shot into the lift faster than it took Isabel the time to swivel back to her computer. The key jangling stopped as Mike moved to perch on the edge of her desk. Isabel sprang up from her chair just as her phone started ringing. She grabbed it, stretching the cord around him so that he was forced to back away. Mouthing the words, "must get this," and "will come and see you in the morning," she turned her back on him only answering when she could see his shoulders swallowed between the huge CH of the Archid lettering that was glazed onto the surface of the entrance doors.

"Archid Associates" she said impatiently, now desperate to go home herself.

"Good evening," said a voice. Isabel caught her breath. For one, crazy, wild wonderful moment she thought it might actually be her cousin Ricardo. "Hello?" he said again.

"Hi," said Isabel composing herself but more coolly than she meant to sound. "It's me."

"Hi me," said Tim his tone audibly relaxing. "You done?"

"Not quite," said Isabel and for some perverse reason, the very reasonableness of his voice made her change her mind about meeting him.

"What's the matter? I hear you hesitating." *And* he could read her mind.

Cradling the phone under her chin, Isabel shifted the cardboard box into her briefcase.

"The thing is, a new proposal has literally, just landed on my desk. I can't explain why but I really think it's important I read it over. I mean by the morning, which I can do, but just not if we have dinner out. I'm really tired. Do you ... do you think we could meet tomorrow night instead?"

There was silence the other end.

"Have you thought any further about *my* proposal?"

No she hadn't, she wanted to say, but she knew someone who had.

"That's fine," said Tim curtly. "Why don't you call me when you're less busy."

"Oh Tim don't –" began Isabel but he had already rung off.

She felt that familiar, sinking feeling she always did when people were displeased or disappointed in her. It was childish she knew- not to be able to say what she really meant, even to say no without her heart pumping faster, her hands going clammy. She could be clear in business but not so in relationships. And yet it wasn't all her. Tim was on the defensive a lot of the time. When he was busy at work she was expected to understand. Why not the other way round? Except that she *had* been busy a lot recently. ... and the man *had* asked her to marry him. So why the sudden, unwelcome panic?

She was about to redial Tim's number when she stopped. She wouldn't be forced to decide like this. Not, when as if from nowhere, Ricardo's name had broken through the wall of her psyche. Not when the idea of that scorpion logo made her pulse race inexplicably and especially not when the night before she had dreamt of Val Negra. That scorpion... where on earth had she seen it before? She mentally shook her head. She couldn't work it out at all. But what she needed was to go home. She would light a fire and open a bottle of the wine her new client had sent over and she would read over the intriguing proposal. Again she could picture the bloated scorpion but in a different context and yet with the same curious sense of deja vu. And then, a little guiltily, Isabel admitted to herself, she would have forgotten about Tim entirely...

*

It hadn't always been like that of course. In the beginning, Isabel had wanted to spend all her time with Tim. They first met at a party a week after Isabel came down from Oxford, in one of those typical, double fronted houses in Fulham. People seemed to be spilling from every window, door and balcony. Men were drinking on the pavement in front of the house and there wasn't an inch of space left on the tiny patio. Isabel elbowed her way into the hall as guests pushed past. There was talk of Wimbledon, Ascot and the weather and some girl's striptease at a pub the evening before. Plump girls with sunglasses perched atop died blonde hair, with piecrust collar shirts and thin, inherited pearls laughed too loudly. The men wore blazers, chinos and rocked backwards and forwards on chunky suede shoes, tipping beer glasses with steady rhythm to wet lips. After what seemed like hours of waiting, someone thrust a drink in her hand. Automatically she raised it to her lips.

"You don't like it."

Isabel looked up to find a man smiling at her. Unlike the other men in the room he did not wear the uniform dark jacket and his shirtsleeves were rolled up at the elbows. Something about his expression made her nervous and she was uncharacteristically blunt.

She shook her head.

"I've never liked Pimms. But it's only drinkable if it's really cold. This tastes like Ribena."

"Does it?" The man seemed taken aback. "It's been a while since I had Ribena. I'm not sure I even remember what it tastes like. But then you are a bit younger than I am."

Isabel flushed, "It's just that Pimms is so ... *English.*"

She pressed herself against the wall to let a couple squeeze past. "Anyway it doesn't matter. I'm not going to stay long."

"And presumably you're not? English, I mean?"

Isabel looked at him curiously. He was so tall she had to crane her neck to see his face, an almost impossible movement given the crush. His eyes, though small were of a particularly vivid blue and crinkled at the corners when he smiled. He was smiling at her now as if they were good friends, as if he knew precisely when to indulge her. And he was unusually tanned with a deep golden tan that reminded her immediately of Ricardo. She felt an unwanted lurch in her stomach. She frowned.

"No."

"What? No you're not English or no you don't want something else?"

Isabel faltered, "I mean I'm only half English."

"Well then I'm happy for you. It's obviously a problem, your Englishness."

She looked up to see if she had upset him but she appeared to amuse him and this intrigued her.

"I didn't mean-"

"Yes you did. Look you don't have to have Pimms. There's other stuff."

Isabel's relief was clear. "*Is* there something else? I would love a gin."

He raised an eyebrow and she smiled.

"I know," she said sheepishly. "But there are *some* things I like about being here. And I'm sorry I was rude. There are just so many people and I didn't really want to come out tonight and then the drink was ... I'm digging myself in aren't I? You must think me an incredible pain. Really, I'm not usually like this."

"Oh I do hope you are!" His hand momentarily touched her shoulder. "Don't apologise," he said. "I understand. And don't move. I won't be long."

She watched his retreating back and wondered if she should leave. She felt self-conscious standing alone and it was late. And yet something made her hesitate. She wanted to see if he would smile at her again and if when he did, she would feel that funny lurch in the pit of her stomach. She had forgotten what it was like to be wanted, to see that look of appraisal in a man's eyes. People were beginning to leave and it was cooler now. The French doors were open and she stepped on to a stone patio. At the far end was a Cherry tree that seemed to have outgrown its small space. She leaned her head against the warm brick of the outside wall and closed her eyes. A firm, cool hand shaped her fingers round a glass and she caught her breath. He was watching her with a look that made her heart race. The fluidity of his movements excited her. She didn't know anything at all about this man and she didn't care. His physical strength alone attracted her and suddenly she wanted him to obliterate any thought of Ricardo or of Val Negra or of the past.

"I didn't think you were coming back." Her tone was more accusing than she intended.

"Couldn't find the ice and knowing now that you like your cold drinks to be really cold, I didn't dare turn up with a warm G&T! I can't begin to think what you'd have had to say about that!"

She clung to the glass as if for dear life and took a huge gulp.

"It's delicious. Thank you."

"Well Thank God for that. We'd probably have got off to a better start if you'd had that in the first place. Better?"

"Much. You must think me awfully spoilt."

"I might have done if I hadn't been warned."

Isabel's eyes were wide.

"Who on earth?"

"Kate." And then in answer to her quizzical expression he added, "As in flat-mate Kate, school friend of Convent days Kate? She says you're best friends."

"Oh that Kate." *I'll kill her* thought Isabel. *This time I'll really kill her.* She took a hurried gulp. " I didn't know you knew each other." And then as the penny dropped she flushed. "Oh my God," she said. "This is *your* party isn't it? And this is *your* house." Her eyes slid back to his face. "So what else has Kate been saying?"

"Not nearly enough by the sound of things." His eyes were on her lips. "Like I said - that you and she are old school friends and that you've been sharing since you came down from Oxford." His voice was muffled as he lifted his glass to his mouth. "What will you do now?"

Her head was beginning to swim as she desperately tried to remember just how rude she'd been about his party.

"I've no idea."

He looked surprised. "You weren't snapped up on the milk run? No merchant bank or solicitors?"

"No. Not yet at any rate. And you?"

"Oh the usual. Cambridge and accountancy."

Isabel's eyes danced. "That's probably why," she said. "I want to make the right choice."

And suddenly he stopped smiling and took her glass out of her hand. She met his gaze. Why *had she said that about making the right choice? What on earth was the right choice? What do I want? Except, perhaps at this moment, not to have to think.* She looked away aware that he was still watching her. Her heart thumped. She knew that she looked good and she was glad she had worn her new dress. It was deceptively simple and expensive. Her hair barely brushed her tanned shoulders. She was tall even in flat shoes and as her thigh brushed his, she felt an overwhelming urge to touch him.

"I should go," she murmured.

"No!" His arm shot across, touching the wall and barring her way. "Everyone's almost gone."

Isabel raised an eyebrow. "And Kate?"

His face was close to hers. "Haven't seen her all evening," he said softly. "Have you?"

"Didn't your mother ever tell you that you should never answer a question with a question?"

He drew back slightly. "Why ever not?"

Why indeed. Why anything? Isabel's legs began to tremble, she wished that whatever was to happen were over.

"So you're not exactly a stranger. You knew who I was."

"I know exactly who you are," he said quietly. "I'm going to get rid of my guests."

Suddenly the house was empty and very quiet. She heard the front door slam shut and the sound of rapid footsteps. Every sense in her body was alert to his presence. She could hardly breathe and her heart thumped so loudly she was amazed he couldn't hear it. She closed her eyes trying to steady herself. *If he wasn't standing in front of her by the time she counted to ten she would go.* Another door slammed. *Ten!* She began to shake. She didn't hear him come up behind her until his hand was at the nape of her neck. She felt her knees buckle as he pulled her against him. His mouth was on hers. She took a deep breath. *Yes,* she thought. *Let it be now, let it be him. Anyone. Only let him once and for all obliterate the memory of Ricardo.*

She reached for him blindly not daring to look at his face.

*

"I'd never have thought it," he said later, reaching for a drink.
"What, that I was a virgin?"
They lay in the dark, she wrapped in his sheets, her hair spread against his knees.
"I'm amazed you weren't raped at Oxford."
She made a face. "I had other things to worry about."
"Evidently," his voice was dry. He sat up and moved to trace patterns on her skin, his fingers combing her hair. "You're quite dark you know," he said.
"I told you, my mother was Spanish. But it's strange because when I was little I was teased for being so white." She glanced down at his fingers on her skin. In spite of his tan, she was still darker. " Do you always ask women to stay after your parties?"
"Only if I'm certain they will."

His face was very close, impassive. He imprisoned her wrists and when he kissed her again she knew she was in love.

The next day Tim told her that he was actually on R&R from a posting in the Middle East and that for the remaining six months of his contract, he wanted her to be with him. The months that followed were the most consistently happy she had ever known. It seemed the most natural thing in the world for her to pack up and leave with a man who was virtually a stranger. Perhaps it was the fact that Kate seemed disappointingly unmoved by Isabel's news that was particularly reassuring. All Isabel knew was that she trusted Tim instinctively. And she fell in love with Muscat, the Omani capital and their villa covered in bougainvillea overlooking the sea.

While Tim was at work, Isabel swam in the pool and in the afternoons when he came home they made love. She revelled in the pleasure Tim gave her and the well being of living once again in a hot climate. She hadn't read a newspaper or listened to the radio for weeks - a fact which both shocked and delighted her. Being out of touch with the rest of the world made her feel cocooned, absolving her of all responsibility.

Twice, maybe three times a week, she would go to the souk where she bought incense and ripe mango or shrimp for their supper. In the evenings they went to the fashionable Al Bustan hotel. An entire village had been relocated in order to build it and now it stood like a huge white albatross on the edge of the sands. In the blistering heat, its large marbled reception was a cool haven. Sometimes they would swim to one of the adjacent islands where they watched the sun set and then return, guided by the moon's shadow as it raked out paths along the water.

"I'll take you to Salalah," said Tim one evening, as they lay entwined on the sand, her legs through his. "The Queen of Sheba set sail from its harbour, her boats laden with frankincense for Solomon. It's very different from Muscat," he added motioning to the line of dusty hills that edged the Arabian Sea. "It's very lush after the rains. The ex-pats love it, reminds them of home I suppose."

He glanced down at her trying to read her mind, trying to see her objectively. Her hair was wet from their swim, her eyes emerald green in a smooth face. Just watching her inflamed his desire but he would not make love to her now, he thought. He would force himself to tell her what had been niggling him for some time.

"Where is home for you?" He asked quietly feeling her start against him and the pulse in her neck beat more quickly. She pulled back but he held her securely in his arms feeling the length of her against him, her hands in fists on his chest.

For a long time she was silent as her thoughts whirled filling her with panic. *Home? God, why did he have to start on that again? Ricardo was home if he really wanted to know. Ricardo.* But up until now she hadn't actually thought or dreamt of him and therefore had enjoyed a certain armistice. She could hardly bear to think of Val Negra at the best of times let alone now when all her energy was channelled into surviving, channelled into just living for once and not thinking of the consequences, not being *haunted* by the consequences. No matter how grateful she was to Tim for bringing her here, she was not ready to tell him anything at all about Ricardo.

She moved so that through the crack of his arms she could focus on the gently lapping water and waited for the moment on the horizon when the twin fortresses that guarded entrance to the old port, turned pink as the sun passed over them.

"England is home," she said.

"You don't fool me," said Tim trying to keep the disappointment from showing. "I know almost nothing about you. You reveal so little."

"I don't mean to," she said contritely. "I'm not used to this, to a relationship. But does it matter? I would have thought it was better *not* to know too much. Then when we walk away there's –"

Tim gripped her roughly.

"No one's going to walk away," he said. "Look at me Isabel." His hands moved to her shoulders forcing her to face him. He tilted her chin so that her eyes were level with his. "I don't want you to tell me things you don't want to but I always feel that I'm prying. You never tell me anything about yourself spontaneously. On the other hand you don't seem too curious about me either! You never ask me about my friends, my work- what I want to do, even what we're doing here!" His hands slid down her arms. " But no matter what I ask you, I always get the impression that I'm intruding."

"I'm sorry," said Isabel. "I don't mean to be secretive."

"You're holding back from me," said Tim. "I want to share things with you. We've been living together now for some months and I still know virtually nothing about you. I know you're half Spanish and a friend of Kate's but that's really about it." His eyes flicked over her bathing suit. "And despite not having an obvious job, you wear extremely expensive clothes! When I was young, new graduates didn't look like you. They didn't wear Armani."

"Don't you like my clothes?"

"Yes of course but Isabel that isn't the point."

"What is the point then?" said Isabel gently. She uncurled a fist and covered his hand with hers. "I've been studying a long time. I'm enjoying myself. I suppose I haven't wanted to well … gush."

"Gush?" Tim burst out laughing in spite of himself. "What sort of word is that?"

"I can't bear people who tell you their life story thirty seconds after you meet them. You can't have any kind of intelligent conversation now that doesn't involve all kinds of trivial information. And you end up hearing about their children and dogs and their entire medical history before you've even introduced yourself."

"Well no one could accuse you of that! I *want* to know more about you. I'm used to girls making demands on me. I've come to expect it. But then you aren't like other girls. I don't want to sound as if I'm complaining because I'm not. It's just that I want to share everything with you. I want you to trust me."

"I do trust you."

"Then talk to me."

Isabel swallowed nervously, "I thought we did."

"We make love. It's not the same."

"What – what do you want to know?"

Tim ran his hand down her cheek.

"You look so worried. I don't want that either. What I really want is for you to be happy. I want us to be close."

Isabel closed her eyes imagining for a minute Ricardo's fingers on her face.

"I'm sorry," she said at last with effort. "I haven't meant to keep things from you. If there's anything you want to know, just ask me. I love this country and I'm happy being here with you. I'm sorry if it sounds clichéd but it's true. I just haven't wanted to think about anything else. Don't you want me here? Do you think it's time I went home?"

Tim pulled her to him roughly. "Christ no," he said his mouth on hers. "I want you more than I've ever wanted a woman and I'm prepared to wait for you. I want you to love me because I've fallen in love with you. You move me," he whispered his breath rough against her cheek.

"Then don't ask too much of me," she said. "Just let me by myself. All my life I've tried to live up to … well, to other people's expectations. I've never really wanted to be myself and now for the first time I don't yearn to be someone else. I don't yearn for something I can never have. I'm sorry. I sound incoherent," she added seeing his bemused expression. "Just give me time."

And to be fair to Tim, he had given her time. More time than it was right to give a woman who wasn't in love with him. He accepted, unhappily at first but later with restrained resignation, their separate living arrangements and never probed, questioned, or doubted, but had been there for her always. And over the years he never wavered in his support. Eventually, he left the large company he had trained with to set up his own accountancy firm while she climbed the corporate ladder at Archid. When only last week he had asked her to marry him, instead of being happy her head, eardrums and heart had filled with blood so that she thought she would pass out. He had held her hand tightly so that she clung to it not because she reciprocated the feeling but because without it she feared she might fall to the ground. Out of foggy depths she heard the words "family" and "children" and "not wanting to waste anymore time." Her whole body had frozen in shock, the shock of reality, the shock of knowing absolutely and definitively that she could never love him or any man just as long Ricardo continued to haunt her dreams.

Chapter 2

Isabel
Winter
Winchester 1997

    Lost in thought, Isabel hurried across the street to her waiting car, the cold biting her cheeks. She pointed her key in its direction, inwardly thrilling as the headlights automatically switched on and the ignition unlocked. The novelty of owning and having paid for her own car had not worn off. She smiled to herself as the last vestiges of guilt associated with Tim disappeared completely at the prospect of driving home alone. She loved nothing better than driving at night enveloped in the anonymity of the hour and the sleekness of the vehicle, moving towards her house, her peace. The streets were silent and empty. Deftly negotiating the one-way system (an unresolved mystery to bewildered strangers to the town) she weaved her way through narrow lanes before emerging onto the St.Cross road. To the left and above, St.Catherine's Hill was a mound of dark against the winter sky. Within another five minutes she had reached The Cottage.

    "It's a garden with a house," Kate had exclaimed when she came to inspect the property shortly after Isabel moved in. Her blue eyes glinted with an unreadable expression. "However, I'm beginning to think that the idea of you and I sharing a flat is jinxed. No sooner do you move in with me than you flit off to Oman with Tim. You come back, again to share with me and out of the blue you inherit a house! Maybe *I'm* the one with bad karma. But either way, darling, it's a bijoux of a house and it suits you."

    Isabel had smiled back acknowledging the compliment silently. It hadn't always seemed such a "bijoux." Inheriting The Cottage when she did had seemed like the worst kind of luck and Isabel hadn't the faintest idea what to do with it. She had just started a new job and was working in London. Her time in Oman with Tim had been wonderful but she had confused desire with love and when she realised this, the heartache was worse than ever. And so she returned to England ahead of him. To her enduring surprise she had quickly found a job at Archid. Kate was completing her pupil age at the Inns of Court and had recently purchased a bright, airy flat in South Kensington not far from Tim's house. Isabel enjoyed working and it was fun sharing with Kate. They had slipped into their old friendship, with Isabel showing just the appropriate degree of deference to the older girl that she had shown her at school. It was a carefree and exhilarating period in their lives and although they worked hard, Kate, Isabel soon discovered, knew how to play hard too. For Isabel it was also a release. For the first time ever, she had money of her own to spend. She went to parties where she met interesting people. She went to concerts, theatre and travelled to Europe on business. She loved London but most of all she loved being free to do as she pleased with no one, with the exception of Kate and very occasionally Tim, looking over her shoulder. But what she didn't love was the notion of any kind of responsibility. She didn't want to be tied to any one place. Secretly she liked the idea that she could up and leave at any given moment. Apart from clothes, Isabel didn't actually *want* to own anything. And she loathed the image of the English country living – that of weird sounding names like Barbour and Lurcher.

Isabel did not accept the news of her windfall, if it could be called that, gracefully. She railed against the heavens (and more specifically her Spanish family) for allowing such a gift. She found it hard to believe that they knew nothing about the house, especially when she discovered that The Cottage was where she herself had been born. And more importantly that all the while she was growing up, a slice of her history lay buried in the English countryside.

So, for some months Isabel did nothing at all, hoping that if she ignored the whole Cottage issue, it would simply go away. But after a year and consistent badgering from both Kate and Tim, she finally agreed to go and see it. Refusing their offers to accompany her, Isabel drove down one weekend in May. It was a bright clear day, the air just cold enough to accentuate the smell of the earth. She located the village on her map and turned into a country lane. There was a church and school and village shop where she asked directions. Only the trustees had said nothing about the house being thatched. If only they knew how she disliked thatched cottages! She should have gone with her gut instinct and sold the place months ago. Nonetheless, she parked her car in the lane and walked the remaining distance to the house. She paused in front of an iron gate whose sign was rakishly twisted from its chain. A large bay tree hung over the gate and a thatched barn sat at right angles to the house. A path led up to the front porch and through the arch, sunlight streamed onto herbaceous borders. Isabel's heart gave a lurch in spite of herself. The trees moved in the breeze, branches of yew rustling and dry.

"So this is where my father lived," she thought to herself without sentiment, "and the mother I have never known."

She stepped back to take a good look at the large timber framed building, unlike any cottage she had ever seen. Thatch dripped over the walls, like melting scoops of ice cream on a tiny plate. A huge beech tree framed the upper windows of a wide balcony. She walked round the garden, the grass still damp with dew, through a series of outdoor rooms. Some were formal, others less so and revealed the owner's sense of fun. Around a pond large enough to swim in, were yew bushes clipped in the shape of ducks. There were yew peacocks as tall as the house and swirls of box that appeared unexpectedly behind sombre borders. There were beds filled with white roses and lavender and a lower lawn, brilliant and green and smooth as silk. At the end of one of the many brick paths that shot off in all directions, was a statue of Pandora. On either side was a border bursting with scarlet phlox, tulips and peonies. Geraniums unfurled towards the paddock and under the mulberry tree in a carpet of blue, like cells spreading beneath a microscope. Boule de Neige roses tossed their scent wantonly with dianthus and lilac. Lavender grew beneath the casement windows. And at the very end, behind a pink gazebo, was a bench that faced the fields and the valley beyond. Isabel sat there for some time trying to conjure up an image of her father, wishing for the first time in a long time, that he were there to guide her. But there was no atmosphere, no sudden chill, only an immense sense of peace in the warm sun.

After that first day, Isabel returned most weekends to The Cottage. At first she only walked round the empty house, occasionally peering in. Cobwebs hung from oak beams and the curtains that could be glimpsed framing the windows, were in tatters. There was clearly much to be done in order to make it habitable once more. The garden, by contrast was in much better condition. But then, knowing virtually nothing about gardening anyway, Isabel wouldn't have been able to distinguish a weed from an exotic plant. But to her untrained eye it looked tidy enough. Only the grass in the orchard grew to waist level and there were dandelions among the daisies. But she still could not bring herself to enter the house. She felt safe in the garden where there were no ghosts to close in on her. She was afraid of going inside, afraid of what she would feel. However, if she was secretly hoping to find the history of her parents' life together, she was disappointed. There were a few good paintings and furniture but no photographs. There was no lurking presence of an ethereal mother.

Later when she was offered the job in Winchester, it seemed that fate had indeed intervened. A huge amount of work had to be carried out on the house but it seemed as if The Cottage had been waiting patiently for Isabel to come and live in it. And every time Isabel returned to The Cottage and especially if she had been away on business, her heart leapt at the beauty of the garden and the delicious knowledge that it was hers. It was also, she knew, the main reason that she did not commit herself to Tim. She could not bring herself to share it with anyone and yet she would never let it go.

Gravel crunched beneath her feet as Isabel hurried into the house out of the cold. She switched on the lights in the kitchen flinging her coat on a chair as she did so. Without stopping to check her post or telephone messages, she made a beeline for the drinks cabinet in the drawing room. She kicked off her shoes and padded on bare oak floorboards as she went through the hall. The polished surfaces gleamed and there was a scent even in winter, of fresh flowers. She poured herself a gin and knelt beside the grate to light a fire. Isabel curled up on the large sofa and sighed with satisfaction. It was a serene, uncluttered room inspired by the pink and sea green colours of her grandmother's house. On the walls were the paintings left by her father. At one end was the baby grand piano she had purchased after her first pay rise. Photographs of her Spanish cousins stood in silver frames on the mantelpiece. She flicked a remote control at the CD player and Julio Caccini's *Ave Maria* immediately filled the room. It was, at the moment, her favourite piece of music and she listened to it repeatedly. This was another reason why she did not want to marry Tim, she thought. They simply didn't share the same taste in music. But Ricardo did. Yes Ricardo did... But she mustn't think about him. Not now. Not when she had work to do and was tired. She took another long sip and closed her eyes. It was such a long time ago, such a long time since she'd been back ...

'Ay juventud, Divino Tesoro' her grandmother Avia, was always quoting when Isabel told her she wasn't coming home after all. Or equally when she told her anything that was unpleasant or disappointing. 'Ah, youth! Always dreaming your golden dreams.'

And just why hadn't she been back when she missed them all so much? But so much had changed. Her grandfather was dead, her cousins long grown up. Isabel took another swig of her drink. The truth was that she was afraid of going back. It was one thing to occasionally dream of Ricardo and sometimes to think of her childhood in Spain but it was quite another to face it all in reality. It had taken her a long time to order her life and to feel secure again. She never again wanted to feel the extremes of emotion she had done when she was much younger. She never again wanted passion and pain to rip her apart. Here in England her life was pretty much routine but it was safe. Besides, she hadn't entirely lost touch with her Spanish family.

"Our Spanish-English girl, how like that other Isabel you have become" her grandmother had said once during one of their infrequent and unsatisfactory telephone conversations referring to the Cervantes character. Her voice was frail, failing and Isabel could hear the sadness over the phone, travelling over countries and it made her fearful.

"Nonsense," Isabel replied tartly. "It's just my work, you know. I travel a great deal –"

"Pero no vienes a casa, aqui no vienes. Yes but you don't come home. Even though you tell me you're constantly travelling, you never come to Barcelona. You never come to visit anymore."

"No."

"Don't you want to settle down?"

Isabel bristled, "Grandmother, I am settled. At The Cottage."

"Ah yes, this famous Cottage. Entrapment is what that is. It's a mirage. It's side tracking you from getting on with your life. And children? A husband? Where in your busy life is there room for them? What about this *Teem?* He won't wait for you forever. He must want children. He'll be too old soon never mind you."

"Men can have children well into their eighties if they want to!"

"Ay! *Hijita.* God forbid that you should wait that long! What is it with today's youth? Always dreaming your golden dreams! You waste time chasing rainbows, when all the happiness in the world is right here …" and Isabel could imagine her grandmother tapping the palm of her hand. "Only here."

"You don't understand!" protested Isabel taking a bite out of an apple so that the following words came out sideways. She had already dropped the phone once much to her grandmother's annoyance. Habitual guilt was rapidly replaced by irritation.

"Are you there? What are you doing?" Her grandmother's voice was sharp. "And another thing, you don't call me Avia anymore. Why is that?"

Emotion welled up in Isabel at the use of the Catalan word for Grandmother. For as long as she could remember Isabel had always called her that. She felt tears prick her eyes.

"Are you there, Isabel?"

"Yes Avia. I'm still here," said Isabel. "I don't know why. I don't know why I don't come home. I have to work. It's not as simple as it was. When I was at university I had longer holidays. I know what I want now. I think I always have."

There was a small silence and just when Isabel thought her grandmother had not heard her, Avia replied in such a low tone that Isabel had to press the receiver hard to her ear and stop chewing.

"It can be a disadvantage in a woman," said her grandmother at last. "I was like you once, so sure, so in love." Again the little silence but if Avia thought this might initiate a heart to heart she was mistaken. Isabel took the opportunity to finish her apple and let her grandmother talk.

"And what about your faith now that we are having this little chat?" she was saying. "Have you given up that along with your nationality? The religion in England might be similar. Oh I know it is a Christian country but it is not the same. You must not forget you were brought up to believe in one, Catholic and apostolic church. Even your father, with all his faults, God rest his soul, was a Catholic. You did not know? And you –" Isabel could imagine her grandmother peering down the phone, as though perfectly able to see the disgruntled form of her grand daughter. "You must not let your faith die. It's not always easy. You have to work at it. As you do with anything, a marriage for example. But going to church, a CATHOLIC church ... " here Avia enunciated the words " ... keeps open that link between God and his people. If you break away, it is very difficult to go back. So your faith will fade and one day you will forget that you ever believed in anything. You must it keep it alive."

Isabel held the receiver away from her, raised her eyes to the ceiling and took a deep breath.

"Absolutely."

"Are you happy child? I only want you to be happy. I want you to know a great love, a love to carry you through the difficult times. One you will always remember. Are you happy with this man *Teem?* You must bring him to meet me. Tell him to come with you next time."

Isabel watched the purple flames of the fire, sparks flying up the chimney. She sipped her drink feeling its warmth flood through her limbs, the soprano's voice relaxing her every muscle. Gradually her mind stopped spinning with the problems of work and tension seeped away. When the CD came to an end Isabel refilled her glass and reached for her briefcase. Maybe getting her teeth into this new proposal would lift her mood just as easily as it was to lift the book from its box. Seeing the bloated scorpion, Isabel once again frowned with the uncanny recognition of it. She traced patterns on the suede cover, her mind struggling with a sudden onslaught of half remembered images. Absentmindedly her fingers moved to the embossed logo, the tips of her fingers reworking it into her mind. Suddenly she stopped and her heart skipped a beat. Her hands began to shake, as at last, the colliding pictures skidded to a halt in her head.

Hermanos Bazan, Castillo Bazan, Val Negra, she read. Of course how could she not have connected the scorpion with a family she knew almost as well as her own? She closed her eyes. Was it the power of suggestion? The fact that she'd dreamed about Ricardo the night before? Was desire distorting her ability to think logically? She took a deep breath, sat up, covered the title page with one hand and even put on her reading glasses. Could she have drunk more than she thought? She breathed slowly and opened her eyes. The words remained. Val Negra! But how was it possible? Who but she knew of this place and of all the places in the world! She shuddered with longing. *Val Negra.* She spoke the words lovingly aloud. *Val Negra...*

And then the significance of the proposal froze all romantic association and her professional side took over. Well, she could go to bed with a clear conscience. There was no work to be done on this job spec after all. She had grown up with Benito and Fernando Bazan. Indeed Fernando was married to her cousin Marta. Unless her grandmother, and she wouldn't put her past it, was somehow responsible for putting the Bazan brothers in touch with Archid, it was nothing more than an extraordinary coincidence. The brothers must have been a target client. She was sure that had they really been interested in Archid, the brothers would have said something to her personally. And if they weren't, a slick campaign would not persuade them to spend the kind of money that Archid demanded on redesigning a product. The Bazan brothers probably had little concept of what strategic designers even did! They'd probably never heard of Archid. Catalans considered themselves to be at the fore of design technology. She couldn't imagine them approaching an *English* company for advice! She was amazed a site visit was in the offing. Not that any of that mattered now. It was a closed case.

All the same ... the brothers Bazan ... who would have thought their name would crop up here? It seemed no time at all since they had played together and squabbled and been friends. And now, here they were all these years later, on the brink of negotiating in business as they had so often done before, in childhood games. And there was Val Negra. Isabel couldn't discard that memory as easily as slotting the Bazan proposal back into her briefcase. How could she have forgotten that emblem, that bloated scorpion that was carved into the iron gates of the house and every stone surface of the house? Val Negra was her youth, her secret bond with her cousins. It was everything. It was also part of a memory that could not be neatly sifted through. Once disturbed, it would take time to settle. And as for the brothers Bazan ... well they were as part of that time as the house and vineyards, as her grandparents and Ricardo. And while Isabel would sometimes indulge herself by thinking about them all, by dreaming about Ricardo, it was many years since she had thought specifically about Benito. But this evening she would allow herself that luxury.

Isabel found it embarrassing to remember how pathetic they both were. She had been a plump little girl, badly dressed, with braces on her teeth. He was even shorter but thin and had a face covered in the most repellant acne she had ever seen. But he was the first boy to befriend her. The more she confessed to feelings of awkwardness the more he reassured her to the contrary. Their mutual gawkiness drew them together. Benito growing up in the shadow of his brother Fernando, who by contrast was gifted, handsome and popular, recognized an outsider when he saw one. And Isabel was not like her glamorous cousins. Recently orphaned, she was a bewildered child who could not speak the language. Benito was the gasp that people gave when they realised he was related to Fernando. And yet, in spite of seeming to have so much in common, their friendship had not survived adolescence. A few years later, when she had lost weight and the braces, she felt Benito's indifference. Instinctively she knew that there would be no metamorphosis for him. Suddenly she was no longer his only friend and boys sought him out, not for his company, but as a means of getting close to *her*. Gradually, their conversations became less frequent and their occasional meetings were clumsy and self-conscious. Soon there was nothing left of their friendship at all.

Only once did he attempt to win her round. He told her that he had news that would interest her, gossip he had overheard in the village square.

Benito was taking a chance. Isabel had become an exotic creature and bore no resemblance to the ungainly child he had known. She terrified him. And just when he had convinced himself that she would not come, she walked into the local bar as though she had never been away and the old men playing board games looked up and whispered. When he sat her down on a tall stool, her long legs swinging in front of him, sun tanned and beautiful, Benito almost fled. She wore a mint green cardigan slung across naked shoulders. Her face was open and happy when she hugged him. He remembered smelling sunflowers and wanting to touch her skin.

"So what is it? What is all the gossip?" her eyes twinkled and all at once they were children again. They chatted easily. He told her about his brother's romance with Marta, how Sigi, Isabel's favourite cousin had grown into a reckless and crazy thing and how the entire village was talking about her exploits. He said that Bea, the youngest child wanted to become a nun. He added how sorry he was to hear of her grandfather's death. And then he told her that Ricardo had called off his wedding to Sonia de Cana. Isabel couldn't hide the hope that leapt in her eyes.

"But why?" she whispered conspiratorially as the interested bar tender glanced in their direction. Benito hesitated frowning. His spotty face contorted.

"No one is saying anything at the moment. Not even your Avia. Perhaps they haven't told her. But they can't get married now. Sonia won't marry him. She's turned him down, sent back the ring and a room full of wedding gifts."

"So why?" Isabel was insistent. Benito's momentary courage failed him and he looked away.

"It's because Ricardo has cancer."

*

Isabel shivered and realized that the fire had died some time ago. Unsteadily she got to her feet and switched off the lights. She went into the kitchen to make a cup of tea. Yes, she could safely say that she knew the Bazan Brothers of Castillo Bazan all right, but not as potential clients. The steaming kettle distracted Isabel from her thoughts. She moved slowly round the kitchen taking a mug from the pine dresser and a slice of cake from the fridge. She sat at the scrubbed, bleached table sipping her tea feeling slightly winded, slightly wounded, her head whirling with half formed conversations and images of the past. She bit into the cake hoping that food would dull her overactive psyche and looked around her. She rarely sat in her kitchen and now in the silence she examined it absentmindedly. She finished her tea and pushed away her plate. It had been a long day. She had to get some sleep. She went up the turned oak staircase, overcome with a nostalgia.

Isabel stood for a moment at the balcony window without turning on the light. The air was icy on her cheek and she peered through streaks of darkness trying to make out the skeletal shapes of her garden. Only the tall cypresses on the lower lawn and the gazebo were visible. In a sudden ray of moonlight, the topiary and Pandora seemed to move in an extraordinary game of chess. These smells and the cold could never be confused with those of Val Negra she thought. Even now in the dark, one winter cannot be exchanged for another. Somewhere a wood owl hooted, a branch snapped. Isabel let her hand drop as the curtain swung into place. That very evening while driving home she had heard John Williams on the radio playing a Catalan folk song. The surprise of it had almost caused her to career into a light post. It was a song she had not heard since she was a little girl.

Que li donarem a la pastoreta?
Que li donarem per Isabel balla
Jo li donaria una caputxeta
I a la montanyeta la faria ana…

dadi dadi dum, da dumm, di dum …

What shall we give the little shepherdess?
What will it take to make her go and dance?
I would give her a hood
And send her up the mountain.

She began to hum the tune under her breath as she shoved her feet into slippers and padded downstairs. Through the casement windows, the full moon was so bright that it illuminated the topiary ducks round the fish pond. Pandora too was translucent beckoning her outdoors. Isabel always found huge comfort in her garden, especially at night and had spent many a dawn huddled in a blanket checking over a proposal. She used her garden rooms as an extension of the house, no matter what the weather. It was where she could think. She poured herself a whisky and took the bottle with her through the French windows that opened onto the terrace.

The water in the birdbath had frozen over and she coughed as the cold air hit her lungs. Carefully she picked her way along the empty herbaceous boarder with its mutilated Hebe and rosebush. A single winter jasmine curved along the brick wall behind. Isabel perched on a stone step beside a cracked, lichen-covered Pandora. She sipped her drink studying the ragged flowerbeds from this new perspective.

All at once she longed for warmth and sun and the spring and Val Negra. She longed to see the first hesitant signs of re-growth in the tightly coiled sprigs of alpine flowers. Above all she longed for the dew-drenched scent of gardenia pushing through meadow pathways. She sighed looking up at the outline of the thatched barn with its decorative birds perched on top, black against the pale sky and the moon hanging above it. This on the other hand was such an English setting Isabel thought with some affection. The country garden with its stone and flint house was far removed from the turrets of Val Negra. Isabel had spent many years longing for and then hiding from her Spanish family. She had successfully balanced, or so she thought until now, the schizophrenic legacy of mixed parentage. She had a secure, if emotionally bland life here in England built upon the solid base of a good education and her own ambition to succeed. So then, how was it that with a dream and the arrival of an unexpected proposal, that all her confidence could evaporate? Perhaps it was the moonlight playing havoc with her emotions but whatever game the gods were playing, Isabel's English pragmatism dissolved and she was whirled into the past, to the beginning, to Val Negra …

Chapter 3

Sigi
Chile
Summer 1997

On the other side of the world, in an expensive psychiatric clinic, Isabel's cousin, Sigi could not sleep either. Drug induced nightmares had given way to a restlessness she had grown to hate almost as much. In an attempt to control her own detoxification and to somehow slow the subsequent decline into madness, she had become like one of Borges's characters, condemned to eternal wakefulness. However, unlike *Funes el Memorioso*, Sigi remembered not the extensive detail of her surroundings but the intricate fabric of her past. She was haunted by her childhood to such an extent that she knew with certainty that she would never leave this place. The present no longer interested her and the future held no meaning. Sigi began to scribble every thought, every rambling memory down on paper and the act of writing became not a step towards recovery but a tool with which to dig even deeper into her history.

At first nothing happened. She imagined a rush of memory or an implosion of feeling would drive her pen. She thought that random words would be the key, that images would zoom towards the inner lens of her psyche and that the process of regeneration would begin. However, the reverse was true. With each fresh sheet of paper and with the mere mechanism of forming those words, all memory was blocked. Instead, she marked the blank paper with stab wounds and chips of pencil hearing the whispers, the Judas kiss that hung above her bed. She knew that the nurses were scornful of her ramblings, that even as they smiled they would increase her medication. Along with the pills, Sigi absorbed their contempt. The nurses treated all patients as though they could not comprehend the limitations of their illness; that Sigi more than most, no longer had the ability to feel, to formulate speech, to create. During the day, they could be forgiven for thinking this, as Sigi lay inert, staring out through the bars at the strips of sea that surrounded the hospital. But at night, breaking free from her concrete island, she soared. Skyscraper words, silent by day, crowded in on her. Voices, shouting to be heard, overpowered the dull stream of consciousness that medication endeavoured to enforce. At night, Sigi would submit to a journey forgotten by morning. It was at night that Sigi, like her cousin Isabel, could remember …

Chapter 4

Sigi
Journal

    I want more than anything to write about my grandmother's house. I want to resolve for myself and for the last time all that happened. I want to return to a time that no longer exists, to a house that was much more than a house. It was a world and a way of life that is long gone. And yet I know it to be true. It is the place that I know best and the place where we were all of us happy. It is a house that I carry in my heart, whose endless rooms I know better than this tiny cell, whose ancient walls form the unshakeable structure of my memories.

    My grandmother's house stands on the top of a steep hill overlooking the sea and the city of Barcelona. It seems incredible, that when I was a child, there were only two houses and the convent at the top of this hill, this kingdom, my grandmother's, we called 'Mialma.' Recently, several bungalows have sprouted along the root-like paths at its base. But when I was small, Mialma could only be reached by a winding track, which veered sharply from the cobble stone paths of the village below. In those days, by virtue of its remoteness, Mialma was a world of its own. As we climbed the treacherous hairpin turns, grandmother's house seemed to be the last earthly stop before heaven. Mialma rose majestically before the final peaks of the mountain, out of cloud and palm tree - an oasis of sudden, fertile land.

    Grandmother's estate was a sprawling complex of buildings. Besides the manor, there were stables, a coach house and a convent. The Moors had left an enduring mark throughout, their craftsmanship evident in the arched pillars and trickling fountains. Bulging orange trees framed casement windows and wisteria cascaded over the balconies. Bougainvillea fought an unrelenting battle with ivy, vying with it, for a ray of dappled sunshine. From the main gate, whose spearheads seemed to have been idly dipped in gold, a tree lined drive lead to an arched portal. There were immense stone flagons and gargoyles hung, expectant, from crooked alcoves. Round the corner of each secret place seemed to lurk the vision of a troubadour. And once, when he still believed in them, my brother Ricardo imagined he had seen The Three Wise Men. My brother said these *reyes magos* stopped beneath his window, struggling to balance their sumptuously wrapped gifts of toys, with that of their native frankincense.

The house itself while domed and beamed in places, was full of light. Unobtrusive colours shielded the walls from the destructive sunlight and shutters flanked the windows. Nothing competed with the other for attention, but receded into the background as though it had always been there. Despite its history, there was a freshness about the house. There was a sense of constant renewal, as though its very foundations were able to churn the soil to regenerate growth and modernity. Over the years and because my grandmother disliked Spanish oak, she had replaced many of her inherited artefacts with lighter French pieces. In my grandmother's house, the windows were always open, muslin curtains fluttered in the breeze, beckoning me in. But then, paradoxically once indoors, the scent of gardenia would propel me just as quickly outside. And outside were endless "rooms" all as gracious and restive as those internal ones. While neat lawns surrounded the house, wilder orchards tumbled towards the sea. And everywhere, the soothing sound of water spilling through marble fountains masked the beauty of indrawn tides.

My family (our parents: Nuria and Tito, the twins: Ricardo and Miguel and us girls: Marta, Beatrice and I) lived in the coach house. When my parents married, the coach house was completely dilapidated, little more than a shell, ravaged by the civil war. It had never been intended as a home but if nothing else Tito did possess vision and he set about modernizing the house with gusto. A team of builders virtually rebuilt it and what stone had survived this latter day onslaught, was polished and artificially enhanced until it was ivy clad and gleaming. For months, the tranquillity of Mialma was disrupted by the constant flow of architects, decorators and landscape gardeners who braved the laborious path up the mountain from the city below. Hushed paddocks were replaced by noisy topiary and absurd nymphs frolicked in Rococo fountains. The lemon groves were pushed back along the ancient Pilgrims walk to form an unnatural boundary. And where the vegetable garden had once been, a large fluorescent swimming pool shimmered beneath the Mediterranean sky.

And then Tito tackled what was to be the house itself. Walls were knocked down at whim, ceilings raised to gigantic proportions, and marble was spread like butter over every available surface. Local craftsmanship was eschewed for the cutting edge of Madrid. Bizarre characters with delusions of Dali-like grandeur arrived by helicopter. And for a time, as these mavericks pirouetted their wares before him, Tito allowed his forming tastes to be guided. But then he grew impatient. Within the year, the anorexic, moustachioed team of artistes was dismissed and Tito himself took command. And today it is the courtyard that survives as a spectacular and lasting tribute to our father's imagination. Here, mediaeval stone was replaced by granite and the whole area enclosed by a huge glass ceiling. To complete the impact of this intimidating entrance hall, Tito shipped in a huge sweeping staircase from his estate in Cuba. This piece de resistance was rebuilt step by marble step and at vast expense. Emerging like a phoenix, Tito's house sprawled beneath the clouds. Dark and menacing, it was a defiant monument to the Fallen. It became his Armada against the faded elegance of the manor and all it represented. And his family became a weapon in his relentless battle to gain recognition. Because, although Tito's ancestors had made a great fortune in Cuba, he could not shake the parvenu Caribbean dust, that still clung to his name.

But while Tito was free to unleash the demons of his imagination on the coach house, the 12th century convent was sacrosanct. Standing alone and even higher up the mountain than the manor, the convent and its farm were well hidden from Tito's restless eye. It was a disarmingly small building belying the wealth of original Alberti frescos that were to be found inside. Originally, it had been the chapel to the estate but since the civil war, when a number of Carmelite nuns had taken refuge there, it had evolved into a fully functioning cloister. At the head of this order was our great aunt, Sor Carmen. Sor Carmen was not only a magnificent cook but also an inspired gardener. As a result, the cloister itself was now drenched in Turkish roses and behind the cemetery, tea trees shaded gardenia from the far-reaching roots of the poplars. Rosemary and bay jostled alongside camomile and thyme in knotted herb squares. It was an intensely romantic place for an adult but when we were little and because it was generally out of bounds, we thought it spooky and mysterious.

Even so, the nuns - that silent, yet formidably efficient sisterhood - were very much part of our lives. Even though we did not see them, their influence hung over Mialma just as forcibly as the smell of their freshly baked bread did as it wafted down the mountainside. They were under no illusions as to the nature of the man they had to deal with and their sympathy lay entirely with our mother. And so they set about making her life as easy as possible. Access to the estate had always been difficult and getting supplies up to Mialma was a challenge in itself but the nuns solved most of these practical problems by providing us with virtually everything we needed. Our vegetables came from their immaculately tended kitchen garden and our dairy produce (including *mato* - a kind of curd that Tito hated) from the farm. And they had said their prayers and baked their own bread before any of us had even got out of bed!

As if displaying all the attributes of Renaissance woman were not enough, the nuns were also artistic, known throughout the country for their fine embroidery. Grandmother, tired of seeing our mother traipse into the city on shopping expeditions only to return empty handed decided to add dressmaking to the list of their accomplishments. But while embroidering the odd altar cloth was one thing, creating and designing an entire wardrobe for five growing children was quite another. It never occurred to Grandmother that this might be an unreasonable thing to ask. After all there was nothing, it would seem, that the nuns could not take in their stride. But it was soon clear that the nuns could not cope. They were painfully slow at altering or mending any of our clothes. As often as not, by the time the garment in question was returned, we would have outgrown it anyway. Their needlework was undeniably exquisite, but the boys wore sailor suits long into their teens and we wore party dresses to climb trees.

There was another drawback to this arrangement. Sor Carmen and her merry band of sisters belonged to an order of nuns called Carmelites and while these nuns hadn't exactly had their tongues cut out as Bea believed, they had non the less taken a vow of silence. This detail had not hindered the smooth delivery of farm products in the past or in any way interrupted the regular flow of baked goods that were left for collection. However, lack of proper communication with the nuns became a very real problem when it came to making our clothes. Because, not only were the nuns not heard but they were not to be seen either. They had withdrawn from the world and that meant from being in any physical contact with any other human being that was not one of their own. The nuns didn't have telephones, television or radio. In fact there was nothing (in theory) at the convent to deflect them from carrying out God's will. Nothing that is, except for our mountain of mending. Now this mending, (together with messages, letters or the regular post) was always left in the convent vestibule on an enormous turnstile. The mended clothes and answered letters were also left for collection in this way. What was not clear was how we were to be fitted for clothes if the nuns could neither see nor feel us. Grandmother had thought long and hard about this and had come up with an idea. It was decided and on the strength of some spurious looking dishcloths she had made herself, that Lupe, our failing, octogenarian nanny would cut out calico mock-ups for our clothes. These "toiles" would then be left at the convent for the nuns to convert into wonderful children's clothes. At any rate that was the plan.

Unfortunately, it was also up to Lupe to work out our measurements. Marooned high upon a nursery stool, we would wait for what seemed like a lifetime for Lupe to shuffle into the room, brandishing an enormous pair of scissors and a rusting iron measuring tape. Her arthritic hands, shaky and uncertain, would tremble all the more as she muttered to herself through a mouthful of pins. I think her measurements were always inaccurate because out of fear we would hold in our stomachs, hunch our shoulders, and lock our knees together. Then she would scuttle round us emerging triumphant to examine her handiwork- squares of muslin, virtually pinned to our skin. Everything about Lupe at that time was unreliable including her eyesight and she was more than capable of taking a chunk out of your neck should the mock-up of a collar be required as well.

But this was only phase one of the laborious process. Once the onerous task of taking our measurements was completed, plans to visit the nuns were set in motion. These "plans" changed daily due to the unpredictability of our mother's mood swings. Nuria's mood changed constantly. She could be happy during the gloomiest time of the year while a beautiful spring day, or merely being reminded that she was a mother, could set off one of her '*mala epocas*' or bad phases. Weeping, lamenting the passage of time, she would burrow into her room not to come out for days. When she finally did emerge, not a word about children or new clothes was spoken. More often as not the toiles had to be put away for a good few months by which time we would have outgrown them and the whole process of measuring and cutting had to begin all over again.

Assuming however, that both Lupe and Nuria coincided in a bout of sanity and the go ahead was given, Pepita, Grandmother's hefty Andalusian maid, was summoned. This was a sure sign that a visit would really happen and we pleaded to go too. But the decision as to which of us would accompany Pepita was entirely random. When they happened, these visits were always exciting. Furtive and infrequent, they transformed the dullest days.

Sometimes, if there was too much laundry even for Pepita, Grandmother sent along Jose. Jose was officially her driver but now that she no longer went out much, he was more of an odd job man. He would arrive still in his impeccable chauffeur's britches but with his hat tucked under his arm. These were the best visits of all. Pepita and Jose would flirt and sometimes kiss which we found both fascinating and disgusting. We would walk along the narrow, flower filled paths up to the convent. On the way back, Jose would play games with us, removing his jacket and tie and rolling up his sleeves. His pockets bulged with sweets and we would shriek with exaggerated delight at their discovery. If there was time he would tell us stories about the civil war, the *only* stories we heard as children. But he was also knowledgeable about the wildlife and the mountains. Those afternoons with him were happy but charged with a sexual tension we could know nothing of and it excluded us yet again from the adult world.

As we approached the convent gates, no matter how chatty we'd been up to that point we would fall silent, both curious and fearful at the same time. And as if by magic the gates would open and we would enter a long covered cloister. At the far end of this cloister a door led into the vestibule. Here the walls were white washed, the floors bare. A single wooden chair and the enormous turnstile were its only furniture. On the wall hung a particularly tortured looking Christ. When we were very small, this frightened us so much that we would huddle together, our heads bowed in apparent piety. Even when I was older I found it hard to look at the figure directly. Pepita immediately sank to her knees. Her eyelids appeared glued shut, her lips moved mutely. Later I realised that the time she prayed usually corresponded with how long she'd spent kissing Jose on the walk up. We knelt beside her, not daring to look up at the crucifix. Then without any warning, she would suddenly leap up so that we would all bump into each other. We would place the baskets of clothing on the table and ring the little silver hand bell that was left for that purpose. We would crowd round, peering into the darkness, waiting for someone to come out. But no one ever did and the clothes vanished and new ones replaced them on the turnstile. Miguel once said that he had heard someone cough but Pepita assured him nuns had more self-control than that. For days afterwards our imaginations ran riot, wondering what really went on in that deep well of silence behind the turnstile.

For the most part, Mialma, with its convent and farm, was self-sufficient. With brothers and sisters to play with, we didn't need other children for company and Grandmother's house, as we grew up, became an enthralling extension of our domain. There, we were allowed to run and touch and play in a way that was discouraged in our own home. We were cosseted and loved and fed, until we were quite literally sick on the steaming chocolate drinks and bilious buns that were produced from the kitchen. We had only to appear in Grandmother's drawing room for the bell to be rung, Pepita instructed and the cook to set pots brimming on the massive stoves. No matter the weather, the hour of the day, our state of health, Grandmother was of the opinion that all children needed fattening.

"During the civil war," she would say at almost any mention of the word food, perhaps in *wonder* that such a thing had ever been possible, "I lost 40 kilos."

"Yes," my brother Ricardo would mutter under his breath, "and she's been making up for it ever since!"

Grandmother would shoot him a withering look. "*Reu meu*," she would say, which meant "little king" in Catalan. "You have no idea what it's like to be hungry, I mean really hungry. No idea at all. Your poor mother was hungry all the time and there was nothing I could do to fatten her up. She was so thin! She looked like a spider – thin and long and growing thinner by the minute. Poor little mite, she was still hungry at bedtime. But she never complained. We gave her what we could, but some days there was only a roll of bread or thin parsnip soup that didn't fill you up for a minute. There was none of the *jamon serrano* that you boys seem to thrive on, or the endless rounds of brioche and cake. And certainly none of Pepita's hot chocolate or fresh orange juice! You children are all spoilt! You haven't had to want for anything."

And she would look past him at some nebulous point on the wall.

My grandmother, or Avia as we called her in Catalan, had love and patience for us children that our parents did not. As a grandparent, she understood the anxieties that consumed Nuria but was wise enough not to interfere and indulged us instead. When she accused us of being spoilt, it was half in jest. She had an idea of what life at the coach house was really like and to compensate for the lack of love we were given there, she engulfed us with affection and food and most importantly, her time. It was Avia, not our mother, who taught us girls to cook and mend and it was at her knee that we learned our catechism and Catalan history. She, like everyone of her generation, could be easily coaxed into reminiscing about the civil war. Her stories greatly appealed to us, as they were never censored like Jose's. They were also a welcome alternative to the politics that saturated conversation at home. They might not have been the most suitable subjects for young children, but they were infinitely better than our father's obsessive talk. Without television or cinema or even school to distract us, we were word perfect in Avia's civil war fables.

"You see," Grandmother would say, lowering her voice furtively, "the same people who wanted to kill your grandfather during the war and who had actually signed his death warrant, were the first to welcome him back to the government. They would send me large bunches of flowers, boxes of chocolates, truffles, even tickets to the opera. But your grandfather, Avi as you call him, made sure I returned everything. Sometimes Pepita would ask to be allowed to keep just one small box and I must say I was often tempted." Avia smiled sweetly, in a modest, self-deprecating fashion and would spread her fine, long hands by way of explanation. "But of course I did what your grandfather asked."

She did not have to add that it was all blood money, bribery for the treachery they had witnessed during the first, chaotic days of the war and atonement for the brutal way in which Avi had been treated when Franco headed the first government. Our grandfather's old world chivalry had been at odds in the new Spain and his loyalty was regarded as treason.

"And did Avi really drive in a bullet proof car?" asked my brother Miguel.

Miguel was as different from his twin as it was possible to be. While Ricardo was dark, pensive, more interested in books than girls, Miguel was blonde and garrulous. From the time he could walk, Miguel had wanted to be a soldier. Any time spent indoors was too long and now his deep blue eyes darted back and forth from the open window. While the other children were draped languidly over Avia's furniture, idly fiddling with plaited hair, or like Ricardo, flicking through the pages of a National Geographic magazine, Miguel stood poised for flight, his knee twitching with impatience. Marta stopped examining split ends to flick her hair over her shoulder. One tanned leg swung easily over the arm of a chair.

"Do tell us Avia! Please tell us again about the early days, when you first heard about the war! That's my favourite bit. I like the part when Grandfather was away and you were all alone!"

Even with the heat, Marta looked cool and immaculate. She was eight years older than me but a generation ahead terms of sophistication and worldliness. Both Beatrice and I fought for her approval. She winked at me as if to say, "Let's indulge the old girl. You *know* we've heard this all before!" But the truth was that we all enjoyed hearing it, no matter how many times it was told to us.

"Tell us, tell us, tell us" said Beatrice mantra like. She sat cross-legged on the cool marble floor, chin cupped in one plump hand, her skirt like an upside down tulip around her. Ignored most of the time, Bea as we called her was a graceful child, trusting and affectionate and young for her years. She cradled a toy animal that she had dressed in nappies and layers of clothing that I pointed out would be far too hot for our climate. The weather in her imaginary games was always cold. She pretended that we all lived in Norway or Sweden where there were few hours of daylight and she could wrap herself up in fur. Avia smiled at us approvingly. I could tell she thought us charming – the girls at any rate, grouped together as we were in our matching white dresses (a rare success in terms of Lupe's measuring.) The twins I thought looked absurd in their regulation sailor suits.

"*Verdad que lo quereis oir otra vez*? Do you really want to hear it all again? Surely you'd rather I read you a story or we played a game?"

"No! No!" we would cry enjoying this part as much as we would her story. "Please tell us. We *really* want to hear it."

"*Por favour . . . porfi . . .*" Bea began mantra like again so that I kicked her. She almost always said each word three times. It was a new and annoying habit.

"*Bueno pues . . .*"

And that was it. Avia was off. She sat bolt upright in her chair, determinedly putting away her needle, and reaching for her fan.

"*Asi es entonces*. This is what happened then. When the civil war began, your grandfather was on business in Yugoslavia. Because it was summer I had already gone to the country, to Val Negra. I had had no contact with Avi during the time that he was away and now with a war on it was difficult to get messages through. The border with France was closed and for a long time I wondered if I'd ever see him again. But of course we did see each other."

Avia hesitated. She never knew how much to tell these children, how much they would find boring and she never wanted to trivialize what had happened. She did see her husband again but what was the point of saying that it wasn't for many years, that it wasn't until the war was over? More importantly how to explain that when Ildefons reached the Spanish border he was forced to enter Spain on the Nationalist side and that this simple act would almost destroy his political life later on?

"So he walked all the way from the border didn't he?" asked Miguel, shifting his weight, hands shoved into his pockets. I could see the bulge of a hidden cigarette packet.

"Yes," agreed Avia. "He walked through the Pyrenees, hiding by day, walking all night. He was only ever safe at night."

"And did you... and did you... and..."

"Oh for Gods sake" hissed Miguel. "Speak normally!"

Bea bunched her eyes shut tight but when she spoke again it was in a remarkably fluid sentence.

"Avia, did you really have to hide your treasure in a metal box and plant it under the fig trees?" This was the only part of the story that really interested her. Grandmother smiled at her fondly.

"Our treasure?" she echoed. *"Tesoro,"* she repeated her voice edging over the word- an endearment in Spanish.

"Bebe!" teased Miguel. "Buried treasure! What on earth are you on about? What does that have to do with the war! This isn't one of your learn-to-read stories you know. Jack and Jill went up the hill to fetch . . . what? A pile of treasure?"

There was a pause and then a large tear began to roll down Bea's cheek. She buried her face in her teddy.

"You don't have to *cry!*" hissed Marta and then to Miguel she said, "You don't have to be so *mean.*"

"Well actually Beatrice is right," said Avia gently. "Do you remember? I told you once about it before."

Marta wriggled in her seat.

"I remember," she said triumphantly. "The 'treasure', was your jewellery. You put it and all your money in a box. And you buried it so that if Avi didn't come back or if the soldiers came, you'd have something left. Mother says the real reason was that you didn't want those horrible Nationalist women getting their hands on the Roble jewels."

"Well she was right," said Avia.

Miguel looked up.

"What do you mean horrible Nationalists?" he asked coldly. "Tito's a Nationalist. Or hadn't you thought about it? And what do you think Franco is, *idiota?*"

"Oh I know," replied Marta sweetly enough but I could tell she was annoyed. "You're going to say what a great leader he is, the bravest man you know - a knight in shining armour!"

"He doesn't look like any of the knights I've seen," I said under my breath finding it hard to marry the lean glamorous images I'd seen in picture books with the tubby, bald figure that sometimes came to the house.

"Well he *is* the bravest man," said Miguel, his voice high-pitched, petulant just like our father's. "He was a great soldier. He was a general at the age of 32! Are you saying you *don't* support our leader?"

"No. *Yes!*" Marta shook her head. "I *know* all about Franco. And don't call me an idiot!" She brushed an imaginary fleck of dust from her dress. She flashed him a taunting look, a smile playing on her lips. "If you're so clever, try explaining this: If Catalonia was committed to the Republic why did we end up *opposing* the Nationalists? The Republic supported autonomy after all and isn't that what we're always bleating on about? Anyway, I know we were Nationalists at the *beginning* of the war. So what happened? Why don't we support Franco now? Why did we change?"

"We didn't. We still support Franco. At any rate this family does," said Miguel.

"We don't *all*," I said.

Miguel glared at me. In our family it was only the twins or Marta who ever entered into discussion. Bea and I were considered too young to have an opinion of any kind. I blushed, wishing I'd kept my mouth shut. Predictably Miguel elbowed me in the ribs. But Bea stopped sniffling and Ricardo for once actually looked straight at me. It was Marta who realised I was being serious.

"At the beginning of the war, Catalonia gave her support in exchange for complete autonomy. Do you understand what autonomy means? It's basically what we want now. We want to be able to control our local government. We want to hold elections and most importantly to speak our own language. Anyway we *had* our autonomy and Catalonia became the stronghold of the Republic. But the *Leftist* Republicans were basically thugs and we didn't want to have anything to do with them. So even though we didn't agree with the thugs, we sided with the Nationalists. There was no choice not until later anyway. Do you see?"

Ricardo raised an eyebrow.

"*Vaya* the civil war in a nut shell," he said. "It's a shame you girls don't go to school. There's obviously a brain in there somewhere."

She stuck out her tongue at him.

"Well can you explain it any better?"

Ricardo looked from one confused face to the other. Mine in particular. He cleared his voice and began in his "older brother" tone.

"You've summed it up pretty well," he said. "Naturally our family supported the legitimately elected government. Isn't that so Avia? We were loyalists if anything. *Of course* we wanted home rule, every Catalan does, but not if it meant being Communist. We were also Catholics, so we were caught and all around us was chaos and there was no one in command. No one who was any good at any rate."

"Until Franco," said Miguel.

"Until Franco," agreed Ricardo.

"And then?" I prompted.

"And then he was a hero. He seemed to be on our side. He was all for the traditional values of family and church and as you say Miguel, he was a great soldier."

"So what's the problem?" I was more confused than ever.

"The problem is," said Ricardo, "that Franco is a fascist. We did support him but that's because anything was better than anarchy. But it soon became clear that in uniting the country, Franco was also declaring war on separatists."

"Well what else was he supposed to do?" Miguel was frowning now, an expression that transformed his benign, baby good looks into one of implacable aggression. "It was war *hermano*. You can't have it both ways. How could he champion local politics and unite the country at the same time? He saved Spain from the Communists. You said we were against them. You *said* there was chaos. Well Franco restored order."

"Yes, by executing anyone who's against him," said Ricardo grimly.

Miguel made a dismissive noise.

"He had to. Franco could hardly risk *another* war! You have to show you mean business. You have to be strong."

"But he's still killing people and not just killing – garrotting them- and the war's been over a long time."

"Oh please Ricardo, you sound so pompous."

"If I *ever* get into law, that's one thing I shall spend my life trying to change."

Miguel smiled without humour.

"What? And put an end to a national pastime. Why it's expected of us, together with bull fighting and flamenco dancing-"

"But...but...but...Catalans don't dance flamenco!" Bea piped up ingeniously. Marta kicked her.

"That's the whole point *idiota*, Miguel's trying to be sarcastic."

"Well I don't understand," said Bea. "I want.. I want.. I want.. to play outside."

Miguel watched her mouth as if he was doing his best not to stuff something in it. I had to admit the almost stutter was becoming excruciating to listen to. His blue eyes settled once more on his twin.

"I don't know why you're so ready to criticise our leader, Ricardo. We should all be thanking him. He saved Spain and … Tito's ass for one thing."

I shot Marta a look and we smothered a giggle. But this only seemed to encourage Miguel all the more.

"If Spain," he went on, "had produced more men like Franco we'd never have lost, well, Cuba for starters!"

At this Marta could no longer contain herself and she burst out laughing. I began to giggle too and then Bea who laughed on cue anyway and I could see Avia struggling not to smile.

"And Tito's family would have been even richer you mean," said Marta smiling broadly.

"Well that *is* how they made their money," replied Ricardo airily. "All that sugar cane!"

"What about Cuba?" I said wondering where on earth this was all going.

"Cuba was Spanish," said Ricardo impatiently. Then he frowned. "You must know that."

"Er . . . yes . . ."

"And that Tito's family owned a few sugar plantations?"

I shrugged.

"And that they lost a small fortune when Spain surrendered Cuba?"

Grandmother smiled.

"I do so like the use of your 'surrender'. I can see r*eu meu*, that you will make a splendid lawyer."

And *I* could see Miguel's sapphire eyes glint with resentment at his brother being called 'little king' and that he knew little more than I did about Cuba's history.

"You know nothing of military tactics," he said coldly, trying to switch the conversation back to more familiar ground.

Ricardo dismissed this becoming bored with the conversation.

"It doesn't matter though does it, what I think or whether or not Franco was a great soldier? You have only to look around you. Look at Spain now. Look at her leader, her *saviour* as you put it. Franco's a fascist and has no intention of reinstating the monarchy. We are isolated from the rest of Europe and the world and neither has the faintest idea as to what really goes on here. More importantly, Franco has banned us from speaking Catalan, from teaching it in our schools, from dancing our national dances, from using street signs in Catalan, from publishing our books and newspapers. Need I go on? He has totally suppressed our freedom of expression. He has bought the souls of the wealthy in return for their silence. Franco is completely corrupt. And as to Catalan –"

"But we're a *country!*" interrupted Miguel his face flushed and animated. "We are part of Spain. Catalonia can never ever be a separate region! You're mad if you think she can survive without Madrid. It's people like you who want to turn back the clock! Every country in Europe, including our own has spent centuries fighting for unification. The Catholic Kings brought about ours, why would we want to pull it apart? We can't have all these petty dialects and over sentimental notions of regional patriotism! That was all right two centuries ago - fine in your feudal Cuba, but not now. We've got to stop thinking ourselves in the middle ages and that's something we'll never do while dreamers like you and morons like the Basques –"

Ricardo's eyes narrowed and I could see that at last he was angry.

"So you really don't believe in Catalan autonomy do you?" he said staring at his brother.

"Do you know something," he continued and again his words were meant only for Miguel. "I feel deeply ashamed that our family ever supported the Nationalists. If I had been alive then, I would have fought with the International Brigade. Those men recognized this war for what it was. Not a single so called *Spaniard* has been able to do that!"

There was silence and then I jumped as Avia's fan snapped shut. She was very still, her violet eyes watching us intently.

"That's enough," she said firmly. "We must concentrate on thoughts that unite us, not divide us. We must never be divided as a family again."

"But –" protested Miguel.

"No, listen to me. Especially you Miguel." Avia pointed her fan in his direction. "I can see that you all have an opinion, very strong opinions in fact but don't ever romanticize this war. It was a *civil* war and that is something I hope you never live to see. It wasn't as if we were united as a country and knew our enemy. We fought against ourselves. You seem to forget this. Brothers fought against brothers, children who had grown up together were divided by their beliefs. Ricardo? Can you imagine what it was like? Families turned against each other; people you had known all your life become your enemy and there was no one you could trust."

Miguel flushed. Avia held up her fan.

"Let me finish. You boys are young men now and you too Marta are clearly old enough to understand these issues but you must know a lot more before leaping to conclusions. You must temper your passion with reason." Her voice was fierce, her eyes darting from one face to the other. "I know we talk endlessly about the war," she sighed. " But then that's because for those of us who survived, it burns still in our memory." She paused, her voice gentler now. "It was bloody," she said calmly. "No war is ever pure and a civil war is all the more terrible. At the end it's hard to remember what it was all about. Sometimes it's easier to make a decision and stick to it no matter what. Life isn't like that though. At the beginning it may have seemed one thing and by the end nothing but survival was important. You'll understand one day. If you really want to know about what happened, then read, study but I don't want my house to be the forum for these kinds of discussions." Avia smiled. "I love your youth and your spontaneity but I will not," and at this her voice became firm again, "I will not tolerate this kind of aggressive bickering. If there are differences, keep them to yourselves. And certainly to the outside world we must never appear to be anything but united. Surely you see how important this is? Please don't stop loving each other. Oh darlings, it may not seem so now but life is so short! You will grow up so quickly. You boys are already grown. You may not even live near each other when you're older. Just think of that. Don't say things you don't mean now and will only remember with regret. You only ever have each other."

She put away her fan and took up her sewing, reaching for the old tea box that housed spools of colourful Cuban cotton. I half rose to get up thinking it was time to go home.

"There is one more thing."

Miguel groaned but as Avia's eyes narrowed in his direction, I quickly sat down again. She was clearly not in a mood to tolerate fidgeting children.

Ricardo moved as far away from Miguel as it was possible, to sit on a sofa beside Marta. I knew him better than to think he wasn't still warring inside but he had our grandmother's ability to compartmentalize issues and now gave the appearance of total indifference. Miguel's face on the other hand was still pink with the exertion of mental combat. He tapped his foot staring out of the window. Beatrice was now utterly bored and lolled unattractively, her legs akimbo, sucking her thumb.

"*Sentaros. Tu tambien,*" instructed Avia and reluctantly, but obediently, Miguel eased himself onto a low oak chest.

It was growing hotter by the minute and Avia called for her maid to lower the blinds. Shadows of vertical stripes were cast along the milky marble floors, smooth beneath the ball and cluster legs of the furniture. I lay back amongst plump sofa cushions, soporific in the heat. Wonderful pastels of delicate children, flowers and nautical scenes graced the limestone wall. An oak tall boy with a huge crimson tassel, hanging from a key, sank majestically in a corner. A revolving bookcase competed in another with a love seat. It was an elegant room and yet still calming and comfortable. Sumptuous silks tickled my cheek as I swivelled to watch my grandmother. When the maid had gone, Avia set aside her sewing. She sat back in her chair, her head leaning to one side, her arms resting fluidly, as though she were about to enjoy a beautiful piece of music. So nothing prepared us for the shock of her next words.

"I should have told you this before," she said. "I was always waiting for the right moment but there's never a right moment. But I can see now that you had a right to know. Interest in the civil war and the past never stops does it? There was so much to explain that I put it off. Now I can't do that any longer."

Avia's tongue wet her lips and she passed a hand over her face as though she were washing it. It was one of the peculiar gestures she made from time to time. When her face emerged once more it seemed revitalized. We sat suddenly absolutely still without fidgeting hanging on her every word. It was so quiet you could hear the sudden velvet thud as a lemon fell from its branch.

"The fact is," continued Avia. "The fact is …" she stared at our upturned faces as if still unsure what to tell us. She swallowed. "The fact is that you have an English cousin called Isabel Pelham. English of course, in the sense that her father was English. Clara, my youngest daughter who you never met was Isabel's mother. Well the point is that Isabel's father has now also died and so she is coming to spend the summer here with us. And many more after that I hope. Isabel is an orphan but I don't ever want her to feel that she doesn't have a family." And then under her breath she added, "our very own *Espanola-Inglesa.*"

I sat up, shaken from my drowsiness. An English cousin! What on earth was going on? I didn't dare look at Marta. Miguel opened his mouth to speak but Avia's expression silenced him.

"We have decided that Isabel will continue her studies in England. For some of the shorter holidays she may well stay at her school – the English seem to have many more holidays than we do- but in the summer she will live here. I want you all to welcome her as though she were a sister, to be generous in your love, to accept her as one of our own. I know this has come as a surprise but you are young, you must learn to adapt, to take things in your stride. And please … don't ask too many questions. It is a difficult time for Isabel. Clara, her mother Clara … your aunt, she … died shortly after …" Avia stopped suddenly and we stared at her, startled by the emotion on her face. She hardly ever showed emotion, or not with regard to herself in any case. And then her face cleared as quickly as it had been overcome and resumed its inscrutable serenity.

"We are the only family left to her and Isabel has never been to Spain. She doesn't as far as I know speak our language." Avia's mouth hardened and the words were clipped. She scanned our faces. "She's your age Beatrice or perhaps a little younger. But I'm sure she will be a friend to you all."

I glanced at the twins. I could see they were thinking that this Isabel wasn't going to have anything to do with *them* if they could help it! They had absolutely no interest in some cousin they had never met. Avia's news was disappointing. They'd thought it would be a lot more dramatic. What they wanted to do now was to escape out doors for a smoke.

"Doesn't she have friends?" piped up Bea. "This English cousin? Can't she stay in England? Or does it always rain?"

Avia smiled. "I'm sure it doesn't rain all the time," she said. "But I know she'll enjoy our sun. You must all show her lots of kindness and love. Do you understand that Beatrice?" Avia's face was still. "It would make me very happy. I know you are good children and capable of great charm."

Marta flashed her most brilliant smile her beautiful eyes tawny and entrancing.

"But we've already got enough children in our family!" she said sweetly. "What shall we do with another baby?"

Beatrice frowned, uncertain. She didn't like the sound of the word Baby. A tear hung in the corner of her eye.

"Baby!" hissed Miguel so that Bea began to cry in earnest.

"She doesn't have to come with us to Val Negra does she?" insisted Marta looking at the twins for support. I thought of Val Negra as she said it, our gracious and beautiful summer home with its quiet river and surrounding Monseny Mountains. "What about our friends? Will we have to share them with her too?"

Marta smothered a giggle and Avia's mouth tightened. "Didn't you hear anything I said? I want you to make Isabel welcome. I do want you to share everything. Yes even your friends. Isabel is as much my grandchild as you are. You are of the same blood. We've been talking about families and the importance of showing a united front. Well you can try and do that now. How would you like it if you were left without a mother and father?"

The twins looked at each other, sharing the same wicked thought. Bea never had her own thoughts but she began to cry anyway.

"Oh do shut up Bea!" said Ricardo.

"Prou!" said Avia sharply in Catalan. "That's enough! I can't tell you how disappointed I am in your reaction. You haven't listened to a word I've said. Apart from showing yourselves to be unreasonably selfish, not one of you has shown the slightest trace of compassion and it makes me very sad. Still I suppose you're only children …"

Avia rang for her maid. "I think your mother will be wondering where you are. I'll see you another day when you've had time to think about what I've said."

"Come on you lot," said Ricardo taking charge. "Let's go home."

He pulled me reluctantly from the soft sofa. One by one, we said our goodbyes. Avia lifted her still silky cheek for a kiss but already she had withdrawn. When I looked back over my shoulder her hands again covered her face and she had disappeared behind them.

Chapter 5

Sigi
Journal

We followed the twins sheepishly down the corridor, aware that somehow we had done wrong. Avia was unhappy with us but we weren't sure why. Pepita ushered us down the long, marble hall into the blazing noonday sun and we soon forgot about any cousin called Isabel. Jose, on the pretext of cleaning grandmother's car, hung around the courtyard, a cigarette dangling from his mouth. Pepita's face broke into a grin when she saw him.

"Yuck!" said Marta as they kissed. "Come on we can walk home without either of those two! I don't know why mother insists Jose wait for us, he's absolutely useless!"

"Sh!" I hissed. "He'll hear you! Besides it's too hot to walk."

"Well Jose doesn't seem in much of a hurry and I'm thirsty. I want to go home now."

"So tell him."

"You tell him."

I glanced at the couple whose faces were glued together.

"Maybe you're right."

Marta clasped Bea's hand. "I'm not waiting Sigi, we're going. Besides we'll be home by the time Jose notices we've gone. Where are the twins?"

I shook my head.

"No idea."

She shrugged. "Then we'll see you later."

"I'll catch you up."

Marta prodded a drooping Beatrice and the two of them stomped off towards the main gates.

I shielded my eyes from the sun. It was blazing hot, the sky brilliant and cloudless. I crossed the cobblestone courtyard, making my way through the arches to the path that led from the convent gates. There was no sign at all of the twins although I knew they had to be near by if they'd stopped for a smoke. Crickets chirped in the dry grass and my footsteps sounded crisp among the daisies. The path narrowed. On one side a low wall prevented the fig trees from sinking down the slope. On the other, the wild meadow fell away to the sea. Walking became easier as the path evened out and in the clearing I caught sight of the twins, still some distance away, but perfectly audible. There was the unmistakable hiss of tobacco and their conspiratorial laughter. Instinctively I held back torn between not wanting to eavesdrop but unable at the same time, to show myself.

"*Joder* it's hot," said Miguel letting out a mouthful of smoke. "Do you really want to go straight home or shall we bother the nuns?" He referred to the game we used to play, when we were allowed out, where we'd ring the convent bell and then pretend there was no one there. Ricardo made a face. I hung back in the shade of the fig trees. Beneath their large leaves it was cool and I was loath to emerge into the withering heat. But the longer I stayed hidden, the more difficult it would be to move. There was an endless silence while my brothers enjoyed their cigarette and Miguel traced patterns on the sandy path with the toe of his espadrille.

"No wonder Spain had a civil war," said Ricardo lightly. "When you and I can't even agree."

Miguel looked up at him through a heavy fringe of hair, smiling guiltily.

"Yeah sorry about that. I suppose I over reacted. It's the heat. Avia's house –"

"That's all right. Funny we always end up talking civil war when we're there and rowing too."

"It's the *only* thing we ever talk about."

"Why is that? Do you think people in other countries are as obsessed with politics as we are?"

"Probably not. But then they don't have as weird a family as ours. Or live in a country that's as strange as this one," said Ricardo and I could hear the smile in his voice. "And we're *living* our politics. That's the difference.

People still haven't got over the war and as for Franco, well you have to hand it to him, he's a constant topic of conversation."

"Oh please let's not start that again!"

"You know what I mean though."

I peered at them between the branches. Both my brothers were tall, with similar physiques, and both still dressed identically. I wondered if our mother realised they were no longer boys. There was a pause.

"It's Mialma. I'm always afraid I'm going to break something. And Avia seems - oh I don't know, so *calm*. It's not for real. Not that the Coach house's any better with Tito marshalling the place like a penitentiary!"

"I'd have thought you could relate to that. But you're right, calm is something our parents are not."

"Mother is having one of her *malas* and Tito's on my case at the moment. He never leaves me alone. He's always interfering. Their lives must be sooo boring-"

"Well Mother's is!"

They laughed.

"Do you think our parents are jealous of us? It's as if they feed off our excitement."

"What excitement would that be?"

Miguel inhaled deeply then coughed.

"Mierda que fuertes son estos. Mas que los otros cigarillos. Woh … these are strong! Where did you get them? And by the way where on earth do you learn all that history stuff? I mean the actual facts- like about Cuba?"

Ricardo leant casually against a tree, shoulders hunched. I remembered some vague warning of Jose's about smoking under trees but it was not one that my brothers seemed to remember now. As he tipped back his head, I was startled by how different he suddenly seemed. It was not just the fact that he was smoking which made him appear older, but he seemed very confident of himself. It made me feel, by contrast, more of a child than ever.

"Dr. Mantua," replied Ricardo. *"Igual que tu.* Same as you."

Miguel frowned. "But you remember it."

"No. I learn it. That's the difference. You could too once in a while."

"I admit it adds a certain *gravitas* to the argument," said Miguel, imitating our old family priest and their tutor.

"I like him. I like him a lot. We're lucky Avia persuaded Tito to let us have him, especially as he is *her* friend. You know how Tito likes to produce his own people. We might have had no education at all except for what we pick up from mother. Look at the girls, they're virtually uneducated."

"Oh I wouldn't say that. Marta seemed to know a bit about the war."

Ricardo shrugged.

"She listens to Avia's stories or to Dr. Mantua. That's not an education."

"Does it matter?"

Ricardo dealt Miguel a mock punch.

"Now we *are* going to have an argument *hermano!*"

"Seriously, you don't think it matters do you?"

"Seriously I do."

Miguel kicked the ground with this toe.

"Why? It's a waste of time. Girls marry and have babies. It's their … like destiny."

Ricardo puffed at his cigarette and considered his brother thoughtfully.

"But don't you want your wife to be clever?" he said. "To be able to share your interests? To really talk?"

Miguel burst out laughing.

"Absolutely not! I don't think I want my wife to talk at all."

"Very funny."

"I'm serious."

Ricardo blew smoke rings.

"So am I. Can you do this?"

There was a pause as my brothers seemed to find it amusing to blow smoke into each other's faces.

"Not like that!" said Ricardo after a while. "Like this! Have you seen the way Jose does them? Especially when Pepita is around?"

Miguel began to splutter and Ricardo thumped him on the back. Then there was such a long silence that I wondered if my brothers had finally managed to set fire to the Seringa tree. I pushed aside the branches to get a better look. The heat seemed to be rising from the very earth. The sun high and brilliant scorched everything it touched. Only the sound of crickets broke the blockade of heat. Sweat trickled down by arm.

"God how I *long* to get out of here!" said Ricardo stubbing out his cigarette and stretching his arms. "It's stifling me. Mialma is stifling me. They treat us like babies. Why do we have to do everything with the girls anyway?" He all but spat the word. "Why can't we do things on our own?

Why do they always have to come with us? They've got Lupe to look after them. Don't the parents realize that she's practically senile anyway and that we're men now, never mind being teenagers?"

"No," replied Miguel confidently. "They're only interested in what Franco's up to. And Mother tries to keep ahead of Tito *and* Franco. It must be exhausting. No wonder she's always been … delicate."

Ricardo looked at him in admiration.

"You surprise me," he said. "I didn't think you were the intuitive kind."

Miguel was pleased. "Well cheer up," he said kindly. "It *must* be time to move on to Val Negra - it's hot enough today. There we *do* have more freedom. It's always easier when we're in the country. Everyone relaxes. Even Tito."

My legs were beginning to cramp and I was just about to come out of hiding when Miguel said, "Or is it Sonia?"

I froze. Sonia? Did he mean Sonia de Cana whose family estate bordered ours in Val Negra? The blonde, delicate beauty we were all secretly in love with? I had never heard the twins talk about girls before. Not specifically anyway. It was weird to think of my brother liking a girl. My heart began to thump. I couldn't wait to tell Marta!

Ricardo picked up a stone and Miguel and he took it in turns to see who could throw the farthest -not an easy thing to do with a cigarette grafted to your face. They stood together facing the sea and the mountains ahead, their shapes black against the sun and the olive trees beyond. Lemon groves, which marked the boundary of our land made a thin line of yellow in the distance.

"No it's not Sonia," said Ricardo. "I feel restless. I just wish we could go somewhere else for a change. I mean alone. Not necessarily the whole tribe. Oh *you* could come," he added quickly. "But every summer we go to the same house. We see the same people. We play with the children of our parents' friends as their parents did before them, a handful of families repeating the same pattern, generation after generation. And guess what? They marry each other too and have children of course, and return to Val Negra!"

"But don't you find that reassuring? To know there's continuity, that there's a place for us? I don't want to make an effort to meet new people. I like the fact that everyone knows who we are and thinks the way we do. Everyone there behaves in the same way."

Ricardo stopped abruptly and stared at his twin.

"That's exactly what I hate." He threw his last stone. "Come on we'd better be getting back."

But Miguel held his arm.

"Tell me quickly about Sonia," he said.

"There's nothing to tell," said Ricardo gruffly. "She's ok. More than ok. But that's the problem. She's the bait to keep me here. If I marry her I'll be doing all the things I told myself I never would. I won't have moved away, I won't have done anything for myself, I won't have *chosen* for myself. Even if I wanted things to be different, the force pulling me towards Val Negra and a certain way of life is so much stronger than my mere desire for change. I find it very frustrating. To be honest, I'd rather be anywhere this summer than at Val Negra."

Miguel let Ricardo's arm drop.

"I don't get it. You've got the hottest girl in the *pueblo* after you and you're wondering about *choice*! You know what Ricardo, you think too much - you're always *thinking*. You should think less and do more. More *accion* hermano! Maybe this summer you'll get a chance to."

"I know. But I don't want to get married. Not now. I want to read law. I want to have a girl friend without getting married. But that's not allowed is it? I'm too young. We're both too young. I want to live a little –" Ricardo stopped abruptly. "What did you mean when you said I'd get a chance to this summer?"

"W-ell ..." Miguel made an irritating face, one Beatrice and I knew only too well. Ricardo held him back.

"If you know something, tell me."

"Let go," he smiled sweetly.

"Tell me."

"There's nothing. I don't know. I mean not for certain. But I heard Tito on the phone the other day. He's planning the *Mili* for this summer."

Mili was slang for Spain's compulsory military service. For three months every year, boys of the twins' age group were sent to different regions in the country for training. Ricardo had never wanted to go because it would take him away from his studies. Needless to say Miguel couldn't wait. But he added pleasantly enough.

"Look you know that Tito doesn't know the first thing about the *mili*. It makes him look good, that's all - Sons of the Republic doing their bit for "*La Patria*." He can't resist having us both in uniform, showing us off to Franco. You said you wanted to get away," he added lamely.

"Yes but not like this."

And then in answer to Ricardo's hopeful expression: "No he's not going to get us off. I heard the priest say something about your studies but that's enough to persuade Tito."

Ricardo looked up.

"You enjoy all this soldiering stuff."

"Yes."

Ricardo eyed his twin suspiciously. "And we're supposed to start university in the autumn."

Miguel looked guilty.

"You mean *you* are. I can't see myself tied to a classroom. Come on it's not that bad! Early morning runs, cold showers, wet socks!"

"*Callate!*"

"Have another smoke," suggested Miguel. "Before we go in." Miguel pulled out a packet of coveted, imported, Du Mauriers from his trouser pocket.

"*Jollines!*" exclaimed Ricardo impressed. "Where did you get those?"

"Pepita's sister knows a girl who knows a guy – the usual thing – who works in the Port. He's able to get all kinds of stuff off American ships." His eyes twinkled. "Just think of how much I could make in the *mili*- I could-"

"You're screwing her." Ricardo's tone was flat. "Pepita's sister."

Miguel looked uncomfortable. Ricardo took a step closer to him and Miguel instinctively took one back.

"So what if I am?" he said his voice petulant. "Country girls are so gullible, so grateful. Have you noticed the way they call you *Conde?* Even in bed? I love that."

Miguel began to walk ahead but Ricardo jerked his arm.

"You should be ashamed of yourself!" he hissed. "You can't behave like this! And how have you managed it anyway? You've let me ramble on about wanting to get out of here when all the time – for goodness sake these girls trust us!"

Miguel smiled sweetly. "I know and it's rather touching. It does make me aware of my … responsibilities."

"Responsibilities!"

"Well, what are we supposed to do? Stay virgins till we marry?"

"Of course not! But for Christ sake not with the *chicas*! It's not fair to them. Most of them are just young girls from their *pueblos*. But you know this. If they're disgraced they can't return to their villages. I only hope that you've been careful. And what do you think Tito would do if he found out!"

"To tell you the truth that thought has only added spice to the whole thing."

"Be serious!"

"I am!" Miguel took a last drag on his cigarette before carelessly throwing it into the bush.

"Well that wasn't clever!" hissed Ricardo.

"Look keep your hair on Ricky. It's no big deal. It's just one girl! I bet you wish you could fool around with Sonia only no one can get close to that monument of ice. It's all about choice, you said so yourself. Well I'm making mine. This is what I want."

For a moment I thought they were going to hit each other and then to my relief and surprise Miguel burst out laughing.

"Have you ever thought?" he said between loud guffaws of laughter "How ridiculous we look in our sailor suits!"

Ricardo made a face.

"You especially Casanova," he said.

Ricardo hugged Miguel round the neck.

"Come on," he said. "Race you back!"

I was now very uncomfortable and as I stretched my cramped legs, I must have made a noise because he turned.

"Hello! What was that? Is there anyone there?" I held my breath.

"I can see you," said Miguel. "Come out at once!" I took a deep breath and stepped from behind the bushes.

"Oh it's you!"

"Sigi what on earth are you doing? Why didn't you go back with the others? Where *are* the others? Have you been eavesdropping again? Well have you?"

I shook my head vigorously.

Miguel moved towards me. "Because if you have–"

And then I was saved, quite literally by the convent bell striking the quarter hour.

"*Mierda!*" said Miguel. "Come on!" He jerked my arm. "Let's go!"

My brothers began to run and I pounded, panting behind them. Nettles stung my legs and sweat poured down my sides. My dress clung to my back. And then at last, in the shade of the plane trees, we came to the door of our secret garden. The door was hidden by clematis and to the undiscerning eye seemed part of the boundary wall. A key dangled from a long chain, through a grille at the top, so that the door could be unlocked from either side. Most importantly it meant that the run back from Mialma was shortened by a good ten minutes and that entry to the house went undetected. Some years ago Ricardo had found the door and soon realized that Tito knew nothing about it.

Now Miguel sank to the ground looking for the key. He pulled apart the long grass, digging in the dirt.

"Got it!" he announced triumphantly. Within seconds he had unlocked the door and pulled me behind him. Ricardo took the key and threw it clear into the bushes. Our secret garden was overgrown with wild roses and ivy smothered its brick.

"That was close," said Miguel.

I nodded in agreement staying close to Ricardo but Miguel reached behind our brother to pull me to him. "Not so fast *pequena*," he said. "I want to know why you were hiding. Were you spying on us?"

My heart began to thud. "Of course I wasn't spying!" I said indignantly. "I didn't hear anything. I Promise. I- I lost Marta and Bea. I thought I was supposed to wait for Jose. And then, and then I couldn't find anyone."

Miguel frowned unconvinced.

"So why didn't you come out right away?"

"I did," I lied.

"Look – " interrupted Ricardo but Miguel shook his head.

"Get hold of that nice chocolate – you know the Swiss stuff Tito brings back and I'll pretend this never happened. Ok?"

"Ok," I agreed reluctantly. I pulled away from him.

"All right then. But don't let me catch you hovering around us again."

I followed my brothers into the house and we in the hall. It didn't look as if we were late after all as the door to Tito's study was still closed.

"Your breath smells *hermano*," hissed Miguel. Ricardo immediately put his hand to his mouth. Miguel fished out a menthol-flavoured sweet from his pocket.

"Here have one," he said.

"You think these work?" he said.

Miguel shrugged. "They're American. Suit yourself but I've never had him smell smoke on *my* breath before."

It was wonderfully cool inside and for a moment I sank against the marble wall. I pressed the small of my back against the cold stone and flattened my palms along its ridges. As I debated whether to go up to the nursery or straight into the dining room, the study door was flung open and Tito appeared clutching his pocket watch. Our father was a short, stocky man and although bald, his face was unlined and youthful. Too fleshy to be called handsome, he had a long aquiline nose inherited from his mother and small suspicious eyes. He trusted no one but his mother and like her, had a sixth sense for sniffing out mischief in children. He was fastidious about his clothes and obsessive about personal hygiene. He hated the smell of body sweat as much as he detested women's perfume. Every morning he cleared his nostrils with eucalyptus.

"Miguel!" he beamed completely ignoring Ricardo and me. I shrank even further into the wall but I was invisible enough in my father's eyes. At the sound of Tito's voice I felt the familiar mix of excitement and fear. Miguel was the only one of his children Tito seemed to like.

"Hombre! Donde has estado?" Do you know it's almost been too quiet here this morning! Not a cackle from the hag in the clock tower either. Come in my boy, come in."

Tito thumped Miguel heartily on the back and made as if to draw him into his study but Miguel in loyalty to his twin, if not to me, held back. Tito's mouth, which was pulled into a huge smile over tiny teeth, fell instantly into place.

"Que! You don't want to come in? You have something else to do? It's lunchtime soon. *Y hay noticias!"*

"So that's why you're all excited," said Miguel in the bored, insolent tone he reserved for Tito and babies although Tito didn't seem to mind. Tito admired Miguel's spunk. Miguel was the only one of his children who dared answer back, who even spoke to him. But then he was the only one who was at all like him. Tito clapped his hands together.

"I've got something that will cheer you up! A young man like you needs a cigarette. Come, *hijo mio."*

"A cigarette?" Miguel said feigning exaggerated surprise.

"Toma!" Tito turned and went back into his study leaving the door open. He unlocked the door of his bureau and took out a large carton of contraband Du Maurier cigarettes. He tossed my brother a packet and Miguel caught it easily with one hand. Ricardo and I looked at each other.

"News like mine deserves a smoke, even before lunch. Come I'll join you."

For a moment their heads were bent together over the single flame. Already Miguel was a head taller than our Father, with powerful shoulders.

His neck muscles flexed. From the back, he was clearly no child even if he was wearing a sailor suit. Tito blew out the match.

"What's happened then Father?" asked Miguel. Tito's eyes narrowed as he inhaled and then blew out a steady line of smoke that wafted towards us. Again I was compelled to listen, even as I longed to turn away.

"Franco's just 'phoned!"

"And?" Miguel's eyes were wide disrespectful.

Tito ignored his tone in his eagerness to share his news.

"Grimau was executed this morning! Franco wasted no time in this instance. He's a strong man but he must not hesitate to rid the country of its enemies. I'm afraid the ugly face of communism is rearing its ugly little head again and that Grimau fellow was one of them. *Viva!*"

Tito made the fascist salute. Miguel answered by an upwards flicking of cigarette ash. I smothered a giggle. Ricardo was not so easily amused. He sucked in his breath sharply.

"What are they talking about? Who's Grimau?" I whispered.

"Just a man, a poor peasant," said Ricardo sadly. "You wouldn't understand. I doubt Miguel does. I wonder why Tito's even bothering to tell him. Poor Grimau, he was no hero but he *was* courageous. He was prepared to die for what he believed."

"*Si, pero quien era?*"

Ricardo glanced at me absorbed in his own thoughts and I had to repeat my question a couple of times before he answered.

"Have you heard anything about the miners' strike?" he replied at last. "Maybe Lupe has family there?"

I shook my head. Ricardo leant against the wall beside me folding his arms.

"Look it's complicated but the thing is that strikes are illegal in this country," he explained. "Franco won't have anyone criticizing his government. Anyway this Grimau was a miner and like many of the miners here he had to work in truly awful conditions. So he complained which of course Franco didn't like. He also just happened to be a Communist. So he was killed. The point is Sigi, that everyone has a right to complain, to say what they really think."

What I really thought was very simple. I'd had enough of my gloomy brothers and their boring boring talk. As Tito propelled Miguel into his study I breathed a sigh of relief. Never had the nursery seemed so appealing. I turned to go but Ricardo seemed so depressed that I hesitated. I racked my mind for something amusing to tell him and then I remembered Avia's news.

"What do you think about Isabel coming for the summer?" I asked brightly.

Ricardo frowned. "Isabel? Oh, you mean the Spanish-English girl? Christ what do I care?"

I bit my lip.

"I just thought - I don't know a new face – I thought …"

Ricardo looked at me as if I were retarded. "I'm going for a swim," he snorted. "This house and everything in it makes me sick."

He turned on his heel and ran up the wide, marble steps, taking them two at a time.

Bewildered, I watched him go. Much later I understood how Tito's indifference had affected Ricardo. In many ways our father was still a child himself, exuberant one moment, downcast the next, with little control over the gamut of his emotions. He was delighted by his own fantasies and bored by other people's. His children were tolerated only if they amused him, which mostly they did not. He was obsessed with politics and passionate about Franco. Tito was governed by eclectic delusions that changed daily. We in turn, were innocent, fragile souls upon whom he attempted to stamp his own vibrant personality. The artistic held no place on his stark, abstract palette. He had seen what weakness could do to a nation and so he did everything he could to eradicate it from his own family. Those of us who survived, grew up to be disparate, lonely beings and the schizophrenic face of Spain was mirrored in us all.

I stood alone in the great marble hall, listening to the gentle drone of voices coming from the study. Only Miguel had ever been invited into Tito's sanctuary. Not even our mother was allowed in. I was confused by Tito's behaviour. He disapproved of smoking and would have severely punished any one of us had we been caught. And yet I had just seen him offer my brother a smoke and have one himself! And not any old tobacco either but the coveted, contraband Du Maurier which was the same brand Miguel had offered Ricardo earlier. Had Miguel even got his supply from Pepita's sister? Or had he made the whole thing up to tease Ricardo? Tito and Miguel were always playing games with the rest of us. They excelled at playing one sibling against the other, pretending to favour one, while secretly indulging the other. But Miguel continued to be Tito's darling. I don't remember Miguel ever being punished for anything. In front of adults, Miguel was always charming and could slither out of most situations. And in the end, it was always someone else who took the blame.

Somewhere above me a door slammed. I looked up at the immense cupola that had been painted with gruesome scenes from the lives of the saints. Tito had been particularly pleased with that of St.Sebastian and the detail of the hundreds of arrows imbedded in his body. Blood seeped from horrible wounds and his guts spilled onto his belly. A fierce vulture hovered larger than life, with tiny beady eyes and you could almost hear the sound of thunder from the gathering storm clouds. As a result, these monstrous murals quite diminished the beauty of the Cuban staircase. Instead of an edifying climb, it was a sinister journey to the top floor rooms. When we were very small, we screamed so much at bedtime as we were carried higher and higher towards these swirling grimacing contortions that the nursery had to be moved to the clock tower and only our parents' bedrooms and the guest apartments were housed in this wing. The rest of the house was equally cheerless. The hall in which I stood, opened onto a vast dining room hung with oversize paintings, all depicting biblical scenes. There was no place here for a floral study or tranquil landscape. No charming portrait soothed nor welcomed the viewer. Instead, he was invited to contemplate the expiation that awaited him in purgatory. A massive dining table was moored to the centre of the room. It would have been better suited to a boardroom but then everything in the house was too big, and the result was an uncomfortable marriage of Spanish bodega to American Country club.

There were few photographs of the family and remembering Avia's conversation, I searched for images of Clara, the aunt we had never known. There was a single wedding portrait of my parents looking as if they already anticipated an antagonistic union. Beside it, the twins smiled wanly at their First Communion day - wanly no doubt as they had been forced to wear white gloves with which to hold their bible and a lily. But there was nothing else. No fuzzy, aged picture of a fat baby that might have been our cousin Isabel, no anonymous sister alongside our mother. As I searched for the aunt I would never meet, the housemaids entered through the swinging doors, to lay the table. At mealtimes, they changed into black dresses, white aprons and gloves. They went about their chores swiftly, coming together to shake the billowing cloths high in the air before smoothing them onto the table. There were always four maids at meal times, one for each corner of the room. While we ate, they stood to attention, alert to the slightest change in Tito's expression. Lupe, who had been Tito's nanny when he was a boy, hovered in the kitchen scrutinizing the dishes that passed before her. She was deeply suspicious of anyone who cooked for her precious boy. She still thought of him as a child. Like Miguel, Lupe was not afraid of him and did not hesitate to speak her mind. If there was something Nuria wanted badly enough, she always got Lupe to prime Tito first.

Now Lupe's arrival signalled that lunch was about to be served. As the clock struck 3.30, Tito emerged from his study, wringing his hands. No one was ever late. The children slid into their places waiting for Tito to say grace. Nuria was the last to sit down, easing her slim frame onto her velvet chair. Tito's voice echoed in the large room and after he had crossed himself he added the words: *"Viva El Caudillo."*

Mother's eyes blazed but she held her tongue.

"So what do we have today?" he asked Nuria. I could see that even before she had time to reply, she had already displeased him. His eyes swept over her drawn face, the violet shadows across her cheek.

"Arroz a la Cubana," she replied unenthusiastically. "Rice and then steak."

Asking what was on the menu had become a joke. We always had steak for lunch. It never varied. For the first course there was either pasta or this Cuban dish that Nuria loathed. Tito of course loved it and expected us all to do the same. He smiled.

"Excellent my dear. You must have known that today is cause for celebration."

Nuria frowned, a pulse beating at her temple. The vein stood proud against the dark hair. She fingered the cutlery nervously, her hands as white as the cloth.

"I know it's Saturday. We always have this . . . on Saturdays." Her eyes darted backwards and forwards, trying to register if there was cause for alarm. His words seemed innocent enough. We ate slowly, alert to any sudden change in the temperature bubble that surrounded our parents. "No other reason," she said slowly. "Should there be?"

Tito waited until the maids had served the platters of rice on which nestled fried eggs and small platane bananas. Freshly made tomato coulis was served with this dish and woe betide any child who spoiled the table cloth with a speck of red. It was a trial to the youngest of the children and concentration alone, guaranteed total silence. The clock ticked and I held my breath. Nuria's apparent reserve was not indicative of her true nature. In reality, she was defiant and rebellious. She was spirited, quick tempered and rarely knew when to hold her tongue. As two bright patches of red appeared on her cheekbones, I could see with misgiving that she was spoiling for a fight. She looked very beautiful with her black hair in its elegant chignon, enormous pearls at her throat and ears. I willed Tito into thinking the same. There was a moment's silence while Tito swallowed a mouthful of food. He set down his fork, the prongs facing upwards.

"I thought everyone knew by now," he said enunciating every word.

Nuria rested her elbows carefully on the table, clasping her hands in a deceptively casual way.

"Knew what?" she said glacially.

Tito's nostrils flared. He sat ramrod straight, his eyes never once leaving our mother's face. And all the while the colour came and went so that we watched her transfixed. There was a pregnant pause. He snapped his fingers.

"Don Luis."

A maid, in this case Pepita's sister, appeared at his elbow, arms behind her back.

"Bring wine," he commanded. "We shall have a toast. My wife appears to be even more dim than usual today. Bring a good *tinto* -a Domecq or Osborne. Ask Lupe if you're not sure. But do not make a mistake. And be careful on the cellar steps. I almost slipped on them myself the other day."

Our mother's eyes flashed.

"How dare you!" she hissed as the maid disappeared through the swinging door. "How dare you speak to me like that in front of the servants!"

Tito smiled pleasantly. "I can speak to you any way I chose," he said. "Stop eating."

We obeyed him instantly.

"Don't!" said Nuria. Again obedient, we picked up our forks. It might have seemed farcical if we weren't all too aware of Tito's violent mood swings.

"I wish to propose a toast," my father said reasonably enough. But Nuria's blood was up and she would not give in. For a moment our parents glowered at each other.

"Very well." Nuria pushed away her plate and sat back dramatically in her chair. "Play your little games if you must. I'm listening."

Pepita's sister appeared with a bottle of wine, still dusty from the cellar and Tito uncorked it, slowly twisting and polishing the bottle. I longed to finish my food but didn't dare annoy Tito. His plate was empty but we had only just managed a tiny bit before he had told us to stop eating. I wished somehow I could devour the food without lifting my fork. But Tito was intent on enjoying the wine. He poured himself, Nuria and Miguel a glass, ignoring Ricardo and Marta.

"Now drink!" he commanded. Nuria lifted her glass and sipped greedily in a deliberately provocative way. But she spluttered when she heard the rest of Tito's toast.

"To Franco," he said. "Death to all traitors. And may Grimau rot in hell!"

"You can't be serious." Her eyes were enormous in her pale face. Troubled and full of pain she drew us all in with her. I held my breath, no longer hungry but very frightened. But then, instead of bursting into tears, she began to laugh. She laughed so much that tears streamed down her face until she sank back exhausted. I didn't know what to do. Were we supposed to join in? From Tito's thunderous expression, I supposed not. And then, just as I thought the whole giggling episode would begin again, she sighed deeply and took another sip of wine. She wiped her face delicately with her napkin and once more composed, ran the tip of her tongue around her lips. Father's eyes followed her mouth, the line of her throat and all the time they grew darker and smaller until they looked like two hard little coffee beans.

"I weep for Grimau!" said Nuria dramatically. "Poor man! His only crime was to defy the authorities, to stand up for what he believed! He wanted to make a difference, he *has* made a difference! He will be remembered for his courage. I've heard about the way men like him are treated. Dr. Mantua says they work all night in those mines. The conditions are intolerable. They are treated like animals. He could bear it for himself but not for his sons. They say one of them was executed before him, that he was made to watch. What kind of leader does that?" Nuria reached for the wine. Delicately she poured herself another glass ignoring the maid who moved to serve her. "And he wasn't given a fair trial," she continued. "That court marshal was a travesty of justice. Do you think the outside world won't condemn it? You'll see. News *will* leak out somehow or other. One day the world will know what goes on here. The courage of men like Grimau cannot be quashed. Franco can't keep his iron fist around us forever. I could weep for Grimau," she took another swig of wine tossing back her head so that the pearls at her ears shook. "If only the sight of you wasn't so hilarious!" And with that, to my horror, she collapsed into more giggles.

Appalled, we stared at our plates watching as the fried eggs on top of the sticky rice, congealed and grew cold. There was absolute silence, the four maids stood like statues in their corner. I hardly dared breathe. And then our mother spoke rapidly in Catalan so that the Spanish servants would not understand.

"I shall never drink to Franco's health while there's breath in my body," she said. "Not at your table, not ever! *Visca Catalonia!*"

My knees began to tremble and I clenched my hands together in my lap. I couldn't look at the others. Tito punched the table spilling water and wine onto the cloth. The red stain spread rapidly, gobbling up fibres of Cuban linen.

"Now see what you've done! You ungrateful witch!" He beckoned to Pepita's sister.

"Change the table cloth and clear the plates. We shall go on to the second course."

This was even more appalling.

"*Pero Papa,*" whined Beatrice. "*Tengo hambre, mucha hambre.* I'm starving! I'm really hungry! Hungry, hungry, hungry."

Tito considered his youngest child as if she were insane. His lips spread over his teeth in the facial tic his mother must have told him once would pass for a smile.

"Then you shall have steak. You must learn patience Beatrice, even a sub human like you must learn characteristics you can never hope to have naturally... Patience is always a virtue in women, together with their silence. It is not good to expect things, to assume they will happen, in this way you will never be disappointed. The rice is cold anyway." He held up his hand and the maids began to clear away our lunch. "This dish is only ever good when it's really hot. It is spoilt. You have to be Cuban to understand about cooking rice." He gulped his wine. "I shall celebrate." He looked at Nuria. "Don't ever speak to me again in Catalan. It's a peasant language."

"Well you should know." Nuria retorted. Tito flushed.

"Ah, of course. We're back to the age-old topic of your precious nobility. Well let me tell you Nuria, I don't care this much" and he slammed his fist on the table. "For your so called blue blood! It has become the most boring thing in my life– hearing about *it* and Mialma. Have you thought about *who* you might be without it? What exactly do you do anyway except waft about the place like a ghost? You are defined by Mialma! Your tiny mind is contained within its sinking walls! And you think you're so aristocratic, so much better than the rest of us! Well look around you, *mujer! Look* at the weak, spineless, snivelling offspring that you have produced. It might be blue but it's *your* sickly blood that runs in their veins not mine! They're all neurotic, useless people. Are they something to be proud of?"

I cast a furtive look at my siblings' shocked faces. "I take your silence to be an admission of guilt."

Nuria's head shot up. Her eyes were ebony chips in her ashen face.

"Thank God it *is* my blood and not yours that runs in their bodies. I'm glad they've inherited my looks – " her gaze lingered on Tito's wet lips and fleshy face, "not yours."

*

And so it went on, the squabbles and the fights, until at mealtimes we learned to block out conversation and to think only of the food, provided we got it, that passed through our lips. Lunch brought the family together alright but it was the battlefield of our childhood. It was ugly and cruel and later I would cry silently in the bathroom until I heard mother's bedroom door slam shut and it was time to go out to play.

Mealtimes at our grandmother's house could not have been more different. To begin with, I don't believe a dish had ever appeared twice at her table. Tito thought her obsession with food typically precious, indicative of her class. His gaze would linger on her plump face for rather longer than was polite. He would then raise his eyebrows in mother's direction as if to say, "You see what I mean? See how fat she is! That's what too much rich food does to a person. It's not healthy."

"It's because of the war. You know that!" Nuria would retort. "They never had enough to eat. She can't help herself."

Avia loved food, they all loved food in her family and an aunt of hers had published a collection of family recipes. It was called *Tia Victoria's Spanish Cookbook.* To the family's surprise this book became the cornerstone of Spanish cooking. Avia herself referred to it religiously. Brought up on a diet of either pasta or the infamous *Arroz a la Cubana*, Avia's lunches were a mouth-watering banquet. We tasted dishes we never knew existed: Mediterranean Merou, Hake Croquettes, *Pigeons a la Espanola*, Quick Rabbit and Chicken Soufflé. And the puddings were something else entirely: Gypsy's Arm, Spanish rings, Marzipan and Rum *Torrijas*. Tito did not allow dessert at home and when we were small we looked forward to lunch at Avia's purely for the sweets.

Tia Victoria's Spanish Cookbook was another thorn in Tito's side, for as our mother never failed to remind him, her family might be aristocratic but when the need arouse, it was not afraid of making money. Tito had been scathing: "You can hardly call cooking work!"

He was forced to eat his words when he saw how well the book did.

Conversation at Avia's table was fun and stimulating and we were all encouraged to contribute. Afterwards while Grandfather snoozed, Avia would play games with us or tell us stories. She wanted to know everything. She was interested in and remembered the names of our friends, what books we were reading, our likes and dislikes. She listened intently when we poured out our troubles to her.

On Sundays, the Carmelite chapel was open to the public and villagers or peasants working the nearby fields would walk up the mountainside to hear mass. Afterwards, we had lunch at Avia's and even Tito was forced to behave himself. He never stayed for coffee leaving just before the last course on some pretext or other. My mother would wave goodbye to him cheerfully enough, a gesture, she believed, convinced Avia that her marriage was a happy one. Sundays were happy days. We had our mother and grandmother to ourselves and we would chat or sing songs if Miguel could be persuaded to play the guitar.

Around seven in the evening Avia would say, "Let's have tea as they do in England," and Pepita would bring in the tea tray, Earl Grey that had been sent from Harrods and a proper earthenware pot. There would be an almond sponge cake, lady's fingers, Spanish cream buns and apricot doughnuts and a mere two hours after finishing lunch, we would begin eating all over again. I remember the teacups especially. They were tulip pink limoges edged with gold. Only when the cup was empty could the tiny pimpernel be seen on the bottom. There would be much laughter and gossiping. Nuria and Avia seemed able to talk endlessly about clothes, dressmakers and the ghastly arrival of a new phenomenon called *Pret a porter* and of course food. Although unfortunately, Nuria never had the opportunity of preparing the recipes that Avia carefully copied from her cookbook and which Nuria took home with her, promising to tell her mother how Tito had enjoyed them.

Tea over, we gathered in the drawing room to say the rosary, the twins muttering under their breath that they would rather go straight home. Then we would line up in single file, to kiss Avia goodnight. The twins were out of doors in a flash hoping to smoke a cigarette. But the pink light from the oriental lamps and the soft breeze as it moved through muslin curtains, made me reluctant to leave. I loved the stone flag floor with its Persian rugs, the rose wood table in the centre and the huge vase of flowers that scented the air and welcomed you in. And on the wall directly in front, hung my favourite picture. It was of a young girl dressed in mint green, her straw hat tied with a wide pink bow. One hand twirled a parasol, while the other grasped her skirt as she stood at the harbour's edge. Behind her, the sea and sky blended together in different shades of blue. Waves lapped against the jetty. Sails and streamers flapped in an imagined breeze and seagulls hovered on the horizon. I could have stood in front of that picture all night but eventually I was called out into the still evening where the lights of Mialma behind me, illuminated the Barcelona skyline.

Chapter 6

Sigi
Journal

All Sundays were movable feasts of my childhood but the Sunday that Isabel came to stay was the greatest feast day of all. The morning had been a rush from the very beginning. The intolerable heat was beginning to affect my parents who needed little to ignite their short fuses. Tito was a bubbling, boiling raging bull irate because Grimaus' execution ("the little communist") had not been the expected political coup. News, as my mother predicted had indeed leaked to the foreign press and the result was a flood of unprecedented international condemnation. The phone had not stopped ringing all night. Nuria was tired and irritable and every time she came within inches of my father she could not help snapping: "I told you so."

Tito stormed and shouted, alternating between summoning his children to him and sending us away. The nursery was in uproar. Lupe was in no better spirits than our parents. On the pretext of sweeping the nursery, she crawled up and down the stairs like a scorpion, her broom an extended stinging tail. She swiped at us if we came too close, muttering unintelligible, cross words. Marta and Bea were already changing in the bedroom and my blue linen dress was carefully laid out on the bed, together with matching hair ribbon and soft kid pumps. The Carmelite nuns had been responsible for these exquisite concoctions. As beautiful as they were, to behold, they were hideously itchy to wear, especially when it was hot.

"No, No, NO!" I protested *"No me lo pondré!* I don't care what Tito says. I hate this dress and I hate wearing the same clothes as Marta and Bea!"

Lupe covered the ground between us, her extended tail banging into the furniture. "All the same, you *will* wear this, *condesa,"* she said through

67

gaping gums. Wisps of hair I noticed for the first time, stuck out all over her chin. I was momentarily distracted.

"Your father wants you to look pretty. Just in case Franco turns up."

"*Y Que?*" I said rudely. "So what! Mother doesn't even like Franco and I've heard Avia say that she's mortified that the man is even associated with our family. Besides Mother doesn't mind what we wear. It's too hot to mind about anything much."

"You know that's not true! Your mother does mind and she likes to see you nicely dressed. Now please do as you're told and stop this nonsense. You've become very cheeky recently. You're all spoiled, the lot of you. When your father was a small boy children were different. Your mother spoils you. *His* mother was a lot stricter - *Abuelita* would know how to handle you. Not one of you takes after your father, more's the pity."

"So everyone keeps telling us."

"I won't stand for your cheekiness."

Lupe moved towards me, extended tail erect.

"*He dicho que no,*" I said stubbornly. "I said no! That dress itches. It sticks out too much."

I was already taller than this diminutive woman but I began to tremble at her expression. For a moment we glared at each other before she struck me.

"Ow! That hurt. I still won't wear it." Marta and Bea who were already dressed in their blue linen frocks and sat on the end of the bed swinging their legs, smiled. Encouraged I lifted my chin.

"I don't see why I can't wear another dress. We don't always have to be the same."

But Lupe was adamant. "*Pues hoy, si.* Today you do."

I rubbed my arm. "Well I might get dressed," I said slyly. "If ... you tell us about Clara, as in *Tia* Clara, our mother's sister, as in The Aunt No One Ever Talks About - Isabel's mother? You must know something, you must remember something - you've lived here long enough."

Lupe was as surprised as if she had been a real scorpion that I was about to crush. Slowly she lowered the suspended broom. She was absolutely still, her knotted fingers gripping the stick until I thought it would snap. And then she raised her head from hunched shoulders.

"You wear the dress regardless," she said. "And the ribbon and the shoes." She seemed suddenly deflated. So much so that she sat down abruptly on the edge of the bed. Bea and Marta wriggled away from her. But she wasn't deflated for long. "Why do you want to know about Clara?

Who's told you about her? Why now? Who's been talking? Tell me." She fired questions one after the other.

I shrugged. Lupe moved to get up.

"Avia. Avia told us. Because of Isabel, I suppose, the cousin who arrives today. Her father has died and she has no one else. She's an orphan." I pronounced this new word carefully. I'd never met anyone who didn't have lots of brothers and sisters, not to mention parents.

"So," said Lupe softly. "The Senor Pelham is dead. What a doomed thing their love was."

My sisters and I looked at each other. "Who's Senor Pelham?" I asked.

Lupe sighed and put her hands over her face as if she were washing it in the same way our grandmother did. Maybe it was the sign of a secret society! When she looked up she looked tired, less like an old witch and more like the little old woman she really was.

"Senor Pelham," she said quietly, "was Clara's husband. He was here in Spain during the war. He came to fight our cause. He came all the way from England and he stayed till the very end, or almost the end. What a handsome man he was! He had yellow hair, like straw and deep, grey eyes that reminded your grandmother, so she said, of English rain. Your grandmother hid him at Val Negra. For some weeks he came and went as though it were his own home. And then he left and never came back. Only he was not alone, Clara was with him."

"What!" I exclaimed.

"And she's poor," said Bea, her eyes huge. "All orphans are poor."

"They're not talking about Isabel, silly," said Marta. "But about Clara, her mother."

"Well I don't understand," said Bea beginning to whimper.

"It doesn't matter Bea," I said impatiently. "Tell us more Lupe. What else do you remember?"

But the spell was broken, Lupe's mood interrupted. She moved from the bed.

"Nothing else. There's nothing more. You get dressed now. No more mischief. I shouldn't have to put up with this sort of thing. Not at my age."

"But what was she like? This Clara? Surely you can tell us that! Was she ugly? Did she annoy you the way we do? Did she walk with a limp? Why aren't there any pictures of her?"

Beatrice giggled. "Maybe she had a wart on the end of her nose like Pepita does."

Lupe snorted.

"She most certainly did not! Clara was a perfect, beautiful creature. If you've never seen a photograph of her it's because your grandmother couldn't bear it. She was grief stricken when she left. For a time, we thought she would lose her mind. Grief can do that, you know, make you mad. But your grandmother is a strong woman."

"But what was she as a person? What was Clara like?"

Lupe wiped her eyes.

"Clara? Clara just … was … She's almost impossible to describe. She was so … different from the rest of you - gentle for one thing and graceful. Above all I remember her patience. She was never in a hurry, or hurried. She just made everything somehow brighter. Everyone loved her. But the one that SHE loved more than anything was to dance. Especially Flamenco, which was strange because it was not popular at the time. She said your Catalan dances didn't have the passion that Flamenco does. She would practise in the ballroom at Val Negra. I remember her sliding and stamping down the marble floors, hair flying, quite wild. I think she made most of the steps up herself but it didn't matter because she carried it off so well. And then she met the Englishman. Dr. Mantua brought him to Val Negra. It was during the war and they hid him, the priest and your grandmother. Clara fell in love with him and they ran away together. After that I didn't hear anything more for some time. All I knew was that many years later, when she was no longer young, she had a child and died."

"Because she was old?" asked Bea.

"Because she was having a baby silly" I said wisely.

"And Isabel?" Marta asked.

Lupe frowned.

"I know nothing about Isabel. I did not know the sex of the child nor whether or not it had lived."

"But don't you think that's strange? That no one talks about her? About either of them?"

Lupe shrugged, stooping to pick up a discarded piece of clothing and smooth the bedclothes.

"It's not my place to ask questions, *condesa*. It's not yours either. Now, *el vestido por favor, ves que mona estas con el azul.* Now the dress if you please. You'll see how pretty you look in blue."

*

We walked slowly up the path to the convent. The skirts of my stiffly starched dress chafed my thighs. I walked like the farm workers from Val Negra, lumbering from side to side. I was incredibly uncomfortable, sweat trickled under my arms and my hair clung to the back of my neck. Marta, skipping on ahead, was a vision of loveliness, seemingly oblivious of the heat. Above the stone wall of the lower garden, the oranges hung like abacus beads against the brilliant sky. As the church bell tolled, we crossed the courtyard to the Carmelite chapel. The twins were nowhere to be seen. We stood in a row waiting for our parents, withering in the heat. Finally, Tito's car appeared and Nuria got out, bending to protect her head which was covered by a mantilla and a huge Spanish comb. She was dressed entirely in black, the austerity of her dress relieved by what appeared to be her entire jewellery collection. Spikes of sunlight ignited the diamonds at her hands and throat, so that she glittered in front of us. She seemed especially tall that day in her high heels. A full-length lace veil cascaded down her back. In one hand she held a rosary made of precious stones. She looked every bit as terrifying as a Cervantine knight setting out to joust.

"Where are the twins?" Her voice was alarmingly shrill.

Not one of us dared speak. She scrutinised our clothes and hair. Her tongue clicked in annoyance.

"Well it can't be helped. In you go and no fidgeting! Not because of Franco, you understand. I couldn't care less. But there may be press. I don't want any gossip getting back to me about the way my children behave in church. *Esta claro? Beatrice?* Is that clear?"

"*Si, si, si,*" said Bea three times, so that even our mother wanted to pinch her.

"Well in you go then. And remember. I have eyes in the back of my head. So does Avia. We see everything."

So does that scorpion, I thought to myself watching a small red creature scuttle under our mother's shoe but we nodded, sobered by Nuria's electric mood and bumping into each other in our eagerness to escape her. The church was deliciously cool, fragrant with the scent of gardenias. Behind a large screen sat the Carmelite nuns, who on Sundays emerged from the seclusion of the convent, to hear mass. It was a tiny chapel crowded with local villagers who carried baskets of bread or pastries that they would take home for their Sunday lunch. Our parents liked to sit in the front row where they could be admired. A handsome couple, people would say, with five lovely children. Marta and I would enjoy the whispers as we walked down the aisle knowing that the women were commenting on Mother's jewels. In Spain, it didn't matter what you did, what kind of person you were, as long as you looked good. The most hardened criminal could be forgiven provided he was *guapo*. Normally the steady buzz of chatter was only be silenced by the priest's arrival. But on this occasion the Spanish women were strangely quiet. There was no rustling as mantillaed heads strained to catch sight of our mother. Only the click of fans as they opened and shut, dissected the silence.

At last, heads pivoted as Tito appeared in the archway, his face expressionless. And beside him was the infamous man himself, our *Caudillo*, Generalisimo Francisco Franco, the tubby little man whose head appeared on our coins and about whom my parents and the rest of Spain fought constantly. I was disappointed. I didn't know what I expected but it wasn't someone who looked … well, so ordinary. I suppose the problem was that there didn't seem to be anything in the least *extra* ordinary about him. Or frightening which was strange given that he was the most feared man in the country. For one thing he was just as bald as our father, for another he was even shorter. He was dressed all in white with an enormous blue sash that flapped about his fat belly as he moved. They made a comical pair as they lumbered up the aisle together (Franco holding his sash away from his groin) and our mother who was much taller than either of them, hovering like the angel of death (her mantilla a billowing black cloud) above them. The fans stopped clicking in unison. A hostile expectancy greeted the newcomer as Tito pushed his way to the front. The priest appeared on the altar. I held my breath.

"In the name of the Father, the Son and the Holy Ghost," said Dr.Mantua. "May the grace of our Lord Jesus Christ and love of God and the fellowship of the Holy Spirit be with you all."

"*Y Cum spiritu tui.*"

I breathed out slowly. I had half hoped that Dr. Mantua would refuse to say mass, take out a gun or at best hit Franco over the head with his bible. Dr. Mantua made no secret of the fact that he loathed our leader but today he did none of those things. If anything he seemed even more controlled than usual. There wasn't the slightest flicker of emotion on his face. I crossed myself and sat down to listen to the first reading.

While our father read, enunciating every word as though the congregation was deaf, I studied the seated form of our priest. Dr. Mantua, a Jesuit priest and Monsignor no less, was known by his medical title. During the war, he had helped many hundreds of men to cross to the other side. "Ask for the Doctor," was what these men seeking help were told and somehow that title had stuck. He was also, rather grandly, known to be Avia's confessor, not that we paid much attention to that claim to fame. What we *were* impressed with was the fact that he knew karate and had more than once had occasion to stand up for himself when an unsuspecting mugger had tried to rob him. (The mugger had come off rather worse.) He, above all men, we knew to be extraordinary. It seemed there was nothing that he could not do or had not done or if he didn't, would soon learn to. He played the piano, fenced, rode and had degrees from the most prestigious universities in Europe. He had studied at Oxford and the Sorbonne before deciding on a career in medicine. He was a voracious reader in more than one language. Best of all he was a magician, the man who could make everything better. In our family, if there was a crisis, medical or spiritual, you called Dr. Mantua.

His head was bowed in contemplation, his hands absolutely still in his lap. I wondered if he had ever fidgeted in his life. But then he didn't look the type. He was the most dignified man I have ever met. When I was little there was not much that I did understand about him. We children were not aware, for example that he had been tortured during the civil war. For us girls he was merely the priest who came with us every summer to Val Negra. And so we set about systematically ruining his holiday. We put frogs in his bed, sewed up the sleeves of his cassock, coloured on his beautiful books. Only once, did I realize that we might have gone too far. Beatrice had drawn a moustache and glasses on the shiny pictures in a book that had only just arrived from France. We had no idea that this novel, curiously entitled *La Peste*, had been smuggled through customs by a colleague, nor of the difficulty of getting hold of any foreign literature. We didn't know of the stringent censorship laws in force in Spain at the time but on that occasion we did realize that we had over done things. Dr. Mantua never mentioned the incident again but the blatant disappointment on his face, the hurt in his eyes, was punishment enough. And Scorpion Lupe who saw and heard everything, knew exactly what we'd done.

"You leave the poor man alone!" she scolded when the priest sadly examined the torn pages of his book.

"You wicked children! You shameful creatures! That poor man has suffered enough! When will you learn to respect your elders? Just be thankful I don't tell your Father! He should give you the beating you deserve. Now run along and don't let me catch you doing anything like this again."

When we were old enough to make sense of such things, Scorpion Lupe told us that it was also thanks to Dr. Mantua that the vineyards in Val Negra survived. He had salvaged the disease-ridden fruit and walled up the cellars so that the best Cuvees could be hidden. He had grown vegetables when everything in the garden looked beyond resurrection and he milked the anaemic goat so that they could make *mato*. Scorpion Lupe said that it was during this time that our grandmother and the priest became friends. Theirs evolved into a symbiotic partnership. Spiritually, Dr. Mantua was Avia's mentor. Once the day-to-day business of survival had been sorted out however, they became ambitious. She, as the autocratic landowner of a famous family was the perfect foil for his undercover operations. She was too powerful to be touched and her opponents could not risk her death turning her into a martyr. And so under the very nose of the enemy, they took in the enemy. Dr. Mantua escorted hundreds of young men to the Pyrenees from where they could cross into France. One day he was captured. Part of his torture was to blind fold him and shoot at him with blank bullets. But he did not betray my Grandmother, nor did he go mad. When the war ended, Grandmother encouraged Dr. Mantua to take on her parish and he was duly appointed Monsignor. This had infuriated Tito, eager for a priest from a new movement, called Opus Dei, which wanted to sweep away old style Catholicism but which merged traditional piety with new the world creed of success. Dr. Mantua remained in situ. Any ambition he may once have had to rise in the church's hierarchy had long been thwarted by the war and the founding of the Opus. He was content to end his days in the neat, middle class parish in which he was born.

"Have you ever forgiven anyone?" Dr. Mantua' voice brought me back to the present. His light pale eyes, eyes that sometimes seemed completely transparent, came to rest on my mother.

"Do we ever truly forgive?"

No, he wasn't looking at Nuria anymore, but scanning the faces of the congregation. When his gaze fell on Franco's bowed head, however, it became utterly blank. No one could have said what he was really thinking. He pulled himself to his full height. His body was still fit. Lupe said women found him attractive.

"Is it enough to turn the other cheek as Jesus would have us do? If we are to be true Christians then we are encouraged to let bygones be bygones and not to pay back evil with evil. The act of forgiveness is something very difficult to achieve. But with the grace of our Lord Jesus Christ we can be released from our sins. And we must endeavour to forgive each other for all wrongs, imagined or otherwise. We must try not to harbour small slights nor be quick to take offence, not allow these remembered things 'to sink in our hearts like a stone'. The Original Greek word used in the Gospels for forgiveness means: 'to let go'. Never was a more necessary action needed than it is today. Our government …" he paused. There was silence in the church. Not a fan moved.

" …Our government needs our prayers now more than ever. If our politicians are misguided then we must not allow emotions to cloud our judgment either. We must pray for men who are weak. God alone knows the evil that lurks in the hearts of men but the day of judgment will come, of that there can be no doubt. So until then, let us show one another mercy. And love." He cleared his throat. "Above all, let us show one another love. Let us pray."

Marta and I got noisily to our feet. There was a great deal of shuffling as the collection came round. Bea dropped her money so many times that she was forever bobbing up and down and then insisting on retracting the coins marked with Franco's face.

"But they *all* look like him *idiota!*" Marta hissed. "He's on all the money!"

"I know!" whispered back Bea. "But they're *not* all the same. I only want the ones that show his face! I don't like his body, body,body!"

"I've got the picture. Just put the money in the collection. It's not for you to keep! So put it in!"

Bea shook her head. Marta grabbed Bea's tight little fist and tried to pry open her fingers. Bea began to whimper which was actually preferable to her repeating random words. Someone coughed meaningfully from behind us and suddenly Marta dropped our sister's hand abruptly.

"Mira!" she hissed. *"Sera ella nuestra prima?* Look over there. Can that girl be our cousin? That must be Isabel!"

"Donde?"

"Alla, no la ves con los jemellos! Over there! Don't you see her with the twins? They've arrived together. Wow! Tito will be furious! They've missed the entire sermon!"

"Really?"

I was beside myself with excitement and curiosity. My heart hammered in my chest. We hardly ever had visitors let alone children our age to come and play and the arrival of a cousin from England was the most exciting thing that had ever happened. I wished Dr. Mantua would hurry up and finish. I wanted to rush over and see this girl for myself. I craned my neck.

"Where?" I repeated more urgently this time. "I can't see her. If only Miguel would move his ugly head!"

"She's in the corner," hissed Marta. "You can see her now."

I had to twist my head to such an angle that I thought it would come right off.

"OhmyGodOhmyGod," I muttered. "That's really her!"

Marta stared at me.

"Not you too."

In my eagerness to get a better look I stepped on Bea's foot.

"Ow!" said Bea beginning to cry noisily.

"Oh for goodness sake!" I said pinching her. "Do you have to cry at everything? Just stop it! Lupe is looking at you! You'll be in real trouble now!"

"And stop wriggling!" joined in Marta. "It's your own fault you got stepped on, you can never stay still!" and then to me she said, "Turn around! People are looking."

I turned for one last look.

"Marta!" I hissed and then my voice rose and I could no longer contain my excitement or anything else for that matter. "Marta! Isabel is wearing SHORTS!"

The entire congregation, including Franco turned to have a look at Isabel. Marta and I leaned over each other to get a better glimpse of our cousin. She was indeed wearing shorts, nasty shiny things that cut into her fat legs. Her skin was very white, even whiter than our grandmother's whose pale complexion had made her a beauty in her youth. Her face was damp with perspiration and her thick hair pulled back in a severe ponytail, was wet with sweat. She wore an aertex sports shirt that clung to her torso and rode up at the front revealing an unattractively plump belly. Squeezed in between the twins, she accentuated their colt-like physiques clearly defined despite their ridiculous sailor suits. Heavy framed glasses perched on the end of her nose. I pulled Marta's arm.

"It's really her!"

"Yes"

"She's not very pretty is she?"

We giggled again until the woman behind us nudged us to be quiet. I was beside myself with curiosity. On the way to communion and during the last hymn, all I could think about was Isabel. She was the weirdest looking person I'd ever seen. I'd never seen a girl wearing shorts before. What was even stranger however was the fact that her eccentric appearance didn't seem to bother her in the slightest. You wouldn't have caught Marta or myself wearing such unflattering clothes but Isabel held her head high oblivious of all the attention and she did little to disguise her interest in her surroundings. She looked around her as if the chapel was the most fascinating place she'd ever been in. I couldn't wait to tell Lupe. This Isabel didn't seem to be much like her beloved Clara after all! If only Dr. Mantua would hurry up! There was so much I wanted to know about my cousin. Would she understand anything I said to her? How would we communicate? What did she like doing? My heart quickened as the priest gave the final blessing. I genuflected hastily pushing my way through the crowd.

"Come on Marta!" I cried. "Let's find Isabel!"

With a final thrust we were ejected into the midday sun. Suffocating heat beat against us more violently than the crowd had. For a moment I felt dizzy unable to breath and then I caught sight of Franco. He was surrounded by a wall of men their faces angry and sullen. Men bumped into him accidentally on purpose or stood on his feet. Women hissed, their fans tapping open and shut, shielding their faces from his sight. I blinked, searching for Isabel. In the crush I was pressed up against Tito. Instinctively he pushed me aside, distaste contorting his features. His face was a purple mask and a vein pulsed at his temple. Behind his horn rimmed spectacles, his angry little eyes darted from child to child. Click click. I could imagine his brain receiving images of his children, wondering how to erase them.

"My sympathies." I heard Franco say to him before he was whisked away by his driver.

"What does he mean Father?"

Tito glowered at me fists clenched.

"Shorts in church!" he snarled aggressively. "Shorts! Children don't wear shorts! It's a barbaric tradition but then she's come from a barbaric country! I've never seen a child in shorts before! This Spanish-*English* child has disgraced us - *Clara's* child, damn her! I knew there was bad blood in the Roble family and it was there for everyone to see! And today of all days! She will be the end of me. She should never have come. She is not wanted." Our mother put a hand on his arm.

"Run and find Isabel," she said to me in a surprisingly gentle voice.

"I'd like to but where is she?"

Nuria nodded in the direction of the bay tree at the opposite end of the courtyard. Dr. Mantua was stooped in its shade, deep in conversation with my cousin. The girl's face was pink with pleasure. She was also wearing sandals with knee-length white socks – kiss of death for the fashion pundits. Spaniards never ever wore shoes *and* socks in the summer and certainly not *white* socks. Wherever did she come from that the people had such poor fashion sense?

"You knew my father!" I heard her exclaim in English, as I drew close.

"Oh yes," he said. "He was a charming man and a wonderful pianist. We were very good friends you know a long time ago. We spent a summer once together at Val Negra. Despite the circumstances, it was a very happy time. And I visited him later in England. You seem surprised? He lived in a house quite wrongly called The Cottage. Do you know it? It's in Hampshire? I thought perhaps you were living there now. No? Ah well, one day I'm sure you will visit it. It has a famous garden, open to the public. Now *that* is a strange custom the English have. It is said that an Englishman's home is his castle and yet he is happy to allow complete strangers to trample all over his house and gardens. Still, your father met some interesting people as they walked around his place. I think he met the nuns from your school in that way. But whether or not you think them interesting is quite another matter."

Isabel smiled. "I always wondered how Father found the Convent for me. But I don't know anything about the house and I don't think I've ever been to Hampshire. We lived …" she hesitated. "We lived close to my school."

For once, Dr. Mantua seemed shaken from his usual composure. He looked puzzled.

"Close to the convent?" he echoed. "You did say you go to the Sacred Heart?"

Isabel nodded, "Yes."

"But that's in Surrey."

"Yes," repeated Isabel.

Dr. Mantua shook his head.

"I'm sorry I may have got it wrong. I'm not as young as I was. My memory may be failing me." He frowned. "The Cottage was definitely in Hampshire. I'm sure I visited Julian there. I'm sure it was with Julian." He looked at her closely. "I was so certain you would have grown up there. I can't believe Julian wouldn't have wanted you to have it."

But Isabel was insistent.

"I'm sorry," she said. "I really have never heard of it. Perhaps," she added helpfully, "perhaps Papa spent time there with my mother before I was born I mean."

The priest stroked his chin thoughtfully.

"Of course. That's probably it. Julian must have lived there with Clara. It wasn't any old house you see. It's the most wonderful house, magical place you will ever see and the garden is … well very special." He finished lamely. "It had been Julian's family a long time I can't understand why it's not yours now. I mean it's not as if… your parents weren't married and you have no surviving siblings." He studied her face not seeing it but her mother's. "I do wonder what happened to it. Who can live there now I wonder?"

"So you knew my mother?" asked Isabel eagerly. When she smiled her whole face lit up so that for a moment she was almost pretty.

"Yes, I knew Clara."

Dr. Mantua looked up spying me out of the corner of his eye.

"Ah … Sigismunda," he said using my full name as he always did. I cringed. This was not the cool introduction I'd planned in my head. I blushed pretending not to hear.

"Sigi, *ven aqui*. Come and meet your English cousin. Are you the same age? You can never tell with young people today. Especially girls. No, perhaps Isabel is younger. Anyhow I'm sure you will get along." He took my arm. "Sigi's English is very good," he added.

"Not true!" I protested blushing.

"Well it certainly should be!" he said. "You spend long enough in my classes!"

Isabel laughed. "Anything must be better than my Catalan," she said disarmingly, her eyes luminous behind the glasses. "I'm sure your English is excellent. I've been longing to meet you. You all have such …different names!"

Different was the understatement but then not everyone had parents as mad as ours.

"What was it again?"

"Si-Sigismunda," I muttered. "But *everyone*," I said glaring at Dr. Mantua's back as he moved away from us, "everyone calls me Sigi."

"Sigi is very pretty," said Isabel. "And a lot easier to say! Are there lots of Sigismundas in Spain?"

"No," I said shortly. "Our mother …" I made a gesture. "Our mother was obsessed with a writer called Cervantes when the twins and Marta were born. By the time Bea came along she'd moved on to Dante."

"Oh," said Isabel "I've never heard of them."

"Neither have I. I only know this because … well because of my name. But please you must really just call me Sigi. Have you met Marta yet? I know you've met the twins," I said. "I saw you with them in church."

"Oh yes!" Her eyes shone. "They were very kind. I got lost. Avia sent me on ahead and I thought I could find the way. She explained it but I still got lost. Everything is so big here. I think they must be awfully grown up. They were smoking!"

"*They* think they're grown up." I pulled her arm in mine. "But don't sort of talk about it. I mean about smoking. They aren't supposed too.

Tito knows – "

"Tito?"

"Oh sorry. That's what we call our father. Ricardo nicknamed him that ages ago. He said the real Tito looks just like him only not as mean."

Isabel's eyes were wide and huge in her super thick glasses. Up close she looked even more peculiar with her peculiar clothes and pale skin. Her one redeeming feather however was her hair which, though wet with sweat, was thick and curly.

"He sounds very frightening."

"He is."

"Does he shout?"

I looked at her.

"Sometimes." Isabel's face seemed to have shrunk behind the glasses. "But don't worry. You won't ever have to see him, apart from at mealtimes, that is. But if you don't speak then he won't notice you. And that's a good thing believe me."

"And have your holidays started?"

I nodded.

"So when do you go back?"

"Back? Do you mean to Val Negra?"

"Val Negra?" Isabel's head was tilted to one side. "Is that what your school's called?"

"School?" I said as though she were mad. "Val Negra isn't school! We don't go to school. We have a governess *if* she stays, that is. They always end up falling out with Scorpion Lupe or Tito. Usually we have a novice from the Carmelites, before they take their vow of silence that is. Tito says a stint with us would make anyone want to be a nun but Mother thinks we're doing the nuns a favour. The twins have started going to the Jesuits but only because Dr. Mantua insisted they go to a proper school. He didn't think they were learning very much at home. Our parents don't seem too worried about *what* we girls do. Tito thinks we're probably too dim for school anyway."

"Gosh," said Isabel amazed pushing her glasses further up her nose. "That must be so much fun. Is it?"

I shrugged. "I wouldn't' say 'fun' exactly. It can be terribly boring. I like Dr. Mantua's classes because he never sticks to the subject and if it's too hot we go for a swim instead. He's not at all strict. He always tells us a story. I know Ricardo likes him. And the twins are lucky because they meet other children. We only do when we go to our country home, Val Negra. Otherwise the parents think we have each other to play with and there's no need to see anyone else. Which is true, I suppose. Sometimes Bea, the baby, is well just a baby and Marta doesn't always want to play with me." I stopped suddenly realizing that everything was coming out all jumbled, realizing that I was out of breath and that suddenly nothing seemed as important as having her close to me. "But you'll play with me won't you Isabel, you and I will be friends?"

*

From that summer onwards, from the time Isabel came into our lives, our grandmother's house took on another dimension. It had always been a haven from the domestic strife in our home but now it came alive with her presence. I came to know my grandmother's house for a second time, to see things in it that I had never noticed before. Isabel wanted to know everything and discover every nook and cranny. She wanted to explore rooms that had not seen the light of day in twenty years. It was Isabel who suggested Avia install a light in the corner display cabinet so that its contents, knick-knacks amassed over the years, were suddenly brought to life. Avia's collection of fans, the figurine of a shepherdess and tiny sheep drinking from a fountain, a leather-bound bible and a tiny boat that opened to reveal diminutive Chinese faces, were only some of the forgotten souvenirs. Isabel and I would spend ages peering through the glass, feasting on the opulent colours and textures of those foreign objects.

Isabel was allocated a suite of rooms in the west wing overlooking the sea. It was the oldest part of the house and for many years had been boarded up. It was where the nuns had been housed during the civil war and formed part of the old nursery. I often wondered if the ghosts of Nuria and Clara as children, played strange and unseen games with those of the nuns and soldiers. I would have been frightened, sleeping on my own in those vast rooms but Isabel said she never was. How could you be? She replied. There was nothing to be afraid of when you had the sound of the sea for company and the lilt of waves lapping against the shore.

Isabel's dressing room contained a huge mahogany cupboard that had been converted from an old linen press. Inside were cedar shelves lined with linen that smelt of lavender. I was most envious of this cupboard because she had it all to herself. Isabel didn't have to share anything with anyone if she didn't want to, while my sisters and I had to share absolutely everything with each other. Isabel didn't have pretty dresses or pairs of matching shoes, as we did, but she did possess a bottle of cologne and a huge jar of bath salts. To me this was the epitome of luxury. Tito would not allow Nuria to wear perfume. It displeased him to such an extent that even Avia didn't use scent if she was going to the coach house. But the real treasure was the bottle with a lid like a sweets' stopper. It even looked like a sweet jar with its multicoloured salts. Isabel explained that in England it was the custom to take a bath. Bath oil and salts such as the ones she possessed, perfumed the water. I had only ever had showers and was intrigued by this concept of 'swimming' in your own water.

"But how can you possibly get clean?" I asked fascinated.

"I don't know but you do," was the reply.

*

Isabel reminded our grandparents what it was like to be young again. The sedate pace that routine had imposed on their lives was shaken in a whirlwind of activity as soon as Isabel arrived for the summer holidays. At first we teased her – she wore such ridiculous clothes and was so lumpy and gauche but later it became evident that she was clever and imaginative. And she surprised our grandfather with a passion for learning completely absent in his other granddaughters. She liked the piano and chess and French literature. He began to reread novels so that they could discuss them together and when she was back at school, they wrote to each other. Avia did not censor our reading. We were allowed to borrow anything we liked from her library, so long as it was returned in good condition. But while the library was stocked with the classics, Isabel could provide the latest, banned literature. Even Ricardo looked forward to Isabel's arrival then anticipating the foreign newspapers, magazines and books that she somehow smuggled through customs. Because of Isabel we were encouraged to read in Catalan and to speak to each other in that language. We came to learn once more, the folklore of our heritage.

It wasn't long before we no longer referred to our cousin as 'poor Isabel'. Subtly over the years our perception of her altered. She became known as 'our clever cousin' or if we were trying to impress our friends in Val Negra, we might even call her 'our English cousin' to give us the edge, as if somehow being English, was exotic and romantic. Even Tito, after his initial horror at seeing her dressed in shorts, treated her with respect. I think he was even a little afraid of her. She was a foreign creature in looks and manner and if she had been stupid he would have devoured her. But her superior intelligence and gentle manner won him over. Or at any rate he was wary of her and therefore left her alone.

Avia was in seventh heaven. She could enjoy her greatest passion – cooking – with the legitimate excuse that she now had a child to feed. And feed her she did. Avia spent hours happily organizing menus, pouring over *Tia Victoria's Cookbo*ok and experimenting with recipes that would tempt the most fastidious of eaters. Isabel grew plumper with every holiday and Avia was delighted. Isabel looked exactly the way young girls of her generation were expected to look. Marta and Bea were far too skinny for her liking. Even I was considered too fragile to be truly healthy.

*

"It's so wonderful to be home!" Isabel would cry running from room to room when she first arrived. She would rush through the house, past the painting of the girl in the hall, down the long marble corridor that led eventually to grandmother's drawing room and Marta and I would follow behind, carried along by her excitement. Avia's face would unravel with emotion.

"*Carino, Amor meu!*" she would exclaim. "*Dame un beso, corre*! Darling heart, how *lovely* to see you! *Cuentanos todo*! How is school? How is that friend of yours –Kate-isn't it? You're still friends aren't you? And are they feeding you? Was the food awful on the plane? We'll have lunch as soon as your grandfather gets home. If you can't wait – actually we'd better give you something straight away, a little aperitif before lunch. Sigismunda-" she would tear her eyes from Isabel. "…*se buena y di selo a Pepita que traiga queso Manchego y pan. Mucho pan. Pobrecilla esta tan delgadita.* Be a good girl and tell Pepita to bring *Manchego* cheese and bread. Bring lots of bread. This poor child looks so very thin."

"*Thin?*" I protested incredulously. But Avia's warning look would send me whirling in the direction of the kitchen. Isabel, curled in our grandfather's chair, would soon dispel any twinges of jealousy I may have had.

"I've brought you *sales de bano,*" she would say as if sensing my antagonism and of course I would melt with gratitude. "And you Bea, some paints and a colouring book. And for Marta, a slip, just like the film stars are wearing! Kate says it's what young ladies wear. Oh and by the way, have you seen the film *My Fair Lady?* What about *Cabaret?* It is SO racy!! The nuns had no idea what it was about!"

Isabel reeled off the names of books and films we'd never heard of. Hers was a language of adventure that might have been mandarin for all we understood of it. The films and books that so vividly painted her landscape were banned in Spain and naturally in our house too. Tito was horrified by Hollywood and he considered all foreign literature perverted. The only film Nuria ever took us to see was *A Sound of Music*. Avia on the other hand loved the cinema and whenever possible she and Isabel would scurry off together to see some film that had been pronounced 'suitable' for the Spanish public. Such was the censorship law at the time however, that often innocent films were rendered incomprehensible. Divorce was not recognized by the church and therefore could not be depicted on the screen. The slant consequently given to dubbed American films was often hilarious. We were too young to bother much with the nuances and we envied Isabel her treats. Afterwards, she was taken for *merienda* to a tearoom appropriately called the *Balmoral.*

"You should see the plates of whipped cream!" said Isabel detailing the food they'd had on their latest outing. "You don't have tea here like you do in England do you? We had hot chocolate as thick as soup and a plate of cream in which you dip huge *enseimadas!*" She held out her hands to demonstrate the size of the Catalan snail-shaped pastry. "I loved them! They're so big!"

"No wonder she's getting so fat!" Marta hissed.

"They both are," said Bea.

And it was true. Avia looked larger than ever.

Then, Pepita the maid would lay the table, eavesdropping unashamedly on our conversation. Only much later would Isabel skip down the stairs to the laundry room for a clandestine smoke and a gossip. At home we were not encouraged to talk to the servants but Isabel talked to everyone, and in Avia's house, everyone talked to Isabel.

"They do a quarter of the work when Isabel is home!" Avia would grumble not really minding. She loved the buzz of Mialma when Isabel was there. On that first day home, our grandparents liked to have Isabel to themselves and reluctantly we would go home for lunch but waiting til the last possible moment, wanting to share in the fun of her homecoming. That first meal would be a feast too, with Avia having spent days in the kitchen before hand and we were reluctant to return to our plate of Cuban rice and overcooked meat. But eventually it was time to leave.

"I'll see you out. No don't move, *carino*," she brushed Avia's cheek. " I won't be a moment!"

She would take my arm, as we moved down the corridor to the hall, allowing Doris our maid and my sisters to run on ahead. In front of the painting of the girl in the mint green dress, she would stop to examine it, as if for the very first time.

"I do so love this, don't you? I love the colours, the little sailboat in the background. Her twirling parasol!"

"I'm glad you do. I don't think it has ever meant as much to my sisters as it does to us."

The use of the word 'us' pleased us both. It drew us into a tight circle of friendship, drawn out of blood and loyalty. And then if I moved away too quickly, sometimes deliberately, she would call me back. And I knew what she would say. And it was always the same. A question, posed oh-so-casually, which did not alter in all the years I knew her.

"And the twins? How are they?" she says.

"Oh they're both fine," I reply.

And secretly I smile to myself and she, my Spanish-English cousin, does not know that I am word perfect in the script that follows.

"And …um …Ricardo?" She asks, has asked as a little girl and then as a woman, has asked every year of our lives. "Will Ricardo be at Val Negra this summer?"

Chapter 7

Isabel
Val Negra
Summer 1967

    When Isabel thought back to that first visit to Spain and to what happened afterwards, she realized that everything really began with her father's death. She was seven years old at the time and she could not remember anything before then, as though her consciousness was only born that year. Isabel had been largely unaware of her father before his death and it was only afterwards that she came to love him. Later, she found it difficult to separate her own memories from the many stories she had heard about him. What she had always known to be true however was that her mother was Spanish and had met her English father, Julian Pelham, when he had gone to Spain to fight in their civil war. But when that war ended the war in the rest of the world began. Julian was sent to the Far East where he was wounded during the fall of Singapore.

    When the nuns at Isabel's convent school spoke of Julian Pelham, it was with great respect. A respect followed by the inevitable hush as they discussed his 'Wartime Injuries.' As a result, Isabel began to see her father as a survivor, someone possessing a power that mere mortals did not. She also understood that although he was still relatively young, he looked very old and had what she called 'lions' all over his face. He had hardly any hair and most amazing of all he could take out his teeth and put them back again. This she considered to be his greatest achievement. Later, Isabel learned that her father had been a prisoner of war and had worked on the Thai-Burma railway. When the war was over and he returned to England, Julian weighed six and a half stone and was crippled from endless beatings. He and Clara did not have a child for some years. Children had always frightened Julian. He never knew what to say to them and his silence and their stares reminded him of the uncompromising scrutiny of Japanese soldiers. No matter how hard he tried not to, he always ended up trembling at their sudden, inexplicable outbursts. And it was just as well, he often thought, that they had waited and been allowed those precious years, because when Isabel was born, Clara died.

When Isabel was four, she was sent to the local convent. Local that is, to the small terrace house Julian rented in Caterham, which was as far away from The Cottage as it was possible to be. When he felt well, Julian would fetch her home for the weekend. These were strange days, which Isabel found uncomfortable and she longed for the routine of the Convent. She soon grew to hate the small dingy house with its peeling paint and perennial smell of damp. She hated living on a street where people shouted at each other across grubby clothes lines. Above all, she hated the street youths who banged at the broken windows calling for the 'mad man' to show himself. And then of course he would, her father that is, flinging open the front door shouting in a language she had never heard. His eyes would be wild when he finally came inside, his whole body trembling. These were the worst times of all because then he would drink a great deal from the bottles lined up on the cold mantelpiece. There would be no supper on nights like that and Isabel would cower in her bedroom, the only bedroom and cry herself to sleep.

There were times when Isabel wondered if Julian even knew that she was there. And the problem was that she didn't know what he expected of her. Except that she wasn't to make any noise or go wandering off alone. He didn't talk much and never read her stories like the nuns did although she could see he liked to read. Towers of books almost as tall as she was, sprang from the moth-eaten carpet together with dusty piles of newspaper. Julian was a voracious reader and nothing was ever disposed of. Books and papers were scattered on the floor, dropped precisely on the spot where Julian had read the last page. But there were no fairy tales or picture books. And there were certainly no paints or drawing pencils or even paper with which Isabel might have whiled away the long, wet afternoons. Sometimes, if they had had a particularly trying day, Julian would lie on the floor reading aloud from whatever book he was engrossed in at the time. To Isabel, his voice sounded like a song without music and when she glanced down at the open book there were drawings, not letters, all over the page. After a while, Isabel began bringing with her, a baby doll called Mary, a present from one of the nuns. Julian thought Mary hideous, especially as it could really wet itself. He said the doll was far too life like and that the real thing was bad enough. In other ways he was more understanding. Once, when he found Isabel in tears one night on her way to the lavatory, he had simply scooped her up in his arms. He had sat down quite abruptly on the top step. She was heavier than he imagined, he said, with a charming, lopsided smile. But then he had begun to sweat heavily and Isabel was alarmed, wondering if he were ill again. After much coaxing, she confessed that in the dark, she imagined terrible monsters leaping from the ancient pipes and horrible shapes crawling along the walls. After that the lights were left on all night because as Julian confided, he was afraid of the dark too.

When Julian was diagnosed with terminal cancer it was a relief to them both. He often spoke about meeting her mother in heaven and how there had never been anything to live for after Clara died. He said that he was bored with living and that he anticipated neither death's sting nor victory's grave, words that Isabel did not understand, and said with a cheerfulness she found confusing. And the shaky closeness that was growing between them became something haunting.

In the months that were left to them, Julian suddenly made a great effort to be with Isabel as much as possible. Most weekends he came to visit her at the Convent where he made straight for the music room. He played the piano beautifully, his twisted fingers still able to move over the keys with grace. He was patient with her and taught her simple piano pieces that delighted them both. There had been no evidence of this side to his character in the little terrace house, but at the convent, Julian said that at last he had found forgiveness. This had made no sense to her at the time but he had also added, more memorably, that now that she was six, he would read to her. Isabel's heart leapt at this and she had run off to borrow books from Kate Douglas. But Julian had been disparaging about Kate's collection. The only story that held any meaning, he said, was *The Ballad of the Babes in the Wood.* To this day, Isabel could not think about the two murdered little children without a shudder. And if Julian didn't read aloud or play the piano, on the days when the fever took hold of him, he would recount odd tales of the war. These strange episodes always ended up with an uncomfortable hug or unexpected sob that unsettled Isabel more than his stories did.

When Julian entered the hospice, Isabel visited him there in the evenings after tea. Her father had lost the weight he had gained after the war and his eyes seemed huge in his sunken face. The cancer seemed to spread daily. His liver was diseased and soon his whole body would turn an ochre colour. Isabel was fascinated by the purple bruises on his thin arms and by the drips hanging from the distended veins of his hands. This was the first time that her unflinching stare did not disturb him he said. He wanted to talk to her, to make up for all the time he had wasted. Sometimes he even forgot that she was a child. In his dreams, it was Clara who sat beside him, wiping his forehead, stroking his hand. On those occasions, Isabel sat silently, her hand clasped in his as together they travelled to the future and then back again. She went with him, his thoughts groping along the fingers of memory pulling her through emotions she was not mature enough to understand. Sometimes he was lucid, at other times he merely spoke his jumbled thoughts aloud. Always he spoke of the war.

Later, he remembered childhood holidays in Norfolk — that other country, he said, where time stands still, where the silence is thundering and the isolation complete. He had carried, he told her, the sound of birds and the palette of an English sky to the remote jungle of Kanchanaburi. Sometimes when the suffering in the camp was intolerable and the anger he felt towards his captors threatened to explode, he would think of his brothers when they were small. He could see them clearly he said, as they jumped the marshes looking for crab. And he could see the last light on the water, even now, as they took out their sailboats. When the war finally ended and he was to come home, he remembered asking Clara not to meet him at the boat train. He wanted to return this last time, alone, as he had so often as a small boy from his prep school. He also remembered that for some absurd reason he believed nothing would have changed. It was enough that he had. And yet as the car swept through his village, the first names that he saw on the stone memorial were those of his brothers.

Isabel, stumbling along the morphine induced haze through which her father talked, finally understood him. What was more, at last she could see beyond the decaying body of a hitherto feared and distant parent. As layers of skin fell away and bed sores ate at his flesh, so did the indomitable spirit of the man shine through. Isabel glimpsed the boy her mother had loved, the sensitive and gentle man who harboured no bitterness now for the years of torture he had endured and for the waste of his lost youth. Once, Isabel had seen a solitary tear run down her father's cheek and this had troubled her. She had wanted to get into bed with him and give him a cuddle but he was too weak to hold and the nurse was afraid they might both might fall off the bed. On one occasion she had arrived to find her father in an agitated state trying to find the bell to ring for the nurse.

"I can't find the world service," he muttered panic stricken. Isabel watched unfazed as her father flicked the remote control at the blank screen of the television set.

"It's the radio you want then," she said calmly.

For a moment he stared back at her before her words penetrated. He grimaced.

"I'm losing it you know. It's happening at last. I don't want you to come again."

Isabel sprang forward.

"Oh but I love coming! I want to really I do! Besides, this way I always miss games and I hate net ball more than anything."

"More than fish eyes and glue?" he asked in a strange voice, with the very faintest shadow of humour.

Isabel was startled. She had spent so much time listening to him that she never imagined for a moment that he ever heard anything she said.

"Yes. More than tapioca."

Julian had looked at her as if for the first time, surprised that she was indeed a child, astounded that she was the fruit of his loins. He had obliterated from memory, the circumstances of her birth. For so long he had seen her as the negation of her mother's life. He would have had no difficulty in choosing Clara's over that of his unborn child's. No misplaced morality narrowed his vision. But greater forces were at work to rake over the bloodied field of his heart. Something bittersweet now tugged at his emotions threatening to sentimentalize the little dignity that was left him.

"I have much enjoyed these visits," he said falteringly.

He lay completely still in the hospital bed and Isabel on her chair, her feet dangling a few inches above the ground, could not move. His eyes looked to her face and beyond.

"So little time now, when once there was so much, too much. I longed for death, prayed for it and now I would give anything to prolong my life, if only to see you grow up. There are so many regrets. It's all so untidy and unfinished." He clenched his fist and then just as suddenly his fingers relaxed. "But I am proud of you, you funny little thing. Isabel, my dear this is important so pay attention. I have never told you anything about my family before. There was no need. But now there is not much time and there are some things you should know. There is no one left on my side. I am the last of the Pelhams and I have no son. My brothers were all killed in the war and my parents died a long time ago. Who would have thought that of four sons not one would leave an heir? But you have lots of cousins on your mother's side. She was Spanish and her sister and her husband and their children are all alive. I am going to entrust you to their care. I should have seen to it a long time ago. Still, you will meet them soon enough. And who knows? Perhaps it will be easier for you this way." He lay back against the harsh white pillows momentarily exhausted. When he spoke his voice was so low, Isabel strained to hear it. "Val Negra," he said.

Isabel bent her head and he repeated the words.

"Val Negra," he said and this time his voice was strong. "If there is one certainty left to me it is that nothing will have changed there. I know your grandmother and her family still summer there just as they did before the war. How lovely for you to have it all ahead of you. Val Negra ..."

For a moment, Isabel thought Julian was dead. He was so still she could not hear his breathing. But when he spoke again his voice was clear. "Val Negra is one of the most beautiful places I have ever known," he said. "It will be for you, exactly as I remember. The Monseny hills with the light behind look purple and then again another colour as the sun sets. In the winter they turn black as though a door has been closed on the sky. And ... Mercedes ..." he said softly, lovingly. "Your grandmother will look after you. Even after all this time and in spite of my pride, my stupid pride, she will forgive me. I know that she will love you. And has wanted to. If she ever asks about me you must tell her that it was my fault. Not Clara's and not hers. You will remember? It was only ever pride. But ... please ... don't ever tell her about this ..." he motioned to the bed and the drip in his arm. "Try not to remember this."

But Isabel did remember her father's death. If there were memories that were hers and hers alone, they were these. She remembered everything about the hospice and that last conversation and clung to the memory of Julian's beautiful voice. He had died a few days later and she had never seen him again. That afternoon she was given a special tea and Kate Douglas had sat with her. Her favourite nun had said prayers and then read her a story. "Something innocuous I think," she said. "It must be a Beatrix Potter at your age." Isabel hadn't liked to tell her that she had outgrown Beatrix Potter but enjoyed it all the same. It was about Hunca Munca and a doll's house full of toy food - plaster jellies that would not wobble and a fish as hard as stone. After her father's vivid account of jungle warfare in Burma, where the sticky heat stank with the infested wounds of his men, Hunca Munca seemed rather tame. She had been put to bed with a cup of Horlicks and Chocolate Bourbon biscuits and unimaginable luxury. But the pleasure was short lived. Everything felt strange and frightening. Just as frightening as when she had stood on the landing waiting to run the gauntlet to the lavatory in the little terrace house. She cuddled Mary, her baby doll, but all the time it felt as if she were holding her breath. All she wanted was the feeling to go away. For the first time she wanted a mother to tell her that everything was as it should be and who would still be there when she woke up in the morning.

But in the morning she felt exactly the same as she did when she went to bed. If anything Isabel felt even worse. The nuns kept smiling and saying how it was God's Will, but that they were still very very sorry for her loss, as after all, she was just a child. She became the focus of attention that only made Isabel aware of how different she was from all the other girls. Not only did she not have a mother but somehow she had lost her father as well. And this was what annoyed her. Isabel hadn't "lost" her father. She knew where he was and the last time she had visited she had found her way to his room all by herself and she had recognized the number 6 on his door. And she knew this because she was six years old and had just had a birthday. Why did they keep saying they were sorry she had *lost* him? And if it was her fault because SHE had lost him why were they all so kind about it? It was all so confusing and she wished she could understand and not have all these words and pictures darting around inside her head. And she wished the nuns and the older girls would stop saying they were sorry and leave her alone. And just GO AWAY.

Later that day she was told by the Mother Superior (who once again said how sorry she was that her father had been LOST) that she needn't bother with any more letter formation or reading, in fact with anything for the rest of the term and how wonderful it was because she Isabel was going on A Really Big Adventure – an adventure so big in fact that it involved going on a plane to another country. And what was even more wonderful was that she had a whole family waiting there for her and that because they were Spanish it made Isabel also Spanish- well half anyway. It didn't matter that she had never heard of them before. God works in mysterious ways all the more his glories to reveal, said the Mother Superior and this was one of those fortunate glories (because as she had said to a Sister, they wouldn't have known what to do with a child in the convent all summer.) Not only was there a Spanish family but miraculously there was a Spanish Grandmother and a Catholic one too. The Mother Superior seemed very happy with the way everything had turned out but Isabel had never met or heard of this so-called Spanish family before Julian mentioned them.

And as to Grandmothers ... well Isabel wasn't entirely sure what exactly Grandmother's did. Did they run schools? Were they teachers or nurses? And what was Spain? And what was all this business about speaking another language? How would they understand each other?

"Don't worry," Kate comforted her. "You'll be back for the autumn term. Which is the one after the summer holidays. When you go up to the big class." And then at Isabel's obvious look of alarm added hastily. "Oh but you do the same things you're doing now ... just more ... and I'll send you cards and stickers for your collection if you like."

"Big coloured ones?"

"If you like."

Kate bent down and put her arms around Isabel.

"Next holidays you can come home with me. But this time it's important you meet everyone. You have a family now."

"But I don't want a family. What does it do?"

"It doesn't necessarily do anything but they'll look after you in a way your friends can't. It's a good thing Isabel, not bad. You'll see that for yourself. It will be fun I know it. And going to another country – well that's all wonderful too. And it's warm and you'll be able to swim without your skin turning blue with cold." Kate clasped her hands together dramatically. She was three years older and Isabel's most grown up friend. She was kind and generous with a sunny disposition and had befriended Isabel on her first day at school. But even her optimism failed to impress Isabel now. Isabel loved her convent school and the nuns. She particularly enjoyed the summer term when the girls played tennis and swam and on fine days had their lessons out of doors. The mile long drive from the main gates to the school were bordered by apple trees and in the spring formed a margin of pink against the lush parkland. It was a warm and happy place guided by an intelligent, enlightened teaching order. It had its own farm and each morning large milk urns were delivered to the convent. There was never a shortage of dairy products and the girls were fed on home made ice creams and cakes. From time to time the two Gibraltarian nuns who were usually in charge of Laundry took a turn in the Kitchen and that's when the food really became interesting. Kate, whose brother was at a Jesuit boarding school in the north of England, likened by many of its former pupils to a kind of Borstal and whose beds were a good deal less comfortable, was scornful after a visit to the convent.

"This isn't school!" he scoffed. "This is a health club. Do you actually learn anything? No wonder all the girls are so fat! The only thing the nuns do here is cook and eat!"

"We know," said Kate delightedly. "And we're not complaining! And at the weekends we get to see great films! Some of the nuns are too doddery to censor anything. We've seen all kinds of daring things. Bet you haven't!"

"Have!"

"Haven't"

Isabel could not imagine life anywhere else, certainly not in a foreign country. Not Spain! She knew nothing about it! Was it anything like Burma? She wondered. Would she catch malaria as her father had done? Were there strange and poisonous fruits and huge Darwinesque plants with hideous branches? Would she be able to take her teeth out whenever she wanted? It wasn't something she really wanted to do but you never knew. Her father had wanted to before he went to bed. She just didn't know. There was so much about the adult world that was confusing. She wished she could ask her father. He wouldn't have spared her feelings. He'd have told her the truth painful as that might be. He had said something about a mountain being beautiful and a place whose name she had already forgotten. On the other hand, big people often thought things were beautiful when children thought they were just boring. That night Isabel wished for the hundredth time since her father died, that she had a mother. She hadn't noticed the lack of one before, but now, without either parent she did feel lonely. It was also a feeling of being excluded. All the girls had parents, mothers who sent them packages of sweets and letters during the week. They also had fathers in stiff collars and nodded at whatever the nuns said. It seemed suddenly as if every overheard conversation had to do with the girls' parents and every story involved a mother. Part of her longed to climb into a Lap and be soothed and cuddled. Kate, once in a moment of weakness, had told Isabel about *her* mother's Lap and ever since Isabel had desperately wanted one too. She tossed and turned all night long in her bedroom underneath the eaves.

In the morning Kate came to wake her up and to give her an airline ticket and a passport she didn't know she possessed with the word **Espana** written on the bottom of it. One of the older girls accompanied her to the airport by taxi, a Panamanian sent once a year half way round the world to school in England. The nuns thought she and not Kate a better choice given her experience in the homesickness department. She was a pretty, healthy looking girl with permanently tanned skin and golden hair. Isabel wondered if she wasn't secretly an angel and instead of going home to Panama, flew directly to heaven.

At Heathrow, a BEA stewardess escorted Isabel through customs and stayed with her until they boarded. Isabel had never been on an airplane before and was disappointed. It was very noisy as they walked through the corridor that led directly onto the aircraft. It was just like stepping onto a train. Neither was she impressed when it shot forward, hurtling down the runway into the sky. Isabel was so tired that soon she was fast asleep, only waking when they had touched down in another country. Through the windows of the aircraft, Isabel could see a stark, small building to which the travellers were heading. The words BARCELONA were written across the upper windows. It seemed very dusty and dry, tall trees stood motionless in the heat. There were Policemen everywhere. They had winged, glossy hats that shone like mirrors. The stewardess said they were called Guardia Civil but Isabel found the words difficult to pronounce. Some held rifles, others smoked, they all looked at her as she walked past. The stewardess tensed, staring straight ahead and gripped Isabel's hand so tightly she squealed. She stayed close beside the stewardess, suddenly frightened. Isabel felt dreadfully alone and longed more fervently than ever for the cool hospice room and the comforting, unchanging shape of her father. She longed for the predictability those few months had held and hated her hammering heart and the panic that made her tummy churn. If she had still been five years old and not just six, Isabel knew she would have cried by now. Loud voices jabbered in a language she could not understand. There was a good deal of gesticulating and laughter. The floor of the building was littered with cigarette butts and although a fat woman slowly pushed a mop in front of the ladies lavatories, it seemed to make no difference at all. Red insects with long skeletal bodies darted into corners and large fans swung lackadaisically, redistributing the hot, stuffy air. Isabel's shirt stuck to her skin and her feet in their white socks and sandals had swollen. She had never felt this hot in her life. A cool cheek was suddenly pressed to hers.

"*Hijita* Isabel," said a woman's voice in English with only the slightest trace of an accent. "It is you!"

Isabel looked up to see a tall, plump woman with paper white skin and hair that was perfectly combed but coloured *mauve*. Even her eyes and dress matched to give her an ageless, ethereal quality that was quite mesmerizing. She seemed not unlike one of the convent nuns, albeit without a habit. Best of all, she looked as if she might possess a LAP. Isabel shot her careful looks from under lowered eyes. All sorts of images had crowded her mind during her last night at school. She had had visions of a wicked old woman whisking her off to a wood and leaving her there to die. But this lady was neither old nor cruel. Her skin was soft to the touch and she smelt of roses. Two ropes of pearls hung along a substantial bosom that seemed so soft and inviting that Isabel wanted to bury her face against her. For a moment she was cradled in her grandmother's arms. Isabel closed her eyes and sighed. This must be what a Lap was all about - Kate was wrong. It wasn't overrated at all.

"Ah Isabel." A man's voice interrupted her thoughts. His voice seemed, impossibly, familiar and she half expected to see Julian Pelham standing there. A very tall, thin man in a dark suit was looking at her with undisguised curiosity. Like her grandmother, he was fair with blue eyes and smelt wonderfully. The collars and cuffs of his shirt were immaculate and as her hands brushed the cloth of his coat she fond it to be as soft as velvet. There were tassels on the end of his fine leather shoes and he wore the thinnest looking socks she had ever seen. When she was older and appreciated such things, she learned that the socks were made of silk, the shirts of Egyptian cotton, and the suits of cashmere or Irish Linen, depending on the season. Isabel had never in her life seen such beautifully dressed people.

"Welcome. Welcome." The man grasped her shoulders and pecked her cheek. Again she felt cool, smooth skin on hers. "So you are my little *espanola-inglesa*," he said. "I wondered when we would meet. I began to think we never would. You are not very much like your mother." He cupped her chin in his hand.

Isabel thought of the hospice.

"My father didn't have much hair and his skin was yellow. He looked much older than you," she added in surprise, thinking this might please him.

"Oh God," said her grandmother in a wobbly voice. "Did he suffer very much?"

Isabel considered her.

"I don't know," she replied truthfully. She looked from one to the other. Both seemed even paler than a moment ago and her grandfather was frowning. There was a strained silence.

"What shall I call you?" asked Isabel when she began to think they would never speak again. "I mean you are both Spanish and I shall have to learn the language. I can't very well call you *Grandmamma?* Can I?"

Her grandmother made a funny strangled sound and then regained her composure.

"Our other grandchildren call me *Avia,* which is Catalan for grandmother," she explained. "They call your grandfather, *Avi*. Because you see, we are really Catalans and although you will hear Spanish spoken in the street, we speak our own language at home. Unfortunately we are not yet permitted to speak it anywhere else. Our government at the moment is very strict. It wants us all to speak the same language. No dialects. But it is not something you need to worry about. I know from the nuns that you are learning French which will help you in learning Catalan. Anyway we can try. I am so happy that you want to learn."

Isabel nodded eager to please and hoped they wouldn't go all quiet again. Her grandfather muttered something in this Catalan language that she did not understand and took her arm. He led the way through the crowd and she was glad that he was so tall and walked with such authority. She felt very safe with him. People moved to let them pass, but not in the way they had done when she was with Julian Pelham. Then they had openly stared. Walking with her grandfather gave Isabel a sense of importance. Avi, her grandfather, did not shrink from people's stares as her father had done, nor did the sight of policemen cause him to tremble uncontrollably. She thought Avi quite capable of making other people tremble and shrink from him. As they passed, men removed their hats, some women curtsied and even the policeman at the exit, inclined his head. Within seconds, they were through customs and outside into brilliant sunshine. Isabel blinked. The sun seemed to possess a thousand fingers, all of them reaching for her. She had never felt such intense heat.

"Ah, there's Jose," said Avia motioning to a long silver coloured car, which Jose told her later was called a Hispano Suzie. It sparkled in the sunshine like a small, beached whale. A short stocky man appeared from behind it. He wore the kind of uniform that would have sent Julian into a spasm. Jose waited expectantly.

"Your suitcase senorita?" He asked at last.

Isabel stared at him uncomprehending.

"There isn't one," explained Avia.

The driver's face was impassive. "Very good."

He relieved Isabel of the plastic bag that contained a toothbrush, a change of underwear and Julian's *The Babes in the Wood* -all her worldly possessions. Kate had advised Isabel against taking her baby doll Mary. Isabel wished earnestly now that she had. More than ever she wanted something to hold on to. Jose placed her bag as carefully on the seat beside him, as though it was made of the finest leather, containing the finest dresses. The back of the car seemed huge, much larger than the cab that had taken Isabel to the airport from school. And it was a good deal more comfortable. It was like sitting on a very large, very soft, brown sofa.

"Did you have a good flight? Did they feed you? Are you starving? What do you eat at the convent? Do the nuns cook well? Do you like milk?" (This last, because it was a known fact that Spanish children were genetically allergic to milk.)

Her grandmother's questions were endless. As she spoke she held Isabel's hand, caressing it in her warm strong one. It was a gesture that seemed to relax them both. Her grandfather on the other hand seemed ill at ease, impatient. He sat on the edge of his seat, his long legs stretched out. In profile, his face was thoughtful, the nose aquiline, the forehead high and smooth.

The car purred along the road. Isabel had to sit up very straight and tall in order to look out of the window *and* keep her hand held in her grandmother's. They passed a spindly statue of a bearded man with a very long, pointy stick.

"What is that?" asked Isabel.

Her grandfather snorted. "Made by idiots, to commemorate idiots," he said emphatically.

"Ildefons!" admonished her grandmother and then to Isabel. "It is very *avant garde n'est ce pas?* It's supposed to be of Don Quixote. Have you heard of Cervantes?"

Isabel shook her head. *The Babes in the Wood* formed the rock stone of her literary education, although just before he died, Julian Pelham had begun to read *Jane Eyre* to her. He had been especially pleased when he remembered it was about an orphan.

"Cervantes is one of our great writers," continued Avia. "In fact he wrote a story about another Isabel, about another Spanish-English girl just like you. Only she made the reverse journey. She was Spanish and was taken to live in England."

Isabel's eyes were wide with alarm. "Taken?" she said her voice rising as a cold hand clamped at her heart. This story didn't sound so different from *The Babes* after all.

"It was a long time ago," said her grandmother. "Spain was … well … at war with England." Her voice faded and Avi shot her an amused look.

"Now you've done it my dear." He said folding his arms and waiting to hear what she would say next.

"I want to know about Isabel," insisted Isabel pulling on her grandmother's hand. "Why was she taken and where were her parents? Where was her father?"

Avia's eyes narrowed. "The story is set a long time ago," she said. " In the story England had captured one of our sea ports. You see the English and the Spanish were fighting each other. Unfortunately. Anyway an Englishman found a beautiful little girl wondering about so he took her back with him. I suppose in a way you could say he adopted her. Anyway he looked after her very well. I mean he loved her and wanted her to be brought up as a proper little lady, as an *English* lady, doing all the things that ladies did in those days. She learnt to sew and play an instrument and to sing beautifully. But he never let her forget her Spanish heritage nor her own language. It's a long story."

Isabel's eyes were wide. "But I want to hear it. Where was her mother? What happened to her? Did she see her again?"

Avia held Isabel's hand tightly. "No she didn't," she said. "But this Englishman was very kind to her. He educated her and he allowed her to keep her religion. He brought her up as a good Catholic girl."

Isabel had gone very still and Avia shook her hands gently. "This story doesn't matter now," she continued "I just want you to have fun this summer. Soon we shall go to Val Negra and I know you will love it there. Darling I want so much to get to know you. For you to be happy." Her grandmother paused. " I am very glad that you have been brought up in our faith. We have Julian to thank for that. Have you made your first communion?"

Isabel shook her head.

"Well, maybe you will make it at Val Negra."

Isabel looked up, that was the place her father had spoken of when he told her about her grandmother and Spain. But what was it exactly?

"There's time enough for all that," said Avi calmly. "One step at a time eh?" And he smiled, a warm gentle smile that transformed his elegant features. There was a self-deprecation about him that reminded Isabel of her father. It was as though he were waiting for something or someone and had all the time in the world in which to do so. Like Julian Pelham, he did not need other people to amuse him. He was happiest alone, with his books, his horses and his music. He loved poetry.

"Are you good at learning things by heart?" he asked suddenly.

"I'm not sure," Isabel replied. "I s'pose so."

"Let's see then. This is a poem I like very much. Rather like a haiku- you know those Japanese one liners."

Isabel stared at him. She did not know. Poetry was one thing about the Japanese Julian had never mentioned.

"It goes like this." Her Grandfather held out a finger to emphasize the words. *"Per una vela blanca daria un sceptre."*

"For a white sail," translated Avia, the smile fading from her face. "I would give a sceptre."

"Per una vela blanca i el mar blau, sceptre i palau."

"For a white sail and a blue sea- sceptre and palace."

"Repeat after me."

And she did. But what did it mean? That in exchange for the sea and a sailing boat, a King would give up his throne? What was the world that she had entered? What was this crazy Spanish world all about? And would she be taken from it?

The car slowed as it approached the Diagonal. (So-called Avi explained, because this broad avenue cut straight across the perpendicular streets of the city.) It nosed its way along the Via Agusta where palm trees and striped umbrellas were dotted along wide brick pavements. Isabel spied large villas with Gothic style turrets and the hint of lush gardens through wrought iron gates. They passed endless cafes and pastry shops and one in particular with the large letters FOIX written in gold against a striped green canopy. Its windows were bursting with a rainbow selection of sugary sweets and thin, caramel topped cakes stuffed with cream called *Brazo de Gitano*, which Avia explained meant "Gypsy's arm." Alongside the square in front of a tall thin church, Jose stopped the car and went in to FOIX to buy dessert. Today was Sunday and everywhere couples with exquisitely dressed children, emerged from church to buy sweets and dessert for the family lunch. Isabel sat glued to the window taking it all in. She loved the square with its pigeons and newspaper stand. On the steps of the church, a priest stood in his black robes looking she thought just like a magpie, his lace cassock like the white plumes of his breast. The church bells were chiming, its twin towers pale against the bright sky.

"I want to fit in. I want to be like you," Isabel said fiercely. Avia laughed.

"You will. You do. After all you are half Spanish, half *Catalan*. And you must learn the language, because your cousins unfortunately don't speak good English. The twins should, they've been learning it long enough but I'm afraid they aren't very studious." She caressed Isabel's cheek. "Isabel darling, I know you must miss Jul- your father. His death must have come as a tremendous shock."

Isabel frowned, "Oh no. He was always ill. But when he was in the hospice he turned yellow. His skin, even his eyes, all yellow! Anyway it's what he wanted. I mean dying. He prayed for death all the time."

Avia seemed hardly to move at all.

"He said that?"

"Yes." Isabel took a gulp trying to remember what her father had said exactly. "Julian said that he had nothing to live for when Clara died."

"Wh –what else did he say?"

"That he wanted to be in heaven with her, that it was all his fault. Oh and ... and that you would forgive him."

Avia's eyes were brilliant with tears. Her face was deathly white. Isabel was frightened again and that feeling of having to hold her breath had returned. She gripped her sweaty hands together, wishing there was the slightest breeze.

"Avia?" she ventured after what seemed like a very long time.

"*Hijita.*"

"Will you tell me about the family? My friend Kate says everyone should have one. Do you think I should too?"

"But you do."

"And these cousins? Who are they? Are they my age? Is there someone to play with? And will she like dolls? Not barbies because I don't, but *real* baby dolls like Mary, one that can really drink. Julian didn't like that at all. I don't think he liked children much and certainly not babies! And – "

Avia looked away.

"Slowly! Slowly!" she said to the window and then calm again she put her hands over her face as if she were washing it. "You ask about the family," she said, "so let me tell you. Well, you have met us of course and then there is your Aunt, *Tia* Nuria who is married to Tit- I mean *Tio* Luis. They have five children. The twins: Miguel and Ricardo and then the girls: Marta, Sigismunda and Beatrice. In our family there are nicknames for everyone and Beatrice is sometimes called "Bea." I think she's a little ... what is the word? *Gate* in French. Spoilt. But very sweet, she has a good heart. You will see for yourself. We will hear mass together and then have lunch. In the evening, when it is cooler, we will drive to Val Negra. It is where we always spend our holidays. I was born in Val Negra and when Avi was a boy he lived in a house close by."

Isabel considered this. "Julian said something about Val Negra." She blinked behind her glasses. "So you have always known each other," she said.

Avia smiled at her granddaughter's grave little expression. "Always. Everyone at Val Negra knows each other. There are no strangers. Strangers always stand out." Avi shot her a look. "I'm sure you will grow to love it as we do." Her grandmother added quickly. "For us it is an escape from the bustling city. It is so much cooler there. You will notice the difference."

"I do hope so," replied Isabel with feeling. Her grandmother appeared not to have heard her. She continued almost to herself.

"All year we yearn for the beginning of summer so that we can go to Val Negra. The house is surrounded by vineyards and beyond them the Monseny Mountains. You can see the vineyards from every window sprawling far and wide towards the hills. Sometimes the mountains look purple as though bruised by the sun but it is only the ripe grape waiting to be harvested that gives them colour. In the winter, when the vine is stripped, the reflection on the Monseny is different again. But above all Val Negra is deliciously cool. There are streams that run through the land and wonderful rock pools that the children love. Do you feel the heat little one? We are having one of our hottest summers!"

Avia rummaged in her handbag and pulled out a long black fan and a large piece of lace she said was called a *mantilla* which she draped over her head and shoulders. She said any Spanish lady who knew what was what wore a mantilla to church and sometimes on other occasions as well. She began to fan Isabel. "I must warn you though, Val Negra gets into the blood and never leaves you. If you have visited once, you will want to return again and again."

They had left the square and begun to climb up the mountain along a narrow steep road. The car groaned as it struggled to change gear. Isabel was amazed that it could turn at all and more than once they had seemed to slide backwards down the hill. Isabel hardly dared look but when she opened her eyes she could see nothing of the village they had left behind and above any view of the sky was blotted out by lemon trees. After a while it became noticeably cooler as they entered a pine forest. Avia rolled down the window and Isabel could smell the delicious scent of eucalyptus and citrus fruit. She inhaled the fresh air gratefully. Suddenly the car nosed round the last bend and up a sharp incline, the entrance to which was almost entirely concealed by foliage. Wrought iron gates were propped against thick bushes of mauve flowers that brushed against the car. Gravel crunched beneath the wheels along a path that seemed to lead nowhere. Then suddenly they emerged onto a paved courtyard. A pink stone building with fat marble columns loomed above them. Wide marble steps lead to the most spectacular front door Isabel had ever seen. Cherubs and bunches of grapes were carved along the frame and it had an enormous gold knocker in the shape of a panther. Jose positioned the car carefully before jumping out. After a few moments a uniformed maid appeared. She shook her head and waved her hands.

"No! No! There is no one at home. Tell the *Senor Conde* that they are already at mass – at the Carmelites. *El Caudillo* is with them."

Avi stiffened.

"Then we will not go."

"But Ildefons we must. And now that we are here! We agreed to meet Nuria and the children. Tito will notice if we fail to appear and it will only cause problems for her. You know how he can be. If we are careful we won't have to meet Franco at all. Anyway he is not interested in us anymore, thank God."

"He is always interested in us. He follows your priest Mantua everywhere and that is only so that he can get close to you. Some people have long memories and he's one of them. He behaves as if the war has not ended. He is still trying to settle old scores."

Avia smiled sweetly.

"But Franco's particular *guerra* was with you *querido*," she said. "Anyway his eye is on a much larger ball."

"While Tito's is on Franco." Avi's voice softened. "I can't help thinking that there is some divine judgment in play here after all. Tito is flattered to death by Franco's attention when it is clear to everyone that Franco's real interest lies in a certain Roble woman by the name of – "

Avia snapped her fan and her eyes had turned that steely mauve that Isabel was beginning to anticipate.

"*Pas devant les enfants*," she said.

Isabel's eyes darted from one to the other. Once again her grandparents were engaged in a conversation full of hidden innuendoes and references to a past from which she was completely excluded. It seemed that there was a whole cobweb of family ties and hierarchy compounded by its role in a civil war that no one had forgotten. Equally her grandparents seemed to want to discuss absolutely everything, to actively search for something to discuss. Isabel was used to infrequent conversation. Julian Pelham had hardly spoken to her ever except when he was dying and the nuns encouraged silent prayer above all things. Isabel began to wonder if they would ever resolve the issue of mass that day and if her grandparents had forgotten that it was even the reason for their stop.

"It was a long time ago," said her grandmother firmly. "It is over." She looked in Isabel's direction. "We have to be bigger than this. We have to appear not to mind."

"Why? Why do we?" said Avi. "I have never minded what people think or do not think of my politics. You of all people know that."

Avia perched on the edge of her seat, smoothing her mantilla. Jose immediately opened the car door.

"And you of all people know that I have never cared what people think about anything *I* do." There was a flash of defiance. Avia's face was flushed. But Avi's eyes narrowed.

"I remember," he said coldly.

"In any event we have no choice now. We are so late, we *must* attend mass."

"Very well." Avi replied curtly. "But I'm warning you. We do not speak to Franco. You do not acknowledge him. Is that understood?"

Avia inclined her head and reached for Isabel's hand.

"Forgive us," she said. "This is very confusing for you, I'm sure. I keep forgetting you do not speak our language. Isabel please, you must go on ahead and we will follow shortly. It's not far from here. Look you can almost see it. Just beyond those bushes and through the gate."

Isabel could see nothing but shrubs and a cobbled path that petered out into olive groves.

"Run along child, we won't be a moment," said her grandfather. Isabel hesitated terrified at the thought of being separated even for a short time from her grandmother. She took a reluctant step forward and then shrank back. If she were drowning, nothing seemed suddenly as rock solid as the broad comforting shape of her grandmother. Isabel clung to her hand but Avia let go of her giving her a slight push.

"Go on! You can't get lost! Just follow the path. It doesn't go anywhere else!"

Isabel gulped and not wanting to disappoint her grandmother, walked on ahead. She shaded her eyes against the blinding sun and although it was cooler up here than it had been in the city, it was still hotter than anything Isabel had ever known. Sweat poured down her sides, her nylon shorts were horribly sticky and her feet felt as if they'd swollen to twice their normal size. Her hair felt like a heavy rope down her back. Isabel had no idea where she was supposed to be going. She had lost sight of the building Avia had pointed out and anyway the path here was bordered by grass that grew almost as tall as she was. She could only make out a few feet in front of her. She wished fervently that she were still at the convent.

Suddenly this Really Big Adventure seemed altogether too much of a good thing and Isabel had had enough. Tears formed in her eyes. If she couldn't have a Lap and a living father then she wanted to be back at school with Kate Douglas. Kate always told her the truth about everything even if it wasn't something Isabel necessarily wanted to hear. Like the time Isabel had cut off her baby doll's eyelashes and had gone to Kate hoping she would say they would grow back. Kate had considered the doll and then Isabel and then told her kindly but firmly that there was no way her baby doll's eyelashes would ever grow back but that they could try and make some new ones. Isabel hadn't minded. There was a certain security in knowing just how things were. Here in Spain however she had a funny feeling that people *didn't* tell you the whole truth. They smiled easily enough but then huddled together gabbling away in a different language. She didn't understand anything at all and she could sense that even though everyone felt sorry for her they didn't really know what to make of her. She now began to cry in earnest, tears and sweat mingling together. She came to a complete standstill unable to go on, blinded by the sun and the tall grass that scratched her face. She covered her face with her hands blocking out the heat and the alien landscape and wishing herself home again. And then just as she had made up her mind to go back and find Avia and tell her she wanted to return to England, she was struck in the side by something so forceful that she was sent flying to the ground. Winded, she sat on the dirt track shaking her head. She looked up bewildered as two young men, one blonde the other dark, looked down at her just as stunned as she was. For a moment no one moved and she stared up at them confused. While they spoke with men's voices they were dressed like over large sailor dolls.

"What the-?" said the blonde haired youth running a hand through straw coloured hair. "Who or what on earth are you?"

Isabel looked at him blankly. The other boy held out his hand to pull her to her feet. Isabel wished he hadn't, her hands were clammy. She would have done anything in her power, not to have to touch him but he was waving his hand in front of her face impatiently. Shyly she looked up at him meeting his intense, questioning look. His skin was so smooth and dark she wanted to touch it. His hair was black, spiky now because of the heat and his brown throat was smooth against his white sailor collar. He and the other boy were dressed identically. And that was what was strange, they were dressed as children but when they spoke it was with deep voices. This country was becoming stranger by the minute and more and more like the Mad Hatter's tea party.

"Come on!" he said more kindly now. "I won't eat you."

But still Isabel sat looking up at him dazed.

"Oh for goodness sake!" he said and reaching down pulled her roughly to her feet.

She could feel the other boy's eyes examining her and she flushed.

"Who's this?" he said. "You don't think it could be …?"

The dark haired boy grinned.

"Indeed I do." He turned to Isabel and said in precise, accented English. "You must be our cousin Isabel. But what were you doing standing in the middle of a field with your eyes shut?"

Isabel bit her lip.

"I'm supposed to be going to the church," she said at last. "But I can't find it." And to her horror she felt a solitary tear trickle down her cheek.

"Christ!" said the other boy groping for a cigarette. "Another Beatrice! They're bound to get on! Just our luck! We finally meet a girl from somewhere and she turns out to be just a kid! Don't suppose you know anything about the 'Beatles' do you?"

Isabel didn't understand what he was saying but his tone was so unpleasant that she felt tears falling freely now.

The dark haired boy frowned.

"Don't cry," he said gently. "Miguel and I will take you. We're supposed to be going to mass too."

"Are we?" said Miguel frowning under his fringe. Ricardo ignored him.

"I'm Ricardo by the way," he added.

"As in Ricardito" added Miguel. Ricardo shot him an irritated look.

"No just Ricardo," he said curtly and then unable to resist the temptation of returning the tease he added "and this is my twin Miguelito."

Miguel thumped his brother on the back.

"You big baboon, she won't understand your little joke."

Isabel shook her head.

"Everyone has such strange names and you're right, I don't understand any of it."

"It's just that in Spanish if you add *ito* or *ita* to something, it makes it small. So for example if I called you *Isabelita* it would mean little Isabel only you're not exactly … little." He finished lamely.

Miguel raised an eyebrow as he glanced from Isabel's bewildered expression to Ricardo's uncomfortable one.

"Great now she's to going to cry again!" said Miguel impatiently.

Ricardo handed her a handkerchief.

"No she's not," he said firmly. "Look, I'm sorry about the diminutive thing, it was clumsy of me and I was clumsy for knocking you over. We were in such a hurry we just ran for it. This path is usually empty. You gave us quite a shock!"

"You can say that again!" muttered Miguel.

"Look blow your nose and then we'd better get going. Everyone will be wondering where you've got to."

"I haven't seen Avia or Avi. They said they would catch me up."

"They probably decided to drive because of the heat. But don't worry we'll see them in church. It really is hot." Ricardo smoothed back his hair. "Come on Isabel, let's run together shall we?" He stretched out his hand. Isabel couldn't believe Ricardo would want to risk touching her again, especially as she now knew he thought her fat but hesitating only briefly, her seven year old's heart doing an enormous summersault, she slipped her hand in his.

Chapter 8

Isabel
Barcelona
Summer 1967

And that was how it began. Isabel was only seven years old when she fell in love with her cousin Ricardo but it was as real and strong to her then as it was to her when she was a grown woman. At first, her friend Kate dismissed her feelings as nothing more than a crush, sceptical that a child could feel anything but infatuation for someone so much older. Kate said that Ricardo was a father figure - the older brother Isabel was so desperate to find. As the years passed however, and the intensity of Isabel's feeling did not diminish, Kate had to admit that she might have been mistaken. She said she thought it unlikely that an English girl could feel so strongly at such a young age and that Isabel's passionate nature was entirely due to her Latin heritage. As far as Isabel was concerned, there wasn't a time that she hadn't loved Ricardo. Her earliest memories included him - he was part of her psyche in the way that language was. Ricardo *was* her language. He was her point of reference, the reason why she had acted throughout her life in the way she had. He was pivotal to her memories of Spain.

And she was never sure why it was that she had chosen him and not Miguel. Everyone agreed that blue eyes and blonde hair should have been more familiar to her - they were after all more *English.* Ricardo's looks were nothing special in Spain but to Isabel he epitomized glamour. But it was a confident, casual glamour combined with unexpected kindness that attracted her to him. Unlike the English boys she was to meet when she was older, he was perfectly comfortable chatting and showing affection to a child. He was happy to hold her hand all the way to the church. He chatted to her in his formal English, trying to make her feel welcome, trying to distract her while Miguel stomped grumpily ahead. Isabel remembered stopping once or twice along the path trying to catch her breath. Looking up towards the hills she had spied a tower, lodged high above them. She squinted in the sun.

"What's that Ricardo?" Isabel had asked in a whisper. Ricardo stopped, following her line of vision.

"What is what? Oh do you mean *Tibidabo*? The tower that looks like a rather grand pylon?"

Isabel nodded.

"*Tibidabo* is ... well it's where Catalans believe the Devil tempted Jesus. You know the story in the bible? The one in which the devil tells Jesus that the world can all be his, if he does as the devil tells him?"

Isabel nodded again enthralled by his voice, clinging to the feeling of calm it evoked in her.

"Tibidabo ..." continued Ricardo, "is a corruption of the Latin *Te Deo*, which means *I give you*. There used to be nothing more than the shrine and gardens - now there's a fun fair, restaurants and a cable car to take you to the top. And here we are."

And there they were. The path ended abruptly amidst a grove of orange trees and a small cloistered chapel whose stone was bleached white by the sun, its clean elegant lines in stark contrast to the opulence of the house she had just visited and everything in stark contrast to England. Especially the light, thought Isabel. It was harsh, unforgiving and the colours everywhere appeared that much brighter. And the heat was something she could never have imagined. And if her senses had not been overwhelmed enough, the sight of her cousins filled her with an envy of beauty that she had never before experienced. They stood together all three of them identically dressed in blue linen dresses with skirts that billowed from narrow hips. They wore matching blue pumps without socks that Isabel found very odd. They were extremely thin, tanned darker even than Ricardo and as they moved, their hair bounced off their shoulders, thick and shining and tied with matching blue ribbons. The older two even looked like Ricardo but the youngest was blonde like Miguel with the same eyes made all the more startling by the fact that the whites were so clear. For the first time in her life Isabel was aware of a feeling of unease, of dissatisfaction at who and what she was. And if Isabel thought Ricardo glamorous, then these little girls with their exquisite clothes and confident bearing were the most exotic creatures she had every seen. Isabel ate them up with her eyes, absorbing every detail. She felt a delicious tingling of excitement as she realized that all the girls had their ears pierced! Now that was something worth reporting back to Kate! She wondered instantly if she'd be allowed to have her ears pierced too. What would the nuns say to that?

Afterwards there was so much to remember about that first day. There was the suffocating, all embracing heat that buffeted her body in a breezeless vacuum. There were her terrifyingly beautiful cousins with their extraordinary, unpronounceable names and there was her aunt Nuria whom she grew to love as a mother. Initially she had been aware of soft skin and a cheek brushing the air.

"*Isabel!*" Nuria cried overcome with emotion at finding her real, live *espanola*-*inglesa*, her slavish devotion to all things Cervantine reaching new heights. Nuria had painstakingly chosen her own daughters's names and yet none of them displayed the virtues of their namesakes. Here was the long lost child come home to her at last. Here was another chance to nurture and mould. Nuria did not see an awkward little girl standing in front of her but the exquisite Isabel of the story and was prepared to love at first sight. It was almost irrelevant that she was also Clara's child.

The whispers grew. *Hija de Clara.* Isabel heard the voices buzzing round her.

"Isabel how good it is to have you here! And your name my darling is so perfect! I mean it's just such a pretty name." Nuria hugged her repeatedly as if frightened that either she or the figment of her imagination, might vanish. But she did not examine her in the way everyone else did, estimating her body weight, mentally noting her dreadful clothes. Nuria was delighted and she spun Isabel this way and that introducing her to everyone she knew. When she spoke her voice shook with feeling.

"Children. Here is our darling Isabel. Come and see!"

Come and see was right, thought Isabel. She felt a freak alongside these sleek, elegant beings and all at once the buoyant feeling she had felt walking with Ricardo was replaced once again with homesickness for the convent. She was so confused. One moment she felt warm all over, basking in all the attention and smiles but the next, when she couldn't understand what was being said and when it was so very hot, she longed for the nuns and for Julian. And although she knew that she would never ever see him again, that she had indeed lost him, she couldn't imagine what 'never' really meant. Already it seemed too long. This day in Spain was altogether too long by half. It was every bit the Really Big Adventure that Kate promised it would be, but now she wanted to go home. She would have to find her grandmother to tell her. She was sure that she could be taken back to the airport before lunch. With any luck she might even be home that very evening! Considerably comforted by this thought, Isabel spun round virtually into the arms of the priest. He caught her deftly in two strong hands, holding her against him. The smell of his cassock reminded her vaguely of Julian and for a moment she sank in the protection of his arms. She kept her head hidden in the folds of his cloth wishing that she might disappear. But the priest pulled her forward and she found her cousins staring at her. The little girls had formed a semicircle round her. Her uncle Tito pushed them aside and planted two rough kisses on her forehead, muttering something incomprehensible. Isabel fought back the tears. She simply mustn't cry. Now that she was six, she mustn't. Kate had warned her about this - that no matter how much she was tempted to, she was not to let anyone think she was a cry baby. Well the twins already did, she was sure of it. This made her want to absolutely blub but just as she opened her mouth to howl she caught sight of the middle girl whose cold dismissive stare stopped Isabel in her tracks. She brushed her eyes.

"Now this is Sigismunda," said the priest pulling the girl forward.

And Isabel had turned to meet her cousin. Their eyes locked and Isabel felt a tremor of fear. Marta and Beatrice were beautiful but there was something to Sigi's beauty that made her stand out even amongst her sisters. Like them she had thick shiny hair and skin and teeth that glowed with good health and careful attention. Like them she had a low forehead and arched eyebrows above almond shaped eyes. Her nose was short and straight, her hair so black it looked blue in the bright light. But it was the mouth full and sensual, that gave the otherwise classical face, its vitality. She was tall, long limbed and graceful. But she did not possess the rigid elegance of her sisters. There was something altogether wilder and more dangerous about Sigi and all the more fascinating.

"Do not ask about my name," she said tightly. "And never ever call me anything but Sigi. Do you understand?"

Isabel nodded not trusting herself to speak.

Sigi's eyes swept over her. "Is that the way orphans dress in your country? And you're wearing socks! No one wears socks in the summer! You must be boiling! You certainly look boiling."

"I am rather," said Isabel feeling smaller than the ants crawling between the cracks along the courtyard.

"Still I suppose being an orphan you're allowed to wear what you want. What's it like not having parents? Are they both really dead? I wish I could lose mine. I wonder where we would go if we did."

Sigi raised an eyebrow hoping to have shocked Isabel with her bluntness. But Isabel was unmoved.

"You'd probably have to stay here, with Avia. There'd be no point in you going to England would there?"

Sigi's lips twitched. "Logical, very logical. You see you've had the better deal. Is England very far away?"

"Not really. I slept most of the way. It seemed to take longer getting to the airport from school that it did from England to Spain. It's a lot colder in England and people look very different."

Sigi tossed her head. "*Ya veo*," she said unenthusiastically. "I can see that."

"Everyone looks as if they're going to a party. They're wearing such lovely dresses. I've never been to a party so I've never needed to dress up. This is what we wear for games. The nuns didn't think I should wear my uniform because it would be too hot."

Sigi stared at her cousin as if she were mad.

"We're not going to a party. This is what we always wear. I mean don't you wear dresses to church? I thought all girls did."

"I-I wear my uniform," said Isabel in a small voice. "I just wear what I have. But ..." she added eagerly suddenly remembering. "I do like dressing Mary. She has lots of different outfits and sometimes the nuns make her dresses from left over bits of material. There's never enough to make something to fit me but there is for Mary. They aren't as pretty as your dresses though. I would have liked Mary to have something a bit more frilly but the nuns said it would be 'showy' and that little girls shouldn't draw attention to themselves."

Sigi's fine arched eyebrows shot up creasing her otherwise perfect forehead. "Why ever not?"

"I don't know."

"Does Mary mind?"

"I don't know."

Sigi made a face. "You don't know very much do you?"

Isabel felt tears burn behind her eyes.

"Well didn't you ever ask her?" persisted Sigi. She stood scuffing one toe of her beautiful blue shoes along the edge of stone, her arms clasped behind her. The skirt of her dress swayed as she moved.

Isabel thrust her hands deep in her pockets beginning to shake.

"I can't ask her," she said in a small voice. " Mary isn't real. Mary is a doll."

Sigi's eyes were enormous.

"A doll!" she shrieked throwing back her head so that her hair fluffed out around her shoulders. "A doll!" And just as Isabel really had enough and this time would not hold back her tears, Sigi clasped her arms around her. "But that's even better!" she said delightedly. "How fabulous! We'll be able to play house together. My baby doll is in Val Negra so we can use your Mary this afternoon. Where is Mary? I must see her."

Isabel took a deep breath. "You can't see her I'm afraid. I left her at the Convent. Kate said I shouldn't take her with me as the heat might spoil her."

Sigi frowned dropping her arms. "And do you always do as this Kate says?"

"She's my big friend at school," said Isabel. "She usually knows what to do."

"I see," said Sigi put out. "Dr. Mantua thinks we should think for ourselves. That we should make up our own minds and not follow each other round like sheep. He says the twins are a bit like sheep," she paused as Isabel struggled with the concept. "I still think you should have brought Mary."

So did Isabel. She would so much rather please her cousin than annoy her. Sigi stood with her hands on her slender hips and Isabel knew she wasn't yet sure if they were to be friends or not. They began to walk away from the chapel and along the dirt path that led to Mialma. Sigi walked very slowly stopping every time she said something, her face animated, her eyes flashing.

"Never mind. We'll just have to think of something else to do until we go to Val Negra," she said. "But we aren't leaving 'til the evening. There's a whole afternoon ahead of us."

"What's it like? Living there I mean?" asked Isabel.

Sigi came to a stand still.

"Like?" she said surprised. "I thought you knew. Val Negra is the best place in the world. But you can't say what it's like because it's impossible to describe. But I know you'll love it. Anyone who has ever been there has loved it. And it's much cooler," she added eyeing Isabel's damp hair and shirt. "Everyone is always happier there, Mama especially because Tito goes walking in the mountains nearly every day. Sometimes he's away for a week. Those are the best times of all! She has more time for us too. She says there's nothing to distract her in the country and by that she means all those boring political people that Tito loves. We only have one telephone and the line is so bad that Tito's friends have given up trying to contact him there. We have a kind of freedom there that we don't have in the city. We're allowed really to do as we please. And go anywhere. Mama doesn't mind what we do as long as we don't hover." Sigi looked at her. "That is one thing you should remember about my mother. She can't abide hovering."

Isabel had a vision of the Lap and the perfect creature that was Nuria. She would be very happy to hover around her. Isabel felt a rush of gratitude, temporarily replacing her homesickness. She stopped.

"I know I'm going to be happy here," she said earnestly. "You're so lucky you know, to have brothers and sisters and to live in this wonderful house."

Sigi looked at her in astonishment.

"Are we? I wouldn't say it was lucky to have a brother like Miguel and sisters can be annoying. Especially Marta. We're supposed to share everything but somehow Marta never does because she's the eldest. And lately she's become very bossy. She has lots of dolls that she doesn't even like but she won't let me touch them. And the twins can be really mean. They are so much older than us that sometimes it's like having *three* fathers. I hate having older brothers actually. I don't mind B but she is still a baby really and cries at the slightest thing. But you ..." Sigi considered her thoughtfully under thick curly lashes. "I think that you could be just right."

Isabel felt herself grow hot with pleasure.

"Oh I do hope so," she breathed. "Really I do."

*

Lunch had been very long and very formal. The gigantic table was set with hard, crisp linen and the little girls were not encouraged to speak. Nuria sat far away from them and Tito was at the head. Isabel could have stretched out both her arms and still not reached her cousins' place settings. Maids glided behind their chairs, passing food, removing plates, wiping crumbs of bread with cotton gloves. Isabel was clumsy at serving herself and watched in awe as her cousins were able to grasp the serving spoon and fork in one hand and transfer the food onto their plates without spilling. She might have been eating with chop sticks for all the grace she showed. She felt the sweat on her forehead and was aware of everyone looking at her. The food itself was strange – fried eggs and bananas in tomato sauce – and vegetables were eaten as a separate course. Isabel had never had so much to eat at one sitting and was beginning to feel really sick. Nor could she understand a word of what was said. Tito talked very loudly while her Grand father spoke little and didn't seem to be at all happy. Neither did Nuria whose face was as white as the tablecloth.

"Politics," muttered Sigi darkly. "And Tito's work – it's all they're interested in. Every lunch-time it's the same. It's the only thing people talk about here."

Isabel nodded, her faculties numbed by so much food. Her gaze was drawn to the huge French windows and the curtains billowing in the breeze. Beyond the boundary of land, the sea was enticingly blue, glistening in the afternoon light. But in spite of its beauty and her earlier sense of elation, Isabel felt isolated from this family that spoke and behaved so differently and yet was linked so comprehensively to her, by blood. She was also physically self-conscious in a way she had never been before. She was aware of how she looked and ate and spoke and this made the food sink to her tummy and ache there. She felt soporific and bored. She longed to go out and play and she longed for her doll. She longed to be home. Abruptly the adults left the table and the maids began clearing away. The minute the chairs were scraped back, the twins vanished. But the little girls gathered around their cousin all perching on the edge of an enormous armchair.

"Are we going now?" asked Isabel eagerly.

"Going? Do you mean to Val Negra?"

She nodded.

"Oh no. It's still far too hot and besides the adults haven't had their coffee. We can't go until it's much cooler. Till tea time."

"But it's long past tea time!" she exclaimed. "It's almost 5 o'clock!"

Bea giggled.

"In Spain we have what is called *merienda* – your tea time - at around 7 and supper is at 10."

"But that's when I'm in bed!" said Isabel astonished.

"Things are different here."

Isabel struggled to remember what Sigi had said to her earlier.

"*Ya veo,*" she replied in Spanish but her spirits sank. The evening seemed a year away and the rest of the afternoon stretched dauntingly before them. It was strange to remember how the afternoons at the Convent whizzed by and how the time between tea and bed was never long enough. A shadow in front of the French windows blocked out the sun. Tito, with a cigar stuck in the corner of his mouth, stood in the archway, Nuria behind him.

"*Abuelita* is coming this afternoon," he announced.

"Oh joy," replied Nuria sarcastically. "So we won't be able to leave till really late now. Can't you see how the children want to get going? They've been waiting all weekend for this. Lunch was so awfully long today. I thought we'd never finish. At this rate we might as well not go at all."

"Oh no!" wailed Bea.

"Such an alarmist," said Tito calmly. "Of course we are going this evening. Abuelita was so looking forward to seeing the children before we left. I hadn't the heart to dissuade her. They won't see her all summer."

"More's the pity," muttered Nuria. She sighed loudly, in a resigned fashion. "Right then. We shall have more coffee." She nodded to one of the maids.

"Not for me," said Tito. "I'm off now. Entertain Mummy till I get back."

Nuria spun round.

"What!!" Her voice was shrill. "What do you mean off?"

Tito smiled and in the sunlight several gold teeth twinkled. Smoke slipped from his mouth. Isabel was reminded of a stout, hairy dragon.

"I'm going to *Montserrat,* to hear evensong," he said, delighting in Nuria's annoyance. "I always visit the shrine before we go on a journey, you know that, to pray for the family -for our safe return. We have so much to be thankful for, *verdad?* I believe in a spontaneous expression of joy."

The veins stood out blue along Nuria's arms and neck. She looked very thin and spiky standing behind her husband – spiky and a lot taller.

"Oh never mind that," she said furiously. "*Montserrat* is miles away and the traffic up the mountain will be awful. You won't be back for *hours.*"

"Can't be helped *querida.* Besides you have your wonderful family to amuse you and the new addition –" he nodded in Isabel's direction. "Especially the new addition. Hours of fun ahead of you."

Marta caught Isabel by the arm.

"This is because of you," she whispered. "We're delayed because *Abuelita* wants to meet you. Especially as she is an old girl."

Isabel pulled her arm away.

"An old girl of what?"

"Why of the Sacred Heart of course. She went to your convent."

"A hundred years ago you mean," interrupted Sigi.

"And she just loves English things," continued Marta waving her hands. "And people. She has a teacher who visits her once a week for conversation classes so that she won't forget it. She still thinks she speaks English fluently but Dr. Mantua says it's with a distinctly Cockney accent and that she shocks all the ladies at the British Embassy when she used to visit but could never understand why she did."

"Who is A- *Abuelita*?" stammered Isabel.

"She is our other grandmother, Tito's mother. She's Cuban. She has nothing to do with you. You aren't at all related."

Sigi took Isabel's hand in an unexpected show of solidarity, sticking out her tongue at Marta.

"Meanie! Meanie!" she taunted. "Don't worry Isabel," she said. "You're jolly lucky *not* to be related. We all prefer Avia to Abuelita. Even Marta does really. Marta *has* to be nice to her though because she is named after her. I wouldn't want to be called after Abuelita. She is Horrible."

Bea's eyes were wide.

"And hairy," she joined in. "She has hedgehogs all over her face especially around her mouth. I never want to kiss her again. She's one big prickle."

Isabel looked from one pretty face to the other, as young and fresh as their description of the other was wizened. They were lovely in their blue dresses, the skirts ballooning gracefully around them. With the heat and excitement their faces were flushed, their skin seemingly smoother and darker than ever. If nothing else, *Abuelita's* impending arrival provided a distraction to the long afternoon that lay ahead. But Isabel was once again painfully aware of her ill-fitting nylon shorts and clumsy shoes. She felt heavy after the enormous meal and sank easily into the armchair. The adults sat outside in large wicker chairs under the lemon trees sipping coffee.

"Where – where are the twins?"

"Smoking probably."

"So you know? I mean do they?" Isabel's eyes were wide. "I mean, not just pretend?"

"Of course we know," replied Sigi indignantly. "We know everything about them. They think they're so clever but they aren't any good at keeping secrets. They're always in the clock tower or on the balcony smoking and talking, mostly about girls."

"Boring," yawned Marta.

"Really? So how come you're always telling me about boys! You're in love with Fernando Bazan. Everyone knows that. Even Lupe," said Sigi pulling her sister's hair. Marta blushed.

"I am not."

"You are."

"Not. Not. Not."

As if on cue a door banged and there were footsteps in the hall.

"*Abuelita*!" They shrieked collapsing in a heap of giggles but on hearing footsteps the girls leapt to their feet standing close together in a straight line. Instinctively Isabel hid behind her cousins not knowing what to expect. For a moment they all held their breaths, Isabel longer than anyone else's and then Abuelita staggered, panting and wheezing into the drawing room leaning heavily on the arm of her driver. Isabel hesitated uncertain where to stand or what to do. She didn't want to appear to be hiding when the old lady entered but on the other hand she didn't want to spoil the pretty effect that a row of identical dresses must make by standing beside her cousins. So she hovered behind the armchair half crouching, her heart hammering in her chest. But to her great surprise Abuelita didn't look at all scary. Isabel didn't know what she'd been waiting for but it wasn't this very tiny, very fat woman who wobbled as she walked. She looked rather like Isabel's baby doll Mary, only much older of course. Her hair was done up in lots of little curls and ribbons just like Mary's was but she sparkled in a way that Mary did not, with large brightly coloured jewels. Her chest was immense. It shot straight down from shoulders to plump feet that spilled over expensive shoes. "You must dominate your feet," she was forever telling her grand daughters. "There is no such thing as uncomfortable shoes. If you want to be elegant you must suffer." And suffer she did and it was these toe-pinching shoes that made her so cross and irritable.

"*Nenas! Nenas!* Where are you?" Abuelita's voice was penetratingly high pitched. "What? Is there no one here to greet me? To kiss my poor cheek! And where's my little boy? *Donde estas Luisito? Tito!*"

Marta was pushed forward, a slender blue cygnet sprung from the nest.

"They're all outside *Abuela*," she said bobbing a curtsey. "Except for Father. He has gone to *Montserrat* to pray for a safe journey and won't be back till late."

"Ah Luisito ... such a religious boy! I always thought he would be a priest. He should have been a priest. He is wasted here. No one appreciates him. So many women!" Her eyes narrowed and she looked as if she had fallen asleep on her feet. But suddenly her face was animated. "Then I shall wait," she announced. "And where is your mother? Having coffee I suppose?"

Marta nodded.

"We were late having lunch. Avis had to collect Isabel from the airport. Did you remember she was coming, our English cousin?"

Abuelita's bosom heaved and she clapped her hands delightedly.

"Ah yes! Yes of course. Where is she? Bring her to me!"

Marta reached behind the chair, grabbing Isabel's arm. She was shoved unceremoniously in front of the little woman. Isabel felt huge in comparison and not much slimmer. A prickly cheek reached up to hers and watery eyes bore into her. Like Tito, Abuelita had a hawk-like nose and neat little teeth. Her heavily powdered face was crossed with thick lines. Her makeup cracked with perspiration and an artificial mole was suspended above a pouting mouth. Isabel shrank from her touch.

"Ah the English cousin! Julian's child am I right?" said Abuelita in her peculiar little girl's voice. "You are at the Convent aren't you? What a lovely place. I so enjoy the English climate. So good for the skin! Not like our terrible heat that dries everything up! Now tell me," Abuelita said earnestly. "Tell me, are you a ribbon?"

She referred to the system of merit used at the Sacred Heart schools. The head girl was one, and wore a blue sash around her shoulder, fixed at the waist. Subsequent ribbons as they were called, were awarded for academic achievement, religious duty and good behaviour.

"No."

"Do you expect to be?"

"Not really."

"I was a ribbon," said Abuelita proudly. "Every single year. The nuns said I was an example to the school and that for the benefit of the other children I should be given special privileges. It was a very happy time I must say." And then a propos of absolutely nothing she stated. " I do so like the way the English take tea."

Isabel's mind boggled at the thought of ribboning up Abuelita's immense bosom but said nothing.

"Are you happy there? I mean I know your Julian Pelham is dead but …" Abuelita frowned suddenly flustered. "Oh where is Luisito? It's too bad having to deal with children on one's own. Oh God. Oh God I feel faint …" She began to take tiny steps towards the garden.

"You are perfectly well Abuelita," said Marta firmly.

"Am I? Am I? Do you really think so? Do take me to your Mama. There's a good girl. It's the strain …"

She gestured vaguely in the direction of the children.

"And I must leave by nine at the latest. I like to be home early on Sundays."

The little girls looked at each other. NINE pm! That meant they wouldn't be able to leave for Val Negra till it was practically night time! Now they realised that Nuria hadn't been joking when she said they might not be able to leave till the morning. Despondently they trooped outside, avoiding the area where the adults sat and settled themselves on the grass. The air was heavy with the scent of gardenia. High above them on the patio beneath their tower bedroom, Isabel could see the twins. She shielded her eyes against the sun and Ricardo leaning over the balustrade, waved.

"The girls all like Miguel the best," said Marta. Isabel looked away quickly. "Because of his blond hair and blue eyes."

"Miguel thinks we're silly. He doesn't like us," said Bea.

"That's because we're girls."

"*Little* girls," corrected Marta. "He doesn't mind big girls with big boobies."

Isabel giggled.

"Ricardo likes elegant women. Not the obvious ones," said Sigi. "I heard him talking about Sonia de Cana. He said she was just his type. He likes them to be clever."

The sisters laughed but Isabel was instantly deflated. While they were talking, while they laughed with her, Isabel forgot that she was different. She could even convince herself that by being associated with them, that because they were all cousins, a little of their glamour might rub off on to her. But she was mad to think like that! She wasn't at all like them. She was far too plump and badly dressed for one thing. For another she lacked their effortless charm, their inherent grace. Above all, she didn't have their conversation, that easy flow of words that connected them to other people who thought and behaved as they did - who claimed them for their own. No one claimed her. She didn't belong. The only reason she was here was because of her mother, because of a woman Isabel knew nothing about. Isabel was beginning to be sick of her mother's name. If she heard just one more person say that she was 'Clara's daughter', she would scream! If only she had been born one of her beautiful cousins. If only she had two parents and lots of sisters and brothers who didn't poke and prod her to see the *Inglesita* for themselves. If only, for one day, she could step into their expensively crafted shoes, into their beautiful brown skin. If only…

*

It was dark and very late when they eventually set off for Val Negra in a neat convoy of cars. Jose drove Isabel and the little girls while the grandparents, Nuria, the twins and Tito travelled separately. Isabel was so tired she felt nauseous. Half of her craved sleep while the other half wanted to stay awake. She felt her eyes droop, exhausted with the effort of talking. For a while her cousins chatted, quarrelled and then grew silent. Afterwards, there was only the purring of the car and the squeak of Jose's leather gloves as he spun the steering wheel in his hands. Swiftly they cleared the gorge near Mialma and headed for the Northern provinces. Here the roads were isolated and winding, lit only by the occasional street lamp. Outside was a blanket of darkness. Jose rolled down his window and the air that rushed in was cool and sweet, scented with pine and verbena.

Isabel had lost all sense of time when the cars ground to a halt. In the distance a faint, mauve light trickled along the horizon. She must have fallen asleep after all and now she sat up blinking, struggling to make sense of her surroundings. Tall gates opened slowly in front of them and the cars moved off once again in unison. There was the palest outline of mountain and colour, like silent lightening, streaked the sky. The road was flanked on either side by corn fields and to the South, a purple blush defined the vineyards. And then the house came into sight. Only it wasn't what Isabel would have called a house at all. It had turreted towers just like the castles she had seen illustrated in story books. There was an archway hung with lanterns and long torches whose nocturnal flames had shrunk by morning.

Isabel gasped, "But this is a castle! Who can live here? Is it Abuelita's?" Isabel could think of no other person who might own such a place.

Marta woke up with a start and looked at her cousin.

"I was asleep," she said fiercely.

"I know but we're here!" said Isabel excitedly. "Or at least we've stopped. At a castle!"

Sigi sat up too rubbing her eyes.

"Oh that!" she said casually. "That's Val Negra." She pushed back her tousled hair and opened the car door. "This is home. *Vamos hermanas!*" Marta and Bea sprang from the car shrugging off sleep like an unwanted piece of clothing.

And with her cry the peaceful dawn was shattered. Doors slammed, dogs and people seemed to be everywhere. Light cascaded from windows flung open to greet them. There was the sound of crunching gravel, voices and barking animals. Luggage was unloaded, maids scurried to and fro unloading boxes. Jose helped a weary Nuria to alight from her car. Tito strutted with his dogs, shouting orders to the servants. Isabel studied the mellow stone building with its arches and balconies. It was covered in scented white flowers and the air was cool and sweet. She shivered, cold with fatigue. Someone draped a blanket around her shoulders and pushed her towards the house. Isabel turned with a start to see a little old woman grinning up at her. She had a dowager's hump and hairs grew in odd places over her face. It seemed to Isabel that a lot of old women here, with the exception of her grandmother, had hair on their faces. This woman's thin hair on her head was coiled into a neat white bun a wisp hanging down the back looking rather like a dead mouse. Isabel was grateful for the blanket that hid her sudden shivering. This little old woman looked exactly like the witch in Rapunzel. But to her astonishment, her cousins flung themselves into the woman's arms.

"Lupe! Lupe!" they cried.

"Well what a time to arrive!" replied the old woman with a lopsided smile. "It gets later and later. It's morning now but you'll have to have some rest. You won't be able to go all day if you stay up. Come along now, we'll have you tucked up in bed in no time. And where does this little urchin come from? Is she here to help in the kitchens?"

"Oh Lupe this is no urchin, this is Isabel. Our English cousin, the one we talked about, remember?

Isabel shrank into her blanket, as Lupe stepped forward to examine her. To her relief, Lupe was not interested in her clothes.

"Julian's child? *Hija de Clara?*" she said in wonder and she touched Isabel's face feeling it all over as though she were blind. "So you are Isabel. Why were you not named after your mother?"

"How can she know that?" said Marta crisply.

"She should have been called Clara," insisted Lupe.

"Well she's not," said Sigi. "Leave her alone Lupe she's really tired. She's not used to our hours."

"I'm not surprised. Making her travel through the night. I've never heard of anything so foolish. Still I suppose your Papa knows what he's about although sometimes it's hard to know what he's doing with his life. Follow me my beauties. Your rooms are all made up. You can shower later. Right now it's sleep!"

"Who is Lupe?" whispered Isabel as the children followed the old woman into an immense flag stone hall lit with torches and hung with tapestries. Even if this was summer, a fire blazed in the enormous hearth casting fantastic shadows along the dove grey walls. There were two large sofas on either side of a fireplace piled high with pine cones. A large bowl of mimosa on a table in the centre of the hall gave off a delicious scent. Isabel longed to curl up on the cushions and go to sleep. But Sigi pulled her by the hand as she drifted towards them.

"Lupe's our nanny," she said. "Well no longer *our* nanny. Nuria says she's too old really to look after any one but she has to live here. She has nowhere else to go. She was actually Tito's nanny when he was a small boy and she helped look after the twins when they were born, although Nuria says that Miguel was too much for her! She helps with our clothes and generally potters about getting in everyone's way. The other girls do the real work. She's happy to see us now but that's not normal for her. Just wait a few days! She's really bad tempered most of the time and chases us with a broom. Marta and I call her Scorpion Lupe even to her face. She's quite deaf you know. You can say anything and she won't hear you."

Isabel's eyes grew round.

"She's not a ... witch!" she breathed.

Sigi burst out laughing.

"No of course not although she certainly looks like one. She's not really that bad. Except when she wants you to do something that you don't want to. But she's the only person in the world who orders Tito about and that alone makes Mother says she's worth her weight in gold. Whatever that means. Come on the others have gone up!"

Isabel followed her cousin out of the hall and up a large curved staircase. On the second floor they peeled off in a corner where narrow stone steps led up to the turret bedrooms. There were fat rope banisters to hold on to and narrow casement windows looked out onto the courtyard below. Beyond lay the vineyards sheltering beneath the graceful curve of the Monseny. Somewhere a bird was singing.

"You two are in here," announced Lupe who was waiting for them at the top of the stairs.

"Now clothes off and into bed!"

"Yippee!" exclaimed Sigi. "I thought Mother might put you in with Bea. I used to share with Marta."

"Yes and she's gone upstairs. In a room by herself," said Lupe.

"Oh," said Sigi momentarily deflated.

"But this has been redecorated and look, the beds are new," said Lupe and then seeing Isabel shiver she turned to her. "Yes it's cold here. You'll be glad of the extra blankets."

Isabel looked around her. It was a cosy little room with wrought iron beds and flowered quilts. Rugs were strewn over highly polished floor boards. The sheets were turned down and Isabel could hardly wait to get in between them. She felt weak with fatigue and suddenly the voices thinned and the room began to spin. Lupe took her firmly by the shoulders.

"Better get this little one to bed," she said. "I wonder if she hasn't inherited her mother's delicate constitution."

"*Delicate*!" protested Sigi.

"Ach! This is puppy fat!" said Lupe tweaking Isabel's cheek. "And not enough exercise! It will go in time. As will these," she tapped her glasses. "Besides how people look has nothing to do with what they're like inside. The most ugly people can be really beautiful and no one can see it. I've seen my fair share of children and believe me the plainest ones grow up to be the prettiest!"

"So what will happen to us?" asked Sigi climbing into bed. Lupe groaned as she stooped to pick up the children's discarded clothes.

"We'll have to wait and see now won't we. Not one of us can see into the future …" Lupe's voice faded. Isabel hardly remembered being undressed or getting into bed or even feeling homesick. She was so tired that she fell asleep as soon as her head touched the pillow.

Chapter 9

Isabel
Val Negra
Summer 1967

    Light seeped through the shutters, spilling long triangles of light onto oak beams. Isabel burrowed under the covers still sleepy. For a few moments she could not remember where she was. Slowly she surfaced through layers of unconsciousness. The bed was deliciously comfortable and the sheets were softer than those at the convent and smelt of lavender. It was very quiet. Then suddenly there was a loud grating sound as the wooden shutters were flung open and sunlight burst into the room.

"Are you awake?" hissed Sigi.

"I am now." Isabel kept her head hidden, slowly opening her eyes. Sigi stood by the window in a transparent nightdress, her hair tumbling around her shoulders. Her face was full and soft.

She stretched.

"Isn't it wonderful? I always forget how lovely it is here and how quiet! What's the time do you think? I'm starving. Aren't you?"

Isabel threw off the covers and looked around her. The room was completely different by day. There was a fan overhead and mosquito netting draped around the beds. Under the window was a delicate carved bench with pink striped cushions. There were shelves crammed with books and a cupboard painted with pink and green flowers. Sigi opened the doors to reveal immaculately piled clothes and lovely dresses hanging from padded hangers. Without giving the exquisite clothes a moment's thought, Sigi tore off her nightgown, leaving it in a diaphanous swirl on the floor. She pulled on a white linen dress that had tiny red strawberries embroidered on the skirt. She shoved her feet into red, rope-soled shoes with ribbons that tied around the ankle like a ballet dancer's. Isabel thought grimly of her own clumsy leather sandals that she wore with socks.

"I like your shoes," she said shyly. Sigi had a red ribbon between her teeth as she tied back her hair.

"What! These things?" she said her cheeks pink, arms above her head. "Espadrilles? Everyone wears them here. We've copied them from the peasants. Only theirs are flatter and always black. Come on!" She added impatiently. "Do get dressed. I'm starving!"

Breakfast was laid out in the dining room on a long mahogany table. Muslin curtains fluttered in the breeze and through them, the vineyards seemed like a sea of lavender. There were pretty pictures on the cream painted walls and on the floor a huge needlepoint rug depicted bunches of faded roses. There were great bowls of gardenias on polished walnut furniture and a clock chimed faintly in the background. No one else was about.

"I can't work out if it's very early or very late," said Sigi helping herself to an enormous plate of food.

"It's certainly very quiet."

"Breakfast isn't a very sociable time, thank goodness. You just help yourself and go off when you're ready. There's no fixed time and no one minds what you eat. Mother always wants to know if we've drunk our chocolate milk but that's all." She took a large bite of bread. "Come on. Don't be shy. Tuck in. Afterwards I'll show you round the garden and we can go down to the river."

Through mouthfuls of bread and gulps of chocolate, Sigi chatted happily away so that Isabel didn't feel obliged to answer. She tried the *pantomaca*t – white bread wiped down with tomatoes- an odd thing to have for breakfast – and milk on its own which Isabel soon discovered was laced with sugar and far too sweet to drink.

"What's the matter? Don't you like it?" asked Sigi noticing her little grimace of distaste.

"It's too warm and very sweet!"

"How do you drink milk in your country?"

"Very cold, for one thing and we never add sugar. The nuns say there's enough of the stuff in it already."

"Gosh," said Sigi in surprise. "We'd never drink milk without it. Not that we willingly drink milk. No Spanish child likes milk. You have some peculiar ideas. Have you finished then?" She pushed away her chair. "Now look, before we do anything else, we'll start outside. Then we can cycle into the *pueblo*. Getting there isn't so bad – it's all down hill – but the way back is exhausting! What is it? Don't tell me you can't ride a bicycle!"

Isabel pulled a face. "No. I can, only I'm not very good. Er … does it have stabilisers?"

"No. Beatrice has a tricycle but you wouldn't want to ride that would you. Not with everyone watching! *Que diran!* What would people say?"

"No," agreed Isabel hastily.

"Doesn't matter. We'll take it slowly," said Sigi confidently. "You can push it most of the way if you want to."

Sigi opened the French doors that led onto a large veranda shaded by palm trees and huge tobacco plants. Wisteria and a tangled mass of roses climbed over the pale stone of the house and beyond them a wild meadow careered down to the river. The vineyards sloping to the foot of the Monseny were a purple blush in the distance. Closer to the water's edge, Isabel could trace the outline of supporting stakes. The fruit heavy with dew, made a multicoloured patchwork against the brilliant sky.

Sigi stretched out her arms towards the land. "As far as the eye can see," she announced grandly.

"What is?"

"Why all this," Sigi dropped her arms. "Val Negra of course - the vineyards, the land below the Monseny and the river – it's all Val Negra. The De Cana's *finca* lies to the East, the Bazan's to the West. Those houses are big wine makers. They send most of their produce abroad but ours is only sold locally. Avia isn't interested in real business any more. Tito is always trying to persuade her to expand – to do it properly. Avia says she's too old for all that, that everyone would start squabbling over who did what. She's right of course."

"But then," asked Isabel "who eats all the grapes?"

Sigi looked at her in astonishment.

"Isabel *querida*, we don't *eat* the grape. It's used for wine. You do know how they make wine don't you?"

"Er … sort of …" Isabel's voice was very small. "There's just so much of it!"

"A lot is needed. You'll see for yourself soon, at the end of the summer, when they pick the fruit and squash it down into pulp," Sigi explained. "Women come up from the village to help. You should see them! They stand in trucks full of grape flattening the fruit with their bare feet. If Tito is away, Lupe lets us help. It's brilliant fun and we get absolutely covered in juice and muck! Although if mean, old Carlos Nadal is in charge, then

Marta and I aren't even allowed to watch! He's such a bad tempered old so and so. Avia only uses him when she's absolutely desperate, and only because he knows Val Negra so well. She says she's never trusted him. You'll see him in the pueblo. He's always lurking round some corner. He thinks we're all too spoilt for our own good, except for Miguel of course. But that's because he wants to be a soldier and like Miguel, Carlos Nadal loves the army. He says that Marta and I are nothing but pip squeaks."

"Gosh what does that mean?"

"I have no idea but it can't be very nice coming from Carlos."

"I'd stay clear of him," volunteered Isabel.

"I do."

They made their way along the edge of the swimming pool, through an orchard full of figs and peaches. A narrow path wound its way through a wild meadow scattered with poppies and bunches of damp lavender. The sun, now high in the sky, was warm on their faces. A balmy breeze fanned tall blades of grass. There was a rustle of willow trees and then the sound of water as a clear stream appeared at their feet. Sigi sat down on the pebbled bank and untied her espadrilles. The ribbons lay like bright, tangled blood stains on the dull stone.

"Come on!" she said wading in. She tucked her dress into her knickers and bent down to splash her face. "It's delicious." Sigi's legs were long, shiny and brown and her feet slender in the turning water. Her beautiful hair tumbled from its ribbon down her back. The muscles of her arms were taught and smooth as she bent and stretched. Shafts of sunlight darted between the trees lighting up patches of the stream bed so that the pebbles looked like precious stones beneath the moving water. Isabel hesitated, gasping as much at the feel of the cold water as the sight of her own white, fat legs. After a while though, she stopped staring at her cousin's neat calves and began to enjoy herself. They collected smooth pebbles, bits of willow bark and whatever else they could find beneath the shallow surface of the water. When the skin on their feet became wrinkled, they sat in the sun drying themselves. Lying on her stomach, Isabel fashioned a doll out of a few dried bits of straw.

"Not sure about the face!" said Sigi critically. " And her body is awfully long. But in a funny way I think she looks like one of the *gigantes y cabezudos* you see at carnival time. They're really people walking on stilts with enormous heads. We should call her *Reina del Rio* so that you'll always remember your very first day in Val Negra, the start of your very first summer here." She squatted down by the edge of the water. She cupped her hands so that water ran through her fingers over the doll. "I baptise you Queen of the River," she said.

Isabel laughed. "She's not a Queen, she's only a straw doll!"

Sigi turned to her fiercely, the pleasant expression wiped from her face. "She is a Queen. She's whatever I say she is!"

They waited until their feet had dried in the sun before going up to the house in search of bicycles. Along the way Sigi showed Isabel the stables and cobbled courtyard that led to the family chapel. They found a collection of farm machinery in one of the outbuildings, scooters in various stages of repair and several bicycles covered in cobwebs. Sigi chose two of the least rusty and they dragged them outside wiping the seats clean with their hands. They walked together through the arches of the main courtyard, along the oak lined drive. But once out of the avenue, Sigi shot ahead, red espadrilles peddling furiously.

"Just follow the road!" she shouted. "But try not to go over the edge! You can't get lost. It doesn't go anywhere except to the village!"

Isabel tried not to look down, for the road which she hadn't seen by night, now made her giddy. There was no barrier. Below, the village nestling among the trees seemed small and a long way down. Isabel started down the hill, dragging her feet in case she had to stop suddenly. Gradually she gathered speed, luxuriating in the feel of the sun and breeze on her face and in the smell of eucalyptus. They passed several villas set back from the mountain road.

"That's where the Bazan brothers live!" shouted Sigi motioning to tall, grey gates. An army of scorpions was picked out in gold along the wrought iron balustrade and carved into the supporting stone pillars. "Marta likes Fernando. I think they'll get married when they're grown up. They've always liked each other, even when they were really tiny. Fernando is very good looking but he doesn't say much. He has a younger brother called Benito. He isn't good looking at all but he's a lot friendlier. They're always at the club playing cards. We'll go there afterwards for a drink. And that's where Rodrigo de Montfalco lives," she pointed to imposing black gates. On either side was a stone statue of a dancing lion and in the middle, where the lock should have been, was a painted coat of arms. "No one has seen him for a while. He used to be a friend of Miguel's when they were younger. He studies in Madrid now because his parents didn't think the schools in Barcelona were good enough for him. He's awfully boring. Nuria says the family prefers horses to people. He's very tall and very rich and all the mothers, *including* Nuria invite him to meet their daughters!"

"Does *he* want to get married?"

"Of course not but people here don't get married because they love each other! Marta and Fernando will be allowed to because we've known his family all our lives and they're neighbours. Families here arrange marriages between their children. It doesn't really matter who Rodrigo de Montfalco wants to marry, his parents will decide. They probably already know who it will be. They've been planning it since he was small. And they'll start with you next if you're not careful."

"Me!" said Isabel astonished. "But I'm only little. Besides I don't *want* to be married! Ever!"

"As I've just explained that won't matter. You'll have to marry whom Tito says. Now that you've come to live with us you'll have to. Haven't you heard people ask you if you are *hija de Clara*, Clara's daughter? That's because they're curious. You're someone new to talk about. And most importantly, you're a foreigner. They'd rather their sons marry an *inglesita* than a Spanish girl who isn't a Catalan."

"Why?"

"Because Catalans don't like the Spanish. We don't really want to be part of Spain at all. We are nothing like the Spanish."

"But you *are* Spanish!"

"No we're not. We're Catalans. That is completely different. We speak our own language, we want our own government, we cook different food, we have different dances. We don't even *like* bull fights!"

"What is a bull fight?"

Sigi slowed her bicycle.

"Isabel don't you know anything? I mean your clothes and your glasses, they're all so different. It's as if you come from another planet!"

Isabel blushed.

"I *feel* as though I've come from another planet. It's just ... well I've never thought about myself much before coming here. At the convent we didn't talk about clothes and people and what they did. We went for walks and had tea and read books and drew pictures."

Isabel thought of her school with a pang and in particular of the panelled dining room at tea time, where trays of rock cakes hot from the oven were laid set out on long tables. There were large pitchers of cold milk and steaming pots of tea for the older girls and afterwards she could do some colouring.

"We all look the same at school," continued Isabel. "I suppose you wouldn't like our clothes at all. They're pretty old fashioned really, but somehow it doesn't seem to matter."

"Well clothes are an obsession here. Women talk about fashion, food and children. Men talk about food and politics. And everyone talks about Franco."

"He sounds like a really bad man. No one likes him do they?"

"Not much. Except for Tito of course."

"Why don't you call Tito, Father? It's as though he were a friend, not your family."

Sigi stopped her bicycle.

"Not a friend, Isabel," she said. "Don't ever think of him as a friend." And then quickly, as if daring herself to speak, she added. " Was yours?"

Isabel thought with a jolt of Julian Pelham. She always thought of him by his Christian name and hardly ever as a father so she supposed in that respect she and Sigi had something in common. Although given her limited experience of parents, she was beginning to wonder if he hadn't been a lot more normal than she thought. Well perhaps not normal in the way Kate Douglas would call normal, but certainly in comparison to Tito. And in spite of his eccentricities and ill health, he was hers.

"Yes," she said at last. " I think he was." Sigi shot her another look but before she could speak, Isabel replied hastily.

"I didn't know my mother."

They had reached the pueblo. This was a tiny village square with a baker, a butcher and post office. When she wasn't serving in the shop, the baker's wife sold espadrilles from the front room of her house. The church was set back, up several stone steps, in a clearing of its own. Opposite, was a tiny cafe whose tables spilled out onto the pavement. The pueblo was the meeting point for the servants who waited on the families, who summered at Val Negra. Only the children of these families ever crossed the square, usually on their way to the village club. The adults only descended from their hillside villas to hear mass, if there was no priest available to visit them at home. In a way therefore the pueblo belonged to the children. It was where they played at being adult. Friendships and romantic trysts were begun there and ended. It was safe, they were armed with the confidence of being known wherever they went and they could buy whatever they wanted on credit.

Sigi propped her bicycle outside the baker's shop. There were large *cocas* in the window, cakes and hundreds of boiled sweets in large woven baskets.

"I always come here, on my first day in Val Negra," said Sigi smiling. She walked purposefully into the shop. It smelt of dough, of softness, of sugar. A tall, blond woman in a spotless white apron appeared from behind a curtain of clanking beads. She had hard black eyes and a face that did nothing to hide the resentment she felt at having to pander to the little girls of the very big houses.

"*Bon dia. Que voleu?* Hello and who are you?" she said looking at Isabel. "This is a face I do not recognize, a stranger in our midst? "

Sigi's breath tickled her ear. "You see how curious they are? How they want to know everything?"

"Then tell her."

Sigi took Isabel's hand.

"*La meva cosina. Filla de la Clara.*"

"*Nom digues!*"

Afterwards, Sigi said that Isabel was good entertainment value, that because of her she'd never had so much fun in the pueblo; that above all she enjoyed the moment when she announced that Clara's daughter had returned. She said she loved the gasp of surprise and then the volley of questions. The Baker's wife showed all these things and more. She clapped her hands together.

"I can't believe it," she said examining every bit of Isabel. "After all these years. Who would have thought it? Such a little stranger eh?"

Isabel shifted uncomfortably all too aware of the contrast she must have made with her cousin.

"And I suppose the Englishman is the father?"

Sigi made a strange face and for a moment the Baker's wife and the little girl were locked into an age-old social conflict.

"We've come for your sweets, Senora," said Sigi. "To go on the account as usual." She grabbed a paper bag and began chucking in handfuls of chocolate bonbons and marzipan.

"What would you like Isabel?" She didn't wait for a reply but thrust a paper cone into her hand. "Choose what you like. Have anything you want."

Isabel stood transfixed. She had never seen so many sweets in her life and now that she could chose, didn't want any of them. She was tired of being labelled 'Clara's daughter', discomfited by the curiosity that the mention of her father's name evoked. She was trying not to think about him too much and yet just when she was beginning to feel as though she could breathe again, someone said his name and the tightness in her chest returned. Listening to Sigi chattering away in her own language reminded Isabel once again that she wasn't part of this strange new world. She forced herself to smile but that sinking feeling was back and she felt cold.

"Yes. Yes," the baker's wife was saying in broken English, "much cooler here than the city."

Isabel nodded, eager to be out of the shop.

"You haven't got very much," said Sigi when they were outside again.

"No," replied Isabel in a low voice. They were silent for a bit while Sigi popped sweets into her mouth. She crunched up the rest of her cone and put it in her pocket.

"I know what we could do," she said suddenly. "I've had an idea."

She pulled her cousin back into the shop.

"No!"

"Well you're going to have to suffer to be beautiful!" grinned Sigi. "It's the only way. Now what colour? What colour espadrilles shall you have?"

Isabel's face lit up.

"Oh really?" she said. "Espadrilles like yours?"

"Absolutely. But they don't have to be red. You can have any colour you want."

"No I'd like red, like yours. They've got to be exactly the same. But ..."

"But what? This also goes on Tito's account if that's what you're thinking. He won't even notice. It's the way we always shop here. Even Beatrice knows how to get sweets from the Senora baker. Anyway I enjoy getting things out of her. I don't think she likes me much."

Sigi clanked the beads loudly to attract the baker wife's attention. " Look you can't go around in socks and shoes. No one but no one wears socks in summer! Not even grown men!"

"If you're sure –"

The baker's wife emerged from a back room.

"Ah the young ladies ... again."

Outside the shop, Isabel tore open the paper bag containing her brand new espadrilles. She took off her shoes and socks and put them in the bag.

"I never want to see these again," she said shoving the lot into the closest bin. Isabel's spirits soared. She looked down at her new bright red espadrilles with delight. Her legs were still white but at least she was half way to being dressed like her cousin. They walked back to where they had left their bicycles, Isabel stopping every few yards to examine her shoes. Sigi dipped into her cone of sweets. She studied Isabel critically.

"You know it's a shame about the shorts. And Lupe says she doesn't think you'll always have to wear glasses. And one day you will probably lose weight. But you look a lot better than you did."

Isabel looked down at her feet. The ribbons of her espadrilles dug into her legs. Sigi's, by contrast, only accentuated the smoothness of her tanned legs and narrow ankles, her lovely cotton dress brushing her knees.

"I'm sure Lupe could make you a dress," she added. "Its just that I don't think any of ours would fit you."

"No," said Isabel miserably, all pleasure in her new shoes evaporating. "I suppose not."

"Have a sweet."

Isabel raised her own cone.

"I've got these thanks."

They walked together pushing their bicycles. Just as they reached the road that would take them up the mountain to Val Negra, they saw Marta and Bea. They were playing a game on the dusty patio of a village house.

"Oh good," said Sigi. "They're with the Bazan brothers."

"What are they playing?"

"It's called *caracoles*, you know – oh what's it called –snails that's it."

"Snails?"

"Yes. You draw squares on the ground with chalk."

"Oh you mean hop scotch!"

"You throw a stone and hop on one foot?"

Isabel nodded.

"Then," said Sigi, "*caracoles* is hopscotch. There, you see we aren't so different after all."

She waved as the boys looked up.

"Now what we really want to do is wrangle an invitation to *their* place. Senora Bazan is Cuban. She knew Tito before coming to Spain. But she's a *nice* Cuban," she added hastily seeing Isabel's expression. "She actually plays with her children. She doesn't have nannies to look after them like other mothers. And she lets us cook with her and make things. She's especially good at making sweets. Hers are magical because she uses something called *Bois de Panama*, which makes the liquid froth up when she's cooking. The bubbles are this high." Sigi made a gesture with her hands. "Can you cook?"

Isabel was taken aback. "I don't know. I've never tried."

"Avia likes all of us girls to cook. She's more fun to learn with than Abuelita." She made a face." At least with Avia no matter how many eggs you break she doesn't get cross. Abuelita has to have her maid with her all the time and she won't let us touch anything. And then she goes to bed for the afternoon because she's so exhausted. So I don't see the point. Avia thinks she's a better cook than Abuelita on account of *Tia Victoria's Spanish Cookbook*. She seems to think we're the only family in the world who can really cook. And because Abuelita is Cuban, Avia doesn't think she counts."

"*Bon Dia. Ets tu la inglesita?*" Benito Bazan's squashed, spotty face looked up as they approached. Isabel leant her bicycle against the wall of the patio.

"Yes," she replied stonily.

"Clara's daughter? The Spanish-English girl?"

Isabel nodded.

"I speak English you know," said Benito between hops around the *caracol*. There was something about his eyes, thought Isabel that reminded her of a small animal. They weren't at all curious and hard like the baker's wife. And he didn't seem to mind that she wore hideous clothes.

"I can see," she said sharply and as his face fell she added quickly, "*your* accent is very good."

"That's because we have lessons every afternoon," he replied breathlessly. "Like these girls. Sometimes with Dr. Mantua. He says he speaks the English of the BBC."

Isabel laughed.

"Do you think he does?"

"I – I think his English is excellent. But I haven't spoken with him for long."

"I like your new shoes," he said. "Come and play if you don't mind them getting all dusty. We're going to the club for a while before lunch and then maybe have *Horchata* in the pueblo."

"We've just *been to* the pueblo," said Sigi in her grown up voice. "And I'm sure my cousin won't want to ruin her shoes."

"How do you know?" said Isabel indignantly. She turned to Benito, "What is *Horchata?*"

Benito stopped his hopping and came to sit beside the girls on the patio wall.

"It's a drink they make here in summer," he said. " It's made from the *chufa* nut. You drink it cold. You must try it now as you won't find it later in the city. You can only ever get it in the summer."

"I'd love to," said Isabel.

"Oh very well," agreed Sigi. "But I want a game of this first. You sit and protect your espadrilles."

"No Isabel is going to play too," said Benito firmly. "Then we'll go to the club." He pulled Isabel off the wall so that she landed perfectly on the first square. He kept hold of her hand.

"There you are!" he said triumphantly. "All ready to go!"

Isabel felt warm with gratitude. The boy's hand was smooth and dry and surprisingly strong. He slipped the stone in hers.

"You throw," he said.

They played until they were tired and then sat on the patio steps watching Fernando and Marta finish their round. Fernando was a beautiful boy with cornflower blue eyes and jet black hair. He hardly took his eyes off Marta who skipped and darted before him, equally enchanting in a white dress embroidered with tiny red strawberries just like Sigi's and B's. Marta also wore red espadrilles. Just like mine, thought Isabel contentedly. Hopping on one foot, Marta made the game look like a beautiful dance. The skirts of her dress twirled around her slim, tanned body as she moved. It was getting late so they cycled back to the pueblo, to the youth club, a large yellow stone villa where the young people met daily to plan their evenings, play tennis or cards and for the older ones to meet their girl friends away from the prying eyes of their parents. It was the one place where the adults did not go. Grouped around the swimming pool, teenagers played dominoes or sun bathed. Isabel spotted the twins smoking and holding court to a bevy of pretty girls.

"Look there's Sonia de Cana!" said Bea excitedly. "She's Ricardo's girlfriend. Everyone says they'll get married."

Isabel turning to look in Bea's direction was dismayed to see a lovely blonde creature in a check bathing suit. The girl was laughing, a tanned hand holding back a mane of yellow hair. The twins ignored their sisters as they marched towards them. Undaunted, Marta flirted and joked with their friends while Benito took Isabel for a *horchata* which they sipped under the umbrellas by the bar. It was a delicious drink Isabel decided, after initially thinking it bland and rough. It quenched her thirst and revived her. From where she sat, Isabel could clearly see Sonia and Ricardo as they swam together up and down the length of the pool. No wonder she was his girl friend, thought Isabel. Apart from her cousins, Sonia was the prettiest girl there with just the right amount of demureness and fun. As Sonia swam towards her, Isabel saw that her eyes were as blue as her pretty swimsuit. She caught Isabel's eye and smiled. Isabel blushed feeling stupid. Why did she feel this way? She was just a child and yet at that moment she longed to be older, to be joining in with the twins and their friends, to be as popular. .

Miguel was equally successful with the girls and they hovered round him as he strummed his guitar, pausing only to smoke the occasional Du Maurier cigarette. Girls sat around the bar splitting sunflower seeds with their teeth and throwing the shells on the ground. Soon it was time to go back to Val Negra for lunch, only that it was already the middle of the afternoon and Isabel felt sleepy. The days seemed so much longer in Spain. Tito was away climbing in the surrounding hills and the house was humming with activity. A large table had been laid under the plane trees near the veranda. Maids carried plates to and from the house, dogs barked, Dr. Mantua hovered waiting to say grace. The table was heaped with dishes of fresh vegetables, cold meats and chickens hot from the outdoor spit. The children sat down noisily, chatting all at once, reaching for food, passing around the bread. Sigi and Isabel sat together, giggling with delight at the informality of it all. Nuria was animated, talking easily to the priest and her parents. There was colour in her cheeks and her eyes sparkled. She sipped occasionally from a glass of wine. The trees rustled above them, the sun muted through a canopy of foliage. Behind them, the castle turrets no longer seemed like Rapunzel's tower, but magical and benign.

"Lessons start today," announced Nuria raising her voice against the din. "In the schoolroom. Dr. Mantua will begin with the boys' Latin."

"Oh no!" There was a collective moan.

"I'm sorry children but it has to be. You boys are far too behind as it is. And as for the girls!" She held up her hands in despair. "Dr. Mantua says there's little hope of getting you into a school this year. We shall have to do a lot better - Beatrice you too. No more colouring in books. You're going to have to pay attention."

"But it's the first day!" protested Marta. "It's Isabel's first day ever! There's so much we have to show her! Besides what is she going to do while we have our lessons? She can hardly learn English can she?"

"No cheekiness," said Nuria looking up from a huddled discussion with the priest. But her tone seemed less sure.

"Anyway," continued Marta, "Isabel hasn't been in the pool yet and she's come such a long way – traveling all day yesterday and then virtually all night. She's not used to our hours. Already you can see that she's exhausted. I don't think it's fair on her. We can't all disappear inside and leave her by herself."

All eyes focused on a blushing Isabel.

"I'm all right," she muttered.

"*Porfi.*" *said* Bea working herself up to repeating the word three times. "Oh please."

"And this way we'll be really fresh for tomorrow," insisted Marta. "And by then you will have decided what to do with Isabel. And Tito – I mean Father is away and it's never the same. You know it isn't. Oh Mother … please, just this once. Don't spoil it for Isabel. Let her have a really wonderful first day …"

"Enough! *Se acabao!*" said Nuria but she was smiling. "What a headache you're giving me! What do you think *padre,* should I give in?"

The priest bowed his head.

"Without a doubt. They'll be no good to me today. The journey last night was very long. Let them get it out of their systems."

Isabel wondered what "it" was. Sigi pulled her shirtsleeve.

"Come on! Let's go. We can get down! Yippee! Let's go for a swim!"

"Not yet, you don't!" said Marta over hearing. "You've got to let your food digest."

"Half an hour," agreed Nuria. "But you can paddle your feet if you like. Go and sit by the pool while we have our coffee. And look after Isabel."

She scraped back her chair making space for the maids to clear up. Isabel followed her cousins through the orchard. Sigi paused to pick a peach.

"I've never had a peach that didn't come out of a tin," said Isabel biting into the sweet flesh whose juice ran down her chin. It was the most delicious fruit she had ever tasted. Sigi looked at her.

"You're so weird!" she said.

"I've never seen fruit like this."

Sigi picked figs, apricots and quince thrusting them into Isabel's hands.

"Come on, take as much as you like," she said. "There's so much here. Avia makes jam from the quince which is wonderful. We take it back to Mialma at the end of the summer. Eat! Eat! As much as you can!"

"Then I'll never be able to swim! I feel as though I'd sink to the bottom. I could burst!"

Beyond the orchard and tall grass, lay the swimming pool nestling among more fruit trees and large lavender bushes. It was a smooth blue mirror under the cloudless sky. The children stripped off shrieking with excitement at the unexpected freedom. Self-consciously Isabel pulled on her regulation school bathing suit that was black and heavy and designed to be unattractive. It was already too small for her and the straps cut into her shoulders. Her cousins sat on the grass, dressed in neat lemon-coloured costumes with daisies embroidered round the skirt. Long, tanned legs were folded beneath them as they leant towards each other, dark hair and Bea's blond mass, tumbling over their shoulders. Isabel hugged her clothes against herself. Her fat, white legs chafed against each other and wobbled a as she walked. She took off her glasses and immediately everything looked less perfect.

"Come on!" said Marta. "I'm sure we can go in now." She plunged into the pool. Isabel, close behind, gasped as she hit the icy water. Her ears instantly ached with the cold.

"You dive brilliantly!" Sigi said with admiration. Isabel bobbed to the surface.

"Do I?" she said pleased. "No one's ever said."

"Will you teach us?"

"I can try."

"Oh look who's here!" said Sigi coming up for air, after trying to do handstands on the bottom of the pool. "The Casanova twins!"

Isabel squinted in their direction, grateful that she was in the water and that half her body was hidden.

"Hello," greeted Marta. "We're surprised to see you here. I would have thought you would find home too boring after the excitement of the club – no adoring harem to follow your every move."

"No, just our lovely sisters," said Miguel.

"What's a harem?" Isabel asked.

"Not sure," whispered back Sigi. "But the Spanish Moors always had them. I heard Lupe talk about one the other day. She told Mother that if they weren't careful I was sure to end up in one."

"Golly. Who are the Moors?"

"Africans. Arabs," said her cousin. "They came from Morocco to invade Spain a long time ago and stayed for 700 years. Nuria says they left their mark, on houses, food and poetry. A lot of Spaniards are mixed up. Part *Moro*, part Spanish. But we are pure. At least Nuria is. She says she's not so sure about Tito, that he's little and dark – *just* like the *Moros*."

The twins emerged from the bush they had changed behind. Their heads bent together, deep in conversation about something or other. Ricardo had a newspaper tucked under his arm.

"What's so important?" asked Marta. "Have we missed something?"

"Yes, what's so funny?" asked Beatrice.

"It's this," replied Miguel smirking. "Franco's on his usual war path." Miguel stabbed the paper. "But of a different nature. Just listen to this!"

Ricardo, leaning over his brother's shoulder, read aloud:

"Two-piece bathing suits and bikinis are considered indecent-"

"So what's new about that?" said Marta bored.

"Sh!" hissed Miguel.

Ricardo continued, *"Swimming suits should cover both chests and back adequately. Women's bathing suits should have a skirt and men must wear sport-shirts. Swimming suits may not be worn on beaches, at clubs, bars restaurants, boats or generally outside the water. Bathing suits are intended to be worn in the water only and therefore cannot be tolerated elsewhere. Sun-bathing cannot be permitted unless a bathrobe is worn or unless the beach is completely isolated and the sexes are separated."*

"Got that girls?" said Miguel winking at his sisters.

"But that's ridiculous!" protested Marta. "What are we supposed to do? Go back to wearing those bizarre all in one things that our grand parents wore?"

"Did Ricardo say SEX?" asked Bea excitedly.

"Yes but not in that way stupid," said Miguel." So what do you think Marta? Will they close down our sleepy little club? We sunbathe there all the time. I do hope Tito won't see this and start paying surprise visits. Anyway none of the girls wear bikinis. I've only seen foreign girls wear them. In magazines."

"Let's ask our little cousin," said Miguel who stood chewing his thumb nail. "She's foreign isn't she? Hey, little girl!" Miguel gesticulated to her. "Is it like this in England? Is it as strict? Do girls wear bikinis?"

"I don't know," said Isabel not too sure what a bikini was. She wished that she had something riveting to say. "I haven't been away from the convent much. And I've never been anywhere where it was hot enough for sunbathing, except here of course. "

Miguel looked disappointed but Ricardo smiled kindly enough. "What a grave little expression," he said. "There's no need to look so frightened. We aren't going to bite you. It was only a question."

"Yes," agreed Isabel dying with embarrassment at having being spoken to directly.

"But there's loads going on in London," said Miguel. "What about the *Beatles* for starters. She hasn't heard about them! And what about Carnaby Street, you must have been there?"

"No," said Isabel wishing fervently that Kate Douglas had given her a crash course in what normal people did, what real families talked about. She was beginning to realize that being an orphan was not at all a good thing. "I've only been to London once and that was to the airport to come here. But maybe that wasn't really London. And Kate – my older friend at school never said anything about bikinis. Just about boys really."

"Joder!" said Miguel. "What a life! To have all that on your doorstep and never have been to London!"

"She's only a baby!" insisted Ricardo. "Don't you think we'd be worried if she *had* been to Carnaby Street and *did* know all about the Beatles. I mean Bea doesn't know anything so why expect Isabel to? They're virtually the same age. What did you think she'd come up with?"

Miguel shrugged. "Something," he said.

After swimming they had *merienda* down by the river. *Merienda* was what the nuns would have called high tea and which they had roughly at the time in England when Isabel would be going to bed. The girls carried blankets, trays of *Coca* and hot chocolate down to he water's edge and Miguel brought his guitar.

"Tito would never ever let us do this if he were home," said Marta happily. "Isn't this fun? I love these sing songs of ours. These *secret* sing songs," she corrected herself. "Tito doesn't like us eating out of doors unless of course we're on a proper picnic in *daytime*. He says it's slovenly. And he doesn't like us staying up past our bed times. We could all descend into anarchy directly he says and then where would we be. Especially with this extra amount of bad blood that we've inherited, swirling like chocolate in our veins."

"Did he really say you had bad blood?" asked Isabel wondering if hers was tainted too.

"Oh yes. He doesn't think any of us takes after him at all. Except for Miguel of course. He dotes on Miguel. Look Tito isn't that scary. I'm only telling you things about him for your own good. Like most adults, he's really nice to you at the beginning but then when you get to know him, he starts shouting when he's cross and isn't really very nice at all. As long as you keep out of his way you'll be fine. But he likes to be spoken to. He detests shyness. So when you *do* see him, try to think of something amusing to tell him. It's easy really. Just try not to annoy him because then he'll pick on you. He won't leave you alone and you don't want that."

"N-no," said Isabel nervously. "He's not here very often though is he?"

Marta smiled. "Not at Val Negra."

They sipped bowls of hot drinks and ate brioches stuffed with *serano* and *manchego* cheese. Miguel strummed at his guitar and the girls sang, led by Nuria in strong, clear voices. Only Ricardo was silent. Wrapped in her cardigan, as it had turned chilly under the trees by the water, Isabel hugged her knees. She sat some distance apart taking everything in, overwhelmed by the events of the past few days. She closed her eyes listening to the songs that came rapidly now one after the other.

"These are Cuban/Catalan songs," said Ricardo moving to sit on the ground beside her. He stretched his legs and leant back on an elbow. "Love songs – sailors leaving the only girl in the world, that sort of thing. The Catalan sailors brought them back from their many trips to the island so that gradually they changed and are a mixture of the Spanish and Catalan of that time. They're catchy enough."

"I like them. They're sad."

Ricardo shot her a look.

"And you like sad songs?"

Isabel was relieved he couldn't see her face in the darkness.

"They make you think more. I mean they put you in a mood."

Ricardo smiled. "Or take you out of one."

Isabel said nothing.

"My God everything must seem so strange to you. I can't really imagine what it must be like."

"That's what Dr. Mantua seems to think too, without the God in front of it."

"Then God or no God, we must think along the same lines. I just can't imagine what it must be like for you, having lost your father. However, I *can* imagine life though without Tito. But then I don't suppose that Tito and your father were remotely alike."

"No. Not much."

"Well, you stick with Sigi. She's certainly the maddest but she's the kindest of the lot. She'll look after you." Ricardo got up.

"Where are you going?" she was suddenly alarmed at being left alone in the dark.

"To cadge a cigarette. Don't worry little mouse. I'll be back in a moment."

And he was and the lazy days of summer passed. The mornings were spent swimming at the club or in the pueblo charging sweets to Tito's account. The afternoons they picnicked by the river if Tito was away, afterwards settling down to their lessons. Isabel was given large texts from the Spanish classics to copy out word by word. She hardly understood what she was writing but in this way became slowly familiar with the shapes and words of the language. She marvelled at the strange formation of Catalan sentences, the 'x' appearing in the middle of many words. She was taught how to sound Chinese by reciting a lyric:

"Tinca tanta son que a las cinc tinc son."

Which roughly meant: *"I'm so sleepy that at 5 o'clock I'm sleepy"*

And over and over again, until she knew it by heart, she copied her grandfather's haiku:

Per una vela blanca daria un sceptre, Per una vela blanca ...

When there was nothing left to copy, she was allowed to do what she wanted as long as she didn't disturb the others. One day, Ricardo gave her a pile of Enid Blytons in English that he had discovered in the library. Isabel had been speechless with gratitude. She had read the easier books all summer keeping the more difficult ones for when she returned to England. On Sundays, they went to church and then lunched with their grand parents and spent long, sunlit afternoons playing *caracoles,* while the adults drank countless cups of coffee and Tito bored everyone with his politics.

That summer in Val Negra, Isabel made her first communion in the 12th century chapel at Val Negra and wore the habit-like dress that had belonged to her cousins. Isabel was blissfully happy. Wearing their dress, knowing that it had encased *their* skin, she felt closer to them, felt almost a sister. On that day, she refused to wear her glasses and with her tanned skin, was almost pretty. It did not matter that she couldn't see two feet in front of her or that the mystical expression on her face was one born of acute myopia. She was happy. She sat between her grandparents, hands clasped in prayer as she had been taught to do and believed that this was the happiest day of her life. Avia gave her a large mother of pearl medallion that she pinned to her chest. Afterwards, they had a huge *merienda* of *Coca* and pastries. There was champagne for the adults and *horchata* for the children. The Bazan brothers were invited and Benito gave her a present that he shyly handed to her when all the others had gone. It was a small photograph frame in the shape of an artist's easel. Isabel was unaccountably touched. No one apart from the nuns at the Convent had ever shown her such kindness. By evening, Isabel's glasses had reappeared on the end of her nose and Benito said that she looked like a little old nun. It was the start of their friendship. They would write to each other and every summer his was the first house she visited when she arrived at Val Negra.

September came all too quickly that year. There was that unmistakable chill in the air, the freshness of autumn and the fading beauty of Gallica roses. Already Isabel was speaking a peculiar kind of Spanish- a mixture of Castillian and Catalan with few verbs to link the nouns and prepositions. But every one understood her. The intensity of her magnified eyes behind their thick lenses had a habit of fixing their interlocutor to the spot. She filled the house in a way the other children did not and Nuria dreaded her going. But eventually the day for departure arrived. Isabel packed her red espadrilles and her books and went down to the river saying goodbye mentally to all the favourite places. Sigi had given her the *Reina del Rio* doll and this was carefully wrapped in tissue paper.

"We'll write to each other," promised Sigi. Isabel nodded miserably. She longed to stay behind with them forever, to submerge herself in this new life. And she wanted more of it. She had been given a taste of something wonderful and all too soon it was being taken away.

"*Es mejor asi, carino, amor meu. Te lo prometo,*" Nuria said when Isabel had asked why she had to go back. "It is better this way."

"But if you love me then why are you sending me away? Why can't I stay with you? I don't understand. I'll be good. I'll study. Tito won't even know I'm here. Please let me stay."

Nuria had sat her down beside her and smoothed her hair stroking her head like a baby's.

"*Amor meu*, how I'd love to have you here with me, you have no idea how my heart crumbles at the thought of you going. But you must, it is written," she added mysteriously. "It is part of the plan. You're a good little girl. You don't give any trouble. It's not that. You've already started your schooling. My girls don't really go to school. Dr. Mantua teaches them

English but the rest is very poor. You are different. You are clever. It would be such a pity to waste all that now for the sake of ... well for the kind of family life we have here. I owe it to Cl-your mother, to do the very best for you. And I know she would want you to have the opportunity to study properly."

Isabel shook her head, her eyes welling up with tears. She didn't understand any of it and didn't want to. All she wanted was to be able to stay. Her heart was sinking quickly with that sickening, hopeless feeling she knew all too well.

"Por favor, porfi," she pleaded.

Nuria smiled at her use of the Spanish for please but pulled away from Isabel's clinging arms.

"I know this is better," she said firmly. "It's hard but I know this is right. Tito doesn't believe in girls being clever. It's seems a long way off now but later on you'll want to go to university. Tito would never allow it. You've spent a summer in Val Negra and it all seems wonderful but it's not always sunshine and the country. In the autumn we go to the city, we are swallowed up in the city. I know it's hard to accept but later on you'll thank me."

"But I want to stay here with you," Isabel said stubbornly.

"I know," replied Nuria miserably, "but I must also think about Julian. We must none of us forget him. You belonged to him too. Thank God you are not one of us. Besides," she added, "you can come home any time you like, during the holidays –"

But the next holidays were ages away! thought Isabel, mentally numbering the weeks.

Nuria hugged her again.

"Oh darling, you are so young! Time will pass. I know an hour seems like a week but it all goes so quickly ..."

Isabel pressed her nose against the glass of the car window. It seemed that already her cousins and Val Negra were figments of her imagination. The driver steered the car carefully down the long chestnut drive where delicate gardenia bushes sheltered from the sun and plane trees loomed high above them. The turrets of the castle speared the peppered backdrop of the mountains. The road out of Val Negra wound down towards the pueblo with its stucco tiled rooftops nestling against the vineyards. Men and women ducked between the pendant clusters of grapes upon which so much attention had been lavished over the past year. The grape pickers waved as the car swerved away from the dusty paths in the direction of the city. A priest on the steps of the church paused to look too, his corded sash dangling at his ankles. The shopkeepers rolled down their blinds preparing for the afternoon's siesta and the baker removed his cakes from the window. A few of the pueblo's elderly huddled round cafe tables, finishing tapas and cloudy glasses of vermouth. A collective air of sleepiness now hung over Val Negra as slowly, slowly, it receded and became small in the distance.

Chapter 10

Avia
Barcelona
Autumn 1997

It was the anniversary of Avi's death. Avia sat by the window of the empty drawing room, her prayer book open on her lap. It was autumn and the dying light made the afternoon seem timeless. It was also ten years since Ildefons had died. That first year had been the most difficult but now she was used to being alone. Avia fingered the pages of her book. Inside were prayer cards marking various family anniversaries: first communions, christenings, weddings and burials. One by one she read through them.

Here was Isabel's:

> "First Communion of Countess Isabel Pelham y de Roble
> Student of the Sacred Heart
> Val Negra July 23 1968."

And Avi's:

> "Pray for the soul of Count Ildefons de Roble
> born 17 April 1899, died 7 September 1979
> comforted by the sacrament and the apostolic blessing."

And then Clara's:

> "Countess Clara de Roble de Pelham
> born March 11 1920, died 27 April 1960
> feast of Our Mother of God of Montserrat.
>
> I have fought a good fight, I have finished my course,
> I have kept the faith."

Avia pressed her back into plump cushions. The sun seemed to tumble out of the sky and the room would soon be in darkness. In a moment, she would call for her maid to switch on the lights, even light a fire, for it was unseasonably chilly. But not just yet. She would sit here for a little bit longer, luxuriating at the uninterrupted peace of the house, the magnificent silence. Alone with her memories, she allowed her mind to wander …

That was one of the great indulgences of age, she thought, it could freely traipse down the avenues of memory, down the corridor of that so prized *vida interior*, Spaniards were always talking about. Which of course was utter nonsense. All she had ever possessed was a healthy regard for stream of consciousness and the ability to camouflage emotion. But it wasn't that over the years she had become dispassionate, if anything, she felt everything much more keenly. She was acutely aware now as never before, of the preciousness of life, the agonising beauty of the seasons and the omnipotent and possessive love she retained for her estates. And yet, during the war and the reconstructing years that followed, she had developed an ability to escape pain. It meant hiding in her mind, delving through imagination and memory, for a happier place. Slowly, like a diver coming up from the depths, she would emerge, having assimilated the shocks, to a tranquil and silent sea. Avi had also contributed in this. His reserve and apparent coldness, held in check a passionate and romantic nature. Initially, his diffidence clashed with her impulsive and generous spirit, but in time she began to understand the wisdom of patience and restraint.

They had first met each other properly at the village feast day at Val Negra. Avia was the only child of wealthy and aristocratic parents. She was an adored and spoilt child brought up to expect adulation as a given. She was beautiful but her blonde hair and blue eyes made her all the more distinctive. She was clever, artistic and charming. From an early age she knew how to use her charm to get what she wanted and could not remember an occasion when she had not had her way. She was arrogant and childish but her high spirits and winsome smile, her passion for life made her all the more captivating. Men who could not be bribed in business became breathless in her presence and the women who vowed to hate her on sight had to admit that she was entrancing. She was supremely conscious of her birthright and consequently loved Val Negra with a hunger that sometimes terrified her. Her father, who refused to think of her as a mere female, gave her an education befitting a son and heir. He instilled in her the creed that there was nothing that she could not do. He encouraged her appetite for masculine pursuits so that she was a fearless if somewhat reckless rider and a first class shot. But equally, she could sew and sing just as prettily as any of the girls of her generation. She grew up in a safe, predictable world, surrounded by beautiful things, petted and indulged and greatly loved.

Avia smiled at the memory. She was still a beautiful woman. Even at her incredible age, she had no need of spectacles or a hearing aid. She wiggled her toes in the new inelegant shoes that Nuria had given her for her birthday. They were a far cry from the soft kid pumps that were specially made for her when she was a girl. She had to admit though, that these modern things were very comfortable. But too loose, rather like wearing bedroom slippers. Her *consuegra* Abuelita, would never have approved and Avia wasn't altogether sure that she did either. And then there was this obsession with *prêt porter!* Bea was all for it and for the so-called 'grunge' look. What a word! Why did young people want to look so grubby? As far as she could see, all they wore was black and grey and their hair stood up all over the place, looking for all the world just like the chimney sweeps that used to clean at Val Negra. And the materials were all shiny and harsh, making the body perspire so. Beatrice was always panting when she came to visit and Avia had no doubt at all that it was due to her clothes. Marta didn't care what she wore as long as it was comfortable and Nuria was beginning to look like Lupe at her age. It was ironic that it was only the little foreigner that now dressed expensively. But despite the designer labels and heart stopping price tags, Isabel's clothes as far as Avia could tell, were still off the peg. She would not be persuaded that this little Armani fellow, who made distinctly masculine looking *trouser* suits, was better than couture. Isabel had laughed when Avia expressed scepticism. *But it's the fashion!* She had said. And when Avia replied that she didn't think it very *feminine,* Isabel had said that no one wore skirts to work anymore.

Avia often wondered what Julian would have made of it all - of his daughter, grown up and in many ways so like her mother. But she didn't see much of Isabel these days. Isabel had made her base in England, as was only natural but there were times when Avia wondered if her grand daughter was really happy. Isabel assured her that she was busy enough and always traveling because of work. There had been that strange year when Avia had thought her lost to them forever, when Isabel vanished to the Middle East with a man she had met at a party. Isabel had returned although not married and without much to say for her romantic interlude. She hadn't offered much by way of explanation either and the next thing Avia knew was that she had a job and was living at The Cottage on her own. Who was this Teem? He seemed like a decent enough man and yet they hadn't married. *Why was that?* Avia wondered with misgiving. *What is stopping her?*

She frowned. She hadn't been thinking about Isabel. And she didn't want to, not just yet. No it was something else …Clothes. Ah yes, Abuelita and shoes. That had all been such a pleasure to her when she was young. Clothes that is. She remembered with shivering delight how a new outfit had made her feel- sexy and desirable and full of promise – as if by stepping in to new shoes, she could change her personality. Now clothes were not so much a pleasure as a necessity and she wore them as long as possible. She wore her clothes to keep her warm, to protect her from extremes of temperature but not with the sole purpose of enhancing her natural beauty. Take that ridiculous Granny nightgown for example that Nuria had given her. She would never have been caught dead wearing something like that when Ildefons was alive! *Then* she had gone for exquisite grooming even if it meant wincing with discomfort or freezing to death half the time. Now it was all to do with what was practical –something depressing called drip dry with a percentage of lycra.

Occasionally, when she was feeling sentimental, she would wander through the empty bedrooms fingering the clothes in her wardrobe, which like the prayer cards, were milestones in her memory chest. Here was her wedding dress, a crumpled mass of yellowing silk - the *derni cri* in elegance, designed by Monsieur Worth himself. Her maid had said that it was best to store silk all bunched up like that because for some reason it lasted longer. Avia had had her doubts. What did it matter anyway? What was she saving it for? It wasn't as if Nuria or any of her granddaughters had wanted to wear it. *"Too old-fashioned!"* They had said scornfully. And it didn't look as if Isabel would ever marry this *Teem*. Here was a mauve Christian Dior ensemble that had always been a favourite. She had worn it with the Roble amethysts when the Dowager Countess died and she inherited the family jewels. Ildefons said they matched her eyes. She still wore it. The cut was good and there was still a shine to the material. Isabel especially liked it. Then there was the nightgown she had worn giving birth to Nuria. Really she should have thrown it out. Funny that. It had been stained with blood - large patches of colour seeping into the fine Irish lawn and Pepita amazingly had managed to get the stains out. And yet, by the same token, she had been unable to remove a small fruit juice mark on a blouse. Here were shoes more treasured than friendships, a dancing slipper whispering of her youth, a hat in which she had flirted and then gone to hear mass, turning the heads of the congregation and Ildefons's. There were single gloves she always expected to find the mate to and beautiful cashmere in all the colours of the rainbow. There were neat boxes of amassed textiles that would last longer than she would. And then what? After all her careful hoarding, would some stranger tear through them? Would they be dumped on some recycle heap to end up eventually as men's shirts in *El Corte Ingles?*

Avia closed her eyes. What did any of it matter really? Clothes, possessions they were all trappings, all distractions. In the end nothing could disguise the fact that she was alone. One by one they were all leaving her. The people she cared most about were going. It was ten years since Ildefons had died: ten whole years, a decade, a string on her rosary, digits on a clock, all marking time. And yet for her Ildefons had never changed. For her he would always be the strong, vibrant man of her youth. But then she too didn't think of herself as old. Oh the body might be a little wrinkled but inside her spirit was just beginning. It rattled inside of her yearning to be free, yearning to dance. One day she would jump out of these clumsy shoes and dance away…

Chapter 11

Mercedes
Val Negra 1916-39

It was clothes or rather an *espadrille*, to be precise, that had started it all. The feast day celebrations were well under way. It had been an unusually hot August but now the Val Negra breeze wrapped skirts around her ankles and loosened the blonde tendrils of her hair so that they clung fetchingly to the nape of her neck. The village square was set up for dancing. Long trestle tables held pitchers of *vino tinto* and slabs of *coca*. A group of musicians played the first opening strains of *Sardanas,* the traditional Catalan folk dances. A long line of flares lit the path to the mountains. Mercedes held back, watching the men and women clasp each other round the neck and hop on one foot, first in one direction, then the other. She waved to friends. Strangers who had not yet met her, but knew who she was, saluted her. Mercedes enjoyed the admiring whispers. It was what she expected when she was seen in public. That evening her smile was generous, her excited eyes flicked from one face to the other. She had no appetite. Her right hand toyed with the tortoiseshell comb in her hair. Combing then fixing, combing then fixing.

"No bailas Mercedes?" Mercedes looked up to see the tall, proud form of Ildefons de Roble. He wore an open necked white shirt and the traditional espadrilles. His hands were thrust casually in his trouser pockets. His face was deeply tanned and his eyes, like hers, were blue. They admired each other, mutually recognising the same patrician features, the same inherited genes of careful breeding, the same pride and vanity.

"I've been waiting for the Sardanas to begin."

The long pitched squeak of the Catalan bagpipes sounded as if on cue.

"Well now they have. Come and dance."

But Mercedes was rooted to the spot. She had not seen Ildefons since the previous summer when he was a gauche, adolescent boy. He had returned a man. His voice was deeper and he had the lazy confidence of a much older person. His close proximity made her heart beat more quickly. She could smell the strong scent of saddle wax and soap. Ildefons loved his horses. She remembered how they had ridden together as children. He was the only boy in Val Negra who could ride faster and further than she.

"You've been away all summer," she began accusingly, in a breathless rush not daring to look at him.

"Yes, at the university. I'd almost completed my course when the English decided to go to war."

"And the rest of the world!"

Ildefons looked at her wryly.

"Not us though. We don't fight, do we Mercedes?"

His words were slurred with meaning. She couldn't speak and lowered her eyes.

"It's been fun," he continued. "I've enjoyed being *al extranjero*, but the Jesuits are very strict. And I don't like the food. The English can't cook! They eat disgusting combinations –soggy cake covered in yellow cream and lots of sausages! I've missed everything here."

"Everything?"

"Oh and my friends of course."

Mercedes met his gaze feeling a rush of bravado.

"I suppose you've taken up smoking and girls," she said her chin tilting enchantingly. She felt his eyes travel over her lips and hair.

"Girls, yes."

"Oh!" Mercedes pretended to be annoyed. "Then I certainly shan't dance with you."

"Of course you will," said Ildefons idly studying the bobbing forms of their friends. "There aren't many boys here who are as tall as you are!"

Mercedes' eyes flashed. "You're certainly ruder than I remembered. Living away has taught you some strange habits. Is this the way you speak to English women? I don't know why you bother to speak to me, if it's only to insult me. I think you're more used to horses than to girls."

"Well they don't answer back. I like my horses. They're obedient. And for some reason they trust me. I've always found horses to be more amenable than people."

Mercedes crouched down on the pretext of retying her espadrille. She felt a hot and sudden prick of tears. She had missed Ildefons and had been happy to see him again. Now it was all going wrong. It was true that she was taller than other girls but her height had never made her feel uncomfortable until now. Suddenly strong hands griped her wrists removing them from her shoe. Ildefons retied the long laces wrapping them round and round her ankle, his cool fingers stroking her skin, making her shiver. His face was level with hers. Her lips parted. He made as if to rise and then swooped down, his hands holding her face, his lips brushing hers. Mercedes gasped, her body tensing. And then he pulled her against him, her body folding into his and began to walk her to the shade of a plane tree. In the darkness, she used her hands to see, moving over the smooth linen of his shirt, the contours of ivory buttons. She felt the rough bark against her back, tearing her blouse. Suddenly her hands were pulling at him, her fingers winding the fabric tightly round her fists so that he could not move. He bent her head back so that she was arched against his arm, clinging to him for support. The world under the trees was spinning and faster so that she thought she would fall. And then he stopped. She was disappointed. She wasn't sure what she had been expecting but it wasn't this feeling of loss, of incompletion. She had been on the brink of something, she knew it, and then he had stopped.

"Marry me," he said. She was trembling all over. The combs, her grandmother's tortoiseshell combs had fallen and been trampled on the grass and her hair fell about her shoulders. Ildefons caught his breath. His jaw clenched.

"My God," he said gruffly, "I want to take you now." But he did not move. Mercedes lifted her chin haughtily.

"¿Como sabes que me quiero casar contigo?" Her voice was shaky and hardly convincing even to herself. "And how do you know that I want to marry you?"

He covered the space between them and his mouth was on hers, his hands through her long hair. He shook her. "Say yes!"

Mercedes took a deep breath and found his mouth again efficiently moving over hers, her neck and shoulders.

"Yes. Yes. Yes."

Four months later they were married in the Cathedral in Barcelona. It was a glittering society wedding, the last of its kind it was said, before the war. King Alfonso was there with his young bride and courtiers who hardly ever visited the Catalan city, from Madrid. A ball was held in the evening and Mercedes danced till morning carried away by utter blissful, happiness. Ildefons's wedding present to her was the portrait of another Countess Roble. It was of a young girl standing by the water holding up her skirts with one hand, while twirling a parasol with another. It had taken her breath away. Ildefons said that the similarity was extraordinary, that clearly their marriage was written in the stars, that nothing would mar their happiness.

And for a time they had been happy. They were both young, carefree. In the beginning, their lives were lived without incident. Ildefons was a vigorous lover. It made Mercedes blush to remember the way he had used her body, the way they had lain under mosquito netting, stark naked, too hot to cover their bodies, the way she had desired him, needed him. She could become quite bad tempered if she didn't have enough of him and this amused him. He would taunt her, tease her and then devour her, feeding her insatiable appetite, leading her further and further away from herself so that there was nothing but instinct between them, bringing her to a shuddering, exhausting, climax.

Nuria, much to Mercedes' surprise, was the product of one of these violent and hugely satisfying couplings. Mercedes knew nothing of the facts of life.

"Doesn't it concern you that you might became pregnant?" Ildefons had asked once. She had not dared admit her naiveté.

"Por que?"

He lit a cigarette watching her dress, enjoying her long limbs and taut stomach.

"I just don't see you as a mother."

Mercedes was stung. "But I love children!" she had protested. "And I'd want yours." she blushed feeling her belly. "More than anything."

"You couldn't hunt for a while or ride. No tennis tournaments."

"I know," she said uncertainly.

"Aren't we happy the way we are?"

Mercedes nodded.

"Then maybe you should think about it."

Ildefons stubbed out his cigarette and threw himself on the end of the bed. He reached for her so that she fell heavily against him.

"Just as long as you know," he breathed hoarsely, twisting in a way that made her ache just to think about it. And his actions had obliterated everything but the feel of their bodies sliding against each other.

A few months later the nausea began and in the mornings she was sick. Ildefons eyed her quietly but said nothing. Eventually, Mercedes went to the doctor. On the way back, she had stopped at a new milliners a friend had told her about, only to suffer the indignation of being sick on the way to the cloakroom. She was pale when she returned home. Ildefons was in the stables. His favourite horse had been brought, that morning, from Val Negra. Ildefons ran an experienced hand down the stallion's flank smoothing, rubbing. The sight of his wrists on the horses skin would ordinarily have made her go weak at the knees but now she felt she might wretch.

"I'm pregnant," she announced angrily.

Ildefons sucked in his breath and his eyes lit up but at the sight of her smouldering expression, his own hardened.

"I know."

Her head jerked up.

"Darling child don't look so surprised," he said continuing to wipe down his horse. He kept his voice steady enough but every muscle in his body was hard, expectant. "It is one of the consequences of so much …pleasure." Ildefons paused and his tone was steely. "So what are you going to do?"

Mercedes leant against the brick wall of the stable, feeling the cold cement beneath her hands, trying to ward off the hideous spinning sensation that threatened to send her tumbling to the ground. Ildefons's aloofness encouraged her to be more abrasive than she felt.

"What can I do except have it of course?" she said icily. "You didn't tell me! You shouldn't have let it happen!"

In one swift movement Ildefons ducked under his horse's neck and was beside her. He gripped her shoulders.

"Look at me!"

Reluctantly she lifted her chin. Her eyes were ringed with dark circles and full of tears.

"I want this child," he said fiercely. *"Nuestro hijo.* You're frightened that's all. I'll help you. I'll be with you. There's nothing to be afraid of. You'd think you were the first woman in the world to have a baby! It had to happen and I'm happy it has now. But you'll have to slow down. You've been doing to much."

He held her against him stroking her in much the same way he did his animals. Gradually her sobs subsided. From time to time she tried to push him away but he would not release her. At last she was still, her face buried against his clean white shirt, comforted by the horse, soap smell of him.

"Better now?"

She nodded like a child. He led her out of the stable, holding her the length of his body as they walked towards the house.

"You need plenty of rest and quiet," he was saying. "Fresh air. Perhaps we should go to Val Negra?"

Suddenly the thought of the vineyards and the river lifted her spirits. Like a balm it smoothed out the wrinkles of discontent, beckoning her to the river and the Monseny. She thought of the vineyards, rows and rows of tiny fruit melting against a background of endless sky. She smiled.

"Yes. Yes I'd like that," and then she added which was unlike her, "I'm sorry for being – "

His mouth was on hers, his hands in her hair under her short jacket.

"I know," he mumbled. "I know."

*

Avia winced ashamed of that memory. Of course she had loved her baby and Ildefons had understood this. He had always understood her. That was the problem. She could never hide from him. While others credited her with all sorts of qualities she did not in truth possess, Ildefons would always smile that secret smile of his, knowing her to be different. And with him, she was able to be herself. It was a tremendous relief at first, to be able to rant and rave in private, to be as bitchy about people as she wanted – to criticise, condemn or praise and then go out and be utterly charming. But later when she wanted to change, to evolve, to grow up, he would not let her. Their mutual attraction had cantered round her being a spoilt and indulged child. There was no room for a maturing, intelligent woman. He needed her as much as she him. They complimented each other while he could tame her wildness but when she could do this for herself, they grew apart. He began to irritate her. His familiarity was irksome and predictable. She longed for the early, carefree days of their marriage when everything was still new and physical - when everything was a prelude for lovemaking.

When the baby arrived, Nuria's birth sparked a whole new range of emotions. Having previously enjoyed a sunny, even temperament, Mercedes was suddenly prone to conflicting and inexplicable moments of rage and frustration. A frustration not helped by the fact that she realised she was jealous of her baby. And why? The reason was simple. Ildefons had fallen hopelessly and unexpectedly in love with his daughter. Mercedes had not thought it possible that a father could love a child so much and it annoyed her. She thought of her own father who had adored her of course, but whose adulation had still been somewhat remote. An adoration that paled in comparison with the devotion that Ildefons gave this baby. Mercedes, who had always been the centre of attention, was now forced to take second place to a helpless infant and she didn't like it. She was ready to go out again, to see friends and go to parties while Ildefons was perfectly content to stay at home. He seemed to her like some middle aged man or at least how she imagined a middle aged man to be. None of this motherhood business had turned out as she expected it would. To begin with, Nuria was not anything like the village babies she had seen bouncing on their mama's knees in Val Negra. Those babies were all smooth, olive skinned cherubs with huge eyes and curly hair. Nuria was a sombre, thin little thing, with spiky black hair and blotchy skin. Of course Ildefons thought her beautiful. But what about *her* looks? Mercedes wanted to cry. What about *her* flawless skin? Only now he had eyes only for the child. It wouldn't have mattered what she looked like. He didn't see her. She had become invisible and not only to Ildefons. It would seem that she was like a ghostly, unwanted presence in the sight of her daughter. Every time Mercedes went near her, Nuria cried.

"Just leave her," Ildefons would say. "There's no need to touch. She just wants to be left alone!"

Left alone! Not cuddle a baby! What baby didn't want to be bounced and kissed? Well it would seem that Nuria for one didn't want to be and this was something Mercedes would never understand. She was a tactile person. It was second nature to touch as she spoke, to drop the odd kiss. She had a low threshold for boredom and did not enjoy playing with her children, but she did enjoy hugging and kissing them. She needed to feel their warm little bodies against her, their sweet smelling breath on her face, nuzzle into the folds of their necks and plump tummies. She did not comprehend a love that excluded physical contact. Ildefons on the other hand, was perfectly able to devote an afternoon to his children without ever once touching them. He gave them all the time in the world – Mercedes gave them a quick hug was off.

Mercedes became increasingly dissatisfied with her home life. As the days passed and Ildefons's fixation with his daughter showed no signs of abating, Mercedes began to spend more and more time away. She crammed her days with exhausting activities – anything to staunch the flow of neglect that began to flood her world. And away from Ildefons she began to feel free, light hearted, young again. Slowly her feelings for him were altering, shifting in this shaky new world of family life. In the old days, a mere look, the lightest touch on her arm would cause her stomach to churn with desire. Now there were times when she didn't seem to feel his touch at all and in bed she curled up, as far away from him as possible. *How could desire have turned, so swiftly, to loathing? Stay me with flagons, she thought, comfort me with apples for I am sick of love. What had happened to them? To that recognition in each other, of the other?* She had no answers to the many questions that spun round and round in her head. Most of the time she was able to dull the uncertainty but sometimes she was overcome with a depression so destructive, that she was left limp, too weak to get out of bed. She could hardly bare to think of the naive young girl she had been during the heady days of their courtship. She remembered a time when Ildefons followed her every move with his eyes, his mouth, his whole being. She remembered a time when she had wanted sex so badly she would rush in from a day's shopping and seek him out where ever he was in the house or grounds. And he would always know. He enjoyed seeing her rush in breathless, her breasts straining against her dress, pretending that the only reason she was there was to gossip about her day. And he would tease her, play her little game and then take her roughly where ever they might be, in the stable, in the clock tower, on the steps of the rose garden. Sometimes it was hard to believe that any of it had ever happened. Mercedes felt so stifled that she felt like rushing to the top of the Monseny and screaming. But instead, she smiled and withdrew into herself, so beginning the metamorphosis from capricious, wild child to stately matron.

Avia often wondered what would have happened to her if the civil war had not occurred at that point. It was terrible and it was tragic. The boys she had seen dancing the *sardanas* that evening in August, were all dead. The whole of Spain was divided - cousin fought cousin, brother fought brother. Families were ripped apart because of a war that was confusing and misunderstood. The genteel girls she had grown up with, left the serenity of beautiful homes to become nurses and in some cases fighters themselves. Some, like herself who had young children, had no choice but to stay at home. And yet in spite of the hardship, the war years were the happiest of her life. All at once she was liberated – able to draw on the built up resources of courage and stamina that had lain dormant, masked by sexual appetite and self absorption.

Avia closed her missal, the prayer cards scattering on her lap. It was strange how a sudden look, a bar of music, a turn of phrase could transport her so immediately to the days of her youth. The details sometimes blurred but the terror, the exhilarating sheer terror she had felt then could somehow burst in on her again. She had known no other fear since. Val Negra … Even now she sometimes woke in the night and could imagine the muffled sound of guns as hurried footsteps trampled the grounds of her beloved land. The vines were stripped, the fields burned and then suddenly there was silence. The looting and desecration all stopped. The soldiers withdrew and for the remainder of the war, Avia was left in peace. But no one could be trusted. Not even childhood friends were above suspicion. There were terrible stories of servants denouncing their masters, pupils turning against their teachers, priests against their parishioners. The list was long. From being a country that upheld the religious beliefs of the Catholic Kings, whose traditions grappled to rise out of the mire of a century ago, Spain had become a dangerous and anarchistic place in which to live. Once more she was a country plunged into darkness and despair. And starvation.

Mercedes remembered all too vividly what it was to go hungry – scraping the pennies together to walk 15 kilometres, just to purchase a roll of stale bread. At first there was no dairy produce. There was no sugar, flour and the only meat they ate was whatever game Mercedes managed to kill in the woods behind Val Negra. They ate rabbit and wood pigeon and once, because a Loyalist deserter had been discovered hiding in the hills, and a wild boar had been killed in the ensuing gun battle, there had been that unexpected delicacy. Mercedes was 34 years old that first summer of the war. Much had occurred since the tumultuous, early months of her marriage. She had spent, if not devoted, the years to bringing up her children, Nuria and Clara, who were now teenagers. Everything about Clara's birth was different. To begin with, she was a wanted baby and the birth itself was easy. Clara had slithered out of her, causing no tear or perennial scarring and from the very start, Avia had loved her possessively and passionately. She could now understand the overriding love Ildefons held for Nuria. It was as inexplicable as it was bewildering but Mercedes accepted it. Meanwhile, she lavished time and energy on the baby. Overnight it seemed Mercedes turned from a vein and thoughtless young woman to a selfless and devoted mother. Her relationship with Ildefons improved. It would never recapture the mind numbing passion of the early days but they became friends once more. Ildefons watched over her, steered her clear of imprudent decisions, listened when she poured out her heart.

When war broke out, she was at Val Negra with her daughters. For a brief time they did not suffer from food shortages or hardship. It was as if there was no war. Their daily routine carried on easily enough. They sewed, cultivated the garden, made charitable visits and shopped for new clothes. But then everything changed. It became harder to buy basic provisions. Gradually too, news filtered through of the atrocities that were being committed – the terrible injuries, the violence festering against Spain's clergy. And still there was no word from Ildefons. But this did not trouble Mercedes. She knew he was abroad –buying horses in Ireland as it turned out – and would make his way home when he could. After a year however, there was suddenly no food, nowhere to go, no news at all. The young men of the village had vanished, leaving in their wake an eerie silence. Mercedes was wary of emerging outside the confines of Val Negra. She became restless, frustrated and fearful.

And then one day, just when Mercedes was at her lowest, Dr. Mantua appeared, as if from nowhere with a goat, called Cuca, tied to his wrist. Avia knew Dr. Mantua by sight. She had often heard him say mass at Mialma. He was a respected Jesuit known to her family but she had hardly ever spoken two words to him alone and now here he was asking for food and lodging. Mercedes hesitated only momentarily. She was aware of her reputation, aware also that now that the servants were gone, she was alone with the girls. She took in his wiry frame, his intense blue eyes and strong hands. His skin was leathery from too much time in the sun, his hair bleached to the colour of stripped cornhusks. She was aware, as she let him pass into the cool stone hall, that need emanated from every pore in her body. She was a strong woman used to being in control but she was exhausted. For the past two years she had managed the estate almost single handed. She still had no news of Ildefons and fear motivated her every action. She felt the man's eyes on her – kind, neutral devoid of all sexuality – the eyes of a priest and she wanted to fling herself into his arms and weep. Instead she put out a hand to steady herself, the niceties of social convention escaping her. It was such a long time since she had had to welcome anyone to her home. For a moment they stood in the great hall, which was looking less than great, Mercedes thought ruefully. Dust sheets covered much of the furniture, the better pieces having been hidden in the wine caves. It smelled of neglect, neglect and decay. Cobwebs hung where drapes should have been, suspended like a trapeze high above them. Everything looked old and tired, shrunk from lack of sunlight. She had not noticed, until now, just how tired.

"You are alone." It was a statement.

Mercedes nodded.

"Apart from my daughters. I have not heard – " she stopped aware of the need for caution.

He held up a hand.

"You do not have to tell me anything," he said flinching, used by now to distrust and lies.

"No, no," said Mercedes, conscious of having hurt him. Why should she not trust him? After all he had come to her for help. Not the other way round. "I mean I want to tell you. There has been no one else to talk to. No one at all." She laughed a funny little sound devoid of mirth. "What am I saying? You must think – "

"I do not think anything, Countess." He made a curt bow with his head. "I am thankful for your courage. I have been turned away before."

Mercedes flushed.

"Courage is a rather grand word for opening the door to a friend." And then because there was a painful pause and her voice had caught on a ragged sob, she rushed on. "Besides, you have made it easy. You don't look at all like a priest! Come in. Come in. You must make yourself at home, if that is at all possible. As you see we live … more simply than before." *In fact, a lot more simply,* she wanted to add. *So simply that I wonder what on earth I shall give you to eat tonight let alone for breakfast tomorrow. So simply, that we share one candle on the way up to bed and use only the wing of the house that overlooks the vineyards so as not to attract attention to the Monseny. So simply that days and weeks merge with the seasons so that until you arrived I did not realise that I was slowly losing my mind.*

"I am used to hiding and to sleeping in very small spaces," replied Dr. Mantua. "This is a palace, with or without its comforts. It will do very well." And then he added almost embarrassed by his admission. "I suppose you have not heard mass in a while."

Mercedes was startled. Mass was the last thing on her mind. And no, it was true, she had not received communion in a very long time. She wanted to tell him that she lived most of her life committing a daily sin and it was years and *years* since a priest had heard her confession. She looked at him quizzically. He must also know the extent of the danger he was in and by association had put them all in. The clergy was being shot on sight and to harbour a religious person meant instant death.

"Then today is your lucky day!" he smiled broadly at her expression. "We shall say mass. Call your daughters. And then we shall talk. There is so much I must ask you. I would have thought you could do with an extra pair of hands here. Set me to work. I am diligent and do not tire easily."

"You may be diligent but you are also reckless," she replied boldly and then blushed at having spoken to a priest in such a way. Years of solitude had loosened her tongue and now she spoke her thoughts. They came tumbling out, disjointed, inconsequential and ragged with tension. "I don't think you are aware of what has happened to us. I don't think you understand at all. I wonder if you know what you are doing by coming here. The men in the village have mostly fled but in their place – "

Swiftly the priest crossed the small space between them and his hand covered her mouth. The humour vanished from his face. His eyes darkened, darting from space to space.

"I know that walls such as these have many ears," he said quietly. "From now on if there is anything that you must say, say it only when you are certain that we can not be overheard."

"I think I know my own house," she replied piqued. "We had a few problems to begin with and the vineyards as you will see, have been trampled. But the orchard was spared and we grow vegetables. By and large I have been left alone. No one has troubled us. We keep to ourselves and do nothing to draw attention to the house. No one comes near. Not even the villagers. I hope that they won't now."

His hand dropped and again he made the bow.

"I apologise Countess, " he said. "I underestimated your intelligence and the loyalty in which your people clearly hold you. Only you see, from where I have come, no one can be trusted. I have forgotten what it means to be in a house where one can still speak freely. I have been a soldier for too long."

"The soldier priest?" Her lips curled sweetly, all irritation vanishing. But the eyes that met hers were suddenly dull and she knew it was no idle confession. Later she was to realise that everything he said was deliberate, that there was no impulse to the man, only an ever measured, ever present sense of duty. And much later when she knew him better, she chided herself for having been so naive. She was to learn what those words, so lightly spoken, so taunting when she repeated them, really meant. It was only when the war was finally over that she learned that he had been badly tortured, that some Basque woman, before the fall of Madrid had nursed him back to health, back to the front. His apparent health, his ruddy skin and bleached hair, disguised a body ravaged by cruelty, a body that like her father's, was falling apart.

"The soldier priest," she repeated but this time she did not smile. She held out her hands to him. "I am beginning to think your arrival is no accident," she said. "Not only have you come in time to salvage what little faith I have left, but as you say, there is work to be done. And you were right. These walls *do* have ears. Let us talk in the evening."

And so began a friendship that was to endure many tests, many secrets. When her daughters were finally in bed, Mercedes and the priest sat in the candlelit hall, shivering in their shawls while the leaves outside rustled along the courtyard and a mouse scurried into a corner. They both looked forward to the evenings, exhausted from their work, exhilarated by each other's company. Often there was nothing to eat, but for drink they had Val Negra champagne, its labels dusty and faded and they talked into the early hours of the morning, oblivious of time, galvanized by the ambition of their plans. In the strange light, the familiar and loved shapes of her rooms became blurred and eerie. But together and a little drunk, they were an island unto themselves, feeding each other with their dreams.

By day they resumed their habitual roles. Mercedes turned with renewed vigour to the running of the estate, attempting to produce food from desiccated land and to stimulate production. Slowly too, deserters appeared at the door – young boys, soldiers, old men. Men and women came to her from both sides. The steady stream of people in need of shelter seemed to coincide almost to the day, with Dr. Mantua's arrival but Mercedes never questioned anyone or anything. In other areas, Dr. Mantua proved to be invaluable. Not only did he seem to have practical ideas as to how they might best feed and clothe their 'visitors,' but he also recognised the sense of restoring the dilapidated vineyard.

"But what does it matter?" said Mercedes turning away, bored by talk of grape. "It has never meant anything to me, even less so now. Let it all go. There's no point. It's wasted away. Let it go. *Dejalo todo.*"

Dr. Mantua was shocked.

"*Estas loca mujer?*" he said striding after her, pulling her by the hand, so that she faced the mess of mildew eaten leaves and shrunken fruit. "If you don't take care for the vine there won't be anything left. You'll never have another vintage worth anything. And with the rate we're working through the cellars, that *will* be a problem! Not even Franco's army could consume so much!"

Mercedes raised her eyes. But he continued, gesticulating to the plants, moving her this way and that so that nothing escaped her.

"I'm perfectly serious. Provided we can start spraying the healthy vine - at least what's left of it - we're in with a chance. Any treatment has got to be preventative. This spring was unusually wet and then the summer was scorching. Just the kind of conditions for disease to thrive."

"Then you do it," she said ungraciously. "I'm not interested."

And he had. Dr. Mantua along with the wounded and convalescing had treated the sickly shoots, often waking up in the middle of the night to spray them. Mercedes looked on as the elderly worked together, slowly and persistently, stooping in the healing sunshine to remove dead leaves. New vines were reproduced by grafting and manure carried on Cuca the goat, nourished the impoverished soil.

"When the war is over," the priest informed her, "you will have to grow the vines in straight lines. I've been wondering if we could start doing it now, but we simply haven't the manpower. The old dears aren't really up to what I have in mind. I've seen it done in France. It's so simple and yet so effective. I wish I could claim the credit!"

"Straight lines Monsignor?" Mercedes shielded her eyes, a smile playing on her lips.

"No I haven't gone mad Condesa. And yes, it's called the *en ligne* system – a new way of cultivating. This mass of vegetation – " he waved his hands at the clumps of fruit growing higgledy pigged, like a patchwork quilt over the terrain, "won't work for much longer. It's impractical. You see how the men can hardly move about? There are no paths and it's virtually impossible to get Cuca into the denser areas. You won't always have these poor old souls to help. When the war is over you will have to invest in some machinery."

"But I'm not interested in it!" protested Mercedes. Dr. Mantua ignored her.

"The *en ligne* system will appeal to you," he continued. "The vines are grown in neat perpendicular rows, it makes them easier to see and treat. More importantly it means that after the vintage is over, all the stakes don't have to be taken up by hand and then reinstated in the spring. Imagine the work it will save! I'd do anything to have it now! Still we can't complain. They're all doing their best."

Mercedes smiled at his enthusiasm. Dr. Mantua wiped his forehead with the edge of his sleeve. He wore Ildefons's clothes, gabardine trousers rolled up at the bottoms and a peasant's shirt. On his feet were the traditional espadrilles. He could have been any of the village men who helped with the harvest.

"You love the idea of growth don't you," she said, "of creating."

"I hate the idea of waste more. Besides it is therapeutic not just for myself but for all of them." He nodded in the direction of the workingmen. "It takes their minds off the war. They have something to work towards, and seeing the small shoots gives us all a sense of achievement."

"Fruit of the vine and work of human hands," she murmured.

Dr. Mantua shot her a strange look.

"That sort of thing."

"I wish I had your sense of purpose," she said wistfully.

"Then work with us in the vineyard. Your problem is, that now that I'm here, you have too much time to think. Save that for our evenings. You've got to start doing something that you love, so that at night you fall in bed exhausted. And I don't mean from having looked after the girls and their needs, or working out what it is we're going to eat. I'm not underestimating your skill at running things here under impossible circumstances. But the difficulty at housekeeping here is no excuse. Don't float along waiting for the war to end. We have to use every day that comes. Do something for you. Start here with your land. There is no better opportunity. Little by little you will grow to love it."

Mercedes was unconvinced.

"Maybe," she said. "But what will I do when you go back to the front? All these men help because you are here. Some of them will be well enough to travel in a few weeks. Then it'll be back to square one."

Dr. Mantua leant against the stake he had been inserting. A thick leather pad protected his chest so that he could heave his full body weight against it. He groaned with the effort.

"Ask the Nadal family. They've got a few hefty lads left. One has been wounded I know, a certain Carlos. You could try him. Even the old man is as strong as an ox and by God you have to be do this. Ugh – "

He released the stake, panting.

"The sooner you change this system the better!" he said testily.

"But how will I pay them?" asked Mercedes suddenly remembering. "All my money is frozen in Barcelona. I came away with nothing. I know your Carlos Nadal. He used to deliver groceries from the pueblo and if I remember correctly a bowl of soup and a hot tub won't be reward enough. I've never liked him. There's something shifty about him and he lives in such a scandalous way! They say he never marries and-"

Dr. Mantua made an impatient gesture and turned to begin the process of inserting another stake, to which he attached a vine, all over again.

"I didn't think you were a gossip and now isn't the time to worry about a person's morals. You may not like him but he'll do a good job and you may not have a choice. Involve Nadal in the grape collecting. Offer him a percentage. I don't know you're the clever one. You think of something. But I *will* see this vineyard produce a noble wine yet!

When your daughters marry, they will drink this year's vintage! Now go away if you're not going to help. You're distracting me."

And then one day, towards the end of the fighting, Dr. Mantua disappeared. He was gone for a month. He left without a note, not a single word of explanation. The evening before had been just as amusing as always and there had been no hint that he was planning to leave. There was no trace of his presence, as if he had never been. Mercedes was so shocked that for a few days she could hardly speak. She realised then how much she had grown to depend on him and how lonely she was without him. She missed him more than she had ever missed Ildefons. It was as though she had lost a brother. She wept at night, unable to sleep and in the morning woke, more exhausted than when she had gone to bed. Everything the girls did irritated her with the result that she left them mostly to their own devices, completely abandoning any attempts she had made to keep them abreast of their school work. She had never known such anxiety. Not even Ildefons's silence affected her in this way and after a while she was certain that they were both dead. Fear and panic gripped her entrails. She wandered aimlessly from room to room, down the paths of the vineyards inspecting, without seeing, the work of human hands. She found it impossible to sit still and moved about all day long, achieving nothing. Afterwards, Dr. Mantua told her, that his silence had been designed to protect her. But she had been hurt. She thought that they trusted one another implicitly. She knew that had she been the one to leave, she would have told him. She never expected to see him again.

Chapter 12

Mercedes
Val Negra 1936 -

Days and nights passed, so many of them that she lost count. One night as she lay awake in her bedroom, she heard the unmistakable sound of footsteps running down the secret passage that connected her bedroom to the chapel. She sat bolt upright thinking immediately of Ildefons, for he was the only one who had ever used it. When they were younger, he had thought it amusing to surprise her in her bedroom and on the odd occasion it had had its uses. She had quite forgotten about it until that moment. It was not a corridor that she would ever have ventured down alone, fearing that she could easily be trapped. She reached for her hunting pistol from under her pillow and positioned it with trembling hands at the trompe l'oeil door beside her dressing table. The footsteps grew louder but more hesitant. It was clear to her that who ever was on the other side of the wall was not sure how to get out. It could not be her husband. Quietly she got out of bed and tiptoed to the wall. Someone on the other side was pushing hard but to no avail. She took a deep breath and pressed a painted rose on the descriptive wall hanging. Instantly the partition sprang back. Mercedes pointed her gun aiming carefully as a dishevelled Dr. Mantua all but somersaulted into the room, into a trail of moonlight. Mercedes gasped as the priest looked up at her dazed. Behind him, stumbled Julian Pelham.

Mercedes had not expected to fall in love again, not after that first love with Idefons. Sometimes however, she found it difficult believe that the young boy she had known then, was the husband who had been absent for eighteen months. The two were hard to connect. She recognised neither. Nor did she recognise much of herself for that matter. There seemed little left of the young bride and mother she had been. Nor had they anything in common with the woman she was fast becoming. She often thought back to the early days of her marriage with a shudder, a mixture of longing and dread. She cringed at her naiveté and the humiliation of having revealed herself so completely to Ildefons. So when she saw Julian Pelham in the shadows of her bedroom, beneath fluttering muslin curtains and a moon suspended above them, all the pent up frustration of the years, her disappointment and loneliness, triggered something in her and brought her back to life. It was as if the years with Ildefons had never been, as if she were a girl again. She saw Julian Pelham and wanted him as she had so often lusted after Ildefons. She felt herself trembling with an uncontrollable urge, a desperation that had to be satisfied. She wanted his comfort and she wanted to anaesthetize all the pain she had ever felt, would ever feel. This was her time. She would never have it again and later she wanted to be able to live off it, feed off it and grow old with it.

After the initial hilarity had worn off and Mercedes had recovered from the double shock of seeing Dr. Mantua in her bedroom and falling in love, Dr. Mantua explained that the man with him was English. They had to help him escape – the only way that was open to them, through Port de la Selva and over the Pyrenees, to France. As he spoke, Mercedes hardly took her eyes off the stranger. This Julian Pelham, she suspected, was several years younger than herself, but with the confidence of a beautiful woman she knew that she would charm him. She smiled engagingly as she lit the way from her rooms to the hall. Dr. Mantua suggested wine and disappeared off to the cave in search of champagne. Julian's Spanish was amusing- fluent enough but with an odd intonation that marked him as a foreigner. It fluttered over her nerve strings as a prelude. She found him clean clothes and boots and then showed him the library. His face lit up at this and he thanked her profusely. She remembered the sight of his wrist under her candle as it fell away from his jacket, reaching to touch the books. Avia had always had a thing about a man's wrist and she stared at it transfixed noticing the expensive watch, the hairs covering the skin, the threadbare cuff. His hand moved along the spines of the books, long lean fingers, supple and strong. His shyness touched her. She longed to press herself against him, feel his arms around her. Instead she smiled modestly and told him a supper of sorts would soon be ready.

He was grateful – relieved she wouldn't wonder at being left alone. Perhaps he was wary of her? But why should he be? She felt confident that Dr. Mantua had told him nothing unflattering about her. Mercedes was used to being praised, used to being popular. No doubt he would pay her the same compliments. But he didn't. To her mild surprise Julian was consistently shy at supper. He sipped the venerable wines slowly, appreciatively. From time to time he spoke about their adventure, but in a cryptic way that could not be misconstrued and of which she knew nothing. Not once did he look directly at her. Neither the priest nor the boy made any attempts to properly include her, careful of their words, speaking as if she was the one who could not be trusted. Mercedes felt left out, disappointed and all at once horribly deflated. She wanted to lash out, jealous of their intimacy.

"What's the matter?" hissed Dr. Mantua when Julian was out of earshot. "You're behaving very oddly. Don't you like him? Our new recruit?" And then his eyes swept over her seeing her tenseness, her flushed cheeks. "Oh no," he added quietly in a different tone.

"I don't know what you mean," she replied stiffly.

"You can't hide from me. I know you remember? I know every mood, every suspicion."

"Well it doesn't mean you own me!" she flared and she snatched the candle from the table leaving him stranded in the darkness. She scampered up to her turret bedroom, angry with the priest and the stranger, but even angrier with herself.

The next morning she went down to breakfast, her head pounding from too much wine and little sleep. She felt generally out of sorts, her limbs lethargic as though she had a fever. All at once the war seemed endless and everywhere, poisoning everything they did. There was nothing to look forward to anymore. She was tired of poor food, of racking her brains to find the money to buy essentials, of constantly having to rustle up meals from meagre provisions. She heard laughter coming from the kitchen, her daughter's laughter. It was a long time since she'd heard that. She pushed open the door and immediately there was silence. She felt as if she were intruding in her own house. As if her presence signalled the end of fun. She was used to silence when she appeared, but it was usually as a result of the effect she caused. Strangers were always stunned by her beauty, in awe of who she was. This silence was different. For the first time in her life, Avia suspected that she was not wanted. She bowed her head shyly struggling to maintain her composure. She wanted to run out of the room, back to her bedroom, hide from this treacherous, shifting world of which she was no longer sure, no longer its centre.

For a moment, it was her turn to be blinded by physical beauty. Mercedes saw the Englishman clearly as she had not, in the dim light of the night before. He was a tall man who did not stoop, but held himself erectly, with a casual arrogant grace. His shirtsleeves, in spite of the cold, were rolled up and his arms were tanned and sinewy. His hair was short, dark flopping on one side. But it was his face that struck her the most. It was clear and young and innocent. The forehead was broad, the nose prominent, the jaw square, the lips not too full and the eyes were a dark blue, like the blush of vineyard beneath the Monseny. She caught her breath, her stomach contracting. When he spoke the arched strokes of his eyebrows spread across his brow and he ran his hand through his hair. But he was not looking at her. He leant against the kitchen dresser, a cup of coffee in his hand, while he talked, his face animated and charming, to her daughter Clara. Clara sat at one end of the table an empty plate in front of her, staring up at the Englishman with a look Mercedes knew only too well and her heart sank. Clara's face shone, her smile was open and wide, ready for love. It was a smile Mercedes had used herself with Ildefons, the night of the Val Negra feast day almost twenty years before.

Mercedes went to the sideboard, peering at the young people from out of the corner of her eye. She reached for a cup and saucer and then set them down abruptly as they began to rattle in her hand. She took a huge breath, gritting her teeth as she asked him the usual questions. *Had he slept well? Had he found the extra blankets?* She kept her voice toneless. But Julian still would not or could not, look at her. He seemed to be enthralled by whatever it was Clara was saying, whatever it was, Mercedes had interrupted. And yet how could Clara be so riveting? How had she failed to notices the change? But then during the past few months, Mercedes had been so preoccupied with her own problems that there had been hardly any time for anyone or anything else. All her energy had gone into Val Negra. Any time left over she gave to her priest. Mercedes looked at her daughter closely. Surely she was still a baby, *her* baby. She wasn't old enough to be thinking about men. Or was she? Mercedes eyed her critically for the first time and felt the bitter, guilty pangs of envy. Clara was just fourteen wasn't she? No wait she was *fifteen* soon to be *sixteen*. For Gods sake how long had they been here? How long had this war been going on? How could Mercedes have failed to notice the budding breasts, the narrow waist and smooth, luminous skin? The elasticity had gone from her own face. Anxiety was sketched along the edges of her eyes. Her mouth was tight. Everything about Clara was fresh, untried. Mercedes knew that she was still beautiful but she was no longer young and there was nothing that she could do about it. But how had it happened? She wasn't ready to grow old. *I feel young, or most of the time I do. And I am young inside!* She inwardly wailed. *Look at me damn you! I'm the one who makes heads turn. Not her! Besides she is me. She's a part of me. I'm the one you want. She's my daughter! She doesn't know anything about life. She doesn't know anything about anything! How can she? She's never been anywhere but here. She knows nothing of the world.*

Mercedes slid into her chair, staring miserably at the weak, mud coloured concoction they proudly called coffee. How she longed for the real thing! She nursed her cup in her hand pretending it had just arrived, steaming from the kitchen, its smell rich and sweet. How weary she was of all the greyness and the cold! They had begun lighting the odd fire again, but only in the library. The rest of the house was like being at the top of the Monseny in December. When she knew the house was being watched, Mercedes hadn't dared do anything that might attract attention. She hadn't even let the boys chop wood. Recently however, she had become careless. When the priest was away, she had sat drinking champagne in front of her fire, dreaming of the past. But the blue flames were never hot enough to warm her thoroughly, she could never, it would seem, get close to the heat. She was so very tired of the war and even of Val Negra. She was weary of this exhausting land of hers that seemed to drain as much as it invigorated – this passionate land with its red earth, dry and barren in places, fertile and lush in others, with the river running through it and the vineyards sloping down from the Monseny. Above all, she was weary of ownership and the huge responsibility that went with it. Occasionally, she allowed herself to think about Mialma. She knew from Dr. Mantua that it was safe now. At the beginning of the war, the anarchists had ransacked the house, looting and burning what little furniture they had not stolen. But later when it was forgotten, and the path up to the hills was overgrown and treacherous, she knew it was safe. An order of nuns who had not forgotten the road up from the village, had set up camp round the chapel, hiding by day, praying by night. Mialma's very own guardian angels. But where were hers? If only *she* could pray, she thought. If only she had Dr. Mantua's faith, his peace of mind. She didn't think she had ever been at peace with anything or anyone.

She looked through the casement windows edged prettily with snow, to the evergreens lining the drive. It was a peaceful scene totally belying the bitter cold inside the medieval building and the warring guns thundering in the distance. She knew her war had been easier for her than it had for most. Even the danger she had been exposed to in harbouring so many clergy, deserters and loyalists, was minor to that experienced by her fellow countrymen. Dr. Mantua's own torture was testament to appalling suffering and the stories he sometimes told her in the dead of night were enough to curdle the blood. She shivered. The house was freezing. The sun, struggling to gain height in a watery sky was weak and inconsequential. The day loomed before her endless and without reason. Julian and the girls' chatter droned in the background but she could not make out the words. She imagined a deaf person must feel like this when there was more than one conversation going on at once. She struggled to understand the barrage of sudden sounds. She pulled her thin, cashmere sweater around her. Once it had been much thicker and new. She remembered ordering it from Harrods and it had taken ages to arrive. She had set aside her husband's clothes for Dr. Mantua, while sharing out the rest of their personal belongings with the people who most needed clothing. But this cardigan she had kept. Her fingers caressed its folds.

They all came to Val Negra one way or another – hungry and wounded – wearing the very clothes they'd been shot in. Men, who survived the first ever blood transfusions, appeared, grotesque, more dead than alive, in their sanguineous rags. Mercedes and her daughters set up huge tubs of boiling water in the courtyard with makeshift shower curtains made from bed linen. Often the men were covered in lice and sores – some gangrenous and stinking – as their flesh rotted away. Without a doctor, many died and they were buried in the family churchyard behind the chapel –butcher, engineer and plumber lying happily bedded in death, with Roble Counts and Grandees.

It was some months since they had had any new visitors however. There was a strange, expectant silence that settled over the place with foreboding. Mercedes realised with a degree of astonishment that she had never spent so much time at Val Negra. Her family had only ever used the house as a summer place. Consequently it had an abandoned, out of season feel to it. It was beginning to look and feel impoverished. Mercedes had seen the seasons come and go, felt her loneliness blow through the empty rooms. Even at night she could hear the rustle of leaves scratching the dusty corridors. Val Negra, proud and beautiful seemed to be wilting beneath her own wanting.

Above all it was cold. None of the furnishings had been designed for warmth. There never seemed to be enough blankets on the beds and the sheets always felt damp to the touch. The rooms were draughty and fires lit in reluctant hearths, were never sufficient. Mercedes shivered at the thought. Often she could not concentrate on what people were saying because of the cold. A few cool months in August had not prepared them for a winter, or several winters, at Val Negra, which reminded her: *Mantua will have to chop more wood. Perhaps this Julian will help him. Or was he to be hidden by day, only allowed a life of sorts in the silent midnight hours, like some of the others?* She had no idea when his escape was being planned. It was strange how they all seemed loath to talk about the war. And then she realised it was *because* the war had become a way of life, a continuous present. But surely it would have to end. Dr. Mantua said it could only be a matter of weeks now. Julian, the evening before, had recounted what news he had heard on the BBC. The Republicans had been driven back over the Ebro. The Catalan front was broken. The fall of Barcelona was inevitable.

"Can we mother? Oh please? I know it's dangerous! But we only have today and it's quiet. I've not heard anything, no guns anyway, in days. Dr. Mantua says it will be all right."

Clara's earnest voice broke into her thoughts. Clara's beautiful eyes, almond shaped and slanted were magnets of crystal light. How *could* she be so animated? And all because of a stranger she barely knew. What did an innocent of fifteen- all right *sixteen,* know about anything? How could he want her? Clara was h*ers.* She had given birth to her, nursed her, spent sleepless nights by her bed when she was sick, loved her. What could a stranger know of that?

"Dime Senor Pelham," Mercedes said icily. "Why have you become involved in our war? What does an Englishman find here to amuse him? I should have thought there were enough problems in Europe to keep you busy. After all it doesn't look as if Mr. Hitler is going to be kept at bay much longer. Or have you enjoyed observing how we die? Is that what you came for? Because if it is, you won't have long to wait. You yourselves will be at war before long. I am certain of it. And when war comes to you, it will be a much bigger affair. This will seem child's play in comparison."

Clara's face fell. Julian's eyes blazed and then just as quickly were calm. He bowed his head.

"I don't know why I came actually."

He fumbled for a packet of cigarettes and after asking permission to smoke, lit one. Mercedes again noticed his hands, long, graceful as they flicked the match.

"Except out of a misplaced sense of something, although I'm not sure of what exactly and because I am young enough to believe in causes. Especially lost ones. I believe there are some issues that are worth fighting for, no matter what one's nationality. Or I thought I did," he smiled, lazily, charmingly. Mercedes blushed in spite of herself. Clara hesitated, her eyes darting between the two, sensing nothing of her mother's tension. "I sound extremely pompous don't I? I think the truth is that I came here to spite my twin."

"Your twin? Is he here?" said Mercedes her heart leaping at the idea that there could be two Julian's.

Julian shook his head. "No. No. He's in England. I do miss him though. And he'd love to hear me admit it. It is the first time we've been away from each other and it feels very strange. And yes, before you ask, all the clichés about twins are true. I can vouch for them. We had a bet, followed by an argument and then I left. But I don't regret any of it."

"Are you identical? Twins I mean?" Clara faltered enchantingly. Julian's gaze softened.

"No. He is by far the better man, in every way. He's more intelligent, more charming, better looking – altogether the golden boy. He's good at everything and everyone adores him. Our own mother dotes on him."

"Do you have any sisters?"

"No. Three other brothers besides John."

"Dios Mio, five boys!" exclaimed Mercedes. Julian stretched out his legs under the table.

"One of my ancestors had eight. Must be in the genes."

Clara rose from her seat and began piling the breakfast dishes. Remnants of soda bread lay on the plates and the only palatable aspect of the meal – fig jam, made from the orchard fruit.

"We wanted to go on a picnic," said Julian springing to his feet. "Would …?"

Mercedes smiled, hope jumping foolishly in her breast. And then she noticed his embarrassment.

"Oh go," she said ungraciously. "Do whatever you want."

*

Later that afternoon she came upon Julian in the galleried hall studying a large family tree that hung on the wall. The top of his head held a halo of light from the candle above. Her stern expression melted. He was, after all, very young, too old for Clara, but still very young.

"Family sagas have always fascinated me," he said.

She came to stand beside him, hands thrust deep into the pockets of her cardigan. He wore a rough tweed jacket that had belonged to Ildefons and which still retained his horsy, soap smell. She felt a pang of remorse that her husband wasn't with her. How just like Ildefons to leave her alone when she needed him most!

"How can you see a family saga from that?"

His fingers traced the embossed coat of arms, down the branches, lines, ladders of children, marriages and deaths. Footnotes added snippets of history – a daughter who danced with Napoleon, an heiress who became a nun, an adopted child who inherited a fortune.

"Well this Roble had twenty children, two sets of twins," explained Julian. "This one had six sons and not one reached maturity. We forget the high percentage of infant mortality, no penicillin to stem the tide of childhood disease. There's an irony that breathes through the generations. Look these cousins have married, these died on their wedding day. Ah…" Julian looked up and he touched her shoulder to focus her attention. "We are linked…our families…'Honeymoon of Enrique Roble and one Clara de Pena. Cruise down the Rhine – had to hurry home when the Franco-Prussian war broke out.' You see, then, as now, Spain was a battlefield that divided Europe. Do you think members of our families have met before? Did your grandfather dance with my great-grandmother do you think, at some military ball in Biarritz?"

"Who knows?" Mercedes shrugged.

Julian turned away, reaching for the candle. "Why are you so unhappy?" he asked.

Mercedes' mouth gaped.

"I-m …not."

"Of course you are. Any moment now you'll be weeping. I noticed it the moment I first saw you. Your eyes were full of tears. Just waiting to spill over. Is it your husband? Don't you know where he is?"

Mercedes shook her head vehemently. She did not want to think, let alone talk, about Ildefons. She did want to feel guilt. Gently Julian leant down and wiped away a tear, brushing it with his thumb.

"The war will soon be over – much sooner than we dare think. The guns are silent. Dr. Mantua was right. There won't be any more fighting up here. Now that Barcelona –"

"It's not that!" her voice was harsh, ragged. He bent his head.

"Then what?"

The light from the candle enveloped them in a tidy, dark little world, in which the boundary around them had ebbed away. Mercedes felt as though she were standing on a narrow ledge on the edge of the world, one wrong step and she would fall … Suddenly there was nothing but this man's rugged face above her. She reached for him, pulling him down to her. His lips were gentle, soft, then hungry and abrasive. She pressed her body to his, knowing, leading.

The candle dropped from his hands on to the marble floor.

*

The next day they were gone. A tearful Nuria alerted Mercedes to the fact that Julian and Clara had not slept in their beds or anywhere else for that matter. Alarm and panic rose in her throat and she felt sick to her stomach. Mercedes searched the grounds, running through the burnt out flower beds and vineyards, oblivious of the frozen soil, the withering fruit. She ran through the rose garden and along the river, tears streaming down her face, panting like an animal. Her hesitant, disbelieving cries soon became hysterical. At last she stumbled into the chapel throwing open the doors, screeching her pain. Dr. Mantua looked up startled from where he was lighting candles. He caught her as she hurtled past him.

"Es Culpa mia. Culpa mia. It's my fault! Oh God. Oh God. I've killed them!" she cried over and over again. She pulled at her hair and her clothes like a mad woman. The priest pulled her to the stone floor, in the archway of the open door, the wind searing their necks. He struggled with her and then at last she was still and he held her in his strong, capable arms.

"Start again," he said calmly. "Tell me everything."

Her breath was jagged and sharp, her voice unattractively rasping. "It's my fault – you were right of course – I did want him. Lust after him, after Julian I mean. And he wanted me. A woman, not some innocent, young love! He wanted a real woman!"

Dr. Mantua shut his eyes, suddenly exhausted but he did not release her.

"Yes Father, dear Dr. Mantua, or plain old Edmondo, I have sinned. Will you hear my confession or will it shock you? Will it?"

Her voice rose hysterically.

"No, it will not shock me," he replied quietly.

"He's different. Julian is different from the men I've known. How could he? How could they?"

She shook her head so that her hair was tangled in her eyes, in her mouth. Her face was swelling with the effort of so much crying, a rash had broken under her nostrils. And then she began to sob uncontrollably, the anger seeping from her, like pus from a wound.

"Who is 'they'?" he asked gently.

"They've gone. Clara has left …with HIM! Oh God! How can she love him? She's a child! How could she run off with him! She doesn't know him!"

"And what makes you think that you do?" said Dr. Mantua rationally. For a moment there was only the sound of her panting between them.

"Because I do," she said wringing her hands. "Because – " the words were torn from her. "Because we've made love! I'm older. I understand him. I know."

Dr. Mantua prised open her fingers and held them between his hands, hands that were surprisingly warm, given the bitter cold.

"Pray with me," he instructed.

"You pray!" she snarled. "It's what you're good at!"

He dropped her hands. "Fine!" he said angry at last. "You come here for my absolution! You want a magic wand, words of comfort! You want me to somehow justify your …your fornication! For that is what it is, forgive my bluntness, but we know each other too well for niceties. Spare me the love story, Mercedes, please. You cannot understand your own daughter's love for this stranger and yet you expect me to sympathise with yours! Well I won't! I won't do it. I will not make your *obscenity* pure! I will *not* soothe your breaking heart. You have only yourself to blame."

He sighed heavily and sat back on his knees, rubbing his bloodshot eyes. When he looked at her again his anger had gone and was replaced by his usual affection. He shook his head sadly.

"You've been moping around the place for ages! I've seen it coming, or *ought* to have seen it. If it's anyone's fault it's mine. I should have explained where I was going, what I was doing. I shouldn't have left you on your own. I know I could have prevented this nonsense. You are lonely and tired. You have been brave for so long but you are not super human. You wanted comfort. We talked so much and yet I failed to strengthen your faith. I failed to notice. I'm sorry."

Mercedes was crying quietly to herself. "Oh God," she said. "Will they ever forgive me? What if they're killed? You were supposed to arrange their route? Where on earth will they have gone? Who will have helped them? How will they have got to Port de la Selva? How – "

"Sh!" Dr. Mantua took her hands once more in his as she sank against the church door.

"You must have faith. Someone will have helped them. I am certain of it, just as we have helped so many. They are young and fit. I know Julian, he will not take unnecessary risks."

Mercedes' eyes were huge in her wan face. "Forgiveness," she whispered. "Do I have yours?"

"It is not mine to give," he said. "Now pray with me," he said making the sign of the cross. "Pray Mercedes. It is said that the vertical stroke is symbolic for the love of God and his people, that the horizontal one stands for the love man has for his fellow man and where the two strokes meet, is perfect love. You must look for that love, Mercedes, not only in your own heart but also in the way you live your life. Follow your faith. Seek out your inspiration."

"But how can I when I have made such a mess of things? I've been a bad wife, indifferent mother, friend to no one."

"How can you say that? You have helped so many –"

"*You* have. I just happened to be here. I couldn't have done it alone, it wouldn't have occurred to me to anything at all if you hadn't come here. Besides it's easy to be heroic. A one off gesture requires very little, what is much more difficult is to survive the drudgery of every day – a loveless marriage, a daughter who shrinks from me …"

"I know. But you have a chance now to make things better. Clara is a woman. The war has changed us all and she is grown up –"

"She's just fi-sixteen!" protested Mercedes beginning to cry again.

"And how old were you when you met Ildefons?"

"Sixteen."

Dr. Mantua shrugged. "And you did not think yourself a child did you? It's time to let things be, Mercedes. You are a beautiful woman. You are not old but it is time to work on your soul. Your spiritual life will be long and rewarding and long outlive your physical beauty. Surely you don't want to become shrivelled and old out of bitterness? Your husband loves you. When he comes back, be kind to him. Open yourself up to new things as you did as a girl. And then there's Nuria. She needs you more than ever before and in a way that Clara never did. She's not as strong as you think and has always hungered for your love. She feels your neglect so much. After the war we will all need our friends. We will need a great deal of love and most of all the ability to truly forgive."

He stroked her shoulder as her sobs subsided and she began to cry quietly. Dr. Mantua continued almost to himself.

"The Greek word used in the Gospels means simply to let go," he said. "But we can only do this for ourselves. We are human. We are imperfect, but somehow we must refrain from *retaliation* and seek *reconciliation*. Clara loves you and because she does, Julian will too. They will come home, when they are ready. Your insecurities are natural, but do not let them twist and change your perspective, your faith. You must cling to it now more than ever."

Mercedes stopped crying and sat up wiping her eyes with the corner of her sleeve. She looked at him strangely and then taking a deep, shuddering breath said, "do you battle then? To preserve it?"

"Of course," the priest replied. "Every day of my life. I would not be human if I didn't."

"Then you have doubts?"

"Undoubtedly," he smiled at his own pun and then was serious again. "Yes. As do you, I know, in your marriage. As we all do. I am always seeking, questioning, battling. But I am always sure of God's love. That is my rock."

Mercedes was calm once more.

"When you were tortured…?" she asked quietly.

"Especially then."

"No me mueve, mi Dios, para querete, el cielo que me tienes prometido," she quoted softly.

Dr. Mantua studied her thoughtfully and touched her *face*. *"Ni me mueve el infierno tan temido para dejar por eso de ofenderte."*

"Will you hear my confession?"

"In the name of the father and of the son and of the holy ghost."

"Amen."

*

Avia reached to pick up the scattered prayer cards before placing them firmly between the sections of her bible.

"I have fought a good fight, I have finished my course. I have kept the faith."

Had she?

Chapter 13

Sigi
Chile
Journal

    There are days when I don't think about my Grandmother's house at all. Whole sections of time are blanked out. These are restful sequences when I am not assaulted by searing pain pulling at my heartstrings, drawing me back.

    At other times, I may be thinking of something completely different, when suddenly I see myself as a child once more, in her house. Then again if I am very bored, I travel in time through the rooms recalling the smells, the sometime stillness. When we were very small, there was always someone working somewhere – a maid in the laundry room, cook in the kitchen and Jose, endlessly polishing Avi's car. I remember the sound a visitor's footsteps made as he or she followed the butler down the corridor, waiting to be announced. We would wait excitedly, wondering whom it might be, trying to guess by the trip trap of footsteps. Abuelita was always the easiest to guess. She was very slow, her expensive shoes scraping along the marble floor as she leant heavily on her driver's arm. But her voice made up for the lack of animation in her feet. It was very shrill and inappropriately girl like, leaping up and down, flitting from one subject to the other. Even before we could see her, she would be calling to our grandmother. Of course there was no need to announce Abuelita, but the butler's formality when others came to visit, was a source of great amusement. We would dissolve into giggles when he bowed saying,

    "Condesa."

    Avia would nod. "Who is it Gomez?"

And Gomez would then announce the guest. We would stare at them mercilessly, enjoying their discomfort. Abuelita was never uncomfortable about anything. But she knew how to make us squirm.

"*Escolta Mercedes.* Now look here," she always began and what she had to say nearly always had to do with our behaviour - our bad behaviour.

As we grew up however, it became harder to find maids and butlers. The large hotels being built in the city, created many job opportunities. Women like Pepita who left their villages as young girls to devote their lives to their employer's families, were now leaving to work in the hotel industry. They were encouraged to have flats of their own, to leave the families they worked for and to become financially independent. Mialma, which had previously been home to several families, often generations of the same family, and a hub of activity, was suddenly quiet. Gone was the large staff and with it, a way of life that would vanish forever. Although there were now many empty rooms at Mialma, it was not neglected. At one point Avia had all the sofas re-upholstered because she said the drawing room was looking 'tired.' The kitchen was modernized because it no longer solely belonged to the cooks although Avia was scathing of the latest fad to tart up a room that would always be just a kitchen. It struck her as absurd, she said, that the same women who spent so much time and energy trying to liberate themselves from domestic duty, should be the first ones to spend much of their earnings on a bespoke, hand crafted kitchen. American decorating journals were full of amazing kitchen extensions inviting women to spend even more time in them. 'The heart of the home' is what they called it. 'A prison' more like, said Avia. 'Nothing *pero un carcel.*' Everything else at Mialma remained the same. The guest room with its faded yellow daisies embroidered on Swiss cotton eiderdowns was exactly as I remembered it. The shutters scraped against the outside wall as they had done when I was little and the right hand tap dripped in the bathroom.

Even when I was grown up, I could not help the excitement I felt every time I went to see Avia. As my footsteps took me down that long corridor to her drawing room, I could feel myself visibly shrinking. With each step I became smaller and smaller until I was a child once more, visiting Avia after mass on Sundays or coming to find Isabel at the beginning of the summer holiday. The maids would greet me with a welcoming: 'Condesa' and I felt safe, secure in the knowledge of who I was and what was expected of me. And that was little enough. Provided we were polite and looked pretty, no one seemed to care what we did. In the street if we were out with Lupe and a friend paused to greet us, the fact that she called us the 'Condesa's grandchildren' was enough to make me feel important. I would tilt my chin, puffed up with pride – a gesture sure to provoke yet another one of Lupe's lectures on the seven deadly sins. But it wasn't pride at *what* I was that made my heart beat quicken, it was simply that I was encouraged by the unexpected attention. Complete strangers were curious enough to want to talk to us, while our parents were not. Sometimes, days passed without even Nuria visiting the nursery. I wanted to ask my parents why they had bothered having children at all. But we all knew that Tito didn't like anyone's children on principle, least of all his own.

I often wonder if we loved Mialma too much. It was an all-embracing world, an oasis of stability in the midst of a turbulent adolescence, a haven in adulthood. At twilight, it was especially beautiful with the perfect light dancing off the ever-changing colours of the sea. I could not imagine a time when it had not been gracious and serene, when the orderly passage of the seasons did not reflect the fulfilment of the lives within. Often the sound of the chapel bell haunts me still and I remember the summer evenings and the scent of orange blossom. I know every cobbled courtyard and path, every broken love seat. Blindfold, I could trace archways, narrow columns, or any of the secret gardens on an invisible map. My only point of reference might be a sunken birdbath or the folly by the lemon grove.

I remember the last time I stayed there although I did not know then, that it would be the last. It was autumn and the light of early morning was pale, translucent, bathing the stone in a yellow glow. High above the city, in my turret bedroom I listened to the birds, the sounds of the day, the maids opening squeaking shutters, pulling back furniture. I could feel the house still drunk with sleep, kick started into life. Wisteria brushed against the balcony and I stepped out onto the terrace, the breeze making my nightdress billow out behind me. Below were the gardens and beyond the gardens, the sea. Above and all around, the mountains were a pearly haze in the early light. There was a hint of the cool weather that awaited us but the sun, embracing the horizon rose steadily and strong. And although I did not know it then, I know it now. Mialma was a constant harbour to which I returned again and again. It was a world within a world and its inhabitants became destructively self-sufficient, clumsy at relationships. We strove for nothing, for we needed nothing. We thought we had everything. We had no expectations and no dreams.

*

Everything here reminds me of another place. I think so much about my childhood that it is a shock to wake up and find that I am not at home, that I am not nine, ten, twelve years old. And while I wallow in those memories and in the image of the nice little girl that I must have been, I recoil from memories of my adolescence. Childhood was safe – what came afterwards was full of terror, the swirling insecurity of what I was fast becoming. Childhood meant holidays with my cousin Isabel, Val Negra bathed in sunshine, the excitement of picnics by the river and later the Bazan brothers. It meant treasure hunts which extended all over the village, afternoons spying on the twins at the club and glorious sunny mornings as we trampled through dew drenched meadows to collect flat stones with pretty patterns. It meant being admired and indulged, constantly reassured as to how wonderful we were, how wonderful we *looked*.

And then suddenly at the age of fifteen, it was not enough to be beautiful or beautifully dressed. People started asking questions, wanted to hear us speak. We were invited out to parties in the evening, to see friends of our parents. We were expected to amuse, to dance and flirt but not too much. We were taught to be enchanting and never ever make anyone feel uncomfortable. But the people I met, expected something from me that I did not know how to give. They hoped that I would be witty like Marta or cute like Beatrice, but I had nothing to say. I was tongue tied in front of strangers. My hands would go all clammy and the hairs rose at the back of my neck. I could think of absolutely nothing because I had nothing to say. I was not clever, like Isabel, at talking about things. I couldn't speak as she did, about the books. Our education was patchy. We were never taught much about anything except religion and I never enjoyed reading anyway. We were never taken to museums or to the theatre or to concerts and I needed so much to be inspired. I felt inadequate, not stupid and yet not quite up to the mark either, as though there was a conspiracy around me of which I knew a little.

"But aren't you curious?" Dr.Mantua asked once at the end of his monthly visits.

"What about?"

He removed the glasses he had recently acquired for reading and massaged the bridge of his nose. He seemed both frustrated and disappointed at the same time.

"Don't you want to learn, to read, to find things out for yourself? There's an entire, glorious library both here and at Val Negra. It is crammed with wonderful books. Your grandfather has access to magazines, Franco would crucify him for and yet you're not interested. I can point you in the right direction but the rest is up to you. You have to *want* to learn. And I *want,* more than anything, to make you curious."

Curious. He had said it again. It seemed to be his favourite word. I didn't feel curious or anything remotely approaching it, only very small, shrivelling inside by the minute, as though I had failed before I'd even begun. I hated when Dr. Mantua sounded cross. I always looked forward to his classes but now he too wanted something more from me. I was at a loss as to what it was. I chewed my nails.

"Why don't you tell me what I should read?" I asked in a small voice but this only seemed to anger him more.

"But that's the point!" he almost shouted. "I don't *want* to have to tell you anything! I want you to take the initiative. I want *you* to tell me something for once in your life! I would love you to come running up to me, fired with enthusiasm, bursting with ideas, questions, thirsting for knowledge, just as you should be doing at your age, just as any young girl would be! Just like your cousin –"

He stopped short.

"Just like Isabel you mean."

"No. Well, yes."

"But I'm not like Isabel am I?"

He sighed.

"No. No, you're not."

And that was the beginning of what I called the 'greyness,' a mood that began slowly and consistently to destroy me. It was a grey, damp cold that could descend at any moment without warning. It could be the loveliest day in the world and rather than soar, my spirits would crash. I became increasingly quiet, not that anyone noticed. Besides, Tito had never wanted our opinions on anything – never wanted to hear the sound of our voices at all. Now he very much wanted to hear us. And so did his friends. And then it occurred to me that we were being paraded around the city in search of husbands. We were taken like specimens of village sausage, to the grand houses of Barcelona to be sampled and to perform. And I couldn't. The sight of spoilt, young men standing behind fat mamas who looked alarmingly like Abuelita, was enough to make me clam up for days.

One Christmas, however, I *did* discover something that made me feel better when the 'greyness' descended. A whole lot better in fact. It was the only Christmas Isabel ever spent with us and she arrived in a flurry of activity, showering gifts and laughter and noise.

("Gosh, how can you remember everything?" – this from a delighted Bea and a cheerful Isabel replies: "I make lots of lists! I have to – there are always so many requests!") Even Miguel was pleased because Isabel had at last made it to Carnaby St and brought him back a poster and a Beatles record.)   She had slimmed down since the previous summer and was looking surprisingly pretty. Her skin and hair, which had always been good, were bursting with vitality and her eyes sparkled with the usual excitement of being home. "Do you realise that this is the first time I've ever been to Spain in the winter? This will be my first ever Christmas at Mialma. It's going to be fabulous, I just know it. You must tell me everything that's being going on and what you do.   It's amazing nothing ever seems to change here."

"But *you* change," I said truthfully. "Every year you are different."

"Really? I don't feel it," she said embarrassed and then went back to what she really wanted to talk about. "Is Christmas truly lovely here? Is it wonderful?" she kept saying over and over again and my sullen, "S'pose so," didn't seem to arouse any suspicions.

She had become such a chatterbox, blabbing on about her great friend Kate Douglas and how thin she was and how she could eat loads and loads ('a bit like you actually, Sigi') and never put on weight. She told us about everything – the fashion for 'drain pipes' and how the girls spent every spare moment converting slacks into skinny, clinging trousers that were excruciatingly uncomfortable, impossible to put on and impossible to sit down in.   And all to wear at the school on weekends and for each other because the girls never seemed to go anywhere! She described the convent, decorated for the feast of the Immaculate Conception, with holly and candles and branches of yew. She told us about all the books she was studying, mostly Spanish authors, as she was doing her O'level and how she finally understood about our peculiar names (mine especially although she promised never to call me Sigismunda) and how her head fairly swam with the voices of Golden Age Poets. She talked about a James Bond film she had seen where one of the baddies has braces like hers and how the girls had taken to calling her "Jaws." She rattled on about shops and musicals in a land we would never visit. The words poured from her, tripping off her tongue in her funny Spanish.

And all the while I listened, it occurred to me that she and I were like the transfers that children rub onto tracing paper with a pencil – while hers was becoming brighter and whole, mine was gradually fading. I stared at her realizing with a start that she was no longer the fat, clumsy little girl we had secretly laughed at. I could also see that she no longer needed me. She was confident and clever and perfectly at home. There was an added sparkle to her eyes and I knew before even turning round, that my brother Ricardo must have come into the nursery. Someone had mentioned something about a new movement called *Opus Dei*. *Ugh! Not politics again*! I thought although Isabel seemed to enjoy talking about government almost as much as Tito.

"What does that mean? What does Opus Dei mean?" asked Isabel in her most irritatingly buoyant mood. Her eyes were huge and shining, her hair bounced on her shoulders. Her glasses, which had previously made her look ridiculous, seemed coquettishly different – not necessarily glamorous but cute. I felt a pang of something. All at once our exquisite clothes seemed too contrived. There was something approachable and warm about Isabel and I could see my brother was aware of it too.

Ricardo made a bow.

"*Buenos dias Cosina,*" he said in the 'nice' voice he used for Tito's family or when he chatted up girls at the club. I looked at him closely. "Don't you know your Latin?" he continued in a playful tone. His eyes ran over her face, delighting in what he found there. "I am surprised. I thought those English nuns of yours were trying to give you an education."

He stood very close to her.

"And succeeding," replied Isabel tartly. "But I don't do Latin. It's hard enough learning Spanish."

"It would help your Spanish."

They looked at each other. Isabel's face was pink.

"It means…" I said blurting out, "God's work. *Opus* means work, *Dei* means God. Ricardo calls them the Holy Mafia don't you? They're a Catholic group, very big here at the moment. Very Franco."

Isabel moved away from Ricardo as if my speaking had broken a spell. But I rambled on, wanting them to listen to me, to remember that I was here too. Isabel sat on a window seat, her face half hidden by the curtain and her hair. Her legs were curled beneath her. She fiddled with the latch on the window.

"What do they do?" she asked in a distant voice. "Are they a religious order?"

"Both. I mean you don't have to be a nun. You can join and be married and have a family. Like Tito." I swallowed, nervously trying to repeat anything and everything I had heard. Ricardo's eyes bored into me, daring me to be silent. "Just now they seem to be everywhere. They look out for young people at the universities and schools, you know, ask them to join groups and things, meetings I suppose. But they want professional, good looking, well-educated young people - not any old riff-raff. They're after wealthy, handsome candidates to promote this new cult – with an emphasis on the young and wealthy. They want everyone to be taken in by how lovely and happy they all are. How Catholic."

"And how d' you know all this?" asked my brother.

"It doesn't sound too bad," chipped in Isabel.

"N-not bad exactly. It's all very subtle you see. It looks and sounds like a wonderful thing. I mean it keeps young Catholic boys and girls out of trouble doesn't it? They organize all kinds of activities like cooking clubs and walks and reading groups."

Isabel giggled.

"Reading groups? Golly."

I nodded uncertain now.

"It's just that Avi says they're everywhere, at every level of government too – that it's going to be an enormous group soon, a sort of secret society. That it's all done very carefully, starting at school, with young impressionable people. You see these pretty, intelligent, dedicated young people who are also very pious, always eager to please, never look cross or bored and you're supposed to think – Yes, that's what I'll do too –. They have such an attractive image you see, no fuddy duddy nuns in habits. Just beautiful, rich, *devout* young people. And then you think that it's got to be worth a go. Because they all look so happy the whole time and always smile and are always pleasant. But the thing is that once they've got you, they never let you go. They're a bit like the masons – all secrets and funny hand shakes."

"What on earth do you know about funny handshakes!" exclaimed Ricardo and Isabel smiled.

I felt the tears prick my eyes and I hated the way Isabel simpered, in that traitorous way. I hated the way she sided with Ricardo.

"Well that's what Avi says. And he's very serious about it. He says that if we're not careful, we'll all end up brainwashed and all over a nice cup of coffee and a sing song!"

Isabel did burst out laughing then and I could hear a rumble or grunt from Ricardo.

"Brainwashed! Surely that's a bit strong!" protested Isabel.

"No it's exactly that," I insisted wishing I'd never opened my big mouth. " They are all charming, attractive petits bourgeois, well that's what

Nuria calls them. And because Tito loves them so much she tells us to stay clear. Come on Ricardo you tell her. You know it's true."

Ricardo looked as if he could throttle me.

"I don't know about the handshakes," he said in a clipped tone "But Sigi is right. There's an element of secrecy to it. But Isabel doesn't want to hear all this," he said, eyes boring into mine. "It's very dull."

"Oh but Isabel does," said Isabel shoving her head in front of the curtain. Ricardo grimaced.

"It's a Holy Mafia," he said tightly. "For the rich and made up of the rich, to further the interests of the rich."

"Well that explains Tito's interest then doesn't it?" said Isabel with a smile.

Ricardo looked at her sharply.

"Naturally, Tito thinks that the Opus are the new Christian warriors. He sees the movement bringing our country back to National Catholicism. Many people, with the memory of the war still fresh, welcome it. But there *is* an aspect, joking apart, that is worrying. For example, Opus Dei Bishops sit in parliament, Opus professors lecture at the university. In short, Opus Dei members are beginning to hold key positions in industry. You see religion and politics go hand in hand in Franco's Spain. And Opus Dei *is* the new Religion. Anyone who questions it is said to be a Marxist. "

"And yet this Opus really does seem to be an opium," said Isabel thoughtfully. "How delicious. Doesn't Franco appreciate the significance? Has he no education at all?"

Ricardo went to sit beside Isabel on the window seat.

"Probably not. But I'm glad to see that the English nuns *are* teaching you something cosina," he said softly. "And maybe Franco has everything just the way he wants it."

"Not just maybe!"

"Well he has Tito taken in, but then that's not difficult."

"No."

They were silent for a moment. Ricardo's hands were thrust deep in his pockets and Isabel hugged her knees. They're heads were almost touching. I alone seemed out of place.

"One thing never seems to change here," Isabel said looking up, catching me watching her, "and that's all the talk of politics! Time seems to stand still here."

"Yes and in the worst possible way."

"What do you mean?"

"I mean that nothing changes for the better and not just politically. Tito rants and raves just as much as before, maybe more and outside, Franco has created a state of tension. An atmosphere if you will. Every child is afraid of him and yet if you asked him why he was afraid, he wouldn't be able to tell you. He's like the bogey man. We talk about Franco in a way that I'm sure you don't about your own politicians."

"Perhaps not," agreed Isabel. "But I find it rather refreshing after school where the girls seem to be mostly interested in boys."

"That's because England is a free country," replied Ricardo before I had a chance to say anything. "You take freedom as a given. We on the other hand can't do anything. Everything is censored and Franco has severed most of our links with the outside world. We could be any country behind the iron curtain. Which makes it rather ironic – if you'll excuse the pun – because Franco passionately loathes the communists and yet this country is hardly any different from a communist one. We're a 'no party state' run by families of the regime. And culturally –!" Ricardo shrugged. "Well … the only thing that people read is this so called *Kiosk* literature, you know light romances, westerns that sort of thing. Nothing serious. It's only here in Catalonia that there's any kind of avant garde literature. You see how Franco creeps into every conversation? Hardly a day goes by that we're not talking about him."

"Then let's not. It's Christmas, we're here and it's wonderful."

Ricardo lit a cigarette, opening the window behind so that Lupe wouldn't smell tobacco.

"Does everything always seem so simple to you?"

"Most of the time," she said. "You aren't going to change anything you know. Short of becoming a politician yourself –"

"A politician? In this country! You've got to be joking! Besides I'd be just where Tito wants me."

"Then what else can you do?"

"I can practise law and not become a soldier."

"Why not?"

"Because the military is something *he* would have liked. Don't parents always force their frustrated ambitions on their children?"

"I wouldn't know."

I made a face.

"I'm sorry," said Ricardo hastily but Isabel was unmoved.

"I just think you have to chose for yourself. It's your life, not your father's."

"Is that what you will do?"

Isabel laid her head on her knees, a tangle of hair spilling over her shoulders. For a moment she seemed thoughtful. Ricardo watched her through a cloud of smoke, his eyes narrow, his movements stealthy. He seemed completely oblivious of my presence.

"It's easier for me," replied Isabel at last. "I don't have anyone to please. Not really. There's no one watching over my shoulder, except for Kate. But she's not, I imagine, going to be anything like a parent."

Ricardo stubbed out his cigarette and after a final airing, slammed shut the window.

"Never mind," he said patting her knee. "In our different ways we'll work it out. You will achieve whatever it is you want. I think you already do and I truly hope that you will be happy. For us it is not enough to want personal happiness and that isn't supposed to sound patronizing, we have to live our politics. Any intelligent person with an inkling of social and moral responsibility cannot help but be influenced by them. Politics affects everything we do here, every professional or academic decision we take. But I'm optimistic," he added with a smile. "I know things will change. Starting with Tito. I *will* practise law, politics *will* change and our Catalan language and culture *will* survive. We *will* overcome!" he rounded off in Catalan.

Isabel laughed.

"I've never known you to be so passionate."

Ricardo looked at her again with that funny expression, half serious and half playful, in a way he never looked at any of us.

"Then you don't know me *cosina*," he said.

No, but *I* do, I thought and just as I was about to tell my brother to stop being so soppy, I heard shouts from downstairs. Moments later there was the inevitable scream and crash of furniture. Ricardo crossed the room quietly to open the nursery door. Isabel and I followed behind him, peering over the banister at the spiral staircase below and the deep pool of darkness at the bottom. But all was quiet as though the sound of weeping and the cries had never been. We stood together for a moment, silent witnesses pressed against each other. Isabel was very white.

"Is Nuria having one of her *malas,* one of her turns?"

"Not exactly," said Ricardo his eyebrows knitted together. Isabel shrank back.

"Oh it's *that.* I thought he'd have outgrown it by now," she whispered.

"Does a leopard change his spots?" replied Ricardo angrily.

"Why don't you do something? How can you let him? Do you think Avia knows? Why has no one ever done anything?"

"No," said Ricardo "I mean, I don't think Avia knows. When we were little we only suspected. You know yourself what it was like. And now … well I thought it happened less. He'd only hurt her more if we interfered."

"Oh that's an easy answer," she said fiercely. "Someone has got to do something. It can't go on," and she made as if to run down the stairs. Ricardo pulled her back.

"And what do you suppose we *should* do?" said Ricardo shaking her a little. "It's all right for you, you can leave this all behind. *We* have to live with it."

"I know that but it doesn't mean I don't care," said Isabel hotly. "I don't 'leave this,' as you put it, because I want to. And if I stayed I'd do anything to protect my mother from –from –HIM! I'd do whatever it took."

"I'm sure you would, " he said softly dropping her arm. "But it's not as simple as that. It's not as if our mother doesn't have a choice. She could leave, you know. She doesn't have to stay. She's not financially dependent on him and Beatrice is no longer a baby and there's Mialma just around the corner. Have you ever asked yourself why she doesn't leave? No, nor will she. Look, there are things that you don't know about. My parents play a lot of games with each other – some more amusing than others, it has to be said. Sometimes I think they deserve each other. They're both completely messed up as people, never mind parents. As sickening and awful as it sounds, I believe they're still drawn to each other. This is way above your head. Leave it alone."

"No matter what she's like, it doesn't condone his violence," insisted Isabel.

"I didn't say it did."

"Then what *are* you saying? That it's too complicated for me so I should do nothing? There is never any excuse for violence. Never. You think I'm too naive don't you? Is that what you've always thought?"

Ricardo ran a hand through his hair.

"No," he said. "I know you care about Nuria a great deal but our mother is a big girl. By now she's worked out a way of coping with her life. I'm not saying that it's good and that it isn't time to put a stop to our bully of a father. It's long over due. I'm only saying that there's nothing you can do. *Your* outrage isn't going to make the slightest bit of difference. This is *our* problem."

My head began to pound and the greyness pushed through new barriers. I was consumed with anger towards my father. I felt stifled on the landing at the top of the clock tower, hemmed in by my old prejudices and fears. The heavy Gothic pictures that hung all around us on the landing, began to swim before my eyes.

"I need air," I said hoarsely and rushed passed them.

"I'm going with her," I heard Isabel say and Ricardo must have tried to stop her because I heard her jagged voice. "No. Let me go," she said. "I need air too."

I ran down the spiral staircase, my feet clattering on the marble, not caring how much noise I made, nor if Tito heard me. All I knew was that I needed to be out of doors, to feel cold air on my face. I ran as if chased by demons with my cousin Isabel hot on my heels. When I reached the courtyard I leant against a wall trying to catch my breath.

"Like a bat out of hell," said Isabel collapsing beside me and for no reason I found this absurdly funny and began to laugh. Isabel began to laugh too.

"Talk about dramatic!" she said and then at the sound of my chattering teeth she added. "You know what, we have to get out of here. I have an idea. Come on let's go and ask Avia. Besides it's absolutely freezing."

"I'm not going back in that house. Not tonight."

"All right, " said Isabel gently. "You can borrow something of mine. Let's go to Mialma and ask Avia. Come on, I have an idea. We both need some cheering up."

Hand in hand we made for the orchard behind the swimming pool. We brushed against gardenia bushes and rosemary in our attempts to find the key that always hung from a long chain by the orchard gate. I held my breath always fearing that one day, Tito would have remembered this secret entrance and confiscate the key. Isabel and I scrambled about in the bushes and then I heard a loud:

"Eureka!"

"Sh!" I hissed.

"No one's going to hear us out here, " she said deftly unlocking the gate. We squeezed through as it creaked and groaned and overgrown branches snapped into place. Isabel hurled the key through the grill on the other side. "Come on!"

We ran down the stone path that bordered Avia's formal garden. Even in the winter, it was green with the odd jasmine still in bloom. The house in the distance was graceful against the sheltering sky. Tiny stars led a path to the moon. I hung back.

"What's the matter?"

I craned my neck, lost in the magnificence of space and endless blue and the twinkle of lights from the yachts and container ships bobbing on the sea ahead.

"It's so beautiful. Mialma is so beautiful."

"Yes," agreed Isabel leaning her head against mine. "Somehow you notice things like the sky and the hills here at Mialma. At the coach house, it's all, it's all …covered up."

"You mean with lots of pink marble!" I said with a smile. " It's all right you don't have to be polite about it. We aren't. Miguel says Tito must have been on drugs when he designed the house. It's the only explanation. And all those hideous pictures! They're absolutely terrifying. Have you noticed how most of the men look like old women? They're all bald and tortured looking."

"They're very different houses," said Isabel diplomatically.

They crossed the flagstone courtyard to the main entrance. Lanterns were suspended from casement windows and because it was Christmas, huge boughs of evergreen decorated with candied fruit, were draped across the portal. They banged against the heavy oak door making much more noise than was necessary. Within seconds Gomez appeared.

"Ah … *las condesitas* …" he said with a trace of annoyance. We suppressed giggles and ran past him, past the picture of the girl with the twirling parasol and down the dimly lit corridor. Light from grandmother's drawing room flooded the end rooms and we ran towards it, hand in hand, arriving breathless at her door.

"You knock!" I hissed. "She'll be happy if it's you."

"Or you," said Isabel surprised.

"Girls?"

We slid into the room, pressed against one another for support, not yet knowing what it was we would ask. Avia was seated in her usual chair, embroidery on her lap, a fire lit to ward off the shadows of the night. We bobbed our curtsies and bent to kiss her cheek. Her skin was amazingly soft. She was warm, sweet smelling. I wanted to sit close to her but she waved us to the sofa opposite.

"*Sentaros!*" she commanded her eyes flicking over us. "It is late. Any later and I would have been in bed."

She picked up her sewing and held it in front of her face, her tongue flicking unconsciously over her lips as she concentrated. She seemed unperturbed by our presence but wasn't going to initiate conversation. From time to time, she looked up, her blue eyes oblique, patient. Her thimble flashed in the light above her head as her hands moved in steady motion. Sometimes she stopped to place a pin in the folds of her dress, in front of her soft wide bosom. I knew what it was like to cuddle up to it, head pressed against her. She knotted thread by twisting it with the thumb and forefinger of one hand.

"Can – *May* we – " Isabel corrected herself abruptly. "May we *please* go out for just a little while?"

Avia's eyebrows shot up.

"Out?" She was genuinely surprised. "What, now?"

My stomach clenched. *That's it*, I thought to myself. *She'll never agree!*"

"Please," repeated Isabel desperately. "I can't explain why, but Sigi and I have just *got* to go out. I know it's not usual but it's important."

"And where do you want to go?" asked Avia.

"I – I don't know. We hadn't thought you'd agree," stammered Isabel looking at me for support.

"A drive round," I said firmly. "Anywhere. We don't even have to get out of the car."

Avia scanned our faces and then put down her sewing and rang her bell.

"You may have Jose," she said. "If he isn't already in bed. There's a wonderful *Belen* in the old town. It's life size and really beautiful. And then you can cross the Cathedral square and visit one of our oldest churches – Santa Maria del Mar. Jose will wait for you with the car. I hope I can trust you," she added. "This may be seen to be a slightly … unusual excursion. We wouldn't want your father to hear of it now would we? And then Sigismunda, you may spend the night here. I shall let the Coach house know. Off you go and enjoy yourselves."

My heart lurched and emotion devoured the greyness in my head with clean, sharp teeth. I was hardly aware that she had called me by full name.

"Oh Avia," I gushed. "Thank you. Thank you. I just can't believe you're letting us do this!"

"Well believe it," said Avia ruefully. "But you won't disappoint me will you? It is, after all, very late." Then she added almost to herself. "How can a visit to a church go so very wrong?"

Chapter 14

Sigi
Journal

I shall never forget that ride with Jose and my cousin, down the winding track from Mialma to the bright lights of the city below. In the dark, our faces reflected in the car windows, stared back at us, distorted, wide eyed with excitement. My heart, hammering wildly in my chest, seemed to lurch in every direction as the car negotiated the hairpin turns. We were carried further and further away from the house and the dark seemed all embracing. Jose, perplexed at being summoned by his mistress at such a late hour and at his mission, glanced at us occasionally in the car mirror with undisguised curiosity. He turned over a toothpick with a thick, clicking sound as if it alone might reveal the reason for our nocturnal visit. The silence was deafening and the road unlit and untravelled by, was terrifyingly long, leading us further away from the house, into the unknown.

And then suddenly we were down the mountain and on tarmac road, emerging into the little square of Sarria where colour and lights and noise bombarded my senses. We knelt in the back seat, craning our necks and feasting on the marvellous images of Christmas that spun before us. The chocolate shop FOIX was lit up with gold and purple lights and cascading through the glass front were boxes stuffed full to bursting with all kinds of candied fruit, sweets and chocolates. The shelves were edged with frills and ribbons and garlands. Cakes, biscuits and sweet rolls were crammed into baskets and hundreds of little sugared almonds painted silver and gold spilled onto china plates. I rolled down my window, hoping that as if by osmosis, I could imbibe some of the mouth-watering confectionery. The smell of sugar and bread hung heavily in the cold night air. But the car sped past taking us towards more colour and bustle. Exhausted children in elaborate bonnets clung to their parents, men burdened with cake boxes pushed past. Everywhere was a sense of activity and urgency, a tangible febricity.

Up until that point it had been enough just to be allowed out. Just to hear Avia say that we could leave the house was victory indeed. Had Jose merely driven us to the South lodge and back, I am sure that Isabel and I would have been perfectly happy. But now, with the world before me, I was inebriated by the noise and the sight of so many people – of this busy, vibrant world that lay, quite literally, at my feet. A world which in every way seemed more exciting, brave and new than the one, that for a few hours, we had left behind. I was restless and excited. I wanted more, so much more, but of what and whom I could not say. As if reading my thoughts, Isabel groped for my hand.

"Do you think Avia knew what she was doing?" she asked with a giggle. "Isn't this wild? The twins will go mad when we tell them! Look at all the clothes! The shops are full with such lovely things! And everyone is up! I thought it was so late. Mialma is all closed up for the night but down here … well it looks as if the day is just beginning!"

"Yes," I agreed troubled. "But you do see how it has spoiled everything. We're never going to be happy again. At Mialma I mean. Knowing that there's all this just waiting for us. We're going to want more of it. And I can't bear not to be able to do this whenever I want. I never realised it before but we're being smothered at the Coach House. Our life is being stifled before it has a chance to begin. No wonder Nuria is so unhappy, she doesn't go out enough!"

"Just like Rapunzel."

"Like who?

"Rapunzel. You know, or maybe you don't. She's a girl in a fairy tale. She has long blonde hair and is locked up in a tower by a witch. One day a prince comes riding by and he calls up, 'Rapunzel, Rapunzel, let down your hair!' And she lets down her beautiful long hair so that he can climb up. She falls in love with the prince and together they plan her escape. Every time he visits, he brings her a bit of silk with which to weave a ladder so that she can climb out of the tower. Anyway one day, after pulling the witch up by her hair, Rapunzel says without thinking, 'How is it good mother that you are so much heavier than the prince?' Of course the witch is furious and cuts off Rapunzel's beautiful hair and uses it to pull the prince up into the tower, the next time he visits. She then pushes him out of the window and as he falls he is blinded by the rose thorns that climb up the wall. Rapunzel is banished to a desert. Anyway they end up finding each other, he regains his sight and they live happily ever after."

"Oh," I breathed completely enthralled. "How romantic."

"I thought once that Val Negra was like Rapunzel's tower," said Isabel lightly. "One day a prince will come riding by and upset the lot of you!"

"If only!" I replied lightly but I was very taken with the story. I could picture myself quite easily as Rapunzel and Tito as the horrid old witch. But who would be my prince?

The car came to a halt. We had turned down a narrow, cobble stone lane, hardly wide enough for a car to pass. On either side were lanterns and exquisite wrought iron balconies and directly in front, grey and huge, loomed the cathedral.

"This is as far as I can go with the car," announced Jose cutting the engine. He reached for a cigarette. "Ok girls off you go. The church as you can see is just there." He struck a match and lit his cigarette, drawing heavily on the tobacco. He rolled down the window throwing the match onto the pavement. "Now although this looks all right, this is the worst area in the city. It is also the oldest. I'm not sure the Condesa your grand mother, was thinking straight when she asked me to bring you here. By day, this is a tourist attraction, the cathedral, the narrow streets, the Gothic buildings, etc. But at night my girls, it is an altogether different place."

My cousin and I looked at each other and my pulse quickened.

"What kind of place?" I asked in a whisper.

"Ladies of the night," replied Jose emphatically. "But they shouldn't trouble you two," he added with a laugh. He leant back puffing away at his cigarette. "Now you go straight to the church, the *Belen* is at the back and light candles for all the deserving. But in one hour, I want to see you both here. Is that understood?"

"*Si, Don Jose,*" said my cousin with mock reverence. "Anything you say."

For a moment we stood huddled together, uncertain as to what to do, with so much freedom.

"What are ladies of the night?" I asked fascinated.

"I have no idea."

"That's funny, I thought you'd know."

"Well I don't. But whatever they are they sound wonderful. We shall have to ask Avia when we get back."

"Maybe we should ask Miguel instead. From the way Jose said it, I get the feeling they're not people Grandmother would want us to be seen with."

"If they are people."

"What do you mean?"

We began to walk idly towards the Cathedral entrance. And for a moment even I was captivated. A bright and full moon hung above the the front garden which was full of palm trees and fenced on all sides with tall wrought iron gates. Moroccan lanterns hung in the wide flat branches. All around the walls of the old town loomed above encircling the building on all sides. If the rest of Barcelona was European in its architecture, here in the heart of the ancient battlements the feel was distinctly Arabic and it was more than easy to imagine another Bethlehem. The sky was clear and cold but in our excitement we felt nothing but the warmth of our interlaced hands, interlaced in our shared adventure.

"You've assumed they're actual people but they could be the name for something quite different, like *brazo de gitano* is not really a Gypsy's arm but cake stuffed with fresh cream. Or for example *Cabello de Angel* isn't of course –"

"Angel hair," I finished for her. "And then there's *Huesos de Santo.*"

"Which is what?"

"Which is *not* you mean, made out of the bones of saints. The one I really like – the name for a curd cheese – *Teta de Monja.*"

Isabel gasped.

"No! You don't mean to say there's really something called 'Nuns'tits'? Have we ever had it? I bet the twins like that one! Golly I wish I'd known."

"And then of course a *Judia verde* isn't a Green Jewish girl–!"

"– but a runner Bean!"

We laughed hilariously our voices tinkling in the cold while a sudden sea of people pushed us towards the cathedral. Inside, there was hardly standing space. People shoved and heaved to be near the altar and life size crèche. The air was heavy with incense, sickly and suffocating. The scent of men's after shave – namely Lavanda Puig – a Spanish brand, instantly recognisable by its green packaging and advertised on billboards everywhere – clung to the greased back hair of young and not so young, Casanovas. Women clutched heavy handbags and children, using them to propel themselves to the front. Priests and nuns kept a strict eye on the procession, taking every opportunity to reprimand the individual who did not demonstrate the expected devotion. My eyes smarted with the cloudy incense and in suppressing a cough I let go of Isabel's hand. It was only for a moment but in that brief space of time Isabel disappeared in the crowd. I struggled to turn around but I was wedged between a couple bent on going in the opposite direction.

"Isabel!" I cried my voice muffled against the coats and scarves of those around me. I was rocketed forward, blindly groping against warm bodies. Hot breath breathed onto my face, buttons scratched my cheek and caught in my hair. Tears pricked my eyes as I gasped for air and perspiration drenched my neck. The room began to spin and my feet seemed hardly to touch the ground. Above me everything was gold and heavy and drenched in incense. Carved statues of gigantic gilt angels were suspended from the enormous vault. Figurines of the Saints were draped in moth eaten red velvet and plastic flowers adorned ornate Victorian pictures. My mouth was full of rough fabric and the stray hairs from astrakhan coats. The skin on the back of my neck went cold and nausea churned my stomach. I groped for something to hold onto, as without warning, I began to fall forward...

Chapter 15

Sigi
Journal

"Pero bonita, que haces aqui?"

It was very cold. I realised that I was sitting on the pavement outside the church, legs and arms akimbo, back against the ancient stone parapet. My coat was open and my scarf loose around my neck. My hat had fallen off and my dress was bundled about me. I felt like a rag doll that has been thrown carelessly aside and allowed to lie just where she has fallen. I was also frozen to the tips of my pretty suede boots. But at least the lungful of freezing air that stung my throat was incense free. Slowly, the stone labyrinth before me settled into focus. Against a background of distant traffic, I struggled to decipher other sounds.

"Pero bonita, que haces aqui?"

I blinked. The words and the scrape of footsteps were very near and coming closer. Shoes – pointy patent leather and diamond patterned socks – stopped abruptly by my knees. I could have touched the jean clad legs with my face. Without warning, the man swooped down so that his face was inches from mine. I could feel his breath on my cheek and the familiar smell of Spanish brandy and blonde tobacco. A width of cracked leather jacket, a jumble of zips and pockets and those absurdly effeminate shoes blocked my vision.

But there was nothing effeminate about Carlos Nadal. Workers on Grandmother's estate, the Nadals had been linked to Val Negra for generations. The Nadals were born into service and had not known anything but the vineyard or life beyond the boundaries of our land. Sometime after the war, Carlos's father quarrelled with Grandmother severing forever, or so it seemed at the time, a socio-historic link with our family. Carlos's father and uncles (the Nadals were given to breeding only male children) found work in the neighbouring town of Vic, eschewing education on the estate, for a life of the picaresque. For a few years, not much was heard of them although they returned enough times to sustain their claim as tenants. The Nadals did not marry their women and changed partners with alarming regularity. And the women, no matter how enthusiastic to begin with, never stayed very long. Never long enough anyway, to instil any manners or religion or sense of decency in the uncouth, unruly lot they produced. Then, just when the pueblo had thought they had seen the last of them, the Nadals returned – a great many of them as it so happened, mostly male, of different ages and all equally offensive in manner. They were loud, their house stank with the stench of unwashed pets, which like the roving gypsies they had become, they insisted on housing in the front room where they lived and slept. No decent women could be seen in their company. The Nadals were not just wild or exuberant or rebellious. There was a cruelty in their blood and a madness. Most of the older generation had scarred pox pitted faces, the legacy of some drunken brawl or other, and all had a strange cast in the left eye that made them seem not to be looking at you at all. The younger children were prone to all the childhood diseases that others were immune to by dint of vaccination or prophylactic medicine. Many died young. Those who survived infancy in that infirm, germ infested hovel knew that they would survive anything. And so, consequently these men possessed an arrogance that the gentle pueblo could not comprehend.

Nor could it comprehend the foul language that flowed freely from even the youngest members of the clan. Words like *cono or joder* were used liberally. Indeed they were probably the only words that the Nadals were able to pronounce absolutely perfectly. For the Nadals spoke incorrect Spanish. Their vocabulary was poor, their grammar non-existent and yet their swearing was inimitably imaginative. They used words whose meanings we did not know but whose implied obscenity caused us to shrink in embarrassment. If language was ever a barrier between two different worlds, it was certainly so with the Nadals. In the years away from Val Negra, they developed a patois that was understood only within the clan and served to further alienate the village. But while my sisters blushed at the very mention of their name, and while they were outraged if greeted by the Nadal's own peculiar form of acknowledgement of the other sex – a guttural throat clearing – I felt nothing but fascination.

"Dangerous, outrageous without a scrap of loyalty!" raged Avia on one occasion when Carlos's father had particularly annoyed her. "But undoubtedly true of all them. Not a moral gene amongst them. And the degradation that has been uncovered!" She raised her eyes to heaven, hands fluttering to emphasise the extent of the damage. "Well! I can see my family has been just like the communist regime."

"Really Avia?" I asked knowing nothing whatsoever about the communists and certainly unable to draw a comparison between Avia's autocratic hold on Val Negra and any other political thinking. "How is that?"

Grandmother's blue eyes bored into me.

"*Esta clarismo,*" she said as though it were the most obvious thing in the world. "Communism kept a lid on a boiling, festering pot of crime and corruption – not that it didn't exist already – but the *minute* it failed, all that criminal activity rose to the surface. The same thing is true here. While the Nadals worked at Val Negra they were kept in check. I knew then, that they were no angels but at least the status quo was preserved. Now I realise it is a miracle that it was. When Carlos Nadal stopped working for me, his true nature and that of his family's was revealed. And what they were up to! My God there is nothing they have not done!"

"Er ...what exactly, Grandmother?"

Avia frowned.

"*Cosas,*" she said vaguely. "*Cosas.*"

I would soon learn just what those 'things' were but now, in the cold and in the shadows of the Gothic town, if my face registered the shock of recognition, Carlos Nadal's son's did not.

I struggled to sit up.

"No," he said without sympathy. "You fainted. Stay in that position, a few more moments at any rate."

"I've lost my cousin," I stammered. Nadal pressed me, not ungently, against the wall.

"No. You should not move."

I watched him as he lit a cigarette, throwing back his head to exhale. His hair was as black as the sky behind him and his eyes, in too narrow a face, were slanted and small. Like the rest of his family, he had the famous cast that was always disconcerting and, as was not the fashion, he wore an earring in one ear. He might have been handsome in a raw-hewn sort of a way if it had not been for a loose jaw and ill-fitting teeth. When he spoke, there was a whistle behind his words that nonetheless gave him a clarity of speech his siblings did not possess. He had small, tobacco stained hands and lean thighs, the result of years in the saddle. His skin like his father's was swarthy and scarred. He looked like one of the ferrets he was forever poaching at Val Negra. Despite his reputation, I was not afraid of him.

"I am surprised to see you here," I said.

He snorted.

"Not as surprised as I am to see you! I cannot believe the *Con* – your grandmother knows you are here. I am not easily surprised but I confess to being astonished at the sight of one of her grand daughters passing out before the altar. And in the *barrio gotico*, of our illustrious city! I didn't think any of you lot were ever seen in the city except under armed escort."

I flushed.

"Tonight is an exception."

"Being the *Noche buena* and all that." Nadal's eyes narrowed and he exhaled smoke so that it rose before my eyes and was swallowed by the night. "You are too beautiful to be out alone. And of that age – " he inhaled heavily, "which is most appealing to mine."

My heart leaped. Beautiful? No one had ever said that I was beautiful! Beautifully dressed yes, the owner of beautiful things admittedly, but beautiful sitting in crumpled clothes on the ground? I didn't think so.

Again I made to sit up but he restrained me.

"Your cousin will find her way soon enough. She's no fool that one. I wouldn't worry on her account."

"But I – Jose will be waiting. I must go. I have no idea of the time." And yet I didn't move. Couldn't move. Nadal's body shielding me from a cold wind was warm and firm. With a word, with one look, he had chased the greyness from my mind and all uncertainty.

"How old are you *bonita*?" he asked while his fingers traced the features of my face.

"Fifteen and three quarters," I whispered. "Almost sixteen."

"*L'edad de la nina bonita*. We marry our women when they're fifteen."

Ash dropped from his cigarette onto my coat and he brushed it away. I stared as the tiny embers failing to ignite, disappeared in the cloth. His hands, though small were competent and precisely shaped. He threw away the cigarette butt and sat beside me on the cold stone floor. He touched my hair, his movements soothing, caressing. My body swayed instinctively to the rhythm of his.

"I thought the Nadals did not marry."

"Not *por la iglesia*. We marry in a different way. Under the stars..." His hands were under my blouse, my skirt. Everywhere. "Under a sky such as this, under the wind and the sun."

I was mesmerised by his voice, by his hands. Mine responded blindly, mimicking his every action. He expected nothing from me that I did not know how to give and the relief I felt was enormous.

"I always knew about you," he said. "I always knew." But his voice came as if from a great distance and I didn't care if there was any warmth or caring in it at all.

"Really?" I replied ingenuously. "Because we know all about you, everyone at Val Negra knows about the Nadals. Grandmother especially. She says – " I stopped, remembering my manners.

Nadal laughed showing his teeth.

"What *does* 'Grandmother' say about us? Tell me. I can't believe it's anything good. She's never liked us. She probably thinks we're all gypsies. Uncouth, unreliable and uneducated."

"Yes, she does rather. And not only that –"

"There's more?"

I blushed.

"She says you breed like rabbits and the women never stay long enough to see their children walk. But she doesn't blame them, not one little bit. She only feels sorry for the babies until they grow up that is and then she doesn't at all because it seems that overnight they're transformed into proper little Nadals, proper little *franquistas*."

"Ah ... I wondered when politics would come into it."

"And religion," I added helpfully. "Grandmother says you're all heathens. She's heard you say that God is dead and that you don't believe in heaven."

Nadal stubbed out his cigarette.

"We believe in hell though," he said quietly. "And escaping it."

"You do? I didn't think that grown ups had to escape anything. You're grown up after all. Isn't that enough? I mean you can do what you want. You can go where you please. When you're a child living in a family, it's different. You aren't free to do anything. You have lessons, you're told what to think, what to eat, what to wear. You're never allowed to do anything or go anywhere that hasn't been decided by the parents. They even choose your friends for you. When I'm grown up I shall really enjoy myself. No one will decide anything for me ever again. I shall do exactly as I please."

"I wouldn't be so sure. Being a grown up as you put it, isn't like deciding on a new pair of shoes, you know. And it's not something that suddenly happens. It's very gradual. You don't notice until people around you start treating you differently and that's exactly when you realise you want to be a child again. Besides you then have other problems to deal with. Grown up problems. Like trying to find money to eat and smoke and a place to live. And women. They're a real puzzle, a real headache. It's tough I can tell you."

I drew my legs up to my chest resting my chin on my knees.

"Do you think I'm grown up?"

Nadal smoothed a strand of my hair.

"I don't know," he said gruffly. "We'll see shall we?"

His fingers felt for my lips and then were in my mouth, rubbing my teeth as though he were cleaning them and then his mouth was on mine and I didn't push him away. All at once my sensations were dulled and then accelerated and then again more intense than before. There was no pain or anxiety or disappointment. My limbs felt pulled by sleep and pleasure. I was devoid of conscience, of any notion of right or wrong. I wanted only to succumb to this increasing and all consuming pleasure and always, always to remember the detail of his face.

Afterwards, when Nadal slipped away into the shadows of the church as though he had never been, the feeling of unreality continued. I no longer worried that I could not find Isabel and for some time sat huddled on the ground basking in unfamiliar lassitude. Eventually I got to my feet, feeling for the stone beneath my fingers, hugging the wall as I felt my way to the front of the church. And out of the light, lurking in the dimly lit doorways of the surrounding houses, I saw women. There were many women, all in various degrees of undress. Most of them wore very high heels and huge smiles that had been painted with fluorescent lipstick. There were young men with enormous, purple smudged eyes and pierced ears. Some shivered, others smiled yet their eyes were over bright and jeering. Some lay sprawled, half naked, their shirtsleeves rolled up to the elbow. None of them spoke but they stared as I passed and I, in turn stared back, fascinated by their silent conspiracy. Their whispers hung in the air, petrified. There was the odd cackle of laughter, a screech of recognition and then silence as they shrank back against the stone threshold, under the arches of the old town.

And what struck me about them was not the fact that they looked dirty or disorientated or even half starved, but the fact that they were free.

They belonged to a grey world of shadows and pleasure, a single, dull layer coexisting under the very skin of our Gothic opulence. They had chosen a decadent, spiralling, poisoned world and to me on that Christmas night there was no sense of duty or morality but a wholly justifiable pursuit of pleasure. Nothing had ever seemed more appealing.

Even now I remember my beating heart as I stumbled past and through, the gathering throng. I felt exhilarated. I felt alive, as I had never done before. My brain was teaming with a thousand different songs and ideas. I wanted to talk to perfect strangers, to tell them what I had discovered. I wanted to dance between the cracks of the paving stones and stand on my head in the neat sand plazas. I wanted Nadal to come back and flick cigarette off my arm and start all over again. I wanted to follow Nadal to the end of the earth or at any rate back to his house in Val Negra. I wanted Dr. Mantua to question me and thought of the wonderful things that I would tell him and how he would never again believe I was lacking in imagination or anything else. I wanted, for some inexplicable reason, to take off all my clothes and wear my stockings on my arms.

I had completely forgotten about Jose and my cousin and myself. I doubt, that at that point I could have told you my name or where I lived. I crouched on the pavement and thought it tremendous fun to try and pull handfuls of fur from women's coats as they swept by. At first the women didn't notice me at all as they stumbled over my huddled form, but then I became more insistent. I tried to do it with my teeth. And then I heard Isabel's stunned cry as she too fell over me.

"Sigismunda!"

"You said you'd never call me that."

I looked up but her face blurred as I buried my head in her lap.

"I've been looking everywhere for you! I was so frightened that something might have happened. I was just about to go and get Jose. Thank goodness I've found you." Isabel's tone changed from angry concern to one of suspicion as she examined me more closely. "Something has happened," she said flatly. "What did you do to your dress?"

"I didn't do anything to my dress," I giggled imitating her accent. "But I rather believe something may have been done to it." I laughed hilariously, thinking this the funniest thing I had ever said.

Isabel was less amused. She pulled me to my feet and away from the crowds.

"My God," she said stunned. "You're drunk! But how on earth – when?"

"I am beautiful," I insisted ignoring her question. "I am beautiful and of a pleasing age. *La edad de la nina bonita*. And heaven may not exist but hell *certainly* does and we must try and escape. Escaping is beautiful isn't it? I certainly enjoyed my visit. It was just beautiful. I loved every minute. I want it to go on and on and –"

Isabel shook my arm.

"Avia will go on and on if you don't stop this. We've got to find Jose and get you home. But for goodness sake pull yourself together. Jose mustn't find out whatever it is that's happened. It's not fair on him. And it's not fair to Avia either. Can you imagine what will happen if Tito –" Her grip tightened. "How I wish Kate was here. She'd know what to do."

"Kate?" I echoed. "Who is Kate?"

Isabel frowned.

"You know, my best friend from school. I've told you about her before. She knows all about this sort of thing. It happens to her boyfriends all the time. How I wish I'd paid more attention to her. She was always telling me – "

She stopped short.

"Have you been sick? Do you want to be sick?"

I flung my arms around Isabel's neck overwhelmed by a desire to kiss her.

"Of course not. I never ever feel sick. But I do love you Isabel, dearest Isabel – "

"Oh for goodness sake. Stop it! We're never going to get back to the car at this rate." There was panic in her voice. "Look what did you drink? You've got to tell me. Try and remember. It's important."

"I haven't drunk anything," I said stiffly, trying to sound dignified. "In fact I was just thinking how thirsty I feel. Oh dear – " I lurched suddenly to one side, groping for Isabel's arm. It was then that I realised that I must have grown because she seemed much smaller than before.

"Anyway it wasn't drink."

Isabel grasped me round the waist and I leant on her as we struggled forward.

"No?" she said her voice creaking with the effort of remaining calm. "Then ... what?"

"Oh I'm not going to tell you that, my darling," I said enjoying her curiosity. "It's my secret. He said it was my secret. And you know that you must never spoil things by telling." I yawned. "It was wonderful though, the best thing that has ever, ever happened in my whole life. I don't feel all grey anymore, just pink and delicious and awfully grown up. I am older than you Isabel and to tell you the truth it *does* make a difference. I didn't think so before but now I realise there are things that, well, just happen when you're older. I wish you could understand. "

Isabel looked at me strangely, which was even more satisfying. I yawned again. "I'm absolutely bushed aren't you? I could go to sleep – "

"Don't you *dare!*" Isabel pinched my arm. "We've got to get back to the car and you've got to help me. I don't want to know what's happened but you're going to have to be jolly good at pretending nothing's wrong. Now grab my waist and keep walking. You can't go to sleep here!" Isabel's voice rose. "Just walk!"

And then she stopped.

"What?"

"Listen!" Isabel stood transfixed. "The bells," she said "I heard them before, a few moments ago. But I wasn't sure. I didn't think it could be so late. "

"And you say *I've* been drinking!" I muttered.

"It's Christmas!" cried my cousin hugging me when moments before she had told me off for doing precisely that. "It's Christmas day Sigi, it's Christmas day!"

There was shouting all around me as people began hugging and kissing each other. Isabel's eyes were shining, bright with tears. "Isn't lovely?" She was staring at the church, its steeple disappearing against the black sky and the minute sprinkling of distant stars. All at once the spinning world seemed to right itself and I was aware once again of the freezing cold and my breath, warm against her face. I groped for her hand - not for support but in recognition of the great affection we shared. Her fingers moved over mine and pressed them hard. She smiled holding me in her gaze before turning to look once more at the ancient building. For a few seconds we stood together oblivious of everything else but the fact that it was Christmas and that because of it, we were expected to be happy. I did not trust myself to speak, my bravado shrinking with every chime and my heart, hammering in my chest, filled the open spaces with noise.

And as the world came into skidding focus on that Christmas morning all those years ago, so it does here. Every time I wake or at least realise that I have been dreaming, reality is superimposed on delicious slumber, shattering it into irretrievable pieces. The chapel bells chime here as they did on that other Christmas night only I cannot leap to the window in anticipation of a scene that is familiar and beloved. If there is one pleasure denied me now, it is that of flinging open an unbarred window. Again and again I remember what it was like to wake up at Mialma. Slowly, I would rise through layers of sleep, as one by one they were peeled away. With my eyes still closed, my senses groping to translate the tiny, unintelligible sounds, I would momentarily flounder. But then the gentle breeze and early bird song would hoist me from my sheltered berth. As my limbs moved through sheets of sleep, my mind would anchor itself to the creek of other blinds being raised, to the crunch of gravel, a distant shout. The room was pitch black and yet at the far end, like a lighthouse, strips of light seeped through the window slats. Still uncertain, skipping from one foot to the other, to avoid standing on the cold marble floor, I would be guided towards the light. There was always a brief moment of panic when the unknown shadows swarming behind me, threatened to swallow me up. With final determination and racing heart, I would fling open the window as shutter and glass were released, suspended, into the air. Below and beneath was an oasis of sky and water and balmy sunshine. I would stretch forward as far as possible, welcoming the warm air that rushed into the room chasing away. And as I leant out of the window, I would laugh at myself, safe in the warmth and the daylight, ashamed to think that I could ever have been frightened of the dark.

Even here, as I struggle with wakefulness, still sunk beneath the many layers of semi-consciousness, I savour my perfect solitude. With it comes a sense of purpose and renewal, a notion of the possible. Now, if there are windows to be flung open, they exist only in my mind and my thoughts must rise through the veils of memory to the places beyond. Time and time again, my soul scours these planes, darting back and forth from the sweet and the not so, until it settles on the bumpy landing of recognition. Back in my room, in my narrow cot, the dazzling whiteness of the walls causes my heart to hammer in my chest as I remember that while I broke the bonds of my captivity, it was only in my mind. It was only ever in my mind.

Likewise it strikes me with awful irony that drugs have served to awaken, to enlighten and to confine. In the beginning, I was enticed by the mystery and weirdness of a world I knew nothing about – Nadal's world. Addiction to it and to drugs, aborted any original thought or inspiration I may have had. Seduced by a temporary feeling of well being, I was deaf to the warnings that one engulfing greyness might replace another. It is with an ever-present sense of the absurd, that I realise that though physically liberated, my mind was incarcerated and detumescent. And now in my splendid isolation, the trappings of my bondage are everywhere but never has my mind been less shackled.

For then we see through a glass darkly, but then face to face: now I know in part; but then shall I know.

But it is too late.

Chapter 16

Isabel
Winchester
Winter 1997

Isabel shivered in the cold dawn light. Yes, it had been many years since she had allowed herself to think about the past in so much detail. Ricardo dreams brought their share of nostalgia but she had never allowed herself to travel so far back. It was seeing the Bazan scorpion and the names of the brothers that had triggered so many memories. There were so many events Isabel had forgotten, tried to forget and yet now, one after another she remembered them all. And of course, there was Tim. Isabel shivered. She had passed the point of being tired but now every bone in her body ached. Even the statue of Pandora seemed to have turned blue and her face looked decidedly pinched. Isabel got stiffly to her feet and picked up the whisky bottle. She knew she was going to have to give Tim an answer. In remembering the past it confirmed what she knew of the future. She could never love Tim as she loved Ricardo. If she married Tim, life would no doubt continue in much the same way although a bit of her, the Spanish bit, would surrender the passion and feeling for life that was rekindled every time she visited Spain. She raised her face to the declining moon, as if it were the warm Mediterranean sun.

She swayed, breathing in the ragged cold air. What a fool she was to cling so fiercely to the memory of a schoolgirl crush. It wasn't as if she and Ricardo even kept in touch with one another. As a matter of fact, Isabel hadn't spoken to any of her cousins in years. Not even Sigi. Isabel let out a groan. Not even Sigi. How had that happened? How had she grown so estranged from the people she loved? Her heart began to beat faster. In all those years of travel for Archid, those lonely nights in anonymous city hotels when even a random piece of music would bring tears to her eyes, why had she never been back? But she knew the answer to that. Isabel bent her head under the oak porch, letting herself in through the back door where the thatch was so low it scraped the new shoots. Maybe it was merely the first hint of spring, in the form of delicate snowdrops, that was producing this unease.

Isabel deposited the whisky bottle in the dining room, huddling into her dressing gown. No, she thought to herself, it was more the fact that for once she was having to make a decision. The proposals, both of them, demanded some sort of answer one way or another. She closed her eyes suddenly tired. She would tell Tim that very day that she couldn't marry him, that really they should stop seeing each other altogether and she would organize a visit to the Bazan vineyard. But what of Ricardo? Isabel's eyes flew open. What of Ricardo? While she was so consumed in her feeling for him she had no idea what he thought of her. Just *what* exactly had she ever meant to him? Isabel realised with a shock that she had never asked herself that question. If she were to see him, would he even remember? Isabel felt her cheeks flush. He *must* remember. She had spent so many years trying to forget and yet every day of her life she was stalked by his memory. She was sixteen the last time she saw Ricardo. But would he remember that? How could he not? Surely that time was special to him too if in a different way? But how was she to know? It had never occurred to her to ask him anything. Until now. Oh what wouldn't she give to be able to dip into that time again, to hold on to it, alter the bits she didn't like and re-write the script! Well she might not be able to do quite that but she would go to Barcelona and she would see him. She would do everything in her power to see him. She would find out once and for all if the feelings that had dictated her entire emotional life, were in any way reciprocated. And now she would go one step further and allow the yearning to consume her. She would let herself remember it all...

Sixteen ...

Chapter 17

Isabel
Barcelona
Summer 1976

When Isabel alighted from the BEA aircraft at Barcelona airport she lifted her face to the sun feeling its strength and warmth like a caress smoothing, cleansing, healing. She was exhausted mentally and physically. She stood on the top step with passengers jostling behind her, oblivious to everything but the sensation of the light breeze and the bright light. The sky paler now in the early evening was still uncluttered by clouds and the surrounding hills were caramel colour against the sea. She inhaled deeply, closing her eyes as relief flooded over her. Her journey through the academic maze and jungle of Oxbridge entrance was over. She needed this summer to recoup her energies before the start of the next term – the start of a new life away from the convent. An impatient cough behind her catapulted her forward and she hurried towards the terminal building. *Guardia Civil* hovered by the door although Isabel no longer found them as threatening as she had done when she was little. The conveyor belts lackadaisically spewed luggage from the worn leather straps that splashed against a gap in the wall. Activity blurred in front of her as she picked up her small case and cleared customs. The sound of Spanish voices was a balm to her senses transporting, her instantly home, to her childhood. Jose the driver was there to meet her. He beamed his welcome.

"*Condesa.*"

Isabel acknowledged his greeting with a nod, secretly delighting in the emotion the word conveyed. Here at least she was known, if not wanted. For this man at least, she existed, if only by name.

"*I los Condes?*"

Jose explained that her grandparents were at some official function – stricken, of course, not to be able to meet her. He made an appropriate face that made her laugh. Isabel was not disappointed. It gave her an opportunity to catch up on the latest news. She could savour the moments alone before the inevitable inquisition with which she was always met when she first arrived. Once in the car, it did not take long to skirt the city's perimeter and head for the mountain road. Night descended, embracing everything in opulent darkness. The familiar crunch of gravel as they swung through the gates of the house, woke her from a deep sleep. The large open windows above her blazed with light. Isabel stumbled sleepily from the car. Together she and Jose crossed the courtyard and entered the house. Isabel paused in front of her favourite painting. In the dimly lit hall, the portrait of the girl's face was difficult to see but by contrast the folds of her dress were luminous against a reflection of water. Even at this late hour, the usually cool room was heavy with heat. It seemed to penetrate her every pore. Her nostrils were full of its smell and it pushed against her limbs, both somnambulant and pulsating in turn. For a moment everything was quiet. But then, within seconds, doors slammed and noises erupted like small petards, all over the house. Pepita appeared, her large plump hands covering her face as if embarrassed by her delight. Isabel hugged her, allowing herself to be pinched and prodded. But she ignored all offer of food. It was the last thing she wanted. Having wanted to express her happiness only moments before, Isabel felt strangely reticent, heat turning her brain to jelly. She gabbled something about the journey and having to go straight to bed. Too tired to shower or even brush her teeth, Isabel kicked off her shoes and fell headlong onto the bed.

*

Sunlight burst into the room, bouncing off the walls and angles of furniture. Isabel winced as spiky rays of light stung her eyes. She felt grubby, sticky with heat. She was thirsty. Her head thudded and lethargy pulled at her limbs. She felt fragile- not at all rested. She could hear Avia and Pepita muttering their concern outside the bedroom door. It must be later than she thought. Interspersed with questions about her granddaughter's welfare, were instructions for lunch. Just when Isabel thought they had gone, the door creaked open and Isabel quickly shut her eyes pretending to be asleep. Avia clicked her tongue but retreated. When her grandmother had gone, Isabel stretched, groaning with stiffness. She glanced around her room, making a mental checklist to ensure that nothing had changed since her last visit. Slowly she swung her legs over the side of her bed and tiptoed to the balcony opening the shutters. The perfume of gardenia and lilac made her dizzy. It was too rich, too heavy. She could touch the lemon trees, overburdened with fruit, from the balustrade. She broke off a leaf, rubbing it into her skin as Avi had taught her. Nothing moved. There was no breeze. She withdrew into the bedroom and stripped, padding towards the bathroom. After a cold shower, her hair still wet, she felt refreshed and little more ready to face the household. Even so she took a deep breath before opening her bedroom door. Waiting for her it seemed, was every servant in the house and her grandmother. They all began to speak at once. Pepita threw up her arms, crushing her against her ample bosom.

"Senorita!" she bellowed much to Avia's annoyance having wanted to be the first to hug Isabel.

"Pero hijia mia que delgada estas!"

There was instant silence as the women stood back long enough to confirm that this was the case.

"But it's true!" Pepita's eyes boggled. "You are too thin! And no glasses! She is gone!" she commented suspiciously.

"No braces," said the Cook.

"No *Body*," said Avia. "You really are skinny! How can that be? Are you well Isabel? You have utterly, utterly changed. True you did not come last summer but it is only a year – not such a long time!"

"I don't know," replied Isabel squirming under the microscopic scrutiny. The nuns never commented on appearances other than to say whether or not clothes were clean. "The braces had to come off some time. It felt like I'd had them forever! As to the glasses, well a nice optician suggested I try contact lenses. So I did. They really are amazing and I can see so much better. I didn't think it possible."

"I wouldn't think it possible," replied her grandmother. "You have changed so much."

Isabel wanted coffee but she knew Pepita and her grand mother would not be satisfied unless they had thoroughly examined her. Even as Isabel attempted to move down the corridor, curious hands pulled her back. Avia circled her wrist with her fingers.

"No fat!" she said now more concerned than suspicious. She prodded her ribs examined her thighs, her breasts. "What has happened to you? " she said in awe. "Even during the war I was never this thin! Have you caught this …this anorexia? All English girls have it. Too preoccupied with self, is the reason. They should work on the *vida interior*. It needs nurturing."

"Pero que belleza! Que delgada.. Oiiiiiiiii!" cried Pepita.

"Madre mia," said the cook and cleaner in unison.

"It's a fact," said Avia sharply irritated and worried at the same time. "That's it. She was plump as a child, now she is beautiful, if far too thin. That's it. Now back to work. This ridiculous chatter! The poor child needs to eat. They obviously don't feed you anything in that place. Bread and water I wouldn't doubt."

Isabel allowed herself to be propelled towards the dining room where a large tray had been laid out with croissants and steaming hot chocolate which in the heat made the sweat break out on her forehead. She sat down abruptly feeling faint.

"No glasses," said Avia again. "It really makes a difference."

"I suppose so."

Avia leant forward and fingered her grand daughter's hair.

"It seems impossible. But now that you are thinner and your face has sprung clear, I can see that you have the same cheekbones as your mother. Hers were high and wide just like yours. You are so like her."

Isabel swallowed the tail end of a croissant allowing the crumbs to fall on her lap.

"Am I? I have often wondered. There aren't many photographs and I don't remember my father very well either." She glanced at her grandmother, embarrassed by the emotion on her face. But the room was too full of heat and sunlight to reminisce.

"What about the cousins? How are they? How is Nuria?"

Avia paused for a long time before answering. She thought better of further voicing her observations. The change in Isabel had shaken her to the core. The ugly duckling – the plump, ugly duckling – had indeed turned into a lovely swan. Isabel was certainly very thin but there was no disguising the beauty of those perfectly turned limbs – the long slender legs and ankles, the graceful hands. Her large almond shaped eyes were a startling green. The nose although long, was straight and fine, the lips wide and generous. She had seen lips in faces like that – she would have to watch her. And her hair, which even as a child had been her one redeeming feature, was shiny and thick and fell just below her shoulders. However, it was her skin that Avia found entrancing. It was smooth and unblemished, the colour of horchata.

If physically, she resembled Clara, in every other way she was like Julian. Every expression, her smile, the way she gave you her undivided attention – a characteristic that was flattering to both men and women – the way her shoulders sloped and her hands rested in her lap, were all Julian's. And that was what shocked her. Avia could not take her eyes from her granddaughter. Avia, knowing that when Julian left Val Negra in '39, it was for good, now saw Julian in this girl's every gesture. Her former ungainliness had only served to keep Julian hidden from her all these years. She had looked for him everywhere but in his own child. Avia panicked. All the emotion that had lain dormant since then now rose tremulously to the surface. She felt as she had done that night, at Val Negra with the mice and the leaves scurrying along marble floors, the night she met Julian Pelham. She could hardly concentrate her thoughts. She hardly dared ask Isabel about her exams. She hardly dared ask her anything. She felt as though Isabel could read her very soul, that by resembling Julian, she had in some way become him.

Avia put away Isabel's unused napkin. Maintaining a semblance of calm, she opened her tin of sewing threads. The girl was appallingly dressed, as usual, but even this did not detract from her loveliness. The ill-fitting clothes merely accentuated the slender lines of her body.

Avia raised her clear blue eyes in response to Isabel's probing expression.

"So who is here?"

"*Pues* ... no one." Even to Avia, her reply sounded inadequate. She searched for words amidst the scrambled sequences in her brain. Isabel in uprooting her from the past had no notion of the effort it took her to speak. "The girls –" Avia faltered. "The girls and Miguel are in Val Negra." She collected her scattered thoughts, forcing herself with that reliable self-discipline, to continue. "Tito is walking in the Pyrenees. There's only Ricardo. Which will be nice for you, as I believe he's the only one of your cousins you haven't seen in a while. Goodness how times flies. Let me see now ... first he was at university, then abroad and then there was all that ...well that other business. Then he lived in the north for a while and then he came home. He's almost through his law exams. Another week and they'll be over."

"Oh?"

"You'll probably want to go to Val Negra at some point. It's unbearably hot here this summer and we've been in the city longer than usual. Perhaps you can go back with Sigi. She'll be up in the next few weeks. You'll see that there's been quite a change in her. Of course she's always been beautiful but this year she has really blossomed. Rather like you." Avia flicked her a look that made Isabel blush. "I suspect it's because she's in love."

"Yes?"

Isabel felt a pang. It was a while since she'd been in touch with Sigi. They hadn't written to each other as frequently as they had done when they were little and it bothered her that she should have missed out on such momentous news. They were no longer children. The fact that her cousin could be seeing someone only confirmed this. For some reason she had thought they could pick up from where they'd left off but Sigi would be thinking of other things now.

"Who is ... he? Anyone I know? Anyone from Val Negra?"

Avia nodded.

"Well yes and no. The family has always owned property in the region but they're really a Madrilenian family. His name is Rodrigo de Montfalco. He comes from an interesting family. Rodrigo however, is every bit as headstrong as Sigi. That is my only reservation. Otherwise I am delighted. I am much relieved. Her ...energies are now focused in his direction. And he handles her very well."

"I hope to meet him."

"Oh you will. It's hard not to. I mean they are such an exuberant couple. They overwhelm one with their enthusiasm, their zest for living."

"How ... exhausting."

Avia shot her a look.

"I hope, *amor meu*, that I do not detect the green eyed monster. You know how unattractive it is."

"I'm not jealous!" protested Isabel hotly but at the same time feeling unaccountably cross for no reason. "I – I just feel there are things I've missed. Everyone seems to have grown up, changed."

"And you haven't?"

"I don't know. I haven't noticed. I feel the same."

"As I'm sure your cousins do. Don't be envious of love, *querida*, you will have your turn. It might seem a long way off but it will come quickly enough and then you'll look back on this period of your life with great joy. Never again will you have so much time for yourself. Don't be frightened of it. You are beholden to no one."

"Oh it's not that," said Isabel impatiently.

"Then what is it?"

Isabel was silent. She couldn't have explained the unexpected surge of resentment and confusion, even if she'd wanted to. Sigi, from what she gathered, was as good as married, while she Isabel, was still at school. Well not exactly school; from the start of the next term she would be at Oxford, but it amounted to the same thing. And while there was nothing that she wanted more, nor had ever worked as hard to achieve, it didn't seem nearly as grown up as being married. Sigi, as usual seemed to be acting out the more glamorous role. Isabel did feel envious.

"There have also been changes at Val Negra," continued Avia, ignoring her granddaughter's glum expression. "Tito has had builders there for most of the year, doing all manner of things to the poor old place. Oh don't worry," she added hastily. "No Madrilenian designers have been involved in this project and remarkably Tito hasn't wanted to add a Cuban look to anything. He's done a pretty good job. Maybe there are too many shower rooms but the house is certainly a good deal more comfortable than it was. I only wonder if it will ever lose its summer house feel."

"You don't mind?"

"It's no longer mine to mind, thank goodness! It's up to my grandchildren to decide what's best. Perhaps one day you'll want to make a go of the vineyard. I suppose it would be viable. I know the de Canas are keen that we should, although I'm not entirely sure as to why they'd want another rival business in the area. They have always had the Bazans to contend with. Still the estate has been looked after, and thanks to Dr.Mantua, the vineyard is immaculate and up to date. I hardly recognise it these days. I did so love the way the vine grew before the war, haphazardly, with all the informality of an English garden -" Avia broke off abruptly.

"And Miguel?"

Avia was jolted from her daydream.

"Oh all right I suppose. He'll never be an Einstein but he's very practical. He was always good with his hands. He likes fixing things. The shop is very simple but he's happy. He feels needed."

Isabel nodded. She never would have imagined that the carefree rebel she had first known pinching Du Maurier cigarettes, would have ended up too timid to go out alone.

"He wasn't the soldiering kind," said Avia reading her thoughts. "As it turned out. Anyway what he went through wasn't your normal national service. Spain lost El Aun through a war, not peaceful negotiation. It was just bad luck that Miguel's unit was sent. They had absolutely no experience. He'd never been away from home, never even spent a night away, let alone gone to war. And war it was. The conditions in Morocco were awful. He couldn't cope with it. Wasn't prepared. His mind just crumbled. Poor boy, such a good-looking boy too! *Pobrecillo, es una pena.*"

Isabel was silent. Even to her grandmother she wouldn't have confessed that she found Miguel's collapse rather pathetic. As far as she could see, he had completely wasted his life. He had had immense privileges yet there was nothing to show for it. The family should have sent her to war! She at least had been away from home all right. She knew all about loneliness and cold showers. Poor Miguel indeed, with no one to make him his breakfast and launder his clothes! No wonder they had lost that particular battle, if Spain's army was made up of poor little rich boys like Miguel! The fact remained that whatever happened to him in Morocco, had irrevocably altered his character. He returned after only five months in Africa, possessing little more than a child's intellect, and weeping at the smallest provocation – a grown man crying like a baby.

Perhaps she was being too hard on him. No one could possibly know what it had been like – the Green march especially – when unbeknown to the people they were supposed to be defending, Spain secretly sold out to the Moroccans. In exchange that is for sovereignty over Ceuta and Melilla. And what could those young men have possibly have known of war? The boys who joked about sitting out their military service in some barrack in Andalusia, soon found themselves in a very real war. They had no more training than the tribal peoples they had been sent to protect. They were ignorant of the land, the language and the politics. They were rulers for seventeen days, of a land they did not even know they possessed.

When Miguel first returned from the desert, he was incapable of coherent conversation and found it an effort to concentrate on anything for very long. He no longer played the guitar and spent most of his time asleep. After a while, he turned his attention to gadgets, to mending broken radios, tape recorders and coffee pots. Surprisingly he showed some talent in this and soon could mend anything from broken china to welded metal. Dr.Mantua found him a job in an electrical shop in the city near to his church where he could keep a pastoral eye on the boy. They often lunched together: mostly *pan tomacat* and wine.

"You can of course use the pool."

Isabel realised she'd been miles away.

"Thank you."

"There will be no one to bother you. Ricardo is too busy studying. Or should be. Not even Lupe is there now. Nuria seems to need her with her most of the time. That woman seems to be able to handle Tito in a way that none of us has been able to, not even his own mother. Much of the time, I used to think Lupe half mad myself. I suppose country air is best for a woman of her age. Do you realise, " she added coyly, "that we are exactly the same age?"

For a moment they held each other's gaze.

"Of course, " conceded Avia, "Lupe was in service at the age of 12. In comparison my life had been pretty carefree. It makes a difference. And Lupe is still working."

"You look years younger Avia!" said Isabel reassuringly. Impulsively she kissed the older woman's cheek, which was still as soft as a girl's.

"*Y eso ...* that I don't put anything on my skin."

Isabel smiled to herself. Whenever complimented on her youthfulness, Avia was at pains to point out that she never spent so much as a *peseta* on cosmetics. Following her example, it was considered very un-cool in the family to spend anything on face creams although by contrast, the purchase of mascara and pale lipstick was positively encouraged.

Isabel curled up in a chair by the window and studied her grandmother's hands as they worked on the cloth in front of her. There was nothing hurried or impatient about her gestures.

"So *cuenta me* what else has changed since I've been away? Apart from the family and Val Negra? I understand Franco has appointed Prince Juan Carlos as his heir – instead of his father, Don Juan."

Avia made a face. "It is hoped that he does not become a puppet for Franco's beliefs. It may be that nothing changes but the head on our coins. Of course the main issue concerning us now, is whether or not we join Europe. Franco has kept us in the dark for so long."

"Will Juan Carlos take us into the EEC then do you think?"

"*Quien sabe*? Not with Carrero Blanco as prime minister that's for sure and heading a government which is full of Opus Dei technocrats. It's as if a hand of iron is positioned at our throats. We know what we must do, what is good for the country, but we are unable to bring about any real change. It has been such a long time since we have been able to properly choose for ourselves. It has been a long time since there was any true spontaneity to our lives. How I long to be proud of our Catalan heritage, to be able to buy our literature in the book shops, to hear it being taught in our schools and to speak it in the street!"

Isabel gestured to a copy of *La Vanguardia* that lay discarded on the coffee table.

"And yet the press *does* seem to be loosening up. On the plane coming over I got hold of *Cambio 16*. It was full of criticism and hinted at reformists within the regime *and* reported the Pamplona strike. I couldn't believe what I was reading."

Avia shook her head. "Pepita is from Pamplona. We heard everything first hand. Imagine that quiet, conservative town coming to a total stand still because of the strikers! It would have been unthinkable 10 years ago. Franco would have had them all shot."

"I suppose even Franco has to mellow as he gets older. I also hear that Tito has been appointed Spanish Ambassador in London. He must be very excited"

Avia raised her eyes.

"*Al contrario, amor meu*, he's in despair! He believes everything is falling apart, the fabric upon which he has based his beliefs is unravelling before his eyes. There are rumours that Franco is dying and that making Carrero Blanco head of the government was an admission of his inability to govern. No, Tito is not a happy man these days and we all suffer as a consequence. I must warn you that he is even more Opus Dei than before."

Isabel grimaced. "Is he happy about Franco's choice in Juan Carlos?"

"I doubt it. I am only cautiously optimistic myself. Juan Carlos as successor does not necessarily mean a return to the monarchy. We are preparing ourselves for the worst. And for Catalonia."

"Ah …" breathed Isabel. "I wondered when Catalonia would come into it. Always this division between us and them."

"Yes," said Avia with surprising force. "Always."

"Why is it do you think that we are never really objective? There's always this hidden agenda, this underlying hypocrisy."

Avia's eyes were narrow flints of blue.

"Hypocrisy?"

"Perhaps hypocrisy is too strong a word," Isabel corrected herself hastily. "But Catalans have this fierce obstinacy, this fantastic refusal to see themselves as part of Spain. Every time I hear a Catalan talk about the 'good of the country,' I know that first he has decided whether or not it is good for *him*. Autonomy for Catalonia is one thing, and I believe in it, but surely everything else must surely just be romanticism?"

"I don't know," replied Avia stiffly. "You seem to have the answers. As the modern youth would say, you tell me."

"No of course I don't. I suppose I just don't feel quite as nationalistic as you do. Such extremes of patriotism can only be harmful – inhibiting even. Take Tapies, for example. He is an internationally renowned artist whose latest exhibition at the Met in New York was a huge success. By anyone's standards, he is worldly and sophisticated and yet he has refused to design posters with Castilian words for the Socialist party. It's like David Hockey designing posters for the Conservative party, but only on condition that they carry Gaelic slogans. It doesn't make sense! It's not only stupid it's prejudicial! No wonder Spain is such a back water and no one wants her to join the E.E.C!"

Avia was not amused but dimly she remembered Julian and his defence of the International Brigade all those years before.

"You've spent too long in your English convent," she said coolly. "And you sound suspiciously *Francista*. Is this what they teach you in England? Is this what such liberal thinking does? I fear for you going up to Oxford. You are so impressionable. Have you forgotten your roots? Have you forgotten what regime we live under? This isn't an Oxbridge tutorial, *querid*a, this is real life, our life that we're talking about, a life that you are able to dip in and out of. We unfortunately have no such luxury. What do you want us to do? Deny our heritage? Our culture? We *are* different from the rest of Spain. We got here first!"

They both smiled feebly but Isabel was not to be deflected.

"I know. But don't you see –"

"I do see, my little English girl. And I think you are hot. You are not used to our climate. Why don't you swim before lunch?"

"Because I don't feel like a swim!" protested Isabel.

"Very well then," said her grandmother. "Amuse yourself some other way. I have work to do. Today, we lunch at 2.30 in deference to your *English* habits."

Avia rose from her chair in that single, graceful movement Isabel always admired. But she made a face at her grandmother's retreating back and was instantly remorseful. How could she have upset her? And so quickly too! She should have held her tongue. Why did she suddenly feel the urge to question everything? And as reluctant as she was to admit it, Isabel was beginning to see cracks in the perfect family picture. As long as she could remember, the family, apart from Tito of course, had loved to hate Franco for all sorts of reasons. His human rights record wasn't exactly glowing and unlike Tito they did not see his excessive use of cruelty as a positive strength. He had done everything possible to quash Catalan identity. It was inevitable that over time, Tito and Franco would become indistinguishable – both were a focus for personal shortcomings and disappointment.

And now, for the first time Isabel began to examine her memories in a new, much harsher light. She glanced around the room, searching for reassuring signs of continuity. The house, at least was true to memory. Slight alterations were registered according to the season. In summer, the marble floors were stripped of rugs and damask covers removed from the furniture to reveal the bantam linen underneath. The air was heavy with the scent of gardenia. Sunlight streamed through the rooms throwing diaphanous stripes across the floor. A clock ticked on the mantelpiece.

Isabel sank back in a sofa stretching her legs. She felt too lethargic to do anything and incredibly hot. Her hair was damp at the back of her neck and her thin cotton shirt clung to her body. There wasn't the slightest breeze. The thought of the library, which she usually looked so forward to visiting, filled her with apprehension. It was too hot to be cooped up indoors and yet the punishing sun streaming through the windows, seemed to singe everything that came under its powerful rays. Even her mind was dull, an opaque void. What would she find to do every day? While back in England, she had thought longingly of the sun and Mialma, having completely forgotten what a Spanish summer was really like. She now remembered that until she became acclimatized, there was a daily battle with lethargy and dizzying, prickly heat. Just as she had longed for the sun, she now craved the cold and rain. Perhaps staying in London with Kate would have been better after all. Maybe she would never really fit in here. But then she reminded herself that there was always this initial uncertainty, this feeling of being neither wanted nor unwanted- an unsettling feeling of displacement.

"Damn," muttered Isabel aloud. Even her legs were damp and had left a shadow against the linen sofa. Although she could hardly bare the thought of going outside, the idea of a swim was suddenly irresistible.

Her bathing suit tucked under her arm, Isabel emerged from the house as if coming out of a manhole. She squinted in the blinding sunlight struggling to make out the stone walk that led to the Coach house. With the garden wall always to her right she followed its boundary until it stopped at a small gate almost entirely covered by laurel. Crouching down on all fours, Isabel groped for the key that was kept hidden in the grass, between the bars. For a moment, feeling increasingly giddy, she couldn't find it and then just when she thought she might actually be sick, her fingers encircled cold metal. Panting with the effort of having to lie flat on her stomach to stretch an arm through the bars, Isabel sat up abruptly, feeling the ground swirl upwards as she did so. She took a few deep breaths to steady herself but her hands continued to tremble as she unlocked the gate. And instantly, the sight of the swimming pool as it lay, tranquil, abandoned and brilliant amidst a wall of stone and bougainvillea, sent her sprits soaring. Gardenia and jasmine spilled onto paving stones and dull grey salamanders slithered between the cracks. Shaded by palm trees, the pool was an oasis beneath the ominous stucco turrets and shuttered balconies of Tito's house. Beyond it, the lemon groves stretched far and wide, colliding only with a horizon of silver, sparkling sea. Gingerly, Isabel climbed the few stone steps to the pool. The water lay stagnant, inches from her toes, blue beneath a mirrored sky.

Eager now to swim, Isabel changed into the green bikini that Kate had given her. She hadn't dared wear it at the convent and rather doubted that it would be acceptable at Val Negra. But the only alternative was her very tight – according to Kate *indecently* tight – school costume. Kate assured her that the bikini was far less revealing than the black swimsuit but all the same Isabel did not think her cousins were wearing two-piece bathing costumes. "That will wow them!" Kate said admiringly when Isabel tried it on but Isabel had been shocked at how developed her figure had become. Now as she slipped into the pool, Isabel was glad that her stomach was bare, enjoying the feel of the water on her skin. She wet her head, closing her eyes, swimming in a secret sea. She stretched every muscle of her body, reaching as far as she could, until gradually all tension in her dissolved. She swam quickly, kicking her legs till her thighs hurt and she strained through the water gasping for air, awash with memories.

She remembered the summer when she was eight, when the swimming pool was being built, and how in the blazing sunshine she had shut her eyes praying fervently that when she opened them again, miraculously the pool would be finished. But of course it wasn't. The excavated hole remained, as did the concrete and granite slabs twinkling conspiratorially in the scorching, noonday sun. Listlessly she and her cousins had sat under the palm trees, fanning themselves with the inadequate black lace concoctions that Avia resurrected from her cupboard – looking every bit like the daughters in a Lorca play. The dust from the workmen's digging hung like low clouds above the parapet. The sweat clung, then as now, to Isabel's neck. Days later it rained for the first summer in years, and her cousins, all dressed identically in bright red pinafores, climbed into the empty pool, twirling umbrellas and shouting: 'We're Singing in the Rain' from the top of their voices. Isabel had sat watching them, not understanding a word of Spanish, not even recognising the tune, mesmerised by the sight of these exuberant little girls in their exquisite clothes. But that was then …

Eyes wide open, Isabel skimmed the floor of the pool. Down here, beneath the weightless burden of water, it was almost cool. Some of the mosaic tiles were missing and there was the odd leaf embedded in the grout. She touched the edge with outstretched fingers, doubling over to turn around, her feet propelling her forward. She sliced through the water, her ribs concave. She pushed for a third lap, her lungs bursting. She wondered idly what it would be like to drown, to be deaf, aware only of a heartbeat, the shape of words in her head. Was it like this? Like being an eternal, underwater swimmer? She made out the murky shape of the step, hidden behind a veil of floating particles. She scattered them with her hands as they danced briefly before dispersing in the water. Unable to hold her breath any longer she catapulted out, shaking her head so that her long hair splayed in strands across her face. Her ears blocked, she did not hear a man's surprised grunt as he was doused in water. As she raised her hands to her face, she was caught by the wrist and pulled unceremoniously out of the pool. Gasping for breath, she cried out, as iron like fingers dug into her arms. Isabel struggled to push the hair out of her eyes but her arms were forced to her sides.

"*Que hace aqui? No hay derecho*!" said the man. "Who the hell are you? And what are you doing here? This is private property! How did you get in? The walls are high enough. Christ, you people are all the same!"

"Ow!" groaned Isabel as her head was jerked sideways. She could hear her own ragged breathing thunderingly loud as one of her eardrums became unclogged and the sound of his heartbeat beneath her cheek. Her hair was pulled tight under the man's arm and the buttons of his shirt dug into her back. One of his legs imprisoned hers. She sank helpless against him, gasping for breath, a familiar smell of crisp linen filling her nostrils with the faintest scent of lime. She closed her eyes momentarily confused.

"Take your hands off me, you pervert!" she hissed but although her voice sounded fierce to her, the man seemed unperturbed.

"You *are* alone aren't you?" he continued. "Or are there any more? Did you come through the gate?"

"Of course. How else? Now let me go. You're hurting me."

"I'll hurt you a lot more if you don't tell me what you're doing here. Are you from the gypsy camp or did Nadal send you? He certainly likes them young! You won't last long though. They never do. And in case he hasn't told you everything, this is *our* land, not his. We don't like strangers wandering in uninvited. Or has he told you that we are all *compadres* with the right to roam? Well *are* you?"

"Am I *what*?" said Isabel. "Let me go. I can hardly breathe."

The man slackened his grasp. "A gypsy. Are you a gypsy?"

Isabel made a half choking sound.

"Don't be ridiculous!" she said.

And then he'd spun her round so quickly, the straps of her bikini slid to her elbows. She noticed with detachment, that the front of his shirt and trousers was wet.

"You've spoken in English," he said abruptly letting her go but not before his eyes had flicked over her half-naked body. He frowned. "You speak Engl –"

"So do you. Oh my God. *Ricardo?*"

There was a pause. The man peered at her closely, disbelief clearly visible on his face. His eyes swept over her again so that she blushed. He ran a hand through his hair.

"*Isabel?*"

"I'm sorry," she replied nervously "I've got you all wet! Even your shoes! I should have called. Avia said that I could use the pool. I – I didn't think there was anyone here. I didn't mean to disturb you. I know you've got your exams. I'm sorry. I would never have taken advantage. I mean of the house being empty. I would have called." Her voice faded at the strange expression in his eyes. Ricardo touched her arm turning it towards him. The impression left by his fingers could be clearly seen on the pale skin.

"It is I who should be sorry," he said gently. "I've hurt you." He held her wrist in one hand while the other felt the marks. "*Disculpa.*"

"It's nothing," she whispered. For a moment he drew her close. Once more she smelled the lime scent of his laundered linen. She struggled to concentrate on what he was saying. Her sight was full of his fine lawn shirt, the pulse at his tanned neck, his mouth as it moved. He was darker than ever, his eyes the colour of cognac, his toned physique belying the serious illness she knew he had suffered. It took all her strength to fight an insane urge to press her face against him. Her heart hammered in her chest and there was a hollow feeling in the pit of her stomach. Again she felt as if she could not breathe.

And then abruptly he let her go. He reached for her towel and threw it at her. "*Toma!*" He said gruffly. He groped for a cigarette, lighting one quickly. She heard the hiss of tobacco as he inhaled.

"You didn't recognise me."

"No." His smile was lopsided. "And in case you're wondering I don't normally welcome my friends by hauling them out of the pool like that!"

"Then who did you think I might be? Who are these gypsies?"

He inhaled again sharply.

"We've been having problems here recently. A gypsy family has been camping along the border with Val Negra. Only it's no ordinary family," he said answering her questioning look. "There are around fifty people there now, including women and children. They claim to be relatives of the Nadals. Carlos Nadal says they have the right to roam – a point which is debatable. What, is not however, is their right to live here. But we're powerless to do anything about it. We've taken out countless injunctions against them but so far have been unable to make them stick."

"But surely you can do something. I mean if anyone has contacts it's Tito and - and you of course would know what to do," she finished lamely remembering his law studies.

Ricardo shrugged. "The whole issue of the homeless gypsies has always been a sensitive one but it's especially true now given Tito's recent appointment. The press has been sniffing around here as it is. To be honest, we hadn't even seen the families but in the past few weeks they've got braver. Nadal's men have begun poaching our wildlife and the women have come up to the house to beg." He shook his head, his forehead creased in a frown. "I know Nadal is behind it but I'm not sure why. I don't know what he wants."

"Does it have to be anything?"

"What do you mean?"

"I think Nadal gets enormous pleasure from causing *dis*pleasure to our family. It's what makes him tick. He doesn't *want* anything in return. Not in a material sense."

Ricardo blew out a smoke ring. Isabel used the towel he had given her to dry her face. He watched her closely.

"How do you know this?"

"I don't. Not for sure. But I always thought there was something sinister about him. He hates us all, our family, our name – even Avia, especially Avia. He resents everything we stand for. Do you remember the way he used to spit on the pavement if we walked passed him? It used to make Sigi and me giggle. He was the rudest person we'd ever met. Then maybe I'm exaggerating."

"No," replied Ricardo slowly. "No you're not."

"But fifty people! That's not just a gypsy family!"

"No and there are problems now with sanitation. There's also the increased risk of disease given the heat. The whole thing could turn into a complete nightmare. It would just take one outbreak of cholera –"

Isabel shuddered.

"What does Avia say?"

Ricardo looked uncomfortable.

"She doesn't know."

Isabel tilted her head, a smile playing on her lips.

"A secret from Avia? That must be a first."

Ricardo flicked ash from his cigarette.

"I agree she's not the person you want to have secrets from but we haven't wanted to worry her. Besides you'd never notice the encampment unless you made a point of looking for it. Avi rides out there every morning to keep an eye on things and Tito of course knows what's going on."

Isabel made a face.

"I just wouldn't want to be you when she finds out. And she always finds out."

Ricardo frowned. "I know that but this really is for her own good. She's not as strong as she used to be and if we can sort it out without her knowing …" he paused. "I studied a similar case once," continued Ricardo thoughtfully, "where a widow who lived on her own was kept a virtual prisoner by gypsies camping on her land. She was too frightened to leave the house. Not," he added hastily, "that we've had trouble like at least not yet but when the old lady finally died no one wanted the house. Her children certainly didn't but they couldn't sell. The gypsies are still there and I believe the estate is still in probate."

"That mustn't happen here," said Isabel forcibly. "I'm surprised Tito hasn't taken the law into his own hands."

Ricardo snorted.

"I'm afraid he's about to."

Isabel shivered suddenly and Ricardo immediately stubbed out his cigarette.

"You've got goose bumps," he said touching her arm lightly. "Come on let's go and sit in the sun. Besides I haven't asked you anything about you! I launched into my tirade against the gypsies when all the time -" He smiled lazily, his eyes tender. Isabel felt herself flush.

"I don't know how – how I can have goose bumps I mean," she said quickly. " I don't remember heat like this."

She slung the towel sarong style around her hips and gathered up her clothes. Ricardo followed her movements with his eyes.

"When did you get home?" he asked leading the way up shallow steps to a stone table under the olive trees. The pool lay beneath them, vacillating under the intensity of the sunlight.

"Just last night."

He stared at her his eyes boring into hers so that she looked away embarrassed.

"You've changed so much. I'd never have recognised you – well I didn't."

"Have I?" she said uncertainly, anxiety knitting her brow. "Well, I've already managed to row with Avia. That's not something I used to do. I wish I hadn't now."

He shrugged sympathetically. "It's another generation. You've just got to listen to her and try not to contradict. I've found that it works best that way. " Ricardo frowned as if thinking of something else. "You got into Oxford didn't you? Congratulations."

Isabel flushed with pleasure. Shadows from the overhanging tree marked the smooth skin of her cheek. She blinked, holding up a hand to shade her eyes, eyes that seemed achingly clear and innocent to him. Without thinking he reached to smooth a strand of hair from her face.

"No one else has said anything," she replied breathless as her stomach did a funny flip when he touched her. "Avia hasn't. It's as if my getting in were a given. As if they never expected anything else. But I did! I never really believed it would happen. And now it has, I can hardly wait. It's the only thing I've ever really wanted," she added shyly.

For a moment she held his look. He smiled, leaning back in his chair a leg crossed casually over the other. He wore leather shoes as was the custom in summer, without socks and the tassel on the end of one jigged as he moved his leg.

"Which college?"

"Oh Somerville, of course. You don't think the nuns would let me apply to a *mixed* college do you? However, Somerville has a very good Golden Age tutor - positively *ancient* so I'm told, but still the definitive word on Cervantes. But then I've always had a head start in that direction. My name alone, *all* our names ..."

He looked at her quizzically, his gaze again so strangely tender that her heart lurched again.

"What's in a name? A rose by any other name ..."

"I always forget your English is so good," she said suddenly breathless. "I don't think I could quote poetry in another language."

Ricardo inclined his head. "Dr. Mantua was a good teacher. Sure you could. There's Avi's peculiar haiku for a start. But thank you all the same."

He reached for another cigarette, tapping the box and for a moment they sat in silence. She watched him inhale, throwing back his dark head his eyes half shut. He was very still and Isabel wondered desperately what he was thinking. Was she boring him? Should she say she was needed at the house and go back? Did he want to be alone? She played with her hair, shaking it over her shoulders so that it would dry in the sun. When she looked up he was watching her.

"Still you have to wonder at the name thing," said Isabel chattering to disguise her nervousness. "I mean I *am* a Spanish-English girl and my name *is* Isabel. Don't you think that's weird?"

He raised an eyebrow. "No, not weird, a coincidence. There must be quite a few Isabels in the world, of mixed parentage like yourself. Besides I thought you didn't like being reminded of the Spanish-English thing."

Isabel smiled. "I don't but I thought I'd mention it myself before it came out. As it always does at some point."

"Oh dear," said Ricardo with a mock sigh. "What a hard life! However, I don't see why you have to go to Oxford to learn about Cervantes. You've grown up with him."

Isabel sat up pulling the towel tighter around her waist. "That is kind of what I meant. I won't only be studying Golden Age though. I shall read Modern Languages. So French too."

Ricardo replied in English.

"I always find it amusing, the way you English 'read' your way through your degree."

"And you Spanish, don't?"

"Not in the same way."

"How are your exams going?"

"Bastante bien," said Ricardo switching back to Spanish. "I've had so much time off with the chemo – " He made an impatient gesture. "It's all over. I'm fine. I've been clear for a couple of years – just had about quadruple the amount of time to complete the course that every one else has. If I don't pass these exams then there's not a hope! But then we all seem to be taking a while to catch up."

"I heard about Miguel," said Isabel lowering her eyes. "I'm sorry."

Ricardo shrugged. "There had to be casualties. I mean of this family." He looked away towards the sea and the line of horizon caught between and then he turned to her the expression on his face quite different. "*Cuentame*, what did you argue about with Avia?"

Isabel ran her fingers through her hair, shaking out the last droplets of water. She closed her eyes, enjoying the hot sun on her face. She had always loved the Spanish for 'tell me'. Tell me all about it – *Cuentame*. Her grandmother said it when she first came home, wanting to hear all about her term at school.

"Oh this and that." She made a face. "Politics I guess."

"That was unfair," said Ricardo gently.

"I know. And Ricardo, it had nothing to do with politics."

"I didn't think it did."

"I suppose I just wanted to be noticed. For Avia once in her life, to say that she is proud of me – to acknowledge what I've done, not what I look like. The academic side of school was never a problem but it doesn't mean that I haven't worked my pants off to get to Oxford. It wasn't completely without effort. I just would like her to notice."

Again his eyes swooped over her.

"You *are* noticed."

Isabel blushed. "But not because I've lost weight! For me."

He leant forward his fingers skimming hers. For a moment he struggled with thoughts he thought better not expressed. Isabel felt the shadow of his touch and wondered if it had ever been. Suddenly he scraped back his chair.

"How 'bout lunch? Then we could drive up to Tibidabo. As we did as children."

Isabel's face lit up and then instantly fell.

"I'd love to," she breathed. "But I told Avia I'd be back. Besides I've nothing to wear. I mean besides my shorts and I don't think you wear shorts yet in Spain."

He smiled. "Nor bikinis, although I'd love to see – " he cleared his throat. "Why is it you never seem to have any decent clothes?"

She stood up, shrugging on her t-shirt and baggy Bermudas. She tied her hair back with a shoelace.

"I'm beginning to wonder that myself."

"Well Doris can sort out Avia. She never needs an excuse to go and see Pepita. We'll send her over now. Luckily your shorts aren't too short if you know what I mean. Anyway they'll have to do. You look fine. More than fine actually."

He smiled.

"What is it?" Isabel asked alarmed. Ricardo took her arm as they made their way up the narrow rocky path to the house.

"Nothing *cosina*. You're just such a surprise. Clever and beautiful it would seem. How my sisters will hate you!"

Isabel stopped short. "Oh I do hope not," she said earnestly. "*They're* the beautiful ones. They always were. And they're so wonderfully dressed! They were so lucky!"

"Perhaps not quite so lucky now," said Ricardo thoughtfully. "Come on. A drive first and then lunch. No. I have an idea. You go on up. I'll meet you round the front."

He ran on ahead, taking the steps two at a time. Isabel followed more slowly, mindful of the heat and the sun blazing directly onto her head. Above her loomed the Coach House shimmering and pink against a cloudless sky. Surrounding the house, the etiolate hills formed a false horizon with the sea and neat white sails punctured the bleached expanse of sand beneath. Isabel skirted the kitchen garden and waited for Ricardo on the steps of the house. His car was parked casually along the half circle of gravel, the roof down. Within seconds he emerged from the front door armed with a *jarra* of wine and a cloth wrapped bundle.

"*Pan tomacat* and *Jamon serano*. You have to start out here in truly Catalan fashion."

"*Naturalment.*"

Ricardo tossed the bundle onto the tiny back seat.

"Get in. Only mind the debris," he said sweeping empty cigarette packets and magazines onto the floor.

"Gosh this will annoy Avia!" giggled Isabel.

"I expect it will," he agreed and they sped off in a screech of gears, leaving a cloud of dust behind them. Isabel sank into the buckle seat, stretching out her legs. Once they began to climb through the hills, it was noticeably cooler. A welcome breeze drew out her hair behind her and she inhaled the scent of pine and the lime scent of her cousin's clothes. High above them the craggy formation of Tibidabo seemed inaccessible and a great distance away. She was silent, overcome with an unfamiliar shyness. Ricardo's eyes never left the road and for a while Isabel wondered if he had forgotten she was with him.

Well before the exit for Tibidabo, he turned off the tarmac and for a few yards they bumped down what appeared to be little more than a donkey track. The car squeezed through bushes of gorse and lavender. A couple of times he cursed as a branch scraped the paintwork. Eventually he pulled over and parked under a giant eucalyptus. He reached over her shoulder for the picnic, his shirt brushing her cheek. Then, not bothering to open the door, he vaulted over, motioning towards the path ahead of him.

"This is a good place to stop and eat, " he said. "Besides there's something I want you to see first."

Isabel thought it best to follow suit, attempting a far less agile leap over the car door. She stumbled before jolting up right with an apologetic laugh.

"You made it look easy," she said under her breath to Ricardo's departing back. He strode on ahead through tall grass, bending under branches of mimosa. Without warning, the path broke onto a large, smooth clearing at the edge of a cliff. The sun was warm, illuminating the plain in a halo of light. Above, the rocks jutting out from the mountain, scraped an electric sky, and here and there, the criss-cross of metallic telegraph wires twinkled in the afternoon sun. Pulled in by these shiny ropes, the surrounding sea seemed little more than a gigantic fish suspended by this monstrous net. Tiny daisies were scattered like jewels on the inch long grass. There was no house or building of any description in sight and the view even of the sea, was unmarred by ships.

Isabel stretched out her arms towards them.

"What is this place?"

"Land I've bought," said Ricardo simply. Isabel spun round.

"This is yours!" she said. "It's so beautiful, so remote, so … undisturbed."

"That's what appealed. It contrasts somewhat, don't you think, with the … loucheness of the Coach house? I love the light, the clarity here - the fact that you don't see anything or anyone for miles. And yet it's still within striking distance of the city. But I've not told anyone, anyone at all and least of all Tito. You're the first one to see it. I shall build a house here one day," he said.

"It's wonderful. Truly."

Ricardo stood close to the cliff's edge. His shirt billowed slightly in the breeze. In profile his face was still, calm. She moved to stand beside him, her heart thumping so vigorously she was amazed he couldn't hear it. She felt a visceral pleasure at simply being with him.

"It's strange," he said without turning to look at her. "I feel I've known you all my life."

Isabel swallowed and took a huge shaky breath before answering lightly.

"But Ricardo you *have* known me all your life."

They sat on the grass with the wine and huge chunks of bread scraped with tomato and olive oil, the pips, anaemically pink against the white crust. Ricardo raised the jug to his lips tilting it as she had seen the peasants do at Val Negra. It came out in a thin, straight spurt, sliding easily down his throat. Ricardo drank without spilling a drop.

"I wouldn't try this, if you want to keep your t-shirt white," he said passing her the *jarra*.

Isabel held it between her hands, caressing the rough pottery.

"When we were little," she told him, "Sigi and I were constantly hungry, or greedy or bored. I'm not sure which. But we ate all the time. Just after lunch we'd set off on an excursion with a *merienda* of huge sandwiches and cakes and then eat the lot almost immediately."

"No wonder you were chubby!"

"Well it's not surprising with the amount Avia used to feed me! She was convinced the nuns starved us. During the holidays her sole ambition was to make me gain weight. She spent the entire time thinking up food that I might like and then preparing it. All we used to talk about was food."

"It was because of the war," said Ricardo.

"Not in my case!"

"No of course not. Growing up, our mothers never had enough to eat and after wards well … I suppose they made up for it. I can't believe Tito ever went hungry though. Even then he must have been wheeling and dealing, extracting the last peseta out of some poor wretch."

Isabel sipped the warm *vino tinto* feeling it float through her limbs and her mind.

"Tell me about Sonia de Cana?" she blurted out too quickly. She had wanted to pose the question casually, in a grown up way but it came out breathless and a little too earnest. "I thought you were going to marry her."

Ricardo lay back on the grass, eyes shut, arms cushioning his head. "So did I," he replied easily.

"But weren't you madly in love with her?"
"She was the first girl I ever loved, yes."
"She was very beautiful."
"*Cierto.*"
"And clever. I remember she spoke fluent English."
"Mine's better."
"So?"
"So. You don't marry someone who is dying of cancer." Ricardo's tone was matter of fact.
"But you're not. I know I would."
"I know you would," he said quietly. "You see she didn't know I'd be cured. I couldn't hold her to our engagement when the future was uncertain. At the time I was spending most days in hospital. It was unfair on her. She was very young. I couldn't ask her to sacrifice her youth, her sense of fun, when no one could predict the outcome. Sonia is happily married, I hear, to a friend of ours from Val Negra – a man much better suited to her way of life than I could ever have been. Anyway I'm only just beginning my career. It would never have worked."
"But you loved each other!" Isabel protested.
"Yes I loved her. But who's to say that the strain of the past few years might not have killed any love she had for me? I couldn't have worried about her as well. I had my own battle to fight. I had to do it alone."
"I had no idea," said Isabel. "I still don't see how she could have left you. How could she have left you when you were so ill, when you needed her? How could she have married someone else if she loved you?"
Ricardo's hand shot out and clasped her arm as roughly as he had done pulling her from the pool.
"It's over," he said firmly. "It doesn't matter now. It's over. I don't want to talk about that time anymore. Why not tell me about you? *Cuenta me* about this Kate of yours. Has she introduced you to any boys yet?"
Isabel choked on her wine feeling herself flush. Ricardo raised his head.
"Aha!" he said smiling. "I've touched a nerve."
"No. No you haven't. It's just that I don't think you can imagine my convent at all. It's very isolated. Occasionally the older girls are invited to dances at a 'neighbouring' Catholic boys' school. But you see 'neighbouring' means a two-hour drive after supper, on a freezing cold Friday night. I went once and I hated it."
Ricardo touched her arm.

"What, a pretty girl like you hating a dance? You must be more English than I thought."

Isabel looked away embarrassed.

"I do like to dance." She said in a low voice. "But-"

"But?"

"Well I was always cold for one thing and I don't think the boys really wanted us there in the first place. They would have been just as happy having a few beers and watching a game of football on the box."

Ricardo looked genuinely puzzled.

"I hope you're joking."

Isabel shook her head. "No it's true and the worst bit was that the nuns would vanish as soon as we arrived so you couldn't leave even if you wanted to. Actually I always wondered about that, you'd have thought they'd keep a close eye on us but anyway they didn't. I didn't enjoy it."

"No I can quite see that."

"I suppose it was all right if you found a boy who did want to kiss you but otherwise you spent the next five hours roaming around a dimly lit, unheated monastery, not knowing what to do with yourself, mortified that a boy didn't like you and wishing you were back in your own room asleep and still having at least three hours to kill! Of course Kate always had a boyfriend so it wasn't a problem. And she was older so she knew what to do and say and was never in the least bit shy. But if you weren't like her, it was excruciating – especially on the coach trip back when the girls would talk about their success, their conquests."

"Where is Kate now?"

"In London. She left last term. I suppose it was a good thing otherwise I'd never have passed Oxbridge. She's great fun but quite a distraction. I expect I shall see her less now."

"Yes but just wait till you get to London!"

Isabel glanced at him a pout forming on her lips.

"You're laughing at me. I know you are."

"Of course not. Tell me more," said Ricardo lazily.

And so, in spite of herself she did. She prattled on telling him all about Kate's adventures on the hockey field and elsewhere. She described Mrs. Simpkin, the tutor who prepared Isabel for the Oxbridge entrance exam– a large red headed woman with a broken nose like a rugby player and a jaw like an ox. And she told Ricardo about the scandal that was caused when the Latin mistress was discovered in the Laundry room kissing the little nun from Gibraltar. She tried to depict the beauty of the grounds and in particular the rose garden where the nuns were buried and where in springtime, primroses crawled untamed over crumbling tombstones. She told him where he might find the cedar walk, the old Pilgrims way that led up through the hills to the town.

"It's a wonder your friend didn't get pregnant," observed Ricardo dryly.

"Oh she was very careful," said Isabel blushing and Ricardo noticed with amusement how the colour came and went on her cheeks every time he embarrassed her. But what Isabel did not recount, was the memory of long cold, winter nights when she cried herself to sleep, or the night her father died. Her face clouded. She grew silent and hunched her knees to her chest.

"You've experienced so much more than any of us," said Ricardo gently. "I don't think we really knew anything about you."

"Oh no," said Isabel. "Everyone was always so kind. I'm so grateful."

"You don't have to be," replied Ricardo harshly. "You don't owe anyone anything. I don't think we did enough. Did anyone ever buy you a stitch of clothing for example and with all the clothes my sisters possessed, did they ever offer to lend you any?"

"N-no but I was far too fat! And Sigi did buy me some espadrilles once that I kept long after I'd outgrown them. I loved those espadrilles."

Ricardo snorted.

"You mean the red ones? For some reason I've never liked red shoes."

"Thanks a lot," Isabel made a face. "I was so thrilled with them but I expect they looked ghastly. I mean on me."

Ricardo shook his head. "I don't know why you're so loyal."

"It's got nothing to do with loyalty. I was just so ... ugly. I'd have looked just as hideous in pretty clothes as plain ones. Anyway it's something else that doesn't matter anymore."

"But it does matter," he said and then suddenly Ricardo leapt up and reaching down pulled her to her feet. His gesture was so unexpected that she was thrown against him her head reaching below his chin.

"Ricardo."

Aware of her skin against his and the smell of her hair he made a supreme effort to let her go. He longed to lie back on the grass and hold her, to forget about the past and who they were. A muscle ticked in his cheek as his jaw clenched. He wanted to kiss her. But that wasn't possible.

It couldn't be. And yet he couldn't stop touching her. He took her by the hand. She was little more than a child. He felt her fingers, trusting in his. She was barely sixteen. Christ.

"Come. To Tibidabo. Do you like the dodgem cars?"

"I've never been on one."

"What!" he exclaimed in disbelief. "But surely you went to Tibidabo when you were little? Surely Nuria took you with my sisters?"

Isabel shook her head. "No but you told me about it the first day I arrived. I still remember that day when you crashed into me when I was lost walking up to the convent and later we walked on and you told me all about the Devil tempting Jesus. I was totally terrified and confused and excited all in one."

Ricardo looked uncomfortable. "Yes I remember that too. I don't know, I'm either knocking you off your feet or pulling you out of the water. I'm going to have to make it up to you somehow. We'll go to Tibidabo then."

"Yes," murmured Isabel smiling sweetly, "show me what all the fuss was about."

"Um …" muttered Ricardo inaudibly.

Chapter 18

Isabel
Barcelona
Summer 1976

Isabel had never had so much fun in her life before. She loved whirling around in tiny cars banging - *deliberately* banging - into other drivers. Ricardo had had more fun. He was acutely aware of men staring at her. He was right, it wouldn't matter what she wore. Isabel's tatty clothes only gave her a charm, the chicest girls did not possess. With her gleaming skin and flowing hair and the sheer vibrancy of her smiling face, she was stunning. Men wanted her. *He* wanted her. It was an undeniable relief to feel once again, the pleasure of desire. But he was appalled, stunned and invigorated by the strength of his reaction. Only this morning he had been entirely focused on completing a paper on a new Anti-Terrorist Law. He was spurred on by the intoxicating pleasure of seeing his work in print. Not only did the subject engross him – a law that would revoke the death penalty in his country – but Tito's reaction to seeing the de Roble name blazing through the pages of *La Vanguardia* was a truly delightful proposition. Ricardo was not sure what excited him more; the fact that his work was to be published or the prospect of antagonising his father.

And now, here he was, whirling round some funfair like the teenager he was not, thinking of Isabel. But why should that be? Until today he hadn't given her a moment's thought. Oh she'd been a harmless enough child; gentle and quiet if at times a little too self-effacing and he had always admired her quick mind but that was as far as his interest in her went. But today he recognized something of himself in her. And that realization was both disturbing and exciting. They were both outsiders – different from other members of the family while at the same time intrinsically linked with each other.

But he had only ever thought of her as a sister. And as with his sisters, he had been oblivious to their growing up. Only Isabel hadn't just grown up, she had blossomed into an exquisite creature. And what was even more surprising than the change itself, was the fact that there had never been the slightest indication that such a metamorphosis was possible. He remembered her only too well as a chubby little thing and now here she was, the most beautiful girl in the world. She was also the youngest. Sixteen. Her age drummed itself in his brain. Sixteen. She was a child. He punched the steering wheel so fiercely he winced just as the closing gong sounded.

"Wasn't that brilliant!" enthused Isabel pulling him by the arm and dragging him from his dodgem.

"Yes," he said flinching at her touch. She really could look hopelessly young. Her cheeks were flushed, her eyes green flints. His own eyes narrowed.

"How much wine have you had, exactly?"

"What do you mean, exactly?" she said and giggled.

"Oh God," he said. "Avia really will kill us or rather me. Come on."

He marched her firmly away from the funfair back to the car. It was early evening and the air was cool on their faces as they drove slowly down the mountain towards Mialma. Ricardo had no desire to speed and he took the turns measurably, savouring the view as the lights came on all over the city. Isabel, curled on the seat beside him, smiled at her own secret thoughts.

"Why are you smiling?" he asked gently.

She started.

"What is it? What are you hiding? Tell me." His voice was deliberately gentle but he was curious. He reached to tickle her but she caught his hand and for a moment held it carefully between hers. Then she looked away and was very still.

"That thing you said about coincidence, there being lots of Isabels and all that. I mean I know it's a coincidence but-" She bit her lip.

"Go on."

"I can't."

"*Cuenta.*" He pretended to be stern and his voice was deep.

She held his hand tightly.

"Promise me you won't laugh," she said earnestly.

"I won't laugh but I may crash the car. You're going to have to let go of my hand."

She dropped it at once.

"Oh my God, I'm so sorry."

"It's all right. Go on, you were talking about coincidences. " He concentrated on the road not daring to look at her, not daring to take advantage of that wide, warm look in her eyes. In a few more seconds he would stop the car altogether and-

"It's that thing about names. In that story, *the* story, *my* story you know the one – the *epanola-inglesa-* well Isabel is taken to England during the sacking of Cadiz by the English sea Capitan and brought up as an English woman-" Isabel remembered how the very word 'take' had sent shivers up her spine when she was a little girl – "but she never forgets her roots or her faith or Spanish."

"It's Cervantes' essay portraying the political and social differences that existed between England and Spain at the time," said Ricardo. "It's probably still valid today."

Isabel touched his sleeve.

"I *know* you know the story," she murmured softly.

A hand clutched at his gut. He knew what she was about to say only too well. He'd been waiting a long time for her to draw the parallel.

"Yes?"

Isabel ran a hand through her hair coiling it over one shoulder.

"I think you're deliberately making this hard for me." Her lips pouted. "You're enjoying this!"

"*Cuenta!*" he commanded gruffly.

"Well, " said Isabel in a low voice, "apart from obviously identifying with the other Isabel, I– I've always been struck by the fact that *La espanola inglesa* is also a love story. The English Captain who takes Isabel to live with his family just happens to have a son and that son is called Ricardo. Isabel and Ricardo grow up together and eventually they … fall in love." Her voice dropped so that Ricardo had to lean close to hear what she was saying. "And when Ricardo falls ill," she whispered, "and is about to die, it is only his love for Isabel that saves him. Do you still call that coincidence?"

Ricardo could not reply and when he looked down at her again, Isabel's eyes were closed although he doubted she was asleep, her face half shrouded by strands of hair and the moonlight spilling, soundless, over her shoulder.

*

Avia *was* furious. Isabel had never seen her grandmother angry before and over something so seemingly trivial. Doris, Nuria's maid had informed Pepita, Avia's maid, that the condesita would not be home for lunch and all hell had broken out. It was not as if Isabel had merely vanished without a word. Isabel could not understand what all the fuss was about.

"Mealtimes are *always* spent at home." Avia raged. "You do not *picnic* anywhere except at Val Negra! I do not care if you were with Ricardo or not. He should have known better. What was he doing *picnicking* anyway? This family, with the exceptional circumstance, does not picnic! I mean, *que diran?*" What will people say!

"Oh come now, Avia," said Ricardo pleasantly. " I can't believe that you've never eaten out of doors!"

Avia's face was thunderous.

"Of course I've eaten outside but out of necessity, not out of choice! The place for picnics is in the country! What if you'd been seen?" She stopped, her blue eyes glaring at Isabel. "Your mother *picnicked* all right," she said contemptuously. "And *you* were probably the result!"

Isabel smothered a nervous giggle.

"It is a ridiculous informal habit practised by foreigners," Avia raged on. "And on your first day! Your grandfather wanted to see you. Instead we were so worried!"

"But why?" replied Isabel mystified "We told you what we were doing."

"Not *we*," said Avia acidly, "Doris told Pepita who informed me."

Isabel spread her hands helplessly.

"It was impulse."

"Ay si. No me lo tienes que decir! Juventud, juventud, divion tesoro. Pensando en sus suenos dorados. Youth golden youth, always dreaming your dreams!"

Ricardo winked at Isabel. They both knew the quote by heart.

He turned smiling charmingly. "It's all my fault, Avia. I apologise." And he made a curt bow. "It was thoughtless when you had lunch waiting."

"And your exams, dear boy, had you no thought of them? There's only a week left."

"Quite."

"You're not worried?"

"Not really."

Avia grunted.

"Juventud!"

Chapter 19

Isabel
Barcelona
Summer 1976

    Whenever possible Isabel escaped to the Coach house. Even when she knew Ricardo was studying, it gave her an enormous sense of security to know that somehow he was near. She could savour the luxury of being completely alone knowing that he might suddenly appear. Sometimes he would sit under the plane trees, with his books. Whenever she looked up, she would find him watching her as she swam. If she were very early, she would swim as quietly as possible, her eyes trained on his bedroom window, anticipating the moment when he opened the shutters. They spent many afternoons together by the pool. Isabel would shrug herself into the long towel dressing gown she had found in the changing room and knew to be his and curl up in a chair under the palm trees. Her chin cupped in her hand, she hung on his every word. Later when she was alone, she would replay every conversation in her mind over and over again. And when they swam together, she could feel her heart muscle tighten so that she could hardly breath and she would have to swim very quickly and seldom alongside him, so that he wouldn't see the longing in her eyes.

    These were the happiest days she had ever known – days that were entirely different from the early, exciting and sometimes awe-inspiring holidays spent at Val Negra. Now, instead of being propelled forward in the wake of a destiny determined by her parents' death, she felt in a small measure, in control of her own. She was full of hope, the never-ending promise of what could be and what was possible. She felt cocooned by the walled gardens, the band of sea, her history and their shared blood. When Ricardo waved in greeting or put aside his books to listen to her, she felt really wanted for the first time in her life and the feeling was intoxicating. She did not dare analyse too much. She was painfully aware of the difference in their ages. She was careful not to bore him and she could not help wondering why he should spend any time with her at all. And yet, surely she could not have mistaken the warmth in his voice when they talked, the casual way in which he touched her arm in order to emphasise a point? After so many years of feeling inadequate and lonely, Ricardo made her feel secure. And she wanted nothing to change.

"They're over!"

Isabel looked up from her book to see Ricardo's elated face. She had never seen him look so unreservedly happy. Any emotion he showed was always chased by a margin of wariness as though he were constantly holding himself in check. Isabel dropped her book on the stone patio.

"I'm so glad for you."

"No more studying," he smiled. "While for you it is only the beginning."

"Yes but for me studying goes hand in hand with freedom and I long for mine!" She stretched. "You have no idea how much."

Ricardo pulled up a deck chair so that they sat, sunken, together. Isabel's feet reached for the edging of grass fanning it with her toes. He offered her a cigarette but she declined.

"You know I don't smoke. I tried it once."

"I forget you're so young. Everyone in Spain smokes. How long will your course at Oxford be?"

"Four years including a year out because I'm 'reading' languages. I have to spend that year abroad somewhere. I can't wait. For the first time in my life I even find Mialma stifling. I never used to. I used to long to come to Spain. It's the one thing that kept me going."

She looked up at the open shutters of Ricardo's window and the tiny turrets of the top floor.

"But now, I feel restless. I want to be able to do what I want, *when* I want. I want to live alone without the backdrop of talk and commentary, without people knowing my every move. Without being constantly reminded that I'm English, and above all without being interrogated on the state of my soul!"

Ricardo drew on his cigarette. "The grandparents aren't used to having young people around the house. You've been away for a while now. It takes time to adjust. Even my sisters haven't visited as much recently. They're all growing up. Things are changing. When Miguel and I were small, Lupe went everywhere with us. Our relationship with Avis was much more formal. The very fact that you live abroad invariably means that when you visit, you see much more of Avis than we ever did. I never got to know them as you have. Be patient. It's only a few more months and then you'll be away studying. You'll have your freedom." Ricardo paused. "Why are you smiling?"

Isabel shook her head, still damp from her last swim. Her skin was tanned and Ricardo could see the swell of her breasts bound by the white towelling of the robe she never seemed to take off.

"I remember the first time I met all of you. You and Miguel were always slouching off for a smoke or trying to pinch cigarettes off Tito."

"And you gave the old trouts in the village something to talk about by wearing shorts in church!"

"I didn't have anything else. The Gibraltarian nun – the one I told you about from Laundry – made them for me. They were awful! I felt so out of place. Your sisters were always so beautifully dressed. I so longed to be like them. When I was little, I would have done anything to change places. I wanted to BE them."

"And now you've got everything we could ever want."

"Have I?"

"Oxford. A chance to escape all this." He gestured to the house waving his cigarette so it streamed smoke.

"And yet 'this' as you put it, is all I ever wanted. It would have made me happy."

"I rather doubt it. You're too intelligent to be content with this alone. At some stage you would have wanted more and then you'd have come up against Tito and HIS wishes and that's when the fun begins. The Coach House, our funny little world here, was never enough for me."

"But now, at last you're doing what you want, aren't you?"

"A little later than planned," he sighed. "But yes, at last, I am. But there's still so much more that I want, that I need to achieve. Gaining my law degree is only the beginning." He inhaled shortly. "And yet look at the rest of us –" he continued. "Miguel's a basket case, Sigi thinks she's Marilyn Monroe, Marta's on the brink of marriage because- well because and B, in a move that must surely indicate the ultimate negation of self, has decided to enter a convent."

Isabel laughed. "Wait! You've lost me! What did you mean about Marilyn Monroe?"

Ricardo grimaced. "It's not actually that funny.' He looked at her his expression sombre. "A lot has been happening here recently," he said. "And most of it to Sigi. I wish I could pinpoint the moment when she changed, not that there probably was one specific moment. It's been an accumulation of things. The truth is, Sigi has been unwell for some time and no one noticed or if we did we were too selfish to draw attention to it and away from ourselves."

Isabel felt suddenly cold.

"What do you mean by unwell?" she asked in a small voice. Ricardo was silent for a few minutes as if thinking how much he should tell her.

"Sigi has always been wild," he said. "She's always shown a special kind of enthusiasm for life and that's what makes her such fun to be with. But last summer she was completely out of control. The Spanish keep late hours as you know. Everyone goes out all night and there's nothing at all unusual about coming home in time for breakfast. But Sigi was out every night. Sometimes she didn't come back until the evening and then only to change before going out again. Isabel, I know she was taking drugs."

His voice trailed. She heard the sharp intake of breath as he drew on his cigarette. "Of course the parents haven't a clue what's going on, which even in our household is quite an achievement. Then again I suppose Tito's away half the time and Nuria still thinks she's a character in a Cervantes novel but there are other things that they should know. It's been pretty stressful hiding it from them. I've been studying so it's really Marta and Bea who've had to cope with it all."

"What else is there?" said Isabel, trying not to remember a certain Christmas Eve, when she had found Sigi, a sodden, druggy mess lying on the ground in front of the Cathedral.

Ricardo frowned and his face was dark with controlled anger.

"Sigi not only takes drugs," he said spitting out the words. "But she's been seen in the *Barrio Chino* with Carlos Nadal. One of the reasons she's up all night is that she travels into Barcelona with that odious man. I know he's supplying her and I suspect he's sleeping with her. The sad thing is that she's lost touch with the people that really care about her while she hangs out with pimps and drug dealers."

"My God," breathed Isabel her head spinning with his news. "I can't believe it. But why are you keeping this from your parents? Maybe Nuria needs to be shaken out of her fantasy world. Maybe you should tell Tito. I know he's not easy to talk to but-"

Ricardo threw away his cigarette.

"You don't understand," he said abruptly. "Carlos Nadal is a very clever man. He's using Sigi just as he's always used the rest of us. It's very simple. If we don't evict the gypsies then he won't go to the papers with the sordid little story about my sister."

"And this is just the kind of scandal that would prevent Tito from becoming ambassador," finished Isabel.

"And more than that," said Ricardo. "This is the first time that a Catalan has been appointed to such a position. It's significant for us. Whether you actually like Tito or not, it's irrelevant."

"How Nadal must hate us," she said softly. "Oh poor Sigi. She probably knows what this will do to us all. How can you go from this – " she again motioned to the house, "to – to the *barrio Chino*?"

"This house has a lot to answer for," said Ricardo grimly.

Isabel pulled her knees to her chin.

"Avia said Sigi was engaged to the Montfalco boy. Is that not true then?"

"Oh it's true enough."

"I don't know how you're keeping it all going!" said Isabel in admiration.

"I don't know how Sigi is!" replied Ricardo with something of a smile. "It could be quite funny. God knows what she tells Rodrigo when she disappears to Barcelona."

"Perhaps he knows."

Ricardo looked at her sharply.

"God I hope not."

Isabel touched his shoulder.

"Why didn't she tell me?" she said. "Why has this happened? How do you explain it?"

Ricardo shrugged. "*Quien sabe...* perhaps it's as a result of having a father who never loved her and made sure she understood that he didn't. And as for Nuria ... well Nuria was so busy in her Cervantes fantasy that she had no time for reality. Our parents buried us alive in this house in winter and smuggled us out to Val Negra in summer. Why else do people do crazy things? For attention! I'm sure that Sigi feels more loved in the *barrio chino* than she ever did here. But she'd be wrong. The only thing, people in the *barrio* love, is money. They think she's a *pija*. Once she can't pay her way though, she won't be nearly as popular. You won't be able to help, if that's what you're thinking. You'll be sucked in."

"But she's so young. So beautiful."

"Yes."

Isabel stared miserably at her toes.

"How could I have not known? I'm almost afraid to ask. Tell me about the others. What about Marta?"

"Ah my lovely sister Marta ..." Ricardo closed his eyes, his face tilted to the sun, a sardonic smile playing on his lips. He stretched his legs in front of him, kicking off his shoes. "Marta is beautiful and intelligent and she's engaged to Fernando Bazan. I like Fer, we grew up together but he's the first and only boyfriend Marta's ever had. I think she should see something of the world before settling down. Still she's old enough. They want to marry next month in Val Negra."

Isabel raised her eyebrows. "Isn't that a bit soon?"

Ricardo held her gaze.

"Yes."

"Oh. Oh I see."

"So that's Marta. She's already lived her future. She spent years fiddling about and was only just beginning to sort herself out. I thought she might have gone back to studying."

"She still might."

"Maybe. But it's a wasted place now. Of all my sisters, she's the one I thought wanted more than domestic bliss. She used to talk of what she would do, of what she was capable of. I'm disappointed for her."

There was a long silence.

"Aren't you going to ask about Beatrice?" said Ricardo cheerfully.

"I don't think I dare. I hoped you'd forgotten about her."

"How could I? In some ways what *she* has done is the most spectacular. Especially coming from a little mouse like her." Ricardo stretched, stifling a yawn. "Bea, it has to be said, was never very bright but what she's done now is bloody moronic. She's as beautiful as her sisters and just as wilful."

Isabel made a gesture.

"Y?"

"And nothing. Bea has decided that she wants to be a nun and what Bea wants, Bea usually gets. However this time, even Tito is a little reluctant to indulge his second to favourite child. Because Bea does not wish to be any old nun! Oh no, no, no! Bea wants to enter the Carmelites!"

Isabel twisted in her chair. "Not the mute ones over the road? I thought they were all dead or something."

"So did we. And they're not called mutes, *querida*. At least call them by their proper name. They belong to what is known as a *closed* order. I rather like the term myself. But you can imagine Tito's rage! As pious and devout as he wants us all to be, it is quite another thing to have his favourite daughter wanting to lock herself away forever. Of course he blames Nuria and Avia too for our friendship with the nuns. He now says it was absurd that we should have ever heard mass there at all, given the fact that we have our own chapel, that we should never accepted their gifts, had our clothes made etc. etc and that we should never have been encouraged to visit there in the first place!"

"I remember. It was quite an adventure. Scorpion Lupe would send us up with the laundry and mending."

"There's more. It turns out that Bea hasn't been going to school for the past six months after all. She's spent every day, *in silence* with Sor Carmen. *In silence?* What were they thinking? She always had that irritating way of repeating words, do you remember? Generally I think most people talk too much but if there's one thing, Bea needed to do was to practise talking, not stop. And she's hardly any better at writing. She wrote Nuria a letter that was riddled with spelling mistakes and was half Catalan, half Spanish. Talk about the ramblings of a half-hearted mind! Still if you've been sitting in that gloomy, dank hall for six months, contemplating that hideous cross of theirs, I suppose it's a miracle she's not stark raving mad."

Ricardo ran a hand threw his hair.

"And you?" said Isabel hardly knowing whether to laugh or cry. "What about you? How do you see yourself in all this?"

"How else?" said Ricardo impatiently. "I'm as sick and perverted as the rest of them. You talk about coincidences. Do you think it's a coincidence that we ALL have problems? I can just about accept that Miguel was unhinged by the Sahara. And Sigi ... well it happens, as they say, in the best of families, but that we should *all* be so flawed? Now do you envy us so much? All you see is the superficial trappings - the clothes you keep harping on about – beautiful houses. It doesn't mean anything if people aren't happy. It was all a cover up for the misery underneath. I can tell you one thing. I *never* want children!"

Isabel felt sudden tears prick her eyes. There was no disguising the force of his feeling. A frown was etched across his forehead - his eyes were narrow, dark, impenetrable. But far from feeling closer to her because of it, Isabel sensed he was angry at having revealed so much to her in the first place. She could sense him emotionally withdrawing from her and the easy confidence between them was broken. He collected his cigarettes and lighter from the small table beside him thrusting them in his trouser pocket. He threw a remaining cigarette butt with a final, violent gesture into the bushes. Somehow, without their knowing, they had drifted into forbidden territory and she was to go no further. It was not *her* suffering, Ricardo made that clear. Isabel got up suddenly from the deck chair and ran down the steps to the fruit orchard. She so wanted to comfort him but somehow Ricardo made her feel inconsequential. Even the experience of her father's death seemed little to go on given the complexity of these family problems.

She ran towards Mialma seeking its serene, peaceful gardens and the shade of a courtyard. Water trickled from fountains and the stone was cold to the touch. Isabel leant with her back against a pillar, closing her eyes, instantly soothed by the sound of water and the feel of sunlight on her face. The palms of her hands lay flat against uneven mosaics. This was not the way she remembered things. She had been aware, of course, of many frictions. There were things that she did not always understand but in her mind's eye it was all still perfect. Her own dreams were built on images of a past she needed to be alive and complete. With his revelations, Ricardo had somehow cast a shadow over it all. For he was hinting at life within the Coach house that was far harsher than any she might have imagined. Isabel's heart began to race. What exactly did she know of any of it? After all she spent most of the time with her grandmother at Mialma and then in the summer they were all at Val Negra. Perhaps she had got it all wrong. But if it was somehow wrong, if her memory was not justified, how then was she to explain a life long obsession? It would be hollow comfort to follow her memories, to be healed by them, as she had been so often in the past, if they were not true.

Her memories of Spain focused on hot summers and beautiful children playing happily in the sunlight – children who played *caracoles* on the terrace at Val Negra and who shaped the Queen of the River out of straw and a dry leaf. Those friendly, familiar yet ephemeral images had accompanied her on many a solitary journey. They had been with her in the stillness of a frosty dawn, in the warmth of a summer's evening. Somehow they had always been close to comfort and draw near. While other things in her life changed, they were unaltered. But without them where would she be? More importantly *what* would she be? Her psyche was composed largely of a pattern and sequence in which she also played a part. When she looked back to that time, Isabel saw herself as one of those ghost children.

In that picture she too was one of the cousins, never an outsider, but one who merged completely with the family. And she belonged to that family and was heeled and comforted by it. She drew her strength and ambition from its unity.

But now it was a tremendous shock to realize just how fragile this cobweb, whimsical family had been. It had been no more constant and much more fickle than her nightly dreams. By recounting what he had, Ricardo had severed her ghostly friendships, misshaping them forever in her past. They were flawed, she saw that now, flawed by their suffering and by a mental anguish she knew, with regret but with intense relief, she did not possess.

Isabel heard foot steps and Ricardo call her name and as he drew closer she shrank into the shadows. She gasped as she felt his hand clasp her outstretched arm.

"I could see you very clearly even if you think you're hiding," he said gently. "Look your shadow is huge on the stone." He pulled her around the column till she stood in front of him. He was right, her shadow looked like a giraffe's. She felt his breath on the nape of her neck. Gently he lifted her chin wiping her tears, smoothing her cheek.

"Lo siento," he said.

"Por que? No es culpo tuo. What for? It's not your fault. You don't have to be sorry."

He hugged her. "Well I am, for spoiling the illusion. I wish I could tell you I was happy here. But there's no use pretending. I just don't want you to be deceived by all this. It's not perfect."

"But Mialma is." Isabel spread her arms as if embracing the courtyard with its roman arches, trickling fountains and the heady scent of gardenia. She closed her eyes. "Mialma is."

She felt his hands hold hers.

"All right," he said softly. "Mialma is."

Isabel opened her mouth to speak but Ricardo touched her lips with his fingers. "No, we've said enough. We – I'm supposed to be celebrating. Let's go out. There's a bar on the way to Tibidabo, at the foot of the climb. I need a drink and although you're too young and I shouldn't be encouraging you, I think you could do with one too. We can go there."

Isabel raised tearful eyes. "But wouldn't you rather be with your friends? Surely you –"

Ricardo put his hands on her bare shoulders, allowing himself the dubious pleasure of feeling her soft and naked skin. "I want you to come with me," he said seriously. "But you're going to have to change. For once you're going to have to change out of my dressing gown."

Isabel blushed. So he knew! But what she didn't tell him was that by wearing his robe she imagined his towelling arms wrapped around her.

"Don't tell me," he said, "you've got nothing to wear!"

"I haven't. And I don't want to go back to Avia's. If I do, she won't let me out again. They'll be so much cross examining it'll take forever."

Ricardo considered this. "Ok, we'll send Doris. Hopefully she'll do a better job than last time. You can borrow something of Sigi's. Marta locks her cupboards to stop the others pinching things so I'm afraid you won't have much luck there. Sigi is closest in age anyway although I shudder to think what she's wearing these days."

"But won't she mind?" protested Isabel, secretly delighted at the prospect of seeing her cousin's clothes.

"Probably."

Isabel followed Ricardo across the courtyard, into the dark cool house their feet barely sounding on the marble floors. The huge oil paintings hanging from every available space were just as menacing as she remembered. The house was quiet with a morbid expectancy, the shutters tightly closed to keep the rooms cool. Consequently the tapestries on the walls had lost little colour over the years. The red and gold fought for victory with the intrepid light seeping through the cedar screens. Isabel paused at the foot of the steps. It was strange to know a house so well and yet not to have really been part of it. Ricardo put a reassuring hand on her shoulder as if sensing her reluctance to go up.

"You know where the girls' rooms are," he said. "I'll change too and I'll wait for you outside."

Isabel nodded and opened the door to her cousins' apartments. Her cousins shared a large sitting room but they all had their own bedrooms and bathrooms and dressing rooms. All rooms led on to a large, deep balcony shrouded by pink saponaria, its green leaves long and pointed, pretty against the cream stone. She threw open the balcony doors feeling the sea breeze on her skin. Almost reluctantly, Isabel turned her attention to Sigi's cupboard. This was immaculately stacked with every conceivable article of clothing. It was just as Isabel expected it to be. There were exquisite linen blouses, stacks of trousers neatly folded, divided according to colour, new looking shoes kept in shape by velvet shoe trees and silk dresses which swirled in the breeze when she took them off the rail. Isabel caught her breath. She felt like a child in a sweet shop. She felt as if she were stealing. She ran her fingers hesitantly over the materials, feeling the weight of luxurious fabric. She was riddled with doubt. She had never borrowed anything from her cousins before, not even the odd t-shirt. Ricardo had told her to take what she wanted. The thought of Ricardo decided her and she chose an ankle length cream silk dress slit to the thigh. She ran a comb through her hair and bit her lips to give them colour as she had often seen Kate do before a dance. With a final glance at the cupboard, she went onto the balcony.

Ricardo was below her, by the swimming pool. He had showered and his hair was still damp. It made him seem more approachable – more vulnerable. She waved as he looked up. As he approached she could see he was frowning.

"Is something the matter?" she asked puzzled as he drew nearer. Framed as she was by the saponaria flowers and wearing Sigi's dress, she had never looked more beautiful. Her skin, smooth and tanned gleamed and her green eyes sparkled with happiness. The thin silk clung to her thigh, her throat was smooth, inviting.

"It – it fits you, " he said clearing his voice. He didn't want to say she looked stunning, that she was more desirable than any woman he had ever known, that he wanted to forget she was his cousin, that she was only sixteen, that all he could do was stop himself from taking her against that wall and crushing her with his strength, obliterating everything but his need for her. And yet her crest fallen face revealed she had expected more of a compliment. But he couldn't help it. He couldn't encourage her in any way. It was difficult enough as it was.

He patted his pockets, searching for cigarettes. He shouldn't be seeing so much of her. It was wrong for both of them. And yet he enjoyed her company. She relaxed him. She was so much more intelligent than the other girls he had met who lived at home with their mamas thinking only of getting married. These were women who did nothing but have their hair done, shop and socialize. Their fathers bought them cars and paid for their clothes. If they worked at all, it was at some fashionable gallery or boutique where their presence was nothing more than symbolic. These were not girls who had to work for a living and when they married, their weddings were large, lavish and spectacular. Their fathers paid for their first ultramodern apartment in which to set up home. These were girls for whom politics meant Real Madrid beating Barca at football and culture meant nightclubs and shopping. Isabel was a bolt of fresh air. She made him feel starved of female company – the right female company. He had forgotten how much he enjoyed being with a clever woman. She revitalised him – made him forget the years of suffering both physically and mentally, dared him to hope in a future.

"Should you smoke so much?" Isabel's voice was crisp.

"What? Oh that. It makes no difference."

Isabel turned on her heel shutting the doors behind her. Within seconds she had joined him outside the house.

"Did you have wild parties here when you were younger?" she asked as they pulled out of the drive. Ricardo made a face.

"No, I thought not."

"We had each other," he explained as he nosed the car onto the road. "That's the problem with large families, your parents don't think you need other children. But of course you do. We never saw anyone outside the family. Tito was always so manic about order and routine. He didn't want to have anyone at home who wasn't family. He's never enjoyed socializing unless of course it's political. I think he should have stayed in the seminary, not that he'd have made a particularly sympathetic priest. But I don't think he should have married and had children. He just isn't a family man. Children especially make him feel frustrated because, despite his efforts he cannot wholly control them. They're like weeds growing wild in an otherwise ordered garden. I don't think that fundamentally he's a bad person, just a very spoilt one. You've seen Abuelita. She dotes on him. He was always allowed to do exactly as he pleased." Ricardo paused. "Why do we always end up talking about my –our family?" he said quietly.

Isabel leant back in the car. The lights on the dashboard lit up in the sudden darkness. She felt perfectly safe. She could sit here forever with him, locked in this moment of time with no future, no past. There were times when she felt too innocent. All she knew of life was the convent. Did he think her very unsophisticated? He was probably disappointed by her dullness. She didn't even smoke. She bet Sonia de Cana smoked. She touched his arm.

"Probably because it's so completely insane. We could talk about it forever and never get bored. Oh all right," she agreed seeing his face. "No more talk of family. We could pretend that we don't know each other at all!"

Christ not that, thought Ricardo. *Family is safer*. He glanced down at her. The slit in her skirt revealed a long tanned thigh. His jaw was taut. Isabel traced his cheek with the tip of her finger.

"Don't do that!" Ricardo spoke sharply and Isabel withdrew, stung by the expression on his face. They had reached the cafe at the foot of Tibidabo and now Ricardo swung the car into a parking bay under the trees.

"I'm sorry," Isabel said jumping out, avoiding his eyes and hurrying ahead.

"Isabel!" Ricardo caught her arm pulling her back into a pool of shadow. She caught her breath, almost stumbled.

"Ricardo," she said scarcely above a whisper. "I –" But no words came.

She watched as his eyes scanned her face caressing her lips, her nose. And suddenly his hands were in her hair pulling her roughly, crushing her mouth with his. She struggled to free her arms and then they were round his neck responding hungrily to his. She pressed every muscle in her body to his, feeling herself sink with the swirling motion in the pit of her belly. She did not care that there were voices and people drinking at tables close to where they stood. She was oblivious to everything but the all-consuming fire in her body. She felt him hot against the thin silk of her dress, felt the steely strength of his arms and thighs as they imprisoned her under the trees. In the shadow and protecting darkness, his mouth moved endlessly, more insistently over hers. Inexperienced, her hands felt hesitantly pushing his neck to her, her cheek against the tangle of hair at his chest. His hands slipped through the wide gaps between the buttons on her dress. Isabel arched her back and groaned a muffled moan as Ricardo's hand flew to silence her. And then he stopped abruptly so that she fell against the tree grazing her back.

"Christ," he said his breath ragged. "I'm sorry."

"Why? I don't want you to stop," she said shakily. "Ricardo I –"

"No don't say it," he said running his hands through his hair. He leant over as if he'd been winded. "I'll take you home."

Isabel caught his hands. For a moment he held her tightly.

"This shouldn't have happened. You've got to forget that it happened."

"Why? I won't. I can't. I want you Ricardo. I want you to make love to me. Please. Why not? I don't understand."

Her face was flushed with desire, the lips red and full. It took every discipline in his body to stop him from crushing her to him.

"I'm too old. And you! You are definitely too young. We're cousins. There can be no future. And I have reached the stage where I would want a future. I've messed about too much in the past and it doesn't bring happiness. And in our family … do I have to go on?"

Isabel's eyes filled with tears but he did not dare touch her. *"Pero te quiero."*

Ricardo looked away. "I love you too," he said quietly and truthfully. *"Yo tambien te quiero."*

*

Isabel sat in miserable silence on the way back. Her head was spinning and not as a result of too much drink. Ricardo had thought better of more than one gin and tonic each especially as the measures poured by Spanish bar men were about four times that of their English equivalent. And at the same time she felt as if everything were happening in slow motion.

Later, she would recall every detail of the evening – the faded patch of blue on Ricardo's jeans, the way his hair grew above a broad forehead, the gesture of his hands as they beckoned to her when he spoke. The gin had saved her, given her a rush of joviality that hid her anguish, her desire. Ricardo hardly spoke to her in the car. His jaw was set in a determined line and his gestures were overly precise. She wished she had not told him she loved him. She was mortified at her frankness. She sat huddled in the car suddenly tired. Ricardo rounded the corner of Mialama, the car screeching to a halt.

"Que Diablos esta pasando aqui!" He exclaimed staring at the illuminated house. Every shutter was flung open. The gate was unlocked, maids scurried to and fro unloading the cars parked in the inner courtyard. In the ensuing commotion, their arrival went unnoticed.

"I'd skip home while you can," said Ricardo gently. "It looks like Tito's back although I can't imagine why. Not only Tito, " he added observing the number of people he could see through the open window assembling in the hall way, "but the entire population of Val Negra. Not the grandparents however. So now would be a good time. You won't have been missed."

He touched the air above her shoulder. She tried to catch his hand and then froze. The easiness between them had gone, replaced with tension and wariness. No gesture, she feared from now on, would go undetected. Without another word he turned away. Avia's house was also open so that Isabel entered, slipping past the painting of the girl with the parasol and went straight to her bedroom. She sat for a few moments in the dark, her heart pounding. Suddenly there were voices. Pepita burst into her room switching on the lights.

"So you've been here all the time! Why didn't you come? Your grandmother has been asking for you. What a time for this to happen! What excitement! What fear! Everyone wonders what will happen next. Your uncle has arrived from Val Negra. No one could get through to the house. We went over several times but the Senorito Ricardo was not at home. El Senor Conde has been trying all evening to get the British news but there is interference, as with the Asturian miners strike in the '60's. You won't remember, you were a child, but the only news came from the BBC. But this time it is a fact. Franco is dead. The English news will not say different."

Afterwards, Isabel was guiltily relieved that such a momentous event occurred when it did. She was able to hide behind the bustle and activity. She was in turmoil and no one paid her the slightest attention. Her grandparents didn't sleep that night. Avi spent the evening glued to his radio, interrupted only by Pepita who brought him flasks of camomile tea and *bizcocho*. From time to time, he issued bulletins, to correct and stem, within their community, the flood of speculation and gossip that had already begun to circulate. There was a steady flow of visitors to the house which kept Avia occupied in the kitchen, ensuring there were enough refreshments. Sor Carmen, hungry for news, released B and summoned Dr. Mantua who wrote it all down and passed sheets of typed papers through the turnstile.

Isabel sat in a corner of the drawing room, ignored by the family, yet at the same time finding comfort in being surrounded by so many people. Catalan voices droned in the background as Isabel slipped in and out of sleep. Even plans for Marta's impending marriage were eclipsed by the politics of the day. The Bazan brothers appeared briefly, the eldest ever salacious of his bride's health. Marta, pale and overcome with morning sickness, languished on a sofa until her mother scolded her for not going home to bed. In the morning, Tito left for Switzerland on the pretext of mountain climbing but the family knew full well he had business with his banks. Over the years, Tito's trips to Switzerland were a source of much amusement. Clandestine and protective of his business affairs, he often told his friends that he was on 'an excursion' abroad. Sometimes the maids were told to simply say that he was 'away'. *Esta fuera* was the information given out and then the whole of Barcelona knew that Tito was in Zurich.

Meanwhile, on a mission of her own, Avia dispatched Pepita and Nuria's girls to buy sugar.

"As a precaution," she said in answer to Isabel's enquiring look.

"She's always thinking about food," hissed Bea. "It's in case there's trouble. In the event that food is rationed. Avia can never forget the war."

"And sugar is the most prized commodity?"

"Absolutely."

"But there isn't going to be rationing," said Isabel scornfully. "Adolfo Suarez has assured us that the transition to democracy will be a peaceful one. Spain will be a constitutional monarchy, just as we have hoped and prayed it will. All this melodrama is misplaced."

"Says the *espanola-inglesa*," said Miguel showing a glimmer of his former self. He sat with his sisters flicking through photo albums, waiting as they all did, for news – for some indication as to what they should do next. Isabel, glancing at the photos, smiled as much at the sight of herself as a child encased in a spectacularly unbecoming swimsuit as to be still considered an outsider.

"I do say. Franco spent too long grooming Juan Carlos as his successor for him not to be King now. He will succeed. It will work."

"*Y para Cataluna?*"

"*Tambien.*"

It seemed in the days that followed, that Franco's death could not have occurred at a more auspicious moment. There was now no reason to prevent Marta's marriage from being brought forward. Except that a constant state of nausea was making even the simplest plan difficult. But that was something Nuria refused to think about. Marta would simply have to pull herself together. The sooner her daughter was married the better. The air of political uncertainty was pumped for all it was worth. It was thought that holding the wedding in Val Negra would be more discrete. (This from Tito who lamented his leader's death noisily and acutely and was all for postponing it indefinitely.) A quiet service was thought most appropriate for the neighbouring families of Val Negra. Nuria felt certain that no one would notice the slight swell of Marta's belly and for once the gossiping ladies had other and more engaging matters with which to occupy themselves. To pledge loyalty to the new King or not, *that* was the overriding question. So while Tito grieved and plotted his financial and political situation and Avi collated BBC information, Nuria and Avia endeavoured to execute the wedding as quietly and discreetly as possible. Dr.Mantua was engaged, wedding clothes were purchased and barely one week after the Caudillo's death, the two families set off once more in convoy for the hills and Val Negra.

Isabel had not seen Ricardo since the night Franco died. It seemed easier to refer to that evening in that way. By doing so it glossed over the agony of Ricardo's silence, his lack of communication. They had resumed their relationship of old, in that they were back on nodding terms. At mass, he nodded in her direction, he nodded in greeting should she come into the house and he nodded when he came to sit down at the table. But that was all. He seemed unable to look her in the eye. She wished fervently that Ricardo had not kissed her. That she had not responded. Otherwise they would be chatting and joking now, or discussing the repercussions that a change of government would bring. As Ricardo was soon to be employed by one of Spain's largest banking corporations, Isabel knew that he would feel the brunt of Franco's legacy. Instead, they elaborately ignored each other, going to extreme lengths to avoid coming into contact with one another. Or rather Ricardo ignored her. Her eyes pleaded for acknowledgement, a word of kindness, anything to make sense of his coldness. But there was none. If she were already seated in a room that he entered, he left it immediately on some pretext or other. Even at mealtimes, he made certain that he was finished by the time she sat down.

It was only in the library at Val Negra, that Isabel could be certain of being left alone. She wondered if it was used much any more. She doubted that Sigi even knew of its existence. She had spent hours there as a child, delighting in its utter quiet and its beautiful, age worn books. It was wonderfully gloomy, neglected even, not at all like the library at Mialama that was all light and comfortable sofas and tranquil watercolours. The Val Negra library was atmospheric and dark with casement windows high off the floor and steep window seats that could be climbed up and into. The books were leather bound, some torn and eaten by mildew. Most of them were in German and Catalan. There were very few in English, except for the obvious classics. One side of the room was devoted entirely to equine matters a subject that Isabel was not remotely interested in. It was a room that could devour the reader. A room that was difficult to leave. Isabel spirits sank. It was also draughty.

Ricardo's indifference was almost more than she could bear. He had awakened an imagined longing in her only to leave her unfulfilled, poised for flight. She had never been in love before. Never been kissed before and now she yearned for him. She could feel the taste of his mouth on hers and the strength of his fingers as they pulled her to him. She could feel the pulse at his neck under her hands as she brought his head down to hers and his breath on her cheek. Her knees went weak as she remembered the way his thighs had crushed hers and the heat of his body as he searched.

All the talk of weddings did little to lift Isabel's mood. As usual, she had nothing to wear. While her cousins were outfitted in dresses which, while no longer matching, were nonetheless as ravishing as the ones they had worn as children, it had not occurred to anyone that Isabel might also need something to wear. She had no money of her own to speak of. At least not enough to buy a dress with and yet pride prevented her from asking her grandmother to help her. On the odd occasion when she almost had, Avia had seemed so preoccupied that it seemed excessively vain to mention the subject. But she knew the difference that pretty clothes made. Ricardo had liked Sigi's cream dress. Now she wanted him to notice her again. And there was another reason. Sonia De Cana was bound to be at the wedding too. Isabel wanted to shine. Isabel wanted to be as beautiful and elegant as her rival. She wanted Ricardo, if faced with a choice, to choose her.

As the day of the wedding drew near and the possibility, now that they were all installed in Val Negra, of buying anything grew more remote, Isabel became increasingly depressed. There seemed nothing to look forward to. She would return to England and Oxford. The summer, which had seemed to stretch before her, wonderfully vibrant and new, was all but over. Isabel seemed to have fallen into her childhood role of following her cousins around, trying not to be a nuisance or get in anyone's way, of gradually becoming invisible.

Avia and Nuria were quick to lose their temper. Marta was constantly sick and the strain of hiding her condition from Tito was beginning tell. Even the news that Ricardo had passed his law exams made little impact on the women, consumed as they were by the unfolding drama. The library was cold enough to warrant a fire, but the grate was swept clean, empty of kindling and logs. And it was summer. They didn't light fires in the summer. Unseasonal rain splashed, unrelenting, against the window panes. The days seemed never ending, turning hours into years. Without the sun to entertain them for at least part of the day, time weighed heavily. Isabel had out grown the club and the small village cinema showed only one film a month. Isabel for the first time in her life felt suffocated and bored and boredom made her listless. Lupe, who was not deceived for a moment by Mata's nausea and the indecent haste with which the wedding had been arranged, grumbled and scolded and had to be confined to the upper regions of the house least her careless tongue give the game away. And most disappointing of all, was the lack of rapport Isabel seemed to have with Sigi. Sigi, beautiful, and aloof, spent her days chain smoking and waiting for the phone to ring. When the phone call came, she would disappear upstairs to do her face and within seconds of the sound of mangled gravel, she would be outside, seated pillion on Montfalco's motorbike.

"Well maybe one of your daughters will marry well, Condesa," grumbled Lupe loudly and unhelpfully as day after day, Nuria watched her daughter waft down the stairs and out the door and glue herself to the Count's back.

"It's a disgrace sitting like that! Legs akimbo! Like the something she is not."

"Like the something she is," muttered Lupe.

"That's enough!"

Nuria's voice cracked with weariness and concern. Her head ached all the time. Her problems whirled round and round even at night, even in her dreams. She had developed a nervous twitch and lines etched her once beautiful eyes.

"Talk to her!" suggested Avia.

"How can I? I never see her except as she gets on that – thing and when I confront her she doesn't listen. I suppose we can comfort ourselves with the knowledge that we know his family."

Lupe snorted. "We know as you put it, the Bazan boys and Marta still managed to get pregnant! Fat lot of good it did knowing the family. Count or no Count they're all the same. He wants Sigismunda all right, but he won't marry her."

"That's enough!" All Nuria and Avia all but screamed in unison.

Isabel closed her eyes and leant against the library wall, her hands finding the cold stone behind her. Count Rodrigo de Montfalco was indeed a most desirable "catch." Intelligent, wealthy and famously good looking, his family had only recently (as in the last twenty years) moved to Barcelona and so was considered a little 'new' to the Val Negra set. He was staggeringly tall, over six foot with dark swarthy looks and a strength that rippled through the muscles of his lean limbs. But he was gentle and kind and nothing of the playboy his looks implied. Best of all he seemed genuinely fond of Sigi. But her cousin had become so distant and secretive Isabel could get nothing out of her. Ricardo's claims that she had grown into a wild, troubled teenager seemed completely unfounded. Sigi seemed perfectly happy to be herself and didn't appear to have any of the personality disorders that Ricardo suggested. But then again Isabel never saw her.

They didn't chat as they used to. There was an inexplicable estrangement between them which saddened Isabel. While the girls still shared their old room with its brass beds and the little birdcage in the corner, Sigi came home when Isabel was asleep. If that is, she came home at all and when she did, Isabel was up and dressed and ready for breakfast. It seemed that Isabel was losing the two people she cared about most. Marta was totally preoccupied with her impending marriage and Bea, with God.

Isabel's head ached. The sky seemed permanently black and often the house was plunged into darkness as a result of power failure. Isabel went out on to the porch that led from the library, escaping the arguing voices inside. Rain dripped systematically over small, scented flowers, dispersing a heady scent. It was the only good thing that seemed to have come out of so much rain, this and the wonderful scent of Eucalyptus. Gallica roses tumbled over the banisters, a crisper white because of the rain, their petals scattered over the drenched steps of the loggia. The garden in Val Negra was greatly neglected. It was permitted to run wild and this appealed to Isabel - there was a wantonness about the place. She sank against the wall, shaded from the rain. She had often waited here as a child, waiting for her cousins to finish their lessons.

"*Has estado llorando.*" It was a statement. "You've been crying."

Isabel sat upright, in the half-light, dazed. She must have fallen asleep and now it was dark. Ricardo stood above her frowning, arms crossed.

"I didn't realize," she said wearily. Her face was pale and there were shadows under her eyes. She looked so miserable he longed to take her in his arms and away from the house.

"So have you got your dress organised? It seems there's little else my sisters can talk about. Never mind the fact that Franco has died and we're entering a whole new political phase of our history. Clothes are evidently more important." He hoped his tone was light. He wasn't in the mood for any more histrionics. He still had Lupe's latest scolding ringing in his ears.

"I'm sure the indomitable English style will prevail," said Isabel. "Perhaps I'll opt for those navy shorts that caused such a stir all those years ago."

Ricardo's eyes narrowed. "Good idea. I have to say I'm not much in the mood for a wedding."

"No."

"Too much has been happening." Isabel dropped her eyes. She felt it inappropriate to bemoan the fact she had nothing to wear, when, as Ricardo pointed out, their country was in the flux of such change.

"Incredible ..." continued Ricardo, "Franco's death has ended nearly forty years of dictatorship. The whole face of Catalan politics could change! We might at last become significant players."

"If that is, you hold out for autonomy. And certainly Jordi Pujol can be relied upon as head of the Catalan assembly."

Ricardo glanced at her. "My clever Isabel. Yes. You're right, Pujol has been promoting home rule for the past few years. We have a unified movement, lead for once, by an intelligent and affluent president. At last there can be change – "

Isabel saw Ricardo's face, his moving lips and all she could think about was the fact that Sonia de Cana would be at the wedding and that she, Isabel, had nothing to wear. Ricardo could think what he liked but at this moment the clothes issue *was* more important than Franco's death.

"You seem miles away," said Ricardo. Isabel blinked.

"They say Franco died clutching the mummified arm of St. Teresa of Avila - the one who is supposed to have written that poem, you know the one Nuria is always reciting."

Ricardo laughed and then was serious. "You mean, *No me mueve, mi Dios para qurerete, e cielo que me tienes prometido?* Perhaps that's because even old Franco had doubts at the end as to what he had accomplished. Conceited bastard. What ever made you think about that?"

"I don't know. It just struck me as weird. And please don't say that it's my heathen-English side coming out! When I read that bit about Franco, I just couldn't help thinking that I'd rather be holding someone's hand –you know – when they're **alive,** not some skeleton. Ugh!"

Ricardo smiled and moved to sit on the surrounding patio wall. "Why aren't you with my sisters talking weddings?" He lit a cigarette inhaling deeply.

She shrugged. She felt very small and alone. Ricardo talked as if nothing had happened between them. And if this was the way things were going to be then why hadn't he spoken to her sooner? Why ignore her so obviously? Why did he decide to speak to her now?

"As you said before, not really in the mood. I've never been to a wedding though," she added. "I suppose there will be lots of Val Negra people."

"Yes."

"Friends you might not have seen for ages?"

"That tends to happen at family weddings."

"Cousins and. things."

"Mmmn ..."

There was a movement in the shadows. The burnt end of his cigarette, like a glow-worm, leapt about in the air.

"Isabel," he said very quietly. "What are you trying to say?"

"Sonia de Cana," blurted Isabel.

"Oh God, not her again. What about her?"

Isabel took a huge breath. "She will be there tomorrow. Won't she?"

"I really don't know. I can't get a lot of sense out of any of the females in my family. If you want to get anything meaningful out of anyone you have to go through Scorpion Lupe and somehow just now I'd rather not. But I expect so. Ah ... I see now."

"If Sonia were free would you choose her again? Well, would you?"

"Isabel!" His voice though low was firm. "That's enough! Sonia is married as you very well know."

"Why don't you want to talk about her?" Isabel couldn't stop herself. "You must still love her."

Ricardo was so still that in the darkness she was suddenly frightened that she had gone too far. Ricardo had always had an ability to fade out – to self-obliterate. He could sit in the midst of quarrelling and commotion and remain aloof. He hated confrontation. If something displeased him he withdrew mentally, the shutters came down. He had confided much. He had always been intensely private. If he chose to talk about himself it was to release bits of information he felt able to share. He usually countered probing with humour or sarcasm. Now, she was afraid she had gone too far. With his silence came recognition. What was she doing here? She was no longer a child in need of a home for half-term or the summer? She was grown up. Grown *away* from this family. Miguel was right. Try as she might to be accepted, in their eyes she would always be the *inglesita*.

Anyway Ricardo didn't love her. One kiss didn't constitute love. Or did it? All she knew was that she had always loved him. But surely, secretly, he must still love Sonia, as she would always love him. How could she have expected otherwise? Carried away by one kiss, she had seen a future stretch before she had never dared dream of and for the space of that kiss everything had seemed possible. Now in the dark, reality glared. Maybe this was what love was all about? A kiss and then you suffered. She knew that she was little more than a child. Ricardo must be thinking of his career. They might not see each other for years. Her heart sank. How she wished she were more like her friend Kate. Kate would never allow herself to get so sentimental. Like Ricardo, she was capable of turning a situation to her advantage. Kate wouldn't have put herself through this masochism. *Why can't I just do what I want, what I really feel. Why this reserve? This constraint, this suffocating reserve that binds me to my inner self. Why can't I just go over to him and kiss him? Why don't I suggest we go for a drink? Why am I not fun to be with? So, amusing that he never wants to leave me, never again hesitates in the dark, or is still as he is now...*

"Of course I love her," said Ricardo suddenly, his words brisk, efficient. "She's entirely tied up with my past, with growing up in Val Negra. I can no sooner divorce her from that than I could Miguel or the girls. But she's part of that time. And it's over. And as I grow older the past seems to belong to another person. I view it as I would a film that is strangely familiar and yet devoid of emotion. As to the other question," he smiled gently. "I can't answer it. Right now I'm concentrating on my job and having a working life for once. It's long since overdue."

He stubbed out his cigarette with his heal and leaned down to kiss her cheek. "I've got to go."

She lifted her face and he touched her shoulder, his fingers lingering. "*Cousin,*" he whispered.

He had never in all their childhood ever called her that in English and it was more sexually charged with emotion than any endearment could have been. She caught her breath, her stomach suffocating in her throat, her hands clammy, her eyes swimming. She was suffused with unbearable longing and yet stifled by the exterior her. She touched his arm.

"Where?" her voice croaked.

"Drinks... made plans with some friends." His eyes were inscrutable, impassive. *Stop him* a voice from within her said, *He'll be gone in a moment. He'll be gone. Then after the wedding you'll be leaving and you won't see him for ages. When will be the next time? But maybe he doesn't want you. He could have suggested you go too. You think you're smarter than you really are, more attractive? But there are so many pretty girls. But blood is stronger. We are linked. We are linked.*

His fingers caressed the nape of her neck and then roughly pulled her up so that she moaned half with pain and fell against him.

"Christ Isabel," he said between clenched teeth. "What are you doing to me?"

She caught her breath, a strangled sound. Her heart exploded all around her. His mouth found hers bruising her lips and she responded, pouring all the feeling and words she dared not speak into this response. Her arms wrapped round his neck and on tiptoe she shaped her body to his, her breasts thrust forward, desire blinding and desperate. The strands of her hair fell over his hands and arms and he bent her back as though sucking her life's blood. At last he gave in to his lust, not rejecting her to protect himself but turning so that her back was to the wall, he wrapped himself around her his tongue searching, finding, his fingers between her legs, her thighs. His strong arms supported her as she fell limply giving herself to the darkness and his burning mouth. But still he caressed her till she was panting pulling his head, arching.

"I want you, I want you, I want you," she whispered. Somewhere footsteps sounded and a door slammed. Ricardo's fingers pinched her thigh so that she cried out. His hand covered her mouth instantaneously.

"Sh!" he said fiercely. He paused, pulling her body to his once more and then he froze.

"God," he said, his voice ragged.

"Don't stop," Isabel whispered shakily, trembling. "Please."

"What am I doing?" He closed his eyes, the muscle in his cheek clenching. Gently but firmly he buttoned her blouse, smoothed her hair. "I can't do this, not to you," he said firmly looking away and lighting cigarette. He inhaled so deeply Isabel thought he would choke.

"Why not?" she said shakily. She heard her grandmother's voice calling her. Isabel closed her eyes. "I love you," she said calmly. "I've always been in love with you."

"It's not right," he said wearily. "You've got your whole life in front of you. It shouldn't begin like this. I know you're fond of me but you'll meet someone else. You've got to want all the things that other girls want - children and a home. At least you should have the opportunity of wanting them. I don't want to take advantage of you. You're so vulnerable, so innocent. Anyway, amongst other things, I have a habit so I am told, of messing people up."

"What are you talking about?" replied Isabel miserably. "I – " she took a step forward but as if to protect himself, as if not trusting himself again, Ricardo moved to open the veranda door.

"I'm sorry," she said her fingers shaking she smoothed her clothes. "It was my fault. It's coming back here. I don't feel myself. It won't happen again."

"Isabel!" Avia's voice sounded closer than ever. Isabel winced.

"Go!" hissed Ricardo. "The kitchen door is still open. I know because I had a run in with Lupe."

Isabel's eyes were wide with alarm. "Lupe? Thanks a lot."

Ricardo's mouth twitched. "Well Lupe will be easier to face than Avia." He shrugged. "Take your pick. You can stay with me --"

He moved towards her as Avia's footsteps stopped behind the door. "Or …"

But Isabel had fled.

Chapter 20

Isabel
Val Negra
Summer 1976

It was raining when Isabel woke the next morning and the sky was grey and bleak. In the corridor, water dripped from a leak in the ceiling into large tin buckets. Isabel felt light headed through lack of sleep. Words, criss-crossing through her self-conscious were only partially distinct from the reality of the morning. She wished she were anywhere but in Val Negra and had it not been Marta's wedding day, she would have hotfooted it back to the city and on to a plane England. The tall Cyprus trees swung precariously in the wind, too near the house and the slates on the verandas squealed with protest at the weight of over hanging branches. Isabel felt utterly forlorn and rejected. Injured pride had replaced desire. She was convinced that Ricardo did not love her or at least not in the same way that she loved him. There had been a moment when he was tempted and for a moment she felt that she really mattered but only for a moment.

The breakfast table was a scene of chaos and hysteria. Lupe, who had not stopped protesting the marriage since Marta's engagement was announced, was more quarrelsome than ever while Avia, affecting an uncharacteristically pompous attitude, did her best to extol the virtues of married life. The accompanying giggles only added fuel to Avia's tirade.

"I have told you – especially those who come into contact with foreigners," she said directing a penetrating look in Isabel's direction as she slipped into an empty chair at the far end of the table. *"Sobre todo no intentes lo que tiene que ser reservado para el matrimonio solo."* Above all, do not attempt that which should be reserved for marriage alone …

Isabel blushed and reached for the hot chocolate. In honour of Marta's wedding, *coca* had been ordered but it lay, in large oblong slabs, untouched by the nervous women.

"It is God's law and a right your husbands have sole mastery over."

"Sounds obscure," hissed Sigi who had only just come home and was in a particularly buoyant mood. Isabel shot her suspicious looks from time to time but Sigi only smiled at her sweetly.

"Escolteu Nenas!" scolded Nuria for once supporting her mother, too distraught to do otherwise. "Listen to your grandmother who is older and wiser than all of us."

Avia was well into her stride. She sat bolt upright, hands clasped in her lap. She looked at some point in the middle distance above her granddaughters' heads. She paused for effect.

"You must be obedient and good wives," she said in her clear, soft voice that belied the steeliness of her determination. "Be dutiful and comforting. Try never to show your unhappiness or displeasure. Always smile and be gay."

More snickers as Marta kicked Isabel under the table and threw merry smiles at Scorpion Lupe who looked as if she could happily strangle the lot of them. Isabel winced.

"Make your homes a happy place," continued Avia warming to her subject. "If you want to do something that your husband doesn't, then it's your place to give in but I want you to give in *gracefully*." She shot Nuria a calculating look but didn't wait for her daughter to respond. "There's no merit in do something you don't want to if you make life miserable for everyone afterwards. And don't think I wasn't just as headstrong as Sigi in my youth." Sigi's eyes flashed but she managed a nice enough smile. "But later you won't even remember what the arguments were about but you will have remained married and that is important. Stay together. Work at your marriages. I want you all to lead useful and pleasant lives. It becomes increasingly difficult in this age of high technology and self-obsession to learn to hold back and to think of others. Of course you can achieve happiness but only with hard work and understanding. I learned the hard way. I only want you to take the short cut to happiness."

"Que santa!" breathed Sigi, her eyes still flashing.

Lupe, overhearing, made a swiping gesture with her broom. Sigi ducked. "Anyway," she added in a loud whisper, "Marta gave in all right and look where it got her!"

Isabel sipped her chocolate studiously. *Oh to be anywhere but here! Anywhere in the world!* There was a lull in the squabbling only for it to be renewed in earnest when Lupe suggested that Marta had put on weight since the last fitting of her wedding dress. Marta and Nuria burst into tears, Avia scolded Lupe, who promptly dropped the tray she was carrying and declared that she would not work any more that day and Tito, entering the room at this point and taking stock of the state of things, lost his temper so successfully, that within minutes everyone was either shouting or crying or both.

It was a seemingly endless day. Although it was a little warmer, the house was still damp. It was grey and tense, full of unwelcome shadows – a summer place caught out of season. The maids made every attempt to dry out the rooms and chase the smell of damp from the hall. Isabel wandered aimlessly from room to room. She was too lethargic to go for a walk, too restless to nap but anxious to avoid her cousins. There was not even the pleasure of something new or nice to wear for the evening. She dreaded the performance to come – all that forced gaiety. The evening would begin with a nuptial mass, cocktails, a long dinner and dance to be rounded off with a wedding breakfast of chocolate and *churros* at anytime between six and seven the following morning! However, given Franco's death, perhaps things would be more subdued. Isabel had no intention of staying up all night and planned to slip away at the first opportunity. And there was all the commentary! Many of the guests would come for the food alone and to get a good look at the house and what people were wearing. And of course they'd want to know all about Isabel.

"And the poor little Isabel?" She could imagine the voices saying. "Did she have a good time? Don't you know which one she is? Why she's the little orphan girl from England, yes that plump little thing with the white skin? *La has visto? Su vestido? Mas boba ella.* Her skin so *Blanquilla! Mas blanda* que *mantiquilla. Pero dulce, dulce y bueno como el pan.* She stands out for her skin alone, have you ever seen skin so white? She never sees the sun, that one. Poor little *Inglesita*, she had skin that's whiter than butter."

Isabel knew these people too well. It was better to be hated than pitied. She groaned inwardly. It would be awful. In the past, at this sort of event, Miguel had been her salvation. He could be counted on to be rebellious, wild and amusing and he always asked her to dance. At family gatherings, he shielded her from the glittering entrance that her cousins never failed to make, with their beautiful clothes and lively wit. But Miguel was changed forever. If he spoke at all now, it was in simple sentences and often he was oblivious to his surroundings. Sometimes there were cobweb movements of his former self, a flicker in his eyes, an understood smile.

That left only Benito Bazan. Remembering how they had got along in the past, Isabel brightened a little. With the thought of him in mind she ventured out of her room. There was an unconvincing silence about the house as if at any moment, doors might open and all hell break loose. Isabel tiptoed down the stairs just in time to see Avia and Dr. Mantua emerge from the library. Isabel bolted back up the stairs hoping she had not been seen. She opened the door of the first room to hand, momentarily disorientated. The room was in total darkness except for light coming from its balcony. She fumbled for the light switch but the familiar groove in the wood's architrave was missing. And then to her horror she realised that she had entered the wrong bedroom and worse still, that she was not alone. On the balcony, under a clear moon that cast a trail of stars along its surface, a girl's face was transfixed with pleasure. It hung like a smaller reflection against the drooping branches of wisteria. Sigismunda lolled against the stone balustrade, her eyes closed, mouth parted, panting loudly. Her beautiful dress was slashed to the waist, the fragile silk, creased and stained. Above her a man's body held her impaled among the ancient statues that decorated the parapet. Isabel froze.

"Rodrigo, Rodrigo!" she heard her cousin cry. For a moment Isabel was rooted to the spot, certain that the whole house had also heard Sigi but nothing happened. Isabel didn't hesitate a moment longer but turned on her feel and ran.

Back in the safety of her own bedroom Isabel struggled to control her ragged breathing as relief flooded over her. She switched on the light and sank on to her bed. But instead of being cushioned by a soft eiderdown, she felt something hard and angular. She sat up twisting round. And there on the bed beside her was a long white cardboard box tied with an enormous taffeta ribbon. She looked at it in astonishment. The box was a present in itself but how had it got there and who was it from? More importantly, who was it for? Isabel pulled it towards her. She felt all over the box. If this was a gift then it was the very first she'd ever received and she it wanted to enjoy every bit of it. Her heart skipped a beat. Nestling in the folds of ribbon was a small blue envelope with her name printed neatly on the front. She slit open the envelope with trembling fingers and took out a thick cream card edged with gold.

It was written in a formal, flowery Spanish that Isabel recognized immediately. The first lines were from Cervantes' novel, "*La espanola inglesa*" and they read as follows:

"Hermosa Isabela, tu valor, tu mucha virtud y gran hermosura me tienen como me ves.

I hope this will be better than the navy shorts. *Un beso* Ricardo."

Isabel read the words over and over before placing it to one side. My beauty? She thought to herself, my integrity have captivated him! Carefully she untied the beautiful bow making sure to roll it up for safekeeping afterwards. And then she lifted the lid. There were layers and layers of tissue paper - so many pieces in fact that Isabel wondered if it were all an elaborate con and that the box was really empty. Losing patience, she threw handfuls of the stuff onto the floor and shook the box upside down. And there, fluttering onto a bed of paper slipped a sheath of green silk. Isabel leant down to gather up the material that was pumped up by yet more tissue paper. She shook out an exquisitely simple mint green silk dress holding it up against her. It clung to her hips, perfectly shaped to fan out along the floor. Spaghetti thin straps held up the low cut front and back. The material slipped easily through her fingers rippling in a sea of changing colour.

Isabel could have wept with joy and suddenly the evening ahead was full of promise. She spun round and round with the dress in her arms. Then hearing one of the many clocks begin to strike she began to panic. She'd had all afternoon to get ready and now there was just time for a quick shower. Laying the dress gently on the bed she kicked open the bathroom door and began to pull off her clothes. She washed her hair quickly but there wouldn't be time to dry it properly. But that didn't matter. Nothing mattered now that she had this lovely new dress to wear and that Ricardo had given it to her with his love. With his love ... She closed her eyes allowing the hot water to splash down her face. She felt fresh and invigorated when only a little while before her melancholy and the cold seemed to have penetrated her very bones. She grabbed a towel drying herself roughly. As she slipped her feet into flat ballerina pumps, her only shoes, her spirits soared. She wanted to throw back her head and scream her happiness. She wanted to skip and dance. Isabel stepped in to the dress pulling it carefully over her shoulders. It fitted perfectly. It fitted as if it had been made for her, skimming her hips just as it should, clinging to her thigh and falling to the floor in gentle folds. Tiny, covered buttons did up under her arm. She twirled so that the skirt moved away from her body and then sank and billowed as she walked towards the mirror. The colour brought out the green of her eyes and lit her skin. She liked what she saw and she hoped that Ricardo would too. Glancing at her reflection one last time, she slipped quietly from the room.

The house was very quiet and the first floor corridors dimly lit. She held her dress carefully as she descended the narrow spiral staircase noticing as if for the first time how each step was inlaid with different wood and how the stone banister at the bottom was carved with opulent flowers and fruit. How many times had she and Sigi sprinted up these stairs without noticing their exquisite craftsmanship? But then tonight Isabel was seeing everything in a new gorgeous light. She had quite forgotten the image of leaking ceilings in draughty vestibules. Isabel even hesitated on the huge landing that led on to the main staircase, the medieval staircase - the staircase that in order to preserve the ancient oak was only used on occasions such as this. Below her in the great hall, flames fluttered from silver candelabras and from torches suspended along the beams. Huge bunches of roses and ivy spilled from urns and the staircase itself was draped in garlands of gardenia. The scent was overwhelming and Isabel stood there transfixed. The cousins were gathered at the foot of the stairs waiting for the bride. Refracted light was trapped along the glittering surfaces of polished wood and gold. Mirrors reflected inlaid marble and semiprecious stone. Even the detumescent paintings seemed to gleam with extraordinary life.

Isabel felt as though *she* were the bride. Her blood seemed to sing through her veins. She was elated yet terrified by the reaction her appearance would cause. But whatever happened, it would not go unnoticed. She, for once, would not go unnoticed. Tito and Dr. Mantua who were in deep conversation, looked up as she floated down the stairs, their mouths falling open. Faces that from above had seemed clear and recognizable, now merged with the suits of armour, the tattered banners, the ropes and tassels of other campaigns. Bloody battles had been fought and won on this very place. De Roble blood had been shed here and in foreign lands in the name of unimaginable causes and yet no challenge was more real to Isabel than the one she now faced. She saw Ricardo emerge from darkness, as remote and expressionless as the portraits of their ancestors, his starched white collar mirroring the ruffles of the men above him. His face, like theirs had the same inscrutable tenacity, the same nose and mouth. His clothes as theirs did, blended perfectly with an opaque background. Only his skin, darker, than theirs could ever be, hinted at the life within. In the pool of candlelight, there was a glimmer as his onyx cufflinks caught the light. Their eyes met briefly, hers leaping with excitement while his remained unmoved. There was a collective intake of breath then a silence. No one moved. No one, for a moment seemed able to speak. Isabel was suddenly frightened. Perhaps she was a Cinderella who was not meant to go to the ball after all. She searched their faces. Sigi's in particular was strange, almost mad with an emotion that had nothing whatsoever to do with jealousy. Tito's for once was stunned and even Dr. Mantua seemed to have lost his habitual cool. Only Bea, in her new nun's habit, found her voice.

"Isabel, *carino*, you look lovely, lovelier than I would ever have thought possible. You've quite taken our breath away. We'd none of us noticed you before. You've grown up! I think you are in danger of stealing the show! Let's have a proper look at you before Marta arrives! Gives us a twirl. The dress does something wonderful when you walk."

"Never mind that, Bea," said Sigi suspiciously. "I'd like to know what's going on. You can't just change like this overnight! It's just not possible. Something's happened without any of us knowing. I think Isabel has a secret. I think she's in love."

"Well *you* would know," retorted Bea.

Sigi made a face, but it was clear she was puzzling something in her mind. "And that dress ... where on earth did you get such a thing? It looks like it cost a small fortune. It looks very like the latest catwalk. It looks exactly like Chan – "

"A present," cut in Isabel joyfully. "I don't think I've really ever had one before. Not a proper one and nothing like this. Isn't it glorious?"

"I don't know about glorious but it fits you – better than that actually. Is it couture? You sly thing! And it's not any old present is it? Besides it's not just the dress," insisted Sigi. "It's everything about you. You've lost weight! You don't wear glasses, or braces. You're *tall!* You've got long hair! I just don't understand it. It's just not possible to change like that."

Sigi began poking and prodding, twirling Isabel this way and that.

"What *is* possible," interrupted Dr. Mantua gently, "is that you just didn't notice. None of us did. I think Isabel has been changing over some time but we've all been too busy to notice. I must say it is a very welcome surprise. You look very beautiful my dear," he finished gallantly looking at Isabel.

Isabel blushed, bobbing him a curtsey.

"I still think we haven't heard the whole story," said Sigi. "There's more to this than meets the eye," she added darkly in English.

"Oh give it a rest," said Baby Bea. "Anyway here comes the bride!"

And indeed there was Marta poised for a moment on the smooth polished landing beneath the candlelight and roses in a cloud of Brussels lace. Her black hair was pinned in a simple chignon and held in place by the Roble tiara. The Bazan 'scorpion'- a huge diamond broach which was loaned to Bazan brides on their wedding day- sparkled at her breast. Hands by her side, she waited as was the Spanish custom, for the best man to present her with her flowers. Miguel kissed her cheek and handed her a bouquet of gardenias. On his arm, she came down the stairs, ghostlike beneath the stained banners and relics of the past.

She turned to Isabel.

"I wondered what all the commotion was about. I thought Miguel here had done something silly like pick a bunch of weeds or die the flowers purple!"

"I'm sorry," said Isabel "I didn't mean to –"

"Don't apologise for your beauty," said Marta burying her face in her flowers. "I'm glad that you are so lovely, at last!"

"And I hope you'll be very happy," said Isabel thinking how trite the words sounded and then added lamely. "You deserve to be."

"Do you think so?" Marta was suddenly serious. "Sometimes I wonder. Sometimes I think that I'm only getting married in order to escape from Tito and even I know that that's not reason enough. Sometimes I think I brought the whole thing on myself that somehow, subconsciously – "

Isabel touched her arm.

"You don't have to justify anything," she said. "Besides it's no good looking back now. The main thing is that you love Fernando. You *do* love Fernando?"

Marta looked away.

"That's the joke of it," she said, a catch in her voice. "I know Nuria hoped I'd marry some exotic creature - not that Fernando isn't exotic – but I mean someone *other* than a Val Negra man. But the truth is that I've only ever wanted to be with Fernando. I love my life with him and I love Val Negra. All the things that I know Ricardo hates about this place are the very things that make me feel secure. Fernando and I think alike. We *are* alike and we know what to expect of the other. He looks after me, and no, before you start *analysing* what I'm saying, he's not a father figure! Besides he's too young and far too childish himself. The truth is that I've loved him all my life. I can't imagine a world in which he did not exist."

Isabel felt the tears prick her eyes.

"Then I'm so happy."

"Didn't you think I loved him?" Marta said genuinely surprised. "You of all people should know me by now."

"Yes," said Isabel. "I should. I suppose I'm beginning to realise that I don't really know any of you. I've kept everyone petrified in a past that never really existed and I've been afraid to let go, to accept everyone for what they really are."

"We're just as guilty of that. Look at you!" Marta glanced down at Isabel's dress, her eyes flicking over her hair and skin. "I nearly fainted with shock when I saw you, really saw you. We, none of us, notice the things that are staring us in the face. I didn't notice Fernando, not for a long time, I mean not in that way. But he was always ... there."

"I'll miss you."

"It's time to move on. We can't live in our father's house forever. You've never had to break away. I mean," she said quickly, "you had a bit of a head start. But it's not easy to leave. It's one thing to talk about being independent and telling Tito to go to hell and quite another to actually do it especially when he's the one with the money and none of us girls have had much education. I think Tito likes the fact that we're so dependent on him because that way we'll never leave." She sighed. "Well now I shall be free of it all and I'm going to make up for it. It's a tremendous release, you know, to be free of Tito. I only wish I'd had the courage to leave sooner." She kissed Isabel, the faintest trace of lips brushing her cheek. "You do look lovely Isabel," she added. "Bea is right. We never noticed. I'm sorry for that and for the fact that we weren't always as kind as we should've been. I don't know what happened to us here. I hope we won't be self-absorbed and inward looking. Today we start again. You'll see, from now on things really will be different."

Isabel was conscious, as she walked into the chapel, of hundreds of tiny candles winking from every corner and of the many pairs of eyes reflected in them. For the first time in her life she walked down the aisle with her head held high, gloriously aware of the gasps of surprise. For the first time she did not shrink beside her cousin Miguel, nor hide behind Benito Bazan or wait till it was almost too late, to slip into a pew from a side entrance. She walked down the aisle alone, her beautiful dress sweeping the carpet, brushing against the garlands of flowers that were tied to the pews. The altar was ablaze with candles that illuminated the frescos behind and the plates of gold and silver. Huge bunches of wild roses teetered above statues of the saints and fat satin ribbons hung from the chandelier. Isabel genuflected before her place feeling every pair of eyes bore into her back. But instead of the usual snicker there were audible sighs and she could all but feel the women crane their necks to get a better look at her.

She could hear the rustle of voices indistinguishable from the movement of silk – echoes of: *"Sera ella? No puede ser? Hija de Clara verdad? La que vive en Ingleterra. Se llama Isabel verdad? Verdad? Verdad?"*

Voices spread like Chinese whispers. Isabel bowed her head, partly to hide her smile and flaming cheeks, partly to gather strength. She felt as if the whole village knew her secret, as though it were written boldly on her face. Her mind was alive, excited, she could hardly formulate a prayer. Her feet were ready to take flight, her whole being floated above this place.

Someone was playing the organ, the slow, haunting hymn – *Rosa de abril* – a *Catalan* hymn, being played for the first time in public in nearly forty years. The voices were triumphant, jubilant. This was not only the celebration of a marriage but of a victory. The air was drenched with the perfume of Tuber Roses. Everything around Isabel seemed exaggerated - the colours were more vibrant, the music that much sweeter. Ricardo loved her! He had said as much. Cervantes words spoke of love: "Beautiful Isabel, your virtue and your honour have moved me …" He cared enough for her to give her this dress! Whatever else he might say, his action sang of love.

In the pew in front, Avia and Bea huddled together in prayer, the shape of her grandmother's high comb and mantilla throwing a strange elongation upon the wall. There was a sudden rustling of papers, the click of fans. Isabel turned to see a whirling blur of red satin and a shawl's fringe that hit her in the eye. Sigi threw herself down beside her so that Isabel was squished into a corner the voluminous skirts of her dress covering her own.

"Sorry," she said as Isabel dabbed her smarting eye.

"You've changed your clothes."

"I didn't like the other dress. And seeing that you'd made such an effort …" Sigi's full red lips pouted perfectly. Her hair was piled in huge curls on top of her head and an enormous comb only served to accentuate her height. A black lace mantilla fell dramatically over her shoulders and her dress was cut so low Isabel wondered how she managed not to fall out of it completely. Magnificent diamonds glittering at her throat only drew the eye downwards. Sigi might have stepped out of an El Greco painting. She looked the epitome of a Spanish lady – albeit a rather daring one. She opened and closed a large fan, hiding Isabel entirely from the congregation.

This was one time however, when Isabel wanted to be seen. She realized as a matter of fact that she was the only lady not wearing the traditional Spanish comb.

"Are you hot?" she asked incredulously pushing Sigi's fan away from her face.

"Of course not," retorted Sigi flicking it back. "But it's such a pretty thing isn't it? Did you know that there's a language of fans?" Her eyes darted around the chapel looking, Isabel knew, for her lover. "Avia always said that you could tell a lady because she could speak with fans."

"Is that what you're doing?"

"No. I was trying to talk to God but there are so many distractions. It's impossible to pray at family gatherings and then the locals always make one feel so self-conscious."

Sigi made a final and elaborate movement, tossing her head. She sat back, spreading her skirt so that Isabel had to sit sideways on her seat. She felt like a chlorophyll deficient stem, to her cousin's resplendent poppy.

"I think I know who your admirer is," said Sigi. "I mean you don't have to be too clever to work it out. If my mind hadn't been on other things, I'd have noticed him years ago. I haven't worked out where he got the dress from though. Unless of course it wasn't a surprise at all and that you were fitted for it. I'm surprised he would know about such things. But still, he's a clever man."

"Oh?"

"Oh don't go all doe-eyed with me, Isa dear. It's me, you're talking to, remember. Still I have to admire your guts. I don't think even I would be quite as daring. But then I'm very happy with my – "

"Just say it Sigi."

A lady behind them coughed.

"I'll tell you later," she whispered.

"You'll tell me now."

Sigi made a face in the direction of the altar. Isabel blinked.

"What? Dr. Mantua?"

Sigi nodded. "He says you look just like your mother. I heard him tell Ricardo when you came down the stairs. Gave them all a shock I can tell you. Scorpion Lupe said it was like seeing a ghost. A rather *green* one."

"Thanks Sigi."

"Apparently he had a thing for her, I mean for Clara your mother. That's what Nadal – well that's what they say in the village. It's why she ran away so suddenly and was NEVER SEEN AGAIN." Sigi hissed the last words menacingly. "Maybe, Pelham wasn't your father after all."

"Don't call him Pelham," said Isabel shakily. "Don't do this now."

"Well it's possible ..."

"Anything is possible. But it's not the truth and not very logical. I wouldn't be in love with my own *father!*"

Isabel was surprised at her own calm but she wanted nothing to spoil this day for her. She would not think about Julian. And then thankfully, just as her cousin drew breath for more, Rodrigo entered the church flanked by Miguel and Ricardo.

"Oh I love that man," she declared passionately.

So do I, thought Isabel glancing in Ricardo's direction. The men were seated, as was the custom in Spanish pueblos for weddings and funerals, apart from the women on the opposite side of the aisle. But Isabel was as aware of him physically as if she'd been sitting beside him. In profile, he was as inert as the effigy of the saints on the walls around them. He was composed, unfathomable. It was impossible to read his mind, to know whether he was in any way moved by the occasion, by its social and political significance, by the cracks of coloured light fragmented in the stain glass windows. She sat equally still, but her blood raged, her soul dancing within her. Isabel wished the mass would go on forever, that she could sit forever in her green silk dress, lean forward ever so slightly, forever, so that she might see him, so that he could see her, that they might always be smothered in this scent, this candlelight.

And then in came Nuria, unescorted, slender in yards of chiffon that fell about her like a widow's weeds, her comb like a crown of thorns upon her head. Her face, a frozen mask of makeup, looked as artificial as the surrounding statues, her jagged jewellery igniting the deadness of her eyes. Afterwards, outside in the dark, it was difficult to see who everyone was. Avia seemed to have completely vanished although Isabel did not see her leave by the chapel door. Torches along the path, concentrated the light in deep rings around their base so that between them was a long channel of dark. A stormy sky once more threatened to erupt and a sharp wind whipped mantillas around women's faces so that they appeared like nightly gargoyles, their shadows twisted and strange. Only their incessant chatter hinted at the festivities just celebrated.

Isabel looked for Dr. Mantua, who like an avenging angel stood on the steps of the church shaking hands with the guests. She kissed his cheek.

"Filla meva," he greeted her. "This is indeed a happy day. A wedding, a return to the monarchy, what more could we want? We have said a mass in Catalan and sung our hymns. Glory Be to God who is surely in His heaven but what about you? There is an admirer lurking. Are you going to tell me who it is?"

Isabel blushed thinking how mortified he would be to hear Sigi's thoughts on the subject. "I think it is only that," she said. "Admiration I mean."

"Oh dear I do hope not." Dr. Mantua studied her thoughtfully. "Do you love him?"

"Oh yes."

"Does he love you?"

"I don't know. Sometimes I believe so. I dare to believe he does. But there are so many obstacles. He – I – it's not possible. Not now." Her voice dwindled.

"Ah … you Roble women," he said more to himself than to her. "It's extraordinary that you should all be the same, that with each generation comes a new, obsessive love for a man. And not always for the right man either! I had hoped the chain might be broken. I've been waiting, watching, praying. And now you, it's your turn. I wonder what will happen."

"What do you mean? About obsessive love?"

The priest looked away from her seeing beyond the dark. "First your Grandmother, then Clara and now you. They both had what the Romantics call, A Great Love - *Un Amour Fou*. Is that what yours is?"

"I have nothing to compare it with."

"I see."

They began to walk towards the house, pausing beneath each compass of light. Isabel struggled to hold her hair and her dress, Dr. Mantua his cassock, as the wind whipped them round.

"You, you're not thinking of giving up your place are you? You will still go up to Oxford, won't you?"

He hesitated and beneath the torch Isabel could see how he had aged, the skin leathery and lined, his eyes a little watery.

"Of course not," she said gently touching his arm. "It's not like that. Nothing has been said. It may not exist at all. If only in my mind."

"Oh I think it is real," he said covering her hand. "It will be. I only hope you'll be careful. It's useless giving anyone advice about anything. I've come to learn that you can spend hours counselling and then the person goes off and does precisely the reverse of what he said he would. I don't know why the old bother telling the young anything at all. But at least I'll feel better knowing that I've said my bit." He looked at her intently his hands moving to rest on her shoulders. " I know when you Roble women love it governs everything you do," he said. " I'm not underestimating that at all. But your generation has so many more opportunities than ours did. So much is better. But the most important thing of all is that you have your education and no one, no lover can take that away. Don't sacrifice that for love. Your degree may seem an ephemeral thing to you now, an abstract obstacle even but it should be everything. If this man loves you, he'll wait. Do all the things you dream of, but have your career. Youth lasts such a short time. Accomplish what you can when you are young. Afterwards ... well it is just so much harder. Everything requires more energy."

"You sound bitter," said Isabel gently.

"No, not at all. But I am at the end of my journey while you are at the beginning of yours. Try and make it a fulfilling one."

Isabel took a deep breath.

"And if it's at the risk of a great many people's unhappiness?"

He looked at her sharply.

"That's up to you. That's on *your* conscience." He dropped her shoulders, his hands disappearing inside the wide sleeves of his cassock as they walked on. He smiled kindly at her anxious expression. "But I don't believe that you will do anything to hurt us. You were not brought up without example. You have only to look at your Grandmother. She has lead a Christian life, a life of great self discipline. It may not be fashionable to be religious but you must remember its value. It won't come easily. Faith does not come easily. You must work at it, keeping open the link between this material world and the next. I know it is more difficult in this modern age of choice and liberal living but in your heart, you will know what I am talking about. I have confidence in you. You are intelligent and you have the tremendous advantage of having lived in different countries amidst diverse cultures. You have seen what it was like here under a dictatorship. Equally while your cousins have to ask their husbands permission to vote, you are free to do as you wish. Not only free, but from the moment of your birth it was your right. All this has given you a unique perspective. You think in a different language from the one you speak. That is a gift. But you must use it. Do not bury your talents, little one, use them wisely and know that you go always with God."

Isabel swallowed. "I don't know if I can live up to your ideal. You make it sound so easy when I know how impossible it is."

Dr. Mantua snorted.

"Well that wasn't my intention! And I never said it would be easy! Why is it that the young think they're the only ones to suffer, to have loved?"

Isabel smiled. *"Divino tesoro* and all that?"

"Precisely."

"You say you older people shouldn't tell us what to do, but you *are* wiser, you have lived so much, you have more experience than we do- it must make it easier. Nothing can frighten you any more."

They had reached another torch. Dr. Mantua removed his glasses, wiping them.

"The civil war taught us many things," he said. "We suffered physically of course, and we saw human nature stripped to its essential greed, its instinct for survival. We saw betrayal and love and sometimes loyalty. But for every twenty evil men there might just be one whose goodness and honour shone through and gave us courage to face the darkest times. Your grandparents were the few good men, Isabel. Ildefons never betrayed the man who hunted him every day of the civil war, a man to whom your father had never been anything but kind. And afterwards, when Franco came to power and everyone was denouncing everyone else and you were sickened by the hatred and cruelty, he still kept silent. And as for your grandmother, Mercedes hid hundreds of young people, from both sides, sharing her food with them, knowing that if she were caught she would be executed. Remember all this," said Dr. Mantua replacing his glasses and putting his arm around her lightly. "Remember their example. I don't believe you'll go wrong. Don't be so fearful of life. It's for the living. Embrace it."

They were close to the house now. Ahead of them walked Rodrigo de Montfalco and her cousin Sigismunda.

Dr. Mantua looked up sharply hearing a rustle of branches. "Embrace life," he said wryly. "But not like that. Your cousin," he added. "… will have to be careful if she means to keep her little Count."

"What do you mean?"

"The de Montfalcos do not marry the local good time girl."

"It's not like that," said Isabel stiffly. "She's not a 'good time girl' as you put it. They are very much in love."

"Then all the more reason to wait. Tell her that. Village gossip has killed more than one budding romance. And of course there's the other matter —"

They had reached the house. The wide front steps were laid with red carpet and torches blazed above the portcullis. Flares lit the path from the drawbridge to the surrounding gardens where smaller lanterns were scattered through the trees. It was romantic and magical and every bit the fairy castle awoken from a hundred year sleep. Isabel smiled to herself. If only the wedding guests could have seen it earlier with its pails of water and leaking ceilings! Isabel let the skirt of her dress fall to the carpet running a hand through her windswept hair. Waiters hovered with trays of drink as the clink of glasses and buzz of voices rushed to meet them. The priest hesitated as a plump gentleman in a tight coat held out a glass to him.

"Monsignor, a word," he said.

"We'll speak later," said Dr. Mantua.

"Yes, later." Isabel bobbed a curtsey and then remembering something called after him.

"Let him go," said Ricardo quietly.

Isabel spun on her heel delight in her eyes.

Ricardo caught his breath. "You look very beautiful," he said softly.

She flushed.

"It's the dress. It's exquisite. Everyone says so."

"No it's not the dress. Although I have to say I'm extremely pleased with my choice. It's you *cosina*, you are beautiful." He handed her a glass of champagne and watched as she took a sip. "I wish I'd known you were going to be so beautiful …"

She looked surprised. "Why, what would you have done? What could have been different?"

"I wouldn't feel I had wasted time. I want to be alone with you."

"We can be."

"Not here. Not tonight." His eyes expressionless, fell to her lips and she ran a tongue over them nervously. "There are too many people watching, Lupe for one. She watches you like a hawk although you'd probably never noticed."

"No." Isabel took another sip, then frowned remembering. "What did Dr. Mantua mean about Sigi? You heard that last bit didn't you?"

Ricardo took the glass out of her hand, his fingers lingering on hers, his breath on her face. In the crush of other guests, he had every excuse to stay close. He steered her into the ballroom where a band played local folk songs and the odd waltz.

"I've never danced with you," he said taking her hand. He held her lightly, guiding her deftly around the dance floor.

"Tell me what he meant," insisted Isabel. Ricardo spun her round so quickly she all but lost her balance. In her flat shoes, his thigh held the length of hers. She could hardly breath. She pulled his head so that he was forced to look at her and the smile was wiped from his face.

"*Te quiero,*" he said.

"Tell me."

"Why? Every conversation we have seems to revolve around my siblings. I'd much rather talk about –"

"Tell me."

Ricardo turned her so that her back was to him, his arm crossed beneath her chin, his mouth at her ear.

"I already have," he whispered. "Before. It's that same small problem she seems to have with drugs. Not so small tonight though, something tells me."

Isabel followed his gaze as Sigi whirled passed them. Her head was thrown back, her eyes half closed while her body swayed to the music. Her dress, which now hung precariously from her shoulders, exposed an entire breast. It was only her untidy hair that stopped her from appearing completely naked. Isabel wondered what had happened to the diamonds, mantilla and comb. She also seemed to be missing her shoes. She held the voluminous skirt of her red satin dress in one hand while the other caressed her long, tanned legs. She laughed very loudly especially when she collided into the other dancers. She seemed oblivious of everything but Rodrigo.

"The barefoot Condesa," said Ricardo under his breath.

"Why don't you speak to her? Do something?"

Ricardo jerked her forward so that she gasped. "Enough *cosina*," he said. "Enjoy the music."

Isabel tilted her head to look up at him and for a moment his eyes devoured her.

"Another sad Cuban tango?" she asked playfully.

"No, this is Catalan. A song about a prisoner on the eve of his execution saying good bye to all the things he has enjoyed, even his life of crime."

"And what did he do, this naughty man?"

"This naughty man as you call him stole from his wealthy employers -jewellery, from the big house."

"I bet Carlos Nadal wishes he could."

"He probably already has. Anyway he's done far more damage than lift a few trinkets. But he's one man I'd hang if I could," said Ricardo forcefully.

Isabel tightened her fingers around his.

"You really mean it."

"Yes." He tilted her chin. "Look, I won't have you being serious. Not tonight and I forbid you to talk anymore about my sisters, any of them."

"All right, " smiled Isabel. "I like this song even if it is sad. It reminds me of Miguel and of when he used to play the guitar and we'd have Cuban coffee, do you remember, wrapped in blankets, sitting outside by the river? But we were always terrified that Tito might come out and spoil the fun."

"He was good at that."

"Yes."

Ricardo's gaze was penetrating and Isabel lowered her eyes. His fingers seemed to burn through the silk at her waist. When she raised them they were narrow with desire. She took a deep breath.

"I dare you to kiss me," she said her voice so low he had to bend to hear her. "Here in front of everyone."

Ricardo caught her in his arms whirling her easily round the floor. She could smell the lime scent of his shirt. His head was bent to hers, hovering above her mouth. For one terrifying, exhilarating moment she actually thought he would kiss her, which was after all what she had asked him to do. And then suddenly as they neared his father who stood watching the dance, Ricardo stopped. He let her go, his lips brushed her hand.

"I would not insult you by doing that," he said sternly. "This is no game. I think you should dance with Tito now."

"What?" Isabel raised dazed eyes but Ricardo was smiling at his father.

"She's all yours father," he said and then she heard a mumbled something about going to find Sigismunda.

"Yes she's definitely Sigismunda tonight," said Isabel under her breath.

"Where's your mother?" Tito grimaced. "She has a lot to answer for. It's what you can expect when there's weakness in the family, a genetic flaw." He glanced at Isabel. "You on the other hand, my dear wouldn't appear to have any flaws at all. I must say you have surprised us. I could never have predicted this." He waved a hand at her dress, examining her keenly. "Come, let's dance."

Isabel, instinctively held back, grabbing a glass of champagne from a near by table. She drank half of it in one go.

"Out of respect for the *Caudillo*'s memory," she said, wincing at her own words. "Don't you think it would be better if we didn't dance?"

"But you were dancing only a moment ago – " protested Tito.

"I know but I must find Sigi too. I think it would better if I went. And I'll try and find Nuria if you like."

"Thank you." Tito spoke the words with an effort. He took a fat cigar from his pocket fingering it between his fingers. "Ah Ricardo, a word, Sir."

The tempo of the music had changed. The band began to play flamenco and the women swooped on to the dance floor with delighted cries. Isabel took another swig of champagne. The music pulsed through her body, pounding out its sensual rhythm in her head. Sigi too had rejoined the dancers. Her hair was now completely loose and there was a large tear in her skirt. All eyes were upon her as she danced the intricate steps weaving between the men twisting provocatively. Rodrigo de Montfalco stamped his expensive feet as the men began to drum their heels. Men and women danced between the tables, in the corridors and in the Great Hall. Isabel set down her glass kicking off her shoes.

"Reach for the apple!" She remembered her Flamenco teacher telling her and now she threw back her head as the other women were doing and watched her hands high in the air, surrendering herself to the beat. "Now pick the apple from the tree, take a bite out of it and throw it away!" The words went over and over in her mind as the beat and thundering heels grew louder and louder till there was nothing but the wild tempo, this thrust for life.

"Is there no end to your accomplishments," said Ricardo moving in front of her, his face skimming past as he joined the other men. They stood in an immaculate line in front of the row of women who rustled their skirts, flipping them from side to side. Isabel smiled, curling her fingers, fanning and spreading them out, still above her head.

"Or yours," she taunted. "I thought Catalans only danced *Sardanas*, such a nice country dance, where men and women hold hands primly in a circle. A dance that is nothing at all like this… one."

"I am full of surprises. But I think Franco has had the last laugh. Here we are, all Catalans together and yet we have chosen the epitome of Spanish dancing for our celebrations. He would have argued that his 'colonisation' of Spain has succeeded."

"Except that Flamenco is also regional."

"But what is more symbolic of Spain than a Flamenco dancer?"

Isabel smiled sweetly.

"You're a coward Ricardo, for leaving me with Tito like that."

The band now began to play: *Perfidio, Amor, Besame mucho* and all the other Latin American songs that were as romantic as the Flamenco was physical. Ricardo pulled her by the hand so that she fell against him.

"Yes. But not in the way you think. I'm struggling with what I know to be right and what is so obviously not."

"And what is that?" Isabel whispered. Their bodies were close, his arms wrapped round her neck as he walked her through her paces before flinging her away as the dance dictated.

"I think you're a little *boracha*," he said amused.

"Perhaps and it's wonderful." There was only the music and this moment. She could not think beyond this moment. She wanted to revel in her youth, the unknowing of it all, her sense of wonder.

"I've changed my mind," she whispered as her hips swayed against him. "I don't care what happens."

He manoeuvred her away from him, shielding her with his broad shoulders least anyone see the naked expression on her face or the pulse at her throat which made him want to take her there and then on the cold marble floor in front of the entire village of Val Negra. Instead his movements were controlled and calm.

"I want you to make love to me. I don't care about anything else. I want to live now. Let me decide. I know you think I'm too young. But I'm not. I know what I want. I can't bear to think that this might all pass us by, that the greatest passion of my life would have slipped away. I feel time is running out – our time. I don't care about the Val Negra gossips, or Tito – only you. At this moment nothing is as important. I don't want to come back here, not in ten or twenty years and only then have the courage to say what I'm saying now."

A muscle tensed in his cheek. His fingers gripped hers and then he smiled, lightly, deliberately.

"Clearly the priest's little speech made absolutely no impression on you."

"So you were eavesdropping?"

"No but I heard the bit about following Avia's Christian example."

Tears pricked her eyes.

"I'm serious Ricardo."

His fingers brushed her lips, his touch electric.

"I told you not to be."

"Oh stop teasing me! I understood what Mantua said, Ricardo, but also what he left out. I don't want to have any regrets, ever. Maybe what I want is wrong but I want to find out for myself. I want to be able to chose, to make my own mistakes."

"Well I hope to God I'm not one of them," he replied wryly. But it took her by the hand.

"Lets go down to the river. We can talk."

"I don't want to talk."

"You've definitely had too much to drink."

They emerged as if compelled towards it, onto a veranda at the back of the house. French windows draped in wisteria led onto an immense terrace. Roses spun a lover's knot along the walls. Comfrey and Toadflax sprouted through the cracks, spindly and coarsely toothed. Wicker chairs were scattered beneath branches of jasmine. Moonlight chased the clouds, in ribbons, across the sky.

"This is not the river," she murmured following him in the dark. "... *y que you me la lleve al rio creyendo que era mozuela.*"

Ricardo halted, his fingers digging into her wrist.

"And are you ... *a mozuela?*"

"Do you have to ask?" she whispered.

"No," he said hoarsely and pulled her into his arms. *"Me porte como quien soy, como un gitano legitimo.* I behaved as I should," he translated and then murmured, "which is something I can not do." His lips were in her hair. "This is all wrong but I can't fight you any longer. I've never wanted –"

His mouth crushed hers. He touched the soft skin of her throat and shoulders his tanned hands like large butterflies on the green net of her dress. He kissed her hungrily, drunk with her scent, her hair, her stillness. She seemed to him so gentle, little more than a child and he was consumed with longing and a need to protect her. The boundaries were down. He wanted to possess her, let no other man come close. She clung to him, holding him to the present. He hesitated but her fingers laced themselves behind his head pulling him closer. He held her tenderly and then his hands moved skillfully, pulling her dress to her waist, holding her head. The stone balustrade pressed against her back and her face was crushed against the rough linen of his jacket. Her body arched. But still he held back, until her hands moved his away impatient, and he smiled amused by her insistence.

"I love you."

Who had spoken?

How many times had Ricardo spoken those words obligingly to other women, knowing he did not speak the truth, knowing, they knew this. And now the knowledge that he was the first with this girl, this woman, leant him an intensity of feeling absent from other acts of lovemaking. He touched her tenderly aware of her vulnerability and innocence. Her fingers traced his mouth, trustingly.

And he understood.

Suddenly he froze and then pulled her quickly to her feet. Protected by his broad frame, she swayed but his hands gripped her arms steadying her. Slowly reality swung into place as the balcony doors opened and guests laughing and drinking, some dancing with borrowed guitars, spilled onto the terrace.

"Bring light! *Luz trai luz! Aqui estamos en oscuras!*" Tito's voice boomed as he commanded maids to ignite flares and place them the length of the veranda. Ricardo cursed but he continued to hold her wrists.

"You recover swiftly!" she said and began to tremble. He spun round to face her.

"Don't ever think – " He cleared his throat. "Are you all right?"

She nodded tossing back her hair. Suddenly he stared down at her bare feet.

"Christ!" he exclaimed. "Where are you shoes?"

"I kicked them off when I was dancing. I've no idea."

"Let's hope Avia doesn't notice or we'll be answering for something, sadly, we did not commit. You won't smoke will you?" He groped for a cigarette.

"No. But at this moment I wish I did."

"Ricardo, *hijo mio.*" Tito's beaming face identified his son in the crowd.

"Mierda," muttered Ricardo. "He really does know how to spoil things. He's not usually this happy to see me. I thought we'd had our little chat."

Tito bore down on them his smile enormous. A light film of sweat coated his forehead and upper lip. He wouldn't have noticed Isabel's bare feet anyway. At the forefront of his mind was the need to speak to Ricardo. The veranda was full now with dancing couples. Waiters squeezed through the guests attempting to pass plates of *turron* and drink. Ricardo reached for a glass of champagne placing it in Isabel's cold hands.

"Drink this," he said gently.

Below them on the lawn, despite the cold, Marta danced. Guests cheered from the veranda.

"Viva la novia! Visca Catalunya!"

Tito frowned. Instinctively Ricardo moved closer to Isabel, wishing he could take her to the river, away from the house, away from Val Negra. But instead he stood rooted to the spot, smoking his cigarette.

"Ricardo hijo mio. Isabel." Tito nodded in her direction. Isabel gripped her champagne glass.

"Ten cuidado o lo romperas." Ricardo unclenched her fingers "You'll break it."

Tito helped himself to another glass.

"Ah ... that's better! This Val Negra *cava* isn't bad at all. I might have known Avia would have some decent stuff hoarded away. It's pre-war and from an extremely good vintage. I will never understand why she doesn't capitalise on the wine making here. There's a small fortune waiting to be made." He took another sip. "However, talking of wine, de Montfalco says it's too late for cutting this year. The buds have begun to move. Perhaps an experimental grafting however, with another vine might do the trick."

He swirled the drink round his mouth, then swallowed.

"Where've you been Ricardo? One minute we were talking and the next you'd vanished. I've been looking for you everywhere – impossible to see in this damn house – couldn't find Sigismunda either. Seems she vanished along with B and Miguel. Who would have thought it could be so cold eh? Never mind, give them enough to drink and people are happy. And I suppose if you're dancing ..."

He shot Isabel a suspicious look.

"You don't seem cold though."

"I'm not."

"Always the problem with a summer place. Still Val Negra has known its days of glory."

"Some two hundred years ago!" smiled Ricardo.

Tito did not smile back.

"Not to be mocked," he said silkily. "Not to be mocked. Besides I think the time has come for a little restoration. The house is too damn cold even if it is summer and the kitchens are a disgrace. I'm amazed we have haven't all died from food poisoning. I think it's time to call in the boys from Madrid don't you?"

Isabel and Ricardo exchanged horrified looks thinking of what Madrilenian designers had done to the Coach House.

"In short," continued Tito, "the house could be made into a comfortable, all year round sort of house." He shivered, breathing out cold air. "A few more weeks will make all the difference here. The autumn is often so much warmer than late summer. It's still too early, too unpredictable with these thunderstorms from the Monseny. But then how were we to know that our dear *Caudillo* would …" Tears came to his eyes. His eyelids sank. Ricardo motioned to Isabel and she made as if to tiptoe away. Tito's eyes flew open.

"The King is to be crowned tomorrow," he said clearing his throat. " Do you not think, Isabel, that such a gesture shows little, if any respect? A certain … insensitivity?"

Isabel opened her mouth but no sound came.

Ricardo glanced at her. "I think it shows leadership," he said.

'How so?" Tito's attention turned to his son.

"Well isn't obvious?" said Ricardo impatiently. He spoke rapidly, anxious to get away and not at all in the mood to talk politics with his father. "Coming in swiftly like this doesn't give the opposition too much time to think. This way we have a leader from the start. Especially as old Don Juan must be wondering why *he* isn't on the throne instead of his son."

"I always forget about Don Juan the Pretender," murmured Isabel. "I can't help feeling sorry for him – for the man who will never be king."

"Franco always made it clear that he favoured his son, Juan Carlos," said Tito pulling out a large, immaculate linen handkerchief and blowing noisily and efficiently into it "He has been very generous in allowing the restoration of the monarchy. I bet not even your dear Avia thought that it would actually happen."

Ricardo ignored the jibe.

"Agreed," he said smoothly. "But it's important that things are settled quickly. The whole of the world is watching us, just waiting for Spain to collapse. And I can't imagine we're too popular having just executed those ETA members. It makes my head spin to think how quickly new laws are implemented here. If we're going to uphold a democracy then we're going to have to accept that you just can't kill off your opponents when you don't like what they have to say."

"But *hijo*, those ETA members, as you call them, were nothing but terrorists - *animales!*"

"And they were garrotted as animals. They were terrorists but they still had the right to a fair trial. But then I suppose fairness isn't something we've seen here for a while." And then he added absentmindedly fingering the cuff of his shirt. " I don't know where you'd go to find a lawyer who isn't corrupt. Look, I'm not defending them. Their activities were illegal. But they shouldn't have been executed. I don't believe in it. Do you?"

Tito's face was flushed, his notorious quick temper getting the better of him.

"Just listen to him!" he flared at Isabel "What does this son of Nuria really know about politics? He hasn't the faintest idea of what Franco had to do in order to keep this country together! You talk about settling things quickly – I wonder what you'll have to say when the communists take over, which they will if we're not careful. Leading a country such as ours is no picnic! Trying to drag it into the 20th century has been a Herculean task. Franco kept a lid on all the warring factions and if he had to use capital punishment as a deterrent then so much the better. I can't think of a more effective one. At least we are respected."

"Feared, Father. We are feared. Franco was feared."

Tito glanced at his son coldly.

"Well what would you know anyway? Franco was a great soldier. I – " he thumped his chest. "I too have known war. Your own twin fought for his country. And you? You preferred your books, your poetry. What did you ever do in the army except have flat feet!"

Ricardo smiled in spite of himself and despite his father's apoplectic raging. But he was irritated that once again he'd been prevented from being with Isabel. He had no desire to quarrel but Tito always stirred unpleasant memories. And those altered his mood.

"*Tiene razon padre.* You are right, Father," he said inclining his head. He took Isabel's arm turning away from Tito. "I didn't go to Africa. I didn't participate in the unfortunate Green March but what I have been is consistently loyal to my party and to Catalonia."

There was silence.

"What does that mean?" Tito's eyes were shrivelled, small and black.

"It means," said Ricardo coldly. "That at least I would have fought with Catalans. I would have fought for my family."

Tito took a step forward clenching his hands. Isabel shrank against Ricardo.

"Let's just go," she whispered but Ricardo turned back to his father.

"But what do you care Father?" he said provocatively. "Does it really matter what I think? Anyway you know my politics – or should do, if you'd ever listened to me. You know that I think the King will settle Spain's regional problems through *peaceful* negotiation - less exciting than the way Franco would have done things but legal non the less. No doubt not all the old guard will be replaced. I'm sure you'll find someone to influence. Besides which you might turn. You might even direct your energies to the King. Anything is possible."

Isabel looked in horror from one face to the other, expecting Tito to lunge at his son but to her huge relief he smiled.

"You feel happier do you, now that you've got that off your chest?"

Ricardo took a step towards his father. Isabel moved between them. She motioned to the dancers on the lawn below them.

"Now, *Tio,*" she said smoothly. "Let's not quarrel, it's Marta's wedding. This isn't the place for this kind of talk. Come on *Tio* I'll dance with you now if you like." She held out her hand to him but his next words froze her.

"This is exactly the place for what I came to say," said Tito softly ignoring Isabel and directing his words to his son. "Not to talk politics, nor to ask your opinion but to give you a message from Sonia."

"She is here?"

"You see? I knew you'd be interested."

"Why should I be?"

Tito smoothed his balding head, as though patting it down with cologne.

"Don't you think it is time your cousin married?" he said to Isabel. "I mean all this time without a girlfriend, without a *novia!*"

"Oh I've had girlfriends," replied Ricardo shortly.

"Really? That is news."

"I don't think –" began Isabel suddenly feeling extremely cold and tired and no longing finding the sparring between the men in the least bit amusing. "I don't want-"

"Don't go!" They both said at once.

"I mean, you must do as you like, of course," said Tito with a stab at good manners. "But what I have to say might be of interest to you too."

"And what would that be Father?" Ricardo's tone was weary. "Isabel is tired and – "

"And *Sonia*..." Tito barred his white teeth. There was a flash of colour from a gold filling. "...Sonia has been asking after you. What a lovely girl she is. Rather I should say, what a lovely girl she *still* is. Motherhood definitely becomes her. She has two children. Boys I believe. But unhappily, the husband is ... well the marriage is to be annulled."

"But she has children!" protested Ricardo. "I know her husband. He's a perfectly decent man. I thought they were very happy."

"I knew you'd be receptive to this." Tito smiled again, his eyes twinkling, his lips spreading from ear to ear. He lit a cigar and began to puff steadily, rocking on his feet, pacing himself and then he made a dismissive gesture.

"Actually whether Sonia was happy or not before, is entirely irrelevant. Well not entirely I suppose. Let us however, be absolutely clear as to the significance of what we are talking about, so that we can *concretar* our options. Sonia has always been an exceptional creature, that goes without saying." He let out a stream of smoke, throwing back his head to blow it away. "And as you know, her land borders ours here in Val Negra. The De Cana wine production, like that of the Bazan Brothers, is very profitable. I am told it has exceeded all expectation, that even our new King is partial to their Cava."

Isabel began to feel giddy. Her thin dress was now inadequate to keep out the biting wind. Her skin prickled and she had the surreal sensation that Tito was drawing her towards something she could not understand. At the same time, while wanting to run away, she was compelled to listen. Ricardo had ceased to be protective. He seemed alien to her – unpredictable, a keeper of many secrets. She felt alone and very cold. Her feet on the marble were frozen. She could hardly feel her toes. Tito's voice droned on and he was drawing pictures in the air.

"To the west, lies the Bazan vineyard." His cigar drew lines of smoke. "To the East, the De Cana *finca* nestles along the other side of our river. We, at Val Negra are right in the middle." He smiled triumphantly. "But the river, *both* sides, is ours. Unfortunately, we have our fair share of arid fields. But again I digress." He sniffed. "It's your interests, I have at heart, naturally. You have always mistaken my intentions. Now, given the events of the past few days I have been forced to think about the future, your future Ricardo. You could for example, work in government. With your law degree, being a Catalan, you would be the ideal person and I do, as you rightly pointed out, have contacts. You could come with me to London if you wanted. And don't worry I don't think your fanatical honesty should be a hindrance to promotion. However in all of this there is a small – " Tito drew on his tobacco, " – but significant requirement. I can only be blunt. You need a wife. You need to dispel any rumours – you know the kind I mean – the usual ones that are whispered about bachelors. The fact that you say you've had girl friends is very encouraging."

Ricardo raised his eyes to heaven and turned to go. Tito barred the way.

"I haven't finished. Pujol, who incidentally is to be the next president of our Catalan government, is a stickler in such matters. This new government must begin with a clean bill of health."

Isabel heard Ricardo's laughter, cold in the cold night air.

"You can't be serious!" And then she felt herself spinning or was it the veranda? She felt Ricardo's hand on her arm, his face anxious.

"I really must go," she whispered.

"No you will not!" Tito gripped her other arm. "I insist you meet Sonia. She is a great anglophile and adores talking English. She wants to meet you. She remembers you from your times here as a child. She knows all about you. You do know that she and this son of mine were engaged once don't you? Well why shouldn't it happen again? They know each other so well. And she has been trained in every aspect of the wine business. " The words came tumbling out as if Tito could not stop the ideas and plans that poured from him. His hand bit into her arm. Isabel felt as though she were about to be torn in two. Her eyes darted from one to the other but Tito and Ricardo were locked in some private duel of their own.

"Sonia will do for Val Negra what your grandmother has failed to," he continued. "She will make these vineyards profitable. While Ricardo brokers his policies in local government, Sonia can take care of Val Negra. It is perfect. A marriage not only of convenience but of mutual need. And the bonus of course …"

Ricardo let Isabel go abruptly.

"Don't!" he warned his father.

Their voices seemed to fade in and out. The faster they spoke, the more difficult it was for Isabel to understand what they were saying. The flamenco music was deafening and Ricardo and Tito were virtually shouting at each other. A wave of nausea washed over her, the hairs at the back of her neck were damp. She had to get away. But she could not move. The scent of gardenia was putrid. But still she could not take a step.

"The bonus would be *children.*"

There was an oasis of silence, a soundless pool of clatter and ringing in Isabel's ears. She tried to decipher the disjointed words, words that held no meaning.

"And why ... would they ... be a bonus?"

Ricardo's voice was anaemic. He moved at the same time, as if to shield Isabel.

"With Sonia at your side you could go far," persisted Tito. "The *generalitat* would be a ... useful place to work."

"But you know I start with *Spanish Country Bank* next month."

Tito ignored this.

"Married to Sonia and with children, there would be no hint of gossip. Either way. Not as a womaniser, apparently your category, nor as a fag. But the bonus, as I like to call it, the handsome return, the dividend, would be children. Children inspire stability. People like a politician to be a family man, don't you agree Isabel? Or is it different in England? Well no doubt you can discuss that with Sonia. But here, much emphasis is placed on the family. It is respected. A man, whose seed has implanted in fertile ground, has grown, been seen to flourish – this is something we Latins appreciate. You can hear it in the music, *verdad*, this pulse of life ..."

Ricardo stood so close to her that Isabel could feel his heartbeat.

"What is a man without children? How can he be a true man? It is after all the simplest function. *Therefore shall a man cleave unto his wife and they shall be one flesh.*" Tito moved away speaking very softly now, very clearly. "Their creation fulfils the purpose for which we have been put on God's earth and by the grace of God, one which we accomplish with vigour and strength. The good seed of Val Negra crossed with the gentle but sweet De Cana and Bazan is a good thing. At least this is as it should be. Only sometimes nature has a nasty, vindictive way of reacting."

Tito all but spat the words. "So Man is forced to use his cunning and a little artifice." His eyes narrowed, his lips became a thin, cruel line.

"I would advise you to adopt Sonia's children immediately. Give them you name."

Isabel turned to Ricardo, bewildered.

"And as you cannot, as you will never ... " Tito stressed each word, delighting in their impact. "...Never *father* your own children, I see hers as a bonus."

The ringing in Isabel's ears was deafening.

"Y que yo me la lleve al rio creyendo que era mozuela ... The flamenco music seemed to be drumming Lorca's words. And Tito's: *I see hers as a bonus ... As you will never father your own children ... I see hers as a bonus ... a bonus ...*

Isabel's blood curdled, congealed, turned to ice. Crashing noise and headless words propelled her headlong into oblivion.

Chapter 21

Tito
Val Negra
Summer 1976

Tito lay awake in the colossal Napoleon III bed in which he had been conceived. It was a spectacular sleigh bed, made of walnut. The headboard was carved with cherubs, harps and cabbage roses with sequoia inlays found in the Americas. It was so large that there was no room for any other furniture. Steps helped him to climb up and into it. Abuelita had given Nuria this bed as a wedding gift but form the moment Nuria saw it, she viewed it with suspicion. One evening in summer, shortly after they were married, Nuria felt the bed move, felt it lurch from side to side as though it were trying to disengage itself from its rocker. The windows on to the balcony were wide open and the moon hung like a huge pearl oyster embedded in its nightly shell. She sat bolt upright feeling herself sway, banging her face on the wooden slats. She knew that if she ever slept in it again, it would whisk her away somewhere beyond the stars, to the Monseny. Tito believed her mental instability started then, when she dreamed her ugly dreams. He, on the other hand, always slept like a baby.

Tito liked to joke about his conception. He was conceived on the evening of January 6, the feast of the three kings, the day Spanish children receive their gifts after placing an empty shoe by the fireplace. He called himself a *regalito de Reyes,* a little present left by the Kings. He never celebrated his real birthday. Sleeping in the bed in which he was born had begotten his own children he slept as if in the womb. At night he would climb into it, rounding the corner of this colossal wreck, defying all mortals to despair and dream like Ozymandais …

Tonight, Tito was especially pleased with himself. The wedding had been a success, the alliance with the Bazan brothers a shrewd manoeuvre. His next, would be to facilitate the marriage of Ricardo to Sonia de Cana. Not only would Val Negra then become the principal wine producing *finca* of Catalonia, but that of the whole of Spain. By annexing the de Cana land, Val Negra would extend from the Monseny to the coast. The rigours of winter that can cause vine branches to burst could be tempered with the favourable climate and soil of the de Cana estate. No longer need they worry that summer rain might drench the grapes or a late spring frost kill the fruit. Such varying micro-climates within the same region could only be an advantage. Wines of differing types required to produce the final blend, would all come from Val Negra. Tito felt wide awake, fired with his ambition. His mind raced. He already knew which red grapes from the de Cana land were most suitable for making Cava, exactly which white ones when blended, would give the juice its body. He knew that a good Cava consisted of red and white grapes derived from as many as fifteen different vineyards. There would be ample choice: the Bazan brothers in the Northern area of the region known for their single red grape and the de Cana for blending different vines and vintages.

It was immaterial that technically, Tito did not have ownership of Val Negra. For a long time the summer place had not interested him. He had been occupied with local government, politics and Franco. But now that those days were over, Tito displayed characteristic foresight. Spain would return to a democracy and if Tito were not to be exiled, he would have to find something worthwhile with which to occupy his time. The dormant vineyard of Val Negra in itself did not excite him but the prospect of expansion did. The opportunity to acquire so much land was too good to miss. His acquisitive nature thrilled at the negotiations that would come into play. The schemes, the Machiavellian interacting, the necessary corruption were all inherent to him. Besides, he had never believed his children capable of managing the estate. Avia was a fool to have bestowed such a potential gold mine on them. Miguel, in whom he had placed all his dreams, was of no use and Ricardo, in his opinion, lacked ruthlessness and business acumen.

His thoughts returned to Miguel. *Pobre* Miguel ... Tito allowed his son a moment's compassion, recoiling from the image of a blond, small boy playing with a sailboat. How he longed to pluck that child from the past and protect it from an unforgiving future. Tito choked back a sob. Still, there was no altering the past. He must concentrate his energy on this project of his. He must not be diverted from the task in hand. And he would have to accomplish this alone. He did not seriously consider Ricardo as a player. It was Sonia de Cana he was banking on. She could be manipulated as easily as most women. With Ricardo out of the way, Tito would have full reign of the Val Negra accounts. He would establish a famous house of Cava that would dominate the region. His opponents would no longer label him the Cuban upstart nor would they question, as Ricardo was beginning to, his role in the civil war. He would never again be branded with the word *traitor*. The whispers would cease. He would become untouchable.

Tito turned his face to the pillow, wrinkling his nose in distaste at the subtle scent of lavender.

Within moments he was asleep.

Chapter 22

Sigismunda
Val Negra
Summer 1976

The following day, the newspapers were full of reports about the King's coronation. Juan Carlos was called a 'motor of change' and all Europe looked on astounded as democracy came to Spain. In the first elections under the new constitution, Spanish people would vote for moderation, believing that democracy could pave the way for a new era of peace. The tumultuous months prior to Franco's death, culminating in the worldwide outrage at the execution of five ETA members, to which Ricardo had referred, were over. The series of strikes and Carrero Blanco's assassination were landmarks of a past administration. A mere 'scratch of the skin, powerless to uproot the evergreen tree of Catalan identity.' *La Vanguardia's* tone was optimistic.

Sigi, lying on Rodrigo de Montfalco's cluttered bed, viewed the newspapers scattered on the floor with a disinterested eye. She stretched, luxuriating in the naked feel of skin against lavender scented sheets, sheets that were changed every two days. Here, clothes were hung up and suitcases unpacked as if by magic. At the Castillo de Montfalco there were twice as many maids as there were at Val Negra. Rodrigo had his own valet, which Sigi considered the height of luxury. Somehow, Lupe's slap dash administration did not compare favourably with the slick efficiency of Rodrigo's man. Rodrigo's room was large, masculine and *heated*. There was a large stone fireplace in every bedroom and pure wool blankets on the beds that Rodrigo's mother had purchased from Liberty's of London. The de Montfalcos had no daughters. Their baronial castle had the feel of a hunting lodge. There were faded Afghan rugs on the broad oak floors and the antlers of wild boar killed in the Monseny, hung from the walls. Rodrigo and his brothers were all keen horsemen, as passionate about wildlife as they were of women. Girls were called 'fillies' and the finer their legs, the more they were appreciated. Sigi possessed the kind of legs that the de Montfalco men admired – long, slender, tapering to narrow ankles. Her face with its short straight nose and low forehead would have been coldly classical had it not been for her warm, chocolate coloured eyes. She was vivacious, affectionate and kind. There was nothing she wasn't game for, nothing she would not attempt just once.

And there was nothing virginal about her, the look in her slanted eyes promised to deliver.

Rodrigo's brothers were boisterous, hot headed and arrogant. In the beginning Sigi had preferred the youngest boy, Enrique, but it was Rodrigo who had pulled her into his arms at a Club dance and kissed her. Later, he dared her to try cocaine and they had ended up in his bed, in this very room. Sigi sighed remembering.

While Sigi contemplated the merits of wealth and central heating, Rodrigo in his hot shower thought of Sigi. Of all the qualities that could be attributed to his lover, he thought with satisfaction, the greatest was her stamina. To put it crudely, Rodrigo told himself, Sigismunda could fuck a man senseless.

Rodrigo showered with the bathroom door open, so that he could see her naked, enjoying the sight of the long, smooth flanks, the nicely covered torso. Despite Rodrigo's veneer of sophistication, he was a man of base tastes. Sigi was not in the least surprised by this. She had grown up with men like him. He behaved, after all, no differently from Tito. She expected nothing from him. She never complained, seeming to enjoy perennial good humour. She took no time to make a decision and could throw on yesterday's clothes at a moment's notice, with the greatest panache. She was an excellent horsewoman, a prerequisite for all de Montfalco women and she could drink as much as he could without becoming tearful. Recently however, she seemed to have thrown caution to the wind and was mixing amphetamines with alcohol. Last night her behaviour was wild and erratic and if there was one thing that had been drummed into Rodrigo and his brothers, it was not to draw attention to the family. A frown knitted Rodrigo's immaculate features. Sigi had danced like a mad thing, exposing too much breast and thigh even for his liking. His brothers had commented. Still, it had to be said that she had more than made up for it this morning. She had been particularly accommodating. He felt the stirrings of an erection at the very thought of it, which lead him, indirectly to remembering something else.

"What happened to your cousin?" he called over the sound of the shower. "Not Abuelita's lot. I mean the English girl. Did you see her faint? What a mess with all that broken glass. She fell into a waiter carrying drinks."

Sigi sat up. " My God. Was she hurt?"

"No. Where were you by the way? Everyone saw. Ricardo was beside himself. I've never seen him so … expressive. A cool one your bro but it was strange, almost as if he cared, you know more than just being polite. Is she pregnant too?"

"Don't be ridiculous!" said Sigi indignantly. "What do you mean, *too?*"

Rodrigo switched off the tap and wrapped himself in a towel. He shook out his wet hair like a dog after a swim and stepped into the room.

"If I ever saw a filly in foal it's that sister of yours. Four months gone, I'd say. That Bazan boy is *such a* dog. *Que bestia!* But your English cousin, now *she* would be a challenge."

The sight of Sigi's full breasts as she turned towards him distracted him. "When did she become a beauty?" he continued absent-mindedly. "Such fine bone structure, luminous skin, exposed so that you can almost see the bone beneath. Highly strung I shouldn't wonder, but then the best fillies always are. Does she ride? What I wouldn't give to see her mounted! She's different from the rest of you."

"Muchas gracias."

"I was quite taken by her. I admit it."

"So it would seem. Well don't get any ideas. She loathes horses and most men I suspect. And she's absolutely not pregnant. What a thing to say! She doesn't even have a boyfriend, although there *is* the dress she was wearing. I still haven't found out who gave it to her. I would know if there was someone special. We're close. *Were* close."

"Une petite vierge. How enchanting."

"Don't even think about it," said Sigi sweetly but she was alert now, cautious. She reached out a long slender arm, tanned and hairless, touching the edge of his towel. "Isn't there something to be said for experience? You always say that a woman improves with practice."

She pulled away the towel taking pleasure in his toned body, the recent memory of his skin in hers. He grunted and brushed aside her hand pushing her into the bed. Straddling her, he pinned her to the mattress, a hand on her throat. She made a feeble attempt to fight him.

"It's the chase that's important," he said against her. "You know that about me. It's what I enjoy most about new relationships. Nothing can replace it and to think that I might be the first – "

"Marry me Rodrigo."

He stiffened momentarily and slipped down to tease a nipple with his tongue. Then he rolled off the bed.

"Never," he said lightly.

When they had breakfasted on hot chocolate and *churros*, Rodrigo sat back, preparing to read the newspapers at leisure. He spread the pages wide and high obliterating her from his line of vision. His dismissal of her was absolute. Sigi flushed, annoyed as much with him as with herself. She could have kicked herself earlier on, for mentioning marriage. It had just popped out and not because she'd been thinking about it, not to do with them anyway. And if he had made a joke of it, she wouldn't have given it another thought but the strength of his response, the finality of that resounding "Never!" had stung her. *Why wouldn't he marry her? Was she not good enough? Her family was far more distinguished than his in spite of his manservant and string of polo ponies and his membership of a Madrid club. All that talk about how he liked a girl to be forward, uninhibited – had that been just to get her into bed? Did he really mean he would never marry her? Or was he like most men, the minute they got what they wanted, they no longer wanted it?* She hadn't thought so. In the beginning he was sweet and gentle and – her blood raged. The smiling face of the new King and Queen, '*Los Reyes de España*' stared back at her. She flexed her fingers and as if they possessed a life of their own, Sigi felt them curl into a fist. A punch cut a hole through the Queen's teeth.

"Christ!" exclaimed Rodrigo shaking the paper. "What was that for?"

"You didn't answer me," she said coldly. "Good manners dictate you answer a question."

"You call that, good manners?" he said smoothing out the newspaper. "Which question did you want me to answer?"

"You know damn well which one."

Rodrigo flinched. He crossed his legs neatly, one Italian leather shoe mirroring the other. He steeled himself for an argument. He knew it would have come sooner or later, and as much as he hated these kinds of scenes, he knew from experience that it was always better to deal with them straight off. He studied her thoughtfully, seeing her in a new light. He hadn't noticed, until now, the vulgarity of her language, nor her distinct lack of subtlety. There was a crudeness about her that he was beginning to find offensive.

They were seated on the terrace. Diego, Rodrigo's manservant hovered in the background attending to their every need, pouring the hot chocolate, removing and replacing ashtrays, clearing the table. The rest of the family was abroad, either competing or buying horses and apart from the servants, they had been alone all summer.

His mother Ines, the Duchess of Montfalco, rarely visited the house. It was her husband's territory. She preferred her elegant villa in Barcelona that over looked the Montjuich Park. At the Villa San Jaume, she entertained politicians, artists and foreign diplomats. During the Franco years, painters such as Tapies and Miro were frequent visitors. Those who had spent that time in self imposed exile, would return gratefully now to her patronage. It was no secret that she considered her husband and sons a breed apart. Their fascination with horses bored her and were it not for her commitment to family and religion, she would have petitioned Rome for an annulment. As it was, she and her husband lead separate lives and it suited her that the men chose to spend so much time in the country. As children, she had tolerated her sons. She had enjoyed dressing them up, parading them before her friends, imbibing them with literature. But as they grew, they evolved into alien, dreary creatures. Not one of them learned to appreciate music or art. The only beauty they saw around them was in women for whom they developed a rapid and insatiable appetite. At the age of fourteen, Rodrigo had been known for his sexual prowess. The boys' affairs were infamous and numerous.

Beautiful and intelligent, Ines de Montfalco was completely devoid of humour. Having long ago lost interest in them, she was now socially ambitious for her sons. Now that Juan Carlos was king, she set her sights on the *Infantas*. They would do nicely for her younger sons. Neither one was overly bright but they radiated strength. They had been brought up to do their duty. Ines was not blind to her sons' lack of charm, but her own marriage was one of convenience and her sons knew what was expected of them.

Now, as Rodrigo watched his lover kick off her shoes and swing a leg over the arm of a chair, he thought of his mother. Sigi, Countess of Roble was not a woman the duchess would have approved of. His mother would never have sat as Sigi was doing, much less take off her shoes. He frowned. Nor did she swear. All at once the habits he had found endearing in Sigi, grated on his nerves. He observed her painted toenails with distaste. *There was such a wantonness about her*, he thought. *But then you had only to look at her family. Mad the whole lot of them! What could you expect with a mother who had a permanently crucified air about her and a father who was nothing more than a Cuban sugar planter?*

It was a relief to know he was no longer in love.

"We should speak in Catalan," he said jerking his head in Diego's direction. He cleared his throat. "You should always address me in Catalan."

Sigi stared at him. "You son of a bitch," she said quietly. "You hypocrite. You've never had any intention of marrying me, have you? All your posturing, that macho display of virility and really you're just a Mummy's boy. You'll end up marrying who ever *she* chooses. A *virgin* of course."

Rodrigo looked uncomfortable. "Not necessarily."

Sigi's eyes shot up. "So there *is* someone."

"Perhaps. Look I don't see why you're so upset. It was just a bit of fun. You said so yourself. I didn't know you wanted to get married."

"That's because you never asked me! Who is it?" she said miserably.

"Sonia," he muttered. "Sonia de Cana."

Sigi's eyes widened with disbelief. Sonia was *Ricardo's* girl. He had always been in love with her. For a moment she was speechless, then surprise gave way to anger. "I don't believe you."

"It's only business. Sonia is getting a divorce – well an annulment in fact. You know how important the de Cana vineyards are. They've been an issue among all the wine producing families for years. It's the most profitable estate in the region and now that Franco is dead, the movement of money will be easier. There can be foreign investments. The opportunities are tremendous."

"Since when did business ever mean anything to you?"

"Father says – "

Sigi gave him a withering look. "Oh I see; *Daddy's* pulling the strings. What about Val Negra? It has a vineyard and a river running through. Aren't you interested in *my* property?" Her voice rose shrilly.

"But that's exactly the point. Val Negra isn't yours is it? It's your Grandmother's or maybe Tito's, I'm not sure."

"Actually it isn't," said Sigi stiffly. " Not anymore. Legally, it belongs to all of us children. Tito is wrong to imply he has any stake in it. He can't do anything without our permission."

"Really? Now that *is* interesting."

"But not enough to want to make you marry me."

"I need to make money. Quickly." He reached for more coffee avoiding her eyes. He stirred sugar into the cup and then sat back calmly, taking short sips.

"*You? I* didn't think the Montfalcos were short of cash."

Rodrigo made an impatient gesture. "Not the family, *tonta*, but me personally, acutely as it happens. Our little habit doesn't come cheap. I can't borrow any more from Father unless I do so against my inheritance and then he'd probably charge me interest! Mother would never agree to it anyway and it all takes time. My father isn't back in the country until next month. I can't wait much longer. I owe that odious Nadal a small fortune and my other debts – "

Sigi waved this aside. "But Sonia will be a divorced woman. Your family would never allow it."

"Not *divorced*. The marriage will be annulled."

Sigi shrugged.

"Same thing isn't it?"

"No it's not, as you well know." He finished his coffee setting down the cup carefully on the glass table. "That reminds me, Dr.Mantua is a family friend of yours and I'm told just the man for the job. He has contacts in the Opus."

Sigi bristled. "You've got him all wrong. He won't do it. He's not like that. And he loathes the Opus."

"Everyone will do something for a price."

"Your family perhaps," Sigi replied icily.

"And yours."

There was a hostile silence between them.

"I resent that," she said at last. "I can assure you that Dr.Mantua will not do this thing for you. There are some people," she added haughtily, "who answer to a higher integrity. Don't look so perplexed, Rodrigo. I wouldn't expect you to understand. Beyond your horses there's not much that you do understand is there?" Sigi swung her feet off the chair and sat bolt upright. "Besides, Sonia has children. It's much harder to obtain an annulment if there are children."

Rodrigo appraised her coolly. Any affection he had felt towards her had evaporated.

"That's incidental. I have no doubt that in due course we shall produce our own."

Sigi blanched, her fingers dug into the palms of her hand, her eyes turned yellow. Rodrigo had seen hunters look like that, moments before they pulled the trigger. He looked away.

"Do you love her?"

Rodrigo snorted. "I don't even know her!"

"And that's an excuse?" Sigi said angrily "That's supposed to make me feel better? I thought you loved *me*. Besides what if Sonia won't have you? Have you thought of that? Sonia de Cana can have any man she wants. Why the hell should she choose you?"

Rodrigo recoiled from her twisting face. "For the same reason you did!" he said.

"Ugh!" Sigi lunged towards him. Instinctively he jumped to his feet fending off her blows but she was stronger than he anticipated. She fought him like a mad thing, biting his hands and his neck, scratching his face. She felt the unusual, giddy sensation of tight flesh giving way as her teeth sank into his cheek, then the spurt of blood. She pulled his hair, his clothes, she twisted back his fingers, stamped on his expensive shoes, tried to rip the buttons off his shirt.

"You bastard, you bastard!" she cried hysterically. Rodrigo grabbed her arms holding them to her sides. She struggled, kicking his shins. He doubled up in pain and when she leapt at him again, he slapped her. All at once she collapsed in a heap in a chair. With shaking hands, Rodrigo smoothed his hair, adjusted his trousers and belt. Blood oozed from a bite on his cheek. He wet a napkin in a glass of water and dabbed at his face. Sigi was crying quietly, large tears splashing onto her fine silk dress. Eventually, exhausted, she stopped. She wiped her face with the back of her hand, shook out her hair and got unsteadily to her feet. Rodrigo did not look at her. Cursing, he shouted for Diego.

Without a word, Sigi walked away from him, into the house.

*

Rodrigo was not a man to dwell on unpleasant incidents. Once a matter was settled, he moved swiftly forward. He was too proud to acknowledge defeat of any kind and he had never had to apologise for anything. The admission of weakness was not part of his psyche and he had grown into the easy habit of finding other people lacking. A reputation of wealth leant him many virtuous attributes that he did not in fact possess. If he spoke little it was because he had little to say and his mild unassuming manner was mistaken for gentleness. He needed people to add colour to his inherent dullness. The wilder, the braver, the more audacious the exploits of his friends, the more attractive, by association he became. Traces of his exuberant adolescence followed him into manhood but the suspicion began to grow that sexual proficiency might be his only talent. He was undemanding of relationships. He did not wish to explore or to be explored. He required sexual gratification, entertainment and physical exercise.

However, there was one thing that he was clear on and that was a loathing of excessive displays of emotion. Any hint of volatile behaviour in a woman and he disappeared. Thank God, he'd had a glimpse of Sigi's true nature sooner rather than later. He had to admit that he had been fond of her. There was a time, albeit brief, when he thought they might marry. She was comforting to have around, rather like a favourite dog and like him she did not feel a burning desire to communicate her every thought. When they first met, Sigi was a refreshing change from the prim senoritas at the Polo Club. Here was a girl who was prepared to give all and was game for everything. She was, in short, a man after his own heart. But she had changed. She had become erratic, unstable and flamboyant. To his alarm, she was already addicted to amphetamines. Her beauty no longer stirred in him the emotion of which he was sometimes capable.

The end of the affair troubled him less however, than did his association with Carlos Nadal. In a shockingly short time, Rodrigo had accumulated an enormous debt and most of it was due to him. This in itself did not pose a problem. Rodrigo was used to owing money and bought virtually everything, including women and horses, on credit. It never ceased to amaze him how quickly vendors were willing to advance him money the minute he gave his name. Money was not something he had ever had to think about. Until now that is. Nadal was not impressed by who his father was and demanded payment in *efectivo,* cash.

Rodrigo lit a cigarette with shaking hands. He winced as his broken lip came in contact with the tobacco. And then he sat down abruptly, feeling dizzy. It was the shock he told himself. One minute he'd been reading *La Vanguardia,* and the next he was assaulted by that mad woman. Christ he'd been lucky. A bloody narrow escape is what he'd call it. Still there had been moments and the sex was good, better than good. Rodrigo thrust the memory from his mind. He was not used to such an intensity of feeling. Part of him longed to confide in his mother, the other wanted to show her that he could sort out his own problems. How proud she would be of him when he announced his engagement! He could just imagine her face when he told her. He must waste no time in talking to Sonia but he would have to handle the potentially explosive area of his finances, with all the skill he could muster. He must do everything in his power to keep his small 'habit' and Nadal well and truly hidden. Besides, he comforted himself, it was only a temporary blip. Sonia, like the rest of the county knew that he was his father's heir. It was only at this particular point in time that his account needed an immediate and very large injection of cash, preferably in American dollars.

He thought again of his mother. Ines de Montfalco would be proud to have Sonia de Cana as a daughter in-law. She was everything that Ines admired – sophisticated, elegant and cultured which if he were truthful was not altogether his type. Rodrigo was more comfortable with girls like Sigi. It really was a pity that things had not worked out. There was no faulting the Roble lineage. Recently however, Rodrigo found it difficult to connect Sigi with her illustrious forbears. And she could never have helped him financially in quite the way that Sonia could. If only they hadn't started on the heroin …

It was no good regretting the past and it was uncharacteristic of him. Now he must put into practice his family's motto: *Forward*. And there was never such an auspicious time as now for doing just that. Franco was dead, the monarchy returned to Spain and it was time for families such as his own, to take their place in society. Rodrigo called for Diego and instructed him to saddle *Manzana*. After he had changed, he would ride out to the de Cana estate and see Sonia. Arriving on horseback would strike just the right note, a white knight on his charger – the lady in distress – a latter day El Cid. Literary associations aside, His Excellency Don Rodrigo Gabriel y Galan, Count de Bofill, heir to the Duke of Montfalco, always made his most lasting impression when he was mounted…

Chapter 23

Sigismunda
Val Negra
Summer 1976

Sigi let herself out. Unnoticed, she slipped through the front door and out into the cobbled courtyard. A dog barked and under the fig trees, chickens lifted their muddy feet, marching towards the road. Sigi pulled at the heavy creaking gates taking one last look at the house where she had been so happy. Now it seemed as though its silent occupants conspired to bring about her eviction. The windows were bolted, the shutters pulled tight. Beneath a grey sky the stone appeared dank and menacing. The tiled turrets spiked overhanging clouds and as if on cue, a roll of thunder rumbled through the valley. No time had been taken in closing the house for the season.

Sigi felt as though her heart were breaking. It was painfully clear that Rodrigo had never thought of marrying her. He did not love her enough for that. No man had ever really loved her, not her father, not her brothers, not even that wretched priest. And yet, from as early as she could remember, she had wanted men to notice her. She craved their attention and sometimes went to extraordinary lengths to attract it. She was always disappointed. The harder she tried, the more she was deceived. And while she loathed this weakness in her, she had not the strength of purpose to overcome it. She realised, with a resigned bitterness that her whole being was shaped by this insatiable urge to be reassured. Only this time, she had gone too far. Where Rodrigo was concerned, she had made herself too available and it was clearly not what men wanted. Not what they married.

Follow and I will flee, Flee and I will follow - words Isabel had quoted to her only the other day. Sigi hadn't understood them at all then but she did now.

And why should that be? Why should men and women be forced to play these silly games? She never had. If she'd wanted something she had said so. Men liked that about her. They said it was refreshing to meet a young lady who was so 'enthusiastic.' In the beginning, she'd had nothing but fun. While her girlfriends spent their days with their hair in curlers talking about boys, *she* had gone out to meet them. Her friends had warned her about her over familiarity with men, they said she made it too easy, that men actually liked to think you weren't interested, but Sigi hadn't listened. She thought they were just jealous because she had so many boy friends and they didn't have any. She began to wonder if her friends hadn't been right after all. Maybe the only way to get a man to marry you was to pretend you weren't interested. Just look at that Sonia de Cana for instance. She'd never heard her say two words of interest to anyone and yet all the men, including her own brother were besotted with her. And she was still married! She wasn't even free and every male of marriageable age was making a fool of himself over her.

What had gone wrong? Sigi had thought they were so well suited. Rodrigo liked her boldness. He said, in a rare moment of revelation, that she made him feel less shy. Well he couldn't be feeling shy now thinking of marrying someone he hardly knew! He'd even made fun of girls like Sonia de Cana. He said he enjoyed Sigi's company more than that of any girl he knew, that being with her was just like being with one of the boys. Rodrigo had told her that he admired American girls for being so 'liberated' and that Sigi's attitude to sex was just like theirs. If he admired her so much, why wasn't he marrying her? What was it that Scorpion Lupe had said to her on the morning of Marta's wedding?

"Men have a good time with girls like you, Sigi, but they don't marry you."

She began to sob, short, rhythmic sobs that accompanied her all the way from the dirt track alongside the Montfalco land to the border with the de Cana vineyard. She could see the water tanks scattered round the wine field used to pump out insecticide spray at the first sign of shoots. The newly hoed vineyard hugged the hillside, neat and pubescent. It was noon and the church bells from the Val Negra chapel chimed the angelus. Two workers in a neighbouring mustard field stopped to cross themselves, their arms silhouetted against the sky. It was very quiet, clean after the weeks of rain. Sigi dropped to her knees picking at the red earth, letting it flow through her fingers, over her face and hair like water. She rubbed it into her cheeks and teeth. She felt distended, disorientated, unrecognisable to herself. Sleep pulled at her eyelids and despite the cold, the wet earth and the fact that she was miles from home, Sigi lay down and slept.

Later she got to her feet, stumbling. *Where would she go? What was she to do?* Her mind was a blank. For a moment she could not even remember where she lived. *Was she in the old town in Barcelona? Where on earth was she?* Slowly the spinning of her head righted itself and she remembered with sickening clarity about Rodrigo. She also thought of Carlos Nadal and with him in mind, she began to run. Even when she knew she should go in the opposite direction, her need propelled her towards the village. It was so quiet. Of course, she remembered now, it was the King's coronation day. Apart from the field workers, there was no one on the path to the pueblo. Only the rumbling of thunder and her sliding feet broke the silence. She walked barefoot, the mud squelching between her toes. Well, she thought grimly she had left Rodrigo with a momento. Her shoes! She imagined they were still underneath her chair on the terrace. Would Diego discover them? Ricardo had called her, 'The barefoot Condesa.' That's what she was now all right, with her feet caked in soil. It was downhill for the rest of the way. Her feet moved quickly, she watched them independent of the rest of her body, pushing through the grain. She cut across the last vineyard – Bazan territory this time, where the vine was in flower. She stepped on the odd root, cursing. And then she emerged onto the road that led to the village. Catalan banners were everywhere. An old man grinned toothless. *"Viva el Rey,"* he said and *"Visca Catalunya!"*

"Visca!" she echoed.

Up a little back street, past the shoe shop and post office, past the blind basket weaver, her soundless feet propelled her on. The putrid smell of rotting vegetables, cats' urine and excreta did not deflect her from her mission. She parted the beaded curtain of a tiny shop, the beads clattering as she entered. A radio played, blasting its beat around the tiny room, breaking the collective silence of the village. Paint peeled off the walls, cigarette butts lined the saw dust floor. There was an unmade camp bed in one corner, the sheets soiled, beginning to shred. Sigi hesitated. A voice in her head urged her to leave and yet she was weighted to the floor. It was too late to turn back. She heard him belch even before she saw his face. Carlos Nadal parted the beads, pushing his head through the strands. He wore his uniform: stained singlet, hair from his armpits migrating to meet those on his chest and grubby trousers rolled above the ankles. His dirty feet were forced into flip-flops. His greased back hair made a shiny helmet, not a single strand escaped. He sucked a toothpick. Bloodshot eyes were raised to hers.

"*Condesa*, what an ... unexpected pleasure."

He made an elaborate bow. "What can I do for you?" He emphasised the word 'do' while his gaze lingered on her mouth and dirt streaked face. He took in her muddied dress, tangled hair and came up with an erroneous conclusion. Nonetheless, what he saw pleased him. He scratched his groin. The toothpick stopped twisting in his mouth.

Chapter 24

Carlos Nadal
Val Negra
Summer 1976

When Carlos Nadal was very young, too young to understand his family's politics and before everything changed, he had been happy to deliver groceries to Val Negra. His earliest memories were of being lifted onto his father's donkey to ride with him up to the house. His feet rested on stuffed baskets of food while delicious smells of freshly baked bread and roasted coffee filled his senses. He sat in front of his father, feeling the wiry strength of him, the smell of horse and leather, the scratch of his moustache against his cheek. He rode like a King, like Jesus through Jerusalem and all before him lay the smooth, green vineyards stretching to the foot of the Monseny hills. They rode through endless camomile lawns, by narrow streams, stopping to drink the clear water. He pretended that he was master of the land, that he could choose his destiny. His father, saying little, drew on the rough tobacco which he smoked blended with beetle nut. He remembered entering the huge gates and being terrified by the enormous bronze lions that stood on two legs, their paws clawing the air, their jowls open wide. But instead of continuing down the rainbow gravel path, they swerved to the left of the house. It was the first time Carlos was aware of a difference between himself and the people who lived in the *castillo*. The second was when the pretty girl with the blonde hair and green eyes laughed to see him riding on a donkey.

His father was in awe of this noble family. He had been brought up like his father before him, to serve it unquestioning, unfailingly, while there was still breath in his body. From the moment Carlos set eyes on Val Negra, however, he felt nothing but resentment. A thousand questions crowded his brain and on the way home he bombarded his father with some of them. He could not accept that an accident of birth should create such a division, that the *Condes* of Val Negra should be entitled to so much, while the likes of the Nadals could look forward to so little. He was not happy to slip into a role that would require his devotion and commitment to a family he neither liked nor respected. Blood raged within him and every time he was propped on the unfortunate mule with its thinning hair and festering sores, Carlos, planned his revenge. As he grew, so too did his resentment, until all he could manage was a grunt of greeting when he delivered the weekly round of supplies. He had inherited none of his father's gentleness or his sense of history. Carlos respected no authority other than his deepest impulse.

After the war, bitterness motivated his every action. He had done his bit during the war, unlike Tito and many of the affluent youths he had grown up with. Tito had spent his war as a deserter, in the relative comfort of the country while he, Carlos, had fought like a pig. Carlos had fought, suffered and been wounded and had returned to fight with renewed vigour. Each new battle fuelled his revulsion for the ruling class. He had killed as many priests, women and children of the aristocracy that he could get his hands on, in the blunted hope that their deaths would calm the turbulent pool of self-loathing within him. He raped young girls, sodomised nuns, revelling in their screams of agony but nothing defused his fury, until the day that is, many years later, when he first saw Sigi in the Cathedral in Barcelona. And afterwards, when she stood beside Rodrigo de Montfalco, so utterly out of place in his squalid back room and her eyes widened in recognition and something else he did not understand, he knew that in another world, he would have loved her. The thought made him angry. Her destruction would be his final victory.

On that occasion, Carlos was all subservience.

"*Si Senor,*" he had bowed obsequiously, rubbing his hands. " Yes of course, total discretion. Whatever you like. And may I congratulate the Count on the beauty of his mistress."

Don Rodrigo had looked up sharply and Nadal had smiled quickly, least he had caused offence. "I mean the *Condesa* is known – " he wanted to say to himself, but thought the better of it – "… to be a beauty. You are a lucky man." And then once a certain comaderie had been brokered, Nadal had made a crude gesture, a risk to be sure, but one that Don Rodrigo had appreciated. It had made him laugh and Carlos had smiled, more from relief, than anything else.

And he had not been discrete. He had dropped a hint in the clever Jesuit's ear. Nadal had noted the names of his clients – names that would prove salaciously shocking when the time came to expose them. He was not sure when, but he knew that some day, those names would be worth real money.

"What do you want?" he turned his attention now to Sigi. The girl's skirt was torn to reveal a strong thigh, her face was dirty as if she had been crawling in mud and yet never had she seemed more desirable. He liked her best when she was not playing the role of Senorita, when she behaved like one of his kind. Absentmindedly, Carlos scratched his crotch then leant back against the concrete wall, patient, watching.

"I – I thought you might have some speed or *coca*, and I don't mean the cake with pine nuts, a few grams not much, whatever you can spare." She wiped her hair from her eyes. She was so tired she was finding it an effort to speak. Her mind was cluttered with voices and loud abrupt sounds. Carlos lit a cigarette and inhaled slowly, blowing out smoke rings that made her cough in the small, windowless room. After a while he nodded.

"I have some acid, not coke but it's more expensive. But you don't shoot heroin do you? If you wanted to try this time …" He scratched his stomach and his hand moved downwards inside his trousers. He continued to watch her, excited by her aloofness, her sense of detachment and her voluptuous body. "It will cost you however, *dia de fiesta* and all. I was not due to supply Don Rodrigo till next month. It is a little earlier than usual, no?"

Sigi nodded. Carlos waited. In her torn, expensive clothes, waiting, as she was, uncertain of her fate, he was once again reminded of the early days of the war. He had enjoyed making his victims wait, as she was doing now. He was thrilled at their humiliation, their soiled clothes and their lowered eyes that did not dare meet his. He had liked, afterwards to dress up in a priest's clothes, twirling round in a cassock. He chose men and women at random but nearly always they were easy victims, identified by their decent clothes. He saw most of the war from a small village outside Valencia where he remained happily killing and pillaging until the fall of Barcelona. There might have been a time when he actually believed in the politics of the war, that he really was part of the people, trying to free itself from a repressive regime. He rather doubted it though. He enjoyed the sensation of killing too much. If there hadn't been a cause, he would have had to invent one.

But Sigi did not have the eyes of a victim. She looked straight at him, with a deep unfathomable look that excited him all the more. As he watched her, she too embodied a lifelong struggle against the hated upper classes and he drew his own parallels. His vision blurred as did her features. They no longer seemed sensual and inviting but adopted the arrogant disdain of her grand mother. *The sins of the father,* he thought to himself, words that had rooted themselves in his twisted heart, words that had stayed with him completing the paradox within.

Even before he moved towards her, he knew what he must do.

"I – I'll have the ... other." Sigi's voice rose above a whisper. Her limbs were trembling. All she wanted was that swift release that cocaine gave her and then to leave and to sleep. "Give me the acid." Her voice was firm, the controlling voice she used with the servants. Carlos's head jerked up.

"Not so quickly, *bonita,*" he smiled. "I said it would cost you."

"Well- how much?" Sigi's mind raced. It was then she realised she had no money of her own. She met Carlos Nadal's penetrating look. "Whatever the price. It doesn't matter," she said haughtily. "Don Rodrigo will pay you after the holidays. He's ... away for the weekend. When he gets back, I will ask him to pay you."

Carlos picked at his teeth and shook his head as if greatly amused.

"I don't think you understand. That is not the way I do – forgive me – *we* do business. If you want something, then you must pay for it. Don Rodrigo is a man of honour, I know, but girl friends come and go – if you catch my meaning? How do I know he'll pay me? He may say you had no authority to buy the stuff on his account."

"If I say Rodrigo will pay, he will," said Sigi angrily. "How dare you insinuate –"

Carlos crossed the small space between them. "I insinuate nothing," he said coldly. "If you want the stuff then pay for it. Otherwise, get out!" He was so close she could feel his hot, beer sweet breath, his sweat.

"But I must have it." Her teeth were clenched. "Please. I promise to get you the money, later on today. Never mind about Don Rodrigo. I promise I will get the money."

Carlos picked his tooth. "No," he said softly.

"But then I can't ... pay you."

"No?"

He ran his tongue round his lips. He touched her cheek. Sigi watched as his crooked, dirty fingers moved from her neck. He touched her breasts. She shivered. His leg pushed hers apart till she toppled against him and he held her easily with one hand. The other ripped open her dress, his hand felt between her thighs. She offered, he was surprised, no resistance. He felt her full breasts greedily holding them in his hands. She groaned. Then he stopped and reaching by the bed, found the needles he kept in a tool box. He sucked at the triangle of white in the crook of her arm, sinking a line into her arm. She shuddered and he pulled her head roughly, beginning all over again and then she smiled, slowly.

"*Puta,*" he whispered softly. "Now do you think yourself so much better than the rest of us? Eh? Your instincts are as simple as ours. You like to be fucked just as we do."

He turned her onto her stomach. "*Te gusta asi. Di que si. Dilo,*" he whispered.

Sigi soared, landed, was disconnected from reality. She responded to the assault on her body, oblivious of his presence, seeking only pleasure and release. Carlos's frustration gave vent and he used her over and over again, hoping to arouse some protest, some sign of disgust. But there was none. She seemed to enjoy herself as much as he did, even as the violence increased. At last exhausted, he moved off her, enjoying the sight of her half naked body, her parted legs.

"*Puta, realmente una puta,* " he said to the inert figure.

Sigi closed her eyes and slept in the filthy bed of that tiny *colmado* store, wrapped in dirt stained sheets, swaddled like a baby.

It was not the first, or last time, she would sell her body for drugs.

Chapter 25

Isabel
Winchester
Spring 1998

Isabel sat at her desk examining the overlarge mock-ups for a bottle of cava. She even stood up to walk round the 2 metre high structures looking at them from every angle. Repeatedly she compared them with the ice blue and green colour photographs of Cava's current advertisements.

In pillar box red, the word **NOW** dominated the page and then below, in smaller stick capitals:

'From the International house of Cava

EL CONFORT

The first sparkling cava to offer

YOU

Nature's light Delectable grapiness

El Confort is the Cava for everyday enjoyment, morning, noon and romantic night. El Confort is a sparkling blend offering finesse and elegance from a noble cultivar. An unforgettable experience derived from a fragrant table grape. Share the sparkle with someone special. Share it now!'

In the background a motorboat zoomed towards the middle distance and in the foreground was the life size picture of a bottle of El Confort - ice cold with gleaming droplets - and two glasses. The photographs were accomplished. They made the viewer share in a wealthier, more enviable lifestyle and enticed him in to thinking that by drinking Cava, the boat and the sunny climes could be his. He was not only buying a moderately priced bottle of sparkling wine, but he was also buying into a higher echelon. It was both original and sophisticated. Archid could not hope to do better. Isabel turned back to her computer. Automatically she typed the opening lines of the standard proposal.

> *'Archid Associates offers success in industry. Effective management means eye catching design. Efficient planning of business organization; optimizing production and distribution are the challenges faced by corporations world wide. Archid Associates has proved that it can cope with such challenges by introducing skilful consultants of the highest calibre. Together we can make a team.'*

She hit the keyboard in frustration. It was all rubbish! How was she going to persuade Rodrigo de Montfalco and the Bazan brothers to spend £50,000 on a new design strategy when their brochure was perfectly adequate? Well perhaps it was a teeny bit soppy - especially the bit about *'Finesse and the fragrant table grape,'* but it worked. The Bazan brothers thought so too and they saw no reason to change it. Except of course that they wanted their family logo of the scorpion to dominate the logo. Isabel had tried to tell them that while of course it was instantly recognisable it could also be slightly sinister. They hadn't agreed and said as much at their recent meeting in Barcelona. Only now she was faced with two problems. She had repeatedly told Mike Fagan that targeting the Bazan estates was pointless, but now that they had, she had her own reputation to consider and she hated losing a pitch. In the past she had been some 80% successful. On paper her proposals were concise and sensible while her visuals were slickly polished. Her personal charm and linguistic flair was often the clinching factor in a deal. But now if she didn't secure the tenure, they would think her incompetent – out of her depth more like. She did not want either the Bazan brothers or the Montfalcos to think she was not up to the mark and especially as Ricardo was involved. He had been present at their talk at the *"Up and Down"* club and seen her present visuals and client portfolios. Flushed with pride, she had sensed his approval. She could not let them think she was merely toying with them. And more than anything, she had no desire to reinforce their already antiquated enough notion that women had no place in business. And an English woman to boot! *It was all about being the typical inglesita, thought Isabel, the fact that we were only ever good for bedding and there had been plenty of that…! Ugh!* It was bad enough dreaming about Ricardo when she *hadn't* seen him but now that she had …

"Damn." Isabel knocked over a cold cup of coffee. She leapt to her feet trying to soak it up ineffectually with a small handkerchief. She pressed her buzzer.

"Sam!" she all but hollered and prepared herself to wait an age but to her surprise Sam was at the door within seconds a damp jay cloth in her hand.

"How did you guess?" said Isabel in surprise her eyes flicking over her secretary's face searching for evidence of newly pierced skin but there was none.

"Well it's already happened a couple of times today hasn't it?" said Sam grimly.

Isabel made a face.

"Sorry," she said sheepishly.

"No problem," said Sam tartly. "And I'll bring you another cup. Tea this time?"

"Please," replied Isabel gratefully. Sam looked uncharacteristically sympathetic. "This one not so easy?"

Isabel shook her head. "I'm not inspired. Can't think of an angle."

"Woh! That's a slick design. Actually I know the drink. It's really good and not too pricey. I bought some for my Mum on her birthday. You can even get it at our local."

Sam pulled the Bazan glossies towards her. "Is the new thing?"

Isabel grimaced. "No. This is the product we're trying to *revamp.*"

Sam's eyes widened. "Why?"

"Precisely. See what I'm up against?"

Sam mopped up the coffee and piled the brochures and budget sheets together. Isabel found herself staring at the girl's bare stomach and pierced navel as she leaned towards her. She couldn't help wondering if Ricardo would find that sort of thing exciting. It would certainly be provocative.

"Sam?"

"Yes?"

Sam's face had lost its habitual bland expression and for once she seemed genuinely curious. Isabel seeing the girl straighten and how her tummy flopped unattractively over the broad rim of her trousers changed her mind. Thoughts of Ricardo were playing havoc with her concentration.

Sam hesitated her hand holding the wet dishcloth away from her.

"Oh I almost forgot. Kate Douglas called earlier. She wants you to ring her back before five."

"Thanks."

"And Tim phoned several times. He's at a client's all day though, so you won't catch him till the evening. Wanted to know why you spend so much time in the field. Said he thought that wasn't your job any more and that the whole point of being a director was to direct. Then he went into this big hu-ha about the failings of companies and that it all boils down to management and good management means good delegation. Didn't think you could be doing much of that if you were out and about as it were."

"Mmn ... " muttered Isabel unenthusiastically. "Sounds like he got an attentive ear on that one. Is the boss around?"

Sam looked disappointed that she wasn't going to have a heart to heart on the subject of Tim.

"No. He's in London for the day."

"Thank God for small mercies. He's Easter shopping I expect."

"There are lots of sales on at the moment. There are *always* sales on. But there you go, sign of the times."

"Yes," agreed Isabel but thought that a slump in the economy wasn't at all the case in Catalonia where several multinationals had recently established bases in the region together with Europe's largest Savings Bank. Business was booming. "That tea would be wonderful."

Sam slunk towards the door.

"Yeah, coming up."

Isabel glanced at the screen as if by magic the words seemed to have written themselves:

'Archid has years of experience in research and investigation. With our extensive network of worldwide offices we can rapidly transport mock designs to the comfort of your own premises. We have experts in the field well versed in the language and customs of a wide range of countries. Our staff offers specialist skills in state of the art technology and design strategy. Archid is your number one choice in the competitive world of Design Agencies –'

Isabel was once again distracted by the bustle of Jewry Street below. It was already dark even though it was not yet four o'clock. Mothers hurried their children along as they darted in and out of shops. A double decker bus skidded unceremoniously to a stop virtually in front of the building. She heard the bus driver swear and the double doors swung open. A delivery van pulled up behind it to unload large paintings for the Antique shop opposite. She saw large gilt frames covered in dust sheets carefully manoeuvred out of the van and lifted through the narrow shop door. The owner smiled making way for the men. Sam returned with a cup of tea and Isabel pretended to be absorbed with the screen, loath to be drawn into any more conversation.

When she was safely out of earshot, Isabel dialled Kate's number and sipped her tea. After several rings the switchboard answered. Kate now worked for a well-known accountancy firm in their corporate tax department. It always amused Isabel to wonder what a client's first impression of Kate might be. She certainly wasn't the stereotype accountant. She was fun, sexy and immaculately dressed. She also possessed a formidable head for figures and an intellect that sliced through the more torpid areas of corporate legislation with remarkable agility. Her flirtatious manner with men was often misleading. Her love life was notorious and she had a conveniently unromantic attitude to sex. She never allowed a dinner companion to pay for her and she wasn't interested in commitment. She was amusing and warm and men loved her. Best of all, she had never been known to mention marriage. She did not whine when a love affair was over, with the result that all ex-lovers were always made very welcome when they occasionally wandered back. Those who didn't, remembered her fondly. But she had a low threshold of boredom and was contemptuous of stupidity. Her man had to be good in bed and intellectually compatible. Currently, she was seeing an American commodity broker several years her junior.

Kate enjoyed a more than comfortable lifestyle. She owned a luxurious flat in Chester square, drove a BMW cabriolet and was a member of the Harbour Club. She went to Ascot, some opera and in late summer headed for the South of France. She loathed skiing but in February took herself off to the Caribbean and returned tanned and relaxed ready to tax the world. Kate was never bad tempered, depressed or unduly worried by anything. Above all, she was a loyal friend and although Isabel saw much less of her than she had done when she first began working in London, there was never any difficulty in breaching the gap.

"Kate Douglas," said a familiar voice.

"Hi. It's –"

"Isa!" shrieked Kate so loudly that Isabel had to hold the receiver away form her ear. "Where on earth have you been? I haven't heard a peep from you in ages! I thought you'd left the country or got married or had a baby or died even – "

"I've been away – work related. Spain this time."

"But wasn't that in January? I saw you before you left remember."

"Oh, that's right," said Isabel guiltily. "I'd forgotten. Things have been a bit hectic here. I'm in the middle of a proposal that I should have got out weeks ago. I just don't seem to be able to get down to this one though. It's partly the subject. I almost know it too well. I'm bored with it."

"What's the time scale on it?" said Kate.

"There isn't any."

"Oh? The client not in any hurry?"

"No."

"So what *do* they want?"

Isabel sighed. "That's just it. They don't."

"Wine growers like yours?"

Isabel nodded. "Yes."

"But more successful."

Isabel smiled to herself. "You could say that. They make top of the range sparkling wine. The EU won't allow them to call it Champagne but the production method is virtually the same. Recently they've done extremely well and sales have increased steadily. Last year they sold two million cases to 85 countries worldwide! It's particularly popular in the States."

"Why is that?"

"Well it's cheaper than French Champagne for one thing and it has enjoyed a good reputation *and* it's been around for a while. The Bazans were clever even *before* Fernando and Benito. The family capitalised on the inability of the French to export their wine during two world wars. By the time the French were back in the market, Cava had carved a nice little niche of its own."

"And now?"

"Now the company has a turnover of some 34 billion pesetas and the possibility of new contracts in the Far East. Or that's how Mike Fagan sees it. Especially when I had to tell him of my connection with the Bazans. He was thrilled of course and I have been designated as chief minder, salesperson, PR rep, translator, events co-ordinator - you name it and if it bears any relation to Cava or the Bazan Brothers, then I'm your woman."

"Sounds good."

"It could be if the Bazans were at all interested in us, but they're not. They have a wonderful design team in Barcelona which I visited, a great product and they simply will not spend X amount of pounds having it all changed. And certainly not by me."

She could imagine crossing her legs and leaning back in her chair.

"There's something you're not telling me here pumpkin. Something that just doesn't hang."

Isabel hesitated only briefly.

"You're right," she said swiftly. "The fact is that I know the Bazans. More than know them. My cousin Marta is married to Fernando Bazan and I grew up with them both. Their land neighbours ours in Val Negra. It's got complicated though and it's entirely my fault. I sort of encouraged the boss to send me out there but really it was only to see-"

"Ricardo?"

"W-e-ll..."

"Ah... Incidentally Isa, what did you say to Tim?"

Isabel studied her new suede shoes. They had tiny buttons running down the middle and were sleekly elegant.

"About?"

There was an irritated silence.

"Tim did ask you to marry him a few months back didn't he?" Isa could hear the tap of keys as Kate continued to work on her computer while still talking to her. Isabel held the receiver closer to her mouth.

"But see that's the strange thing," she said in a whisper not wanting to be overheard. "I told him that I couldn't marry him which he accepted, although he says that there's no reason why we shouldn't be friends. I sort of understand that as we've known each other such a long time but now he's behaving as if nothing at all has happened. He calls just as much as he used to and asks me out as if we were dating."

The tapping on the computer stopped. There was a brief pause.

"What exactly happened when you were in Spain?" said Kate quietly.

Isabel hesitated remembering the *Up and Down* club. She had thought of little else since she returned. She switched off her computer with one hand and then took a gulp of now tepid tea.

"Ok," said Kate her attention now fully engaged. There was nothing more riveting to her than affairs of the heart. Even the challenge posed by the more orphic areas of the law, palled with the complexity of sexual relationships. "This is all to do with Ricardo isn't it? God girl will you never change?"

"You'd better come on up. Look Chevy Chase is out for the night so I'm free. Get the train. Leave your car at the station. Get the train and you'll be up in an hour. We'll have supper and you can spend the night. Tell Sam you'll be late in. Come on we haven't seen each other for ages! And it sounds like you need my expert advice."

"I know what you'll say, Kate. You'll want me to have them both."

"Of course not," said Kate shocked. "That's only for me. I can't have you running around seeing two chaps at the same time. Even if they are in different countries! You've got Tim to think of. No. No it won't do. We've got to talk. After all you and Tim have been together forever!"

"It certainly feels that way."

"I know," continued Kate cheerfully. "I'll get some of your famous Cava. If nothing else, we can always study the packaging!"

Isabel laughed. It was awfully tempting. The thought of an evening's interrogation by Tim seemed suddenly too depressing to contemplate and the alternative was drinking lots of whisky and moping about the house alone. At least if she drank too much Cava, it would be with Kate.

"OK," said Isabel. "I'll do it. If I leave now I can make the 6:10 and be with you around 7:30. It'll be good to see you."

"So did you?" Kate's voice was low, conspiratorial. Isabel, already grabbing her bag and pushing notes into her briefcase, paused.

"Did I what?"

"You know, with Ricardo."

"Oh shut up," said Isabel sweetly. "See you later," and she rang off before Kate had time to probe further. There would be enough of that when they saw each other.

It had been a close thing but Isabel had caught the London train in time. The only draw back to going up straight from work was that she hadn't had time to fetch her night things and she didn't have a change of clothes for the morning. But it didn't matter. The impulsiveness of the moment excited her. Just like in Barcelona. She shut her eyes as the Inter-city train pulled out of Winchester, crowded with commuters. She was lucky to have found a seat. These days you paid a ticket but it didn't guarantee you'd be able to sit down. Barcelona. She could think of nothing else …

This time, when she returned, she had felt more than ever that she was going home. Never before had she felt so at ease with the language or the people. The changes in the city since her last visit some years previous, had been phenomenal. With the Olympics the infrastructure of the whole region had improved. Nine billion dollars alone had been spent on improving the decaying old port area. Now there was a marina, seafood restaurants, updated tapas bars, walk ways, an aquarium and a shopping complex. The new Barcelona airport, with its apricot marble floors and countless glass doors was a far cry from the ramshackle building over run with Guardia Civil Isabel had known as a child. Everywhere was evidence of a more democratic and liberal Spain ruled by the most popular monarch in Europe. Not only did the kiosks bulge with foreign newspapers, but the latest films were advertised on Cinema billboards. And the streets abounded with people talking on mobile phones. Even women walking their dogs seemed to find some excuse to chat. In a status- obsessed nation, this was the latest must-have gadget. Now, looking at the neat green fields and the gentle sloping cornfields as they whizzed past her carriage window, England seemed the foreign country.

The train jolted to a standstill and with a start Isabel realised that she had slept for most of the journey. Waterloo was buzzing with commuters who were either rushing to make their trains or waiting for information in front of the Departure boards. People crowded in front of kiosks to buy coffee and sandwiches and the newspaper vendors shouted the evening news while stacking their change in neat tower coins. The central area was like an obstacle course as commuters darted in and out of the crowd trying to create a small, private space in which to await their train. Everywhere was the smell of hot pies mingled with tobacco. Isabel pushed her way out of the station glad of the crisp air. Spring was on its way but at night it was still cold.. At this time of the evening, it would take longer to get to Kate's by taxi but Isabel could not face the hot, over crowded tubes. As the taxi spend along the embankment, she felt the first rumblings of the excitement that always gripped her when she came up to the city. She enjoyed seeing the scenes played out by day, converted to night time. Shoppers still sauntered down the streets as though it were the middle of the morning, oblivious of the cold, under the cover of darkness. In the square young people gathered before hitting the pubs. The feel of spring was palpable and contagious. Isabel felt her heart soar despite her confusion.

The taxi stopped, its engine still running, in front of a large, wide building. Behind was the dusted greenery of communal gardens. Isabel loved to gaze up at the dimly lit interiors. She paid the driver lingering for a moment before ringing the bell. There was row upon row of pretty rooms but Kate's drawing room was the loveliest of them all. Ivory silk curtains framed a double window and a winter flowering jasmine crouched beneath it on the outside. Through the window could be glimpsed the polished surfaces of good furniture, the subtle colours of a rug, the corresponding water colours. Bowls of flowers and small silver objects crowded occasional tables and in the window as though someone had only recently brushed past, lay the scattered petals of cut roses. A fire burned in the grate, a sofa on either side and in between them was a large rectangular ottoman. On top of the ottoman was a silver tray laden with crystal and tempting things to eat. With a bottle of Cava catching the light, the whole scene could have been a photo shoot for one of Archid's brochures.

"Darling!" The door was flung open and Kate threw her arms around her friend. The hall was well lit, the carpet thick and spotless and the whole enlarged by a beautiful gilt mirror that took up the entire length of one wall. Isabel dropped her coat and briefcase on a chair and followed Kate into the drawing room. She was wearing a very short skirt and black tights. Her shoes lay discarded by the sofa where she had been sitting reading.

"Managed to find the fizz," she said motioning to the bottle of Cava. "Come and sit down. You must be exhausted."

"I am and I don't know why. I don't seem to manage much work at the moment."

"Not pregnant I hope."

Isabel grimaced.

"Hardly."

Kate studied her thoughtfully. "Drink first," she said firmly.

Isabel sank into one of the over stuffed sofas, her body pressing against Aubusson cushions. No expense had been spared in converting the place into a luxurious and cocooning apartment. Chairs were covered in the finest fabric, trimmed with the most luxuriant braid, the walls on close inspection revealed many layers of a laborious paint finish and the curtains were double lined, standing proud. Scented candles flickered on round tables, Herend figurines and bronze statues were placed alongside first editions of books bound in leather and graceful lamps with hand made silk shades lit up welcoming corners of the room. A picture of a child with a kite dominated the mantelpiece and a tall boy on the facing wall was topped with blue and white china. It was so warm that Isabel could have stripped naked.

"This is blissful," she said.

"Isn't it?" Kate uncorked the bottle and poured out the champagne. "To us," she said lifting a glass.

"How's the American?" Isabel asked after they'd made the appropriate sighs and settled down with their drinks. There was no sign that anyone else was living in the house, no stray pair of shoes, no unfamiliar papers. But then there was no stray anything. The place was immaculate.

"Scout? He's fine. Nice boy. He's kind to me. Good lips."

Isabel shook her head. "You're unbelievable."

Kate laughed. "Why? Because I know how to have fun? You have to know how to pick 'em though."

They sipped their drinks for a moment in silence. Isabel felt the tension in her ease and she too kicked off her shoes, stretching out on the sofa.

"And work?"

"Oh much the same. Too many late meetings. I was in the office till 10:30 last night. I've headed up a new division but that doesn't stop my old clients thinking they can still call me for advice the minute something goes wrong. And I've got a temp who's useless and out to lunch – I mean literally – half the time I need her. Getting good support staff is so difficult."

"Good management too. Tim is always on to me about it. Sam isn't much good either, but just when I think we've had enough of each other, she perks up and then I wonder if it's worth training someone new and then the time has passed and I find we've rumbled along for another half year! And the body piercing! Ugh! I can't tell you how difficult it is explaining that to my Spaniards! She does make my tea just the way I like it and that has to count for something!"

"I know. I know. It's not as though you can even fire them very easily either. Everyone has all these rights and then they threaten you with unfair dismissal. It's a pain."

They nodded in agreement and drank another glass to compensate for the difficulties facing women in the work place.

"Tim is worried about you," announced Kate at length.

"Tim?" Isabel echoed in mild alarm. "What do you mean? Has he said anything? Since when did you speak to each other?"

Kate held up a hand.

"Hey steady Isa. It's mostly to do with work. We've overlapped in the past."

"Until now."

"He's concerned."

Isabel took a gulp of cava.

"He has no right to go about discussing us – "

Kate balanced her glass carefully on the smooth, damask cushion beside her. "He hasn't. It's only that he says he hasn't seen much of you recently. Even as a friend Isa. But then none of us has."

"I've been busy."

"We're all busy. It's not an excuse."

Isabel took another swig, feeling the drink spin through her head deliciously, her mood uplifted by it.

"Look I don't know if there's room any more for Tim," she said easily and then was shocked by how little it mattered. "I don't love him any more. I don't think that I was ever really in love with him."

"Well you could have fooled me," snorted Kate. "I remember the whole Oman thing. You seemed in love then. You're not like me, remember, I'm the one who gets rid of the good men. Tim loves you. That's got to be worth something. Besides you've been together ages and it's not so easy meeting people when you're at the stage we're both at. The grass isn't always greener you know. You can't just end it!"

"Yes I can."

"But why?"

"Because I've out grown him. I've grown out of love. It's as simple as that. I'm no longer attracted to him, there's no passion any more, no excitement. He's become more like a brother than a lover. We don't live together anyway and there are some weeks I don't see him at all and then when I do – look I don't want to disappoint you but just because you've been with someone for ages doesn't mean you have to marry them and I don't. I'd rather be alone than marry someone I wasn't in love with."

"I don't believe you. You're the romantic, sentimental type. You go all soppy and introspective when you're alone. Look what's happened to you now and it's only been a few weeks!"

"But that's because I'm still 'attached' to Tim and he's the wrong man. When I'm free of him, I'll be perfectly happy."

"Perfectly?"

Isabel nodded.

"I thought you loved him. I know you did. Remember that party? The one where you first met? And then you ran off to the Middle East. You spent a whole year there. You must have felt something. If *that* wasn't love, what was it?"

"Lust. I don't know. I was very young. I was confused. Swept along. I didn't know my own mind."

"And now you think you do?"

"Yes. I know what I want. Or at least what I don't. And right now I know that I'd be happier on my own."

Kate shook her head, her expensively bobbed hair falling around her face.

"Yes but for how long? It can get pretty lonely you know, not having someone to come home to, someone to tell about your day. You never thought Tim was the wrong man before. What's changed? You can't have excitement, you know, all the time," said Kate reasonably. "No matter whom you're with, it palls after a while. That's the reality. The alternative is to go for endless one-night stands and you don't have the character for it. Or the stamina! And I speak from experience."

Isabel shot her a glance.

"I'm sure you do."

"And?"

"And what?"

"It's feeble. Your excuse is feeble. I don't understand how you've suddenly 'fallen out of love.'"

"It wasn't sudden." Isabel looked uncomfortable. "I have felt this way for a while."

Kate looked at her closely.

"I'm really quite shocked you know, Isa" she said.

Isabel smiled.

"I don't see why. You fall in and out of love all the time. Why can't I?"

Kate's eyes narrowed.

"So – you're out of love with Tim but 'in love' with someone else. Is that it?"

"N-no. Not exactly."

Kate's glare was penetrating.

"I just don't I love him anymore," said Isabel knowing how weak it sounded. "I don't know what the fuss is. I'm fond enough of him but when I meet – well when I meet *Spanish* men for example, he just seems so terribly English. And so *boring!* Everything he does annoys me. I know he's good and kind and all that but he's not really very sophisticated, he doesn't have much conversation that doesn't revolve around work and the pub. He doesn't really understand women."

"And Ricardo does?"

Isabel flushed.

"I wasn't talking about – "

"Yeah, you were."

"I wasn't! But now that you mention him, then yes, Ricardo is a lot more exciting to be with than Tim. He has suffered for one thing, with the cancer I mean. But even if it hadn't been for that, there's a different dimension to him. And he understands women. But then Latin men do. They appreciate women, they want to talk to them, be with them. English men want to talk to other men, in a pub and sometimes, if they're feeling really adventurous they may actually want to make love. It's not guaranteed though. They're terrified of showing emotion. Latin men aren't. They're 100% confident in their roles. They know who they are and aren't afraid to be macho, or sentimental or emotional. They aren't afraid of showing their feelings."

"Some might see that as a weakness."

"I see it as a sign of strength."

Kate pursed her lips.

"And this ... Ricardo understands you? Your being Latin?" she raised her blue eyes wide and clear. "And being your cousin."

"Yes. Yes, he does."

"What an impossible thing to compete with then. Ricardo I mean. How can Tim shine against a man who has stared death in the face and overcome? And there's the fact of your shared past. There's nothing quite as seductive as a shared past. Poor Tim, he hasn't got a chance."

Isabel's cheeks flamed as much from the heat of the fire as the admission of unspoken thoughts.

"It's not that simple."

"Of course it isn't."

Isabel poured herself another glass feeling the floor slide off to an angle. She blinked.

"We just get on. Ricardo notices me."

"He's your *cousin*."

"All right but when was the last time an Englishman wanted to really talk to you, took pleasure in being with you simply because he enjoyed being with a woman? You say yourself that most of the men you meet are hopeless louts."

"Yes but then I'm not too bothered about conversation. I don't want to talk poetry or anything remotely like work. I get all that during the day. I don't want to have to waste time with all the romantic stuff. I don't want to talk at all."

"Well I do. I'll say one thing though. The one way to get an Englishman's attention is to talk about his mother or his dogs. Especially if that dog is a Lurcher."

Kate smiled. "Well the men I meet certainly don't want to talk about their mothers! You don't half exaggerate Isabel. You've completely fallen for him haven't you? Then again I don't know why I'm surprised. You were always mad about him. And then every time you come back to school, it was the same old dilemma of you wanting to be Spanish, of not feeling that you fitted in. I want to meet this Ricardo. He has a lot to answer for."

Isabel bowed her head. "Only this time it's worse. It was wonderful being in Spain." She closed her eyes, her head pressing deep into soft feather cushions. "I was dreading it. I hadn't been back in such a long time, years even. I thought it would have changed, that the magic would have gone. But it hadn't. I loved every minute of being home, of returning with the success of Archid under my belt and the confidence it has given me. I realise just how proud I am of my work, how important it is for a woman to be independent. Some of the restraints I felt as a child have gone."

"And Ricardo?"

Isabel kept her eyes closed, trying to conjure up his face in her mind. She was afraid to talk about Ricardo. She had never told anyone about him. Kate knew instinctively that there was someone other than Tim but it was an unspoken secret. Kate knew and Isabel could refer in abstract terms to her visits to Barcelona, knowing that Kate understood. But now, to actually speak his name aloud was to trespass on something intensely private. She was frightened that by speaking about him, the dream would vanish. And yet what was she afraid of? He existed didn't he? As did her feeling for him.

"I saw him."

"Yes?"

"I love him. I always have. But – "

"But you haven't heard from him since you got back."

Isabel shook her head miserably. "I can't understand it. It was so wonderful or at least I thought it was."

"And you're wondering if he isn't really like all men and if this lifelong obsession hasn't been a figment of your imagination? And if it is, what or who will you love now?"

Isabel nodded. "It's more than that. If I could only throw myself into my work it would be all right but I just can't concentrate. Everything seems so dull. Winchester suddenly seems provincial and middle-aged. At work all I do is quarrel with the boss and outside of it, Tim and everything else seem ... well ... boring. I used to love The Cottage and my garden but they don't seem enough now either. When I think of what life could be like in Barcelona, I just feel I'm wasting my time here."

"And what would life be like in Barcelona?" said Kate. "You have a good job here where you're known and respected. You have a lovely house and you used to find working in the garden therapeutic. What exactly would you do in Spain? What kind of work could you find? I know you have your languages but so do most people nowadays. Don't you think that after a while you'd go straight back to being dependent again with the hang ups and insecurities you had then? Look we always want what we can't have. No job is endless fun. I happen to love the law but tax can be stale and lifeless. Sometimes I just want to lie in bed and read Cosmopolitan. I'm sure it's the same with you. You need a break. You're just jaded."

"Perhaps."

Kate yawned.

"I think you need a change of scene," she said. "Why don't you rent out The Cottage and come and work in London for a bit? The problem with you is that you're not really a country girl. A spell up here would do you good. A bit of stimulation is what you need – healthy urbane living. There are hundreds of men around. I bet you don't meet anyone in Winchester! I mean it's a pretty town and all but you're right, it is middle aged. I think we've cracked it you're simply bored with village life."

Isabel's eyebrows were knit together. "It's not that," she said, wishing now she hadn't said anything at all.

"Tim is a good man," Kate persisted. "He's loyal and strong and he'd make a good father."

Isabel choked on her drink.

"Excuse me?"

"Well he would."

"So would lots of men. What's your point?"

"W-well," she replied guiltily. "I know he'd like children."

"So you're really been talking about me!" said Isabel testily.

"No. A bit. Look Tim loves you. Why don't you marry him, move to London for a year or two and have a child."

Isabel put down her drink and stared at her friend in amazement. "You can't be serious? Why would I want a child? My life is complicated enough as it is and why would I want to live in London? I've lived here once before, remember. The issue here is whether or not I should move to *Spai*n and not with Tim. And anyway for once your argument is completely flawed. Most of my friends with children are moving *out* of the city. Besides I don't want children."

Kate looked horrified. "Of course you do. One day. You're just fantastically messed up. I just didn't realise how much."

"Thanks."

"It's being half and half," she said smugly. "It does your head in."

Isabel sighed. She was beginning to feel drowsy and her mouth was dry from all the champagne they had managed to drink. She felt uneasy talking about Ricardo. She felt as if he were everywhere and at the same time out of reach. She began to doubt almost everything about their last meeting. What if it had all been part of her imagination? What if she had created a man and a love for him that didn't really exist? What if Kate was right and she threw away Tim's devotion and loyalty and the possibility of a good future together, for something that she had never really had? And yet those few days together had to have meant something to him too? She wanted to believe that they had. Her gut instinct couldn't be so off course, or could it? The needlepoint cushion was rough against her skin and she was reminded because of it, of her grandmother's house.

"Of course I could carry on just as I have been, " Isabel said thoughtfully. "You're right I haven't really thought about what I might do in Barcelona and I enjoy Archid, at least most of the time, too much to let go of it completely. I know now that I could never *not* work. So why not have both? I could live for part of the year here in England with Tim and see Ricardo when I visit Barcelona! I don't see why I should have one to the exclusion of the other do you?"

Kate was nonplussed. "And you say *my* argument is flawed? You know what's wrong with yours?" she said crisply. "It never works. You can't see two people. One always wants more than the other. It sounds all tidy and workable but invariably you'll yearn for continuity. You'll want to spend more time with one. You'll have your favourite shoes in England when you want them for some dinner with HIM. It's just not practical. It's too emotional for one thing and for another I don't think either Tim or Ricardo would agree to it."

"They wouldn't know."

"I don't believe I'm hearing this."

"But you see lots of men all the time!"

"Yes but one at a time. And even then there can be the occasional sticky moment when one relationship hasn't quite ended and it overlaps with another. It gets awkward. And someone inevitably gets hurt. It's simply not worth the agro." She frowned. "Aren't you tired?"

"I was." Isabel considered her foot clad in its expensive Wolford tights. "The thing is that I like the way Ricardo makes me feel. I like the way he makes me see myself. Tim makes me feel impatient and unkind and then ultimately I feel guilty and then the whole thing starts again. I like myself when I'm with Ricardo. I can stop trying. He knows me so well, knows my childhood. I don't have to explain all the time or justify my every action. And he understands the – my Spanish side."

"Then he's dangerous," said Kate emphatically.

"Why? Because you think he loves me?"

There was a long silence before Kate answered quietly, "Because I think he may not."

Isabel's heart lurched. So Kate didn't believe in it. Why was she so sceptical? Isabel was beginning to wish they hadn't started talking about Ricardo or Spain or anything to do with that time. Isabel felt more confused than ever about Tim. The lovely glowing feeling that came when she had drunk too much and indulged herself by thinking about Ricardo was wearing off and Isabel was suddenly tired and afraid. Kate had grown bored of the subject too and announced that it was time for bed. She turned off the lights and led Isabel upstairs.

The guest room, like the rest of the house was comfortable yet simply furnished. No expense had been spared in the exquisite attention to detail. It was wallpapered in a blue toile de Jouy with heavy ivory silk curtains at the windows. The bare oak floorboards were highly polished. There was a four-poster bed and a Windsor chair by the fireplace. The scent of Tuberoses wafted from the adjoining bathroom where fluffy white towels were piled floor to ceiling in an alcove framed by mirrors. Books filled the shelves. There was a small crucifix in one corner and above the fireplace hung a charming painting of two children playing on a beach. Isabel smiled. It was all so inviting – a physical haven for the tempestuous and conflicting emotions that fought within her.

Isabel lay for a long time in a hot bath, her every sense heightened by her longing for Ricardo. She felt his presence everywhere, as though she were already enveloped in his embrace. Her mind, her skin was impregnated with thoughts of her cousin and the memory of their time together in Barcelona. She longed to be curled up against him, her cheek on his chest, with his arms around her as they talked or were silent, were still. Did he think of her? What was he doing at this moment? How she longed to disengage from the tangled net of her life with Tim. She longed to come clean, to be free and free to talk about him or not, as she saw fit but not to feel as she did now, as if she harboured a guilty secret. By the same token, she was surprised at how calm she felt towards Tim, how remote, not even disloyal or guilty. She knew she would always be fond of Tim and grateful, she supposed, for having taken her on, for having believed in her to the extent that he did. But she did not feel any more than that. Every emotion that she had ever felt for him was used up. Her attachment to him (she could not bring herself to use the word love) was an arid wasteland, seared of any understanding. She could anticipate everything about him, every mood and reaction with the result that she felt as though she had long over taken him. Tim already seemed part of the past. He could not awaken in her, any more desire or unexpected surge of emotion. She felt as though she had been drifting, only half alive for some time and had it not been for this Barcelona trip she probably would have continued to do so, unsuspecting and complaisant. She sank into the water, holding her breath as her face went under. She felt on the brink of something new and exciting. No one was responsible for her actions but herself. She had the power to change things but it was up to her.

Chapter 26

Isabel
Winchester
Spring 1998

    Isabel woke from a deep, unsettling sleep and struggled to remember where she was. The house was quiet and dark. Kate had left for work some time ago. Isabel scrambled into her clothes feeling grubby in spite of the bath the night before. The house was cold. It had the morning after a party feel to it. The light outside was grey, full of unfamiliar sounds – the odd police siren, the chug of a taxi. Isabel pulled back the eiderdown, checked that she hadn't forgotten anything and hurried down stairs. She locked the front door and pushed the keys back through the letterbox. She flagged down a taxi and sank gratefully into the seat, adrenalin racing through her body at the thought of the day ahead. She had failed to recharge her mobile phone so that she was unable to call Sam at work to tell her she'd be late.

    It was a day that went from bad to worse. The cab driver cursed when all she had was a £50 note, she stepped in a puddle splashing her tights and skirt having just decided that she did not have time to go home and change, and to top it all there had been a security alert at Waterloo so that all trains were running some 45 minutes late. When it did arrive the Inter-city was full of disgruntled commuters. Isabel eventually got to work at midday, testy and uncomfortable. She hated appearing less than immaculate and was painfully conscious of her wrinkled suit. The building buzzed with activity. The designers on the third floor were busy, for no obvious reason, designing a miniature psychedelic bikini that they had pasted onto huge cardboard sheets. There were also several mock-ups of champagne bottles and the current advertisements for Bazan Cava. Alternative glossy photographs depicted mellow toned soft focus bunches of grapes, alongside quaint sketches of wine barrels. The bloated scorpion dominated every label.

'Cava. Methode traditionnelle,' it read, *"if giving is in your nature…"*

Isabel almost laughed aloud.

"Let me share the joke." Isabel's boss, Mike Fagan's unmistakably oily voice spoke in her ear. She jumped.

"I thought you were still away," she said unoriginally. She ought to have gone straight up to her office. Likewise she regretted not having breakfasted on the train. Her tummy rumbled and too much Cava the night before had left her feeling listless after an initial spurt of energy. Her head ached. Already she had second thoughts about having confided in Kate. Long after it no longer mattered her friend would have remembered their conversation in detail. It might still come back to haunt her.

Mike laid a casual hand on her shoulder.

"Come up to my office," he said loudly. "You can bring me up to date on the Cava account."

"Sure Mike," she said her heart sinking. She had wanted to be better prepared the next time they met or at least less emotional. She shouldn't have been angry with him. She was also achingly conscious of her splattered tights and slept-in looking clothes. He stepped back, ever courteous, to allow her to pass and she slipped by him and was halfway up the stairs before he could catch up.

"Isabel, my dear, you seem a little, how shall I put it, unsettled?" He was breathless as he followed her into his office. He patted the back of the chair in front of his desk.

"Coffee?"

"Please."

She could not have sounded more grateful if he had offered her a pay rise. Within seconds his secretary had brought in two steaming mugs of freshly ground coffee, not the instant mess that Sam made. Mike's girl appeared significantly more efficient too. Isabel frowned. maybe Tim had a point. Perhaps she wasn't very good at managing her staff. But how was it that men always got women to do their bidding? Whenever she asked Sam to do something it was always accompanied by several reasons as to why it shouldn't be done. She really ought to get rid of her.

Mike sipped his coffee thoughtfully. It was pleasure enough just to be with Isabel. He had missed her. His busy schedule and her trips abroad meant that they hadn't seen each other for some time. Similarly he understood women sufficiently, or so he flattered himself, to sense that she was preoccupied and not by work. For once, emotion seemed to have leaked to the surface of that immaculate reserve. He contemplated her pale face – the dark shadows under the eyes that made them look even greener than ever, more intractable, than ever. She aroused him and now he was deliciously unsure as to which Isabel attracted him more – the chilly ice maiden or the hesitant schoolgirl. If he offered her a shoulder to cry on, if she could see him in the role of protector ... Mike surreptitiously opened his tissue drawer, hand poised at the ready.

"Delicious coffee," she said and then cringing inwardly added quickly, "as good as you get on the Continent. And this is not an ad line."

Mike bowed his head gallantly. He was beginning to feel unexpectedly optimistic. Perhaps their last banter had been nothing more than a wholly feminine ploy of playing hard to get. *And* she hadn't asked her secretary to be with them as she had threatened to! She was all smoke. He smiled warmly.

"My pleasure. I want you to know Isabel, that I can be your friend. If you ever need to talk, if there's anything you want to tell me ... well ..." he shrugged. "You can confide in me. I am always here to listen."

"Thank you Mike." Miraculously the caffeine had given her a boost and the Dutch courage she needed. After the smallest hesitation she pushed the chair back and rose to her feet.

Mike felt for the tissue box pulling one halfway through its pouch. But instead of the tears that he anticipated, (oh hope against hope that she might even perch on his lap) she actually smiled. Dry-eyed, she launched, not into a woeful explanation of her personal problems but a vigorous synopsis of the Bazan account.

"Things have changed overwhelmingly since Franco's death and Spain became a democracy," she was saying by way of introduction. "Especially for Catalonia. Barcelona, its capital, is now the driving force of Spanish economy. Catalonia accounts for 20 percent of Spain's GDP, a quarter of her industrial output and a quarter of exports. And since the peseta recovered, she has had an annual increase in exports of 30%."

Mike blinked and he slammed shut his desk drawer.

"G-good heavens," he stammered.

Isabel shot him a withering look   "Put succinctly," she continued hardly pausing to draw breath, "Catalans enjoy the reputation of being the best business people in Spain – a business acumen inherited from their ancestors, who, in the Middle Ages were the great merchants of the Mediterranean. But what we should really focus on is the fact that Catalonia is world leader in the production of sparkling wines."

"And the Bazan brothers?" muttered Mike his head reeling. "Where do they fit in?"

"With 200 Cava bodegas in North-Eastern Spain, that's where," replied Isabel more tartly than she intended. "They employ some 3,000 people. Last year 142 million bottles were sold worth 57 billion pesetas. The Bazan brothers also have their own vineyards in Chile and have just approached the Malagrida vineyard which currently produces a fine Brut Nature, with a view to trading."

Mike Fagan just caught the notes Isabel flung at him: maps of the region, photographs and glossy brochures. She stood like an avenging angel, hands on her hip, warming to her subject. She explained that Germany was the largest consumer with 14 million litres, followed by America. As Cava became respected in its own right, sales to Europe similarly increased because of its price versus quality ratio. She argued that Cava was just as good as French Champagne, while some French Champagne seemed in her opinion, more acidic.

And as she talked, Mike became more and more excited and determined to secure this rogue Bazan as a client and Isabel in his bed. Bazan could prove to be his most lucrative client to date. There was huge potential, not only in its immediate sector, but increased contract distribution would necessarily demand Archid's expansion as a company. Work on the account would involve even more travel, if that were possible and possibly extended periods living abroad. Mike could hardly contain his elation. For some time now, he felt that he had outgrown the South-East operation. It had ceased to provide a challenge and he had grown dissatisfied and restless. He had long felt that his skills were being wasted in this tiny conglomerate. He had often envisaged himself in Japan or the Far East, and in securing the Bazan account, this dream would be realised. He knew he was personable - could demonstrate some charm even- and was a shrewd negotiator. Together with Isabel, they would make an unbeatable team. Adrenaline pumped through his body. He knew he could go far. He had been waiting for an opportunity such as this, to make his mark and now it was being handed to him on a plate. Mike had always been driven by ambition ever since his uneasy student days at a minor public school. He had not made Oxbridge but Reading University instead. Cambridge's refusal to accept him had sown the seeds for an inferiority complex that had never left him. But now was the time to redress the balance – make the world see what a success he had become. He felt himself gripped by the familiar driving force of ambition, the dizzying feel of power, like a sexual urge. His eyes travelled hungrily over Isabel's body, lingering on the stretch of thigh as it strained against the soft material of her skirt. This new, dishevelled look was more inviting than her chicest outfit. Perhaps it was another signal that she was ready to make amends. Tonight he would make a move. Enough of this coyness! They were adults after all, not clumsy teenagers.

But what was she doing now? She leant over his shoulder jabbing at the paper in front of him. He could smell her skin. Her presentation was incredible, even for this informal meeting. She must have rehearsed for days. He admired such professionalism. Yes, things were looking good. His heart thumped as his glorious future unfurled before his eyes. He felt omnipotent. He could have anyone and do anything. He could buy into a dream that was a fingertip's reach away. He frowned, wasn't that a jingle from one of Archid's design campaigns? He giggled to himself. No matter, essentially it was true – clichés in general were true. No joke existed that did not convey some truth. What was it that he had memorised at school? *'Our deepest laughter is one that tells of saddest thought.'* How wise he felt, how philosophical! He could actually feel the length of his future and what it held. It was dazzling, intoxicating highlighted along the way by accolade after accolade, media tribute after tribute and light-years from Winchester. He felt giddy. More hysterical laughter gurgled behind his throat.

"And that about wraps it up."

Mike heard the pause, waited for the climatic moment that would surely come. She stood exhausted by the talk, her body spent, as he imagined it might be, post coitus. His look was full of anticipation and approval. Now, came the moment when they wrestled, metaphorically, about fees.

Isabel stood with her hands splayed against the back of her chair resting one new shoe against the other, but gently so that the suede was not marked. The weight of her breasts was clearly defined under the roll neck of her cashmere sweater.

"And that is why ..." she stated calmly, "... the Bazan brothers have absolutely no intention of changing their packaging, design or financial system. They wish to remain a Catalan concern which they have been since the 17 century and which I have endeavoured to illustrate against the background of the new Spain. They have naturally stressed how impressed they were with our presentation but they do *not* wish to employ us."

Mike could hear a buzzing in his ears. Suddenly the blood seemed to be bursting through his brain and he felt a pins and needles sensation in his left arm. His tie seemed to strangle him and he stumbled to his feet. Knocking over the proposals: brochure, coffee mugs and whatever else lay in his wake, he slumped across his desk.

Isabel froze in horror. For a moment she was paralysed with shock and then common sense got the better of her and she swung into action. She ran 999 for an ambulance, shouted for help and loosened his clothing trying desperately to turn him over. She had barely managed to manoeuvre him into the recovery position when the medics arrived. Relinquishing the honour of escorting him to the hospital to his secretary, who covered his cheeks in kisses and could not stop sobbing, Isabel slipped out of his office. Archid was all at once heaving with personnel, media and curious pedestrians. Isabel instructed security to lock the front doors and encouraged the translators to leave once they had printed out any material still in the system. Even so it was a couple of hours before Isabel was able to leave. The phones had seemed to ring endlessly and no one could be bothered to answer. She responded in robot fashion, cancelling appointments and reorganising Mike's diary. At last she was free to go.

Chapter 27

Isabel
Winchester
Spring 1998

 Somehow Isabel found herself home again. She had little recollection of the short drive through her village or of having switched off the alarm as she entered the house. The scent of paper whites hung in the air. Never had she been so happy to get home. Isabel dumped her brief case on a chair and made straight for the drinks cabinet. Her hands shook as she poured herself a generous whisky which made her think she was more shocked than she thought. Surely she couldn't be entirely responsible for Mike's heart attack? What was going on that in trying to be clear and truthful she was causing such chaos to those around her? The medics had done their best to reassure her that Mike had an ongoing heart condition but Isabel was riddled with remorse. She'd been too harsh. In her desire to quash the Bazan proposal she'd ignored all the warning signals. She refilled the tumbler and took it out with her into the garden.

 The air was sharp, clear and very still in the weak evening sun. She took a couple of deep breaths trying to keep her mind blank. She would walk around the whole of the garden and concentrate on nothing else and she would start at the North end, pausing for a moment under the arch of yew in order to see the whole expanse of lower lawn across to the valley. Through a Yew gateway she explored the pond that was flanked by nine topiary ducks. In the summer there would be pond lilies and fat pink tea roses growing between the hedges. From there, uneven stone steps led down to a croquet lawn and gazebo. A gravel path wound its way behind the orchard to an ivy-covered grotto. Isabel picked her way through the rock garden with its pools of leaf-drenched water, along the brick path that lead back to the herbaceous border and Pandora.　She leant against the statue's base. Pandora was looking a lot happier now that the lychen had been removed but the cracks through her face retained that quizzical look that Isabel always found encouraging.　Contrasting scarlet berries made her appear as if she were picking her way through the thorns.　Form here, Isabel could just make out the iron silhouette of the Victorian green house although she could not remember the last time she'd been inside. Curiosity propelled her on.　Glibly, she stepped over the ankle- high, boxed hedges of the parterre. The door was open.　She ducked under the ancient vine that covered the doorway.　Here, was a secret world of potting plants and indoor graftings. Everything was fastidiously organised.　Carefully wound rope and hose hung from purpose built hooks. Packets of seed and weed killer were stacked alongside fish food and insecticide.　Shelves groaned with gardening books and weekly magazines.　A kettle and mug patiently waited on a tray, together with a pair of gloves and a trove.

Isabel was astounded.　She had thought her contribution to weeding and the odd de-heading of roses, significant.　She was ashamed to admit that gardening even featured as a hobby on her CV.　But it was clearly inadequate when compared to her gardener's immense knowledge of the subject.　Carefully labelled notebooks were piled by his expense ledger and once again Isabel was astonished by the care and time devoted to them. She flicked through pencil references to lawn scarifying and illustrations of rare plants.　A large drawing block and a child's set of crayons were amongst the paraphernalia. She turned the pages.　There was a deceptively simple sketch of the parterre that was clearly visible from the green house.　She glanced up comparing the formally patterned box hedges to the pastel drawing.　In darker hues he had accurately depicted the chamfered corners designed to give the central area an illusion of space.　He had drawn each box hedge and listed the plants and flowers that were to be filled in each area.　Then he labelled each box: A, B, C and D. In his wobbly, spider writing he had written:

A= Rosa (wind rush), Lemon, Hips, Pink Cornelia, Boule de Neige.

B= Nepeta (grey and blue), Forget- me-nots, Lobelia for summer or Love In A Mist, Campanulas and Geraniums

C= Santolina(pale lemon), Dianthus – Mrs.Simkins (white), Artemisia and Lavender.

D= Verbascum, Tulips(white) or Anemone (jap), Digitalis(pale pink)

'End of summer,' she read, 'cut back Nepeta, pull out Forget- me-not, leaving seedlings for next year. Geraniums stay in — cut back dead leaves after autumn colour. Under plant Roses in Section B with winter flowering pansies to extend interest in the autumn. Remove or cut back when spring growth re-emerges. Dead head roses until end of summer when Wind rush may be allowed its hips!'

Isabel folded back the drawings. No wonder her gardener hid here on rainy days. She could think of nothing more pleasant than to sit sketching, while outside rain splashed against the windows. Now in the cold and enclosing twilight, it could not have been more peaceful and she felt the shock of the day slowly recede. She only regretted not having brought out the whisky decanter. She felt too lazy to go back into the house and anyway it would soon be too dark to read. Even Pandora's face, usually luminous at night, was beginning to recede into the shadow of trees.

Lost in thought, she did not hear the crunch of gravel as Tim's car swerved and then skidded into the drive. It wasn't until she heard him calling her name that she ventured out of the green house. He stood trapped on the other side of the box hedges, breathing out cold gusts of air. He waved, wrapping his thick yellow cashmere scarf around him. She had never liked the colour. It was not something Ricardo might have worn. Tim stood for a moment staring at her with the barrier of box between them. He took a step forward and Isabel held up hand as if to warn him off, not wanting him to intrude on her newly found haven.

"I've been calling for ages. Didn't you hear me?"

Isabel looked up, bristling at his tone.

"Oh hello," she said.

He raised his eyebrows.

"Just hello?"

The minute news reached him of Mike Fagan's heart attack, Tim had cancelled his partners' meeting and rushed to The Cottage to be with her. He envisaged Isabel nursing a drink by the fire, listening to Mozart and greeting him warmly. He anticipated a relaxed evening, eating in and talking – something they didn't seem to be able to manage much recently. Instead, he had spent a good twenty minutes trying to get into the house. He was now freezing cold and hungry.

She ignored the jibe. "I've been in here. Sorry, must have been miles away. I've discovered Mr. Pebble's notes. They're fascinating. You'd be *amazed* at the attention to detail and the drawings are really good. He puts me to shame. All the time I've fancied myself as a gardener and he's the one slogging away. I really am going to try and be more involved with this house."

Tim shook his head in disbelief. "Who the hell is Mr. Pebble? You don't mean your *gardener?*"

Isabel bit her lip distractedly. "I'll show you his work sometime. Even you would be impressed. By the amount of time he's put into it if nothing else –"

"Never mind Mr. Pebble," exploded Tim, "what about Mr. *Fagan?* I came as soon as I heard." Tim's toes seemed to have fused with his shoes and he was becoming increasingly irritated. "Aren't you cold?" he added petulantly.

"Not really. Oh Fagan is all right. It was only a small heart attack. Scared him more than anything. Over stressed and under fit is what the doctor said. He'll have to take it a bit easy. But he'll be fine."

Again she seemed to concentrate on the leaf of a viburnum bush. Everything about her was seemingly off hand, disinterested, in him, that is. His heart sank. Isabel did not seem at all happy to see him and he'd had a lousy day. He had been up early for a 6am breakfast meeting. Then there'd been an error in the set of accounts he had been due to sign off on and a recent recruit was threatening to leave. Only the thought of seeing Isabel and warmed by the memory of happier times had cheered him up. Now he turned away in disappointment. There was nothing appealing about hovering in the grey half light while the frost crept slowly in on them. The facing casements windows were welcome beacons of warmth and he desperately wanted to be inside.

"You must be in shock. Let's go in. I could do with a drink to be honest. It's been a hell of a day and for you too. Come on you can tell me all about it."

"I'm not," said Isabel, wishing he hadn't come and willing him to leave. "I mean I'm not shocked – I was obviously at the time, it happened so quickly. But now that I know he's going to be OK. Anyway there's nothing to tell. It was quite funny really. Mike thought he could get his leg over AND secure the Bazan account and I was in the middle of telling him that they weren't interested, when suddenly he grabbed his neck, rather than me and fell over. Luckily his desk broke his fall otherwise he might have cut his head. I couldn't help much. He was too heavy to move. I had no idea it was a heart attack. At first I thought he was just pausing for breath before crucifying my campaign." Isabel started to giggle. "It could have been **so** embarrassing."

"You seem to have coped very well," Tim said coolly. "But I expect this will mean big changes to Archid. You'll have to carry his workload while he's convalescing."

"I suppose so. I hadn't thought that far."

"Still I expect his clients will allow some room."

Tim thought about the holiday he had been planning. The chances of things ever going back to normal seemed more and more remote. He realised his coming here had been a mistake. If only she would meet him half way but she seemed so absorbed in her own thoughts. He turned to go.

"Isabel, I love you. But I can't wait for you forever. I asked you to marry me and I understand why you said what you did. But I know you didn't mean it, not really. I'm getting old and I've reached the point where I'm tired of games. I want to settle down and have a family. I never thought I would but I do now, more than anything. I will ask you one last time but if the answer is no then I want to call it a day. Do you understand?"

Isabel swallowed.

"Come into the house," he repeated and then more gently, "we'll talk inside."

"No!"

The word came out like a gunshot. Isabel had not meant it to sound so violent. Her head was beginning to spin with the day's events. She just wanted to be left alone, for her no to mean just that.

"I'm sorry Tim. I just can't – "

"Can't marry me or can't decide?"

"I – look I'm sorry," she said with an effort. "I'm tired I-"

"I know." Tim was instantly contrite. "What can I do? Shall I make supper? Let me stay – "

Isabel's eyes widened and his heart sank.

"You're shutting me out," he said. "Literally. It's freezing. Let's go in and talk."

He attempted to pull her into his arms but she was tense and unyielding.

"Isabel I love you. I want to marry you. Doesn't that mean something to you? I don't understand what the problem is. If you love me as you used to say you did, then surely you'd want to marry me. Either we get married or we end it."

He felt the tension in her stiff body. He released her. Tim was right of course. If she loved him … but it was a big If. He forced her to look at him but there was little warmth in her eyes.

"I know this is a difficult time for you at work. But work can't be everything. You've got to have something outside it. You're becoming obsessive. It doesn't have to be all or nothing."

"Doesn't it?" she flared suddenly. "I've spent years trying to get where I am. I like my independence. But you know, not all that much has changed for women. I still come under unbelievable scrutiny at work. They want to know everything about me, my private life, where I shop, what I wear. Everything. And now that Mike is off sick there will be even more to do. I'm away half the time as it is. I have to be just that much better than my male counterpart, to get half, no a quarter, as far. And now that I have, I'm not about to chuck it away."

"Not for me obviously," said Tim quietly.

"Oh Tim," said Isabel impatiently. "It's not that. Don't you see how difficult is? Everyone is demanding so much from me. I feel I'm torn at work, you pull me in one direction, my friends in another. If I try to be tough, you say I'm aggressive. If I try to soften up, you say I don't exert myself enough. I just want people to stop wanting me to live up to *their* ideal. I have to be myself."

"I'm not criticising you Isabel, I'm only asking you to marry me."

"Yes but you want my time. And that's all I have left for me."

"I'm sorry you see it that way." His voice was distant, cold. He searched her face for any trace of affection, any softening of her mood but there was none.

How had they become these two sparring partners with nothing to share but resentment and bitterness? There were times when he thought she actually disliked him. Those balmy days in Oman when he believed she loved him seemed nothing but a distant memory. He was proud of what Isabel had achieved but now he realised it had been at a huge cost. He had not appreciated how determined and self-absorbed she had become and how the stronger side of her character had evolved to eclipse a fragile ego. The uncertain but gentle girl she was then had gone. He didn't want to acknowledge the fact, but she was fast turning into any number of the hardened professional women he met on a daily basis through work. He shifted his weight in his expensive Church's shoes and almost groaned with the pain. He was sure he had frostbite.

"You know what your problem is, Isabel," he said. "You want everything to be just like one of your advertisements, smooth and clean-cut, beautiful people in well groomed situations – no flaws. But that just isn't life. This is the reality. We go on and on. Life doesn't just stop at the end of a photo shoot. We make choices and compromise all the time. There is no plateau when everything stops and the curtains are drawn and it says The End. You have one chance of getting it right and if you screw up that's too bad. Only you aren't giving us that chance. You're bored with this relationship because someone has told you it's not quite perfect, all of the time. And if Kate is your guru I wouldn't pay too much attention to what she says. Of course she has great relationships because the minute she's bored she moves on. But that's not commitment. And it won't make her happy. It won't make you happy. Ultimately you'll end up an embittered old woman and very much alone. I don't know what more you want from me. I don't know what you want full stop. But not even you are worth the wait. Not any more. "

He wrapped his scarf more securely round his neck and taking careful steps, walked away from her.

Isabel huddled against the low wall of the green house watching the car headlights disappear down the drive. She noticed that winter roses were growing along the path. It was strange to think of the winter months in a garden as being dead ones, for in many ways, and it only occurred to her now, it was very much alive. Beneath a frozen exterior, life in its various stages, beavered away, biding its time until the Spring. It was now, when the garden was stripped of its perfume and foliage, that the elegant bone structure was most apparent. The distinctive yews shaped its structure, drew out the boundaries of her land. A barn owl hooted from the direction of the orchard. The moon, bright and full, swung above the pond slicing the grass and obelisk topiary in half. Pandora gleamed, smiling secretively.

If only you could tell me, thought Isabel, scraping moss from the statue's marble sandals. *If only you could speak, tell me what I should do. Am I throwing away my one chance of happiness? Am I being a complete fool? After all, what am I holding out for? It's not as if Ricardo has actually said anything, as if there's the remotest hope that he might love me, whereas I did love Tim once. Or thought I did. I feel gutted to think I may have hurt him and that this time I may have gone too far. And he loves me better and more compassionately than I have a right to be loved. God knows I've tested his love, made him suffer for it, given little in return. I've depended, to some extent, on him always being there in the background. And now that he may not, it should matter but it doesn't. Despite the pain I've caused him, it doesn't seem to matter.*

Isabel sat back against Pandora. That was the awful truth of it. In spite of all Tim's love and the carefully nourished hope of a shared future, it didn't matter. Slowly but completely, her love for Tim had died. Try as she might to breathe life into it, it was gone. And she was more confused than she had ever been. *And colder!* She felt very tired.

What was it Sigi had said to her once in the San Juan Hospital during that disastrous visit when Isabel had wanted so much to help her? *'The good I would I do not, but the evil that I would not, that I do.'*

Well, Sigi had been wrong to say it about herself.

Chapter 28

Sigi
Journal

    My grandmother's house stands on the top of a steep hill over looking the sea and the city of Barcelona ... How often I have seen it in my mind's eye and travelled there in the wrangled wreck of my subconscious. *Visualisation,* they have said, *is the key to recovery. Try and picture a scene, an object, anything that might be a source of inspiration and comfort,* which had made me laugh – the only images I can picture are those of needles and cavorting figures on a bed! The only peace I have ever known was one derived from self abuse. In the beginning, those drugs were replaced with these tranquilizers and such was the effect that it was difficult to think about anything let alone *visualise* it. But slowly the fog cleared and eventually some of the more violent images receded. I began to remember, at first, only the early days of my childhood. Much later, when they were confident I wouldn't stuff the paper down my throat or stab out an eye with the pencil, they gave me writing material. I was terrified by the whiteness of the sheets. There was nothing but white. Everywhere. The walls, the floors, the bed and the nurses were all *white.* I stared for hours at the paper uncertain as to what was expected. It was as though I were stranded in a desert of white waiting for the Little Prince to say:

    "If you please ... draw me a sheep!"

    But no one said anything. Was I to write my name, which some days I could hardly remember, and if not my name, then what? After some days had passed, letters did appear on that immaculate white paper, that Tabula Rasa of the mind. Stick letters appeared as if my fingers were detached from the brain, with a will of their own. I used the pencil as a book binder might his tool, carving out the word as if it were gold leaf impregnated onto fine leather. I scratched out the name Rodrigo, over and over again, until there was only the margin left to write on and the words:

I love you, I love you, I love you.

And after that, there was nothing. Emptiness. (*The mind is its own place and it alone can make a heaven of hell, a hell of heaven.*) Until they give me more paper. Only this time it is a whole fat wad like a sanitary napkin and again I stare at it unable and unwilling. And they begin again …

"*Try to visualise an image, water for example …* "

"The sea," I say, as much to my surprise, as theirs and it is their inordinately enthusiastic response that silences me once more.

"Yes. Yes. The sea so what does that mean to you?"

But again there is nothing. Days follow days and nights are all rolled into one long whiteness – days in which I recognise nothing in myself that is familiar. These are days that hold no memory of the past and no future and are filled only with disquiet and unfeeling. I am consumed by a numbness that paralyses my thoughts and automates my physical responses. Rodrigo. *Mio Cid* and I know that if I succumb yet again, as I have been doing repeatedly, if once again I am prescribed benzodiazepines, I shall never emerge from this place – never ask for paper, never be able to even formulate such a request. With the greatest effort of will, I thrust these fragile images away. Instead, I cling to the sanity of the scene before me, that of the great ocean, below and above and the thunder of the waves to soothe, to calm and obliterate feeling …

*

My grandmother's house stands on the top of a steep hill overlooking the sea and the city of Barcelona. The hanging gardens of Babylon must surely have inspired the terraces that sloped from East to West, down to a murmuring sea. There was a Moorish influence to the bathing pools and the fountains that trickled water from fish that leapt in the air to capture the light. There were pathways and arches supported by fragile columns, patios in unexpected places and an alcove beneath an orange tree. There was room upon room of sculpted loggias, mosaic screens through which to hide from a world that had hidden us away. And suspended everywhere was the scent of white gardenia, thin spiked palms and tuber roses. There were fruit trees of all description: fig, peach and pear and wisteria that twisted its boughs round columns of jasmine. In spring its scent was carried with the Sahara breeze into the garden rooms, whispering and inviting, full of summer promise.

The evenings in this place are long. Although they give you drugs to sleep and then again in the morning to wake you up, the long quiet hours till morning seem filled with the collective nightmares of my youth. Sometimes I dream that I am once again at Mialma and I awake sweating, disorientated by the misleading layers of whiteness that surround me and only the sound of the sea below offers a glimmer of beauty in this ugly and sterile place. Sometimes, if I am very lucky, I dream that I am once again with Rodrigo, during the early months of our courtship. I cling to those dreams, not daring to open my eyes against the cruel glaring light of the day and the interminable hours of morning. I blot out what has gone before and what came after and I concentrate on recalling the summer months when we first met …

In many ways, Rodrigo was very like my father. Like Tito, he had had a thorough, if unimaginative education. Rodrigo was not interested in the arts. Despite the fact, for example, that his mother was one of its patrons, Rodrigo had never been to our city's great Opera House, the Liceo. He had never read a book that was not about horses. But he was easy to be with and uncomplicated. The parameters of his world were defined long before he was able to make a conscious choice. And what remained was governed simply by nature and the wildlife around him. There was no subtlety to the range of emotions he experienced but he was articulate enough to describe them. He was happiest however, with his horses. Equally, he was unhampered by self-doubt. He had not stumbled towards adulthood, as I had, racked with uncertainty. He had not been crushed by a father's genuine dislike of his child. He was not consumed by needing. And he loved me, I believe in the beginning. I thought we would write our future with the stars that nothing would mar, the intensity of our loving.

When it was over I wanted to die. Every morning I woke not knowing if it was day or night, with no desire to ever wake again. The pain was like a hundred knives thrust into my heart. It was always there, shadowing my sleep. Sometimes there was nothing I wouldn't have done to make it go away. When I lost the baby, my agony was total and the bloodied sheets were nothing to the mangled wreck that come from my body, from my mind. It is then that I cry, the tears choking back the pain of memory. I cry for the foolish girl I was then, for those lost years, for not having had the wisdom to listen, to know that I could change. I know we could have been happy, Rodrigo and I. But I was too proud. When I walked out of the gates of his *finca*, the morning of the King's coronation, I did not really believe that I would never return.

And I yearn for him still. When the mosquito netting flutters in the breeze and the sea turns azure blue in the heat and if I close my eyes, I can just pretend that we are together again in the tower room at Val Negra. I can feel him beside me, the weight of his arm across my shoulder, the sound of the chapel bells at dawn.

The whiteness of my room is disconcerting. Sometimes I see black blobs, like ants creeping from the cracks in the plaster and I turn my face away. This colour or non-colour, isn't soothing. I thirst for restive light, for undulating shades of blue or sea green or even pink but this white, that reminds me of the Carmelite chapel at Mialma, is nauseating and ageing. There are no mirrors or pictures on the walls. I laugh to myself to think of the Coach House where every inch of space was given to pictures. When the blankness of the walls equals only the terrifying emptiness of the paper, I amuse myself by recalling those paintings and traveling mentally through all the rooms of the house. I begin at the massive hall with its furious portraits. I travel up the gilded staircase to the balconied rooms of the first floor. Here you can see the "modern" painters: de la Serna, Abreu, Tapies and Miro. Not everyone likes these of course but they are still notable examples of Post-Francoist art. Ines, Rodrigo's mother would have approved. Only Nuria's rooms are unexplored. Perhaps fear stopped us from pushing open the heavy doors onto a world of such loneliness, it was unbearable to contemplate. We respected the little privacy she had, knowing that if denied her sanctuary, we might lose her altogether. It was in these rooms that her children were conceived and born and then carried away to the nursery to be cared for by Scorpion Lupe.

From the balcony of the house, approached by emerging onto the flat roof and then in again along a narrow passage and up a spiral staircase, you could just glimpse the twin towers of Mialma. After Isabel came to live there, that first summer, Marta and I would scramble up to this rooftop to shout our goodbyes. It was where the twins came to smoke, Marta to be with Fernando and Baby B to recite her catechism. It was my favourite spot, the only place you could safely be alone. It was where the Sahara breeze brushed your cheek in high summer and the scent of orange blossom wafted along the night air in springtime. It was the only place I ever prayed, the night I lost the baby …

*

I have made awkward, small dots with the tip of the pencil all over the white page. They remind me of the snowflakes in the paper weight Tito gave Lupe once as a present. She was thrilled with her toy and she made a special place for it on the shelf in the nursery. Carefully cupping it in both hands she would bring it down to show us. She would shake it gently so that the snow scattered filling the sky. We had never seen snow and Marta and I would marvel at this miniature world enclosed in the palm of our hand. On the same occasion, Tito had given us a globe of the world and a storybook in English by Hans Christian Anderson. In this book there were drawings of China junks laden with tea chests and there were small children dressed as we were in Sailor suits, sporting hats made out of newspaper. There was a picture of a King and Queen dancing in their bedroom slippers and Grenadier guards marched up and down the pages beating a drum. Whenever Isabel was home and came into the nursery, she would give the globe a great push sending it spinning round and round so that I was afraid it might come off its stand. Then suddenly she would slap down her hand, making it stop abruptly.

"There!" she would say triumphantly as if having just conquered the place herself. "Vanuatu. Tell us, you Miguel. Tell us what you can about the place – its latitude, population that sort of thing in less than, let's see now, one minute!"

She was intense about everything she did and the expression on her face made us laugh. Miguel would make up some ludicrous story about cannibals in grass skirts eating chocolate bars for breakfast. She would spin the globe again.

"Now tell me about Manila, Western Sahara, Algeria, Bhutan, Sikim, Saskatchewan!"

"Which isn't a country," interrupted Ricardo. "You've listed countries. Saskatchewan is a province."

Isabel hesitated.

"Where?" asked Bea.

"Canada stupid," replied Marta sneaking a peak at the globe.

"She's right," agreed Isabel and then to my brother she said, "No wonder you want to read law, you're pedantic enough."

But rather than be annoyed, Ricardo seemed pleased by this observation. Isabel spun the globe again flashing him another look. "Don't you want to see these places?" she asked dreamily. "The names trip of the tongue like a balm. They're so romantic! Just think Hong Kong, New York, Oslo even Sevilla sounds wonderful."

"Well you'll just have to find a rich husband," said Lupe in her usual, disgruntled fashion, dumping a basket of laundry unceremoniously at our feet. "And a husband who will want to travel. Most men want their women folk home producing babies."

"You mean like our mother," piped up Bea helpfully.

"Ugh!" Isabel made a face. "*Not* like Nuria. I have no intention of getting married."

"You don't?" Baby Bea's eyes were as round as saucers.

Isabel shook her head. "No rich husband for me. No husband at all. I'm going to make my own money. I shall work. I'm not going to rely on anyone to feed and clothe me."

Lupe cleared her throat loudly and began to fold clothes draping them all over the spare chairs and over the desk where Marta was writing. She looked up pushing a shirt out of her way clicking her tongue in annoyance. I held my breath. Lupe's eyes, scorpion fashion, had narrowed menacingly. Our mother was having one of her *malas* and Lupe didn't look in the mood to discuss anything let alone the rights of woman. But Ricardo sat back in his chair watching our cousin thoughtfully looking as if there was nothing he wouldn't discuss with her.

"Then what will you do?" asked Bea who had been brought up, like the rest of us to believe that a woman's place was in the home. It had never occurred to her to think she might do anything else. Isabel stopped the globe.

"I don't know yet but I shall start with university. Maybe I'll teach. I'm not very patient though. Or I might consider publishing. I like books. I'd love to be surrounded by books all day. It would be heaven."

We stared at her in amazement. Lupe's tongue darted in and out of her mouth, wetting her thin hairy lips, which I could have sworn had turned green in the process.

"University!" she scoffed hands on hip, toothless gums pushed forward. "You're dreaming my girl! Women don't study! Learning to cook would be more useful. I'd get hold of *Tia Victoria's Cookbook* and study that! What man wants to eat books for his dinner? A man wants a woman who can run a household and put a decent meal on his table, bring up his children and keep a tidy home. He doesn't care whether or not his wife likes to read!"

"Not necessarily," interjected Ricardo mildly. "I think Isabel *should* go to university if that's what she wants. It *is* as important for girls as it is for men. Even Spain is slowly changing. You do exactly as you please, Isa. Don't let anyone put you off."

But Lupe wouldn't let the matter rest. She swooped down on the laundry basket like a pelican looking for fish. Her arthritic knuckles clutched at our clothes as she folded them in piles, shaking them out roughly – a fisherman casting his net.

"And who is going to pay for this foolishness?" asked Lupe. "We all know that good for nothing Englishman didn't leave much. And poor Clara, well her money wasn't hers anyway – "

Isabel's head shot up and her eyes were green flints behind concave spectacles. I had never seen her look angry.

"I have never asked anyone for anything," she said quietly. "If I go to university," she paused to correct herself, *"When* I go to university I shall do so on my own steam. You won't have to worry about money. I shall never ask this family to pay for anything. There are such things as scholarships, Lupe, and that's what I intend getting. I have always come top of my class and I have never had to repeat a year. You can laugh all you like but *I will* get to university."

After that we were all a bit wary of Isabel. None of us had ever questioned Lupe's authority before. But Isabel had. We had always thought Isabel to be a bit 'bookish,' odd even but on this occasion she manifested an ambition to succeed that was alien in the rest of us. She was as warm and loving as before but now we respected her. In spite of her abysmal clothes and clumsiness, she clearly possessed what Spaniards respected more than anything, a *vida interior*. She had revealed a passion, a secret life. Suddenly it became important to have her respect.

Even Nuria was to say in later years that her daughters had not been ambitious enough. Isabel had bided her time, had known what she wanted. She never complained. Perhaps we were insensitive to her feelings. But the truth is that we never gave her a moment's thought. We didn't know if she minded being plump, what her likes and dislikes were – apart from studying and my brother Ricardo that is. There was something aloof about Isabel even as a child. From the moment she came into our lives she was apart from us, always on the edge, always looking in. She watched us keenly, studied our mannerisms, the way we spoke, the way we did our hair, as if storing the knowledge she gleaned for future reference. We were flattered by the attention, amazed that she should genuinely want to be like us. So while we fretted about our clothes and whether or not Pepita had ironed out the creases in a blouse, with no thought beyond the evening's fun, Isabel was shaping her future, vowing even then that she would never be without money or physical comfort. As we grew up, she was a mirror image of how not to be and we prided ourselves on being thinner and prettier, more loved and more feted. We surrounded ourselves with mirrors, limiting our world even then to one of appearance and artifice. It should not have come as any surprise, therefore, that when Isabel finally left, she took one gigantic step forward, leaving us bereft, and light years behind.

So many images crowd my mind and are clumsily translated on the page. They are a collage of fragmented time, self-imposed on this white paper. Isabel would not have approved, nor Rodrigo for that matter. They both had that in common - a desire to keep order, as if by imposing order they might control the uncontrollable. As if they might govern fate by will. Shadows clutter snatches of conversations punctuated by syntax and still it means nothing. Only the crashing waves of the Pacific Ocean hold any meaning. I can hear the waves beating on the white plaster walls of the clinic and see the long stretch of beach below. It is a beautiful place. The location at least is beautiful. Funny, that in all her spinning of the world, Isabel's hand never landed on Chile. Perhaps she did have some control after all. Would I have shrunk from that name? Would some shiver of revelation have passed over me? Would I have had a sense of deja vu? Sometimes my grip on the day's reality is so tenuous that I feel I am clinging to time with my fingernails, a sensation I have to say I never knew when I took speed. Everything was clear then, vivid, even though it wasn't real. During the brief dreams, I dreamt when I was awake, I felt confident and happy. Now I tread water and one unfortunate slip, and I shall go under, to be submerged in the shadows.

If only I could see my little boy. I need to touch, be touched, held in arms that bind and comfort, arms that hold me from myself ...

*

They say there has been a relapse. Or at least I have reached a plateau from which I will not budge. *Would you?* I long to scream at them, w*ould you volunteer to move from the safety of oblivion, to abseil down the drop of memory? I have come a long way but the road I took was the one least travelled by and that made all the difference.* But I cannot or will not walk that extra mile. Sometimes I sink effortlessly to the bottom of my subconscious, as I would if I had plunged into the sea. Then there is that delicious drowning feeling as my arms move above my head. But still I can stop it. I know I can. My ears are logged with water. There is silence and thunder, booming cannons under the sea's surface. Silence. I remember the strangest things – the tapered candles at the Carmelite Convent, the thick incense which made the air heavy, impenetrable. I remember the black virgin of Montserrat whose face is plastered on every postcard of Barcelona. Watery faces float along the surface in rainbows of colour like oil in a puddle of water – faces that I should recognise, that are familiar and strange. These have androgynous smiles that do not match the eyes, maimed limbs and heads, all engaged in this sinister fight for recognition.

Rodrigo? Is it you? Is it *your* voice and that of our aborted child that constantly haunts me? Is it? Rodrigo? What form do you take now? Are you all the voices of my childhood? The house at Val Negra, the walled garden down to the sea? Which is it? Why can't I remember?

But I know your name. And it surfaces again and again. It will not be deleted. Rodrigo. *Mio Cid.*

Only the margin left to write on now. I love you. I love you. I love you.

The next morning is Sunday. I know this because of the silence and the tolling bells. It is April and the winds from the South Pacific are chilly. People talk of moving to Santiago. I will not be moved. I want to be near my son. I know he will come and visit. A child always wants his mother, as a mother yearns for her child. He must be curious to know what has happened to me. He must want to see me. What have they told him? What does he remember?

I will never forget the morning he was born. Six o'clock on such a morning as this and I wanted to shout for joy, to tell the whole world I had a son. I wanted to ring every church bell. I felt my heart was bursting with happiness. That morning was like no other in the world, new and innocent and all my sins were wiped away. I was overwhelmed with emotion as tears ran down my cheeks and he – I stop. Who is *He*? Not Rodrigo? It was not Rodrigo. I struggle to remember. The shape and sound of his voice is so strange, not really loved and not beloved as was Rodrigo's. His voice does not arouse the surge of passion I feel for my son. *Then whose is it?*

Again an aqueous film floats before my eyes. I smooth the page, another white sheet of paper to begin on again. Every time, they say, is a new beginning, but can I trust them? What if they are lying? They wear too much white and merge with the walls. I long to splash something – whisky perhaps, caramel coloured, over their neat white clothes. Then they would look just like the ice cream Sundays, the South Americans are so mad about. When I first came here, I couldn't get enough of them either. The feel and taste of that creamy, cold smoothness as it slips down your throat is irresistible.

'*If you eat too many of these you'll get fat and I will divorce you,*' he had said spooning the delectable concoction down my throat while helping himself to whisky from a crystal decanter. There was always an abundance of crystal. If a glass was accidentally chipped, it was thrown away, instantly replaced by another.

I was chipped. I was flawed.

Whisky.

Ah yes. Now it is clear. His face, the face of the not so loved one, emerges, father of my living child. It is not important, I realise now on paper, that I did not love him. There was only ever room enough in my heart for one man, in spite of all the men I have known.

But now his face emerges from the shadows.

All is revealed …

Chapter 29

Sigi
Journal

    The years after Rodrigo left were not easy. I do not remember much about that time except that I spent most of it asleep or stoned or both and certainly much of it I was already addicted to heroin. What I do remember is an overriding concern for money and how I would continue to finance my habit. Sometimes my sisters helped me, sometimes Miguel. They say I tried to kill myself once (once?) and that I threw myself into the port claiming to be Marilyn Monroe. I do not believe it. I never cared for Marilyn. I found her looks too blousy and I thought her fat. I much preferred Ava Gardner or Vivien Leigh. Leigh in *Waterloo Bridge* was so poignantly exquisite. I have never seen anyone so beautiful. I ask the nurses here if they have ever seen *Gone with the Wind* or *That Hamilton Women* or *Ship of Fools* or indeed any of her films but they only ever watch American TV, hardly ever go to the cinema. They love B*ewitched* for example and *Get Smart*. I pity women as beautiful as Leigh. Imagine seeing that beauty every time you looked in the mirror? Growing old would be so hideous. How could anyone have been so perfect? I always cover my eyes at the end of *Waterloo Bridge* when Leigh throws herself in front of a lorry and you hear the terrible scream of brakes. What an agonising way to die. On the other hand I think I would gladly kill myself if I could come back looking like Vivien. That's a joke by the way. If you say things, *write* things like that, they prescribe a short electric shock treatment that takes weeks to recover from. I can do the Lithium even a session in psych but not the shock thing. But it's true. I mean that I never tried to kill myself, nor think that I was Marilyn.

Isabel came to visit me in the mad house they call the Hospital of San Juan. If there was ever a place that looked like a cloistered convent, it was that Gaudiesque building on the outskirts of Barcelona. It was years since I had last seen her, not since Marta's wedding. I think she was genuinely moved to see me. I had been tied to the bed the night before and my wrists were bruised. Her eyes filled with tears that did not fall to her cheeks. I wanted to reach out and catch them. I have to say I hardly recognised her and we faced each other as strangers. Gone were the old inhibitions and constraints that had grown up between us around the time I started seeing Rodrigo and she had her 'admirer'. Alone in this sterile place, we saw each other as we really were. *Through a glass darkly and then face to face…*

A beautiful creature, elegant and poised, had replaced the clumsy child we had loved to hate. She was expensively dressed. Her hair, immaculately swept from a pale face overcome with emotion, was expertly cut. Her hands were manicured and she wore good jewellery. She busied herself courteously but firmly directing the nurses to arrange the flowers she had brought, to open the windows, pour us glasses of water. She emptied tempting pastries onto a plate and placed two packages on the regulation blankets. The way in which they were wrapped was a work of art in itself. Layer upon layer of crisp tissue paper gave way to overlong satin ribbons and hand blocked wrapping paper. Large clocks in vibrant colours leapt all over the paper, wriggling, some on legs and hands. They made me laugh, inside that is. I could not bring myself to smile. I stared at the delicate silk undergarments in confusion, uncertain as to what I was supposed to do with them. She brushed my cheek and I could smell sunflowers and sea air and the pine needles of Val Negra.

I realised that my past was deprived of all sensory sensation. Tito forbade our mother from wearing perfume because he didn't like his taste buds distracted when he was eating. Now, I could not take my eyes off my cousin and longed to bury my face in her hair. She was a metallic streak against the sombre backdrop of the psych ward and more importantly she was a link with my childhood. She chatted aimlessly as I ate my way through an entire box of chocolates from Foix. As children we had visited that shop on many occasions charging sweets to Tito's account. Even the bold gold writing on the package hadn't changed from when we were small. Her every gesture was graceful, measured. She was supremely in control, sure of herself in a way that we would never be. For a long time I was speechless. I let her talk. She seemed to want to. She spoke of Marta's children, her gallery in the old town that had had some success. She talked of our grandfather's death some years earlier and how marvellous Avia was at coping. How beautiful she still was how the house was just as pretty. She spoke of Dr.Mantua. Had he been to visit? And Miguel, and how he still worked at the little electrician's shop in the square not far from the Cathedral. She did not speak of the past or of Ricardo, as I knew she would not. Nor did she talk much of her life in England, the house that her English Father had left her, her job with an advertising agency or a boyfriend, if indeed she had one at all. With consummate skill she steered clear of any subject that might cause pain. At last she paused, exhausted no doubt, by my lack of response. After a while though, she recovered and became animated once again.

"I almost forgot. I've brought *Horchata*! It's almost too late to drink it. I found some in Sitges yesterday. I had a meeting with some clients, the San Miguel people actually. Have you heard of them? We're trying to persuade them to have a new design package which is a bit of a joke really as they spent a fortune revamping their non-alcoholic beverages only a couple of years ago. But that's the kind of business I'm in. Anyway one of the bars along the waterfront was selling Horchata."

She whipped out a carton of the drink from a large paper bag together with two plastic cups.

"But they had some in Sitges?" I heard myself speak the words hesitantly.

"Yes." Isabel managed a smile. "Don't you love it?" she said smacking her lips as though she were wine tasting.

"No. But you do."

Isabel almost choked on her cup.

"This is after all, about you."

Isabel finished her drink unperturbed although I noticed her hands shook slightly. I felt a strange spurt of pleasure. It was such a novelty to be the distributor of torment rather than its recipient.

"You swan in with your fine clothes and successful life when it suits you. You never tell us when you're coming and then expect to be greeted like the prodigal daughter. It's always been like that. Some holidays you came to Val Negra, others you did not and only if it fitted in with your plans. Were you bored in England, is that why you've come back after all this time? Or is it to gloat? Well, here you see me, this is as good as it gets!"

I turned my face to the wall so that she would not see the joyfulness in my eyes. She was so quiet. At last out of curiosity, I turned round. She was standing with her beautiful tailored back to me. Her legs were long, smooth in expensive stockings. One suede shoe with its faultless heel leant against the other, her hair hung like a curtain, shiny and dark to her shoulders.

"You're right of course," she said soothingly. "Except that I haven't come to gloat. You have suffered so much. Why don't you come back with me?" She turned slowly. There was nothing but affection in her eyes. "To England I mean. I work long hours so I couldn't take all that much time off but you would have your days to yourself. If Nuria wanted, she could come too although I know she hates flying. Otherwise I have a woman who comes in daily. She's a tremendous gossip. She drives me mad but I suppose she might be some company and then in the evenings I'd be home and we'd have the weekends together of course."

I spluttered with laughter. I couldn't stop laughing. She seemed so earnest, in just the way she had as a child – so desperate to make amends, so completely out of place here, with her simple extortionately expensive clothes and natural glamour. She was part of the world I had fought so hard to reject. But Rodrigo would have loved her. She exuded all the breeding and sophistication of his beloved mother. Oh how wrong we had all been when we were children! This ugly duckling had grown to be the most accomplished of swans! It was priceless. I rocked with laughter. Months of repression burst like a dam inside me. I could not stop laughing. All at once her perfume was sickly. I swept the presents from my bed, spilling the pastries onto the floor.

"Go away!" I said between giggles. "Go back to your safe job and house and life. You're not wanted here. You never were. Don't you remember that first day at Mialma when you were dumped on us? Not even Avia wanted you! Why do you think you spent so much time with us at Val Negra? No one could be bothered with you, just as they weren't remotely interested in Clara. They were well rid of her when she married that *Ingles*, that Pelham character!"

I did not see my cousin's blanched face or the way she gripped her hands together. I was too immersed in the waves of pleasure that passed over me.

"Let's be clear about one thing. Your mother was a slut, pretty enough but a slut all the same. Even your father had the good sense – poor as church mouse they always were. Didn't you think it odd the way Avia never bought you any nice clothes? You were always so appallingly dressed and she never bought you a thing! That's because you were never loved and never wanted!

So just go away and leave us alone. You're a foreigner. You always were and you always will be. Your accent gives you away every time."

Isabel pulled herself up straight and stepping over the debris on the floor, leant to kiss me so that again I was reminded again, unwillingly of the sea and sunflowers. I had never before known the intoxicating attraction of scent. It confused me.

"This isn't you," she said hoarsely. "It's the illness. I love you and I can be here if you want me. Nuria has all the contact numbers if you should change your mind about coming to England. Look at me!" Her almond shaped eyes were steady. I raised my own taunting ones.

"What?" I said rudely.

She grasped my shoulders. "You *will* get through this," she said. "You're a lot stronger than you think. I may not have been loved and wanted as you say. But you certainly were. So don't forget that. You have a family around you and most of all you have Nuria. You don't know how lucky you are to have known your mother. You have brothers and sisters who care about you. You *will* find a way out of this. You can do anything you choose. But stop blaming other people and get on with your life. You've got the rest of your life ahead of you, so make it count for something. We all make mistakes. Sometimes we do the very things we never thought we were capable of and then worry about the fact that nothing is the way we intended."

"The good I would I do not, but the evil that I would not, that I do."

Isabel stared at me. "Yes. That's exactly what I meant. See? You're not just beautiful but clever!"

"Or well taught," I said bitterly.

Isabel sighed. "You are gifted and funny. How we laughed! Do you remember all the fun we had with Lupe? What a witch she could be! Remember how she used to nag and chase us with a broomstick? She always blamed me anyway for my 'foreign devil ways.' Gosh she was a pain."

"Lupe is dead."

"I know."

"It's no good Isa," I said. "You can't fix everything. There are some things you just have to leave alone. Go back to your English life. I can't really be helped. Too much has happened. I've done –"

She touched my lips to silence me with a perfectly manicured nail. Her hands were soft, strangers to washing up liquid or mud. I was fascinated by her wrists, strong and capable the blue veins prominent under the translucent skin. Good veins, I thought. Her selfless concern grated on my nerves.

"It doesn't matter," she whispered. "Start again. What are a few years in the context of a lifetime? You've learned from it haven't you?"

"Oh sure. I've learned all right, a hundred ways to get high on speed and amphetamines and how to shoot up. There's a new combo called ecstasy. Bet your precious, *pijo*, clients wouldn't want to hear about that! Do you know there are nightclubs in town now where alcohol is banned and the only thing anyone is taking is ecstasy? What ever happened to a good old Manhattan and a Du Maurier cigarette eh?"

Isabel sank on the bed in her beautifully tailored suit. Her throat was smooth as it rose from the soft silk shirt. For no logical reason, I was curious about her underwear. Was it expensive too? I so longed to believe in her, to be transported to her safe, urbane existence and turn my back forever on the sordid nightmares that tormented me.

"Sigi come home with me. Start again."

I looked beyond her at the greyness.

"I wish I could."

"There," she patted my arm. "You'll see, everything will be all right. I promise."

Once again she was composed. I imagined her brushing away the afternoon's unpleasantness, putting it down to bad client management and moving on.

"No it won't," I said furiously. "Oh it's all right for you! You've got your Oxford degree. You can switch jobs the way most people switch toothpastes! I haven't been to university. I'm not qualified to do anything except spread my legs and even that gets a bit repetitive!"

Isabel rose from the bed. "Just stop this," she said suddenly angry. "Stop complaining about how awful your life is! I don't have to remind you that you've had every advantage imaginable. You have a family and wealth and people who love you and you still managed to screw things up! I had none of those things." Isabel brushed her hair back impatiently. Her voice rose and then was low again but frighteningly firm. "Not until, as you so sweetly put it, your family condescended to take me. I love you all and I only want the best for you. But you know something? There was a time when I would have killed to have the things that you did! You were pretty and funny and beautifully dressed and you had two parents! Ugh!" Isabel made a low exasperated sound. "Stop feeling sorry for yourself and get off your backside!" She smiled. "This once."

I gargled a mouthful of Horchata as if it were mouthwash. Isabel took a step back.

"And what about Ricardo?" I said carefully, planning my final coup de grace. "No flutters, no sweaty palms?"

"I don't know what you mean," she said stiffly.

"Oh I think you do. Rodrigo always wondered if you were pregnant."

"What on earth are you talking about?"

"Oh you know what I'm talking about. That night you fainted, the night you caused such a sensation at Marta's wedding."

"If I remember rightly, it was *you* who caused the sensation. And I'm not going to drag Marta into this." Isabel's tone was steely.

"But you were mad about my brother!" I continued. "It was so obvious. You were all over him. You were nothing but a child. A lovesick teenager! God, it was embarrassing. Poor guy. I wonder how he put up with it! On the other hand, he was used to girls throwing themselves at him. But you! You'd have thought you would have had more sense. Maybe even a sense of gratitude. We took you into our home and that was the way you repaid us! Perhaps you thought you might marry him. Was that it? Then you'd get a share of the cake. After all Tito is a wealthy man. You can't have been ignorant of that. How clever you were, *cosina*, even then."

Isabel closed her eyes defeated.

"You see!" I said triumphantly. "I was right."

She swung her Loewe bag over her shoulder, swung 5.000 pts worth of luggage, just like that.

"No," she said quietly. "You were wrong."

She did not look at me again but pulled out a small envelope from her bag.

"I almost forgot." she said.

And without another glance or look over her shoulder she left the ward. Too late I tried to get out of bed. I felt myself sink into the dark, with only the lingering scent of her perfume and the expensive gifts around me. The fans whirled, making a spluttering sound as they were switched off. Nurses on padded soled shoes moved quietly down the corridor administering the night time cocktail of drugs. I gathered up the silk nightdress and dressing gown, luxuriating in the clean swoop of fabric, the wonderful sheen of hyacinth blue. I tried the dressing gown on over my hospital garb. It was so delicate I was afraid I might tear it. There were no mirrors so I could not see what it looked like. I curled up embryo fashion, blotting out the routine sounds of the evening. I opened the envelope and saw the *Reina del Rio*, devoid of her hair but still the same brittle mustard coloured corn husk. *I baptise you Queen of the River.*

Too late I realised I was sorry.

*

That night I dreamt again of Val Negra. Perhaps it was seeing Isabel or gorging myself on the rich chocolate truffles in their plethoric gold boxes, that resurrected those memories. Isabel's visit stirred the restless longing I used, much later, to associate with the spring - those lengthening sun-drenched days when the hazy light thinly engulfs the landscape in preparation for summer. Only the sudden cold air would hint at the winter months that had just been.

It was spring too when I met Jaime Malagrida. Mialma was empty of children. Marta was married with her own little ones, Miguel lived in a small flat over his shop in the plaza near to Dr.Mantua's church, Bea was studying theology in Toledo and my brother Ricardo lived in splendid isolation by the sea. Tito spent very little time in the city and was busying overseeing works at Val Negra. Central heating was being installed, the kitchen modernised and the vegetable garden reclaimed, after years of neglect. The prospect of spending more time in the country did not excite our mother however.

"I like my time alone," she grumbled as endless builders traipsed through the house. Plumbers, electricians and painters, were all united in the common endeavour of prolonging the job for as long as possible. "I shall have your father underfoot all day long. I shan't see Avia as much."

It was always the same. After so many years of looking after her family, she was lonely and alone. She felt redundant. She had long ago lost touch with girlhood friends. The war had interrupted friendships in a similar way that her marriage and motherhood had. Her looks had faded. She had lost her defiance and her sparkle. Together, we paced the empty rooms, spied on by dozens of oil encrusted eyes and dust-gathering artefacts and felt helpless.

"It's strange," said Nuria, "when you were all little, I longed so much for this time alone. I would have given my soul to have days to myself, in an empty house, with countless hours all for me. But when I saw myself in the future it was a young and glamorous me, not an old woman worn out by life, too tired to care about anything."

I stared at her in horror. My beautiful, sometime volatile mother whose fighting spirit had encouraged us all was now withered and old. I saw for the first time, the sagging hips, the lined skin and watery eyes, the thinning hair and only the very faintest trace of the beauty she once was. I looked away more terrified by her than any chimera I'd ever had in San Juan. The wonderful sunny weather outside turned sour and oppressive in the face of her misery. I was speechless.

"I'm sorry. I didn't want to upset you. You mustn't be upset," she said as though repeating a mantra. She squeezed my arm. "Why don't you go for a walk? I'm going to lie down." She laughed suddenly. "Isn't it funny. Here we are together with absolutely nothing to do." She frowned. "You'll have to find some sort of work. It's one thing for me being here on my own, but you're so young. If only we could find you a husband! Oh darling, I simply don't know what's going to become of you." Her eyes filled with tears and she sat down heavily on the top step.

I put my arms around her, deeply shaken.

"You mustn't worry about me. I'm much better now, but what about you? Why don't you go round to Avia's. She's always cheerful —"

"I know," she said gloomily. "I can't face that. Not today. Avia has no patience with this sort of thing. She's always got plenty on."

"Then what about Dr. Mantua?"

Nuria touched my cheek. "You are sweet. Now you run along. Find Lupe. She'll give you something from the kitchen."

I looked at my mother strangely. Lupe had been dead for nearly five years. She rose unsteadily grasping the banister.

"Oh I almost forgot. I think the Bazan brothers are up for the evening with Marta. And your erstwhile brother Ricardo for once has called in. I heard them say something about meeting for a drink at the *Up and Down*. I'm sure they won't mind if you join them. You should get out more Sigi, it would be fun for you. But perhaps that doesn't interest you."

"No. I mean yes. Of course it does. I'll phone them, Marta at any rate. Maybe."

Nuria shook her head. "You used to be so close. What's happening to us Sigismunda? What's happening?"

Nuria only ever used to call me by my full name to emphasise a point or when she had time and this she certainly did. I felt helpless.

"Why don't you come too? We'll *both* go over to see her? "

Nuria lifted a frail, still graceful hand. "I'm rather tired just now," she said. "Perhaps a little later."

I nodded. The day stretched ahead of me long and uncertain. I'd never been much for reading and there was nothing on television. In San Juan I'd had enough TV to last a lifetime. I wondered round the garden, inspected the pool, the orchard and the games room. By the early afternoon I could think of absolutely nothing I wanted to do. The silence of the house was stultifying. I put on a pair of jeans, grabbed my purse and let myself out.

Chapter 30

Sigi
Journal

It was many years since I had walked the streets of my city alone. I had forgotten how beautiful the path was leading down from Mialma to the 14th century monastery. Sunflowers poked their heads over the surrounding walls and the scent of gardenia was all around me. For a while my footsteps were the only sound. But when I reached the square, motorcycles and cars whizzed by, blowing up clouds of dust and noise that disintegrated in the strong sunlight. I bought a packet of cigarettes at a kiosk in front of the church of Sarria. Glancing up I caught sight of Dr. Mantua at his window and he waved. I sat on a bench surrounded by pigeons, like an old woman basking in the sun, soaking up the sounds of the weeks' activities. A woman complained about her daughter-in-law, another her sick child, another berated the fashion of short skirts – the blatant pornography exhibited at most news stands and the decline in moral and religious standards since Franco. There was much comment about Aznar's recent appointment ending so many years of a corrupt socialist government. They talked of Pujol's increased power and popularity. What would this mean for Catalans? Would we be any better off? As usual everything went to Madrid and as before Madrid benefited from our years of hard work. But what was different? It had been the same thing before the war.

I smiled to myself. It was so good to be out of San Juan and on the streets of Barcelona even if I didn't have, as Nuria pointed out, a job or a husband. I bought *pan tomacat* and ate it on a bench in the sun. After a while I grew bored watching children playing, all dressed up in their Sunday best. I lit a cigarette and thought about Isabel. It would be good to see her again. But would she want to see me? I also thought about speed.

I mustn't succumb. I don't want to give in. Not again. With shaking hands I fumbled for another cigarette. I wandered down narrow cobbled streets until I reached the Cathedral square. By day this was a respectable bourgeois haunt but by night it crawled with the low life of the city - pushers and 1ooo ptas prostitutes.

When I was a child the Guardia Civil patrolled this same square. The selling of soft line drugs had not yet been legalised and rigid censorship laws were in place. It was hard to believe that I had grown up under an authoritarian regime where physical violence, long prison sentences and summary executions were daily occurrences. A man's career might be blighted or a doctor's passport withdrawn for no other reason than his opposition to the party line. The common man was denied his freedom of expression. The Ministry of the Interior controlled all public meetings and any opposition or criticism of the government resulted in fines or imprisonment. Now, watching the bowels of the city, hookers, the homeless, gypsies and beggars, it was hard to imagine a time when these people would have been too terrified to show their faces in a public space.

At last I found a telephone that wasn't broken and covered in graffiti. I dialled Marta's number. The maid answered and I don't know who was more shocked she or I. I couldn't remember the last time I'd phoned my sister. Reluctantly the maid let me know that my sister and her husband would be at the club later that evening. I lit another cigarette. I was wearing jeans but didn't want to have to go all the way home to change. Nightclubs like the *Up and Down* maintained a strict dress code. Wrestling with this conundrum, I walked towards the plaza San Jaime, past the immaculate generalitat with its huge flags flanking the entrance steps and down the narrow street of San Sever. I hardly noticed the gathering crowds until I was suddenly pushed against the cathedral walls.

"*Bueno, bueno,*" said a voice that was horribly familiar. A voice that would haunt me as long as I lived. "We meet again. And here of all places! I suppose you could say it's really "our place" but I wouldn't have had you down as a romantic. It's many, *many* years since then. But the first time as they say is–" His tone changed. "You *are* a surprise," he said harshly now. "A pleasant surprise I must say."

"I wish I could say the same about you. I thought you were dead."

"Actually I thought *you* were," said Carlos Nadal, eyes glinting like two hard, little glass beads.

"No thanks to you. They had to give me Norcan to resuscitate me after that stint at Val Negra. I don't suppose it would have meant anything to you, one way or another."

I peered at Carlos in the faint street light. He looked older but he had cleaned himself up a bit. He wore a loose fitting suit and dark glasses stuck out of his jacket pocket. He wore a black tie and Sigi wondered if he had turned religious in his old age. Her eyes traveling downwards saw that he had not given up a penchant for shiny pointed shoes. Even though he was clean-shaven he still managed to look dirty.

"No, no todo lo contrario, bonita," he said moving close. "I much enjoyed our… time together. If I remember correctly, so did you. I don't remember you objecting, in fact quite the opposite. Full counts for enthusiasm. I always feel enthusiasm makes up for technique don't you?"

"You bastard," I said stubbing out my cigarette. "You used me. I was little more than a child. I had no idea what was happening. I certainly don't remember it in the detail you seem to."

"A child? You?" Nadal chuckled. "You were born knowing what to do with men. I'm pained that you don't remember though. I have quite a reputation you know. Women remember everything when they've been with me."

"Sorry to disappoint you." I said trying to squeeze past him. "I'm late."

Nadal caught my wrists and in spite of myself, my heart began to beat more quickly.

"Let me go," I hissed. "I'm clean."

"So I heard. Compliments of San Juan, verdad? It's good you *pijos* have the money. Not everyone is so lucky. You've had time off nothing more. Don't kid yourself into thinking it won't all happen again."

"Get off," I said violently. "And it wasn't time off as you put it. It wasn't something I would choose again. They saved my *life*. It wasn't optional, you know. You left me for dead. In some ways I should be grateful. I've been clean for 18 months. Not even the obnoxious, vile likes of you – "

He put a hand to my lips. "Sh!Little one! What is this? Just admit you had a good time. *Both* times. How are you going to change, if you can't be truthful?"

"Oh and truth is one of your specialties is it?"

"No but I don't pretend to be something better." He put his hand to the nape of my neck holding my hair tightly in his hand, positioning me so that I could not move. His breath was thick on my face and yet I was not afraid. This man, who had always had the power to destroy me, who even now held me pinned like a moth also had the ability to make my stomach churn with excitement.

"Admit that everything is clearer," he whispered. "There is none of your greyness is there? Only beauty and neat angles, *verdad?* You reach a high that is better than sex. A feeling that anything is possible, the world is in your hand and you have only to– "

"Yeah and the downer comes afterwards when you're freezing and your hair hurts and your nails are agony and every orifice shits, vomits, oozes sweat and even your shins sweat –"

"Sh! Little bird, Sh!" Nadal's body was pressed against mine, wiry and unyielding. His hands were like iron cuffs around my wrists. "Don't you remember anything about being with me? I don't mean when you were fifteen but the last time we were together. I held you just like this, my hands just like this." His mouth was in mine.

"Christ!" I spluttered. "What was that?" And then I sank against him, warm relaxed, removed. His voice seemed a long way away. I felt his legs parting mine, as they had done before. Against the church wall, his hands unzipped my jeans.

"It's called Red Rum," said Nadal as his lips caressed my neck. "Much more popular than the old stuff. Much purer – gone from 4% to 35% and you can snort it or smoke it, no more shooting up, no more stigma. No more fear of Aids."

"I thought ecstasy was better," I whispered lamely, luxuriating in the slow rhythms as he rocked against me.

"Pah!" He was dismissive. "Ecstasy is for kids. No, this is pure. Clean. I'll tell you a little secret. Dealers keep it in a little balloon in their mouths, so if there's a raid, they just swallow it. Easy eh? And smooth. Feel good? I thought so."

He thrust himself in and I groaned hungry for more. I was suffused with pleasure. Everything seemed right and good and clear just as he had said it would. I wanted him to go on forever.

"What, you been off sex or something?" he grunted.

"Something like that."

No boredom, no fear, no restlessness. For a moment.

"Well you know where to find me." He stopped and pulled up his trousers smoothing his hair with the little black comb he kept in his shirt pocket. Nadal preening himself was a sobering sight. A clammy hand clutched my heart. I remembered that I was meeting Isabel. I took deep breaths trying to stem the panic that was beginning to flood over me. I had given in after all. I hadn't been strong and at the first opportunity I had allowed myself to be tempted. Part of me wanted to tear my hair out, literally or at least his, while the other tried to implement the steps I'd been taught in the clinic. It didn't matter that I had failed on this one occasion. I wouldn't think about it again and I would move on. *But I must think about it!* No!

I shook my head. "I don't think so. There won't be a next time."

Nadal put on his sunglasses. "Sure there will. You're the dependent type. You think you can kick heroin? You're dreaming! You stop, you start. You're off for what, 18months? That's a joke. You'll fall again. Trust me. You already have." He felt my cheek. "But you know what? I like you. No morals, just a healthy appetite for pleasure and to hell with the rest of the world. What beats me is why you even opted for San Juan. I'd just carry on."

"I didn't *opt* for San Juan," I said stiffly. "I didn't have a choice. I almost died. *You* almost killed me. Just be thankful I never went to the police."

"Don't make me laugh. What *I* could say to *them* would interest them a lot more than your pathetic little story."

I shrugged. "You're deluded. This is not a habit. I've got it under control."

"Yeah, I see that, everything but the habit. Look it doesn't bother me. But don't pretend you're not still addicted. You will be for the rest of your life. Like I said, it's just your nature. You aren't a *pija,* you're one of us. You're a gypsy Sigismunda, nothing but a gypsy. Good screw by the way."

I slapped his face. "Bastard."

He caught my wrist holding my arm behind me. "I heard your friend Don Rodrigo has became a Duke and that he got married. Look around you *bonita* what do you see? Hookers and junkies just like you. You are *all* dependent types and why? Because when the merry-go-round stops and all the pleasure with it, you're left with nothing. Nothing that is but life and you can't cope with that. Do you think Don Rodrigo would want you now?"

His eyes lingered on my torn blouse. He felt between my legs. "I don't think so do you?"

He dropped me so suddenly that I stumbled against the church wall, banging my head.

"Scum. *You* are the low life, people like you, no better than the next man in the street." Carlos picked his teeth with a dirty bit of card. "You *pijos* are all alike. You think that just because you have money and elaborate names, you're better that the rest of us. But there is no difference. None at all."

A woman approached us, painfully thin, anorexic looking, her arms bruised by needle marks.

"Carlitos," she minced.

"*Si carino*." He kissed her on the mouth as moments before he had kissed me. I turned away, lost amongst the dozens of other drug addicts lining the street, caught in the twilight zone of sobriety and illusion.

Just like them.

Somehow I found my way back to the Ramblas. The rowdy noise, the coloured street lights, all forming part of my dream. I could have been floating, for all the impression my footsteps seemed to make on the pavement. The tall palm trees swung in a light breeze. I inhaled petrol fumes and dust. I was full of self-loathing. At last I found a taxi, yellow and black striped with its little green light looking just like a glow-worm, crawling along the ground. I muttered the name of the night-club, oblivious of the odd look the cabdriver gave me.

"You're sure you mean *The Up and Down*?" said the Adaluz driver in his lisping accent.

"Yes," I snapped.

He shrugged, steering the car clear of a mob of teenagers. "*Joder. Vayanse!* Get off the street!" he hollered. "Youth!"

"*Si. Ja!. Divino tesoro.*"

"*Que?*"

"Golden Age of Poetry. Don't they teach you anything in the South?" I snapped.

"*Puta,*" he said good-naturedly stopping the car. "1000 ptas."

I thrust a bank note in his hand and let myself out. A doorman slammed the door.

"*Up and Down?*"

I nodded. Even he looked strange, enormous in his uniform. I felt like Alice through the looking glass, having drunk some magic potion. The huge black and gold doors were open. I had almost slipped through the catch net of waitresses, bouncers and reception, when a firm hand gripped my arm.

"I'm sorry, this is a private club. Members only. And um ..." The night club manager, a tall man immaculately dressed, cleared his throat, managing to convey utter contempt in just one look. "No jeans."

"*Christ!*" I said loudly.

"Senorita." His hand on my arm tightened as he began to steer me quickly towards the door.

I pulled back.

"*Condesa* actually."

The man shrugged. "And I'm the King."

"Get your hands off me," I said. "I'm meeting some people."

The man smiled smoothly, his eyes flicking professionally round the room. Stick thin women, with faces the colour of mahogany, shimmied past us.

"I don't think so."

I dug in my heels. I could almost feel the thick carpet caught underfoot. The music from the dance floor was subtle, the clink of glasses a far cry from Carlos Nadal and his popping Red Rum.

"I'm meeting some friends," I repeated. "I insist you tell them I'm here."

"Then your friends will have told you," said the manager "that jeans are not allowed and no drugs. Now get out before I call the police."

"Then call them. I'm meeting my brother, Ricardo Bacardi, *Conde* de Roble and ... and Fernando Bazan, *Marques* de Bazan." I all but spat their titles.

The man closed his eyes, his face tensing with anger. I made one last desperate appeal, a stab in the dark really. "Tell his grace the *Duke* of Montfalco that –"

The manager's eyes opened suspiciously, wondering I could see, what de Montfalco could possibly have to do with me or at least what he *intended* to do with me, in his night club. But if indeed, I was a friend, he couldn't run the risk of offending a client. Not a Montfalco at any rate. "I don't believe you're a ... guest of Don Rodrigo's?"

"How do you know I'm not?"

The manager coughed.

"Well?"

"All right," he agreed reluctantly. "You may go in." His breath was in my face. "But no trouble. Or I'll call the police."

In the darkness, I felt what seemed like hundreds of eyes upon me. I stumbled against tables, my heart in my mouth. My heels tapped against the marble edge of the dance floor, against shapes of ornate pillars draped in ivy. Elaborate floral arrangements protruded from unexpected places. Low, seductive voices hummed against the uncorking of champagne bottles. Julio Iglesias crooned in the background. Much older men with very young girls who were not their wives, huddled over miniature tables, rubbing ankles with stiletto heels.

"Mierda!" I exploded as I knocked over an ashtray. Instantly three waiters, dumpy little men in tight neru jackets fussed over me.

"It's all right!" I said bending down. "It's all right."

And as I raised my head, the front of my shirt soaking from the spilled drink, on my knees amidst the broken glass, I caught sight of them and froze. Against the velvet wall and huge mirrors, my sister Marta sat ensconced on an enormous sofa. She looked fragile and exquisite, her long legs crossed in sheer stockings. She wore a short black dress cutaway at the shoulders. Her hair gleamed and diamonds shimmered at her ears and hands. She looked more beautiful and happier than I had ever seen her. She was laughing, her hands gesticulating as she sipped from a tall champagne flute. The Bazan brothers, my *cunados*, hung on her every word. I peered at the faces of the two other men beside her. I saw the other one, last of all, in the corner, shrinking into the shadows.

"Hello," I said. For a moment, Marta's face registered shock but she composed herself quickly, and smiled. The man beside her came into view and I recognised my brother Ricardo. The club manager pushed me aside.

"I'm sorry *Excelencia*," he said making a curt bow with his head. "She made such a commotion at the door, I couldn't stop her. She said she was your guest. I told her we don't allow drugs on the premises. They can do that sort of thing in the *Barrio Chino*. But she said she knew you. And you *Condesa.*" He nodded in Marta's direction. " I do apologise."

I swayed. Rodrigo emerged from the shadows, a whisky tumbler in one hand, cigarette in the other. He inhaled sharply before stubbing it out. His face was expressionless.

"She is our guest," he said, pressing some notes into the manager's hand. He murmured something and patted him on the back. Everyone laughed.

"Well if you're sure," said the manager. "But she *is* your responsibility."

Rodrigo nodded and when the man had melted away he crossed the space between in us in seconds. He was taller than I remembered him.

"Christ, Sigismunda," he said shaking his head.

"Everyone seems to be calling me that today. You never called me that when –"

"When what?" his eyes shifted.

"Oh carry on," I said irritated by the others' anxious expression. "I've only come to see him anyway. " I jerked my head in Rodrigo's direction. "And where's the lovely Sonia de Cana? You did marry her didn't you?"

Rodrigo's fingers bit into my arm.

"You're hurting me. Can I have a drink?"

Ricardo took my other arm.

"I'll deal with this." Rodrigo assured my brother. "We're going for a quiet talk. Look after our guests, will you."

"Let me come," said Marta struggling to move past the low coffee table. Ricardo restrained her.

"Let them be," he said. "This is his business. Rodrigo can handle her. We'll only make things worse."

"Come on," said Rodrigo coldly.

"But *mi amor*, what a greeting after so long!"

His grip didn't slacken as he steered me well away from their table.

"Are you ashamed of me?" I said my voice rising. "I *do* want that drink. Why can't I have it with them? Why do we have to go and hide. It's so dark here!"

"Here have mine." He thrust his glass towards me so that the liquid slopped over the side.

"Mmm … my lips on yours …" I murmured. "Tastes good."

"Oh for Gods sake," said Rodrigo his reserve broken. "What are you doing here anyway? I thought you were – "

"*Dead?* In San Juan?" I finished for him. "My goodness news travels fast. I'm beginning to think everyone is a little disappointed that I survived. Everyone seems to know everything about me! And what's with this insistence on calling me Sigismunda? I shall feel grown up in a minute."

"You *are* grown up."

I tossed back his whisky. It curled my teeth. "I forgot whisky was your tipple. Come here often?"

"*No. Que quieres?* Look, what do you want?" He said tersely. He stood stiffly, not unlike the club manager, shifting his weight, his eyes darting around the room, hoping I was certain that no one would recognise us. In another life he *would* have been a night club manager. He could barely bring himself to look at me. He was grey at the temples, deeply tanned, older. Age leant him a distinction and strength of character that he'd never had when he was young. He had filled out, his shoulders seemed broader, his body, from years in the saddle was taut. His clothes hung well, draped casually, in just the right places. He was impatient to get back to his friends. His hand jingled the keys in his pocket.

"I'm fine thank you Rodrigo. It's so good to see you after all this time. My heart warms to know how much I once meant. Above all it's reassuring to know how you care for your own. I knew I could rely on you Rodrigo." I took another gulp of whisky. "What the hell do you think I want? I haven't had a single word from you in all these years. Nothing. Not a peep. Do you know that I almost died thanks to your friend Nadal? No, it probably wouldn't surprise you. What a relief you're thinking, *that* would have been. Your little problem neatly disposed of. Well I think you owed me a little more than just: 'I've got to marry Sonia de Cana, because my Daddy wants more land' kind of crap. You said you loved me."

My voice broke. Everything was becoming confused and jumbled and the awesome greyness was smudging out the dark. My head was beginning to spin. "You never even bothered to find out if I was pregnant."

Rodrigo's head jerked towards me. He took a step forward. "W-were you?"

I saw the coldness in his face, the total lack of interest and contempt. So this was the man I had loved all my life, would always love. How different things might have been! And now he stood in front of me just as I had so often dreamed he would and I knew all he could see was my sweat stained shirt and tangled hair. He did not see me at all, but what I had become – pathetic, dependent, just as Carlos said.

I shuddered, taking a deep breath.

"No," I said shortly. "No I wasn't."

His body sank with relief. He took his hands out of his pocket, signalling a waiter to bring him another drink. He frowned.

"Is it money? Do you want money?"

I closed my eyes. I thought my heart would break.

"Relax," I said shakily drawing my last cigarette from my blouse pocket. "There's nothing I could ever want from you. I wasn't really looking for you. To be honest, I didn't even know you'd be here. But it was worth a try. I was actually trying to meet up with Isabel but that jerk of a bouncer wouldn't let me in."

"Are you surprised?" Rodrigo said a little less harshly. "Just look at you," he said. "Your clothes, your hair …" he made a clucking noise.

"You sound just like my grandmother," I said between puffs, not quite managing to blow smoke rings. "What would your dear mother say if she could see you talking to the likes of me?"

A waiter placed a fresh tumbler and jug of water on the table beside him. Rodrigo swirled the glass, the ice cubes chinking against the edge.

"Oh look. I won't bother you again. I wouldn't want to anyway, you've turned into such a boring old sod."

"Sigismunda." Rodrigo set down his glass, stood to attention, nervously fingering the knot of his tie.

I made a mock bow.

"Your Grace."

He raised his eyes.

"Oh you can go!" I said. "Fuck off back to your friends and your wife where ever she may be."

"Having our son actually."

There was a booming sound in my head as his words bounced painfully back and forth. For a moment I was winded, couldn't breathe. I inhaled sharply.

"I see. And you're here. Congratulations."

Rodrigo swallowed. "Thank you. And it's not like that. It's been a long labour. I came for a meeting if you must know, with your cousin. Sonia told me to come. The baby won't arrive till the morning. I've only popped out. *Dios* why am I justifying myself to *you?*"

"I don't know, why are you?"

There was a moment's tension between us and at last he really looked at me. His eyes boring into mine, until I was the first to look away.

"I've got to go. And so do you. Leave the others alone. It's business. Go home Sigi. It's late. "

"*Too* late by the sounds of it." I took a last drag on the cigarette. "So long Rodrigo. *Se bueno pequeno.*"

Rodrigo clenched his hands so that I thought he might hit me. I closed my eyes preparing myself for the blow, welcoming any emotion from him other than his hideous indifference. When I opened them, he was gone.

I leant against the velvet wall in the darkness. Nadal was right about too many things. The problem with coming off drugs was that all life awaits you. I licked my lips hoping for any trace of Red Rum but it had long been absorbed into my blood. I needed something. The music was louder now as couples spilled onto the dance floor. No one noticed me as I stood like petrified wood against the narrow corridor. Or so I thought.

"Are you all right senorita?" asked a voice out of the shadows. "Forgive me, but I noticed you at once when you came in and then later – " he spread his hands. "I could not help overhearing some of your conversation. It would give me great pleasure if you would have a drink with me."

I laughed sarcastically. *"Great pleasure?* No one has said that to me in a while." I had meant to sound coolly flippant but my voice snagged and then even more embarrassingly, I was forced to apologise. "I'm sorry. I – I didn't mean to be rude."

I peered up at him in the dim light. He was tall, thicker set than Rodrigo, and some ten years older. He wore black tie, his collar immaculate and stiff. His hair was grey at the temples rather like Ricardo's, but his eyes were watchful and full of compassion. His accent was intriguingly South American.

"I know," he said gently. He clicked his heels "Jaime de Malagrida of the Chilean Embassy."

He took my hand as I hesitated. It was cool and strong and I clung to it as if drowning. He seemed to be able to see into my very soul, to understand everything. His eyes did not immediately appraise my body as most men's did. Instead, he studied my face as though I were a long lost friend. I tried to pull my hand away but he gripped it in his, showing me to his table.

"And you senorita?" he asked. I opened my mouth but no sound came out. He smiled patiently.

"It's Sigismunda, Sigi for short."

He raised his eyebrows.

"As in *Persiles and Sigismunda?*"

I gritted my teeth. "My mother had a thing about Cervantes," I said. "No one calls me by full name."

He inclined his head and settled me on a stout sofa similar to the one Isabel had been so elegantly draped upon. There was an open bottle of champagne, a single glass recently poured. He signalled the waiter to bring another one.

"Well I think it's beautiful. Now perhaps you would prefer something else. Another whisky?"

I shook my head vehemently. "No. No Cava would be lovely."

Jaime smiled. "Ah yes, of course you prefer your Catalan beverage to the French. I should have known. I shall change it. In Chile, we have an over zealous appetite for brand names. But, by all means, let us drink Cava."

I smiled. His formality was soothing. I was used to baser conversation with men. I felt he was not looking for an angle or to be cruel and I was grateful.

"It's just that even now my loyalties …" I gestured in the direction of Rodrigo's table that was clearly visible from his.

"All wine trade. The woman is my sister Marta. The men she is talking to are the Bazan brothers. They're the ones with their backs towards us. The other … taller person is.. de Montfalco. I expect I rather upset things."

Jaime sat back in the easy chair opposite me. For such a large man he was surprisingly graceful. Every movement was relaxed and patient. His eyes did not flit about the room studying the people as they entered but were fixed on my face with a tenderness that disarmed and confused me. He made me feel like a child and I yearned for no reason to please this total stranger. I smoothed my blouse, clasped my hands in my lap, hoping that mascara was not smudged half way down my face. For a moment we stared at each other until I looked away embarrassed.

"And the other man? There are four?" He crossed an elegant leg to reveal a beautiful silk sock. There was no margin of skin exposed only smooth silk disappearing down his expensive trouser leg. He lit a cigarette on the sole of his shoe as I had seen men do in films.

"Ricardo, the other man is my brother Ricardo."

"I see. And you are close?"

"Does it look it? Oh I'm sorry. No. Yes. I don't know. I suppose we were when we were children. He was older though. We grew up together. Sometimes I think that's all we did. Now we could all be strangers. I'm sorry this must be boring you but I feel – I feel I can talk to you. Isn't odd, I don't even know you." I took a sip of my drink. "We were all close, once. Everyone has tried to help, I see that now. But I'm not that easy. Not a puzzle to be solved and then neatly boxed. I go on and on and on. They've all lost patience."

"And why are you so unhappy?"

I paused. *Why indeed?* He made everything sound so easy. I smiled. "I don't know."

"Let's dance." He stubbed out his cigarette leaving his drink untouched.

"Oh no. I can't. Not dressed like this! They'll see me and that vile and obnoxious club manager will want to throw me out again. I'm so grubby.

I was –"

"You're not to me." He took my arm determinedly. "It is dark on the dance floor. No one will see you but me. I want very much to dance with you."

I blinked. "Why? Why me, when there are so many beautiful girls and in a place like this? Don't waste time with me. The people here are all rich and beautiful and fun. Look at them, all without exception, having such a wonderful time."

"Not all of them. You are beautiful," he said simply. "I see people like them all the time at embassy parties, political meetings, openings of commercial centres, television spots, countless dinners given by first secretary wives. Do I have to go on? You are not like these people."

"Aren't you the lucky one!" I breathed as he propelled me by the arm.

Jaime was a superb dancer. He had all the rhythm we assume Latin Americans to have. He whirled, pressed, tossed me round the floor effortlessly and I danced not wildly as I used to with Rodrigo, but controlled, melancholy at first and then more carefree as I tried to forget.

"That's better!" he whispered as I laughed, tossing my head and he pulled me into his arms for a slow waltz.

"There aren't any embassies in Barcelona," I said against his shoulder. "You said you were from the Chilean embassy."

"I have been in Madrid for three years. I have come to see friends here in Barcelona before I leave for my next posting. Home as it turns out. I have been recalled to Santiago. I leave tomorrow," he glanced at his watch. "No today. But later."

I froze wondering why it should matter. "But I've just met you."

"Yes."

His voice was low, his accent so different from the harsh Catalan I was used to. It was exotic and mysterious. Our bodies seemed to fit and I relaxed against him although he held me lightly, gently unwinding my arms from his neck. I wished fervently now that I had not been with Carlos Nadal, that I had changed my clothes before coming out, that I had been patient. I swore then that I would never ever do another line of heroin again. Jaime seemed to represent the future, a glimmer of hope, of what might still be.

"You are thoughtful *mi amor.*" He held my hand. "I think it is time to go. It has been a long day yes?"

I swallowed. Somewhere along the line I had lost my purse and had no money to get home. Suddenly I was back to facing my reality, a reality that included the loss of Rodrigo and an ever present threat of Nadal. With Jaime I felt safe and I could pretend to be someone else, the girl I once was. I panicked. I did not want to be left alone, did not want to be without him. And he was leaving. I would never see him again. The thought was terrifying. The nightclub was almost empty. Couples were either draped over each other in darkly lit corners or kissing on the dance floor as Julio Iglesias, back for a fifth run, sang rather less enthusiastically, in the background. Even the waiters seemed to flag as they opened bottles of fizzy water, prepared the odd cup of coffee. Ashtrays over flowed with cigarette butts and lipstick smiles smudged abandoned glasses. The debris of a night-club was mournful. There was no sign of my siblings. As we made our way to the exit a middle-aged man, got unsteadily to his feet.

"Ah Diego," said Jaime "I apologise for keeping you waiting." Jaime took my arm. "I'm sorry," he said in my ear. "One of the disadvantages of the job. He comes with me." He smiled. "Diego's a good man but he hates night-clubs."

"You can tell."

We emerged onto the pavement into the half light.

"Well …" I said my heart thumping.

Jaime turned. "Well what? Why do you hesitate, Sigismunda?"

The seconds were going too quickly. In a moment he would be gone and I knew so little about him. I couldn't breathe. *Don't go!* In a moment it would be all over and I would be on the street trying to flag a non-existent taxi, back to the Coach House, back to the emptiness of life with Nuria. I touched his arm. His tie was undone and it lay like two withered leaves on either side of his white shirt. He stood calmly, patiently as though he had all the time in the world.

"I – " I frowned. "I know nothing about you."

Damn, that wasn't what I'd wanted to say nor would it hold him. I'd known a lot less about most of the men I'd gone off with in the past. Why should it matter now? Why couldn't I be so scintillating and sparkling that he would never want to let me go?

"You know I can dance." Jaime motioned to Diego. "Get the car and drive around the block. We won't be long."

Diego bow-legged and weary, clicked his heel. "*Si Excelencia*," he said ignoring me entirely. There were a few more precious moments…

"Yes. It was tremendous fun."

Jaime had not touched me during the whole evening except when dancing and now he pulled me out of the doorway, into the shadows, his hands lingering on my arms.

"I would not insult you by expecting you to come back with me. I do not ask anything of you. You are very beautiful and you are more real to me than all the politicians and diplomats I have yet to meet. You fill the loneliness in my heart. There is no artifice in you, no guile or malice and that, in the world I inhabit, is worth a lifetime's ambition. It has refreshed me and I thank you for reminding me of such innocence."

I felt the tears prick my eyes. He touched my cheek and kissed me but I turned my face deliberately so that our lips met – mine hungry for affection, his cautious.

"I'm not innocent," I said. "If you only knew-"

"I do know," he said pulling away.

"I want to come with you." My heart was in my mouth but it was only pride that was stopping me from doing what I really wanted. *Only pride of which I have so little left ...*

"Jaime, let me spend this last day with you. Please. I won't bother you. I promise I – "

"Sigismunda," he said wearily. "You don't owe me anything. You are free to leave."

"But I don't want to!" I said my voice cracking. I turned away. "I can't bear to think I will never see you again."

He turned me to face him, gently tilting my chin so that I was forced to look at him. His face was lined and vigorous. I needed his strength. I craved it.

"Nor I you," he said.

Chapter 31

Sigi
Journal

Jaime was staying at the elegant Ritz hotel, not far given the new tarmac road, from Mialma. He had spacious rooms that seemed an extension of my grandmother's house. They had the same sort of paintings, period furniture, the same silence. Time had taken on an unreal dimension. It was as if I had thrown away my watch and was being governed by some other set of ordinance. He turned on a small side lamp and pulled back the curtains, so that the city sparkled around us, grew and took shape in the dawn. The pinks, blues and purples of the early morning smoothed away the rough edges of the buildings to make it beautiful. He ordered whisky for himself and tea for me and sat, still in his evening clothes while I had a bath and tried to scrub away all trace of Carlos Nadal.

Afterwards, wrapped in a hotel bathrobe, I talked and paced the room while he watched me. I talked, as I had never done to any of the psych doctors in San Juan. I bared my soul. I told him about Avia, about my parents, my brothers, about Marta and Bea's irritating habit of repeating some words three times. I told him about Rodrigo and the night I lost the baby. I told him even about San Juan. Jaime drank a good deal of whisky but he made no comment. And when I had finished he undid his cufflinks and dropped them, one by one, onto the glass table. They were round silver spheres with a diamond in the centre. Exhausted but exhilarated, I lay sprawled on the carpet.

"You must sleep now," he said. He carried me in his arms like a child and tucked me in his bed. But he did not stay. He left the bedroom door ajar and I saw him move around the sitting room, opening briefcases and another bottle of whisky and settle down to work. I had never felt safer or more at peace in my life. I fell asleep.

*

It was late when I woke up and I felt utterly refreshed as if the past had been completely wiped out. The bedroom door was closed and voices came from the salon. I opened it a fraction, just enough to peer through and nearly slammed it again in horror. A whole television crew seemed to have crammed its way in and the room teemed with journalists and photographers. Jaime was halfway through an interview with ABC. *La Vanguardia* jostled alongside some Chilean paper I had never heard of, to ram their microphones in front of his face. There was a bevy of secretaries with dicta phones. Telephones and bleepers sounded incessantly. Jaime was formidable in his crisp shirt and immaculate suit. He emanated power and solidity. He did not look like a man who could ever be corrupted and my heart sank. Similarly, he did not look as if had spent most of the night at the *Up and Down* and what remained of it, working. Diego hovered in the background with bottles of water that he offered round.

I tiptoed to the bathroom and washed my face, trying to be as quiet as possible. I brushed my hair with the hotel toiletries and wrapped in a towel, wondered what on earth I was going to wear. I wanted to burn my jeans and shirt, to obliterate any reminder of Carlos Nadal. I padded back into the bedroom but couldn't find my clothes anywhere. With any luck, I thought to myself someone had already disposed of them. What I did find however, was a large shopping bag. Curiosity getting the better of me, I looked inside to discover a simple blue shift dress with matching cardigan and underwear – exquisite, flimsy bits of lace and a flat pair of pumps. I took the lot back into the bathroom. The bra and panties were beautiful and the dress fitted like a glove. I swung the short cardigan round my shoulders, slipping my feet into the soft kid shoes that were as comfortable as slippers. I gave my hair a final brush and smiled at my reflection. I bit my lips to give them colour but it was an unnecessary gesture, my whole face glowed with happiness. No one had ever been this kind to me and I wanted to dance and jump and shout with the unexpected delight of it all. I felt like a naughty child who knows with guilty delight, that on this occasion, she has got away with it. I waited patiently in Jaime's bedroom for what seemed like hours. At last it was quiet. Then the door burst open and I jumped to my feet.

"I'm so sorry I could not stop – to do with my new appointment – my God you are beautiful!"

He seemed breathless, uncharacteristically, less controlled.

I smiled. "Oh Jaime, thank you, thank you from the bottom of my heart."

Jaime laughed. "It's Diego, you have to thank. He's had a busy morning and not exactly the one he had in mind but I'm glad to see he got the size right."

I smoothed my hips. "The dress is lovely."

"Hyacinth blue. It's your colour." He kissed my hand. "Come Sigismunda you must be starving. And again it is late. The day is advancing too quickly. We must hurry if we are to enjoy ourselves at all."

He tucked my arm proprietarily in his. "You are truly beautiful," he said.

"It's because of you."

His eyes bored into mine so that I blushed. "I've booked a table for half an hour ago. We must eat." He kept my hand in his, a large cool hand to lead me to the door.

"We could have gone somewhere less formal," Jaime said when we were seated at a little table in a corner by the window. "But I feel reluctant to waste time getting to and from places and strictly speaking, I suppose I'm still on call. It's always a busy time, moving."

Jaime studied the large elaborate menus and ordered Chilean wine. The food arrived in silver dishes, delicate and aromatic: small scallops in cream of ginger on a bed of saffron rice. Tiny parcels of vegetables in shredded pastry shells melted in your mouth. Raised on a monotonous diet of pasta and meat, this food seemed like ambrosia. Jaime was an amusing and considerate host. The evening's previous restraint seemed to have dissolved and he was more relaxed. He recounted amusing anecdotes of embassy parties. He told me about his home in Chile and its sprawling vineyards. He talked of Vina and the sea. He spoke of his apprehension at returning to Santiago. He had already been posted to Rome, Vienna, London but never Paris and he had greatly enjoyed his three years in Madrid. He liked Europe but the volatile politics of his country made him inherently cautious. He was not ready to return home.

After coffee and the large brandies Jaime had insisted on, I began to feel distinctly light headed.

"It all sounds so exciting, the traveling, the parties," I said.

"You meet interesting people, yes," he agreed thoughtfully. "But there are a lot of idiots too. A lot of it is monotonous and lonely and you're on the move. There is always a new country to get to know, new customs, new toes to avoid stamping on and then the machinations of my governments' policies churn away in the background and we are always the last to know and you're briefed by some fool who has never left Vina. Sometimes it is difficult to make friends. There is always a price."

"I didn't think you were cynical."

"No. Not generally." He pulled me to my feet. "Not today. Now," he said sternly.

"W-wouldn't you like to see the city?" I stammered nervously. "I mean it is your last day. There's the Sagrada familia, the Gaudi buildings, the Miro foundation." I added with a flourish.

"No," said Jaime pulling me out of the dining room towards the lift. "I've seen the sights. Believe me. Countless times. I know the Picasso museum too," he added as I drew breath. But I had deliberately avoided mentioning it, as it was a stone's throw from where I had encountered Carlos Nadal the evening before.

He held me firmly by the hand as he unlocked the bedroom door.

"Where is Diego?" I asked. Jaime shut the door behind us.

"Why?" he asked amused. "Shall I get him? Can he do something for you?"

"I thought he was your shadow."

"He is but not till tonight. He's worked more than his quota this week. We don't do *everything* together!"

Jaime tossed the electronic key so that it fell lightly on a chair and still he did not let go of me. With one hand he removed his jacket.

"Now," he said again holding me so that I could not breath nor dared to look at him. "I was wrong about last night. There is one thing I *will* ask of you. And that is that you always tell me the truth. I don't care what it is or how difficult you think it might be. You must always be honest with me. I can help you but there must be no lies between us. Do you understand? I want you to trust me."

His fingers were rigid, holding my wrists and then suddenly he released me.

"I promise," I said bowing my head.

"Good." But as I moved away, he caught me roughly by the arm so that I gasped.

"God but I want you," he said hoarsely and then his lips were crushing mine, his body bent over me. I buried my face in his strong dark neck, this stranger's skin that smelled of his clean crisply laundered shirt. I felt his face under my fingertips and his hair and the back of his head. His lips tasted of brandy and I closed my eyes. My dress rustled to the floor as I stepped out of it and again like a child he lifted me effortlessly in his arms, high above the darkness.

*

And now all is clear. The rest of my story rushes past in careful pictures. No detail is lost. Jaime emerges like a phoenix from the ashes, stark and strong, the not so loved one, father of my living child.

I remember it all. I am calm as I look out of my window towards the sea, banded by white beach and the azure sky beyond. I see the sailing ships neatly bobbing on the horizon and they seem as unreal as did those illustrations of boats in our English fairy tales when I was a child. I see the globe of the world in our nursery that never stopped at Chile and the water colour of another Countess Roble in my grandmother's house.

One by one, the scenes of my destruction float before my eyes. I remember the early, happy days of my marriage and that first, wondrous journey to Chile. I remember glittering Embassy parties, with the rooms full of flowers and famous people talking brilliantly and of brilliant things. I remember when at last, Jaime was awarded the embassy in Paris and we arrived and dazzled. For the first time people listened to everything I had to say. Women hung on my every word, copied my hair, my clothes, wanted my recipes. Their husbands cut in on each other at dances, all vying for my attention. Jaime beamed with pride showing me off with tenderness and love, wanting only to bask in my light. And I became accustomed to such admiration, yearned for it, *needed* it, grew to expect it.

And when our son was born and Jaime could see his own features in the tiny face, he praised God for such joy and for this heaven on earth. I remember the wonder of holding my baby for the very first time and mourning with renewed vigour, the loss of Rodrigo's child. When little Jaime could crawl he was like a puppy with plump rolls of fat around his neck and chubby hands that swiped the air. Then, when he was older and could ride a bicycle, he would whiz down the marble corridors laughing with delight, and we laughed to see him. I remember exciting trips to London, Rome and Venice and coming home laden with clothes I could only have dreamed of, and expensive toys for our son. I held happiness in the palm of my hand and like soap bubbles, one by one I blew them away.

And I remember shooting heroin in a bathroom at the Spanish embassy in Bonn. And then it was over. I remember the scandal, the newspapers, the photographers, the police, the disgrace. Everything. But most of all and always, I remember the naked anguish on Jaime's face, the wail of the wounded and his look of betrayal and bewilderment – the grey hair and lined face, the now stooping shoulders, not broad enough to weather the hurt I had inflicted. Oh Jaime, why could I not love you the way I loved Rodrigo? You who were a thousand times more worthy, more noble, more honourable in every way. You who tried, so many times, to save me from myself?

I remember the time my son would not come to me but buried his face in his nanny's lap.

And I remember that I am here. No more white paper to write on, no more lines or ink spills to terrify me. I have done that all by myself. And last of all, in the sequence of pictures, as one by one they vanish, and are lost, I see myself as a little girl at Val Negra, surrounded by my sisters and the twins. We sit, dressed identically as we always were, this time in white linen dresses embroidered with yellow daisies. Bea has a large yellow ribbon in her hair that makes me think of a monster butterfly and I try to pick it off with the edge of my pencil. We sit in the school room while Lupe darns socks in a corner, peering and scolding as she sits fit. The governess, who has only recently been hired for the summer, stands behind a pile of books that will be wasted on us. Through the open windows, we hear the river and the falling sound of camomile leaves. With a sudden breeze we smell tuber roses and gardenia. We sit, chin cupped in hands, anticipating only the end of the lesson. In the kitchen, the maids are concocting delicacies for our tea. We are treated like china dolls and the promise of our future is great. At last, the hour is over and we bang down our desks and with shouts of joy rush towards the garden. The Monseny shields our playing fields, filtering the afternoon sun so that it is warm and balmy. Under the willows, our parents in what appears to be a moment's harmony, converse politely. Nuria blinking in the light, looks up, hand to pearly throat and waves while Avia and Abuelita gossip ferociously with no time for distraction, their jaws even at this distance, in fierce activity. It seems, that for a split second, we are all caught in some captive eye's still-life. It seems, that the empty school room echoes with the voices and laughter of childhood years, that their memory is trapped there forever.

Chapter 32

Ricardo
Barcelona
Spring 1998

It was April 23, St.George's Day, feast of the legendary crusader who dipped his fingers in his own wound staining four vertical stripes of blood along his shield. From that day onwards, Catalans had their coat of arms and symbolic colours of yellow and red. It was a day traditionally celebrated by the exchange of a book for the Senor and a rose for the Senora. Ricardo sat at his desk at the Banesto Bank contemplating the mound of documents for review. There were contracts, solicitors' reports, m&a accounts, internal memorandum, files of all description, letters to and from La Caixa, letters to the Generalitat, letters peeping from every possible desk and filing tray. But he had little stomach for it this morning. He flicked through the newspapers – the usual motley collection of local rag and financial news. He glanced at the English Times which had devoted its centre pages to a spread on Catalonia.

Unesco has declared April 23rd as World Book day, he read. There was a large colour sketch of Shakespeare, who shared a birthday with their patron Saint and the caption: *Today he is a Catalan.*

Ricardo smiled to himself. When he was a boy, Catalans were not allowed to celebrate this fiesta at all and certainly no literature was published in that language. Now the entrance to the Ramblas, which he could just see from his window, was teeming with young people, all seeking to purchase a book and a rose at the hundreds of stalls along the boulevard. It was twenty years since Catalans were granted permission to use their ancient language, the Generalitat was restored and its Statute of Autonomy approved by the King. The then Prime Minister had shrewdly recognized the fact that democracy would not be achieved without acknowledging Basque and Catalan Identity. After 13 years in government, the Socialists had been defeated and in order to form a new one, Jose Maria Aznar head of the Popular Party, needed the support of Senor Pujol, president of Catalonia. Pujol, was the father of modern Catalan nationalism and still only answered media questions in Catalan, sending Spanish television scrambling to set appropriate subtitles.

Ricardo, pondering the political changes since Franco, also recognised the fact that he was getting old. He folded the newspapers and rose to pour himself a cup of coffee. Large windows, opening on to the street below brought in the bright April sun. He felt strangely restless and not used to self- analysis, was unwilling to further assess the emotion. He was not overly sentimental or nostalgic. He faced life with characteristic stoicism if not humour and tried not dwell on the past. His illness had taught him that. It was more than twenty years since he had been diagnosed with leukaemia. At the time, he had not cared whether he lived or died. The irony was, that at the beginning he hadn't even felt ill. It was the treatment that nearly destroyed him but he was not afraid of dying. He believed that in a lifetime, everyone has a required ambition to fulfil. For some people this is realized when they are very young, for others not until they are old although the result is the same. But his time was not up and he had survived. He had paid the price of the treatment and a second chance at life.

Ricardo was an organised and dedicated bachelor. He worked long hours and in the evenings would often join a colleague for a drink at one of the local *tapas* bars. Occasionally, he went to the *Liceo* or the cinema and dined out regularly. On Fridays, he brought his bags to work so that he could head for a friend's house, leaving early to beat the weekend traffic. Mostly, he enjoyed the privacy and solitude of his own house with its spectacular views of the sea. He liked to be alone and this was often a point of contention with girlfriends and one of the reasons he had never married. It was only recently however that a disquiet had set in. There had been problems at the bank. Work was not without its stress and colleagues were ever vigilant, anxious to protect their jobs. There was a tension that affected them all. But his sense of personal dissatisfaction went deeper than that. It was the first time since his illness that his infertility saddened him. As he grew older, it was a physical disability that he recognised with increasing cynicism. He could not pursue a long-term relationship without the inevitable question of marriage and children being raised. Ultimately it ended in heartbreak and disappointment, with the result that he told no one of his infertility and enjoyed fraudulently, the reputation of being a playboy. He was always seen in the company of beautiful women, yet no relationship lasted more than a month. He became well versed in sarcastic quips and witty one-liners. He was expert in deflecting emotional probing or sentimentality. In a society where machismo defines the male and the family institution is the pinnacle of a man's success, Ricardo shrank from married friends with children like a salamander loath to emerge from the shade. He surrounded himself with a protective circle of older, single processionals – mostly Foreigners. The Dutch and the English, he discovered, had a more relaxed view of the family and religion. He could converse quite adequately without those twin subjects ever being raised, whereas his Spanish counterpart found it impossible to avoid commenting on both.

All at once the prospect of yet another weekend repeating the same endless routine with some girl he had only just met, bored him rigid. The sight of his *Loewe* bag ready by the door was infinitely depressing. His phone was ringing and he turned back to his desk. Let his secretary answer it for once. Usually he picked up the phone himself. It was one of his betes noirs. He saw no reason why clients shouldn't ring through to him directly. However, it was not a procedure practised by his colleagues, where reaching them was a full time occupation in itself. Ricardo had no time for contrived artifice. And at the end of the day, he maintained that dealing personally with enquiries was both cost-effective and time efficient but not today. He let it ring. That would jolt Carmen out of her day-dreaming. She was probably wondering, along with the rest of the female staff, where her rose was. He sat down heavily in his chair. The very thought of having to review another loan document paralysed him with inertia. Perhaps he should leave even earlier than planned for Tarragona. He knew Tarragona like the back of his hand and even its fine Roman attractions were beginning to pall. A pretty Belgian girl who worked as a compliance officer for a mutual client had invited him to join a house party there. But as charming as she was, she bored him rigid. He only went because her friends were fun. Maybe he would give the weekend a miss altogether and spend it at home – a quick drink at the *Up and Down* and home.

The *Up and Down*.
Christ. Isabel.
A wave of feeling came over him as he remembered his cousin. He moved to pick up the phone just as it stopped ringing. And then he hesitated.

Am I mad? He almost said aloud. She wouldn't want to hear from him. Not now. Not after what Tim had said. He had to confess to be stunned by the Englishman's phone call, by the man himself. And only a few days after... well after she'd spent the weekend with him. He'd had no idea Isabel was engaged to be married. His jaw clenched. He would never have thought of her as dishonest but then he clearly hadn't understood her. But apart from his male pride he was curious to know if he had meant anything to her. Surely you couldn't share what they had and be unaffected? Or on the contrary, maybe you could. Perhaps it had been such a long time since he'd had a real relationship with a woman that he'd lost touch with what the modern woman really felt. Obviously not very much. At least not for him. He knew she had responsibilities, her career, The Cottage. She could, if she wanted, have all the things he couldn't give her – namely children. All the things she could have with Tim. But why hadn't she told him? They'd talked so much over those few days. He thought he knew her. He thought... Even now he could feel her beneath him, her breath on his cheek, her stillness ... She had said she loved him. Hadn't she? And all the time she was engaged to be married...

No, it was better to let things be. It was far too complicated. She would never leave England and his work was here in Barcelona. And just for good measure, like a vulture hovering above everything they did, was the Family. But what irritated him most of all, was the fact that they hadn't had the chance to go further, to develop a friendship that had only just begun. It had ended abruptly, with Tim's phone call. If only Isabel had talked to him. Even in the weeks that followed had she been in touch... but there had been nothing at all. Only this impossible silence. And more importantly this persistent feeling that Isabel was the only woman he would ever love haunted him still. He was left with the bitter- sweet curiosity of what might have been. Ricardo couldn't help savouring the memory. It would stay with him always. It had helped him to face the more stressful times at the Bank and the endless problems that seemed to plague his siblings. And today, because of the sentimental nature of the feast day, he indulged himself and remembered ...

*

It had been on a Friday such as this that she had called. It was a busy time at the Bank and he had worked late the previous night. He was up to his eyes in contracts, meetings with personnel from the human resources department, other lawyers and clients. He had several reports to get out by the afternoon. He was testy, his eyes ached and he had been forced to cancel his box at the *Liceo*. It was bitterly cold even if it was the spring and for once the sun was not shining, a phenomenon that made all Spaniards bad tempered. The phone rang incessantly and he cursed his policy of always answering it himself. He paced his office rehearsing a speech he was to make that afternoon. It was several moments before he finally grabbed the receiver.

"*Si?*" he said curtly hoping it wasn't going to be the Catalan Finance Councillor, Sr. Alavedra who was expecting to sign off on several contracts by mid morning. A mutual client, *La Caixa,* had recently taken two major stakes in *Telefonica* and *Repsol,* an exciting achievement for Catalan economy and one involving a colossal amount of preparation. Lawyers and secretaries alike laboured round the clock to complete the legal work. There didn't seem to be anyone on the line.

"*Digame?*" Snapped Ricardo hoping his tone would put the caller off.

"Ricardo?" Isabel's voice was hesitant. "I didn't recognise your voice. It's me, Isabel."

"*Isa?*"

Ricardo was so surprised he sat down abruptly at his desk. He had not heard from his cousin in years and she had never telephoned him before.

"Isabel?" He said regretting having used her nickname. Perhaps she had outgrown it, perhaps it was too familiar.

"I know you're busy," she said apologetically. "I'll make it quick."

"No. No, I mean I am but it doesn't matter. It's good to hear from you. It's been so long. Is there anything the matter? Are you all right?"

"Yes of course. Thank you. I should have called before – given you some warning but my meeting was only confirmed yesterday. You know what these Spaniards are like! It's hard getting them to commit but now they have I'll be in Barcelona tonight. I'm seeing the Bazan brothers."

"What? As in *our* Bazan brothers?"

He was doubly surprised and then he remembered snippets of news that had trickled down to him over the years. Didn't she work in marketing or was it advertising? Was there a difference? He wished he'd paid more attention.

"And not only Fer and Benito but Rodrigo de Montfalco as well. It's a long story but such a coincidence! The company I work for is targeting the wine trade – Catalan Cava in particular, hence our friends. I say business meeting but it's really just a social. I'm taking them to the *Up and*

Down. I thought – " she paused. "I thought it would be better if I had someone with me."

"You mean a lawyer." Ricardo's tone was dry. He remembered now from a hidden source, the playful way they used to banter and it amused him unexpectedly. He cradled the phone under his chin reaching for a cigarette. He lit it waving the match in the air.

"No. Well yes, it's always useful."

"Just useful?"

He wondered if she were blushing in the way she used to so easily, if he said anything remotely provocative. He could hear the smile in her voice.

"No. Oh you know what I mean. I could do with your … support. There will be other members of the wine board and a Chilean who has vineyards in Vina del Mar. Anyway he has agreed to meet the others. You know how macho you Latins are. I thought it would be better – in fact I *know* it will be, if I have some one of your calibre with me. But it's not just that."

She stopped, her voice so low he strained to hear it.

"Yes?"

"It's been so long since I've seen you. "

All at once he remembered Marta's wedding. Did she remember it too?

"I'll come," he said abruptly. "But it'll be late. I mean even by Spanish standards. I have a meeting. Will you wait?"

"I'll wait." She sounded elated.

He felt overwhelmingly curious – curious and guilty. Isabel. Good God, after all these years! Still …

Carmen opened the door to remind him of his appointment and motioned to the gentlemen waiting outside. He smiled so good-naturedly his secretary wondered if anything was wrong.

"Send them in," he said. He adjusted his cufflinks and walked round his desk to welcome his clients. In spite of the hard work ahead and the cold, the day seemed immeasurably brighter.

*

Ricardo worked long into the evening but had finished by 11.30. He piled documents into a cabinet not bothering to sort them out before locking the door. He binned the newspapers and left a note stuck to his computer for Carmen. He walked the short distance to his car, breathing in the cold air and stretching. He was exhausted but relieved at having met the required deadlines. He flicked off his car alarm aiming the buzzer at the door of his slate-grey Mercedes. He slung his briefcase onto the passenger seat and got in, switching on the CD. He loved to drive at any time but he especially enjoyed it at night, cocooned in the warmth of the car listening to music. He found it as relaxing as unwinding over a glass of *vino tinto* and Catalan *chorizo*. Only tonight he wanted to get to the club as quickly as possible. He accelerated speeding towards the city centre and a mere twenty minutes later, skidded to a halt outside the nightclub. He handed his keys to the doorman exchanging the usual pleasantries.

Ricardo was a regular visitor. He enjoyed a certain comaderie with a friendly but discrete staff and he knew many of the clientele by sight. He liked the fact that there was always a good atmosphere, the perquisite number of pretty girls but also that he could just as easily drink alone if he wasn't feeling sociable. Ricardo nodded to an acquaintance, eyes darting to the empty dance floor. A crooning Julio Iglesias indicated it was still early. He approached the counter where Francisco, the Andaluz barman, greeted him warmly.

"The usual, *Senor Conde?*" he asked placing a whisky tumbler in front of him and a plate of *tapas*.

Ricardo nodded, helping himself to a dish of black olives marinated in rosemary.

"So what do you think of the elections, my friend?" asked Ricardo.

Francisco smiled showing a glint of gold tooth. Ricardo always flattered him by listening intently to his political opinions and according him more intelligence then did his fellow waiters.

"I think the Madrilenians haf to sweat it out!" he said gleefully. "All these years trying to teach us a lesson, thinking they are so *presumido* and now who needs us but the prime minister? Pujol can afford to take his time. He can make Aznar very nervous. If I were Pujol, I would make him suffer. After all, without Pujol's support there is no government."

Ricardo allowed Francisco to pour his whisky, nodding his thanks. He reached for another olive.

"Very true but you are not a Catalan. I thought you hated us"

"NO!" protested Francisco, dark bushy eyebrows meeting in the middle. "I hate those from Madrid much much more!"

"So your support has nothing to do with the fact that Pujol is now in a position to negotiate even more self-rule for Catalonia and to control even more of its income tax, and run his own labour policy?"

The woman's voice was low, melodious. Ricardo noted Francisco's irritated grimace – the one he used for especially attractive women – before he saw her.

"Isabel?" he spluttered almost choking on an olive pit. She gave his back a thump.

"Christ!" he said when he could breath again. "You've grown up."

"I would hope so!"

The green eyes that he remembered, stared out at him in a flawless face. His eyes flicked over her simple black dress, cut away to reveal the new erogenous area of shoulder. Her hair, streaked with a hint of chestnut, was smooth across her collarbone. She brushed his cheek with her lips and he felt the softness of her skin, the scent of sunflowers. She scrunched up her dress to allow her to sit on one of the tall bar stools. Her legs dangled tantalizingly in front of him. She placed a Prada bag on the counter, its material cover disappearing against the granite surface. Ricardo cleared his throat.

"Forgive me. Francisco, this is my English cousin, Isabel Pelham. Isabel, Francisco."

Francisco bowed curtly and Ricardo could tell he didn't believe for one minute that she was related to him. He grunted a greeting but wouldn't look at either of them.

"What will you have? A cocktail or something soft? You hardly look old enough to be in here."

Isabel laughed. "You flatter me. I'm not a schoolgirl anymore. I'll have the same as you."

Francisco deposited another glass none too gracefully in front of her and noisily began setting out *tapas*, his face set in a heavy scowl.

"I don't think your friend likes me," she whispered loudly when the waiter had turned his back.

"He's just jealous. We usually have a bit of a chat before the action gets going. But he hates it when a pretty girl turns up."

Isabel raised an eyebrow.

"Why? Does it happen often?"

"No of course not but it's just that … well modesty aside, I think he's rather fond of me." Ricardo mouthed the words, "A bit possessive."

Isabel's eyes twinkled.

"I see. Ricardo… there isn't anything you want to tell me?"

"Um?"

Ricardo could hardly concentrate his thoughts. Gone was the skittish, colt-like girl he had known, delightful as she was, but a child all the same, and in her place was this sophisticated, ravishing woman. He felt the familiar lurch of desire. He took a swig of whisky.

"I was trying to remember the last time I saw you," he said knowing precisely when it was. "It must have been at Marta's wedding and that's …" he struggled.

She looked away.

"A long time ago."

"Yes." He leant his elbow on the bar so that he was facing her. "I'm getting to the age when everything seems to have happened twenty years ago. You fall into that category. How come I haven't seen you? Surely you've been back since Marta's wedding?"

She swivelled to face him too and again he couldn't keep his eyes from skimming her body. Her arms were slender but toned in the soft light. He could see the swell of her breasts in her low cut dress. She shrugged.

"Not much. Once. I came to see Sigi when she was in the hospital at San Juan but it wasn't a success. I thought I could help. Of course I speak to Avia and we write once a week but what with work …"

Ricardo looked at her thoughtfully. "So the *espanola-inglesa* returns, only I think now more English than Spanish." He touched her glass with his. "*Salut,*" he said. She raised her eyes to his, unwavering. Was it his imagination or had they misted over?

"It's been a while since anyone called me that," she said.

"It used to annoy you."

"Only because I wanted to fit in."

"And you went to Oxford in the end."

It was a lame statement but Ricardo didn't care what he said. He needed to keep her talking while he got over the shock of seeing her again. He couldn't believe it had been such a long time since they'd seen each other – why *she* could have children old enough to be going to university themselves - and yet talking to her now felt as though they were picking up from where they left off. But why hadn't she been in touch? Why had they all grown so distant from each other? It was bizarre to think that this girl who had spent so much time here in Spain with his family, who *was* his family, returned a stranger.

Isabel smiled coolly.

"It *has* been a long time! Yes, I went to Oxford. But it seems years ago. It *is* years ago. I've always worked in marketing and now I'm at a company called Archid. We have a lot of clients in Spain although not in Barcelona until now. That's why I'm here tonight. We're targeting the Bazan Cava account - I can't tell you the surprise I had when I received their proposal." She touched his sleeve. "And of course I wanted to see you. I've missed everyone so much."

"You've stayed away too long," he said gruffly. "It was a mistake."

"I see that now," she said lightly. "And you? You stuck with your bank?"

"Yes. Not very imaginative I'm afraid."

"But it was what you wanted, then."

"Then, yes." He looked away scanning the small tables that were beginning to fill up.

"You must find us all much changed," he said. Her eyes darted to the streaks of grey in his once jet black hair. She swallowed.

"Everything. Nothing. Sometimes I even wonder if I shared in it at all. It was my life, all of you, Val Negra. Avia. It's as if it happened to another person. And now ..."

"It has been replaced by another," he finished gently.

"It's always a little strange when I come home. It takes a while to adapt. Then after a few days I don't want to leave again. It's a schizophrenic existence. Or it was, maybe it's not so bad now. I used to feel it more when I went back to school after the summer holidays."

Ricardo scanned her face. *How could he have let her go? He must have been mad. He hadn't behaved very well but she seemed not to hold it against him. Did she remember that night?*

Isabel smiled brightly.

"And how is everyone? How are Sigi and Beatrice? I don't know if I'll have time to see them. You must tell me all their news."

"Ah." Ricardo lit a cigarette offering one to Isabel but she declined. "I wondered when we'd start talking family."

"It's impossible not to and I'm hungry for news about everyone. Start with Sigismunda," she said. "You know that she was always my favourite. How is she? I know she married and has a child and lives aboard."

Ricardo blew out smoke above her head.

"Yes. It was all a bit of a whirlwind. She married someone she met here," he looked around the walls of the night club. "I didn't think for a minute that it would last. They'd known each other for literally two days before she vanished to South America. I thought Tito would be apoplectic but he and Nuria were just so relieved to have her off their hands. Jaime is a charming man, a saint to take on Sigi that's for sure."

"And does she still have a …problem?"

Ricardo nursed his drink. "Por ahora, I'd say no but you can never know with Sigi."

"And the child?"

"A boy. I haven't see him yet. Jaime travels a great deal but not to Spain."

"And the others?"

Ricardo balanced his cigarette on the edge of an ashtray.

"Let's see.. Miguel is still working in the shop. Marta's married with a girl and a boy. The eldest must be …um … not sure. This high anyway." Ricardo made a gesture estimating his nephew's height. He could never really remember how old he was. Every time he saw him, he seemed to have grown. "Fernando and my sister have been happy. Marta has a shop selling children's clothes in the Paseo de Gracia. But you'll be able to catch up with them later. I think they're on their way."

"I can't wait to see them. And your parents?"

Ricardo refilled their glasses. "Tito lives most of the year in Val Negra. He's completely obsessed with his health. He swims every morning regardless of the weather and does even more hiking than before. Sport has replaced his passion for politics, which I suppose is altogether safer for the country. No more huge plates of pasta in that household. It 's all steamed vegetables and grilled meat."

Isabel shook her head.

"Unbelievable. And Nuria?"

"Nuria … is … well… mellow I suppose is the word. I mean she's no longer obsessed with Cervantes which is a relief but sort of strange at the same time. It was kind of fun having a weird mother. Now she's just normal as in worried, fretting and overly concerned for her children. It's come a bit late but nonetheless the sentiment is genuine enough."

"I'm sorry for that," said Isabel. "I thought that by now Nuria would have made a life of her own."

Ricardo sighed. "Nuria was never very sociable. She hardly sees anyone outside the family but she won't go to Val Negra. She says she wants to be in the city where her children can reach her."

"And Avia? Sometimes I can't believe she's still alive. She's the oldest person I know!"

Ricardo chuckled.

"Well you know how she says longevity is in the Roble genes."

"Nonsense it's because she eats so much!"

Their eyes met.

"But not during the civil war!"

Ricardo smiled.

"I don't know what it is but she's pretty fit. She hears mass daily, often *walking* up to the Carmelites. She only grumbles that because she's lived so long most of her contemporaries are dead. On the other hand, she still lives in the house in which she was born, surrounded by her pictures and books and people who love her. It can't be all bad."

Isabel bowed her head. "I feel so guilty."

"Don't."

"It's just that when I started working at Archid, I buried myself away. I had to make it work and I wanted to succeed. But it meant breaking away from the family for a bit. And then, what with Sigi's problems and Bea becoming a nun, I suppose I began to rethink everything. Nothing was what it seemed. I began to think I had got it all wrong. I was forced to re-examine the past and I didn't always like what I remembered and what I did, I felt I may have exaggerated."

Ricardo felt uneasy. Was *he* one of the things she didn't want to remember? He took a quick slug of whisky. Isabel had drunk hers too and he freshened her glass. Her eyes seemed huge, gentle but in no way accusatory.

"You were very young," he said. "We all tend to romanticise the past."

She touched his shirt-sleeve, her fingers playing absentmindedly with his cufflink. Her head was bowed so that all he could see was the curtain of her hair but he could smell her scent. For a moment he closed his eyes as it transported him back to the days of his youth.

"Yes but I got it *wrong* and I failed to see people for what they were."

She raised luminous eyes to his.

He sighed. "You wanted us to be perfect and we weren't. You put us on a pedestal when we were just like everyone else, only possibly more flawed."

Isabel spoke hardly above a whisper. "I couldn't bear for you not to be. I didn't want to see the cracks."

His hand covered hers briefly before replacing it in her lap. She didn't seem to find it difficult to touch him but he did. The feel of her fingers on his skin was electric. He frowned.

"There's nothing wrong with cracks," he said roughly. "I've always distrusted perfection especially in families! Besides I think if you admit to the flaws you seem more approachable. But you Isa, had the advantage of being able to see our family from a distance."

He noticed a quick hurt look come into her eyes. She sipped her drink quickly.

"I wasn't judging."

"I know that and you don't have to justify yourself to me," said Ricardo harshly. "It's only normal to want to have your own life. "

"Yes." She tossed back her head in a gesture that he recognized at once as being defensive. "Tell me about Bea."

Ricardo scanned the room. "Your people not here yet?"

"No."

Isabel followed his gaze. The nightclub had suddenly filled with people. There was a background noise of clinking glasses and murmuring voices.

"And Bea?"

A muscle tensed in his cheek. Ricardo stubbed out his cigarette. He caught her by the wrist pulling her off the stool.

"Let's dance," he said.

His fingers moved to thread her fingers through his as he steered her to the dance floor. She melted against him, her thigh brushing his. Her hair was under his lips and he had to summon every muscle of self-control to prevent him from crushing her to him. Altogether Isabel was having the most extraordinary effect on him. He hadn't seen her in over twenty years – *Christ was it that long?* And yet she seemed to have changed little. Obviously she was more confident but she wasn't pushy or aggressive like the women he worked with and there was nothing contrived about her. And unlike the women he worked with, she didn't ram the fact that she worked down your throat every five minutes. Furthermore, despite their shared past, she was deliciously mysterious. *Come off it! said a voice in his head, she's only mysterious because you haven't seen her!*

But it wasn't the novelty of seeing her again, of being with a beautiful woman. It was as if the years had fallen away and they were dancing together at Marta's wedding and now as then, he felt the same strength of desire. He might be feeling old, he might have thought that he could no longer really feel passion but seeing Isabel had changed that. It was as if he'd been dead all these years. As if to prove it he spun her round and round the room with an energy he hadn't felt in ages. She laughed breathless, relaxing against him. And ignoring the warning signals then as now, he held her closer than was strictly necessary.

"It seems that whenever I see you, you quite literally take my breath away!" she said laughing.

He inclined his head. "You have that effect on me."

And it was true he thought. He felt light-headed because of her - just as he had done all those years before. Only then, the lovesick girl he held in his arms provoked conflicting feelings of guilt and desire. The older Isabel was infinitely more alluring, sensuous and intriguing. He felt no such guilt now. He was absolutely certain of his feelings.

And before she had time to reflect on what he'd said, he pulled her in the opposite direction so that once again she was laughing, pleading with him to stop.

"Has everything turned out the way you thought it would?" she said at last when they had slowed down. Her words broke into his thoughts. He looked down at her upturned, expectant face.

"Does it ever?"

"You sound bitter."

"Not at all. I've been very lucky. I had my way over Banesto for example. It's just different. I wish I had more time. I wish I could start again."

Isabel squeezed his hand. "I know," she whispered.

Ricardo longed to take her face in his hands, caress the clear skin, absorb some of her calm.

"Isabel – I'm sorry for what happened before," he said suddenly. "I behaved badly and I owed – owe you an explanation. Believe me when I tell you that I never wanted to hurt you. I promise you that with all my heart."

Isabel held a finger to his lips. "Not now," she whispered. She met his eyes but he did not smile. All at once he wanted her more than anyone he had ever met and not just sexually. More than anything, he wanted to spend time with her. She was more beautiful then he could have thought possible and she was intelligent and warm. Other men must think so to. A disturbing thought crossed his mind.

"And in between Oxford and work – haven't there been – you must have known –?" He cleared his throat. "Don't you have a boyfriend?"

Isabel looked at him quizzically. "You're not … jealous Ricardo?"

"No, curious."

"It's complicated."

"Are you seeing someone?"

Isabel was silent.

"It's not a difficult question." Ricardo's grip tightened as he spun her round the room. But the music had changed. "Come let's sit down. I can't dance to this."

Julio Iglesias was still crooning out love songs and had started on *In the Beguine.*

"Too soppy?" said Isabel playfully. He guided her to a table so that they could sit with their backs against the wall, keeping an eye out for their guests.

"No. I'm just too old. I have to pace myself now. It's ok for you young things."

Isabel made a face.

"Not so young."

He touched her cheek gently.

"Young enough."

For a moment she held his hand against her.

"We're trying to catch up on too many years," she said quietly. "Perhaps we shouldn't. But before we start on ourselves, please tell me about Bea."

Ricardo sat beside her, so close he could hear her heart beat. He loved her stillness. So many of the girls he knew seemed to be in perpetual motion – fingering their faces, their clothes, adjusting sunglasses, and most of all their hair, flicking it back and forth, always shifting. Isabel was the very opposite. He had forgotten that she could also be stubborn.

"Tell me about Bea," she insisted. "There must be something you're keeping from me or you wouldn't be so reluctant to talk about her. Come on Ricardo what is it? Is she in Toledo? Is she a Sister by now? Has she completed her training, or whatever it is Carmelites do?"

Ricardo sat back. "No she hasn't done that," he said his face in profile and suddenly distant. "She's pregnant."

"What!" said Isabel stunned. "Surely you must mean Sigi?"

"No," said Ricardo testily. "I mean Beatrice. She went on some Opus Dei course where she met an exchange student – Kenyan to boot. She's not in love with him. They only spent one night together and she's pregnant."

"It only takes one go," replied Isabel flippantly.

"Well I wish to God, she'd realised that," said Ricardo angrily. "It makes me wonder if she knew anything about the facts of life."

"Well Avia never told me if that's any comfort."

Ricardo shot her an odd look. "It's not. So … who did –? Anyway you can imagine the bru-ha. Tito won't have anything to do with her and won't let her anywhere near Val Negra. Nuria says she'll divorce him unless he does. And Marta suggested she have an abortion. Can you imagine that? We're all Catholics and yet we seriously discussed abortion? Needless to say there have been a lot of tears. If only Lupe were alive to see this latest drama! And the Kenyan just probably wants to run a mile and I wouldn't blame him."

"Goodness it's got so Tennessee Williams."

"Very funny."

"Sorry. What about Avia?"

"Nuria and my sisters couldn't decide for weeks whether or not to tell her but when it was certain that Bea was going to keep the baby, there was no alternative. Marta was all for having it adopted and mum's the word, as it were, bad pun I know. Anyway, in the end they had to tell Avia. She was shocked of course but she's been a rock and it has to be said the only member of the family to talk any sense. She doesn't think Bea should be forced to marry this man if she doesn't love him."

"That sounds pretty reasonable. Avia has certainly mellowed a bit since I was growing up! But how does she explain Beatrice to her friends. *Que diran*? I mean what will people say?" Isabel made a face.

Ricardo smiled, his eyes crinkling in the corners.

"Well I suppose it's lucky that most of her friends are dead. Except of course for dear Dr.Mantua. But he's more than a friend. There's nothing he doesn't know about our family! And here's the best bit. After much gnashing of teeth Avia has come up with an ingenious explanation. She has decided that Bea was and is, entirely innocent. Rather like a premeditated crime, Avia says, that as Bea did not *intend* to commit a sin, she's as innocent as the day she was born. She says it must have been a moment's aberration. Avia is convinced that the *Negrito* as she calls the Kenyan, got Bea drunk and had his wicked way. Although she does concede that Bea's volatile nature may have contributed in a small way and wearing a habit when nuns no longer have to."

"What about the habit?"

"Apparently the Kenyan has a thing about nuns."

"You mean he's done it before?"

Isabel giggled.

"I suppose this only confirms Avia's worst fears about foreigners."

"Of course."

Isabel sipped her drink. "And Tito?"

"Tito has taken to the mountains. He's camping at a small shrine to the Virgin of Monserrat. Maybe you remember it? As children we used to go there on excursions and sing a Salve Regina before sprinting down the mountain again in time for *merienda*. Tito has taken a portrait of Abuelita with him and is praying to them both for guidance. At the moment he is unable to forgive Bea for the disgrace she has brought to the family."

"So Avia's theory hasn't managed to convince him?"

"Nope." Ricardo crossed a leg on his knee. "It's not just the baby, Isa, it's the fact that the father is black."

"I see."

He looked at her suddenly weary.

"Do you? Tito is many things," Ricardo said "but he's not a racist. He's a realist and this isn't England. You're used to seeing people of all races because of your colonial history and you English are more tolerant. But here!" He made an expansive gesture. "It's very different. Until recently you'd never have seen a black face in Barcelona."

Isabel's eyes narrowed.

"But what about the Moors? Weren't they black?"

"They'd never admit to that. Then I suppose it depends on what your definition of black is." He smiled. "Look I'm not defending him I'm just trying to explain. People of his generation just didn't see foreigners of any description. Catalans have a hard job getting on with other Spaniards let alone anyone else!"

"So he's ok about it then."

"Well not exactly, no. He thinks she's disgraced the family. He's also managed to have the Kenyan deported."

There was silence. "I'm sorry," said Isabel at length. "I'm truly sorry. I wish I could help."

"Short of adopting the baby, you can't. Now do you see why Nuria hasn't made that life of her own? We seem to lurch from one family crisis to another. My sisters are still overly dependent on their mother. They aren't like you at all. They have no self-esteem and are totally ill equipped for work. Except for Marta I suppose. I'm not sure who needs whom the most. Nuria certainly thrives on being needed. But it's not healthy. I hate psycho-babble but if there was ever a dysfunctional family it's ours!"

Isabel downed her drink and held her glass for another.

"I think dear Cousin, " said Ricardo soberly "you're in danger of becoming quite tipsy. I'm not sure that I should be encouraging you and you haven't even had your meeting yet!"

"I am, you should and at this stage it's medicinal. Oh God I had no idea all this was going on."

"Why should you? You've made your life in England. It's the best thing you could have done. It's easy to get sucked up in the family. Believe me it's hard work keeping them at bay. It's right to be concerned but my sisters have got to stop blaming their child hood and get on with life. No one can do it for them. That's what my parents never taught them. They still place all their hopes and aspirations, in events or a person. They haven't realised that it's down to them. You have."

Isabel was startled. "But I didn't have a choice! It's easier not to, although at the time I hardly thought so. I so longed to be one of you. I envied you – your family, your sense of belonging. Avia took me in of course, but I always felt like a guest, as though I belonged by default. I was shown a great deal of love though, especially at school."

"And we had everything we could possibly have wanted in material terms, but not love. Our parents were not united in what they wanted for us. They argued over each one of us, tearing us apart with self-doubt until what little self-confidence we began with, was completely destroyed. Home was a minefield and each one of us a hand grenade, just waiting to be detonated. Only Tito was the detonator, mad and infantile and utterly unpredictable."

Isabel laughed. "You sound like Miguel. Remember all his talk of the military?" The thought of him sitting in his shop all day fixing transistor radios made her hesitate. "I don't know what the answer is," she said. "I suppose parents just do the best they can. We mustn't criticise them too much. I'm not sure I would do any better."

Ricardo sat back suddenly tired. This was dangerous ground to be getting on to and fatherhood was not a subject he felt up to tackling. Isabel's attention was opportunely diverted to the dance floor as a switch to flamenco music signalled a stampede of women. She leapt to her feet.

"Dance with me!" she said pulling him by the hand.

"Not more!" he groaned as drumming heels deafened further conversation and in spite of himself he felt the gypsy beat flow through his blood. And once again he was transported back to the night of his sister's wedding, when local musicians played *Sevillanas* and moonlight shone brightly above the neat terraced vineyards of Val Negra. Isabel's hair swung as she moved.

Her velvet devore dress clung to her body – cut-out shapes of silk transparent against her legs which flared as she turned. Ricardo felt his stomach knot with desire. And all the time as they paced and strutted in front of each other, her arms high above her head, reaching for the imaginary apple, she never took her eyes from his face. Had it not been for the arrival then of the Bazan brothers and Rodrigo de Montfalco, Ricardo may well have whisked her away. He could still hear the pulsing guitar in his head and the wailing Andalusian voices.

The evening went more smoothly than Ricardo anticipated. He had largely lost touch with the boys from Val Negra and it was a pleasant surprise to see how much they still had in common. Isabel impressed the Bazan brothers with her knowledge of their industry. He felt a mixture of pride and frustration watching her give her talk and an inexplicable strength of emotion. Sometimes when their eyes met, he had the feeling that everything she said was meant for him.

There was much merriment that evening and much of it was due to the presence Isabel's Chilean client. Ricardo found him to be one of the most engaging men he had ever met. Articulate and cultured, the proved to have many talents. Apart from being a wine grower, he was also a linguist and writer. He was able to describe the natural beauty of his country in vivid detail. He told them that Santiago, like Beirut before the war, was one of the few capitals in the world, where you could ski and go to the beach in the same day. He told them about the Atacama Desert with its famous Valley of the Moon and Lake Chungara, the highest lake in the world and about Chile's Antarctic territory which reaches to the South Pole. Appealing to the wanderer in them all and especially Isabel's love of mythical places, he mentioned such names as Easter Island, Cape Horn, Tierra del Fuego, Patagonia and last but not least, the island of Robinson Crusoe.

When he moved on to the subject of wine, his knowledge was no less impressive. He recounted his family's long history of wine producing, highlighting the fact that it had never been touched by the plague that devastated French vineyards in the 19th century. He informed them that his country's Central Valley had exceptional growing conditions: a warm climate coupled with abundant water for irrigation, derived from melting snow from the Andes. The surrounding desert, Pacific Ocean and Antarctica all formed natural barriers against disease. He indicated a keen interest in expanding his business and making inroads into the rest of Europe.

Finally, he produced several bottles of Cabernet Sauvignon that were duly tasted amidst admiring gurgling sounds and appreciative gulps.

"We must compete with our French counterparts with years of tradition and a reputation which paves the way," he said toasting Isabel, "but tell your English friends that we have the advantage when it comes to price. The quality of our wines is first class. We produce a fruity Merlot and our Chardonnay and Chenin Blanc are superb. As you will see the price of Australian wines has increased. Ours has not, while the quality of our beverages is consistently high. We have won countless international awards and because of the interest in our vineyards, we shall harvest new ones over the next few years."

The Chilean had left shortly afterwards but not without having invited Isabel to visit him in Santiago.

Yes it had been a success. And afterwards they had stood outside the nightclub hesitating. Despite the cold, Isabel's shawl had fallen from a shoulder to reveal a gentle swell of breast. His eyes travelled to her throat and he looked away. He had lit yet another a cigarette trying to steady a sudden apprehension.. Isabel tapped her suede shoe. Her leg, fully extended, seemed very long. He glanced at her ankle distractedly.

"Where shall I drive you? Are you staying at Avia's?"

Isabel drew her wrap round her neck. "No. I'm staying at the Ritz." And then she added as if feeling an explanation necessary, "It's only a fleeting visit."

"Really?" Ricardo felt unaccountably relieved and alarmed at the same time. "How fleeting?"

"Oh just the weekend," she said casually I'm booked on the first flight Monday morning."

"I see."

Isabel traced an imaginary pattern on the pavement with the toe of her shoe. He watched it and then her face as she raised it to his. Her eyes were clear and steady.

"I don't want to go back there just yet," she said. "Show me where you live."

"It's late, already morning. Isabel – " Ricardo moved towards her needing her to reassure him as to her feelings but she danced away from him just as the night club door man drove up in Ricardo's Mercedes. Isabel darted into the passenger seat with alacrity.

"Anyway I have to have something to report back the next time I see Nuria," she said when Ricardo was behind the wheel. "Or maybe she's seen your house?" Isabel raised an eyebrow as his silence confirmed that the reverse was true. "Ah! Well that makes me all the keener! Do you mean *that none* of your sisters has seen it?"

Ricardo shook his head. "I can't let them. One step through the door and I've had it. They'll be popping in all the time and with all kinds of excuses as to why they would have to stay. I know them too well. I want peace. I need a refuge, a place where I can repair the damage."

"Is there damage?"

He had meant it flippantly but Isabel's voice was low suddenly charged with emotion. Ricardo glanced at her sharply. It was too late and they were both too tired to start being serious and he was too overwhelmed at seeing her again to begin analyzing his state of mind least of all to her.

"It's tough out there," he said lightly, "being a single male."

"Not with the likes of that bar tender of yours to protect you," said Isabel under her breath. "It's not exactly next door though is it?" she persisted playfully. "I don't think your sisters would just "pop" in if they had to drive half an hour on the *autopista*."

"Can't risk it though," he said smiling. "Now are you sure you want to see where a craggy old bachelor lives?"

She touched his cheek.

"Not so old," she said.

They travelled through quiet streets, dormant before the onslaught of shopkeepers and customers brought them to life. The car purred gently along the smooth road surface as they climbed along the mountainous hinterland. Rugged cliffs overlooked the now dull blue of the Mediterranean. Stormy clouds along the horizon heralded another rainy day. They sat for most of the journey in silence. Isabel was so still that from time to time, Ricardo forgot that she was even in the car. He was tired now. He craved solitude and distance with which to review his thoughts. He wanted her but without the complications of their tangled lifestyles. He didn't want any more games or half hearted, half-started relationships. He didn't want them to start a conversation where they said one thing and meant another. He concentrated on steering the car round the sharp hair-pin bends. The car sank into potholes until the last uneven stretch of path. A narrow road led to a typical Catalan farmhouse surrounded by olive groves and perched precariously on the edge of a cliff. Isabel gasped with delight and opened the car door before it had come to a complete stop. She leapt out and he followed more slowly behind.

"But this is wonderful!" she cried excitedly and then she stopped abruptly a frown creasing her features. She grabbed his arm shaking it slightly. "Ricardo it's here isn't it? This is the place you showed me all those years ago isn't it? Do you remember? You did it! You always said would build a house there, here and you have!"

Ricardo shrank from the happiness on her face. She seemed so fresh in the early morning light, so selfless. *What was he doing encouraging her all over again?*

"Come. I'll show you," he said curtly. He saw the quick flash of hurt and cursed himself. She followed him down a stone path to the orchard and the boundary wall that divided the lemon grove from the cliffs. The wind whipped her hair round her neck and the thin dress around her legs. Behind the house, the mountains loomed above them. She breathed in deeply, thick lashes fanning her cheeks.

"An ideal retreat," she said almost to herself. Ricardo cleared a strand of hair from her eyes. He cupped her face in his hands forcing her to look at him.

"You didn't answer my question."

Dark eyebrows rushed to meet each other.

"Which one was that?" she said.

"Are you seeing someone?" he asked quietly. She made as if to pull away but he caught her firmly by the arm. "Look at me."

"Why? I haven't asked you if you are? I've never asked you about Sonia."

"That's because there's nothing between us. Sonia is happily married to Rodrigo and expecting their first child. But you know that," he added grimly. "Yes I was in love with her, yes I wanted to marry her but then … well then there was the illness. She assumed I was going to die."

"But you didn't."

"No. And Isabel we've been down this road before and you *have* asked me all about her. Sonia wanted children."

Ricardo dropped her arm.

"And I also think you know all about that. If you remember nothing else about Marta's wedding, Tito's little speech will have stuck in your mind. Let's have breakfast," he said wearily. "You must be starving."

"Yes," said Isabel quickly. "No, I mean I'm not starving but yes there *has* been someone. Since I came down from Oxford actually. I'm not in love with him anymore but I'm grateful to him. He was good to me, better than I deserved."

"Gratitude isn't love."

"No but it can be easily confused as such. I've been alone so long that I'm clear about every emotion but love."

Ricardo scanned her face intently but she dropped her eyes. He took her hand.

"Come on," he said quietly. "We'll talk in the house."

He pushed open an arched gate overhung with wisteria and soon they were back on the stone path that led to the front of the house. Ricardo unlocked the door. Isabel followed him into an immense hall. It was open-plan with the drawing room and dining area merging together. One side of the house was entirely flanked by French windows that gave on to a long veranda and the sea beyond. At one end of this vast living space was a huge stone fire place. Ricardo now strode towards it reaching up for the box of matches that he found on the mantle. Within minutes flames leapt in the hearth casting shadows upon the white-washed walls. Suddenly the sand coloured stone floor was brought to life and the deep colours of the haphazardly strewn Persian rugs seemed to glow more brightly in the fire light. Isabel cast an appreciative eye over the locally crafted furniture and the *horchata*-coloured sofas covered with cushions. The walls were lined with bookshelves and a highly polished grand piano was covered in a Paisley shawl. A sprawling iron staircase led to a minstrel's gallery and the main bedroom.

"This is a dream," said Isabel in awe. "It's just perfect. It's exactly the way I would have done it myself. The colours, the views of the sea – it's too lovely."

"I'm glad you like it."

Ricardo went to the kitchen. Isabel glimpsed more pale furniture and ochre coloured walls and blue china pots planted with basil and rosemary.

"A woman's touch." Isabel motioned to the fresh flowers and herbs.

"My cleaner's."

"Ah."

Ricardo carried a cafetiere and two cups to the sitting area, placing them on the coffee table that was strewn with books and journals. Isabel paced the room examining his possessions. There were no photographs anywhere as every available surface was given over to reading material and yet it was paradoxically uncluttered.

"Stop pacing," said Ricardo. "Come and sit down. You remind me of one of my clients who never does business sitting down. You're making me nervous."

Isabel immediately sat down at the far end of the sofa, horribly conscious of the ocean of space between them. Ricardo poured the coffee and sat back undoing his tie and stretching his legs. Small silences weighed heavily between them. He was wary now of her. What had seemed possible only hours before, if only in his mind, now seemed completely unattainable. They both needed to get some sleep. He glanced at her. She seemed uncharacteristically ill at ease and the stillness with which he associated her had momentarily fled. She repeatedly crossed and uncrossed her legs, folded her arms, toyed with the corner of her dress. Was she wondering if she would have been better off going back to her hotel? What had that meant, her wanting to see his place? If indeed it meant anything at all. It couldn't. Besides she had said something about a boyfriend.

"In the Middle East they put cardamom seed in the coffee," said Isabel brightly and when Ricardo turned, watching her animated face with interest she had blushed.

"You've been there?"

"Yes." She cupped the hot mug in her hand. She kicked off her shoes and sat, legs tucked underneath her, leaning slightly towards him. "I spent a year in Oman. But we travelled to the neighbouring countries. Oman for example is very beautiful, much more than the Arab Emirates. It has mountains and sea for one thing. It's not as flat as Dubai. Dubai is just one large duty free airport full of bars and restaurants and the drinking isn't prohibited which is probably why the Brits prefer it."

"Is it very strict? Like Saudi?"

Isabel shook her head.

"No it's the right mix, not as fanatical as Saudi Arabia but not as liberal as Bahrain. It seems successfully to have blended the traditional with the modern. There are areas that are still virtually unexplored, inhabited only by the Bedouin. There are wonderful villages that take a day to reach, perched on the edge of a cliff. The Omani people are courteous and friendly. In the south there is a place called Salalah that is lush and cool. Omanis flock there in the summer – " she stopped. "I'm boring you."

"Not at all," he replied politely, automatically.

She frowned.

"You're teasing me."

"No. It obviously meant a great deal to you."

Isabel paused. "They say that the Queen of Sheba sailed from Yemen into the port at Salalah. Her boats were laden with caravans of gold and frankincense for Solomon. You can see Frankincense bushes everywhere in Salalah which is why they now think that one of the three wise man may have been Omani." Her voice trailed. "I thought Jaime de Malagrida's description of the Valley of the Moon was just as romantic."

Ricardo smiled. "Even as a little girl you loved to hear of foreign places." He drained his coffee. "Is that where you met Tim?"

Isabel's mouth formed a perfect O. "How do you know about him?" she spluttered.

Ricardo enjoyed her confusion. "Avia. Who else? And from the way you talk about the place, you must have been in love."

"So why the interrogation before? If you knew about Tim?"

"Hardly an interrogation, *cosina.*"

"But you knew."

"Verification of the facts. Nothing more."

Isabel flushed and struggled to get to her feet. "I think I want to go now."

"Good heavens, why?" He pretended to be surprised.

"I just do. Suddenly. Now."

He raised an eyebrow.

"Any moment you'll be stamping your foot. Oh sit down and stop being so melodramatic," he added as she continued to stand stiffly in front of him. "Besides how would you get back?"

"Well you might drive me," said Isabel testily. "It's the least you can do"

"You're not going anywhere. Sit down."

She sank back uneasily onto the sofa. Ricardo continued to watch her with a ferocity she found unnerving. There was an awkward silence.

"You don't have to be embarrassed about admitting you were in love," said Ricardo easily after a few moments. "It is, after all quite natural. That's the problem with our family. We've always been able to talk in great detail about the trivial things, but never about anything of any real importance. I'm interested, so tell me."

"I wasn't. I'm not. It's not like that."

"Tim was your first lover. Don't worry about it."

"I'm not!" Isabel sounded suspiciously close to tears. Ricardo shot her a strange look. He couldn't tell what she was thinking. *And why should it matter to him?* She was right about that. *But he needed to know.* She certainly looked very beautiful, her cheeks were flushed and in spite of the fact that she'd been up all night, her eyes glinted like emerald flints. She jumped to her feet and began pacing in front of him.

"You're just jealous."

Ricardo was genuinely astonished. "Jealous? Me? Of what ... exactly?"

"Of ...of ... someone like Tim. He's kind and funny, well sometimes he is. He's like a brother. He's clever, he went to Cambridge and – "

"And he's an accountant!"

Ricardo suddenly threw back his head chuckling. "Isa darling, you really are priceless! How can I be jealous of someone I haven't even met! I'm just surprised you can't be honest about him. You obviously care a great deal. I hope you will be very happy. And you deserve to be. I'd offer to give you away but you probably wouldn't want that."

Isabel stopped pacing. "I'm not getting married. It's not like that."

"But he has asked you, hasn't he?"

Isabel was silent.

"Hasn't he?" Ricardo's tone was like a pistol shot. She nodded. Ricardo sighed heavily. He seemed suddenly deflated and Isabel noticed for the first time, deep lines etched on his face. His hands were thrust deep into the pockets of his outstretched trouser legs. His head sank onto his chest.

"And Sonia?" persisted Isabel. "If it hadn't been for Rodrigo, *would* you have married her? She *did* have the ready-made family, Tito was right about that. You asked me if I remembered the night of Marta's wedding? Of course I remember it. How would I not? There's so much about that night that I was never clear about. I've always wanted to know."

Ricardo was frighteningly motionless but he turned to look at her, his face a frozen mask but she went on blindly.

"Wasn't Tito talking families then? He seemed to think marriage to Sonia a very good idea. I don't see why you let her slip away. Maybe you'd be less bitter now. You always said she was the woman you loved."

Isabel stopped short, a frown deepening. "Do you know?" she said slowly. "It suddenly all makes sense. All these years I've tried to understand what happened." She looked at him, her eyes clouding with an emotion he didn't recognise. "And now I know. You were just using me to get at her. You were trying to make Sonia jealous of ME. That night in Val Negra, you *wanted* her to see us. You were just pretending that you wanted me. I couldn't understand your sudden kindness when you'd spent weeks avoiding me like the plague. You gave me that dress and then danced most of the evening with me. And of all dances you danced flamenco *and* in front of the family so that forever afterwards your sisters couldn't speak of the wedding without referring to the way I danced! Were you just *using* me to get back at Sonia or was it Tito you really wanted to upset?"

Ricardo sprang to his feet in such a rapid, feline movement that Isabel instinctively took a step back. But he gripped her wrist pulling her towards him and shaking her so roughly that she winced.

"Stop it," he said. "This is all nonsense and you know it."

"Is it? I don't think so."

There was a silence as they glared at each other and he continued to imprison her wrists. And just as suddenly as it had flared up, his anger abated.

"We really don't know each other at all do we?" he said coldly. "We seem to have been at cross purposes, always misinterpreting each other's actions."

"Well what do you expect?" Isabel's eyes brimmed with tears. "I was only sixteen! All I knew of life was the convent and Mialma. You seemed so worldly, so sophisticated. You had had girlfriends. You knew what you were doing. And then suddenly you noticed me. You made me feel pretty and wanted and special - as if you liked being with me. I trusted you."

Her voice was choked but Ricardo steeled himself, briefly, against emotion.

"I wasn't using you," he said more gently as a solitary tear ran down her face. He reached down to brush it away as something within constricted. "Isabel, look at me. Sonia is very happy with Rodrigo. I don't know how many times I have to repeat it. My relationship with her ended, God, over *twenty five* years ago and that night in Val Negra *was* special. I do remember it. I enjoyed every moment of it. It is something I shall never ever forget."

"Yes. But did it *mean* anything?" Her voice was very small.

He was so close to her he could see the pulse jumping at her throat - could smell her scent, see the flecks in her green eyes. And suddenly his hands were in her hair pulling her head to his.

"Oh Isabel," he groaned. "Isn't it obvious?"

His lips burned along her throat as she was crushed against him, the buttons of his shirt pressing into her skin. His arms were powerful, insistent, as he gathered her to him.

Isabel stood on tiptoe struggling to wrap her arms around his neck.

"Then love me," she whispered.

*

Later, when they woke to the sounds of rain splashing against the shutters, Ricardo pulled her towards him, wrapped in a long swirl of sheet, so that she lay with her hair fanned over his chest. She could hear the dull even beat of his heart under her cheek. "Like England," he commented.

"*Not* like England," Isabel replied smiling happily entwining her legs through his. "Even with the rain, the smells, the sounds are unmistakably Spanish. It couldn't be anywhere else."

"Do you feel this is home?" he asked. "*Could* this be home?"

"Yes, sometimes, most of the time. Once I've adjusted to the people to the pace, then yes. When I was little, I yearned for Spain. I wanted to be with all of you more than anything in the world. You'll never know how much, but now, well I have my work and my house. I must sound awfully boring! There hasn't been time for anything else."

"Not even Tim?"

Isabel pulled away but Ricardo imprisoned her in his arms.

"I told you. I'm grateful. He's kind and we've been together a long time. Those important years since leaving university were spent with him. I haven't known anyone else. I suppose we've become a habit to each other. There's no passion not like – " she blushed but Ricardo did not smile.

His fingers dug into her arms. "And children? Haven't you wanted children with Tim?"

"You're hurting me," Isabel said quietly her eyes level with his. But he did not loosen his grip.

"The biological clock hasn't begun ticking if that's what you mean. I never really thought much about it. I've never wanted children. I was too miserable myself."

Ricardo's hold on her slackened. "But you will. You say this now but you *will* want children. All women do."

"Then I'll adopt them," she said lightly. Ricardo's hands held her face still against the pillow, his eyes intense and then gentle with the faintest trace of hope. He touched her cheek moving against her and she closed her eyes sinking into the covers.

"It's that confirmation of self," she whispered. He hesitated.

"What is?"

"Love," she said and then as if she could read his very soul she added, "it's not that opposites attract but ultimately one seeks, and hopefully finds, a confirmation of self in another human being."

"And have you?"

She held the palm of his hand against hers.

"Of course," she said lightly. "We are of the same blood. It could only ever be you."

Afterwards they cooked lunch, *pan tomacat* and eggs washed down with Bazan Cava. They listened to the music of her adolescence: Luis Llach, Juan Serrat and Mercedes Sosa. Steeped in nostalgia, they talked about the past, baring their souls, voicing until now, silent dreams. Much later, when she sat by the fire reading, naked except for the Paisley shawl filched from the piano, he had looked up suddenly.

"You belong here," he had said frowning at the admission, surprised that the thought did not disturb him.

"I hope so."

And it was true. She did not bother him. She knew how to be silent and when to speak. It felt as if she had lived in the house from the beginning. The sounds from the sea, the gulls and the drum of the waves against the cliffs were all the more soothing because of her presence. There was no mention of the future, of their work, of anything that existed beyond the boundaries of the farmhouse. Their only reality was time and the hours, minutes, hurrying them towards her departure. He would not think of that. As if thinking similar thoughts she looked up from her book.

"Play some more music," she said. Ricardo flicked the remote control so that within seconds Rodrigo's *Concierto de Aranjuez* reverberated round the room. Isabel shivered suddenly, pinched alert by the dysphoric beauty of the guitar. No matter how many times she heard it, the music moved her, evoking visions of Moorish castles and Castilian noblemen, of unrequited love. No matter how often she listened to it, the guitar seemed to touch every nerve in her body. It was never ever worn with familiarity.

"I remember a boy at Oxford," she said suddenly. "Domingos. He was Portuguese but had grown up in Mozambique until his family was chased out by the revolution. They settled in England. He's dead now. Both he and his brother Antonio drowned. I don't suppose you ever heard about *The Marchioness* disaster?"

Ricardo shook his head. "I'm listening," he said.

"Well, *The Marchioness* was a pleasure boat, hired out for parties on the Thames. Antonio, the successful elder brother, had hired it to celebrate his birthday. Domingos only went because it was his brother's birthday but he hadn't wanted to. Parties weren't his thing. He was very different, much more introvert than his older brother. Antonio was the madly social, gifted financier who'd had four glittering years at Cambridge and then made a fortune in the city. Domingos was much less gregarious and left Oxford to play the piano." Isabel paused. "I don't know why I'm telling you this"

"There's so much we don't know about each other," said Ricardo. "We always talk about the family. Not that there isn't enough material there to last a life time, but we've rarely had a chance to discuss *our* lives, what has happened to us." He smiled, his eyes crinkling at the corners in the way they only seemed to do for her. "Go on," he said. "Tell me about Domingos."

Isabel swallowed. "Antonio invited lots of people to his party on the boat. It was dark. There was an accident – another boat crashed into them and lots of young people died."

"And Antonio?"

Isabel nodded. "Both of them but what I remember about Domingos, is his gentleness and how he seemed so much older than the rest of us because he'd had to leave his country, been caught up in a war. And he had this wonderful voice that was slightly accented, mysterious. His voice made you forget that he was really quite frail, slight even and just a boy." She smiled, shaking her head at the memory. "It's funny I thought him so glamorous and yet he was only a child, he was only 17. I can't remember how we first met. But I do remember walking past his rooms one summer's evening and hearing this music. He had ground floor rooms at Magdalene, his college, with huge windows that opened on to the meadows. You could climb through the windows directly onto the grass. I remember the light that day because it was so beautiful." She smiled apologetically. "Every college in Oxford is beautiful in the evening. But that evening was magical. There were arches, moths caught by the light, a clatter of footsteps as choristers made their way to Chapel, then silence. And then after a while I heard this wondrous concerto. I had never heard anything more beautiful and it was so Spanish, so perfect …"

She turned her head to the fire.

"There is always one person who seems to be able to do that – share the gift of music. For me it was your father."

"My Father?" said Isabel stunned.

Ricardo nodded. "I visited him once in England. At The cottage."

Isabel was speechless.

"You've been to *my* Cottage? In Compton?" she said at last.

Ricardo nodded. "And to the listed garden famous for its topiary."

"But you never said! All the time I've known you, you never said anything!"

Ricardo shrugged.

"I never knew when to bring it up. Somehow there was never a right moment. We were always interrupted," he looked at her pointedly. "One way or another."

Isabel twisted in her chair wrapping the shawl more tightly round her.

"Well ... when was it? I want to know everything! Tell me about it."

"It was many years ago."

Isabel made a face.

"I gathered that."

Ricardo smiled, his eyes traveling over her face.

"Come here," he said hoarsely.

"I'm not moving," she said. "Until you tell me."

"It was only once. I was a boy and it was at a time when Dr. Mantua travelled a lot. Anyway he was invited to lecture at the embassy in London. He asked Tito if he would let us boys go with him and to my astonishment he agreed. Miguel didn't want to come so I had the wonderful doctor all to myself. Nuria and the girls and Miguel went on to Paris where we later met them. I had a wonderful time. Dr. Mantu was the most amazing person to travel with. He knew so much about everything. He made it all into a great adventure which it was anyway of course. He knew everyone, knew wonderful places to visit. One of those places was The Cottage. But it wasn't a good time for Julian. I'm not sure he really liked children. At least not then," added Ricardo hastily seeing Isabel's face fall. "We spent the morning in Winchester seeing the round table and Dr. Mantua told me all about the legend of King Arthur and then we had supper at The Cottage. Julian played the piano afterwards – jazz which I'd never heard before. It was the strangest music and I loved it. He was very frail and looked much older than he really was." Ricardo paused. "You never speak about your parents."

"That's because I don't remember much about them. I do remember *some* things about Julian. But I no longer remember his voice. I tried so hard, **not** to forget it but then one day it just went. I suppose that's why The Cottage is so important. I thought that it would reveal its secrets, that by living there I might learn something about them."

"And have you?"

Isabel shook her head. "No. All I've ever known is how much they loved each other, that they were happy. It seems so unfair. There are so many couples that are miserable together but they weren't. I think about Clara more and more. I'm almost the age that she was when she died."

Ricardo's eyes bored into hers. She lowered hers first. "There's so much I wanted to know – what Clara was like as a little girl, how she met my father – all the usual questions. Avia wouldn't talk about her. I suppose she didn't want to upset me. What she didn't realize was that I knew nothing at all about her. But it must have been painful for Avia. Then I reached the stage when I stopped asking. Now I'm no longer curious or at least not in the same way. It's enough to know that they were happy."

"Yes."

Isabel looked up at him, earnestly now.

"You've no idea how I envied you all," she said, "how I envied your having brothers and sisters and two parents, the security of knowing where you came from. There were never any hushed whispers when you went to a child's party or whenever adults met you for the first time. Whenever I went anywhere there was always whispering and I always heard the word 'orphan' spoken as though it were some contagious disease. You could see people physically recoil. *You* all possessed that tremendous confidence that comes with belonging."

Ricardo came to stand behind her, fingering the fringe of her shawl, his hands skimming her throat and shoulders.

"Well it hasn't done Sigi or B much good, this confidence as you call it. I doubt that they would say they were privileged in any way. Besides, you know that it wasn't all sunshine and laughter. In fact I don't remember that there was much laughter. Other people's families always seem happier, wealthier, more fortunate. You were lucky that you only came to Val Negra in the summer when everyone was more relaxed. But you know what Tito was like. You've seen the other side. It's easy to forget that, now that he's older and we've all moved away. But he wasn't exactly good to Nuria and while my siblings may have forgotten that, I never shall."

"And you ask me if I want children!" Isabel said wryly.

"Of course you do. And we'll go on to repeat the same mistakes."

"Oh God I hope not."

Ricardo twirled the fringe around his fingers and in one abrupt movement, pulled it towards him …

*

And as easily as he had let her into his life, he had let her go. They had talked so much, cramming years into a few days. They discussed Bea and Sigi. Ricardo spoke of his distress at seeing her in the clinic and of the futility of her sporadic attempts at rehabilitation. They spoke of Miguel and how he had never fulfilled the promise of his gifted adolescence. They discussed the recent elections, Pujols' popularity and the immense satisfaction of keeping Madrid waiting, the intoxicating feel of power. Ricardo, in exaggerated detail and summoning all his oratory skills, recounted the day in February, when a minority of the military had initiated a coup d'etat. He chuckled remembering how Avia dispatched her maid to purchase supplies of sugar and flour, just as she had done when Franco died. But the King had successfully thwarted the ambitions of a minority. He had matured into a popular and much loved monarch.

For the first time ever, Ricardo told her about his cancer. He described the harrowing treatment and subsequent bone marrow transplant – the gruesome side effects, one of which was his sterility. He described his work at Banesto and the stress of the past few months. In turn, Isabel recounted her early school days at the Convent, her friendship with Kate, her time at Oxford and her work at Archid. She told him about Mike Fagan's heart attack and a little about Tim.

And then it was Monday and he could not voice his true feelings. They had not dared to speak about a future. He was uncertain. He was not sure that he had anything to offer her. And by Monday anyway, she was making phone calls and e-mailing the world. When he returned from driving Isabel to the airport, with the sky now clear and the sun bursting through the pine trees, the house by the sea had seemed empty and lifeless.

*

Ricardo scanned a letter awaiting his signature. Perhaps he might send Isabel a rose? Or would she think it tacky? Even using April 23 as an excuse, he remained unconvinced. He focused once more on the work at hand but the voices from the street below distracted him. The mound of documents and books suddenly seemed overwhelming. Was this it? Was this the sum of his life's work and ambition? He had everything he wanted in material terms but it was not enough. The phone was ringing and he ignored it. Where was his secretary? Why the hell didn't she answer the phone? He opened the door of his office.

"Carmen!" he bellowed but there was no answer and she was nowhere in sight. She was probably in the toilet, he thought, having a fag with the other secretaries. The phone was still ringing.

Damn would no one answer it? He went back into his room ignoring the phone but still it persisted. Finally he grabbed the receiver.

"*Diga?*" He shouted. There was silence on the other end and then the crackling line of long distance.

"El Conde Roble?" said a women with a marked South American accent.

"*Soy yo,*" replied Ricardo shortly. *Who on earth was this?* And if it was Campsa, he needed the file in front of him. Where the hell was Carmen? Campsa was one client he couldn't bullshit his way through a conference call.

"One moment. While I try to connect you," came the reply and then speaking to a third party she said, "You're through Ambassador."

"Ricardo? It's Jaime, Jaime de Malagrida."

"Jaime! *Hombre. Cuanto tiempo? Como estamos? Que noticias?* It's been so long, how are you?"

"Ricardo. I've been trying to reach you for several hours." Jaime's voice was exhausted and a cold hand of dread reached over Ricardo, so much so that he swivelled in his chair with his back to his desk.

"We've had a problem with the phones," Ricardo lied, playing for time. "My secretary should have informed me. Are you well? Are you coming to Spain?"

"No. It's nothing like that." There was a muffled sound. A sound which sounded suspiciously, much to Ricardo's horror, like a sob." Ricardo waited holding his breath. After a moment Jaime continued.

"Ay …*hermano* … "

Ricardo thought wildly, that he wouldn't have been in the least surprised if his brother-in-law had started to call him *Compadre*. He was on the point of saying something to that effect when a cautionary note made him hesitate. Something told him that this wasn't a time for flippancy. Already he was preparing himself. Already he knew.

"I have the distasteful job – may God forgive me – do you remember your Cervantes? Your *Persiles y Sigismunda?* Which in this case couldn't be more hideously appropriate? *Mesanjero sois amigo, non mereceis culpa non.* You are only the messenger, friend you don't deserve the blame." There was a hysterical giggle and then again that terrible sob.

Ricardo lit a cigarette with a trembling hand cradling the phone under his chin.

"Something terrible has happened – " The words were all jumbled. Jaime's usual eloquence was rumbled. Ricardo struggled to make sense of the words.

"Sigismunda is dead, the baby too."

Ricardo heard his thoughts spoken, as if they were not his own.

"What baby?" he said. *"What are you talking about?"*

Jaime was sobbing now, huge wrenching incoherent sobs – hideous in a man of his usual composure. Ricardo felt a tightening in his chest and stubbed out his cigarette hardly aware that he did so. He loosened his tie. He had known before Jaime said the words.

"Sigismunda is dead. She took an overdose this morning only I did not know that she was pregnant. She was in the *Clinica* where they are supposed to watch her night and day. But there was nothing anyone could do. She was dead by the time the ambulance arrived. I'm so sorry. I'm bringing them home."

Ricardo put down the phone. There was a buzzing in his ears. He stretched out an arm swiping the papers from the desk. Then the buzzing stopped. The world stopped spinning.

He felt for the first time as a man, the salt taste of tears on his cheeks.

Chapter 33

Mercedes
Barcelona
April 1998

Mercedes lay in her bed at Mialma watching the moving shadow of the priest as he bent over her. The purple colour of his vestments was vibrant before her eyes but beyond it everything merged in her *Agonia*. There was no other word to convey the death throws she thought.

In Latin or Spanish, it was self-explanatory, but in English, for that nation of free thinkers and the zealously tolerant, it could never have the same significance. It was essentially a Catholic word. Dr. Mantua had administered the last rites and she knew she was dying. The priest hovered by her bedside. His shape grew and became small in the orbit of her vision.

"It is only a matter of time." She heard the whispers. *La Condesa ha entrado en su agonia.*

A few days ago, when Mercedes had been told of Sigismunda's death, her heart had stopped, quite literally. She had felt the flutter in her bosom and unbuttoning her dress had seen the veins under her withered skin shudder once more into life. But it had been a premonition. Nothing more could matter now.

Years before, Dr. Mantua had given Avia a book of Kahil Gibran that she kept along side her bible. It was a constant source of inspiration and comfort. He had underlined certain passages and she had read nothing else since hearing about Sigi and the baby.

> *Your Children are not your children.*
> *They are the sons and daughters of Life's longing for itself. They come through you but not from you,*

*And though they are with you, yet they belong, not
to you ... For life goes not backward nor tarries with yesterday.
Let your bending in the archer's hand be for gladness;
For even as He loves the arrow that flies,
so He loves also the bow that is stable.*

When Dr. Mantua first gave Mercedes the book, soon after her own daughter Clara had died in childbirth, Mercedes understood none of it. She had been consumed by her own misery.

"Why do you give me this?" she had said ungraciously, handing it back to him.

"Why does my lack of faith concern you? Why can't you accept it? Why won't you leave me alone?"

"I will never leave you alone, Mercedes," the Jesuit replied calmly. "Who else but I *should* be concerned? I left you to your own devices once before and look where that got you! I don't intend to let it happen again. So I shall keep at you for a bit longer. Yes, I am concerned about your faith but not for the reasons you think. I shall be your conscience."

Mercedes smiled at him strangely.

"How nice," she said. "How easy. Like having a resident puppeteer." And her voice was ragged when she next spoke. "*I fled him down the nights and down the days ... I fled him down the arches of the years.*"

Dr. Mantua hesitated only briefly before replying: "*Of my own mind, and in the midst of tears I hid from Him, and under running laughter.*"

Mercedes looked at him in astonishment. "How did you know?"

Dr. Mantua shrugged. "I don't mean to boast, but I *do* have a degree in Comparative Literature. It has always been one of my favourite poems, answering to my own peculiar flirtation with faith and the getting of it. I'm glad it moves you."

"It has. I have loved it ever since Julian read it to me from an anthology we had at Val Negra. My English wasn't very good then. It has meant more as time passes." She swallowed and looked down at her hands. "I try to avoid God sometimes, to act as if he doesn't exist. But then the hound from Heaven is always there, following, following after. *You* are my hound from Heaven, Father aren't you? Never letting go. You never give up. Only sometimes it's your claws I feel sinking into me, never mind your conscience."

For once Dr. Mantua's characteristic patience failed him and he made an impatient gesture.

"Julian!" he said angrily. "Always Julian. Haven't you learned yet? Doesn't your daughter's death signify anything?"

"Of course it does!" she said fiercely. "How can you possibly know what it is to lose a child? I loved Clara more than I have ever loved anyone." Her voice broke and was raw. "That is something you will never experience! Something all your philosophy and years of training will never show you. I loved Julian. I loved Clara."

"Then forget him! He wasn't yours." The priest took her hands. "Look at me," he said.

She made as if to pull away but his grip was strong and she let her fingers sink between his.

"I understand what you feel," he said. "But you aren't a young woman any longer. You have to put away all the childish things. Your pain is real. But now you have the chance to make things right. You have the child to think of, your granddaughter."

Yes, thought Mercedes bitterly, the child. But she was not interested in it. Clara's death had been a cruel, devastating blow but the final gut wrenching twist was living with the thought that Clara had died having Julian's baby. Even now Mercedes could not bear to think of them lying together, of Julian making love to her daughter, of Clara's hands caressing the nape of his neck – that soft boyish skin – as hers had done. She could not bear to think of his smell clinging to Clara's arms, so that if she wiped her hand against her cheek, Julian was all around. And the weeks passed without any news of either of them. She waited for the time when Julian would reappear, would say that it had all been a terrible mistake, that he was coming home. But he never did. There was never any news at all. Not even a letter. Mercedes blamed herself. She knew that she had betrayed Clara's trust. She also wondered what exactly Julian had told Clara about that night at Val Negra. Had he said that she, Mercedes had thrown herself at him? Had they laughed about her when they were together? Mercedes no longer cared what Julian thought of her. She only wanted to see him. But there was only ever silence and her guilty secret. Sometimes Mercedes believed that he too was dead. It was easier to wipe out the abyss of pain and to pretend, especially to Ildefons, that she was blameless. But Dr. Mantua knew and when she was with him, Mercedes was racked with guilt and self-hatred.

Your children are not your children. They are the sons and daughters of life's longing for itself.

Longing ... *Life's longing for itself. What did it all mean?* Yes she longed for Julian, she yearned, screamed for that innocent time, that was not innocent, that one night that was set apart from everything else, that was isolated from all that had occurred before and whatever would follow after. She longed for the Clara she had loved as a baby and she longed for her own youth in the days when she was in love with Ildefons.

The priest bent closer. Mercedes could see his face, as frail as her own, yet the eyes behind the glasses were as intense as ever. *My friend* she thought, fondly. *Dr. Mantua, you have always been my friend.* He made the sign of the cross, his ring twinkling in the light of a candle and for no reason even as her lips mimicked the prayers for the dead, she thought of Ildefons ...

*

Mercedes was a frail and tired woman when she returned to Mialma at the end of the civil war. She was worn out with the strain of secrecy, the responsibility of survival and without Dr. Mantua at her side to boost morale, she felt herself crumpling. Not even Nuria's engagement to the wealthy, though little known Luis Bacardi, did anything to cheer her up. It was yet another reminder that she was growing older, that the girls, she fondly called children, were in fact young women capable of making her a grandmother. She was confused and restless. As restless now as she approached middle age, as she was as a teenager. Nothing motivated her or excited her – not the vineyards, dormant in their expectancy, nor the gardens crying out for attention. Nothing gave her any pleasure.

She had had no news from Ildefons except in the early days of the war when he surprised them with a visit to Val Negra. She was ashamed to say that she had not missed him. Her conscience pricked at the lack of feeling his name evoked in her. The war had in many ways answered her needs. She had been fired with ambition and had experienced more extreme emotions of fear and depravity than she ever thought possible. And now, without a cause, she felt redundant, expiated and hollow.

There was no warning of Ildefons's release. On a hot summer's morning, when she sat listlessly wondering what to do, he had simply appeared as if from nowhere. She had seen him first from a bedroom balcony, long before he came fully into sight. She had seen him – a tall man wearing a beggar's clothes. But she recognised his walk even before seeing his face. For a moment, confused in time, she thought she was in Val Negra and that the man striding towards Mialma, was Julian. Her heart leapt in her mouth and she jumped to her feet. Even as she ran down the sweeping staircase, her worn out shoes barely touching the marble, she knew the man could not be Julian. And still her heart thumped so that she forced herself to slow down and walk sedately through the Gothic archway. And then he had disappeared. He was not waiting, arms outstretched as she imagined he would be, as she rounded the corner. She ran looking for him in the empty stables, the torched gardens, the ruins of her world. Nor did she call out his name, not trusting herself to speak. At last she found him in the only section of the garden that had not been razed to the ground. Ramrod straight with his back towards her, he stood by what was left of her gardenias, looking out towards the sea. He did not stir as she approached.

"I – I thought it was you."

She was forced to speak, as he made no effort to greet her first. His hands were thrust deep into his pockets and he seemed unusually relaxed, as if he had merely strolled out after breakfast, to take a look at the view. She was breathless. At a glance he didn't seem to have changed at all and in profile his face was as patrician, arrogant and aloof as it had always been. It was only his clothes while as immaculate as always, that hinted at change. His shirt was spotless, the sleeves rolled up and he wore to her amusement, a peasant's espadrilles. His face and arms were tanned so deeply he looked Southern Spanish. His hair, unlike hers, was as thick as ever. He did not look as though he had suffered, Mercedes thought in irritation and instinctively her hands went to her thin throat, her sun bleached cotton dress. She scratched her ankle with one leg. She tossed her head back in that way she had when she was either nervous or simply aware of the impact that her beauty would make. Ildefons appeared unmoved. She waited, silent, confused, disappointment mingling with frustration. This was not the way a husband and wife should greet each other after a three years absence! Had he lunged at her, she would have felt revulsion but total indifference was an entirely different matter.

"Hello Mercedes," he said in a flat, new voice she did not recognise. And then when she had still said nothing, not daring herself to speak, he continued kindly enough. "Cat got your tongue? I've never known you to be at a loss for words!"

"I – I'm just –" Irritation got the better of her. "I'm surprised that's all. I didn't know you were coming home."

"What, never? Or just not today?"

Mercedes frowned. "Today –"

"It's all right. I was joking."

He shot her a glance then, seeing her face strained and irritated and thinner, her skin, that prized skin that never saw the sun, tanned and faintly lined. A trickle of sweat had begun to run down the hollow at her neck. Her eyes, huge, pain filled, human at last, clung to his and he hesitated. But then his jaw clenched and he turned away.

"I feel nothing."

For a moment recognition was slow. *What was he saying? Nothing about how much he had missed her or how the thought of her was what had kept him going!* She had been prepared to offer her lips in welcome. Her face froze. *This was not right at all.* Where was the indulgent, patient, loving look he had only for her, no matter how hard she tried to hurt him? Why was he not moved by her beauty? Panic clutched at her throat. Was she not beautiful? Did he find her so changed? And why should it matter anyway when she had spent so much time convincing herself that she did *not* love him. She hardly heard what he was saying.

"This means nothing." He motioned to the manor's ancient walls. In spite of the obvious neglect, Mialma was never more beautiful, rising like a phoenix from the ashes, triumphant in the knowledge that it, like its mistress, had acquitted itself nobly during the war, that it had been loyal and courageous. There were no shadows of mistrust lurking here, no pacts with the devil.

"What are you talking about?" Mercedes voice rose shrilly, pinnacle of her unquiet thoughts.

"This and Val Negra have been the *only* reality. How can you say it means nothing? We've been lucky here. You should see what is left of the Castillo Bazan! They will have to rebuild from scratch. *We've* only lost furniture! Even the paintings were saved. The Carmelite nuns who were here for the duration, hid them in the wine cellar. Oh I know it's all a bit of a tip and the garden's a mess, but the house is intact –"

"That's not what I meant," replied Ildefons quietly. He stretched his arms, breathing in the heavy air. It was midsummer and the heat wrapped its arms around them. She could smell the breeze from the Sahara and the scent of tubular roses.

"Per una vela blanca," he said as if to himself, *"daria un sceptre."*

"What!" Mercedes snapped. "Poetry? Now!" She stamped her foot impatiently in a way she had not done in years. "What the hell has poetry to do with anything? You're talking in riddles. I don't understand you. Why don't you say something important?"

"It *is* important. I'm trying to tell you, if only you'd listen to what I'm saying instead of waiting for my reaction to *you*. I've learned to appreciate simplicity. This view, for example, I *did* miss this. But that is all. I have learned to survive on very little. Everything here is too rich, too opulent, too perfect. We have smothered ourselves in perfection, Mercedes, we've isolated ourselves from the people."

"The people!" Mercedes exploded her face white with hurt and disappointment. "I haven't seen you in three years and you turn up talking poetry and politics! I've seen enough of your so-called 'people' to last me a life-time. You forget that I've been in Val Negra with the children. In order to feed them, I've had to suck up to those ghastly *people* -people like the Nadals for one, who ingratiated their way into my life, forgetting who I am and who they are. Ugh! I want the old ways back and quickly!"

Ildefons turned to look at her. There was a time when the sight of Mercedes, her hair falling over her shoulders, her breasts taut against her blouse and that little girl look he found so alluring would have inflamed his desire. Now he found it hard to believe they had ever shared a bed or that she had born his children, indeed that they had ever laughed or lusted together. They were shadows that once had eclipsed the other.

"It hasn't taken us much time to go back to *our* old ways," he said. " But I didn't come back to quarrel. I came to tell you, before the gossips make our life a misery, that there is to be a court marshal. Technically I am under house arrest."

Mercedes bianched. She swayed but he made no move to steady her.

"I don't understand," she stammered.

She held up her hand to shield her face from the sun. For a moment and only a moment, the old longing returned and he was tempted to scoop her up into his arms, to run his hands through that hair.

"Don't play the sympathetic wife now, Mercedes," he said smoothly. "I couldn't bear that. Please leave us some dignity. There's nothing dramatic about it – impulsive and foolish in the extreme as it turned out and I shall pay the price – but not dramatic. Do you remember at the beginning of the war, that time I came to see you in Val Negra? Well, it would seem that we entered Spain, inadvertently, on the Republican side. It was the only way we could. The border was closed." He sighed. "It's such a long time ago and the war is over. Who would have thought that it would matter now? But it appears that Franco attaches a great deal of importance to such casual actions. He would rather I explained myself to a court. It's a technicality. It is nothing."

"Nothing?" she echoed in amazement. "Have we grown this far apart?"

She sat down heavily on an upturned stone, prickly with heat and at the same time icy cold.

So much has happened to enclose us in our separate worlds, she thought. I can no more explain mine, than he can, his. There is no common ground. Nor do I want to talk to you. How can I begin? I feel so strange, so unfamiliar to myself. I need heeling and peace and oceans of time alone. I can't think about any more danger for those I love. How can I think about Clara? I could hardly cope when she was a child and now I am not ready to grow old. What is there here for me at Mialma without Ildefons? Without the war, the purpose of survival, what will I do? I am alone as I wanted but what will I do without him?

The sun was blinding and sweat pricked the patch between her shoulder blades. She did not love him, or at least not with that physical ache with which she had loved Julian, so why should it matter if Ildefons loved her or not? Her head ached. She felt old, worn out. She closed her eyes.

Did he know something? Had he heard about Julian? Why then was he so cruel?

She felt the butterfly touch of his fingers on her face. She smiled, awash with relief. He did love her. He did want her. She felt a guilty semblance of power and she opened her eyes ready to receive him. *Per una vela blanca*. Perhaps she understood the poem. A little. She certainly knew it, by heart, as he did. She would tell him of course.

"*Per una vela blanca*: For a white sail, I would give a sceptre. For a white sail and a blue sea; sceptre and palace."

She looked up expecting to see his kindly look, feel those familiar hands on her neck as they began their journey downwards.

But he had gone.

*

And the years had passed, some of them unbearable. There had been times when Mercedes had wanted to leave or commit some terrible, destructive act, or both. There were times when the passion of the early days of their marriage returned, others when she could not bear the sight of him. Mercedes would then disappear to Val Negra to recoup some of her composure and sense of perspective. There were times when Ildefons irritated her so much that she imagined herself lunging out at him as he sat impassive, unsuspecting. If his mouth, small and thin, ducked into itself, or if for no reason at all, he was suddenly slow to pick up on an idea or suggestion, then she could fly into a sudden rage and strike out at him. At other times, over come with remorse, she would reach out for him, gently as though he were her child. But always at the back of her mind and between, came the shadow of Julian.

When she was already an old woman, she went on a pilgrimage to visit the allied war grave in Thailand at Kachanaburi, where Julian had been a prisoner of war. She travelled on the small train to Nam Tok up to the River Kwai. She walked in silence through the simple huts that marked a former field hospital and saw the photographs of POWs who had built the railway. In the cemetery, under a hellfire sun, she sat as Thai workers dipped in between the graves caring for the plants and grasses that grew alien, in an alien earth. It was then that she began to appreciate Dr.Mantua' teachings. She remembered that he had once told her that the vertical part of the sign of the cross, symbolised the love of God for his people, while the horizontal one indicated the love man bore for his fellow man and where they met was where perfect love was to be found.

"You have a second chance to make things right," he had said.

When she returned from the Far East, Mercedes was a changed woman. She realised how much she had missed of her children's childhood. She was determined to make up for lost time and to get to know her grand children. There was no more room for remorse or guilt. Gone was the anxiety of those middle years. Her doubts, her fears of growing old, were over. There was nothing left to prove, either to herself or to anyone else. Sometimes she would dream that Clara and Nuria were children again, their round perfect faces full of hope and childish fancies. Through *their* children, she stepped back in time, to undo all the wrong, all the hurt. And with Ildefons, Mercedes also adopted an altered approach. She cared for him, in his last illness, with the devotion that was missing from their early life together. Too late, she learned to hold her tongue, not to take offence, to ignore slights and to let antagonisms slide. She grew into old age with dignity and reserve.

'Until there is commitment,' she read once, 'there is hesitancy.' All her life Mercedes had chased rainbows in the hope that they would bring happiness. She was never satisfied with the here and now and round the corner she always hoped to find something better. At last, she learned not to rely on anything or anyone for contentment. It had taken her fifty years and a visit to a bamboo hut, half way round the world, for her to realise this. She had found peace, amongst the bones of the dead.

*

Mercedes opened her faded blue eyes. They reached for and found her priest.

"Ah ... it is you ..." she whispered.

Dr.Mantua leant over the bed catching the shadows, the shallow breathing, felt the dying pulse.

"Come Holy Spirit, fill the hearts of your faithful," he intoned. "Enkindle in them the fire of your love."

He anointed her forehead, blessing the air above her head. His hands moved through halos of light, closing her eyes as they swept downwards.

"Julian," she said.

Chapter 34

Isabel
Barcelona
April 1998

Isabel stood on the steps of the church, shivering in an unseasonably chilly wind. She was glad she had brought a coat, not that she'd had much choice, as it was the only black garment she possessed that wasn't an evening dress. Despite its length, she felt the cold and her ankles felt naked and exposed. Her face was pinched. Her hair, pulled severely back from her face, accentuated its pallor. There were shadows under her eyes and she clenched her hands to stop them from trembling. She was late. The rest of the congregation was seated, the doors of the church thrown open. Dr. Mantua waited by the entrance of the Lady Chapel, seemingly unaware of the cold in his thin vestments, ready to receive the coffin. A solitary bell tolled. Only the pigeons happily scrounging for food seemed oblivious to the sadness of the day. In Isabel's mournful state, everything appeared grey – the stone walls of the chapel, the courtyard, even the naked trees. The congregation dressed uniformly in black, formed a dense border against the lit candles of the altar. Isabel hesitated, unwilling to enter the church, to initiate the beginning of the ceremony. She was ill equipped to combat the battering of emotions that assaulted her. Every muscle in her body was tense, guarding against the ocean of pain that grew in momentum beneath her frozen exterior. Dr. Mantua descended the steps to where she stood, his Jesuit robe billowing around his thin body in a sudden gust of wind. She shrank from the sight of the purple scarf at his neck.

"*Isabel, filla meva,*" he said serenely, holding out both arms. "I'm so sorry. I know what this will mean for you. I know how close you were, how much she loved you. But you have had a wonderful friend all these years. And an example to follow."

Isabel bowed her head but clung to his hands as if for dear life. When she raised her eyes they were fever bright.

"When I say the words, 'my grandmother has died,' they sound so common place. My colleagues at work were barely sympathetic. A grandparent to them is an old person who expects death. But to me, Avia was young and beautiful! She was wise and vivacious. She had an answer to everything. She wasn't old! We have this absurd obsession with youth! As though once the body is wrinkled and inflexible, somehow the person within has vanished! As though you have nothing more to give if you can not attract a person sexually."

Isabel's voice broke on a sob. She was in danger of completely breaking down. She felt ripped apart with grief. Her eyes blazed wildly. "And so soon after Sigi – I can't bear it!"

Her voice rose shrilly. Dr. Mantua gripped her hands so tightly that she thought he would break her fingers.

"But you *must bear it*!" he said fiercely. "You must. Your grandmother needs you to lead the family with dignity. You must not disappoint her now. She was all the things you said and more but she *was* old. She'd had a good life. And you must move on. I know you'll hate me for saying it but you must control yourself – "

She was interrupted by the arrival of the hearse. Together they watched as the coffin was lifted down and the men who would act as pall bearers, alighted from their cars. Isabel, out of habit, caught herself looking for Ricardo. For a moment their eyes met, hers drowning in the need to be comforted, his puzzled, discomfited. The coffin was cloaked in a blanket of white jonquils that Isabel had carried with her, in refuse sacks, on the flight from England. She had felt like a fool, bulbs protruding from every pocket, but still it had been Avia's request and she was not one to question it. Avia had wanted the daffodils from England, from The Cottage, to cover her in death. Now their delicate scent was contained in the icy air. Ricardo and his twin took their places at the front while the Bazan brothers were at the back. In the middle, but facing each other as they had done one week earlier in Chile, stood Tito and Jaime de Malagrida. Isabel turned away, tears streaming down her face, but Dr. Mantua pulled her back.

"I need your help with something," he said. He motioned to Jaime and Isabel was appalled at how much Sigi's husband had aged and at the same time by her own selfishness. She smiled feebly. But Jaime was looking at his feet or so she thought, until he moved towards her and she could see a small child clinging to his leg. She stared at the child mesmerized by the boy's blue black hair and almond shaped eyes. Sigi's expression was painted in the tiny perfect features.

"He's called Sancho," said Dr.Mantua.

"Sancho?" Isabel gave a strangled sob. "My God," she said not knowing whether to laugh or cry, "the circle is complete! Surely Sigi wouldn't have called her child after Sancho Panza? Is this family never going to be free of a Cervantes obsession? It's so funny! I can't believe Sigi's sense of humour!"

She began to giggle. The priest gripped her arm.

"I'll slap you if I have to," he said stonily.

"So will I," hissed Ricardo as he hovered for a moment on the steps beside her. The indifference of his tone was enough to choke any further hilarity. She stared slightly dazed at her cousin's retreating back and then looked once again at the child.

"This is your cousin Isabel - the lady I was telling you about," the priest was saying kindly to the little boy. "Do not be afraid. There is nothing to be afraid of here."

"What can I do?" whispered Isabel.

"Look after him during the service. There was no one else to mind him at Mialma. I wouldn't have brought him here at all. A funeral is no place for a child but I hope he's too young to understand what's going on. It's a cold and miserable enough day as it is. Maybe he'll just go to sleep, what with the time difference I think they're both exhausted."

Isabel gulped. She had little to no experience of children and none of her married friends had children. She hadn't the first idea what Sancho might want. For a moment they examined each other warily. Then she felt his small, warm hand thread itself in hers and her heart melted. His other fat little fist clutched at a toy train. She crouched down so that her face was on level with his. Instinctively she kissed him, this bit that was left, of Sigismunda. His arms went round her neck and for a moment their skin touched.

"Carry you," he demanded. Isabel smiled.

"Carry me," she corrected.

"*Si*," he repeated. "Carry you."

Isabel swung him into her arms as his chubby legs wrapped themselves round her waist.

Isabel held Sancho tightly as if holding on to the innocence and vivacity that once was Sigi's. It was as if his mother's sprit, worn out and sordid, in him, was given another stab at life. She had forgotten about Ricardo and now looking up found him looking back over his shoulder at them both. She felt the blood drain from her face a second time and she buried her face in the child's hair.

"You may go in now," said Dr. Mantua. Isabel led the mourners up the steps. She made the sign of the cross, wetting Sancho's forehead with a kiss. The congregation rose in silence. Then the Carmelite nuns began to sing the Catalan hymn:

> *Rosa D'abril,*
> *Morena de las Selva*
> *Del Montserrat estel.*
> *Illumineu la Catalana terra,*
> *Gieunos cap al cel.*
> *Gieunos cap al cel.*

Isabel and the child sank to the floor in genuflection. The alter boys swung mesh gold capsules spreading incense like cold ice. The priest began:

"Give them eternal rest, O Lord, and may perpetual light shine on them forever. In him, who rose from the dead, our hope of resurrection dawned. The sadness of death gives way to the bright promise of immortality. And so with all the choirs of angels in heaven we proclaim your glory."

Isabel sat Sancho on her lap and instantly he relaxed against her. After a few moments he was asleep, thick lashes immobile on rounded cheeks. The toy train thudded to the floor. His warm body was a dead weight against her but his even breathing was comforting and she found her lips repeatedly brushing the top of his head. She was scarcely aware of anything else but the presence of this being. She was oblivious to her cousins, to Marta and her boys, young men now or her aunt. Or the men seated, segregated from the women, on the other side of the church. She could not see Ricardo in the darkness. The isle between them was a wide Sargasso Sea, and everything beyond it, unexplored territory. She couldn't recall a word of the glowing homily or the hymns. Only the altar, illuminated at the head of this island, drew her in. Dr. Mantua prayed over the chalice, mixing the wine and water. There was a flash of a jewel. Sancho woke suddenly, rubbing his eyes. He looked around him with interest, fascinated by the candles and the priest with his flowing robes. She smoothed his back, pulling her coat around them both, her cheek against his. She felt his breath on her face and when she looked at him again, he was asleep.

Isabel again saw the flash of the priest's ring as it caught the light and was reminded of a poem that Avia had often recited to her, a Catalan poem called *The Glow Worm*. She wished Sancho were old enough to understand it. Learning the poem by heart, was one of the first exercises she had been set, all those years ago in Val Negra. A bishop, so the poem goes, addresses a poor congregation, overawed by the wealth and splendour of his position. They stare at his elaborate vestments that sparkle in the candlelight. It is a grey and cold day outside but inside the tiny church all is warmth and colour. The bishop seems to these unworldly people, like a King. Real gold, so they believe, lines his vestments, his bishop's staff, and even his coned hat with the streamers hanging down his back. He is eloquent and erudite, beyond their understanding. The words trip off his tongue as silvery and rich as his clothes. When he speaks of heaven, they believe. He dazzles them with his jewellery, which dances and twinkles in the light. When the village folk shuffle up to communion, they get a closer look at their Bishop and once again are awed by his opulence. He looks well fed and rested. They imagine he sleeps on soft, sweetly scented sheets and everything in his house is comfortable. The mass comes to an end and the Bishop raises a plump hand to bless these poor, dirty, humble people. As he does so they catch sight of the most spectacular of his jewels - a huge ruby ring which sends off light in all directions. A wonderful scent permeates the room. Closing their eyes they can smell pine cones, eucalyptus, tubular roses and gardenia. All the perfumes of a garden at twilight wash over them in that instant blessing. The congregation is enraptured but when these simple country people open their eyes they see to their amazement that the Bishop is chuckling to himself. Again he makes the sign of the cross, a large expansive gesture.

> *Y el bisbe rirure,*
> *tothom ha sentit*
> *el perfum del jardi.*

And what they do not know, these simple uneducated people, is that the Bishop owes all his popularity to this one ring. With it he captures, enraptures his audience. Not only is it exquisitely beautiful but it repeatedly reproduces all the wonderful scents of a garden. The bishop is constantly amused by the fact that it is no ruby that sits on his little finger, but a loyal, living creature – a glow worm. *Cuca de llum.*

> *Lliri blanc espolca un raig de perfum*
> *I cau a la molca*
> *la cuca de llum.*
> *Esmeragada viva*
> *d'aquest jardi vell*
> *qui et tingues captiva*
> *en l'or d'un anell.*
> *Teniu, li diria*
> *al pastor mitrat,*
> *I el bisbe et duria*
> *sobre el guant morat.*
> *La gent amb veu forta*
> *diria 'Senyor! quin anell que porta*
> *tan ple de claror.'*
> *I el bisbe riuria*
> *I al n'ar beneir*
> *tothom sentiria perfum de jardi.*

Isabel gathered the child closer to her. Dr. Mantua was right, Avia had left them all a marvellous legacy of memories and anecdotes and family history. She stood up, placing the now alert Sancho carefully on his feet. The mass was over and the pallbearers were escorting the coffin down the aisle.

"*Quiero mi tren,*" said the child. "I want my train."

"*Donde esta?*"

Isabel knelt between the pews and moving feet looking for the toy.

"*Mama* was in a box," he said and then incidentally added. "Do you like trains?"

Isabel swallowed.

"Yes. Yes I probably do. I'd never given them much thought."

His upturned face was full of hope.

"I have lots of trains in *Vina, en casa. Mi tren es muy grande. Era de papa cuando* era *pequeno.*"

"Have you heard of Thomas the Tank?" asked Isabel wracking her brains to remember children's toys."

"*Claro, Mama* bought him for me but I gave it to her when she was in hospital. She has it with her. She can play with it in heaven you know. She'll play with the angels and with my little brother."

And then they were outside once again in the cold, biting wind and people pressed against them. Women crowded round touching the child's face, stroking his cheek.

"*Pobrecito!*" they said kissing his soft round cheek but Sancho viewed them all dispassionately, a small pasha before his subjects. "*Poor motherless babe!*"

Isabel fought her way through the crowd, her arm protectively encircling his small warm body. Jaime de Malagrida stood apart from the others, huddled in his overcoat.

"Sancho." His name came out in a croak. He smiled kindly and with such tenderness, Isabel felt her heart constrict and the world began to spin. She held out the child to him feeling that at any moment her legs would give way. Jaime raised the child up, swinging him high in the air so that his coat was all bunched at the back.

"I – I am so sorry – " she stuttered. "I don't know what to say – how to comfort, I mean about –"

Jaime listened patiently but Isabel froze unable to continue.

"And I must offer my condolences for the loss of your Avia," he said at last.

"Thank you." Isabel touched his arm. "But Sigi – "

Jaime made an expansive gesture tightening his hold on his son.

"It had to happen. I am beginning to think that. I have to believe that no help, no person could have made a difference, that her desire for destruction, for *disruption*, was stronger than my desire for happiness. But I thought we were over the difficult episodes. It came as a great shock."

"She loved you."

"Perhaps."

"I wish I had seen you together."

Jaime, his head bent to his son's, looked up. "So do I," he said sadly. "If only, and this is selfishness on my part, so that others might see that we could be happy some of the time. That while she was clean, she was wonderful." As he spoke his fingers caressed his son's head with a strong brown hand that momentarily hypnotized her.

"*Como estas hijito?*" He asked him. "*Quieres que vayamos a casa?* Do you want to go home now?"

Sancho's head resting on his father's shoulder suddenly popped up like a submarine's telescope that has spied land.

"*Si, pero quisiera que la Senora venga con nosotros.*"

Jaime's voice was expressionless.

"He wants you to come with us. I think we shall go now. He – I – find it overwhelming."

Isabel nodded.

"There are some 400 people, not bad for a 98 year old."

"Not bad at all," Jaime agreed soberly. Sancho, nestling against him, tried to roll his toy train down the lapel of his father's coat.

"You see how it is."

"He's a fine boy," said Isabel a catch in her voice.

"Yes. You'll be at the house later?" He raised bloodshot terrible eyes to hers. There were grey shadows on his face, and his hair was white. Only the hands that held his son, were still vigorous and strong.

Isabel hesitated.

"I'm not sure. I may go back to England tonight. It's a busy time at work and it was hard to get away. Somehow all these people now, at Mi-alma …" her voice trailed. "Well no one knows better than you."

Jaime reached into his pocket, holding Sancho easily with one arm.

"Don't say anything more," he said. "I find it difficult to talk about any of this. After a while, the simplest conversations are the most painful. But these are for you." He handed her a note book. "I suppose this bundle, this corn husk, means something? The journal is self-explanatory. I haven't read it. I have no wish to. But it is dedicated, if that is the word, to you, in as much as your name was scrawled over the front page. I almost threw out the twigs, and then I saw that they make up some kind of doll. Maybe you will make sense of this … *locura.*" There was a flash of anger and then his voice was expressionless once again. "I will never understand it. Never."

"No. None of us will."

Isabel took the book and the tissue wrapped *Reina del Rio* which had already made more travels than she cared to remember and shoved them in her pocket.

"Sigi did love you," she said.

Jaime closed his eyes for a moment, pain etched on his face.

"In her way perhaps she did. The truth is that she could not escape the family. Everything she did was to gain their recognition, their approval. The tragedy is, that while she did everything to alienate them from her, in the end she could not survive without them. I was not enough –" he held up a hand to stop Isabel from interrupting. "I am no fool *hermana*. I did everything in my power to make her happy, but it was not enough. I could not make up for the rejection she felt as a child. I could not give her self-worth. I could not make her love life, *choose* life."

Isabel's shoulders stooped beneath the truth of his words. "Neither could I."

"If –"

They both said at the same time.

"If you ever come to England ..."

Jaime made a bow holding Sancho in front of him and clicked his heels. His lips skimmed the air above her gloved hand. For a moment hers clung to his.

"*Igualmente.*"

And then she too was alone. Sedate talk gave way to animated chatter. Friends and family surrounded the Spanish cousins like a wall around them. Ricardo was nowhere in sight. There was a mass of strangers, friends of her grandmother's she had not seen in years and whom she would no longer recognise. Dr. Mantua stood amidst his colony of parishioners and she could not get close. Already Avia was being forgotten. People, true to form, had returned to the more immediate topics of food and clothes and gossip. They talked about the cold, mentally preparing the evening meal, the forthcoming week. They were moving on.

Isabel turned away. She was not ready to forget. Not quite yet. She wanted to nurse her pain a little longer, to indulge her grief. But she could not face Mialma without her soul. Inwardly she smiled at the pun. Mialma – *My soul*, she thought although it wasn't hers was it? Mialma was and had always been, part of Mercedes. *Her* soul was in the very fabric of the house. And what Isabel could not quite face now, today, was her grandmother's house, crawling with curious, eager visitors. It was inevitable that after a while, when they grew bored, their attention would revert to her. She could just hear their excited, inquisitive voices. '*What, not married yet! But surely there must be a boyfriend somewhere? Time is marching on querida, even for a pretty girl like you. Now what would you grandmother say to this! Que diran?*" Isabel shuddered. No she wasn't ready for Mialma and if not Mialma, then where?

Suddenly and with growing desperation, Isabel knew she had to be alone, alone with this excruciating grief that threatened to rip her apart. She could not face one more friendly face, one more person who had known her mother or who had met her as a little girl. She did not want to have to smile or make small talk or pretend to be nice when all she felt was an unstoppable rage and sorrow at what had happened. Like a hurt animal she wanted to be alone to nurse her wounds. She needed to bury herself away somewhere quite alone, until she was ready to come out. She needed to make sense, or at least attempt to make sense, of her anguish and the loss of Sigismunda. Like a fresh stab of pain, the thought of her cousin made her stumble and she turned blindly away.

Val Negra. And suddenly like a thin ray of sunshine in that bleak day, the thought of Val Negra acted like a lifeline. The thought of the vineyard and of the Monseny and the sweep of blue that stretched along the horizon was an instant balm, a helping hand stretched from above to guide her onward. With a strangled sob she shut out everything but her urge to get to the hills. Nothing else seemed to matter. She would leave now, why wait till later? There was nothing to stop her. Her car was parked just outside the plaza. It would take her no time at all to reach the ronda dalt and then the autopista to Puigcerda. Already her feet began to move in its direction and then she broke into a run clutching Sigismunda's little notebook and shoving the remains of the doll in her pocket.

Val Negra.
She would go home.

Chapter 35

Nuria
Barcelona 1998

Nuria sat alone in the empty church. The buzz of conversation outside was gradually drowned by the sound of the wind and the clanking thud of the doors being locked. She sat bent double, unnoticed in the front pew, an old woman who may or may not, have once been beautiful. A heavy shudder passed through her. She knew this church well. It was Dr. Mantua's parish church and now her mother's funeral had taken place here and was over. Avia. *Her* mother. It was strange to think of her in that way. So many people had sought to claim Avia as their own, that Nuria had long relinquished any right to her. Not of course that relationships *should* be about possession, but they were. All life was about possession now that she came to think about it. The law of the land hinged on the premise of possession while man's inherent nature was all about acquisition. Marriage in particular was about possession and despite the fact that Spanish women were so generously permitted to keep their maiden names when they married - becoming 'de' so and so - the very word 'de' meant *belonging to.* While she would always be Nuria de Roble, she was much more significantly, *de Bacardi*, property of Bacardi or Tito Barcardi to be exact. And consequently parents *owned* their children. It was only death that severed the umbilical cord.

Avia was no exception. They had all wanted to possess her, friends and family alike. Nuria began making a mental list. First and foremost had come her father, Ildefons. Despite rumours to the contrary, Nuria knew that her parents had been devoted to each other. And Avia had relied on Avi's strength, his calm. But she knew that he was not always the easiest man to live with. He could be arrogant and unemotional. His sulks and episodes of silence were merely his way of showing displeasure, of telling HER that he was lonely, that he wanted her attention. Then there was Nuria's sister Clara, almost forgotten now, who had only ever wanted Avia and to the exclusion of any sibling relationship. Nuria often wondered if Clara even thought of her as a sister, as part of HER or HIM, of being linked by blood. From the moment she was born, Clara had behaved as though she were the only child, a fact that was supported by Avia's complete absorption in her second daughter. There was a time, when Nuria peering into the cot and standing on tip-toe so as not to rumple the yards of fussy lace, truly believed that she and this infant would be friends. She even hoped that one day they would unite against the impossibly elegant and unapproachable effigies that had become their parents. But it was not to be.

Even as a baby, Clara was different from other children. She never cried or sulked about anything. There were no cranky evening hours to cause Avia to block her ears and feel the throbbing veins at her temples pulsate with resentment. No, Clara had had Avia's undivided attention from the beginning. With an uncanny and precocious intuition, Clara seemed to understand that there was a price to pay for such maternal devotion. If Clara was unlike other children, Avia was certainly unlike other mothers. She did not immediately bond with her babies and did little to disguise her boredom, fatigue and irritation with the whole business of child rearing. Clara seemed to realize that if she were to keep this particular mother enthralled, she would have to subjugate all baby like tendencies. As Clara grew from the perfect toddler, into the perfect little girl, Nuria by contrast, and out of sheer frustration, was as naughty and difficult as she could possibly be. By the time they had both reached adolescence, Nuria had exhausted herself and everyone around her, in the process.

It was to everyone's huge relief when Nuria married Luis Bacardi. Not that Luis could be added to the list of Avia devotees, she thought ruefully. There had never been any love lost between her husband and her mother but the grandchildren had more than made up for his dislike. From the beginning, Avia had shown them genuine affection. It was as if the past was wiped away and Avia could begin again, *had* begun again, to become the kind of mother, Nuria had always dreamed of. It was with increasing wonder that Nuria observed how her children vied for Avia's attention, thought of a hundred little ways to please her. But that had all come so much later.

And then of course there was Dr. Mantua – *especially* Dr. Mantua, the man of God who in turn appeared to have acquired sole ownership of the new Avia, the now serene, wise Avia with an irreproachable past. There were also the countless devoted friends and families she helped during the civil war and with whom she still kept in touch. There was endless correspondence and visits that kept Avia away from Mialma for extended periods of time. Nuria had wanted her mother with her but these strangers, these names that arrived by electronic mail, had a prior claim.

And lastly, there was Isabel, the little foreigner, Clara's child. And because of the past, *in spite* of the past, Nuria had loved her from the start, until she too had turned to Avia, becoming like Clara before her, only hers …

Nuria covered her face in her hands, ran her fingers through her hair spreading the chill. Her heart was full of bitterness and the unhappiness she had fought so long to suppress, had finally engulfed her. Today was testimony to the final irony, she thought wistfully. *Judge not by how much a man loves, but by how much he in turn is loved.*

It was so unfair. Avia was so loved by so many, so many had wanted her for their own, while Avia had spent much of her life thinking of no one but herself, *loving* no one but herself. And here was Nuria loving till it broke her heart and all the good it did her …

Nuria should have been able to share it all out, not to mind. But she always had minded. She had done all the things, Dr. Mantua advised against. She had allowed the imagined slights to imbed themselves in her heart and she turned them over frequently in her mind. Most of all she minded that there was never any time for her. Nuria was ignored as a child, and then as a young girl pushed aside to make way for her beautiful mother. The *novios* who came at first to court *her,* were captivated by Avia. And if she were honest with herself, Nuria couldn't really blame them. In fact, if these potential suitors *didn't* fall for her mother she was disappointed. Avia was so self-possessed, so amusing, so *brave*. After the war ended, and the full extent of her heroism made known, people came to the house out of curiosity. But they left completely smitten. Avia had survived with dignity, with honour and with her sense of humour intact. And dear old Dr. Mantua could not refrain from extolling her virtues. For those who knew her, she came to symbolise the New Spain. Out of the anguish and pain of those terrible years, she emerged stronger than ever. She was an inspiration to everyone – to the old families of the aristocracy and to the new. Even people like the Nadals could not fault her courage even though they despised everything she stood for.

And yet, said the persistent little voice at the back of her head, Nuria knew Avia hadn't been quite as perfect as she made out. She may well have been a war heroine but at the same time she was a hopeless mother. It was so typical of her to die just when Nuria needed her most! It was a long time since Nuria remembered even wanting her mother, (Avia could fly half way round the world to visit a war grave or comfort a widow but she had never dried *her* tears) but now in the face of new tragedy, there was no one she wanted more, no one to take her place. There was no one to share her burden, no devoted confessor to guide *her* down the labyrinth ways and now that Nuria had lost her faith … She wanted her mother.

A deep sob ripped through her. Today she grieved for everything: for the fact that she no longer believed, for her passing youth, for the hope, long dead, that her life would be different. And most of all, she grieved for Sigismunda. The pain that gripped her heart was overwhelming and for a moment she could not breath. When Nuria learned of Sigi's death she thought that she too would die – had *wanted* to die but her cruel and treacherous body kept on living. It was equally unfair that Avia should have been allowed to die and not her. What God could view a mother's grief so dispassionately? Nuria banged her head on the pew, grateful for the shooting pain. She welcomed it. For a moment her thoughts cleared and then she sank back exhausted.

What a mess her life had been in comparison to Avia's! Who would attend *her* funeral and weep so prettily over the elegant and highly original arrangement of what, Nuria could see, were only English Daffodils? But that was Avia. Her whole life had successfully merged the elegant with the eclectic. It was a poetic fusing of grace and courage with a rounded symmetry to its end. Nuria's on the other hand had been a disaster from start to finish. She had had no relationship to speak of with her parents - even her father whom she had adored as a child had grown distant in later years, her husband was an egotistical monster she despised and her children's lives were the fragmented reminders of her inadequacy as a mother.

If only she could have been more like her sister, more like Avia. Both had been light-hearted and amusing even in the face of danger. Both had been incapable of taking offence, of being stung to the quick by careless remarks. Nuria by contrast, had always been a strange, serious creature whose beauty was marred by a stern disposition. She had never been able to shake off her primness, no matter how hard she tried. Avia teased her and the more she made fun of her, the more self-conscious Nuria became. She was acutely aware that she wasn't fun to be with. Even as she yearned to be quick-witted, her responses would stick in her mouth, her lips freeze in disapproval.

And then unexpectedly, for a short glorious time, she changed. To her delight, Nuria was the bride she never thought she would be. She wasn't in love but then she did not know what being in love meant so it did not trouble her. She viewed marriage as a chance to escape Avia's perfect home, the chance to focus attention on herself. And for a while, she *was* the centre of attention. She was taken to dressmakers, florists and hairdressers. She was taught to cook, to entertain, to keep house. The young Luis Bacardi showered her with gifts. Avia presented her with family jewels and Avi, for the first time in her life, took her out riding. Desired, Nuria blossomed. She smiled more readily, laughed when it would have been her natural inclination to remain silent and became in short, the person she always suspected, lurked uncomfortably inside. The discovery that she enjoyed sex came as a huge relief. But such was her enthusiasm, that Tito wondered on more than one occasion, if she really was a virgin when they married.

And then, just when Nuria dared to believe in a kind of happiness, she became pregnant. Not that this was unwelcome. Nuria had begun to read Cervantes devotedly. Domestic life and a taste for Golden Age Literature made life very pleasant and she was determined to name her children after the great heroes of his novels. She read avidly and she was convinced that her marriage, like that of *Persiles and Sigismunda,* would be based on Christian ideals. And more than that, she headed Cervantes' moral that through a good Catholic marriage the confusion and disappointments of life could be overcome. Why even Luis's catholic fanaticism conformed perfectly to that of Cervantes. However, the arrival of children in quick succession deprived Nuria not only of sleep, but of any desire to read. Once again, she was assaulted by hidden terrors that warped her character. Luis, apart from his talent in the bedroom, soon proved to be a boring, pedantic husband. The small corners of love that had begun between them were soon gnawed away by his cruelty. Now, she would not care if she never saw him again. There was no twinge of feeling for the time they had shared together, for the fact that they had once been lovers.

An echo of hysterical laughter sounded in her ears until she realized it was her own. She had spent so much time lost in a Cervantine infused past, that she had failed to draw parallels with her own. Luisito she now saw, not as the romantic knight of their courtship, but as a kind of Sancho Panza to her aristocratic and tormented Don Quixote. It stung her with awful irony that they had indeed spent most of their lives in the quest of lost causes. Unlike Sancho Panza and although short and dumpy, Luis did not possess inherent wisdom. His vision of the world did clash with hers but without their reaching a degree of mutual love and respect. Both of them however, like Spain herself, presented an extreme of consciousness, two diverse ways of seeing the world. But this absorption in their dreams – hers of courtly love and his with Franco – had prevented them from facing their familial duty.

But this realisation had come too late to help her children. For a moment Nuria dwelt on the poignant memory of the delightful babies they had once been. No one could have guessed their future. She thought of them all: Miguel, named after the great writer himself, who could barely string a sentence together let alone write anything, Ricardo, withdrawn and silent and in love like his literary namesake with another Isabel, another *espanola-inglesa* and here it struck with bittersweet sadness that the greatest love she had ever witnessed would never bear fruit, Marta with her dull, unspectacular children, Beatrice, plain unmarried and unwanted and her illegitimate, black child, doomed to a life of mediocrity. She, most of all, had inherited Nuria's gloomy disposition and the beauty she had known as a child had long withered. And Sigismunda – the heroine of a Cervantes novel ...

Nuria grunted in pain. Her head sank on her chest. No heroine in the end but a sad lonely daughter, alone in a foreign country – what had made her so unhappy that she should take her own life without any thought of her own baby? What had gone wrong? Nuria would never understand it and now she no longer cared. Not even the sight of Sancho had stirred the ashes of love. Nuria felt nothing, as she had felt nothing at the sight of Avia laid out on her bed her hands clasping a wooden cross.

"She looks beautiful," Marta had whispered as they sat through the night together by the coffin.

"She looks *dead*," Nuria replied, suddenly aware that any need for pretence was over. From now on, she would say exactly what she thought - tell it as it was. There was nothing romantic about death – all that nonsense about looking peaceful and asleep! Death was a shrivelled ugly thing and all too revealing: the spirit had left the body and the body was old and detumescent.

Nuria raised her head. It was very cold in the church and her feet were numb. She sat back on the wooden seat, her bones creaking along with the oak. Then slowly an immense feeling of relief washed over her. There was nothing left for her, or to her. But she was free, free at last, free of comparison. No longer would anyone remark on the differences between mother and daughter. No more endless accolades to the Saintly Mercedes. Her mother was dead and there was no one to remember that they were even related. The physical likeness at any rate had vanished. Nuria was spent. The rose was blown.

Nuria struggled to her feet and although she did not genuflect or make the sign of the cross, her lips moved, fighting for recognition. In spite of herself, she uttered the words:

"Oh Lord, into thy hands, I commend my spirit."

Chapter 36

Isabel
Val Negra
April 1998

    Isabel drove slowly through the mountains, the roads twisting under stripped poplars, through woods of pine trees up towards the Monseny. She was glad of the silence and of having to concentrate on the road. The car's heater blew hot gusts of air in her face and gradually she felt her toes thaw. It had been bitterly cold standing outside even for that short time. It was dark now but the avenue trees were well lit under a suspended moon. In the distance, the vineyards formed a linear boundary beneath the mountain range and she knew that she was home. Isabel parked her car in the empty courtyard. She rolled down the window to breathe in the cold, clear air enjoying for a moment the sight of the house, graceful and aloof under the spring sky. Mist hung in pockets over the grounds and skimmed fir trees. She got out of the car, her feet crunching on wet gravel. She wondered if the house was aware that its owner was dead. If it did, it revealed no change. It appeared as serene as always – a place where time stood still, where the shadows of the past danced their passage of life within its quiet walls.
    She walked towards the front of the house, delighting in the silence and in being quite alone. She had forgotten just how quiet Val Negra was. Not even The Cottage could boast this degree of silence. How she had yearned for this moment! Already her heart hammered in her chest in anticipation and she paused just as any visitor to the castle might, to admire its breathtaking beauty. Isabel looked up at the casement windows in whose pale crystals the moon was reflected. She would not have been surprised to see the image of a young girl in a high-wasted dress, looking out at her.

Likewise, she could imagine soldiers thundering through the wet grounds turning them into a river of mud. She could easily imagine these men storming through the rooms, plunging their bayonets into silk tapestries and slashing at plump cushions, their feathers floating through the air. She could almost hear the horses clattering towards the stable block. Lastly, she envisaged the ethereal figures of children, as stumbling, they took their first steps, towards a tragic fate.

Isabel shivered, trying to shake off these violent images and fumbled in her pocket for the fragile bits of willow bark that constituted her doll. In the morning, she would take it down to the river and scatter it over the water, as if the brittle wood shavings were Sigismunda's very ashes. For a moment, Isabel felt herself teetering, as if she were standing on a suspension bridge with the thundering waves beneath her. Reality and illusion, truth and untruth were indistinct as she felt herself tremble with shock. Blackness skidded against her, like the sides of a skateboard arena. Isabel wrapped her coat more closely around her with frozen fingers that felt webbed to each other. How could she bear it? How would she live her life without them? Her consciousness, her ambition, her sense of who she must become, had always been defined by her love for her grandmother and for Sigi. She could scarcely remember a time that it did not shape her every thought and action. Without them she was lost. She was frightened of what might happen without the ideal they represented.

In *their* name she had achieved all that she had. To make *them* proud of her, she had gone to Oxford, joined Archid, cared for The Cottage. For them, much much more than out of a declining love she still held somewhere in her heart for Julian, she had striven for her independence. But all the while she had concentrated on her career and her life in England, she had ignored the fact that they too had changed. They were no longer the beautiful creatures she had so idolized as a child. They had acquired flesh and bone, and with the years had altered beyond all recognition. She could not bear it that their relationship had changed, grown apart, disintegrated even. If nothing was as it seemed, she realised with brutal clarity, it was because she had failed to see them for what they really were. Their physical beauty and wealth and her own perception of their inaccessibility had blinded her to the truth of their own raging passions. Her desire to *be* them reflected only a flaw in her own character. While quick to identify their flaws, she realized that she along with the rest, were all damaged. And the irony was, that while she prided herself on her superior intellect, her independence, her stability, she had got them all wrong, while they had only ever seen her for what she had always been.

Isabel leant against the stone balustrade that led to the formal garden, her world spinning round her. She felt winded by an new understanding of herself. She realised that most of her life had been devoted to recapturing the heady days of that summer when she was sixteen, in Spain, here with her cousins. Those few months, in memory had grown to shape everything that was to follow. Every future relationship, every emotion was compared to what she felt then. She had travelled, worked, loved in order to regain that all consuming emotion, to *retain* just a small fraction of that time when she hardly needed to sleep or eat, when the world was more beautiful, more vibrant than before or since, when everything was accentuated, when her thoughts and inspiration flowed, when everything seemed possible. Even Kate's friendship was important to her, in that it developed prior to that first visit to Spain. Isabel closed her eyes. If this were indeed the case, then what did she really feel for Ricardo? Did she love him simply because he was of that time? Was she drawn to him because, he like no other, prompted her to feel as she did then? What if she had built him up in her mind, as she had done with his sisters, only to protect that mood, preserve for always, those feelings? What if all life was based on just one emotion? What if she spent, what was left of it, reading endless books, writing exhausting proposals, travelling further and further a field, forming unlikely relationships, all in order to feel, just once more, the way she did when she was 16?

This is ridiculous, she told herself, *you're going to go mad thinking like this! You need a drink! Oh Yes*, said Isabel aloud. *A quick blast of something to chase always these cobwebs!* She began to feel, with renewed intensity, the penetrating cold. It was also just as well that there was such a bright moon she thought, as everything was in darkness and she hadn't brought a torch. She walked to the back of the house, through the courtyard, up on to the marble veranda where she and Ricardo had danced flamenco all those years ago. In the far corner by the French Windows, she felt at the base of the wisteria for the key, praying that it would still be there. Panic tingled through her nerves. She had made no provision for it *not* being there. She dug inelegantly in the frozen earth, cursing. And then just as she was already mentally, driving back to Barcelona, her fingers felt something hard and cold. The ancient and unusually large key still hung from a long, rusty chain. She yanked it towards her, as far as it would go. Isabel leant against the French windows, dizzy with the exertion and weak with raw emotion.

She felt with her fingertips for the lock, scooping out dust from the rough grained wood. The key turned with a rusty click. She withdrew it and holding the door open with her foot, threw the chain into the wisteria tree. As she pressed her body to the door, remembering the required heave and twist, it swung back so unexpectedly that Isabel went with it.

"Ugh!" she groaned as her shoulder twisted and she was pulled unceremoniously into the great hall. Someone held her pinioned, someone with a dripping candle that floated above her head. She could feel his fingers pinching her skin even through her coat. Pain sent adrenaline rushing through her body clearing her fuzzy mind. Isabel's heart pounded in her chest as she peered in the candlelight to see who it was, knowing of course, who it was.

"Jaime told me you were headed here." The man's voice was rough, angry. Her stomach lurched. Why did he always have this ability to make her feel utterly discombobulated even when she should be angry? With the greatest effort of will, she forced herself to appear calm.

"Oh hello Ricardo," she said swivelling in his arms. And then gaining strength, she added almost as an after thought. "Isn't the electricity working?"

He released her immediately and for a moment they stared at each other. She could feel the defiance making her eyes bright and the angry response to it mirrored in the dark. His mouth tightened with annoyance. He moved even closer, lifting the candle high so that it did not drip wax. Instinctively she stepped back, hardly able to breathe, hardly able to control a sudden overwhelming urge to throw herself into his arms. She thrust her hands deep in her coat pockets to stop them from trembling.

"That's it?" Ricardo's words were sarcastic, biting. There was no warmth to his voice. It was totally devoid of the affection with which he generally addressed her. His eyes did not crinkle with the weight of the secret they shared, the respect he would naturally have shown a member of his family. In the past, she had enjoyed the feeling of security she had when they were together, bound by the invisible ties of a shared blood, shielded by the umbrella of their common nobility. "Hello Ricardo?" he continued mimicking her. "Is that all you have to say? After all these weeks?"

Isabel ignored him. "I thought Tito was renovating this place. It doesn't feel as if anyone has been here in ages! And there's a horrible damp smell. It's warm enough but what about the light?"

As she spoke, Isabel moved towards the hall table, effortlessly locating candles in the top drawer. Returning to the house in the dark was the greatest test of memory. In spite of Tito's renovations nothing appeared to have changed. The outline of the furniture indicated that nothing had been moved.

"This too is the same, the interrupted electricity." She stood beside him, briefly lighting her candle from his, allowing the warm wax to drip onto her hand. She was acutely aware of his physical proximity, the clean, lime smell of his clothes, his skin. She wanted to feel his cheek on hers, search for something that would take her back to that last time together. He was distant, unresponsive and now she was frightened that he no longer felt as she did. What would he do if she touched him? The thought of rejection, however, was sobering. "I could really do with a drink," she said in a shaky voice. "It's been a long day. I thought for a moment I wouldn't get into the house. I couldn't find the key."

She moved past him, a shadowy figure in her long, black coat. Her silhouette and elongated shape were abstract against the stone walls. Without needing to feel her way along the corridor, she walked confidently towards the library. Ricardo was forced to follow her if he didn't want to risk losing her to the engulfing darkness of the house. She found the drinks cabinet and set her candle in the groove above. The house was well prepared in the eventuality of sudden power failure.

"I'll join you," said Ricardo abruptly. "In whatever there is."

"Of course."

Isabel located a musty looking whisky decanter, wrinkling her nose at the smell. She smothered a giggle. "It must be something leftover from the war! We'll probably have alcohol poisoning as a result."

Ricardo grunted a response.

"Well if it's a Scottish malt then it will be. Dr.Mantua used to drink it and so did our grandfather.. The odd Englishman hiding here would leave a bottle as a gift – " he stopped in mid sentence as if something had suddenly occurred to him. "Drink it slowly," he added harshly. "It might well be the last."

Isabel climbed up and onto the window seat that was set in oak, high below the casement windows. She took a quick gulp and gasped as fire lit her tongue. Beneath her, Ricardo merged with the shadows. She could just make out the outline of his shoes as he leant against the bookcase. But she could not see his face. The alcohol trickled along her throat to her stomach.

"What's the matter?" she asked at length "You're angry."

"Of course I'm angry!" spluttered Ricardo. She heard the crease of his clothing as he uncrossed his legs, the scrape of his glass on the mantelpiece. "Death makes me angry. *You* make me angry."

"But I'm not dead," she muttered suppressing a giggle. There was a frigid silence.

"Why are you, then?" she said in a small voice.

"I don't hear from you in all this time and then you waltz in as if nothing has changed!" He was almost shouting.

"Don't be ridiculous," replied Isabel stiffly. "Everything has changed." The alcohol was empowering her with shallow bravado.

"You know what I mean."

"I don't actually. Anyway if anyone has a right to be angry here it's me! This is the second time I've gone away and you've not been in touch. You never called or anything really. The only news I had of you was what Avia managed to pass on which wasn't much. I never heard a peep from you after that … after that weekend. You could have been dead for all I knew. How do you think I felt?"

"I have no idea." Ricardo's voice was toneless. "You didn't phone me either."

"I wanted to though so much. I couldn't understand why you were so silent. I thought we had something special but I obviously misread it." Isabel made an impatient gesture. "Look it doesn't matter now. But I, well.. I hoped that you of all the family might have been the one to tell me about Sigi. You know how I love – loved her."

Ricardo shifted his weight, she heard the tinkle of glass scraping a cufflink and then a pause.

"I'm sorry."

Isabel felt tears suddenly prick her eyes and her courage began to shrivel.

"It doesn't matter," she repeated hollowly.

There was a strained silence.

"Did you get the Bazan job in the end? You never said." He asked forcing the words. Isabel was surprised, she expected anything but that.

"No. I'm not sure what we were doing there to be honest. Their setup is pretty perfect."

"Indeed." Ricardo set down his tumbler.

"There *is* something I should have called you about," he said tersely. "Something you should have told me during that weekend, as you call it.

And now that we're finally talking we might as well fill in the gaps." There was a tense silence.

"Yes?" whispered Isabel.

Ricardo voice was steely. "Why the hell didn't you tell me you were engaged?"

Isabel was stunned. She followed his voice in the dark.

"I don't understand," she said.

"Oh for god sake," Ricardo said angrily. "Don't play the innocent with me! Look your fiance Tim phoned me. The day after you left actually. I've never met the guy but he sounded pretty angry. He also seems to know you pretty well."

It was Isabel's turn to be angry.

"And did you ask him what I'd said?"

"I didn't have to. He implied-"

"Precisely." Isabel tried to control the mounting anger with the absent Tim, from getting the better of her. How *dare* he call Ricardo and worst of all how could he have lied like that? If there was a final nail it was hearing this.

"You mean he was wrong?"

"Wrong!" Isabel snorted. "I told him that I didn't love him and that I couldn't marry him. I went further than that and said we should really stop seeing each other all together, not even as friends."

Ricardo said nothing.

"You don't believe me." Her tone was flat.

"I'm finding it hard to."

Isabel felt her heart constrict. Ricardo had always thought so highly of her, she hated that now he mistrusted her, that the warm easy feeling between them had evaporated. That he could believe Tim whom he'd never met, over her. She would have done everything in her power at that moment to turn the clock back to that weekend when there had only been mutual love and compatibility. She remembered with a stab how they had sat in companionable silence together after making love, how every pore in her body screamed her love for him, how he had only to brush her shoulder to turn her into a quivering mass of desire. She had wanted that weekend to go on forever and in her heart of hearts had believed it would. Now she faced a stranger and the rejection she felt was complete. She smothered a sob. She heard Ricardo light a new cigarette and watched as its red tip traced patterns in the air.

"I miss her. I miss Avia," said Isabel in a small voice overwhelmed anew by her loss and Ricardo's coldness. "I didn't expect to, not like this."

"Really?" Ricardo's voice was sarcastic, unkind. "It wasn't as if she was overly generous with you when she was alive."

Isabel turned a tear stained face in his direction.

"How can you say that? You know we were close, that I adored her. She took me in. And I spent every summer here. She *did* welcome me."

Ricardo snorted.

"You *do* see life in a perverse way!" he said brutally. "She gave you a home! Not only was the old girl wealthy enough but you *were* her grandchild. It was her duty apart from anything else. And can you imagine what ignoring you might have done to her reputation? Imagine a war heroine of all people, denying charity to her own flesh and blood? It would have destroyed her."

"She didn't have to," insisted Isabel. "I know she didn't love me in the beginning, but that changed as I grew up."

Ricardo grimaced.

"And you never wondered why she didn't give you any presents? I don't mean occasionally, I mean never – not even clothes, for example. I never saw you in anything but that hideous school uniform, while the rest of us were outfitted like princes! Didn't you wonder why that was? Didn't you ever think the perfect Avia just a little bit hypocritical?"

Isabel set down her glass.

"My God you're cynical and no I didn't," she replied quietly. "If you really want to know, I don't believe in hypocrisy. I think everyone acts in different ways at different stages in their lives. With hindsight, it's all too easy to apportion blame. Often the way we behaved in the past seems illogical and inconsistent. But people change, evolve, grow more or less compassionate. In your case I'd say rather less! You're being unkind about her. If I'm not critical of the way Avia treated me there's no reason for you to be. I'm not reproaching you, Avia or anyone else. You've changed Ricardo, towards me especially. Or perhaps I just never knew you …" Her voice trailed but there was no self pity in it only confusion and a desire to understand what had happened between them, or rather what had not. Isabel traced patterns between the diamond shapes of the window that her breath frosted over just as quickly. There was another long silence, broken only by the sound of Ricardo stubbing out his cigarette and refilling his glass.

"So you'll go back to The Cottage?"

Isabel searched for him in the darkness but could see nothing but the quick glint of his watch in the candlelight as his arm raised his glass to his mouth.

"Of course," she said surprised. "I'm only in Barcelona a few days. There's nothing to keep me here. I almost went back this evening." She frowned realising the enormity of the words. She pressed her cheek against the cold window pane and closed her eyes. She felt so very tired.

"You'll have to come back," said Ricardo harshly.

Her eyes flew open.

"I don't *have* to do anything. And I'm not sure I want to anyway."

"Well there's a time frame on this, you know. It has to be settled within three months. Even if there isn't time to sort everything out before you leave, you'll have to come back. You have to decide what you want to do about the house and there's all kind of paper work, never mind the taxes. There are restrictions on the land, but they will only apply should you decide to sell. And then there's the contents, the paintings, artefacts, outbuildings. Even the Convent, I think, comes into it. Do you want to allow it to continue as it has been or do you think it's time the nuns moved away? Do I have to go on? You can't just leave it!"

"Leave what?" said Isabel bewildered. "What exactly are you talking about? If I decide to sell, sell what?"

There was a brief silence.

"I can't work out if you're naturally stupid or merely triumphant, gloating at your good fortune. Either way it's not attractive."

Ricardo's words stung her.

"I truly don't know what you're talking about," she said hardly above a whisper, her throat constricting with tears. "Please tell me."

Ricardo banged down his glass.

"Mialma is what I'm talking about!" he said frostily. "What else? Avia left it to you! Everything. You get it all, the house *and* its contents. Including, in case you're wondering, the painting of a Countess Roble as a young girl, standing by the water, the one you like so much. It's all yours, *Condesa.*"

Isabel was stunned. Sweat pricked her forehead as the room began to spin. She struggled to open a window sucking in the cold air. She shook off her coat, her body suddenly hot and clammy.

"Well that's the longest I've ever known you to be quiet! And for heavens sake shut that window, it's freezing."

"I don't believe you," she stammered at last.

"Well it's true."

"But why? *Why me?*"

"God knows," he said flatly. "Perhaps even Avia could feel guilt or maybe she thought it was time to right a wrong, maybe she just mellowed, grew – how did you put it, 'more compassionate' in later life."

"And that's why you're being so sarcastic and hurtful? That's why you seem so angry with me?"

"Partly. You know the other reason."

She heard him light a match and for a moment his face was illuminated. He was older than she remembered, hardened and there was more grey in his hair and lines around his eyes. She looked away. Had she been wrong about him all these years? Was Kate right after all? Had she invented him, nurtured a ghost? She began to shake uncontrollably. Without him, more importantly without the *idea* of him, what would she do? Even now she realised that what had kept her going was the thought that she would see him after the funeral, that somehow everything would be right between them, that at long last she could set down the tremendous responsibility of her love. She felt stifled by a sense of loss.

"Look," she said slowly. "I don't want Mialma or its contents. What on earth would I do with a Catalan house? Let the others have it. *You* have it, Ricardo if it'll make you happy. And I didn't come home – to Barcelona because of it. I never knew Avia's intentions and I certainly don't know the terms of her will. You are right about one thing though. When she was alive, Avia never gave me a single present or stitch of clothing, but I don't expect anything from her now that she is dead. Unlike you, I have never expected anything from anyone and least of all from the family. I never believed they *owed* me."

She slid from the window seat, shedding her coat like a skin. She bowed her head although she knew he couldn't see her face in the dark. She continued to shake, her legs uncertain as she moved towards the drinks cabinet where she refilled her glass. She heard the sharp hiss of his tobacco and the sudden glow from his cigarette.

"I can't believe we're even talking like this. I thought we were above it," he said. "I'm sorry. Perhaps I over reacted. Everything and everyone seems to have gone mad lately. It's making me paranoid. It would seem that we've both behaved in ways that was open to misinterpretation. I should have been in touch before and I shouldn't have brought this up now. I should have left it to the lawyers."

She smiled weakly downing her drink in one, the alcohol lighting her brain.

"You *are* a lawyer."

"And you needed one once before, remember."

"I needed *you*."

And then when he didn't reply she added softly, no longer caring what he thought of her.

"There *is* one thing I must know," she said taking a huge breath. "If it hadn't been Avia's funeral, would you have ever got in touch? Would we ever have seen each other again, do you think?"

He left his cigarette smouldering in an ashtray and got to his feet. She could feel the words pounding in her head. *Say them. Say them now or forever hold your peace. You have one last chance to get things right. It is only vanity, fear of rejection stopping you. Say them. Tell him what you feel, he will never know unless you tell him. What have you to lose? You will never know what he thinks about anything, unless you tell him.*

And suddenly the thought that she might lose him and this time indefinitely, was enough to decide, even in the midst of her turmoil, that she *did* want him, ghost or not.

"Because you see ... because ..."

"Because?" His voice was gentle.

"Because I love you." Her voice broke. "I have always loved you and I wish you could believe that I was never engaged to Tim."

In a swift movement Ricardo sprang forward, his hand shot out gripping her wrist so that Isabel cried out, falling against him.

"Let go! Please!" she said weakly, breathless. Hunger, whisky and the shock of the days' events caught up with her, making her dizzy and she began to fight him. Her fists punched the air in the dark. "Let go!" She was panting now, her long skirt entangled tightly round her body, her hair caught in the buttons of his jacket. In the dark, she was suddenly panic stricken, blinded, unable to see his face, lost in swirling blackness. His arms were like iron bars against her chest.

"I will not," he said hoarsely. "Not till we've sorted things out once and for all."

She stopped fighting him, tried to twist round so that she could breathe more easily. Her heart was hammering in her chest. She thought she would faint.

"What do you ... want?"

And then there was a shuddering bang, a jolt and the electricity was reconnected. Lights came on all over the house so that virtually every room was illuminated. Isabel blinked. Ricardo slackened his grip momentarily, turning her so that he could see her face. She looked up at him bewildered and he took in her tear-stained cheeks and tousled hair. He also saw the fear in her eyes and his arms went round her again, only gently this time. And then his hands around her waist, began to move, felt her back, the nape of her neck. With a groan his mouth was on hers, insistent, angry.

"Christ, I've missed you," he muttered. His lips were rough, bruising. He pulled her into him. She felt her legs go limp as his stood rooted to the floor, solid uncompromising. She made a feeble attempt to fight him off and then remembered all the longing, of all the years and she wrapped her arms around his neck. She blocked out the events of the past few days, swimming in a secret sea, drowning in the need to be comforted.

"I –" she began.

"Don't!" he said gruffly his lips in her hair. "Enough of everything that isn't us, *especially* the family. I've been wrong. I've hurt you when I only wanted to love you." He swung her suddenly in his arms. "We have time to make up. I am so sorry, for the past, for the silences, No more games *cosina*. I'm not going to make the same mistake again. I let you disappear from my life once before because I was weak because I was a fool to listen to Tim, because I wasn't courageous enough to fight for you. Not again. Not this time. I will not let you go."

He kicked open the library door and carried her into the great hall, now flooded with light. For a moment he looked at her, his eyes travelling to her parted lips, and then he bent his face to hers.

*

Moonlight flooded the bedroom and through the open window, Isabel could see the snow capped hills in the distance, the break of cloud as dawn beamed across the horizon. It was cold and Isabel shivered, stretching a leg against Ricardo's warmth. There was the weighted sound of stillness, of a house, at last at peace with itself.

Ricardo's arm shot from beneath the covers and pulled her against him.

"Why can't you sleep?"

"I was just wondering, you don't think there are any secret passages in a house like this, or even priest holes, do you? Sometimes I think I can hear noises behind the walls."

"That's what's keeping you awake?"

"Well do you?"

"No. And if there are we'll never know now. Avia has taken her secrets with her to the grave." He ran his hand through her hair. "What is it? No regrets?"

"No. Well – "

Instantly he sat bolt upright, struggling to read her expression.

"Oh not that. I couldn't help feeling a little guilty, more than a little, quite a lot actually."

"For heaven's sake, what about?"

Isabel drew her knees up to her chest, slender arms wrapped round her ankles.

"Well ..." she began thoughtfully. "All these years I struggled to be good enough, to be *like* you. No, don't say anything just yet. I so longed to be part of your family, to be accepted. I was so envious of Sigi and Marta and Beatrice. They were all the things I wasn't – pretty, amusing, confident. They always said the right thing, *did* the right thing. And they had each other. They had that bond of sisterhood that no matter how close I got to, I could never really share. I was always the outsider. Anyway, the point is, that I should have known better. I should have trusted in the future. I had so little faith. But Avia had faith. You call her hypocritical, but she was too clever for that. She understood everything. She *wanted* me to be different. And she made sure that I was by denying me things when I was little, so that I *would* struggle, so that I *would* go to university and have my career. Above all, she knew how much I loved you. Dr. Mantua once said that we Roble women were hopeless when we fell in love. Avia was the same. And she realised that what I felt ..." Isabel smiled. "I thought I was so good at hiding it. But she knew and what is more in one fell swoop she has solved everything."

Ricardo touched her shoulder.

"Not everything," he said sadly. "There will never be children."

"Oh but there can be." Isabel reached for his hand. "I've been thinking about that ever since this morning. Ever since I saw Sigi's little boy. I would like to be Sancho's guardian. Oh don't you see?" Isabel voice rose in excitement.

Ricardo touched her knee.

"Not exactly, no."

"I know it's unconventional. I know there's a lot to work out. But I want to be able to share in his upbringing. Jaime has his career. Having a child with him must be difficult when he travels so much."

"The boy should be with his father," interrupted Ricardo firmly. "I hope you're not suggesting he give him up."

"Of course not! Oh nothing like that! I just want him to always feel welcome at Mialma, to treat it like a second home, to know that he can spend as much time as he wants there. I don't mean now so much as later, when he's older, when he's away at school. There will be school breaks and long holidays when Jaime will be travelling and that's when I can help. He could come and stay with me, the way I used to with Avia. I'm sure that's what Avia was thinking when she left me Mialma. She had a vision of how it could be. While we were reeling from the shock of Sigi's death, Avia was thinking of the future. She knew that if she left me the house I would *have* to spend time here, that I would share it all, help everyone. It would mean that Mialma was never sold to offset taxes on Val Negra or fund some extravagant scheme of Tito's. But most importantly she knew it would bring me to you."

Ricardo pulled her into his arms.

"We can't have children of our own," she continued her voice muffled against his chest, "but we can lavish Sigi's child with all the love possible as if he were our own, whenever he comes to stay. Not everything turns out the way we expect. I used to think that if I didn't plan everything down to the smallest detail then nothing would ever happen. Now I realise the details don't matter at all. They never did."

"Then you've decided where you want to be," said Ricardo.

"For some of the year. I can't entirely give up The Cottage. It is my only link to Julian and in spite of my saying that I'm no longer curious about my parents, they seem to live on there. It's almost as if The Cottage holds their secret, that one day I shall find out about them."

"Then we'll work things out," said Ricardo quietly. "I love you Isabel, but I don't want there to be any sacrifices. There have been too many senseless ones already. Of course I want you here with me but only if it makes you happy." He looked down at her, at the hand slightly curled, resting trustingly on his chest. "I've been overly cautious where you are concerned." He tilted her face to his, beginning to move once more against her. "No longer … *Hermosa Isabela, tu valor, tu mucha virtud y gran hermosura me tienen como me ves …*" and his mouth drowned any reply.

Chapter 37

Mialma
Summer.
Later

Ricardo sat watching Isabel's sleeping form, the gentle rise and fall of the sheet, her even breathing. He lit a cigarette, throwing the match out of the window. It was morning. The heat already rising above the sea carried the scent of Seringa along the tops of the orange groves. A sailing boat on the horizon tacked towards them.

"Per una vela blanca daria un sceptre."

Ricardo spoke the words aloud and thought briefly of his grandfather. He inhaled and blew smoke rings, something he had not done since he and Miguel would hide along the mimosa trail for a clandestine smoke. All at once he understood the wisdom of Avia's decision. She had understood everything as Isabel had said she had. Perhaps it was simply because she loved this girl, as he did, with an all-embracing love, which in securing her happiness had benefited them all. There were still pitfalls ahead of them and the way forward was not without risk, but he was confident that he was doing the right thing.

The clock tower chimed the hour with an echoing peel of bells from the Carmelite Convent. Ricardo stretched contentedly and opened the journal that only now, he was in any way ready to read. His face softened at the sight of the surprisingly childish hand.

"My grandmother's house," he read, *"stood on the top of a steep hill, overlooking the sea and the city of Barcelona ..."*

THE END.

Printed in the United Kingdom
by Lightning Source UK Ltd.
115407UKS00001B/79-156